Heretic

The Sanctuary Series
Volume 7

Robert J. Crane

Heretic
The Sanctuary Series, Volume 7

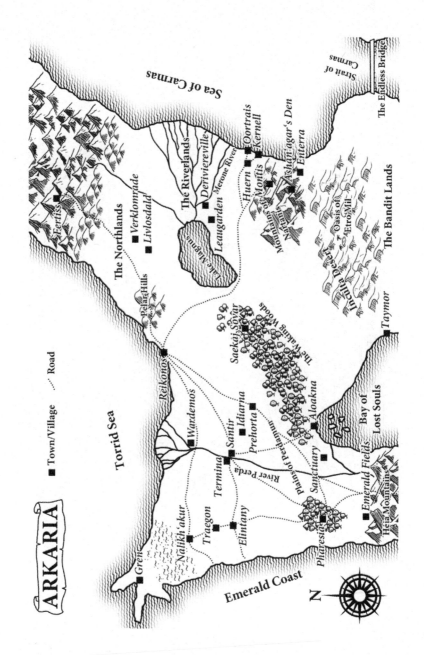

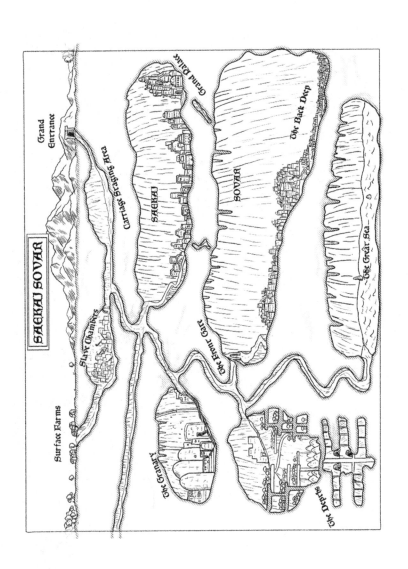

SAEKAJ SOVAR

Grand Entrance

Carriage Staging Area

Surface Farms

Slave Chambers

SAEKAJ

Grand Palace

SOVAR

The Back Deep

The Home Gate

The Great Sea

The Granary

The Depths

NOW

Prologue

"There is no hope left," Cyrus said into the silence of the Council archive, mist starting to seep in as the day began to fade around them. They had sat in silence for some time, he and Vaste, since they had returned to the top of the tower. Clouds were darkening the sky and a thick fog was creeping in over the Plains of Perdamun.

"Ugh," Vaste said, sticking out his tongue as he placed his scarred face in his mighty green troll hands, which were at least twice the size of a human's. "I'm finding it really difficult to be around you right now."

"So leave," Cyrus said, looking out the window at the darkening plains. Shadows played across the hilly terrain, and he surveyed them with blank eyes. A dragon could have emerged from the mist blowing fire and roaring fury, and he wouldn't have much cared. *Though it seems unlikely Ehrgraz would let a dragon come this far north*, he thought idly.

The troll raised his head up, peering between two fingers with a yellow-onyx eye. "Why? So you can drive your sword through your own face over and over in peace?"

Cyrus lifted a hand and a dash of flame burst out, lighting the room brighter than the fire in the hearth. The shadows clinging to the sandy-colored stone walls faded instantly. "I think I can do it a little more efficiently than that."

"Well, I'm not leaving," Vaste said, standing up. He snatched at the leather-bound journal beside him with his wide fingers. Seizing it and stalking over to Cyrus, he shoved the book in his face. Up close, Cyrus could see the subtly pebbled texture of the leather. It smelled of secrets, rich and alluring, the parchment wafting with an unmistakable aroma. Even the ink smelled familiar, sweet, but Cyrus yanked his nose away as though it were something vile. "Read this," Vaste said.

3

Cyrus turned away purposefully, looking out the window, back to the shadows, fog and darkness shrouding the Plains of Perdamun. Nightmares lurked out there, but they held no fear for him any longer. "I don't want to," he said.

"Read it!" Vaste said, more insistently. He thrust the book out at Cyrus again.

Cyrus glanced back at the troll, trying to keep his expression impassive. Vaste's eyes were wild, his lips gently parted, his arm shaking just slightly as he held the book toward Cyrus. *A worthy try, my old friend, but you won't sway me from this course.* "I already have."

"Read it or I'm going to strip my clothes off and dance naked in front of you right now," Vaste said, "and I expect once you see the beauteous curves of my arse, it'll snap you right out of that funk you're in." He gyrated his torso in a suggestive manner that caused Cyrus to take a step back and clank into the wall, his backplate thumping against the edge of the window sill.

"You're the worst company," Cyrus said, snatching the volume out of his hand in resignation after a moment's consideration. *He'll likely do it.* "Do you want me to pick a random passage or do you have a specific—"

"Here," Vaste said, ripping the diary open and thumbing through until he reached a specific page. "This," he said with satisfaction, thrusting the journal back into Cyrus's hands. "Now read, or you get the green arse."

"This isn't why I wrote to you—"

"Read."

Cyrus turned his eyes toward the page and started to read the flowing script.

In spite of all that has happened in the wake of the battle in the Jungle of Vidara, in spite of all we lost, today might, in fact, have been the happiest day of my life.

Cyrus tore his eyes away from the page and looked up into the smug face of the troll standing above him. "You think reading *this* is going to make me want to kill myself less?"

"Just read the damned thing, Davidon, or I'm pulling off this robe and you're going to see what a real troll looks like down—"

Cyrus threw up a hand in surrender and buried his nose in the book, picking up where he left off. There were occasional smudges on the parchment where the ink had gotten wet as the passage had been written. He noted them as he went, trying not to add his own contribution to the pages. As he turned to the next page, the parchment made a rich crackling sound like faint thunder on a stormy night.

> *It was a gorgeous summer day, and we conducted the entire event on the lawn. From start to finish, from sunup to sundown, it was our day, and it was a day of celebration. Not grief, not mourning, not quiet introspection, but our day to celebrate ourselves, to celebrate our love, so labored and long in the making …*
>
> *Perhaps to say that it was "long in the making" is an inappropriate way to describe love, but … well, it's true, and fortunately so, in more ways than one.*
>
> *I did not wear a traditional dress, and my groom did not wear any sort of suit of the kind you might find on a gentleman of Termina, both of us preferring our armor to other finery. It was what we were wearing when we met, it was what we were wearing throughout our relationship—and why change a thing that works, even on a day like this one?*
>
> *Still, I walked down the aisle with flowers in my hands, my sister trailing behind me in place of my mother, and Cyrus stood there at the front, smiling but for the moment when he looked back to see Vaste at his shoulder rather than Andren. We ignored these moments where the loss, the sadness that had so filled our lives threatened to intrude on our special event, ignored it all and made this our day. Our happiest day.*
>
> *Our wedding day.*

Cyrus threw the book hard against the wall. He felt a smoldering within, a dark, crippling sensation of something growing within him—rage, resentment, fury. Common feelings, especially of late.

"Well, at least now you're feeling something other than maudlin self-pity," Vaste said, looking up at him from where he had retreated across the archive, sitting with Alaric's journal clutched in his hands. "That's an improvement, probably."

"There is no improvement," Cyrus snapped. "There is no getting better. Do you not understand?"

"Cyrus," Vaste said, "there is always—"

"NO THERE BLOODY WELL IS NOT, VASTE!" Cyrus

shouted into the archive, his voice rattling off the walls and echoing out the window onto the plains far below. "That's what it means when you have no hope … that it will never, *ever* get better …" He waved a hand out the window. "Not for Arkaria."

"Not for me."

His throat burned, the pain rolling down it as his face grew hot. "And not for her," he said wistfully, "because she's gone … and she'll never come back." He looked up at the silent troll. "The real irony, of course, is that she feared to be with me because she thought that once I died, she wouldn't be able to bear living without me for thousands and thousands of years." He listened to the silence in the archive. Vaste sat motionless next to the hearth, his skin yellow in the fire's glow. "And yet it's I who lost her first. *I* who suffered the cruelest of losses." He sighed, and all the life flowed out of him with the breath. "I who can't imagine living the next thirty or forty or—if fate be so cruel—sixty or seventy years of my pitiful little life-span without her."

He walked to the window and stared out into the rising mist. "So … to go back to your earlier question … no, I don't mean to rebuild Sanctuary." He looked at the stones that framed the window and put a hand on one, his gauntlet scratching lightly against the rough block. "This is their place, our place, where we grew the bonds of fellowship, the place where so … so very many of our friends lived and died, Vaste." His voice grew faint. "I won't insult their memory by pouring new life into it." He turned around and saw the troll watching him with that rarest of emotions, the one Vaste almost never displayed—sadness. "This place … is the closest they have to a grave. It's their tomb. Their mausoleum.

"And I mean to join them in it."

TWO YEARS EARLIER

1.

"Of course you're leaving," Cyrus Davidon said into the silence of the nearly empty foyer of Sanctuary, his quiet voice carrying over the stone and overcoming the quiet crackle of the fire in the long hearth that ran down the entire side of the massive room. It burned like a long line of fire, reminding him of a spell sent forward like a charging knight on horseback, stirring up a straight cloud in its wake. Emotions played through Cyrus in quick succession—the sting of personal insult; the shock of another loss, a pin's prick in a forest of them, before finally settling into the jaded resignation that seemed to permeate the very walls of the guildhall recently. "Sooner or later …" he said, trying to smile, "… everyone leaves."

Carisse Sevoux was a young human ranger whom Cyrus recalled from an occasion when she had delivered a message to his quarters. She had dark hair and a tanned face, as rangers tended to, along with a thin, lithe frame that was mostly hidden beneath her green cloak. When he'd seen her before he recalled a youthful face, but now she looked tired, drained of her vigor and vibrancy. There was no spark of light in her eyes when she spoke, not now. "I am … deeply sorry, Lord Davidon."

"You don't have to apologize to me," Cyrus said, trying to salve the nettled sense of pride he felt run through him. It prickled at his skin and itched at his mind. He forced another smile. "I'm still here, after all. It's you who are choosing to leave, and it's not as though you bound yourself to Sanctuary's service for a lifetime."

"I just need to go home," Carisse said, glancing away from his gaze. She fiddled with the edges of her cloak, drawing them closer, as if to protect herself from feeling guilty. *That's all inside, lass, and adjusting your cloak will do nothing to protect you from it,* Cyrus did not say aloud. She hesitated, taking a halting step toward the door. "Well … I suppose this is farewell, then."

"Yes," Cyrus said quietly, feeling as though he were perhaps channeling the spirit of the last Guildmaster of Sanctuary. "Fare well in your travels, Carisse Sevoux, and should you ever have call to tread back this way again, you will find our gates open for you." Faint though it was, the smile that he'd pressed onto his face felt almost physically painful.

"Thank you," she said, taking his words as gracefully as she probably could and then sweeping away with a flutter of her cloak as hastily as she could within the bounds of good manners. *She might as well be running, though*, thought Cyrus. She certainly seemed to want to, an extra jump to her step as she hurried out the massive door of Sanctuary's guildhall.

"Was that another departure?" The voice that came from behind him was sharp as the sword that rested on her belt. For once, his wife's voice did not make Cyrus Davidon smile.

"It was," Cyrus said, watching the door as Carisse Sevoux slipped out into the grey day. "I've lost count of how many that makes it."

"Thousands," Vara said, slipping up next to him. She swept her gaze over the mid-afternoon emptiness of the guildhall, her blond hair pulled tight into a golden ponytail, her silver armor losing some of its glister in the low light of the foyer. "Many thousands. And with most of the Luukessians guarding the Emerald Fields—"

"This guildhall is becoming as ghostly as its last master," Cyrus said, finishing the sentence for his bride.

Vara studied him carefully, her attention now focused wholly upon her husband. Cyrus could feel her piercing gaze, surveying him, working its way through the cracks in his armor and those in his soul, and he only looked at her out of the corner of his eye, waiting for her to pose her inevitable question. "Did you take this leaving with quiet aplomb, then?" she asked. "With the dignity due your post?"

"Of course," Cyrus said. "Why wouldn't I?"

"I don't know," Vara said quietly, in a tone of voice that told him she very much did know but had chosen not to fight about it. "What did you say?" she asked, moving on.

"The same thing I've told so many others," Cyrus said, turning his head to look at her. Her blue eyes glowed with a quiet intensity. "That if she found herself wanting to come back at some point, our doors would be open—"

"Revolting. You're too conciliatory."

"It's what Alaric would have said." Cyrus maintained his quiet composure. *This is how Alaric would have explained it, too.*

"I heard you say something else," Vara said, a hint of tension coiling into her frame, visible even under the dully gleaming armor. "Something about … 'Everyone leaves'?"

Cyrus shrugged even as he reddened. He felt a strange urge to hide, some childlike urge to retreat from the criticism he knew would follow from her. "There is truth in that, no?"

His wife looked at him so sharply that he flinched as if she'd thrust at a blade at him. "That's a very dim view of the world."

"It's a dim day," Cyrus said, nodding to the enormous circular stained-glass window over the main doors that was barely lit with the sky's light. "And it rings true."

"Your helm will also ring true when I clap my gauntleted hand upon it," she said, pursing her lips in disapproval, "yet I doubt you have any more desire to hear that than I do to see my husband spew forth such forlorn, self-pitying twaddle." Her voice lowered and softened, run through with a gentleness that he did not often hear from her in a public setting. "You're better than this."

"I know," he said, looking away from her again. "You're right. All these—these many leavings—they bring out the worst in me." He ran a metal-encased hand over his cleanly shaven cheek, scratching his face with his gauntlet finger. "I can't help but remember in times like this that my father left, my mother left …" He pressed his lips together hard. "… Alaric … Andren …"

"Most of them died," Vara whispered, her hand touching his shoulder so gently that her gauntlet made no sound against his pauldrons. "It wasn't as though they simply walked out a door and left you behind."

In the silence of the foyer, Cyrus stared at the open door, nothing but grey visible in the sky beyond. "I know I shouldn't," he admitted. "But on days like today, I can't help but feel that way. The idea that … whether they want to or not, everyone leaves. One way or another."

"I won't leave you," she said, now brushing her own fingers across his face, careful not to pinch him between the armor's joints.

He turned his head to look at her pale face, hints of gold that had slipped out of her long ponytail drifting into her eyes. "No?"

"No," she said, and a mischievous light came to her eyes, "I mean to torment you for years and years to come, dear husband. It's chief among the reasons I married you—"

Her mischief was contagious, and a genuine smile blossomed on his own face in response. He was about to make a clever reply, but he was interrupted by the squeak of the door as it opened fully. Vara turned, and they both stared at the shadowed figure that stood in the entry, three smaller, four-legged shapes standing up to hip-high on their master. Cyrus could hear them panting across the room as they stood there silhouetted against the iron clouds in the background behind them.

The Northman's leather armor squeaked as he stepped another foot into the foyer. "Lord Davidon," Menlos Irontooth said tensely, "you're needed at the wall, Guildmaster."

"What is it, Menlos?" Cyrus asked. Vara had detached herself from him at the first sign of company and was now standing just behind him, her shoulder almost brushing his.

"Trolls, sir," Menlos replied. Even though Menlos was cast in silhouette by the light that flooded in behind him, Cyrus could tell the Northman's expression was grim. "There are trolls at the gates."

2.

"Did I just see Carisse leave?" Menlos asked as he led the way across the grounds. The mighty stone wall that encircled Sanctuary stood out in the distance, the giant gates closed to visitors or guests. *They've been like that for an awfully long time now*, Cyrus thought, staring at them as he and Vara followed the Northman to the wall. *Not at all like they were when I first came here, thrown wide and welcoming to all comers …*

"Yes," Cyrus said, looking across the lawn for the ranger. Brown dirt had taken over where lush grass had once ruled the grounds, and it felt very much like a symbol of Sanctuary's decline. "She decided she wanted to seek her fortunes elsewhere. Or perhaps she was just tired of associating with us."

Menlos grunted. "These people leaving, they lack the basic loyalty of a dog." He reached down to scratch one of his wolves behind the ears. It panted appreciatively. Menlos's armor continued to squeak as he walked, his short blade rattling in its scabbard. He had an earthy aroma to him that Cyrus could smell even some ten feet back, and the wolves had an even stronger scent even to them, although their fur was clean and luminous as though they'd been recently bathed.

"Why are there trolls at our gates?" Vara asked as they all stumped along the brown dirt path. The wall was only a hundred feet away now. "And how many are there?"

"Perhaps ten? Twelve?" Menlos said, shrugging, his armor making a noise as he did so, the boiled leather not as heavily worn as it might have been. Cyrus recalled vaguely that the hairy Northman had received it in the Trials of Purgatory some years back. It looked strong and near flawless, well taken care of and probably heartier than many of the weaker metals others wore for protection. "It was tough to tell, they

13

were all bunched together."

"So not exactly an invading force, then," Vara said, sounding slightly mollified.

"Invading force?" Menlos's eyebrow cocked, and he let out a mild guffaw. "No, not according to them."

"And here I was worried for a moment that they were here about that expedition we staged into Gren a couple years back," Cyrus said as they reached the staircase and started to ascend the wall. Menlos's leather boots made noise as he began his climb; Cyrus let Vara go ahead of him, and her metal boots clanked against the stone as she followed the Northman up. "Thought maybe revenge was on their minds."

"Hard to tell what's really on their minds," Menlos said, looking suspicious. "But as for their declared purpose … well, you need to hear it for yourself."

They reached the top of the wall and found the guard that was always on watch along the length of the barrier that ringed Sanctuary somewhat spare. *We used to have more people to man this wall*, Cyrus thought mournfully, looking in either direction along the length of the stone bulwark that guarded the guildhall from assaults across the long, green Plains of Perdamun that stretched out before him to the horizon. *But then, we used to have more people to do just about everything …*

Scuddar In'shara was waiting, wearing scarlet robes and with the scarf he wore around his head pulled down to his chin to reveal that he had shorn his coal-black beard. He showed not a trace of humor as he looked at Cyrus, merely nodding to acknowledge his Guildmaster's arrival. A bare second later, he bowed almost imperceptibly to Vara. "M'lord," he said. "M'lady."

"Castellan," Cyrus said, acknowledging Scuddar by his title. "I hear we have visitors."

"More than a few," Scuddar said in his rich baritone. He led them to the crenellations in the wall, and they peered between the teeth and down some thirty feet to the torn ground outside the gate where a party of green-skinned, wide-bodied trolls waited patiently, their breathing so loud that Cyrus could hear it even at this distance. Beyond them, standing off a ways, was a green-cloaked elven wizard who watched the knot of trolls with wide, worried eyes from atop a brown and white horse.

"Hail," Cyrus called down to them, dropping his hand to rest on the hilt of his sword, Praelior, hanging on the right side of his belt. A surge of strength from the weapon's enchantments ran through him, filling him with the confidence that Carisse Sevoux's departure had stolen away.

Each of the waiting trolls looked to be somewhere in the neighborhood of ten feet tall, taller even than him. They all glanced up at the sound of his voice, and he counted thirteen faces staring up at him, some with black facial hair growing out of their chins and jawlines, others without a hint of it to obscure their complexions, which ranged from bright green to a sickly yellow that reminded Cyrus of a rancid lemon.

Several of the faces wore suspicious expressions, but Cyrus picked out the leader of the group quickly enough, standing at the fore draped in old, rusty, iron armor that exposed the flesh around the troll's smallish breastplate. Dark green nipples were visible on either side of the breastplate, which was strapped rather tightly around his figure. It looked like something a smaller-framed dark elf might wear, but it had been repurposed to protect this troll's heart. He also wore pants stitched together from goats' skins and had ten brass earrings the size of Cyrus's hands sticking out of each ear. His lower teeth protruded from his underbite. "Hellllo," the troll leader drawled, looking up.

"Whom do I have the pleasure of addressing?" Cyrus asked, looking down at the curious assemblage before the gates.

The troll leader cocked his head, puzzling at what Cyrus had said. After a moment he grunted, seeming to get it. "I am Zarnn." He turned slowly to wave a hand at the motley collection of trolls behind him. "These my ... fellow travelers."

"Where are you traveling?" Cyrus asked, sparing a glance for the elven wizard who was still ahorse, standing off nervously from the trolls, apparently hoping he could avoid any association with them.

"To here," Zarnn said slowly, as though it were obvious.

"All right," Cyrus said, trading a look with Vara. She rolled her eyes. He turned back to shout down at Zarnn once more. "Now that you're here ... what do you intend to do?"

Zarnn paused as though to think about it. "Join Sanctuary," he decided, and there was much head-nodding behind him among the other trolls.

"The bloody hell you say." Menlos Irontooth did not bother to keep his voice down. "They're here to join? Like we don't have enough problems as it is ..."

Cyrus tried to hold back his surprise, peering over the crenellations at the group below. "I'm sorry ... you're here to ... become part of Sanctuary?"

Zarnn looked around at the walls and the flat lands around him. "This ... Sanctuary, yes?" His voice was rumbling as he missed words, struggling to string his thoughts into speech in his non-native language, but he had a hint of innocence to him that Cyrus found unsettling. *He's no Vaste, that's for sure.*

"I heard that there were trolls at the gates," came a voice from behind Cyrus, causing him to turn. "I hope you've locked the doors and hidden the keys." Vaste stormed up the steps, his white staff in hand, his deep black robes rippling behind him as he strode across the wall to stand next to Cyrus. He peered down. "Good gods. It's like a little piece of Gren washed up on our doorstep."

"How did you hear that there were trolls at the gates?" Menlos asked, his eyes bulging. "I didn't carry the message past the foyer."

"Don't worry, my smelly northern friend," Vaste said, looking down at the trolls, "the dead carried your words the rest of the way." Menlos stood frozen for a moment before he looked left, then right, self-consciously, and his nostrils flared quietly as he sniffed himself.

"You there!" Vaste called down. Zarnn looked up at him with a childlike expression on his bearded face. "What are you doing here?"

"They say they're here to join," Cyrus said before Zarnn could answer.

"Impossible," Vaste said, shaking his head. "Everyone knows there are no trolls in Sanctuary."

"Aren't ... aren't you a troll?" Menlos asked, more tentative now.

"No," Vaste said, not bothering to look away from the crenellations and the trolls beneath, "I'm a gnome, keep it straight."

"Explains why you vex me so," Vara muttered under her breath, so quietly that Cyrus doubted very much if Vaste even heard her.

"We ... here to join Sanctuary," Zarnn called up in answer somewhere in the midst of the crosstalk.

"Told you," Cyrus said.

"You tell me a lot of things," Vaste said, frowning. "I'll let you in on a little secret—I don't listen to you most of the time. Maybe if you spoke less, I would. I mean, really, it would require something on the order of three whole minutes per day to catch everything you throw at me verbally, and who has that sort of time?" Without waiting for Cyrus to reply, he angled his head to speak to the trolls below. "Why would you possibly want to join Sanctuary right now? Don't you realize we don't like trolls around here?"

A stark silence fell over the wall as everyone seemed to pause to take in everything that was happening. Guards up and down the path along the top stared, watching the exchanges with obvious interest. *Probably the most interesting thing to happen on duty in months*, Cyrus thought.

"You ... troll," Zarnn said, calling back up to them. "You in Sanctuary."

"I'm not a troll," Vaste replied neatly, "I'm an elf."

"Don't you dare—" Vara started, her ire rising.

"Fine," Vaste said, not even looking back at her, "I'm a—" He glanced sideways and caught Scuddar standing down the line, arms folded over his robes, "I'm a man of the desert!" Vaste pulled his robes up over the back of his head, yanking the hem a good foot off the ground as he tried to recreate the cloth coif that was a hallmark of the dwellers in the Inculta Desert.

Zarnn stared up at Vaste and a small rumble of conversation made its way through his party. "You troll," Zarnn finally decided. "You in Sanctuary. We trolls. We want to be in Sanctuary, too."

"I said there are no trolls in Sanctuary!" Vaste shouted back. "Are you calling me a liar?"

Cyrus stood there dumbly, wondering how this could possibly end, and not sure what to say even absent Vaste's distraction. *Troll applicants? Here? Now?*

Why?

"You liar, yes," Zarnn said after another moment's deliberation below with his party.

"Well, then why would you want to join a guild of liars?" Vaste asked, dropping the backs of his robes off the top of his head. "I mean, really. That should settle it for you right there."

"Because ... strength," Zarnn said without consulting his group. "And gold."

A prickling of understanding ran over Cyrus. "We, uh ... there's not much gold around here anymore," he called down to Zarnn. "We don't tend to run expeditions lately, and we haven't taken a mercenary contract in a very long time. You'd be better off joining a company if you're to hire out for coin, or applying to one of the Big Three guilds—Amarath's Raiders, Endeavor, or Burnt Offerings if you're looking to adventure for reward." *Because Sanctuary is presently out of the business of adventure,* he did not say, but he caught Vara looking at him in askance even so. *And there's not much strength around here anymore, either.*

Zarnn seemed unsure of what to say to that, and Cyrus watched him turn back to his party, and they spoke together for a moment before Zarnn turned back. "We looking for … home."

"Gren is that way—" Vaste started.

"Vaste," Cyrus said, putting his hand on the troll's arm, pulling it down from where he'd been pointing to the northwest. "We don't … we don't turn away people who are looking for—"

"If we're smart, we damned sure do," Vaste said, his eyes hard.

"Weren't you the one who once told me I didn't know anything about trolls?" Cyrus asked.

"And you still don't, which is why I'm turning them away for you."

"I'm with Vaste," Menlos said, arms still folded before him. "Send 'em back to the swamps. Better not to invite this kind of trouble into our walls."

"Stop making me rethink my hard line," Vaste said, eye twitching in annoyance.

"Turning them away isn't what Alaric would have done," Vara said quietly, her voice soft and regretful.

Vaste shot Cyrus a scathing look. "Don't you have some insecure reply to that?"

"She's right," Cyrus said. "This isn't … Sanctuary is supposed to be a haven for those seeking a path."

"Whoa, no," Menlos shook his head. "We're not talking about gnomes or goblins that can't find work in Reikonos. We're talking trolls here. Trolls. Slavers. Kidnappers. Twice the size of a normal person, and four times the threat of a strong warrior."

"Which makes them something on the order of fifty-two strong warriors we'd be taking on as applicants," Cyrus said, looking down at the thirteen of them waiting. "When was the last time we had fifty-two of anyone apply to us in a single day? Or even thirteen?"

"Oh, I hear the seeds of my defeat planted in your words, and they sound like … nuts," Vaste said, taking a ragged breath. "As in, 'You've gone—'"

"I caught the implication," Cyrus said. "Though I would have thought you'd say I'd gone soft, perhaps."

"And risk your rather brazen wife tossing out some suggestive witticism about your insatiable manliness my way? No. No. I'd rather insult your sanity, it's safer."

Vara gave the healer a look half as mischievous as the one she'd favored Cyrus with before Menlos had interrupted them in the foyer. "If you'd like—"

"Open the gates, then," Vaste said, coming back from the edge of the wall, sounding utterly resigned, as though he'd lost a fight and received a hard shellacking in the bargain. "Mark this moment in your mind, though, if they go treacherous or dangerous or merely lecherous with the local farm animals—I warned you and you ignored it."

"Those poor animals," Menlos said in a low whisper then whistled, drawing his wolves to him immediately.

"Come on," Cyrus said, already heading for the stairs. "Let's go meet our new applicants."

He descended the stairs under the cloudy skies, the faint glow of daylight making its way through patches of the clouds above like lamps shining through mist. Vara fell in beside him. "You were right," she said softly. "This is the proper course for Sanctuary. This is who we are."

"I haven't forgotten," Cyrus said. "I forget a lot of things, but this … I couldn't forget this."

His boots hit the soft earth as the squeal of the gate hinges and chain of the portcullis being drawn open reached his ears. He stood in the middle of the dirt pathway, watching as the trolls made their way inside the walls and the wizard on the horse followed at a distance. He barely made it inside before the gates began to squeak shut again, pushed closed by the warriors manning them.

The trolls strolled into the open grass-and-dirt space behind the wall, looking around in amazement at the distance to the guildhall. It was not a small area, the space between the walls and the keep; there was plenty of room for a small town to take root between them, and Cyrus had often considered that very idea. *At least I considered it back when the guild was growing, when we were ascendant. I haven't had to think about that possibility in … quite some time.*

"Welcome to Sanctuary," Cyrus said to Zarnn as he and his party came to a halt in front of Cyrus. Green faces looked down at him from a few feet above, the towering trolls putting his height to shame. "We'll need to ask you some questions and have you put down your names on our parchment as we begin the process of having you apply to Sanctuary."

"All right," Zarnn said, nodding once after gauging the response of his fellows behind him. "Good."

Cyrus and Vara exchanged a look. "Good," Cyrus repeated, unsure what else to say.

"No, not good at all," Vaste said under his breath. "It's only good until the shrieking, and the terror, and the murdering—"

"Vaste will show you into the hall and start asking you some questions." Cyrus smirked, sure that a look of horror was spreading across the healer's face. "If you'll follow him …"

Cyrus stepped aside and the trolls sauntered forward toward Vaste, whose head was hung in obvious disappointment.

"Right," Vaste said, bringing his eyes up. "First thing I'm going to tell you about Sanctuary is that trolls get worked like dogs here, having to do all the unpleasant tasks. Also, there are no goats, so if that's going to be a problem, best just leave now." He waited a second, and when there was no response from his audience, he let out a small sigh and started toward the doors to the keep. "Fine. Follow me."

"This isn't a mistake, is it?" Cyrus asked Vara as they watched the trolls following the smaller Vaste away. There was some grunting among them, and Cyrus saw Vaste look toward the heavens, as though expecting a lightning bolt to streak down and kill him. "Is Vaste right?"

"Probably not," Vara answered after a brief pause. "But …"

Cyrus waited for her to finish. She did not. "But what?"

"But the alternative is to trust no one, ever," she said, seemingly stirred back to life by his words. "To hang tight to bonds of old friendship but never make new ones. To grow old, truly, and to watch those around you diminish with you, until you age out of life alone." She glanced at him quickly and then looked away again. "I'm going to help Vaste get them situated."

"I'll—" Cyrus started, but he caught movement out of the corner of his eye. The elven wizard who had come in with the trolls was now standing only feet away from him, leading his horse with one hand, the other outthrust, an envelope of yellowed parchment extended to Cyrus. "I'll be along in a …" He took it from the wizard and spared only a glance to see Vara already wending her way toward the doors, not looking back at him for a response or anything else. "Who are you?" he asked the wizard.

"Messenger, sir," the wizard said primly, casting a baleful glance at the last of the trolls, now receding behind the gargantuan doors of the entry. "I brought this for you from Reikonos. It is a matter of great urgency, I was assured."

Cyrus looked at the envelope, crinkled in his hand. *Cyrus Davidon* was written across its front in a familiar hand. He caught the wax seal on an edge of his lobstered gauntlet and ripped it open, pulling out the missive within. The page crackled as he unfolded it, a flowery scent filling his nostrils as though set loose from the paper.

> *Cyrus,*
> *I need to speak with you immediately. I would not write to you were it not a matter of the greatest urgency, and something only you can aid me with.*
> *Imina*

Cyrus blinked at the words then read them again. His eyes fell out of focus and then refocused on the messenger, whose lineless face watched him for reaction. "Who gave this to you?"

"A young woman, human," the elf said, adjusting the vestments that identified him as a wizard. "She found me in Reikonos Square and bade me come here and deliver it, and to await your reply."

"Describe her for me," Cyrus said. His lips felt suddenly quite dry, as did the rest of his mouth.

The elf's lips became a thin, annoyed line. "She was tall, for a woman, dark hair, skin the color of an ashfruit … she had a green jeweled ring upon her finger."

That's Imina, Cyrus thought, and a little bead of moisture trailed across his head under his helm. "And she wanted my reply?"

"Indeed," the elf said impatiently.

"Can you take me to her right now?" Cyrus asked, casting a look back at the guildhall. The doors were closing. "And bring me back once my business is concluded?"

ROBERT J. CRANE

"For a fee," the wizard said. "Naturally."

"Take me to her," Cyrus said, reaching into his coin purse and coming out with two pieces of gold. He pressed them into the waiting palm of the wizard, who looked at them impassively for just a moment before pocketing the generous payment. He smiled thinly at Cyrus and then closed his eyes, murmuring an incantation under his breath. With a splash of light, the magic burst all around Cyrus, instantly transporting him from under the grey skies of the plains to another place he had once called home.

3.

Reikonos Square bustled in spite of the snow in the streets, the new year only a few days away. The winter solstice would follow, the days growing short, and here it was not clouds that dimmed the skies but the setting sun. Cold, crisp air burned at Cyrus's cheeks and made him regret not returning to the Tower of the Guildmaster for a cloak before embarking on this journey. He let out a slow breath and it misted before him, the filthy scents of the human capital filling his nasal passages and the cold air burning them as he drank in the smells of the city.

Cyrus took a step and his boot crunched in fresh snow. He looked down; he hadn't left Sanctuary in months, and it seldom snowed in the Plains of Perdamun. The wizard, noting his surprise, said, "It's been falling here and there for a month. We received a plentiful dosing the day before yesterday, though. Almost a foot."

"Indeed," Cyrus said under his breath as the frigid air seeped in through the gaps of his armor and crawled over his skin like tentacles of ice. He cast a steady gaze over the crowds that swarmed through the square, treading through the snow and leaving their own prints in the process, long cloaks sweeping and smoothing the soft powder behind them.

"I was told by the lady who gave me the missive that we would find her in the markets," the wizard said stiffly, starting past Cyrus across the square.

"I thought she was going to be waiting here?" Cyrus asked, holding his ground. The wind whipped through hard just then, and he cringed as his cheek numbed.

The wizard turned back to look at him, raising his cowl against the hard blast. "She runs a flower stand. Without her, business halts, so I presume she did not dare lose gold on the chance that you might not come immediately."

"Fair enough," Cyrus said and started his slog through the snow, following in the wake of the wizard. In spite of the steady traffic, the snow still reached a high point around his shins and slowed his passage. The wizard seemed to be having an even harder time of it, but together they trudged out of the square and into the realm of stalls and shops, their cloth hangings covered in an inch or more of snow.

How long has it been since I've seen Imina? Cyrus wondered, trying to place their last meeting in his mind. *Four years? I didn't even recognize her the last time ...*

The traffic thinned as they took a turn down a market street. Costermongers hawked their wares on either side, vivid splashes of color on white-covered streets telling him that the bright cloth dyes of the Dark Elven Sovereignty had made their way into the human city. The new imports seemed to have taken over the market for colored cloth, and a rainbow of hues was spread before Cyrus, muted by the traces of white snow that were draped on the cloth hangings above each stall to protect them from the elements. The keepers of these open-air shops were bundled tight against the elements, with cloak and cowl, misting the air with their shouted bargains.

Cyrus followed the wizard closely, only a couple steps back, afraid he might lose him to an abrupt turn. The wizard was looking back every now and again, apparently concerned about the same, casting careful looks over his shoulder to confirm that Cyrus was, indeed, still there, trailing in his distinctive black armor, as though he might disappear if given the chance.

Cyrus didn't dare, though. Not after that letter. *Not if Imina needs my help.*

They turned a final corner, the traffic hurrying all around them. A woman in a cloak brushed past Cyrus, a look of horror crossing her face as her eyes fell on him. She gave him a once over and scampered away as though he'd cast a fire spell at her. When he turned back to the elf, the wizard was approaching a stall where a woman waited, dark hair curling out of her cowl, which was pulled forward to shield her against the wind. Her stall was replete with flowers tied off against the winter's edge, a beautiful bundle of glowroses fixed in the middle of the small display.

Imina.

Cyrus started to speak, to greet her across the distance between them, but his mind and his eyes forced him to hold his tongue. He swept his gaze over the lines of the woman beneath the cloak, and something seemed ... off.

The way the cloth held her body, loosely, felt most peculiar to him. *Am I just suffering from another failure of memory? Or is there something different in the way she holds herself? The way she—*

"Hello, there," came a grunted voice at his side, low and full of glee. Cyrus turned; he had not even realized that someone had crept in on under cover of the crowd until they were practically upon him, at his side, perfectly positioned to jab at him with a dagger or a sword—

He spun, but not quickly enough. There was a hand already upon him, one that yanked him closer, hard, ripping him off balance and pulling him forcefully toward the speaker. Cyrus grunted, unable to resist, the strength greater than his legs could muster at the notice of a moment, and then he realized, seeing the face with the scars around the man's lips—

It was Rhane Ermoc, warrior of Goliath.

And he had his hand upon Praelior.

4.

Rhane Ermoc stepped nimbly aside as he pulled Cyrus past him, unsheathing Cyrus's own sword as he did so. The speed and strength of Praelior was now at Ermoc's disposal, not Cyrus's, and Ermoc immediately swept his feet with a hard kick to the shins—

Cyrus landed on his elbows in the snow and tried to roll, but without Praelior to aid his movements, he flopped upon the ground with a clank, his vambraces hitting the stone buried beneath the snow, knocking over a wooden stall selling herbs and spices, a mixture of scents threatening to overwhelm him as they fell all around him. Cyrus tried to get up, but a hard thrust of his own blade found his back—

It drove into his breastplate and ran him into the snow, the force pushing through plate and mail to bruise his skin but failing to so much as rupture his armor. Cyrus grunted in pain, and then bucked against the attack, pushing the point of his sword off of him. *This bastard thinks he can sneak up on me and steal my sword without a fight?*

Cyrus rolled over to see Ermoc stumbling back, recovering before he crashed into a nearby stall, Praelior clutched before him in both hands.

I'm going to have to show him how wrong he is.

A hard gonging noise distracted Cyrus as something clanged against his helm. It was followed by another, and he lowered his head against this new attack. Arrows, he knew in an instant. He glanced in the direction they had come from as another whizzed at him, clinking as he turned his head against it.

Orion.

The ranger was in the distance, his bucket-shaped helm as distinctive as a battle standard hoisted aloft on a battlefield. He fired again and his aim was true, his steel-tipped arrow bouncing harmlessly off Cyrus's pauldrons. *If I weren't wearing my armor, he would have killed me thrice by now. As it is, I just need to keep my face away from him, and the plate and mail should protect me until I can get Praelior back and then gut that sonofabitch like one of those man-sized fish they bring in at the Reikonos docks—*

Cyrus reached behind him as Rhane Ermoc came hard at him once more, Praelior extended ahead of the Goliath warrior like a spear. Cyrus turned slightly to blunt the attack and Ermoc landed his blow with full force against Cyrus's breastplate. Again, his armor withstood the blow, and Ermoc's face twisted in surprise and fury. *I guess he didn't realize that my armor is quartal as well,* Cyrus thought as the force of impact smashed him into a wooden stand filled with glass statuary. The shattering sound filled the cold air as Cyrus stumbled to recover his balance. *Ermoc never was that bright.*

Cyrus's fingers grasped the hilt secreted away behind his backplate and pulled the blade he kept in reserve. The sword was shorter than Praelior and had none of its strength or speed-boosting abilities. *But it's better than trying to fight him with my gauntlets while dodging Orion's arrows.*

A tongue of flame lipped at Cyrus from his left and he dodged away as a fire spell burst at him. It faded after a second and he saw a smiling, emaciated figure with terrible teeth leering at him through a ragged beard and sallow skin. *Carrack. He looks about like I last saw him, like he's still suffering from his years in prison here in Reikonos. I should relieve him of his misery.*

"What else does Goliath have to throw at me?" Cyrus asked, barely dodging Ermoc's next breathless attack. Praelior came sweeping in, destroying the hanging cover to a produce stand as Ermoc applied his pathetic swordsmanship to chasing down Cyrus.

"Oh, it's not just Goliath," came a rough, low voice at Cyrus's back, and he didn't quite dodge in time. A hammering blow landed on the back of his head, rocking him even through the quartal. He felt as if someone had dropped an anvil from the top of the Citadel upon his head.

I know that voice.

Cyrus hit the snow, his spare sword skittering out of his grasp under a nearby fruit stand and sliding down a small hill of wet snow. Screams filled the air all around, and Cyrus wondered if people had been crying out all along and he hadn't noticed or if perhaps the crowds had only just realized there was a fight in their midst.

Cyrus's head rang, the blow having done far more harm than Orion's attempts to plink his brains out with arrows at a distance. This was the cry of nerves and skull done harm, a resonating blast of pain that swept into the area behind his eyes and bounced around within it. Cyrus tried to push himself to all fours, but a heavy foot landed upon his backside, kicking him over onto his back. He looked up into the darkening skies and saw a face darker still, with long black hair and a crooked grin. A pale scar crossed it diagonally from forehead to chin.

Archenous Derregnault.

The Guildmaster of Amarath's Raiders.

The man who betrayed Vara and left her to die—

"I hear you married my former fiancée," Derregnault said in a rough whisper as Rhane Ermoc and Carrack lurched up to flank him.

"I figured after you stabbed her and left her for dead, you wouldn't mind," Cyrus said bitterly.

"I don't," Derregnault said. "My business with Vara is settled. My business with you, however—well, it's not personal, exactly. Call it a matter of advantage. See, I lost some face when Amarath's Raiders fled Reikonos during the war …" He pointed his sword right into Cyrus's face, and Cyrus could see intricate carvings all along the blade. "This is my chance to redeem that mistake, and to, shall we say, leave Vara in the dirt once more." Derregnault's lips split into a sinister grin. "I see no downsides to this matter at all."

Rhane Ermoc spat over Archenous's shoulder down upon Cyrus. "Now you're going to get what's coming to you, Davidon, you swine."

Carrack grinned from where he stood over Cyrus. "And don't be thinking you can cast your fire spell against us, either. Lift so much as your hand and I'll cook you as black as your armor."

"You should have joined us when I asked you to, Cyrus," Orion said, creeping into view above Cyrus now, his arrow nocked and pointed right into Cyrus's face. *At this range, he won't miss. He'll plant it in my head and kill me, or near enough to it as not to matter.* "But you had to be the big man, had to go and build Sanctuary up … and why? So you could just tear it down with your own idiocy later?" Orion's eyes danced where they peeked through the metal slits in his helm.

"You're going to do this right here?" Cyrus asked, looking around him. He could see the faint shape of a cloak above him, just out of his vision. *Where Imina was standing.* "Right in the markets of Reikonos?"

"Haven't you heard?" Orion asked with an obvious glee. "There's been a declaration made by the Leagues. You're officially a heretic. We can kill you right here, and not only will we not be punished, we'll get rewarded for it."

"So do it already and stop leering at me like a bunch of smitten schoolgirls," Cyrus said through gritted teeth. *So it finally happened. I'd almost tricked myself into believing that they weren't going to do it.*

"Oh," said the last figure above him, "but that would be too easy." The rasping, high voice was entirely familiar and entirely expected.

Malpravus.

The skeletal dark elf stepped into Cyrus's line of sight, just above where he lay, and looked down at him. Because of the way he stood, he appeared upside down to Cyrus, like a bat hanging above him with a leering grin.

A bat with a lock of Imina's hair hanging out the front of his cowl.

"I hate to say it, dear boy, but you are too valuable to be allowed to go to waste." He reached up and pulled the lock of Imina's hair out from his cowl and let it fall onto Cyrus, who caught it reflexively. "Such a shame that you are so very foolish sometimes, lad. Charging headlong into danger for your friends, for your allies, and even for a past lover … It makes you tragically predictable."

"And it's about to make you tragically dead," Ermoc said with a smug satisfaction.

"There's one thing you seem to have forgotten, Malpravus," Cyrus said, looking up at the enemies arrayed around him. He could see others creeping in at the edges of his vision, clearly part of Malpravus's ambush—a dark elven woman in sharp armor with spikes that marked her a dark knight, some elven soldiers in full regalia, even a few city guards of Reikonos—all waiting, watching, no doubt ready to deliver news of his demise to countless interested parties. Cyrus flicked his gaze to the bony necromancer, who stirred within his robes.

"And what is that?" Malpravus asked, watching him through slitted eyes. *He expects treachery because he is treacherous. It's all he is. It's all he's ever known.*

"I'm a heretic," Cyrus said, forcing a cold smile out upon his lips. The only satisfaction he was going to have today was spoiling Malpravus's mood. He looked one last time at Ermoc, who held

Praelior tight in his fingers. *There's no way I can get it back now, and if I stay, I will die.* He looked back to the necromancer, who had already begun to react as Cyrus mouthed the words, *"Arn-schee, raun-noang, laav-vule!"*

"Stop him!" Malpravus shouted, but it was too late. Blades and spells descended upon Cyrus as the magic of the return spell he had cast consumed him, carrying him back to Sanctuary before their attacks, safe—but without his sword.

5.

"What were you thinking?" Vara asked, the fires roaring on the torches and in the hearth, spreading their warmth around the Council Chambers of Sanctuary. A grim quiet lay over the room, the round table not filled, conspicuous gaps between the occupied seats. An ever-so-faint smoky smell wafted in the air, something familiar and homey, though at present, Cyrus did not feel much at home. The crackle of his wife's voice was faster and sharper than the blade he'd just been forced to leave behind.

Cyrus felt a hard pang of regret in his stomach as he recalled Praelior once more, the squeak of the soft, worn leather on its hilt. "I was thinking … someone needed my help, which, I faintly recall, is something that we render when asked here in Sanctuary." He did not feel compelled to elaborate, having fully explained the entirety of the note's origin to the Council once already.

An awkward silence hung over the room. Vara seethed beside him, now sitting in the Elder's seat previously occupied by Curatio, her appointment to the post still fresh, done less than a month ago. Her blue eyes glistened like the frost on the Reikonos streets. There was a danger there, a wrath he could not recall seeing from her since the day they'd been wed.

"Perhaps we should leave aside Cyrus's error in judgment for a later time." J'anda Aimant spoke softly into the silence. His aged face looked particularly wrinkled in the flickering firelight, and his eyes were tilted down as he spoke. "Say, for your bedchambers when the two of you are alone, and the rest of us need not suffer through watching a very unpleasant marital argument and hopefully, after that, a more pleasant marital making-up."

"They could just do that here," Erith Frostmoor said from across the table. "It might add an element of entertainment to otherwise very bad news." There was a hint of mischief in her eyes as she drew looks from everyone in the room. "Come on. With all the departures, partners of one's own and delights of the eyes are getting harder to come by."

"I cannot even muster the words to describe how much I vote 'nay' on that idea," Vaste said, his head down. "As if adding troll applicants were not enough asininity for one day …"

"How many of them were there?" Ryin Ayend asked, looking slightly sick to his stomach. The human seemed more than a little discomfited by the heresy pronouncement.

"How many … what?" Cyrus asked, looking at the druid. "How many members of Goliath? I counted Malpravus, Orion, Carrack, Ermoc … then there was Archenous Derregnault of Amarath's Raiders," he tried not to look at Vara, but he could see her bristling out of the corner of his eye, "plus some Reikonos guards and what looked like members of the elven army, all waiting around to watch the show."

"I thought Rhane Ermoc was persona non grata in Reikonos," Samwen Longwell said, his ruddy face twisted in concentration. "Didn't he betray them by opening the gate on the dark elves during the war?"

"All of Goliath was an enemy of Reikonos," Cyrus said. "They led the invasion of the city. But it would appear that they've decided to put aside their differences in order to murder me."

"It's a shame about your sword," Mendicant the goblin said, his voice low. "And of course about the heresy pronouncement as well, and the attempt to kill you," he added the last two quickly, as though he'd forgotten them at first.

Cyrus waited for further comment then realized with a start, not for the first time, that every single one of the remaining officers of Sanctuary had just spoken. Even after all this time, the emptiness of the room jolted him every time he thought about it. "Somehow I doubt it'll be their last attempt."

"No, this is almost certainly just the opening gambit," J'anda said, sounding very drawn. "Now the enemies will circle, since the pronouncement has been made. So many it almost defies the counting."

"Goliath, Amarath's Raiders, the Leagues," Ryin Ayend said in a glum voice, "The Human Confederation, the Elven Kingdom …" He blinked. "I … think that's it."

"Don't forget the God of War!" Vaste added cheerily. "You know, I think it might be quicker just to list the people who *aren't* our enemies at this point."

"The gnomes, the dwarves, the goblins," J'anda started, "the dark elves, the Luukessians, the elves of Amti, the trolls and possibly the dragons."

"Heresy makes us enemies of the gnomes, the dwarves, and possibly the dark elves," Vara said quietly.

"No," Cyrus said, "Terian won't join in." He looked around, and there was a pause.

"THE SCOURGE," Vaste announced definitively, slamming a hand down on the table and drawing every eye to him as he broke the silence. "Sorry. The mood was lightening entirely too much. I thought I almost felt a glimmer of hope, and I needed to quash it."

"Well done," Vara said acidly.

"We need to talk to our allies," Cyrus said, feeling more than a little worn. "This is the moment we've been waiting for months and months. It's time to—"

A knock at the door silenced him, quieting the Council Chambers, and Cyrus paused, exchanging a brief glance with Vara, the crackling of the fire the only sound. "Come in," Vara called to the door, loud enough to be heard through it.

The door rolled slowly open, wide enough to admit the tumbling brown hair of Calene Raverle, the human leader of the Sanctuary rangers. Her eyes darting nervously about the chamber. "Uhh, sirs … madams … err …"

"What is it, Calene?" Cyrus asked, leaning forward and brushing his helm, which lay upon the table, a black shadow in the darkened chamber.

"There's a messenger," she replied, her glance still flitting from one member of the Council to the next. Vaste extended a hand straight up and waved at her floridly. A perplexed look spread across her face, but she returned his wave with much more reserve. "They've come from Reikonos …" She looked right at Cyrus. "They say they've come to accept your surrender."

6.

"I hope you told that ponderous idiot it'll be a frosty day in Reikonos before they'll be seeing our madman of a Guildmaster surrender to their tender mercies!" Vaste said, his voice loud and tinged with bitter amusement.

The Council Chambers were quiet save for the troll's ringing voice. Cyrus was the first to speak after that. "I'm sorry, did you say ... my surrender?" he asked, leaning forward in his chair as if to speed up the haste with which Calene might answer him.

"Yours only, in fact," Calene said, nodding. She pointed with a thumb over her shoulder. "I've got the messenger under guard two floors down on the staircase if you want to hear from her. Menlos and a detail are watching her."

Cyrus's brow furrowed. "I ..." He looked around the Council Chambers. "We do, don't we?"

"Why?" Vara asked, sounding severely put out. "So they can make empty threats?"

"With the combined forces of Goliath and Amarath's Raiders on their side—not so empty, I think," J'anda said. "To say nothing of the remnants of the human and elven armies."

"Yes, we need to hear this," Cyrus said, ignoring the scathing look from Vara next to him. "Bring her up, Calene."

"Certainly I want to hear them," Mendicant said with a nod, then turned to Cyrus. "But ... if this person wanted to attack you in the manner of those who just ambushed you—"

"Then she'll die with a lance in her guts and my boot in her face," Longwell said, seizing his lance and standing up, his armor clanking as he moved to stand by the door.

34

"And I'll also commit horrible violence, et cetera," Vara said, her voice layered with icy fury. "I think we can handle them, unless they're so physically imposing we have some cause to worry."

"It's a woman," Calene said, "shorter than me. Surprisingly bold for being in a den of heretics, I think, though. She's got a real fire burning within."

"Well, send her up before she gutters out or Menlos starts to deploy his charms," Vaste said. "Otherwise she'll jump right down the middle of the staircase, and we'll never get all the mess out from between the stones at the bottom."

Calene nodded and left, not bothering to shut the door behind her. Longwell snapped shut his visor and waited, standing silent sentry behind the door.

Cyrus barely seemed to have time to look at Vara, whose cheeks were burning scarlet, before the door opened wide to the chambers and in walked a woman. At first glance, she seemed to be barely half Cyrus's own height, though she was probably taller than that. She had the figure of a child and was all but lost in her oversized red robes. Runes on her vestments marked her as a wizard, and the look on her small face was wary anger, barely contained. Her eyes darted around the Council Chamber, taking silent stock of everyone seated within.

"My name is Cyrus Davidon," he started to say to introduce himself.

"I know who you are, heretic," she said, one step above a hiss.

"She's got charm, like Menlos," Vaste said. "I like her already."

The wizard glanced at Vaste and made a face of obvious disgust. "My name is Agora Friedlander. I am a messenger from the Leagues of Arkaria."

"And what is your message?" Cyrus asked quietly, the events of the day settling like a pall upon his bones and suppressing any instinct for action.

"I am sent to inform you, Cyrus Davidon, heretic, son of Quinneria Davidon, the sorceress and heretic—"

"Whoa," Vaste said, standing up immediately, sending his chair skidding back with a clatter. "Stop right there—!"

A silence lasting no more than a second fell over the Council Chambers before everyone exploded into reaction at once.

Damn, Cyrus thought, catching Vara's worried look at him. They had not told the Council the secret of Cyrus's parentage yet. *That cat just burst every seam of the bag to reveal itself a lion.*

Ryin Ayend's voice came first, choked, "Your mother was the Sorceress?"

Mendicant's voice came almost immediately thereafter, but awed. "Your mother was the Sorceress?"

"What the hell, Cyrus?" was Erith's reply, her jaw almost hanging to the table. "Did you know?"

"This explains why you hated trolls so much!" Vaste said, his eyes wide and focused on Cyrus, the pupils as big as a human hand, "your damned mother was the original slayer of our kind—"

"ENOUGH!" Vara called, her voice crackling over the table and silencing all. Wary eyes were aimed at Cyrus from Erith and Ryin, respectful ones from Mendicant. J'anda had his head down, fingers steepled to cover his mouth. Cyrus did not even care to speculate at the enchanter's reaction to the news. "This is not the time to have this discussion," Vara finished. "We have a guest."

"You knew, too?" Vaste asked, voice cracking with betrayal. "Of course you did. Of course you knew. You look utterly unsurprised."

"We have a League messenger in our midst," Vara reminded them loudly.

"Well, the Leagues should know," Longwell pronounced, startling Agora Friedlander into jumping; apparently the messenger had not noticed the dragoon lurking three paces behind her when she'd entered the room. "I don't give a bloody damn if Cyrus's mother was Mortus and his father was Yartraak." He thumped the end of his lance against the ground. "You come for us, you best bring an army and a load of shovels, because you're going to be digging a lot of graves for your own dead."

"The Leagues don't want to come for any of you," Agora Friedlander pronounced through puckered lips. "None of you are heretics. He's the one who's used magics unlawfully—"

"He wasn't supposed to be able to use magics at all," Vara said, leaning forward, voice arch. "That's the line the Leagues have fed us, in any case. That magic is the province only of those properly trained. So … how does the fact that a warrior can use magic fit with League doctrine?"

"Because he's the child of a heretic, obviously," Agora said, a cool glint in her eyes. "He was taught fundamentals improperly at an early age, the building blocks necessary for him to use spellcraft later in life. She paid for her crimes with her life—"

"I used a spell inadvertently when I was being attacked by the Avatar of the God of War," Cyrus said, staring at the messenger who met his gaze without fear.

"And you used a return spell in the markets of Reikonos just hours ago," Agora said, a small smile of triumph on her face. "The thing about you heretics … you don't stop once you've had a taste of your wickedness."

"By your League standards, Cyrus should have been trained by your people," Vara said, still combative, settling in for the long argument; Cyrus knew that look well.

"But of course he wasn't," Agora said, as though it were the most obvious thing in the world. "No fool would train a child of a heretic in magic. He's fortunate he wasn't put to death as a precaution."

"I was six," Cyrus said quietly. "And your Leagues did try to put me to death. They cast me out from the Blood Families in the Society of Arms. That was as good as a death sentence. I dodged the executioner's axe only because it was clumsy."

"Well, your days of dodging have run out," Agora said, expression stiff. "If you surrender now and come back with me to face judgment for your crimes—"

"She means 'death,'" Vara said, with a cold fury.

Agora Friedlander looked right at Vara, smiling as though it were obvious. "But of course I mean death. This man is a heretic. There is no other punishment for that most odious crime. He has twisted the laws of nature, laws put in place to protect us, the people, from unnatural perversions of magical spellcraft. Imagine a field of warriors casting fire. Imagine the destruction they could wreak in a city. There is a very good reason why not everyone has magic. It is the province of the well-disciplined, the carefully trained, the—"

"The elite," Vaste said quietly, staring straight at the hearth.

Agora looked at him with a pinched look upon her face as though she couldn't quite believe he was speaking. "Precisely," she finally agreed. "It is for good reason that we keep these things under law, under control. It is regrettable that this particular sore was allowed to fester, but the time has come for the boil to be lanced, the pus to be removed—"

"That particular pustule is my husband," Vara said. Cyrus gave her a look and she shrugged in half-apology.

"If he surrenders now and admits to his guilt," Agora said, back to prim and proper, the disgusted look put away for now, "he will be granted a painless death administered by a skilled alchemist via a toxin that will put him into a deep sleep from which he will never awaken. No action will be taken against Sanctuary or its allies."

"Look at you," Mendicant said, his low voice rattling, "so smooth with the offer of the carrot."

"Now let me present you with the offer of the sword," Agora said, her voice gaining the steel of a threat. "If he refuses, the word will spread to every corner of Arkaria of his heresy. Every member of Sanctuary will be excommunicated from the Leagues. That is permanent. They will never be able to join another guild, and they will be unwelcome in every League city, which is a rather considerable number. The Human Confederation, the Elven Kingdom, the Dwarven Alliance, the Gnomish Dominions—all of them will turn their backs on your members, refusing them entry into their borders, and you will be hounded everywhere you go, driven out like the renegade scum you will be … all for harboring this man." She nodded at Cyrus, the look of purest hatred returned to her face.

"That sounds oh-so-familiar," Vaste said, still staring at the hearth. "Didn't you people do that to us once before?"

"This time it will be worse," Agora said. "A decree of heresy will follow into every land. You will not be welcome anywhere outside this guildhall, and soon enough, even these walls will be closed in upon by the forces allied against you." She stared right at Cyrus. "You know of whom I speak."

"I know of whom you speak," Cyrus agreed quietly.

"Give yourself over now," Agora said, "and the question, the agony … it will all be over so very quickly. This is promised."

"Promised by whom?" Vara asked.

"Pretnam Urides himself," Agora said. "He guarantees it."

"Of course Pretnam Urides would send a mere child into danger rather than coming himself," Vara said contemptuously.

"I am not afraid of you," Agora said, holding her head high. "If you kill me, he will get his answer, and I will die for the cause."

"You really are a true believer," Cyrus said wearily, looking at the table. *The entire guild will suffer for my sins. Or …*

Or I could just suffer for my sins and be done with it.

"This is on me," Cyrus said, and started to stand, pushing his seat back carefully. "I acc—"

"You are a duly recorded witness for the Leagues, yes?" Ryin Ayend asked Agora, still staring at the table. "Your word is binding? You speak for them? Witness for them?"

"Yes," Agora said. "I do. And that is why you may be certain that when I make this offer, I speak the truth. It will be recorded. It is guaranteed."

Ryin looked up, and there was an anger in his eyes. "Witness this, then."

He raised his hand, and a force blast gently blew Agora Friedlander onto her backside.

Agora gasped sharply upon the floor as Ryin stood to look down at her. "You—that was a paladin spell and you're a druid—"

"My name is Ryin Ayend and I stand with the Guildmaster of Sanctuary." Ryin unwound the druid vestment from his shoulders and tossed it into her face. "The Leagues are liars and have lied all along, for as long as they've existed. I would not trust your word if you were to promise me that the sky was blue and the season was winter." He extended a hand to point at Cyrus. "You may have this man over my dead bloody body, for I, too, am a heretic, and you may tell your League masters that it is so."

Mendicant jumped upon the table, tearing off his own wizard vestment and tossing it at the feet of Agora Friedlander. He ran a claw over his finger and drew green blood, then his fingers glowed with the light of healing and the wound sealed itself. "If you want a heretic, we will give you heretics."

J'anda stood, clutching his stave, and tossed his own vestment at Agora Friedlander. "I will spare you the display, but you may be assured that if you come for me … you will see a fire spell that will destroy enough of your number to affirm your fear of heresy from now until the end of your days—which I predict will be soon, should you persist in this course."

Erith rose slowly and removed the vestment on her shoulders. "What they said." She tossed it at Agora, who still sat upon the hard stone.

"You face a guild of heretics now," Vaste said, rising to his full height. He reached under his robes, fishing for something as Cyrus watched him, stunned. The troll pulled out a most curious implement that gleamed with the sheen of quartal, freshly mined and smithed, a pointed spear head some foot long with an empty space in its center, as if it were to be attached to something else. As Cyrus watched, the troll lowered his staff with its crystal tip and screwed the attachment upon it, the crystal sitting in the small gap in the middle of the metal, turning his staff into a deadly spear. "No need to pretend anymore, then. If you come at us, we will come at you with everything we have ... and it will be considerably more than what you're allowed, should you hew to your fancy rules." He clunked the staff down and looked like a proper fighter with his spear. "So ... come after this man, and you come for us all. Deliver that message to your cowardly leader who doesn't have the balls to come tell us himself. And take this with you." He tossed his vestments at her like the rest.

"I will tell him what you have said," Agora Friedlander said, her nostrils flaring in fury. "I will tell him what you have become. And you should know ... it will change nothing. We will not stop."

"Neither will we," Vara said, rising from her place at the table. "We have killed gods." She smiled in cold satisfaction. "You idiots couldn't even win your own wars without us. Consider carefully what you do now."

Agora Friedlander's expression of rage disappeared in the twinkle of her return spell, and Cyrus sagged against the table, putting his hand to his face. "That was foolish. Utterly foolish, all of you."

"You're welcome," Vaste said. When Cyrus looked at him, the troll shrugged, dipping the point of his new spear. "This is Sanctuary. Doing utterly foolish things is our specialty."

"That and loyalty," J'anda said, giving Vaste a pitying look.

"Yes, and that," Vaste agreed. "We combined the two, see."

"You've committed us to war," Cyrus said, looking around the table, seeing the last hope of peace evaporate. He honed in on Ryin. "You, of all people ... why?"

"Because they've lied all along," Ryin said, looking up from his spot at the table where he had returned to staring. "I don't believe for a moment they would've offered you a painless death, or that they would have been content with only you. Trust a liar once, and it's their disgrace if they break faith. Trust them again, and it becomes your folly." He straightened up. "I don't mean to be a fool again. They've lied about the nature of magic, they've lied about who can use it, and they would come for us with all they have, sooner or later, because knowing what we know makes us a threat to everything they've established."

"So it's war," Cyrus said, his voice nearly cracking. "Again."

"Sometimes you have to fight," Ryin said, and there was a series of nods around the table. "And this … is most certainly one of those times."

7.

Cyrus and Vara ascended the stairs to the Tower of the Guildmaster in utter silence after the meeting of the Council broke. Cyrus stole careful glances at his wife. He could feel the storm brewing between them. *It's to be hard wind and lashing rains tonight, I suspect,* he thought as he climbed the last few steps and followed her through the door to their quarters.

He expected an explosion when he shut the door; when it did not come, he looked up the stairs to see Vara's retreating back, her silvery armor disappearing at the top of the steps. He followed with some hesitation, listening to her boots strike against the stone floors with a steady cadence as she walked toward the wooden dummy that held her armor when she wasn't wearing it.

Cyrus slowly came up the stairs and looked after her. Vara was shedding her armor now, the breastplate and backplate already unfastened. They clanged against the ground with a hard rattle, and she undid her greaves and vambraces next, the chainmail beneath them rattling as she moved, undoing the latch points.

Cyrus eased up the stairs into the tower. The doors were closed on all four balconies, battened down for the season to keep the chill out. *So it's to be silence before the storm breaks, then.* One of the balcony doors rattled forebodingly in the wind; Vara did not look up from what she was doing even to spare it a glance.

"Are you going to bed?" Cyrus asked, wondering if she would answer him.

She inclined her head slightly, though she did not look back at him. "It's barely evening. Why would I go to bed at this hour?"

"I don't know," Cyrus said, stepping up to the level of the tower floor. "I don't ... know what you're thinking."

"Have you considered asking?" She sounded a little stiff. "It's not difficult, though it takes a small amount of courtesy and consideration for your spouse. Something simple, such as, 'My darling, light of my very life, wife who speaks to my heart itself—what are you planning to do with your evening?'"

"That's a little effusive, isn't it?" Cyrus asked.

"Oh, well," Vara said, still concentrating on her armor, "I find it's generally wise to lay it on a bit thick when you've been monumentally stupid. It helps salve any wounded feelings that might be present in the situation, you see."

"Do you have wounded feelings?" Cyrus did not move closer, waiting to see. He could feel the tension ratcheting up in her voice the longer she spoke.

"Do I have wounded … hah … hah!" Her laugh was low and dangerous, devoid of actual humor. "I think you know the answer to that question."

"I'm sorry," Cyrus said, and after she did not react for a moment, standing still and quiet, he went on. "I'm sorry I lost Praelior—"

"That—bloody—sword—" She rounded on him and threw the vambrace in her hand carelessly as she did. It whizzed past his head and smashed into a painting of a landscape that had hung between two of the balconies since before he'd taken the quarters over from Alaric. "You think I give a damn about you losing your sword?"

"Apparently not," Cyrus said, flinching a little at the wrath that gleamed from her slitted eyes. "So … it's the fact that I went to Reikonos to—"

"It's the fact that you nearly *died* in Reikonos," Vara cut him off, steaming like an old kettle, "and you didn't tell anyone—not me, not Vaste, not the guard, not any—bloody—one—" she tore her last bracer off her wrist and hurled it through the air to the side. It crashed into the paned window in one of the balcony doors. The sound of breaking glass was muffled by the curtain that covered it. "You could have been killed because you walked into stupid trap without any help. And you could have had help. In spite of those trolls, you could have had help. You could have had *my* help." Her lips twisted in pain. "But you didn't want *my* help."

"Forgive me for not informing my current wife when I got an urgent request for assistance from the last Mrs. Davidon," Cyrus said, looking away. "I thought it would be—"

"Well, you thought stupidly in this case," Vara said, "through and through. Do you think I give a damn?" He looked at her and saw the well of hurt and disappointment on her face. "Do you think I would have—what? Been jealous? I don't bloody care. You're not married to her; you're married to me. Keep up a regular correspondence with her for all the damns I give. But don't use me—my non-existent potential jealousy—as an excuse to keep you from sensible action in these times." She looked more thoroughly insulted than he could ever recall seeing her. "If you didn't want to take me because you felt uncomfortable, there were any number of others who would have gladly gone with you—Longwell, Scuddar, Ryin, Calene, J'anda—any number. Hell, Terian would have come from Saekaj with a retinue of soldiers just to meet the former Mrs. Davidon." Her voice dropped and the hurt sounded more evident. "You nearly died, Cyrus. You nearly died because of raw foolishness of the exact sort I used to excoriate you for regularly. I never saw it from you then like I saw it from you today. That was simply stupid. There is no other word for it."

"This is why you shouldn't throw that imprecation around all willy-nilly," Cyrus said, feeling that perhaps the worst had passed. She watched him with careful eyes, waiting for him to finish. "Because when I actually do something deeply stupid, you don't have anything left to deliver. The well of insults is dry."

"Yes, well, I'll work on my reserve after you practice dragging your head from your hindparts," she said sharply. "I'm only glad that no permanent damage was done. It could easily have been otherwise."

"I think damage was done," Cyrus said softly. When she looked up at him, he elaborated. "Imina. Malpravus … he was covered in a cloak like hers, wearing what looked like a lock of her hair. The letter they trapped me with … it was written in her hand."

Vara's eyes fell. "Do you … think he killed her?"

"I don't know," Cyrus said, scooping his helm from his head and holding it in his gauntlet for reassurance. He squeezed it, and neither it nor his gauntlet yielded. "Malpravus and his allies—" he saw a flash of danger in Vara's eyes and knew she was thinking of Archenous Derregnault, "they're not bound by conscience. If they'd received the messenger we did tonight, they would have sent her back without her skin."

"You don't need to tell me about the treachery of Archenous Derregnault," Vara said, speaking the name with loathing, "nor of Goliath. I remember well the many times they tried to fit us for a coffin, to maneuver us into unfavorable circumstances for their own profit. That they've now apparently allied and are moving openly against us, along with a sizable portion of the rest of Arkaria ..." She pursed her lips. "It is cause for great concern. And caution," she added vehemently with a pointed look at him. Her voice softened. "What are you going to do about ... her? Imina."

"There's nothing I can do," Cyrus said. "Every member of Sanctuary is about to be excommunicated by the Leagues; I suppose I could try and hire some outside party to look for her." He thought about it for a moment. "Terian might have someone we could have look into it. But ... there are other problems." He felt himself quiver thinking about the worst of them. "The big one ..." Cyrus said, feeling reticent to even bring it up; it seemed the least of the worries they'd discussed, "... is the sword."

"Yes," she said, shrinking slightly, as though the air were leaving her. "It is a loss, admittedly. A great one."

"A warrior of Bellarum never relinquishes his weapon willingly," Cyrus said, intoning the old saying by force of habit.

"Oh for the sake of ..." Vara rolled her eyes. "One would think that after being nearly killed by said god, and—as you just pointed out—presumably you were supposed to be murdered by the very Society that taught you to parrot some of those ridiculously phrases. You could worry less about your time-honored traditions and dispense with the warrior-ethos guilt."

"Without my sword I'm just another warrior," Cyrus said. "A man in armor."

"A man in quartal armor," Vara said, her face returning to the acerbic look that she wore when delivering a good barb. "But you are also my husband, and, lest you forget, obnoxious and rather pompous."

Cyrus frowned. "You think I'd remember I'm your husband but forget that I'm obnoxious and pompous?"

"Well, of course," she said, showing a glimpse of that mischievous look he'd seen in her earlier in the day. "It is hard to forget me and easy to overlook your own gaping flaws."

"With you about, it's not easy to forget either. I tend to receive constant reminders of both."

She looked mildly affronted. "I think I've been rather good about not emphasizing either, at least until now, when gods know you need a good reminder, Cyrus Davidon." She padded over to him and stood looking up at him in his full armor. It felt dark to him somehow, like the usual blackness of it had become looming shadow, representative of his new role in Sanctuary. *I am the darkness within this place, the curse upon it.* "I know you were going to give yourself over to them—Urides, Goliath, the Leagues."

"It was the sensible thing to do," Cyrus whispered.

She ran a hand over his cheek, the faint stubble rising up on his skin rough against her fingertips. "You've never taken the sensible course. You've always pushed the world in the direction you wanted, not accepting what was handed to you. Don't be afflicted with being sensible now. Not now. To cave to expectation at this moment ... it's the worst possible time."

"I never thought I'd hear you suggest that I should be more unreasonable," Cyrus said with a faint smile that cracked through the darkness enshrouding him.

"Just this once, I think," she said and tugged him down to kiss her. There was reassurance there, in the arms of his wife, and she held him like that for some time, though not nearly long enough to assuage his worries.

8.

Cyrus stood in the throne room of the Sovereign of Saekaj, waiting patiently before the empty wooden thrones that sat at the end of a lush red carpet. Samwen Longwell, Calene Raverle, Vaste and Mendicant stood with him, the occasional cough in the darkness or the shuffling of the goblin's claws the only things to break the silence. They had had a long ride down from the surface after a short walk from the nearest portal. Cyrus had looked out upon a bustling city built into the underground caves of Saekaj and seen beauty in the darkness as his carriage carried him rattling along to the palace.

"How long do you think he's going to keep us waiting?" Longwell asked under his breath.

"He rules a nation now," Cyrus said, feeling the curious absence of Praelior at his side. The scabbard sat upon his belt, but he'd selected a sturdy steel blade as a replacement from the armory, which was still in disarray after the death of Belkan. The blade rattled loosely in Avenger's Rest, the scabbard on his belt, and he was resolved to find the new blade a better holder. *I need to find Rhane Ermoc and get Praelior back*, he thought with a touch of glumness. *Though I doubt he's going to be waiting around for me to come back for it.* "Terian has responsibilities."

"The Sovereign is a busy man," came a woman's voice out of the darkness. Cyrus tensed; the only woman he could think of who might be working as Terian's aide was the one who'd saved him from the wrath of elven king several months back. *But that's not Aisling's voice*, he thought. *It's too ... low, breathy ...*

A woman came striding out of the dark, wearing a blue-green dress. Her hair was dyed to match, its sea green complementing her blue skin tone surprisingly well. She wore a look of amusement as she surveyed the Sanctuary party, her eyes honing in especially on Cyrus's. They were piercing, clearly trying to get the measure of him. "So ..." she said softly, "you're Cyrus Davidon." She paused beside the thrones, cocking her head as she studied him. "I thought you'd be taller."

"I'm ... one of the tallest humans you'll ever meet," Cyrus said, face screwed up in surprise. Her reaction to his height was a not a common one.

She waved him away. "I know, I know, but still ... I thought you'd be taller after all the tales I've heard about you."

"And here I've heard nothing about you ...?" Cyrus said, slightly nonplussed by her candor.

"Oh, Terian hasn't told you about me?" She placed a hand on her blue cleavage, well displayed, and

Cyrus had the impression she wasn't above using her attributes as a distraction.

"Ah," Cyrus said, nodding. "You're his wife."

She nodded, a coy smile perched on her lips. "My name is Kahlee Lepos."

"Does that make you the Sovereigness of Saekaj Sovar?" Mendicant asked.

Kahlee Lepos's smile turned wry. "No."

A door banged open at the far end of the chamber, causing Cyrus to turn his back on Mrs. Lepos abruptly. The Sovereign of Saekaj Sovar himself came storming down the carpet, his axe in his hand, moving with a startling alacrity.

That's how I used to look when I held Praelior, Cyrus thought with a sudden surge of regret that felt like a hole had opened up in his chest. *Dammit.*

"Cyrus," Terian said, slowing his pace as he came closer, slinging the axe over his shoulder and drifting back to human speed. The Sovereign wore the battered metal armor of the Ghost of Sanctuary. He took off the helm and carried it under his arm, approaching Cyrus at a normal pace now, his pointed nose standing out in the middle of his face, undisguised relief writ across it. He placed a hand on Cyrus's shoulder, reaching up to do so. "I'm glad to see you survived the Goliath ambush."

"Not just Goliath," Cyrus said, feeling stiff in his own armor.

"I heard," Terian said, letting his hand drift back down and pacing toward his throne, stopping before he got there. His wife threaded between the gorgeous wooden seats and came up to stand behind her husband. He glanced back at her movement. "Have you met my lady wife?"

"Briefly," Cyrus began.

"I know all your names," Kahlee said with that same coy smile. "No need to delay your meeting for introductions."

"Everyone knows my name," Vaste said, nodding sagely. "Apparently it's not often you meet a troll with such stunning good looks and excellent wit."

"It's very true, Vaste," Kahlee replied impishly, "most of them struggle with even forming basic sentences in the human language."

Vaste sighed. "Oh, you married well," he said to Terian.

Terian smirked, then shifted his attention back to Cyrus, the gloom of the throne room hanging over them as the Sovereign's smile faded. "I heard that squirt of wet feces Rhane Ermoc got Praelior." He did not glance at Cyrus's scabbard for confirmation. *He doesn't even question it; he already knows.*

"He did," Cyrus said, feeling a very taut sensation bubbling back up inside. "I'm sure he's dancing a merry jig right now at his triumph."

"Well, I do hope you're ready to feed that triumph back to him," Terian said, "blade-first, of course."

Cyrus started to speak, but held onto his first thought and sighed. "I would," he said when he spoke, "but this was not a simple attack that merits quick revenge. This was a plotted assassination attempt against me that was followed by a declaration of—"

"Heresy," Terian said, nodding. "I got the notice yesterday after you were ambushed. They wanted me to turn against you, can you believe it? It's as though they haven't been paying attention this last year when we allied against Danay with Emerald Fields." He broke into a smile. "Naturally, I sent their missive back with one of my own."

"What did you say?" Vaste asked.

"I didn't *say* anything," Terian replied. "I did, however, wipe my arse on a piece of parchment after a particularly wretched bowel movement and had it sealed with wax, writing, 'For the Eyes of Pretnam Urides Only' upon the envelope. I do hope he followed the instructions to the letter."

"You are the soul of regal comportment, my husband," Kahlee said.

"Oh, come on," Terian said, still grinning, "these are the moments that make being Sovereign worth the headaches of trying to get this nation to run." He looked at Cyrus. "Like I said before, in the Jungle of Vidara, I'm with you. What do you need from us?"

"Nothing at present," Cyrus said, though he heard Longwell harrumph and tap his lance against the floor of the throne room. "We have enough forces to guard our walls—"

"You have very little in the way of forces left, to my understanding," Terian said. "Cyrus … with the Luukessians helping my army garrison Emerald Fields against the elven threat, you have less than two thousand members of Sanctuary left at the guildhall. And you're going to lose some of them now that the pronouncement has been made."

"You know my numbers better than I do," Cyrus said, feeling the sting of that as well.

"I don't take the departures as personally as you do," Terian said gently. "Though I can't imagine it's been easy watching thousands and thousands stream out your doors this last year."

"Not easy at all, no," Cyrus said, straightening up. "But that's irrelevant. We can garrison Sanctuary itself with less than five hundred, and you know it. The Luukessians would be more than glad to send additional help should we need it—"

"As would we," Kahlee said, apparently pre-empting her husband.

"He already knew that, wife," Terian said.

"When someone is embattled, husband, it's good form to offer support, because the encouragement is needed most when clearly absent from all other sources," she said.

"This is a peculiar marriage," Calene said in a quiet whisper.

"You said it," Terian agreed. "In any case … yes, Cyrus, we would willingly reinforce the Sanctuary guildhall if it comes to that. Say the word, I'll send my best. The civilian council that runs things with me here has already given their approval to aid you as our ally, so … whatever you need."

"Thank you, Terian," Cyrus said, looking away from the paladin's gaze. "I should have known you'd—your loyalty is much appreciated in this hour."

"Forget all that maudlin sentimentality," Terian said. "When are you going after these bastards?"

Cyrus looked up to find the Sovereign regarding him carefully.

"Terian, Goliath and Amarath's Raiders are the vanguard of our enemies at the moment. The Human Confederation and the Elven Kingdom are both standing clearly, if not quite as enthusiastically, behind them, with their immense—compared to ours—armies. And as you just pointed out ... we have about two thousand guild members, if you don't count the Luukessians, and I don't—"

"Ahem," Longwell said behind him.

"—because of their primary commitment to their new homeland at the moment," Cyrus said, casting a look over his shoulder at the dragoon. "With the tension between them and the elves right now, that force is going to have to stay in place for the time being. Those troops are useless to us. Even if King Danay didn't want to involve himself in this little conflict brewing, his mere existence means that we've got a hand tied behind our back. The Luukessians are pinned in place."

"So unpin them," Terian said, a glint in his eyes.

"Perhaps you're not listening," Cyrus said, feeling as though the Sovereign might have missed a step. "Leaving aside the elves for a moment—Goliath is against us. Amarath's Raiders is against us. Two guilds which competed with Sanctuary in size before we lost half our number in the last two years. The Human Confederation sits in their shadow—"

Terian yawned. "And behind them, presumably, in lessening orders of enthusiasm for making war upon you and Sanctuary are the dwarves and the gnomes. I'm aware of the political state of Arkaria most acutely, my friend. I spend most days considering it for endless hours, thanks to my advisors and their incessant desire to chatter about such things. Here's what I also know—the Human Confederation has roughly one hundred thousand troops under muster at the moment, the Elven Kingdom roughly fifty thousand—"

"Like a herd of naked dwarves bursting out of your quarters unannounced, I personally find that worrisome," Vaste said.

"Does ... does that happen to you often?" Calene asked.

"They already have us outnumbered some fifteen to one, even if we counted the Luukessians," Cyrus said, ignoring Vaste.

"Goliath also has some twenty thousand or more, though it's hard to count because they're housing most of their forces in the Bandit Lands," Terian went on, as if reading from a list, "and Amarath's Raiders has a company of some five thousand, a much higher than usual mix of spellcasters mingled in there, possibly as many as a thousand of their number."

"So it's one hundred and seventy five thousand to ten thousand," Vaste said. "Oh, good. That hope I was feeling at your proclamation of support got quashed all by itself."

"It's not that bad," Terian said, "we've got about twenty thousand troops at our command in the Sovereignty, though admittedly many are very young or very old. The war went a little hard on us, after all—"

"Thirty thousand to—" Vaste stopped. "You know, I'm just going to say six-to-one."

"Easy odds," Terian said with a grin. "If you wanted to fight them straight up … though I wouldn't exactly recommend it."

Cyrus's head felt as though it were spinning. "Then what do you recommend? Because all I'm hearing now is talk of armies and comparisons with staggering numbers of troops at a level I can't even conceive of battling against."

"Cyrus," Terian said in disappointment, "you took ten thousand charging Luukessians against a hundred thousand dark elves at the Battle of Sanctuary, and you wiped them out utterly."

"We caught them with their backs to us on a charge," Cyrus said. "It wasn't a fair fight—"

Terian clapped his gauntlets together. "Exactly!"

"You're suggesting we start an unfair fight?" Calene Raverle asked in utter bewilderment. "Oy, between the herds of roving naked dwarves and all the war and defeat, I feel a bit dizzy …"

"You'll get used to it," Vaste said.

"Damned right I'm saying you should start an unfair fight," Terian said. "We set the terms of these engagements and knock them back in pitched battles where they don't even realize they're battles until they're counting their dead with regret."

"I don't think Malpravus feels regret over the dead," Vaste said. "More like fond longing. Glee, even."

"Aren't you a paladin now?" Cyrus asked Terian, feeling once more as though he'd been turned in a circle quite rapidly.

"Paladins protect other people; it's our highest law. Aren't you facing enemies that set a trap for you using your former wife's signature and then stole your sword right off your belt while your back was turned?" Terian asked, now serious. "These people are treacherous dogs and you're *not* a paladin. You're a man who's surrounded by his enemies and is about to be run through on all sides. If you want to try and fight them fair without Praelior, you *can* do that." He shook his head. "But I wouldn't bet on your survival, and neither would anyone else. You need to be the General again, the one who valued his army's lives so much he never got in a fight unless he had six tricks up his sleeve."

"Assuming I—" Cyrus quit his question right in the middle of it, running his gauntleted fingers over his forehead and coming back with their tips moist. "I don't know how I would even approach this, assuming I bought into your conceit about an unfair fight."

"How would you have approached it when you were in the Society?" Terian asked, once more looking especially sly. "This is a fight for survival, Cyrus. They started it. They've wanted you dead all along, now they've just snapped it to highest priority. They will come at you with everything, and it's not just you—it's your guild, it's the people you care about, it's your allies—they're going to come at us, in any part of Arkaria where the Leagues hold sway. You can meet them in honest battle if you want. I know you tried the more deceitful tack with the titans and didn't like the taste of treachery, but these bastards are going to do their best to crush you, and they're not going to do it cleanly or politely or honorably."

"Yeah, but I learned from my mistake with the titans not to buy into unfounded assumptions," Cyrus said. "Like believing that they were going to teleport into the north when they couldn't."

"Do you believe Goliath is *not* going to come for you?" Terian asked, arms folded. "Because I think they'll siege the Sanctuary guildhall the moment they believe they could win. They'll pull the wall down brick by brick, or blow it open with Dragon's Breath, and they'll come in and slaughter everyone, then set up their headquarters there. It's what Malpravus has wanted all along; he didn't even need an excuse to do it before, but now he's got one, and Sanctuary is weaker than it has been since Enterra." Terian took a step closer and looked up at Cyrus. "You'd better get ready. You'd better prepare to do the ugly things. You're not a paladin; you're a warrior and a heretic, and they're going to come at you like you're one. They will beat you any way they can, and they won't care about the high-minded ideals of Alaric Garaunt, even if you do."

"Doesn't that mean I should care more about them?" Cyrus asked quietly.

"Your tribe is growing smaller by the minute," Terian said. "When it's all done washing out, Sanctuary is going to have less than a thousand members. You will be strained. They will attack us—all of us—in ways we can't predict."

"The sidewinders," Vaste muttered under his breath.

"This is the last stand against Goliath," Terian said. "It's going to be you or them this time."

"Make it you," Kahlee said quietly. "I hate Malpravus. You, I like—though I think you should be—"

"Taller, yes, I get it," Cyrus said.

"I was going to say meaner," Kahlee said, smiling at him.

"If you follow their lead," Terian said, stepping right up to Cyrus, "if you wait for them to move before you counter, you will lose. Their attacks will be merciless, their treachery unfathomable. Malpravus ... he knows no law but power, and he will do anything, say anything, to anyone, in order to get what he wants."

"If I sink to that level ... I'll be as bad as he is," Cyrus said. "Do you not recall? I led an expedition that started a war with the dragons in order to smear the titans—"

"*Smite* the titans," Terian corrected. "They ended up pretty damned smited. I'd take that as the lesson."

"We lost—"

"You will lose more," Terian said. "Get ready for it. This is war. You can no longer try and merely be the Guildmaster of Sanctuary, Cyrus. Alaric never attempted to be both, and for good reason. You need to be the General again." The lines on his face softened. "I'm sorry, my friend. I truly am. I wish this weren't so. I wish that all in Arkaria were good and virtuous people, seeking nothing but to live in peace." His gaze hardened again. "But they aren't, and you need to make a decision. Give it some thought. Mull it all over. Talk to Vara about it. These people ... they want to destroy you because they couldn't control you, and now your very existence threatens their control over everything else. They won't let you live, and they won't hesitate to wipe out anyone standing near you for fear that if they let even one live, they'll never be able to regain that control again."

9.

"Where is your lady wife this fine day?" Administrator Cattrine Tiernan asked Cyrus as they walked through the woods near Emerald Fields. There was a rustling sound between the branches, and a flock of birds broke loose from a large oak to their left. Cyrus could see his guard within fifty paces of him, but he and the Administrator were speaking in whispers so as not to be heard.

"She sends her regrets," Cyrus said, "but she's staying at Sanctuary to oversee the defense. We're … running a bit thin on help at the moment."

"Yes, Terian told me," Cattrine said, causing Cyrus to miss a step.

"Terian told you?" Cyrus hurried to catch up, avoiding the natural ups and downs of the wooded path. "You two have regular meetings?"

"As good allies and most favorite trading partners should, yes?" Cattrine frowned slightly.

"Sorry," Cyrus said, shaking his head, "I just had a recollection of the times in Luukessia when you and Terian did not, er, see eye to eye."

"A trip across the seas and a change of responsibilities for each of us has had a wonderful leveling effect on our perspectives," Cattrine said. "Also, he's considerably less of an arse now."

"Indeed," Cyrus said, walking along beside her. "And what does our present predicament look like from your current perspective?"

"Altogether grim," Cattrine said quietly. "At least, on your side. You stand in the midst of all your enemies once more. It is becoming something of a pattern with you."

"I'd love to be standing elsewhere, I assure you."

"Yet you're not," Cattrine said, glancing at his scabbard as the new sword rattled within it at a hard step. "I have heard of your history with

Goliath, and I know of Vara's past with this Archenous Derregnault—"

"You know an awful lot."

"It pays to know much when one's country is so little," Cattrine said, not turning back to look at him. "You would be wise to do the same."

Cyrus felt a stiffness in his chest. "It's not the first time someone has suggested I employ more spies and listeners. I doubt it'll be the last."

"In statecraft, honor is not assured," Cattrine said. "We must deal with loathsome people."

"Like Terian?" Cyrus asked with a smirk.

"Terian is by far the least loathsome of the leaders of the major powers," Cattrine said with a shudder. "Paying tribute to King Danay over these last years has convinced me more than ever that I must never let myself become more than an administrator bound by the wishes of the people. And your Human Confederation—"

"They did pronounce me heretic and cast me out, so I don't think they're really *mine* anymore."

"—and its Council of Twelve, a messy, prideful batch of oligarchs supping on the veins of what was until recently the most powerful nation in Arkaria?" Cattrine shuddered in disgust. "I'm thankful I don't have to deal with them and can go directly to the Confederation territorial governors. At least the dwarves, gnomes, and goblins are more reasonable. Ancestors, even the trolls have more honor."

Cyrus raised an eyebrow. "You deal with the trolls?"

"I deal with anyone who has coin or trade," Cattrine said with a slight smile. "In case you missed it, in the last two years Emerald Fields has risen up to become nearly its own nation, for we are supplying the foods that half Arkaria eats."

"That was fast," Cyrus said, cocking his head as he looked at her admiringly. "But it couldn't happen to a more worthy people."

"Well, we're hardly out of it yet," Cattrine said, clasping her hands together behind her back. "After what the titans did to us last year, we're still building and rebuilding the settlements, but at least our crops are in place. Our prosperity grows, and the armies we have are enough to make good a fight if our putative 'allies' in Pharesia decided to bring one." She looked sharply at him. "We are in far better condition than you at present."

"Everyone keeps pointing that out to me," Cyrus said darkly, "as though I don't already know."

Cattrine stepped closer, her expression guarded. "I can never tell what you know and what you ignore anymore. You built a small nation and a massive army in the Plains of Perdamun, winning title to that place from all powers ... and yet you never treated it like a nation, and now it is fast becoming a no man's land."

"I had ... other concerns on my mind in the last year and more," Cyrus said, laughing bitterly. "The titans, for one."

"I am aware," Cattrine said seriously. "But ... it is incumbent upon you to lead now, and to do the things that leaders do. Even the unpleasant ones," she added with a little bit of a point to her words.

"Did you and Terian discuss what path Sanctuary should take in all this?" Cyrus asked, getting the distinct feeling that he was behind the curve once more. Birds tweeted overhead while he awaited Cattrine's answer.

"We did," she said. "But ultimately, the Sovereign of Saekaj Sovar and I can discuss your course all day and it matters little." She leaned closer, her gaze intense. "We could both counsel war against these adversaries, but you will be the one who has to take up the burden, for you know my state is watching its own borders and Terian's greatest focus is on his. You are the vulnerable one in this, the one who'd need to lead and put himself out front. You are a bold and brave warrior, Cyrus, and you have won many ugly battles against fierce foes, but now you face the whole land turned against you in a way you haven't before, and it comes when your strength is ebbing." She looked away to where a sparrow sang in a nearby tree. "I cannot decide for you to fight this. In fact, I heard your first instinct was to surrender to it, and that does not exactly instill confidence in me or your followers."

"I was trying to spare them—" Cyrus let out a low breath and lowered his head. "Do you know what a heresy charge brings in its wake?"

"I've heard," she said. "It sounds most disagreeable." She snapped her green eyes onto his as she brushed her long brown hair back over her shoulders. "But you are being corralled by most corrupt forces. Two guilds which can only be described as evil, and two nations whose leadership is ... well, let us say, unpleasantly divided."

Cyrus frowned. "What are you talking about?"

"Statecraft," Cattrine said with a sigh, turning away from him. She began to walk off but held up a hand to stop him from following. "I have matters to attend to, Cyrus. You need to decide, and quickly, if your misadventures in the south and your ambush by Bellarum have stolen all the fight from you. For you have a long and dangerous one on your hands, and while we in Emerald Fields are most certainly your allies …" she stopped and turned, looking somehow taller than he could ever recall seeing her before, so different from the woman in the muddied dress he had met years earlier when she came to him to bargain from a position of weakness, "… but we are not fools, and I will not lead my nation into war with a General who has lost all heart for the fight." She gave him a small smile and then walked off purposefully to rule her country.

10.

"That all sounds a bit dismal," Vara said after listening to Cyrus's description of the day's events. They sat on a couch in the corner of the Tower of the Guildmaster, the balcony doors open and a light, chilly breeze blowing in. He'd found Vara on the walls at his return, watching the empty horizon for signs of trouble. A cold, sunny sky had lingered overhead until the last hour, when it had begun to sink over the horizon, the mountains to the south visible out the far doors, the snow-capped peaks turning purple.

"Cattrine spoke to me as if I'd lost all heart for battle," Cyrus said, still stinging from his former lover's rebuke. *From anyone else, it might not have carried the same weight. From her, it felt like a slap, a judgment, a pox on my damned soul.* Vara did not stir, but her face bore a look of great discomfort. "You feel it, too," Cyrus said after a moment's breath.

"You are not perhaps as ... ornery as you once were when it comes to battle, no," Vara said. "I sense no lack of courage on your part to plunge into danger. More a lack of willingness to send your armies into the fight."

"We have lost so many friends, Vara," Cyrus said. "I have sent people to their deaths in more fights than I can count, and the cost has been dear. And for the last few years, we've been taking increasingly harder hits. Narstron, Niamh, Alaric—though he may still be alive, I concede—your mother, Nyad, Odellan, Cass, Belkan, Thad ... Andren ..." He said the last one hollowly. "We've seen good people die in corners of Arkaria where they didn't need to."

"I hear the list of names you speak, but I can't shake my feeling that this is all down to your defeat at Leaugarden, isn't it?" Vara asked quietly.

"It's down to death, everywhere," Cyrus said. "I chose the path of battle, and so did our guildmates ... but it doesn't make it any easier when they die and I live. Until now, at least I had the luxury of knowing I had a sword that helped even the odds in these fights. With Praelior, victory, if not assured, was certainly more likely."

"You are more than a sword, Cyrus," Vara said. "You were always more than a sword. You defeated the Dragonlord without Praelior and led us into Purgatory without the damned sword—and with fewer numbers than any of the Big Three boasted at the time."

"Of course, later we found out Alaric and Curatio could beat the Trials all on their own," Cyrus said bitterly. "And they're both gone now." He cut her off before she could interrupt in protest. "I'm not ... angry or upset or bitter about them leaving. It's just ... Arkaria is changing. Sanctuary is changing. We've lost ground. Everything we worked so hard to build is ..."

"Crumbling," she said, nodding. "I know. I've felt this before, you know, when Archenous stabbed me in the back and left me to die in the Trials, after murdering my guildmaster and stealing *my* damned sword." Cyrus pictured the blade that Derregnault had thrust in his face, the patterns of runes on the blades. "I know what it's like to lose that which you have poured your life into, to feel it slipping like sands between your fingers as you watch in horror, unable to do anything to staunch the flow. If not from that, then seeing Termina invaded and destroyed most certainly awoke me to that sense of loss." She inched closer to him on the couch, her armor squealing as it caught on a pad, tearing it. "Damn these things."

"I know you know," Cyrus said. "And you are right about Leaugarden. I may have lost friends elsewhere, to assassins, to goblins, to the Scourge, to the dark elves, to the dragons, but Leaugarden ... that was the place where Malpravus smashed me as a General. It's a lingering wound. In the Society they taught me not to flinch from the pain, to guard against the fear that came after the blow, because the fear would paralyze you, keep you from fighting against the next and the one after. I've been flinching for over a year. Not in the battle itself, but before it. It was a humbling moment in a way that being pushed back by the Scourge or having to retreat from the bridge in Termina wasn't." He shook his head. "They were an unstoppable force of nature, those ... things in Luukessia. But at Leaugarden ... all I faced was Malpravus and Yartraak, and they …"

"They showed you the lengths they would go to in order to win," Vara said, her head down. "The same lengths our enemies would go to now, incidentally. Sending that dark elven trollop to your bed to spy on you and murder you at their command—that is perhaps the level of viciousness we can expect now." She pulled off her gauntlet and placed a slightly moist hand upon his face. "Are you ready for that?"

"Is there any way to be ready for that?" Cyrus asked with a wan smile. "Terian counsels war against insane odds, suggesting I simply go back to being a tricky general, and Cattrine brings up the same point as you. She fears my willingness to fight this fight, fears that leading her nation into war with me wavering would be foolish. And I don't blame her. I can't see a path to victory from where I stand." His admission rang in the empty air of the tower as the door to the nearest balcony creaked in the night. The sun was down, and now darkness swept into the room, the torches having lit on their own some time ago. "How am I supposed to lead these people when I have no idea what to do? When my only inkling of a plan is to line them all up and charge into impossible battle?" Her hand rested on his face. "What do I even do, Vara? Other than despair, which seems to be costing me more than it is worth in this moment?" She stared into his eyes with her bright blue ones. "I don't know how to win this fight. And I don't know how to even fight it with what we have left."

"Then perhaps it's time to count on your friends," came a voice from near the balcony. Cyrus leapt to his feet, as did Vara, both their swords drawn instantly. A cold tingle of fear broke over Cyrus's skin as his new blade, still foreign to him, rattled in his grasp.

Terian stepped out from behind the balcony door, Alaric's helm clutched beneath one arm, and the Battle Axe of Darkness in his other hand. "Sorry. Didn't mean to interrupt all this grim despair, but we need to talk."

"We talked earlier," Cyrus said, feeling himself relax only an inch at the sight of Terian. His eyes fell to the axe, and the cold chill on his skin did not subside. *With that in hand, and me with this sword … he could massacre us.*

Terian's gaze followed Cyrus's and a flicker of amusement danced across his lips. "I know what you're thinking, but I didn't come here to kill you, dumbass. I'm here to help you." He tossed the axe deftly toward Cyrus, who caught it, fumblingly, with his free hand.

"As did we all," Cattrine said, stepping out from behind the door with Terian, a spell of invisibility casting her in a faded light. Cyrus could see her, ghostly clear, as she lingered next to Terian.

"Who said that?" Vara asked, sweeping her gaze piercingly toward the source of the voice. She murmured a spell under her breath to give her sight past illusion, and then she made a faint grumbling sound. "Oh, it's you."

"Sorry," Cattrine said, the veil of invisibility still shading her. "I can't remove a spell once it has been cast upon me. But ... we need to talk."

"I talked with both of you not but a few hours ago," Cyrus said, clutching the axe in his hand.

"We talked in public," Terian corrected him. "We said things, mouthed platitudes meant to be circulated in rumors that would make their way back to listening ears outside our own nations. Now ... now we need to have a real conversation. Eye to eye, with no outside listeners."

Vara looked at him with practiced disdain of the sort that Cyrus had become very familiar with in his first years of knowing her. "And what do we need to talk about now, in secret, under the cloak of darkness— and how did you sneak into the tower?"

"Falcon's Essence," Terian said with a grin.

"Should have been stripped when you crossed the wall," Vara said suspiciously.

"It was," Terian agreed. "Which is why Bowe recast it before we climbed to the top of the tower, we three."

"How did you get through our guards at the wall?" Cyrus asked with suspicion of his own.

"Your defense is porous," Terian said. "I own the loyalty of several of your guildmates on duty right now." He held up a hand to stifle the outrage that started to pour from both Cyrus and Vara. "Trust me ... this is good."

"It's good that you have spies in our midst?" Vara beat Cyrus to the nasty accusation. "We're your allies."

"Yes," Terian said, nodding, "which is why I've got them watching Sanctuary, trying to find out who within these walls is loyal to other parties."

"This is low, even for you, Terian," Cyrus said.

"This is not the way of the white knight," Vara said.

"I wasn't always a white knight," Terian said grimly, "and I'm not *just* a white knight now—I'm the Sovereign of Saekaj and Sovar—"

"I suppose that absolves you of any need for honor or decency," Vara said, but her voice held little of her usual dagger-point anger. She was more resigned, as though this were somehow expected. "In spite of your new armor and class, you have retained a surprising amount of your old self."

"And you'll be very thankful for that soon, I predict," Terian said, glancing sidelong at Cattrine. "Because I hate to break this to you sensitive souls, but a paladin isn't going to walk out of this ambush you've stumbled into. You're going to need more."

"Which is why you're here to talk?" Cyrus asked.

"Exactly," Cattrine said. "This is why we're having a discussion out of sight. So we can address the things that cannot be talked about where anyone might hear them. So we might talk about how to win this battle."

"Well, you've gone to all the trouble of sneaking up here," Cyrus said, now feeling even wearier than before. "We might as well hear you out."

"I hoped you'd say that," Terian said, smiling tightly. "And I hope you don't mind that we've brought a third, someone uniquely positioned to help us in this matter."

"Your druid? Bowe?" Cyrus asked, starting to move back to the couch to seat himself. "If you trust him, I suppose I do."

"I'm glad to hear you say that," Terian said, and a thin smile spread across his lips. "But it's not Bowe. He's back at the wall."

Cyrus froze, about to take a seat. Vara, next to him, had cocked her head in curiosity.

"Come out," Terian said to someone hiding behind the balcony door, and Cyrus felt a shudder run through him, as though he knew what was coming before it did.

She stepped out into the moonlight, her hair washed out even paler than when last he'd seen it, the ghostly aura surrounding her somehow even more faded than that of an invisibility spell. She shimmered in the darkness as she came around Terian, a little tentatively, her hand clutched on the blade of a dagger at her belt.

Cyrus's eyes narrowed as she halted between the Sovereign of Saekaj and the Administrator of the Emerald Fields. She looked straight at him with those purple eyes, faded to a faint violet under the power of her weapon's ability to cloak its user, and felt his jaw lock as his teeth clenched.

"Oh, you," Vara said with utter disdain. She cast a look at Cyrus, her eyes afire. "Give me that bloody axe, I'm going to—"

"Please don't," Aisling Nightwind said, and she pulled her dagger out of its scabbard and tossed it lightly at Vara, who caught it and stared at her, fury still contorting the elven paladin's features. Aisling stood with hands raised, now solid under the moonlight, washed out, her navy skin paler than he remembered it being under this same light.

"And why should I not?" Vara asked, clutching the dagger, her own skin rippling as she disappeared under the blade's power, fading into a shadowy version of his wife, her golden hair turned white under its spell.

"Because I'm at your mercy," Aisling said, casting a glance to Terian, who nodded in a reassuring way. "Because I mean you no harm … and," she said, licking her lips, a faint trace of fear crackling her voice, making it unsteady, "… because I'm here to help you."

11.

"The problems are simple," Terian said, pacing back and forth, Alaric's old armor squeaking faintly with each step as he made his way across the Tower of the Guildmaster, "we have foes we cannot easily best in a direct fight—"

"And so you bring the Duchess of Treachery to advise us," Vara said, still clutching Aisling's dagger in her hand. Her knuckles practically glowed beneath the shade of the spell the blade cast to turn her invisible to the eye. "You ask us to trust she who once plunged a knife into my husband's back after spying on him for the God of Darkness from within his very bed."

"Perhaps coming here was a mistake," Aisling said. She was leaning against the narrow stone wall between the balcony doors, which were now sealed shut against the elements and other intruders. "They don't want my help, Terian."

"Whether they want it or not is irrelevant; they need it desperately," Terian said, halting his pacing and giving Vara a hard look. "Yes, she slept with Cyrus. Yes, she spied on him. Yes, she stuck a blade in his back and helped cause the most horrifying defeat Sanctuary ever suffered on a battlefield. I was there, I saw it, I partook in it." He drew himself up to his full height, which was somewhere around Vara's own, and yet he looked considerably more commanding now. *It's an effect much like what I saw with Cattrine earlier—these people I've known are becoming more than they were before.* "And frankly, that's the kind of treachery you're facing now, so you might want someone skilled in it on your side." He pressed his lips tightly together and some of the navy bled out of them, leaving them an almost cerulean shade. "Gods know you're not in a position where you can afford to be choosy with your allies."

"Thus far," Cattrine said, stepping up, her own expression guarded, her face shrouded in some of the shadow offered by the torchlight, "you have led Sanctuary nobly and bravely, but you have demonstrated an utter lack of guile when it comes to statecraft. Even your maneuver against the titans, using the dragons as your pawn, was so lacking in secrecy that any other power in Arkaria would have seen through it. The dragons, being insular, failed to detect it and acted accordingly against the titans. Here ..." she cast a sideways look at Terian, who nodded, "... you will find no such advantage."

"Sanctuary has spies within its walls," Aisling pronounced. "Many. More than you could imagine. More than just me."

"Yes, and some of them are traitors who work for the Sovereign of Saekaj," Vara said acidly, looking right at Terian.

"Those 'traitors' will help keep you safe," Terian said darkly. "Others—and there's no telling how many—most assuredly will not."

"If you know we have traitors," Cyrus said, still clutching Terian's axe from his place on the couch, "give me their names." He lifted the haft high. "We'll go forth and have a merry time of lining them up and removing their heads."

"I don't know who the traitors are," Terian said. "I know who *I* own in Sanctuary. And I have spies elsewhere, remnants of a network put together by my predecessor and expanded by me. Some of the people who betray don't even know they betray you. They rumor, they gossip ... innocent activities, but the whispers circulate and fall into the wrong ears, the ones who are intending treachery, and so the word spreads to spymasters across Arkaria." He sighed as he looked at Vara and Cyrus. "Goliath and Amarath's Raiders have spies. Endeavor and Burnt Offerings have spies. The Human Confederation and the Elven Kingdom—"

"Have spies, yes, I get it," Cyrus said, looking sidelong at his bride. The tightness on her face hinted at a steely discomfort. "Is that true?" Her gaze flicked to him. "Does Amarath's Raiders have spies?"

"Of course," Vara said. "Almost all guilds do. How do you suppose that Isabelle knew so much about Sanctuary when first we met?"

"Yet we don't," Cyrus mused quietly, looking at the stone floors of his quarters.

"That was Alaric's doing," Terian said.

"And so you think we should do away with that anachronistic

honorable behavior?" Vara asked sharply.

"Alaric didn't have formal spies," Terian said with a ghostly smile, "but he certainly had ears all over the place. Sanctuary never had a need for formal spies because between Curatio and Alaric's considerable sources, the friends they had all across Arkaria, they were apprised of most threats without a need to become excessively deceitful. You two, being unable to go insubstantial at a moment's notice or having the benefit of ages of sowing the seeds of friendship or using the power of heretical magics—well, incredibly strong heretic magics, sorry, Cyrus—are somewhat lacking in the area of covertly gathering knowledge." He stood stiffly. "Also ... Alaric trusted people, perhaps too much. That is one of the reasons your house is replete with spies."

"Wonderful," Cyrus said, leaning his head back. "Everyone has spies watching us, and we have none. They are well versed; we are ignorant. You're laying out a compelling case for formation of a network of some sort, and yet I feel perhaps the time for that might have passed some time ago, as the gold we have to spread around for such work is running thinner every day—"

"I'm not expecting you to come out four-square in favor of everything I'm telling you right now," Terian said, "I'm merely letting you know that in this place, in this way, you are blind."

"Blindness," Cattrine said, adding her own dagger to Cyrus's heart, "is not an advisable state."

"I ask again," Vara looked at each of the three of the intruders in turn, "what are your suggestions, then? To put ourselves in this harlot's capable and well-traveled hands? This is what you bring us in our hour of dire need?"

Terian looked reassuringly at Aisling and nodded. "This is what I bring you. The most capable assassin in Arkaria."

"Wait," Cyrus said, coming to his feet, "you mean—"

"Calm yourself," Aisling said, looking perhaps as glum as he'd ever seen her, "that's not the only reason I'm here."

"I don't see how we can assassinate our way out of this conundrum," Vara said after a moment, seemingly less bothered by the possibility of assassination than she had been to Aisling's involvement minutes earlier. Cyrus cast a scandalized look at his wife. "Nor am I saying that we should," she added once she saw his look.

"You say that because you don't see Arkaria the way she does,"

Terian said, inclining his head toward Aisling.

"That's correct," Vara said, "I see it on my feet, she sees it on her back, or bent over a strong table, perhaps—"

"You don't see Arkaria," Terian said, ignoring the jibe. Aisling, for her part, merely rolled her eyes. "You see a homogenous whole—a Confederation of humans, a Kingdom of elves, large armies ready to march against you. You see an impassible wall."

"On my feet, yes," Vara agreed. "I suppose on my back I would see the night sky—"

"You would see the divisions in the Confederation," Aisling hissed. "You would see the resentments in the Riverlands, in the Northlands, in the Southern Reaches, and the Western District for having to bear the cost of a war begun by the Council of Twelve to expand their territory, a war which left those territories stripped of troops and in the case of the Riverlands and the Reaches, invaded. You would hear the griping in the public houses and in the fields about how Pretnam Urides and his Twelve are the head of the Confederation in Reikonos and treat everyone outside of it like the rump." Her expression of irritable contempt settled into a frown. "Also, I suspect you spend a great deal more time on your back or bent over a table than me these days."

"With my husband, yes," Vara snapped back.

"Funnily enough, when I did it, it was with your husband, too—"

"Not helpful," Cyrus said, then looked to Terian, who wore a small smile. "What are you suggesting here?"

"Vara," Terian said, looking right at her, "how does the kingdom feel about Danay after the last war?"

She blinked at him, cheeks red, still steaming. "I don't live in the kingdom, how would I know?"

"You're the Lady of Nalikh'akur," Terian said. "You are the authority of the northernmost province. You don't have an assemblage of other Lords and Ladies of the Kingdom once per year?"

"I have not gone in the past several years," Vara said. "Anyway, I don't imagine I'm going to be Lady of Nalikh'akur much longer, as I'm surely about to be declared heretic on my own merits shortly."

"You are the shelas'akur," Cattrine said, interjecting, threading her way in a circular path past Terian. "The nominal governor of a province, at least in name." *She's putting on a show here*, Cyrus thought, *warming us up for something*. "How many other provinces are there?"

"Many," Vara said, shaking her head. "Why—"

"How do you think the Lord of Termina views King Danay at this moment?" Terian asked.

Vara's brow furrowed into deep lines. "How should I bloody know what Oliaryn Iraid thinks of the King? I only know the man in passing, and I haven't seen him in years."

"You should stop into Termina and pay your respects," Cattrine said, smiling. "He'd welcome a visit from you."

Vara narrowed her eyes at Cattrine. "Know that, do you?"

"I do," Cattrine said, eyes glittering in the torchlight with something beyond amusement. "As two of the most economically liberal parts of the Elven Kingdom, we have frequent discussions about trade … and other matters. The Lady Voryn of the Emerald Coast has also been a frequent attendee of our conferences of late, as well representatives of the poor, begotten protectorate of Amti—"

"My gods," Cyrus said, burying his face in his hands, "you're fomenting rebellion within the Kingdom."

"You're damned right we are," Terian said, burning with self-righteousness. "You saw what Danay tried to do last year, to you, when his heir died on your expedition. You know what he did to Odellan after Termina—"

"Gods damn you for bringing up either one of them," Cyrus said weakly, casting aside his gauntlet and rubbing at his own face. The stubble on his cheeks felt rough, like cactus quills sprouting from his skin, a perfect representation of how prickly he felt right now. *Cornered like a porcupine, all I want to do is spike everyone in sight.* He glanced sidelong at Vara, who looked stricken but listened intently.

"This is not a time for delicacy," Terian said with rising fury, "because they are not going to be delicate with us. Danay would have smashed the Emerald Fields last year because you led his daughter willingly into a battle where she got killed. This is a man who is about to put the bulk of his broken kingdom, which he has jeopardized for years by ignoring threats at his very gates, into direct opposition against you. He is capricious and cruel, and I have no qualms about bringing him low." He drew himself up, a shadowed knight in paladin armor. "Do you?"

"I …" Cyrus looked to Vara, who returned his gaze, stricken. "I …"

A knock sounded at the door, thundering and loud, echoing

through the tower. Everyone froze, Terian with a look upon his face that seemed as trapped as Cyrus's had been a moment earlier. "No one can know we're here," Terian hissed.

"Why not?" Vara asked, eyes darting back to Cattrine and Aisling, who were moving to hide themselves in the toileting room built into one of the Tower's walls.

"Because you're thick with spies," Terian said under his breath, moving to join the other two. "Just … keep it quiet."

"Fine," Cyrus said, tossing back the Battle Axe of Darkness. He noted as he made for the stairs that Vara did not return Aisling's dagger, that she merely swept it behind her back, and that a look of utter antagonism was exchanged between the two of them before Aisling disappeared behind the door.

"Who is it?" Cyrus called, coming down the steps tentatively, as though Goliath assassins were lurking behind the door, waiting to smash it in and kill them both the moment he answered.

The pounding came once again, even more insistent this time, and Cyrus looked up at Vara, who stared back with her eyebrows knitted low. He watched her reposition the dagger held behind her, readying it for use. She followed behind him, invisible to the naked eye, shadowing his movements, ready to attack any would-be attacker.

"Who's there?" Cyrus called once more and waited for an answer. None came, and with a last glance at Vara, who nodded, he was decided. With utmost caution, he reached for the knob, clicked open the lock, and began to slowly open the door.

12.

"Hihi!" Vaste chirped, his green face grinning at Cyrus from the crack opened in the door. "Can we come in?"

Cyrus blanched, the still quiet of the Tower of the Guildmaster hanging above him like a blade, reminding him of what he was hiding above. "I ... no. You can't."

"Why ever not?" Vaste asked, teeth bared in an enormous grin.

Cyrus glanced furtively back at Vara, who was still invisible behind Aisling's dagger's effect, and she gave him a look of great significance. "Because we're ... having sex right now." Vara let her head fall back, rolling her eyes.

"That's not really a no," Vaste said, still lurking behind the door.

Cyrus pressed against the barely open door. "What, are you Erith now?"

"Hardly," Vaste said and shoved once against the door, knocking it open to reveal J'anda standing beside him. The enchanter carried his staff, with its glowing purple orb, and Vaste held his newly improved spear his hand. Vaste nodded at Vara. "You're wearing a surprising number of layers to be having sex," Vaste said, shoving gracefully past Cyrus and squeezing past Vara with little difficulty, avoiding her well enough that Cyrus knew he could see her clearly. "Also, I doubt you would bring the dagger of your husband's former lover to bed, no matter how randy you both got." He glanced over his shoulder at Vara, who looked alarmed. "You're not thinking clearly. You're invisible but you're hiding the dagger behind your back. Pointless since no one can see you."

"I can see you," J'anda said, still formally waiting outside the door. He bowed. "Do you mind if I come in, now that Vaste has made

71

himself welcome in your abode?"

"Sure, why not?" Cyrus asked, a tense feeling pooling down his throat and into his belly. J'anda nodded politely as he came inside and Cyrus closed the door behind him.

"Aisling's dagger casts a lovely light upon you," J'anda said, nodding at Vara, who pulled the blade from behind her back and stared at it in frustration. "But then, my dear, you always look good, no matter the light."

"I don't know what you think you're doing here—" Cyrus began.

"We're interrupting your meeting with Terian, Cattrine Tiernan, and Aisling," Vaste said from the top of the stairs. "Terian! You old dog! Come out of the toilet!"

Terian appeared as Cyrus and Vara climbed the stairs with J'anda a few steps ahead of them. Cyrus exchanged a look with his wife, and her discomfort was obvious. "It's all right," Terian reassured them as he emerged, axe slung behind him and his helm under his arms, "these two probably aren't traitors."

"'Probably'?" J'anda asked, plainly affronted.

"Why, I never," Vaste said, nodding to Cattrine and Aisling as they came out of the bathroom behind Terian, a little more reticently than the Sovereign of Saekaj had.

"How did you know we were up here?" Terian asked, a look of wary resignation on his face.

"I was just lying in my bed, dreaming of warm, fresh-baked pie," Vaste said, "when suddenly the spirits around me began to whisper so excitedly that they woke me up. And oh, the tales they told—of how several of Cyrus's lovers, past and present, were currently having a grand meeting in the tower. At first, I thought, *Orgy, best stay away*, but then they mentioned Terian, and I realized that there probably wasn't any harm in at least looking in on things—"

"Very nice," Terian said, lips puckered in amusement. "How much did these spirits tell you?"

"You are forming a shadow council," J'anda said, looking very formal still, leaning upon his staff. "You're going to deal with the dangers we face in a way that we don't traditionally deal with them."

Cyrus felt a pang of guilt. "I hadn't decided yet. I was just listening to—"

"I think you had better decide," J'anda said, cutting him off. "I think you had better agree."

"You, too, J'anda?" Vara asked quietly.

"This may sound peculiar," J'anda said, "but I have no illusions about the type of people we are dealing with. Our armies are insufficient to the task, so other means must be found, unless you wish us to surrender to the coming death." He brandished his staff before him. "Why would you think that I, of all people, would have some objection to employing trickery? It is my mushrooms and suet, as we say in Saekaj and Sovar, my very reason for being."

"And you?" Cyrus asked, looking at Vaste. "I can't remember a stauncher critic against what we tried to do to draw the dragons into war last year. Why would you even consider this? I mean, it's going to be … potentially so much worse."

"Your great bugbear last year was the titans," Vaste said. "They made you blind because you knew what creatures of the God of War could do. For you, it was personal and it blinded you to all other considerations." He sniffed the air and looked at Terian. "For me … the enemy that produces that same effect is Goliath."

"Hear, hear," Terian said quietly in agreement.

"I would do almost anything to rid myself of those jackals," Vaste said, his onyx eyes flashing in the torchlight. "You feared the grand assault of those monstrosities in the south. I fear the silent, whispering steps of those assassins among our old allies. They are liars and cheats, and as I told you once before, they do not come cleanly at you once they've decided to kill you. It's a dagger in the back, a drowning in the night. They've got two of the largest powers in Arkaria already on their side and one of the Big Three guilds." Vaste's face tightened. "In this case, I'm utterly fine with giving Malpravus a bitter dose of his own hemlock. To me, that would feel like justice."

"Still," Cyrus said, looking at the few of them lined up around his quarters—Vaste hugging his spear-staff close; J'anda, leaning on his; Cattrine holding her thin hands one over top of the other; Aisling lurking near the western balcony door as though she wished she could disappear into its curtains; Terian, regal and observant, and finally—

Vara.

Cyrus's wife stood in stoic silence, staring straight ahead into one of the torches on the wall. "What are you thinking?" he asked her, jarring her out of her reverie.

"I think the man who once asked me to marry him, the one who stole my sword, cursed me, killed all my friends and left me for dead has joined with declared enemies against us," Vara said, her eyes shifting, becoming calculated and cunning. "For all these years I have denied myself revenge, thinking … thinking it a foolish pastime, thinking myself a better person for swearing it off. But here he comes again, once more trying to take *everything* from me …" Her voice went low, harsh, and the emotion poured out; for the first time Cyrus realized how much his being ambushed in Reikonos had affected her. "There are weaknesses in the Elven Kingdom," Vara said, nodding once, her decision plainly made. "Cracks that can be made larger. Rifts that we can exploit to either push them into dissension or cause Danay to topple entirely. Either way, they will be … off our list of adversaries for a time." Her face twitched with rage.

"I don't know about this," Cyrus whispered, almost to himself. "The Sanctuary Council—"

"Cyrus," Terian said, shaking his head. "Your Council is compromised. Remember when Goliath turned Arkaria against us years ago? Malpravus had someone on the inside then."

"I don't believe it," Cyrus said, shaking his head. "He could be spying on us with the dead, like Vaste just did."

"Mmmm, no," Vaste said. When Cyrus looked to him for elaboration, the troll merely shook his head. "Trust me. The dead in this place are not on speaking terms with Malpravus."

"Consider this," Aisling said, breaking her long silence at last. "It may not even be an actual council member. One of them may have taken a lover, for example, and simply have a loose tongue in the bed." It took Cyrus a moment to realize that the strange sound he heard was Vara grinding her teeth. Aisling watched her for a moment in mild alarm before continuing. "In the world of information gathering, this is an ancient practice."

"To scheme in this way is dangerous," Cattrine said, returning to the conversation once more. "The people of power in these governments would undoubtedly love to know what we're planning here now, which is why it is imperative that it be kept secret. Even if all goes well, no one in Arkaria outside these walls may ever even know what we have done here. Not only because of reputation, but because the legitimacy of the outcome in some of these cases … well, the secret must be kept." She looked at Vara. "Surely you agree?"

"I agree that whoring is an ancient practice, yes," Vara said, her jaw still in a tight line, her eyes locked on Aisling. "And … yes, if we have a leaking Council … perhaps putting this before them would not be the wisest course if our plan relies on our enemies not knowing what is coming."

"Try and imagine displacing King Danay or Pretnam Urides if they had full awareness we were plotting to do so," Terian said. "They would counter immediately. They are not stupid. They are surely cognizant of the more restless elements within their own houses, but they probably don't see those factions descending to the levels we'd like to drag them to."

"So what do we do, then?" Cyrus asked, frowning. "Stand back and … play dead?"

"We plan," Terian said.

"We scheme," Cattrine agreed.

"We put things in motion," Aisling said. "Toppling these men, these enemies … it's not going to be easy. You'll need to assemble coalitions of the willing against them, make deals at the very top of the power structures of Arkaria. It will take time, and it needs to be done in utter secret or it will fail."

"We just declared war on the Leagues," Cyrus said, shaking his head.

"And you should be seen huddling down," Terian said. "We all should, because we're outnumbered. They know we're outnumbered. They know we know."

"I know almost nothing," Vaste said cheerfully.

"Indeed," Vara said.

"I set that up so perfectly for you," Vaste grumped.

"They know Cyrus Davidon as a man whose first instinct is battle," Terian said. "You've been hit. You're reeling. You need to play into that, but not look so weak that they come at you right away. We need time. Hiding behind the walls provides it." He darted a gaze at Cattrine. "Their first move is likely to try to find a way to sever us from each other. Without allies to come to your aid, you're much easier prey."

"They're going to strike at you, then," Vara said, looking at Terian.

"Very likely," Cattrine said. "At Terian or me, directly or indirectly."

"What are you going to do to guard against that?" J'anda asked.

"We have a plan or two," Cattrine said.

"But it's hardly infallible," Terian said in a warning tone. "Goliath's treachery should never be underestimated, after all."

"They never come at you cleanly," Vaste whispered.

"And they won't this time, either," Terian said. "They will knock the legs from beneath us and strike when we're down." He took a step closer to Cyrus. "You won't see the strikes coming, but you have to be ready anyway. You have to be willing to knock them down with you, to wrestle in the dirt, to fight and scrape and push their faces into the mud. This isn't even war, it's not troops in lines marching against each other." His eyes burned as he stepped right up to Cyrus. "This is the lowest form of combat, a brawl in a dirty alleyway, and the only prize is that you and yours get to keep breathing. Are you ready for that fight?"

"To keep this secret, maybe to your grave?" Cattrine asked.

"You're asking me," Cyrus said slowly, "to subvert Sanctuary. To go against who we are. To compromise—"

"I'm asking you," Terian said, landing both hands on Cyrus's pauldrons and shaking him lightly, "to not be stupid at a time when your very survival requires you to be aware—your enemies are coming in the night, with blades, and you don't know who all of them are." He lowered his voice, and it was thick with emotion. "Cyrus … you need to decide whether you're going to fight for Sanctuary to live … or just give up and let it die with all its people as they close in on all sides."

Cyrus looked at Vara, who gave him a subtle nod. Glancing at Vaste and J'anda, he saw the same approval.

The guild looks to me … and I look to … The quiet in the tower was a palpable thing, every single one of them waiting on his answer. He looked around, not at them but at their feet, his mind awhirl. *This is not what Alaric would do.*

But Alaric has never faced these enemies before.

He sighed, as the answer—the only one—came. "All right," Cyrus said, "let's find a way to save this guild."

13.

"Is this really necessary?" Cyrus asked, straightening his breastplate. The way he'd fastened it, in haste, on his way out of the tower, had caused it to poke into his chainmail and press it sharply against his ribs. If he wore it into battle in this lopsided way, he knew it would result in injury, but he wasn't counting on a battle.

"You definitely need armor for this," Vaste said. "What if they throw things?"

"Don't listen to him," Vara said, seizing the edge and adjusting it straight with one good tug. She gave the troll a searing glare. "You know this is necessary." She looked him in the eyes. "You need to address the guild about these events. It's been elided over for entirely too long."

They were standing in the foyer outside the Great Hall, and dinner was already well underway. The clatter of plates and silverware rattled in the air, and the smell of cooked meat enticed Cyrus even as the prospect of what he needed to do repelled him. Taking up a prominent place close to the door, Cyrus could see the new troll applicants eating rather messily. He glanced at Vaste, who had covered his mouth with his hand. "Gods, that's embarrassing," the healer muttered.

"You'll do fine," J'anda said, giving a look behind him. The rest of the Council lingered in the foyer as well, the Great Hall looking empty compared to what it had been only a year earlier. "Go through the sequence of events, answer questions at the end, and don't forget to be your usual, charming self."

"Yes," Erith called from behind him, "do try to remember to charm."

"Or at least try not to kill anyone," Ryin said, an aura of weary resignation about the druid. "That seems important right now."

"Such encouraging words," Vara said under her breath. She looked up at him once more, and he could see the faint light of hope within her eyes. "You can do this."

"I can do this," Cyrus agreed, sure that she was right. He still felt a sense of unease, stemming not only from all that was coming at them now, but also by his consideration of the plans put forth by Terian and the others only the night before. *I am actually going to do this, to fight this battle ... as I might have when I was a warrior in the Society, on my own. Bare knuckles, whatever weapon I can find.* He sucked in a breath, but his armor did not stab him as it had a moment earlier. "I'm ready."

"Oh, good, because you're the one who really needs to be," Vaste said. "I mean, I could be unready for days, possibly, because I don't need to speak—"

"Truer words were never spoken," Vara said, nodding at Cyrus and stepping up beside him. "Shall we?"

"We shall," Cyrus said and started into the Great Hall before the troll could retort, the officers following behind him. They threaded their way through the crowd, which was packed in knots around some tables with others left empty and abandoned. Cyrus made his way up front to the officers' table, surprised that the Great Hall didn't look emptier. *The Luukessians aren't here ... we have a tenth of the numbers eating tonight that we had a year ago, yet the place doesn't appear utterly desolate.* He caught a glimpse of Larana watching him through the pass-through to the kitchen, eyes intently upon him. When he caught her looking, he smiled. She did not return the smile, but neither did she look away.

Cyrus stopped before the officers' table and waited for the others to file in around him. *We still have a full complement at the walls ... the hall is even emptier than I knew ... at least it doesn't look it. Doubtful that having that be obvious would appear as anything other than weakness to the members we have left.* "Good evening," he called, swallowing once, hard, before he began to speak. "Thank you for coming tonight."

"It'd be hard to miss, given it's dinnertime!" came a rough voice out of the crowd. Peals of laughter crackled through the room and Cyrus smiled, nodding along with the jest. *They're bound to feel isolated, alone, with this recent news. Some of them are probably very afraid. Let them have some humor, and maybe this will go easier.*

"Well, I wanted a captive audience," Cyrus said, prompting a little laugh of his own. He caught a glimpse of Calene Raverle sitting with some of the rangers in one of the front tables. She smiled at him encouragingly when she caught his eye, but he could see that her expression was nevertheless laced with uncertainty. "It's been a long time since last I addressed the guild this way. Too long. Much has changed—"

"Too much!" someone in the crowd hooted, and a chorus of catcalls followed.

"Too much, agreed," Cyrus said with a nod. "And too little of it we controlled. No one enjoys change, especially not change for the worse, and yet that's what we've been presented, time after time, of late." He kept his voice steady and loud, booming out to those sitting in the back of the room. "Well, I don't care for it any more than you do, and I think it's time we—"

"When are we going on an expedition?" a voice—the same one that had been calling since the first thrown jest—yelled. A murmured chorus of assent flew through the ranks, running through the room like water down a steep slope.

"Well," Cyrus said, trying to keep his good humor about him and delivering his answer with as much levity as he could muster, "more or less the entire Council is now declared heretics and are considered persona non grata in many of the major cities. Several very large, very dangerous guilds—Goliath and Amarath's Raiders, for instance—are presently trying to find ways to kill us, so … running expeditions out from behind these walls and our defenses is not a priority until we clear this matter up."

"You don't just clear up a declaration of heresy!" that same voice called again, and again, many others chorused in agreement.

"No, you don't," Cyrus said when the yelling faded. "It's not that easy, but we are—"

"We got no stipend!" came another voice, less cultured than the first. "We haven't been paid gold in nearing a year!"

"Well, we haven't been on any expeditions," Cyrus said then inwardly cringed. *Like they don't know that.*

"So, what, are we working for free now?" came the first voice again. Cyrus peered into the crowd and saw the speaker. He was a swarthy human in his thirties with glaring eyes, and his lips looked like they might not ever have cracked in a smile at any point in his entire life.

"What's your name?" Cyrus asked, looking right at him.

The man stood, and his long, dusty-blond hair fell around his face as he rose to his feet. "Mathyas Tarreau, Lord Davidon."

"You don't have to call me 'Lord Davidon,'" Cyrus said. "And yes … you're working for free. Or for room, board, food, lodging, protection … almost everything except actual gold." He looked around the room. "I know this isn't what a lot of you signed on for—"

"I came for coin!" shouted someone at the back of the room, and a roar of agreement ran through the Great Hall.

"Oh, I am sick of this interrupting arsehole," Ryin muttered under the roar of the crowd.

"I remember when that interrupting arsehole was you," Vaste said, elbowing him in the ribs.

The druid shot the healer a sour look. "When it comes to interruptions, you remain the king."

"I'm sure you did," Cyrus said to the gathering. "And for a time, obviously, Sanctuary had a stipend unlike any guild in Arkaria. Our members practically floated in gold while we took mercenary contracts during the war. But that was never the reason we were here." A silence had fallen, and he could feel his audience listening. "The purpose of Sanctuary was to be here to help Arkaria in its hours of greatest need." A creeping sense of guilt prickled at Cyrus. *Is that what I'm doing now, in conspiring to remove leaders from governments to save my own skin? To save my people?* "We were meant to protect this land against all threats. We were never a mercenary company except when we had to be. We did what we had to do to help the people of Emerald Fields survive, to help ourselves survive. We beat the Dragonlord. We destroyed the tyrannical Goblin Imperium. We knocked back the dark elves when they reached forth their hand for empire. We killed Mortus and Yartraak, have fought enemies … unfathomable enemies to save a people … we have battled dragons and titans, and now we face the governments of men and elves, and allies of old turned against us." Out of the corner of his eye, he caught Vara looking at him. "We have a purpose. We are not mercenaries, though we have taken gold for service. We are not mere adventurers, though we have adventured. And we are not soldiers, though we have fought. This guild is more than any of those things. It is a home, it is our place—" He looked sideways and saw Larana staring at him, now out of the kitchen, watching him in rapt attention, "—and they're going to come for us. And we're going to fight them."

"You're out of your godsdamned mind if you think we're fighting the Confederation, the Kingdom, Amarath's Raiders *and* Goliath, and for free, no less," Mathyas Tarreau said, still standing up in the crowd. Others stood up to join him.

And so we come to it at last. "No one is going to force you to stay," Cyrus said. "As ever, Sanctuary is a haven for those who want to be here. Anyone who doesn't ..." He looked uneasily over the crowd. "You should leave. Before things get untenable."

"That's it, then?" Mathyas Tarreau asked him, looking through the crowd with furious eyes. "You're just ... done with us?"

"We're heretics here, Mathyas," Cyrus said, staring him down. "Arkaria is turning against us. We'll be besieged. Enemies will come for us from all sides." He raised his voice. "If you're here for coin, there is none. If you're here for adventure, all we have is battle, at least for the foreseeable future. If you're looking for a home, and loyalty that runs thicker than blood, that won't abandon you in your darkest hour ... then don't abandon us in ours." His gaze flicked across the crowd, seeing a gamut of emotions represented there. "If that's not you ... then, yes. We're done."

A shocked silence fell over the guildhall, broken by the sound of a chair sliding against the stone floor. Someone stood up in the back, turned, and with hunched shoulders, shuffled out of the Great Hall. Another chair slid out a moment later, then another, then so many of them Cyrus couldn't count them all. It seemed like half the hall rose and started toward the door. He stood in silence and watched, remembering a time when Alaric had done something very similar, and waited, as over half their number streamed out, leaving Sanctuary behind for the cold, dark night and the empty plains beyond the wall.

14.

"That could have gone better," Ryin said once they were safely ensconced back in the Council Chamber, the light of the fire crackling and giving the room a lively tone in spite of the dead silence that had hung over them.

"It also could have gone worse," Vaste said. When everyone looked at him, he said, "They could all have left."

"Did anyone get a count?" Cyrus asked, brushing his helm where it lay next to his right hand on the table. It made a slight noise skidding against the wood, reminding him of the chairs in the Great Hall scooting back all in unison.

"I believe the technical measure is a 'shit ton,'" Vaste said. "As in, 'Those people were shits, and there were a ton of them.'"

"They were our sworn brothers and sisters," Vara said quietly.

"Less than a thousand," J'anda said. "Nine hundred, perhaps?"

"We lost more on the wall," Samwen Longwell said, newly reappeared from where he'd been on guard duty during the meeting. "I had to drag people onto night duty once we closed the gates. It's been a steady trickle since, as well, people coming to regret not walking out with the rest."

"Gods, we're here again," Cyrus said, bracing his chin against his hand. "Time runs in a circle, and now we move back to the beginning."

"In the mood to travel Arkaria to rustle up new recruits?" J'anda asked with a warm smile.

"Even if I weren't likely to be attacked on the road whilst doing that," Cyrus said, shaking his head, "I think that might be a task for a younger man. Alaric sent me, after all; he didn't go himself."

"Oh, he's blaming himself for this," Vaste said. "I can see it in the way he's about to droop onto his hand. The self-loathing is running over like mead in a shallow cup. It's splashing onto me."

"That might just be your own self-loathing," Erith said quietly, her complexion a pale blue. She looked sick, Cyrus thought.

"So, what do we do?" Longwell asked, drumming his spear against the ground. "Close up the wall, obviously."

"Obviously," Vaste said, "since we don't want to pit our—what? Less than a thousand now? Against Goliath's twenty thousand?"

"We should get a count," Vara said, her voice almost a whisper. "So we know."

"We need new officers," Cyrus said. "That's what Alaric did when all hell broke loose last time. He appointed Vaste, J'anda, and me to the Council in order to help bring things back in line."

"And it worked out just marvelously. At least until now," Vaste said.

"We're still not as small as we were then," J'anda pointed out. He looked to Cyrus, warm regard on his wrinkled features. "Who were you thinking for officers?"

"Calene Raverle," Cyrus said, "Scuddar In'shara. Menlos Irontooth?"

"I'm not so sure about Menlos," Erith said, shaking her head. "He's nice and all, but … he seems more like the front line type, not the sort you put on the Council."

Cyrus frowned. "Are you sure? He seems like a leader."

Erith shrugged. "Just my feeling. I guess I don't know him that well."

"I hate to say this, but …" Vara looked around. "We could use Fortin here on the grounds for a time. With our numbers this low, having a rock giant at our disposal would not be a terrible idea."

"Agreed," Cyrus said, somewhat reluctantly. "I'm sure he won't be pleased, but … he'll come if I call."

"So that's it, then?" Longwell asked. "We have nothing else? Hide and appoint a few new officers, and hope that this storm blows itself out?"

Cyrus traded a look with Vara and carefully kept himself from glancing at Vaste or J'anda. Instead he surveyed the remaining few officers that were not in his circle of confidence, his shadow council. "Of course not," he gazed at Ryin, who sat in quiet, obvious desperation, then at Mendicant, who looked rather stoic, all things considered, staring straight ahead like Ryin but without his lethargy. Erith squirmed in her seat, looking as if she wanted to run out and never come back, her blue complexion almost grey in the torchlight. Longwell, for his part, clutched his lance in his gauntleted hand firmly, ready for action that would not be coming their way soon, Cyrus hoped. "We need to wait for now, though," Cyrus said. "In a fight with a bigger foe, one that you can't win through contest of strength, it becomes a game of waiting, of skill. Their guard is strong, but it won't last forever. If they come at us, we may be able to bleed them dry, if we are prepared. Sanctuary withstood a siege of a hundred thousand before—"

"And they blew down our walls," Ryin said, covering his face, his worried eyes, with a hand. "I don't see how we stand against that."

"Ice spells cast from the parapets," Vara said. "A careful watch. What spellcasters we have left that are willing, we should make heretic as well, give them all the abilities we can. Imagine a hundred enchanters at our command, that could switch to wizardry in an eye's blink."

"Most of our spellcasters left in the last months," Mendicant said, sounding oddly indifferent. When he looked up, it was with a curious look. "They, more than warriors or rangers, were acutely aware of the mark of heresy or excommunication and wished to avoid it most assiduously. Still, training those we have left …" His eyes glittered with hints of excitement.

"That's what we'll need to do," Cyrus said, nodding. "We need time. Time to train these people. Time to study the defenses, to anticipate the movements of those would come to us. We'll prepare, we'll watch, and we'll watch for openings. We'll grow stronger, and perhaps they'll lose their resolve?"

"Against heretics?" Erith asked, her voice like ground glass had been run down her throat, choked and lifeless. "Not likely. They'll never forget us. They'll never let up. They will come eventually, one way or another."

"And we'll be waiting," Cyrus said, keeping his eyes low.

"But defending the wall with less than a thousand?" Longwell asked, shaking his head. "It would be … a slaughter if they break through."

"No," Cyrus said. "Because if it comes to that … we'll leave before they get the chance." And with a weight in his heart, he looked at the faces around him, filled with as much despair as he found resting in his own heart at the thought of leaving Sanctuary behind.

15.

The dawn's breaking found Cyrus awake, Vara already dressed in her armor by the time his eyes opened from a slumber he had thought would never find him. He stirred sleepily to see her sitting in a chair on the far edge of the bed, an envelope grasped in her fingers. "Message from Cattrine," she said, fatigue showing in the dark circles under her eyes and the way her hair was still mussed from sleep. "We have a meeting arranged in Termina today."

Cyrus got out of bed, cringing inwardly at the feel of the cold floor beneath his feet. The hearth was quietly burning, nearly down to ashes, but it sprung to life as he got up, a new energy within it, as though it sensed his wakening. "Who brought the message?" he asked as he began to slip on underclothes, soft and clean.

"That druid of Terian's, Bowe," Vara said, still as a statue where she sat. "Apparently he has been vouched for as one of the only people our dear Sovereign considers completely trustworthy in this."

"If he's good enough for Terian," Cyrus said, his chainmail rattling as he pulled it on over his head, "I suppose he's good enough for me." He stifled a yawn; he'd been awake into the small hours of the morning, too many thoughts awhirl for him to sleep.

"Trust does seem to be an active concern going forward," Vara said, rubbing her face, causing her pale cheek to turn red. "For example, with Bowe already gone, we have no way of easy transport to our meeting."

"Damn," Cyrus said as Vara got up to assist him in fastening his armor on. "We'll have to take a druid or wizard along, I suppose."

"Disguise will also be necessary," Vara said, pulling hard the strap to Cyrus's breastplate and backplate, ratcheting it tight against him enough to elicit a grunt of discomfort. "I've already left a message for

J'anda under his door. Hopefully he will be awake enough for us to collect him when we head down."

"I suppose it would be asking too much for them to let us teleport into Santir and walk into Termina as we are," Cyrus said as he fastened one arm's vambrace while Vara tended to the other. He gave her a smile, a thin one that was nonetheless motivated by the grim humor he found in the whole situation. "Though it would be funny to show up, declare ourselves, and then—"

"Die, horribly, at the end of many arrows and swords," Vara said dryly. "There is most likely a garrison in Santir at the moment, though hopefully they will not be at the portal. There is definitely an army in Termina, watching the bridge carefully in fact—"

"And of almost no use now that there is no dark elven army moving across the plains to cross and sack the town," Cyrus said with a hearty yawn. "Armies—always looking to fight the last war."

"It's not as though there's much cause for the elven army to go elsewhere," Vara said, tightening Cyrus's right arm bracer to the point where he felt a numbness even under the chainmail. "I believe the rest of the elven army is gathered south of Pharesia, massed in case the dark elves and Luukessians around Emerald Fields get any imperial ambitions and decide to come north. Or in case Danay decides to make the first move."

"An unsettling if entirely plausible scenario." Cyrus turned his attention to the bracer just fastened by Vara, loosening it slightly as she watched, unamused. "I'll need to meet with Calene, Menlos, and Scuddar later today to inform them of their impending officership."

Vara rolled her eyes. "More people in the Council that we cannot fully trust. This appears to my eyes to be some sort of window dressing, husband. Why do we need more officers now, when our numbers are sunk to their lowest level in years? And as much as you might bemoan the exodus last night, we have lost some ten times more than what we saw yesterday eve."

"Not at one time, though," Cyrus said quietly. "Not all in one go."

"I suppose their exit was somewhat more dramatic than the steady trickle of departures that came before," Vara said, thick with tiredness, "leaving in their ones and twos, often in the middle of the night, without a word of warning, as their hope dwindled. I confess I thought perhaps we were through the worst of it, knowing how many we had lost, but

… yes, from an emotional point of view, seeing that many go at once does leave something of a mark on the soul."

"A little bit," Cyrus admitted, stooping to fasten his greaves. That done, he straightened in silence, sighed, and placed his helm upon his head as Vara reached for hers and did the same. Cyrus cinched his belt, the sword resting loosely in the scabbard upon it, and then turned his head to look for a chest that he'd thought he'd seen stored somewhere in the room. His eyes searched the corners until they fell upon a wooden box in one corner that had been moved with the rest of his personal effects when he'd taken over as Guildmaster. He strode over to it lazily, pausing over the thigh-high chest with its metal bindings around every edge to hold it together, an object clearly made by a skilled craftsman—or two, even; a blacksmith to piece it all together with the metal and a carpenter to make the sides.

"What are you doing?" Vara asked, watching him carefully.

"Placing my thumb on the scales currently weighted against us," Cyrus said, opening the unlocked chest to find exactly what he was looking for within. "To balance things slightly." He took hold of the mystical ball and chain stored away within the chest and began to wrap it around his armor. He started by draping the length of chain around his waist, then crossed it diagonally over his chest both ways, winding the long chain around himself until it ran out of length. At one end was a steel ball covered in spikes, and at the other, a simple leather-wrapped handle, which he hung so that he could easily reach it with his left hand.

He turned to see Vara staring at him, a look of revulsion over her face, warring with her obvious weariness. "I guess you remember this, then," he said.

"It would be hard to forget," she said with a mild shudder, "seeing as you acquired it during our last trip together to Termina. I honestly thought that Unter'adon was going to kill you."

"He had a good chance," Cyrus agreed, taking hold of the handle of the chain and feeling the very slight power imbued in the weapon rush through him. It was no Praelior, that much was certain, but it was better than nothing. He drew the sword on his belt and practiced with a sudden feint, then a forward strike. "Well?"

"You're faster than you were without it," she said, though she sounded almost pained to admit it. "Let's hope you don't find yourself in need of it, however."

"Yeah, against Rhane Ermoc and my own sword," Cyrus said, letting loose of the handle, "it's not going to be as much use. But I might be able to take on a small army with its aid."

"Very small," she said, and he started past her toward the stairs, not wanting to address the sickened look on her face. He knew all too well that the mere sight of the weapon he was now forced to hang around his body for added strength and speed was a terrible memory for Vara. *Too many unpleasant associations with that night.*

Cyrus was halfway down to the door when a gentle knock sounded. "Who is it?" he called, Vara a few steps behind him.

"'Tis I, as bid," J'anda called through the door, and Cyrus opened it to find the enchanter standing there, looking much more awake than he or Vara. "Are you ready to go?"

Cyrus looked back to find Vara a study in glumness. "This is mad, isn't it?" he asked, not sure whether he was speaking to the enchanter before him or his wife behind him.

"No madder than sitting here and waiting for the axe to fall," J'anda said with a very slight smile that, Cyrus thought, perfectly represented the enchanter—wry and encouraging, with none of the desperation that he and Vara were exhibiting. "There is much to be done, my friends," J'anda said with a twinkling of his eyes, "come—let us begin."

16.

The foyer of Sanctuary was quiet, the new troll applicants standing around near the lounge with a few other solitary souls, the quiet morning light streaming in through the circular stained glass window above the doors. Cyrus nodded to Zarrn, who nodded back. One of the other troll applicants gazed unabashedly at him as Cyrus came down the stairs, watching him as he crossed to the great seal. Cyrus stared back, meeting the troll's eyes, and saw a probing intensity there. This particular troll wore a beard as black as the caves of Enterra, and after a long look, he seemed satisfied and nodded at Cyrus, who returned the courtesy.

"Our portal is still shut," Vara said, which Cyrus already knew, having ordered Mendicant to close it months ago, as a precaution when Sanctuary had begun hemorrhaging wizards who knew the spell to carry them and any who wished to come with them right into their hallowed halls. "We'll need to use return to get back."

"Or come in at the northern portal and walk," Cyrus said, peering into the lounge in hopes of seeing a wizard or druid within. Alas, no luck there; three rangers and a warrior in mystical armor were sitting in isolated seats, reading or merely staring off into space, in their own thoughts. "Hmm. We should, perhaps, learn some wizard teleportation spells of our own, I suppose."

"That would make it considerably easier," Vara said. "Though casting fire is one thing; I am not sure I trust myself not to accidentally carry us somewhere beyond the ether if forced to cast a teleport."

"Perhaps we should start by teaching you some illusions," J'anda said with a raised eyebrow. "Those cannot go so wrong. At worst, you might become a gnome instead of a dark elf."

"As though that's not a catastrophe of its own." A half-smile cracked Vara's tired facade, but she abruptly turned serious, her gaze fixed on the doors to the Great Hall. Cyrus looked to see what had stopped her and saw Larana there, her matted brown hair falling frizzed upon the shoulders of her muted brown robes. The vestments of the druid that she habitually wore hidden beneath her hair were cast off, now, and he caught a glimpse of her green eyes looking up at him from beneath worried brows as she shuffled toward him shyly.

"Larana," Cyrus said, greeting her with a nod. She had not, that he could remember, ever approached him of her own accord. She always trailed behind, looking at him with those fearful green eyes, as though he might strike at her any moment. She looked ready to recoil, and even seeing that in her gaze made him want to shy away himself, uncomfortable at what it might indicate. "How goes it this morn?"

She stopped, seemingly taken aback by his simple query. "Very well, my Lord Davidon."

"Glad you're having a better morning than the rest of us," Cyrus said with a sly smile. *At least someone isn't in darkest despair around here, though you wouldn't know it by looking at her.*

"M'lord," she said, bowing her head even further, so that he could no longer see her eyes at all, "I—I am loyal to you. To Sanctuary." Now she looked up, just barely, enough that he caught a glimpse of smoldering sincerity beneath her tangled hair. "Please ... let me help you. Any way I can."

Cyrus regarded her carefully, feeling a tightness within his chest. *This is a woman who, on her own accord, and with her own resources, acquired enough quartal to smith my chainmail. Even if she were dearest friends with the Elves of Amti, that can't have come cheaply.* A question occurred to him presently. "How loyal are you, Larana?" he asked, peering down at her, noting the pinched look on her face as he asked. "Are you willing to do heresy for me?"

The answer came without hesitation. "Anything," she said, nodding sharply.

Cyrus felt the stab of a breath stuck in his chest, and he looked back at Vara, who nodded. "Very well, then," he said, nodding. "Why don't we start with something simple?" And he indicated the doors to the guildhall and led the way out into the day, sunny sky shining down upon them without a single cloud in view. The air was cold and crisp, and

90

they made their way across the quiet grounds to the stable, the only sound muted conversations in the distance being held by the sentries atop the wall.

When Cyrus reached the stables, the doors were already open, and the stableboy Dieron Buchau was waiting, his red hair nearly glowing in the sun. "Lord Davidon!" Buchau called, "I didn't know you were coming. Windrider didn't raise any sort of ruckus—"

Cyrus raised an eyebrow at that. "I won't be needing Windrider today." When the stableboy met his statement with a confused look, Cyrus elaborated. "I need something nondescript. Too many people know Windrider. I need very plain horses for this errand."

Dieron Buchau looked around, staring at the horses around him. "By all means, M'lord. Pick anything you wish."

Cyrus chose a very plain, old brown mare, and the others selected exceedingly ordinary horses as well. Cyrus paused by Windrider's stall and offered quiet words of encouragement. The horse whickered at him in a friendly way, seemingly not at all jealous of Cyrus's choice of a different horse.

With that task done and the horses saddled, Cyrus rode out of the stables and into the day, leading his small party of four to the side of the guildhall, into the shade of a wide-trunked yew tree. When they had all gathered around him, he looked straight at J'anda. "We're going to Termina via Santir. What would you suggest for a disguise?"

"Why are you asking him?" Vara asked with a sniff of annoyance. "Why don't you ask the person who lived in Termina much of her life?"

"All right," Cyrus said, trying to mask a smile. "What would you recommend, my dear?"

"That you ask me next time, and not try to gallop past your failure of intellect by simply sprinkling a 'my dear' upon your error." She gave him an acrid look and turned her attention to J'anda. "Dark elven merchants. They are doing a booming trade with Termina once more, and I think it is not uncommon to see the more well-to-do ones teleporting in from elsewhere to spare a journey of weeks across the Southern Reaches of the Confederation. They would also, perhaps, have cause to treat with the Oliaryn of Termina, if they were sufficiently well-placed."

"Dark elven merchants," J'anda said with a nod. "This, I can arrange. But then, I can arrange much more than that." He twisted his fingers around his long staff, and the purple crystal glowed bright before releasing a spell. It snaked around them and Cyrus found himself looking at three dark elves surrounding him, all in cloth shirts and pants, though two of them were women. Their clothes were much cleaner and of higher quality than any dark elven merchant Cyrus could recall seeing in Reikonos, and they also wore metal bindings that held their cloaks together at the neck. The binding had a logo of some sort upon it, but though it was familiar, Cyrus was unsure where he might have seen it before.

"It is the Seal of Grimrath Tordor," J'anda said when he caught Cyrus looking. "One of Saekaj's highest noble houses, and one that has fared fairly well in the aftermath of the … shall we say … revolution." He wore a smile perched upon his lips that looked somehow impudent even in spite of his illusion, and Cyrus wondered what was going on in the enchanter's thoughts.

"Larana," Cyrus said, looking to the nearest dark elf to him, "We need—"

"I'm not Larana," came Vara's voice from the dark elf he had fixed his gaze upon, mock-offended. "Apparently you can't even recognize your own wife. For shame. This is, perhaps, not your day when it comes to pleasing me."

"I question whether it's ever my day in that regard," he returned, eliciting a snort. He turned to the other dark elven woman. "Larana … please take us to Santir."

The druid, hidden well under her dark elven guise, nodded once, and then raised her hand in the air, twisting the forces of magic to her command. The air swirled in a storm of hard wind, a tornado of magic gathered around them, and with the rise of the force of air, swept them away from under the shaded yew tree on the Sanctuary grounds, hundreds of miles away and to a different land.

17.

Santir was smelly and crowded, and not at all how Cyrus had remembered it. But then, Cyrus's memory of the town had come in the days before it had been sacked and burned completely to the ground by the dark elves, so this was not unexpected. What had sprung up in the ruins was something entirely different, a bustling new city that had taken root around the portal. His horse led the way for their small party of dark elves, his eyes searching the streets for hints of danger.

The streets were dirt, not a cobblestone in sight. The sound of the horse hooves thumping steadily against the ground was soft in Cyrus's ears. On either side of them, new wooden buildings, constructed in the last few years, were already showing signs of weathering, the wood streaked and darkened from the ashen rains. The skies here were clouded, as though the burnt remnants of the original town still lingered in the atmosphere, waiting to be returned with the next downpour.

There were gaps between some of the buildings, vacant lots covered over with weeds or the occasional small garden, with its earth left empty for the winter, tilled and fallow. There was no sign of the snow that blanketed Reikonos, just a bitter chill in the air, much harsher than that around Sanctuary.

Cyrus could see the scars of the war everywhere. The road ahead led through the spare and struggling town, hints of industry springing up here and there. A massive building just ahead echoed with the sound of sawing wood, a lumber mill brought to life, probably charged with taking wood floated down the River Perda and turning it into boards for new buildings.

The residents in the streets seemed to have little life to them. They watched Cyrus and his party with undisguised suspicion. Eyes followed them even as they made their way toward the Grand Span, the massive bridge in the center of the river that led to Termina.

At the bank of the river, the stolid atmosphere of Santir suddenly changed. The river was practically a living thing, so thick with small boats, barges, and other craft that Cyrus wondered if he would even have needed the bridge to cross. It seemed to writhe with activity, vessels navigating past their moored fellows, all trying to squeeze up to docks that were already occupied on both sides of the river. Santir certainly seemed to be getting the lesser traffic of the two, with Termina and the western bank stacked up with barges filled with elves and humans and dark elves and even dwarves and gnomes yelling at each other to clear the channel, each with their own objective for their boat, aiming to deliver cargo or receive it.

"That's more like it," J'anda breathed as they started up the Grand Span, their horses' hooves clicking against the cobblestones.

When they reached the apex of the bridge, the city of Termina lay spread out before them, still a shade of its pre-war glory. Cyrus took in the spectacle, trying to focus on it rather than the uncomfortable memories of where he was presently riding. The bridge was scarred, the cobblestones black in some places from rampant, raging fire spells that had scoured their surface. Cyrus caught his bride looking down at them, forlorn even through her illusion, and he felt his breath catch in his throat. *How could she not be thinking of Chirenya?*

Soon enough, though, all their eyes were on the city. The traffic on the bridge was light, but elven sentries stood in the middle, watching the parties come through, gazes fixed on the horizon. *Watching for sign of a dark elven army,* Cyrus realized with numb surprise. *They'll be watching that way for a thousand years or more after being caught so flat-footed last time.*

Innumerable burned and blackened structures were still dotted around Termina, the wreckage of war obvious in the landscape. Other portions of the city appeared completely demolished, either by fire or intentional razing. As Cyrus watched, an explosion went off to his right, a booming that echoed across the river, and a whole block of houses disappeared in a cloud of dust.

"No cause for worry," one of the elven guards standing atop a makeshift wooden platform at the side of the span called out to the traffic blow. "It is a controlled detonation of damaged housing." He waved a hand, beckoning the suddenly stopped traffic to be on about their way. "Move along."

"I imagine they're having to do quite a bit of that," J'anda said, once they were a hundred meters past the guard post. Another stood ahead of them, more elves waiting atop it, staring at their brethren ahead, the clear start of a chain of relays, where word of any potential invasion could be shouted back into the city within minutes.

"The dark elves held portions of the city for quite some time," Vara said stiffly. "They fought street by street when King Danay ordered his troops in to reclaim it, and they did not yield easily. Var'eton—the lowers—where that house was destroyed—it was the site of some of the most pitched fighting, as I understand it. As was Ilanar Hill."

"Mmm," J'anda said with a nod. "Of course. Someone gave me a mansion there once, though I imagine that that offer has perhaps been rescinded now, given current events."

"Shh," Cyrus said, watching for any sign that anyone had overheard J'anda's snide remark. "They'll take more than that from you given half a chance."

J'anda shrugged, almost indifferent. "They may try. There is little left to take, and the price I would exact before they succeeded would be ruinous."

They rode into the city of Termina by the old Entaras'iliarad, the main avenue into the town. Cyrus had recalled this street bustling with life, and it still did, workers and residents moving up and down it. Ahead, he could see the wreckage of the Chancel of Life, the shrine to Vidara, Goddess of Life. Where before it had been a domed building, a massive edifice in the center of the city, now it stood less than half its previous height, covered over in scaffolding, a modest effort at rebuilding clearly underway. Wooden cranes moved in the circular roadway surrounding the chancel, lifting block and wood up to the heights upon which they were constructing the new Chancel, possibly upon the bones of the old. With the scaffolding in place, Cyrus could not tell if there had been any remainder or whether the dark elves had spitefully dragged it down stone by stone.

From the bridge he'd spied the old sites of the other two largest buildings in Termina as well. The old Bazaar, a massive, square market that spanned an area the size of a small city, nestled in the southern reaches of Termina, had lost its roof to fire and the sack, but the bustle of commerce had clearly returned to it, even absent its ceiling. The government center, though, a squat and unattractive building that had sat in the Olenet'yenaii, the northern artery that ran to the Chancel's square, seemed to have been destroyed altogether. Innumerable tents dotted the square where it had stood.

"Where are we going?" Cyrus asked, looking over the tent city.

"Oliaryn Iraid runs the provincial government out of his own personal manor on Ilanar Hill," Vara said with a barely disguised smile that he recognized as ironic. "Apparently it was one of the least damaged structures in the city."

"I'm surprised the dark elves did as much damage in the siege as they did," J'anda said. "They must have barraged the most important buildings with trebuchet and catapult in order to bring them down."

That's it, Cyrus realized with a start. *They didn't haul down the building brick by brick; they bombarded their choicest targets from across the river and turned them to wreckage over the course of years.* For him it was something of a revelation, going from trying to figure out why an army struggling to hold onto the city would waste time and manpower destroying key buildings just to demoralize their enemies. *They didn't,* he realized. *They just sat back and knocked it down from a distance with their artillery corps, probably once they'd lost control of that sector of the city. All they would need would be some stone, which surely they could drag from the quarries north of Santir. It would be a practically infinite supply of projectiles.*

They passed buildings that had clearly been bombarded, some by massive pieces of stone charred from being doused in oil and lit afire, and others by stones simply hurled in haste, no time or oil wasted upon them. One house had had its red tile roof completely crushed in, all the windows broken and the sky shining through, revealing that every floor had been destroyed. Cyrus could see the projectile that had done the damage, still lying within the shell of the house, probably on someone's list of wreckage to clear, someday.

Work like that was going on all around as they took a right down a wide avenue that cut from the Entaras'iliarad to the square where the government center had sat. The tents were visible ahead, canvas billowing in the breeze, probably a half a hundred of them, of various sizes. Troops were surely quartered within, though Cyrus doubted it was enough to keep the entire army of the northern kingdom here. They were undoubtedly also staying in any number of houses within the city, raising to Cyrus the question of exactly how many residents of old

Termina had returned to this place after its destruction.

The sound of hammers, of pick and axe, echoed through the streets. Shouted commands in elvish and the human tongue drew Cyrus's curiosity. He passed an all-human work crew who gazed at him suspiciously, and he realized with a start that they were Luukessian by their accents, and saw a cloak that suggested at least one was from the Kingdom of Actaluere and a former soldier, at that. *Must have hired themselves out for work here. Though I'm surprised they didn't stay in Emerald Fields to build for their own people …*

They went on, through the wide avenue, and circled around the edge of the tent city in the old wreckage of the government building. Cyrus could recall being led through the warren of corridors in the squarish building once upon a time. The smell of dust and sweat lay thick upon the air, and he could see the faint hints of where the building might once have stood, but it appeared that almost all of it had been hauled away by horse and cart, leaving the empty ground for the tent city.

"There are whole fields that have been filled with the refuse from the destruction of the city," Vara said quietly. "Sifted through for usable stone and wood, the waste hauled off and discarded to help clear the streets. It's left quite a blight on the landscape outside the city, as I understand."

"Hmm," Cyrus grunted, letting Vara lead him. She angled them on a path through the tent city, weaving between the unevenly placed tents and up a road on the other side. They traveled that path north for a time as the buildings thinned and the damage from the war seemed to fade, its intensity nowhere near what it had been in the main avenues of Termina. The smell of dust was fading as they went. They were on a winding path now, heading west once more, and the ground sloped upward, an obvious incline. "This is Ilanar Hill?" Cyrus asked.

"It is," Vara said, her eyes slowly taking in the first of the mansions, behind a low wall to their left. It looked like a white stone building that had collapsed in on itself, the walls forming a V in the center of the rectangular structure. The bare hints of red tile roof that were visible in the mess suggested to Cyrus it might once have been a luxury home, more massive than the Sanctuary foyer, and perhaps more lushly appointed as well. The lawn leading up to the building was brown with winter's touch, and he tried to imagine it green and inviting, with the building standing as it might have in better days. "These were the homes of the wealthiest and most powerful of Termina," Vara said, a hint of longing in her voice. "They were ... glorious, I must admit. Marvels of elven architecture, more stunning even than the beautiful, classic homes of the Old District where I grew up. Every one had its roots in our culture, was designed to be an outward representation of everything the Kingdom had accomplished in all its long years, even before its official foundation under Danay." She looked away from the wreckage. "And just like so many other things ... now they are destroyed."

"Indeed," J'anda whispered under his breath as they went on, horse hooves clopping along the lonely cobblestones. There was no reconstruction here, only quiet grounds, grey skies, and wreckage. The street ahead of them was empty. *And why would it not be?* Cyrus wondered.

They rode another twenty minutes, seeing countless ruined mansions through felled and bare trees on either side of the road. *Was one of these mine?* Cyrus wondered, his eyes flitting over collapsed edifice after collapsed edifice. *Was one of them Vara's? Danay promised us, promised the defenders of Termina each a mansion here. Was this one to be mine?* His gaze fell on a house that had clearly been hit multiple times, only one wall still standing. He could count at least eight boulders the size of wagons lying in the wreckage. *Whatever the dark elves intended to do to the main structures of Termina, it would appear that demoralizing the wealthiest citizens was also part of their plan. Or perhaps these were just some of the biggest targets.*

Finally, a mansion that had survived intact came into view. Its soft lines reminded Cyrus of an egg where it tapered to a dome in the middle of the structure. Two wings swept out, one each to the left and right, more angular but still regal and graceful. He stared at the building, trying to piece together in his head if any of the wrecked buildings he had seen had looked anything like this. He could not recall any of them hinting at the shape of this one, with its marbled walls and stone roof, so unlike the tiled ones he had seen in the wreckage of the other mansions.

They rode through a gate without being stopped, the soldiers on either side nodding to them when they saw the emblems upon their cloaks. They went onward, into a courtyard between the two wings of the house, up to a portico that stretched out over the cobblestone courtyard, clearly designed to allow egress from carriages in inclement weather. Servants stood with their backs straight, not even looking at

Cyrus and his party as their horses trotted up.

"We're here for a meeting with Oliaryn Iraid," Cyrus said as a soft breeze drifted down upon him from over the mansion's northern wing and swirled through the courtyard. The nearest of the servants did not even look at him before nodding and sweeping an inviting hand toward the steps into the mansion.

Cyrus handed the reins of his horse to the servant, who took them silently, along with Vara's, J'anda's and Larana's before tying all four off to a nearby post next to a long, silvery trough filled with water. Cyrus walked uncertainly up the stairs to where two more servants waited, opening the doors for them, faces impassive.

"I wonder if the General of Termina typically meets with dark elven merchants without even inquiring as to their provenance," Cyrus muttered under his breath as they passed into a silent, empty entry hall. A shining marble balcony encircled the room on three sides, and hearths burned on either side of the room, warming it. Lush purple carpets led from the entry doors, which were closing quietly behind them with a soft click, to the massive stairs that split to sweep up to either side of the balcony that ringed the room.

"He does when he's been told who they are and to expect a party that will not be what they appear," Cattrine Tiernan's soft voice came from just beside the stairs. Cyrus had not even seen her there when he entered, but she was there now, without doubt, in a cloak of her own, with the cowl pulled back to reveal her chestnut hair. She wore a tight smile, standing in the shadow of the steps. "I've been waiting for you, as has the Oliaryn."

"I apologize for any delay," Cyrus said, making his way over to Cattrine, boots crushing the soft velvety carpet beneath every step. She shook her head, and J'anda's illusion faded away in an instant, leaving Cyrus standing there in his black armor once more.

Cattrine eyed the chain wrapped around his chest and waist. "That's new."

He did not reply, and she led them forward into a hallway empty of all life. There were no servants here; only silence greeted them, and walls that burned with candles in sconces that emitted a soft, waxy smell as they shed their light. She took them through two turns and finally stopped outside a wooden door that looked new, as though it had been replaced in the aftermath of the sack. It probably had, Cyrus reflected;

while this mansion might not have been bombarded, it had surely had dark elven pillagers coursing through it like blood through veins during the siege.

Cattrine knocked once before a thunderous voice bade them enter. Cyrus cast a look back at Larana. "Wait here," he said, and she nodded once, her eyes downcast. "Keep watch."

He followed Cattrine through the doors into a spacious office, Vara and J'anda trailing behind him. Vara shut the door once they were inside, and Cyrus let his eyes adjust to the brightness of the room. There were at least four large windows, all shut, but allowing the grey light of day to stream in. A hearth burned at one side of the room, and in addition to the large wooden desk that had clearly been carved by elven craftsmen for all its intricacy of pattern, there were countless pedestals and shelves filled with artifacts, weapons, and sculpture, and the walls were covered with paintings.

Cyrus could not help but gawk at the one above the hearth, which dragged his gaze away from the grizzled, grey-haired man in a silken doublet behind the desk. With nary a glance at the Oliaryn he had come to meet, Cyrus found himself drawn to the painting, to the hearth, the warm fire crackling, the sweet smell of smoky cherrywood filling the office and growing stronger as he drew, inexorably, toward the object of his attention.

"You have a keen eye," Oliaryn Iraid said, coming over to Cyrus, who took slow, halting steps the closer he grew to the painting. "To pick that, out of all my collection. Though I suppose you can't help it, can you?" The General sounded amused.

Cyrus stared at the picture above him. The frame was bronze and lined with flowered sculpture at each corner, a work of art in and of itself. Within the frame lay a canvas of careful oils, brushstrokes that showed the mastery of an elf with thousands of years of experience. The skies in the painting were a true-life, as if someone had taken the grey clouds from the sky outside and somehow laid them across the surface of the canvas. Each of the soldiers in the battle-lines that stretched to either side of the canvas looked as though they were real, breathing, and would be charging out of the painting into actual war right there in front of Cyrus.

"Possessing that painting," Iraid went on, apparently expecting no response from Cyrus, "is more than a minor crime, did you know that?

The Leagues, of course, have never hesitated to tell us when we're doing wrong, and I suppose that keeping an icon depicting such a thing … well, it's not right in their book, is it? But I can't bear the thought of them burning it, which they would if I turned it over. So I keep it here, quietly. The Leagues need not worry themselves about destroying art, and I need not make myself sick at the thought of its destruction." Iraid cocked his head, clearly admiring the piece. "Besides … it's not as though merely looking at it could compel one to be a heretic, could it?" He smirked openly at Cyrus. "After all … you're a heretic, and you've never even seen it until now."

Cyrus stared at the painting, at the center. "It's the Battle of Thurren Hill," he said, and Iraid nodded. At the center stood a woman in twilight purple robes, clutching a sword—a very familiar sword—in one hand, the other glowing with what looked like a lightning bolt coming out of the clear sky. The blade she held was curved, unmistakably dangerous, and the look in her eyes was fury turned hot like molten metal, directed in the same place as the lightning, beyond the painter who had witnessed this moment and commemorated it on the canvas in glorious, painstaking detail. "And that's Quinneria … the sorceress."

He swallowed hard, and felt Vara nudge him as she came to stand next to him, her eyes fixed on the painting, and at its center, his mother. She did not say anything for a long moment, but when she did, it was quiet, even though everyone in the room heard it. "Well," she said, her voice low and hoarse, "I suppose now we know what happened to your father's sword."

18.

"Your current predicament is a serious one," Oliaryn Iraid said, once Cyrus and the others were seated around his desk. Cyrus, wanting to remain standing but not wishing to be perceived as rude, had taken the offered seat between Vara and Cattrine across the massive carved oak desk, but he found his eyes constantly drifting back to the painting of his mother in her wrath. He had recognized her instantly, of course, even without the sword and lightning. Even with the anger projected across her face like a shadow in the night. He remembered her differently, with a smile that had grown dimmer as his childhood went on.

"We do find ourselves in rather deep waters," Vara said, "and without a boat in sight."

"Mmm," Iraid acknowledged with a nod. "I am by no means hung up on the tradition of the Leagues. Any thinking man can see through the fiction they've concocted as doctrine. Their game is control, nothing less, and in the name of gods we don't even worship for the most part in this kingdom. But the nominal tie is there, and it is strong, as all traditions are." He wore a ghostly smile, and even paying less than full attention, Cyrus had a feeling that much was being left unsaid by the Oliaryn.

"We appreciate your open-mindedness," Cyrus said, trying to make it sound sincere.

"The trouble coming is, naturally, of concern," Cattrine said, and once more Cyrus got the feeling that true meanings were being couched under seemingly meaningless words. *The trouble coming? Of concern to whom?* Cyrus resisted the frown that threatened to break across his lips. "Arkaria seems to be once more lining up for war."

"Dark times, again," Iraid nodded. "Though, if you'll forgive me for saying so ... the battle this time does not seem quite so lopsided as before, when the dark elves were ascendant under the leadership of a god and all others scrambled to hold them at bay."

"I doubt the dark elves are a threat to your city at all," Cattrine said with the hint of a smile.

"My province," Iraid gently corrected with a smile of his own. "Termina is merely the capital of the region I oversee as both Oliaryn and the Lord of these lands. And you are correct, no military threat lies within sight of us, unless the humans decide to do something foolish."

"I doubt even Pretnam Urides is that dumb," Cyrus said, still fighting off the dark countenance that threatened to spill over his face. "His attention is focused on us, entirely, at the moment, and after that ..." He shook his head. "Who knows? I doubt he'll go starting any more wars in the near future."

"But war always comes back," Iraid said, nodding. "Trust me. I've seen enough of them to know."

"True enough," Cattrine said, still smiling as she leaned toward his desk. "But that's a distance off. Hundreds, maybe thousands of years. A problem for the generations after mine, I think." Iraid nodded subtly. "But other problems are here today," she went on, prompting another nod from Iraid. "Surely, you must see what other difficulties loom on the horizon."

"Of course," Iraid said, a little drily. "Every man has his problems. Though few have them as bad as you at the moment," he said to Cyrus with a chuckle.

"Ah, but in his—and Sanctuary's—problems may lie the solution to your own," Cattrine said carefully.

Iraid did not react to this small suggestion, his eyes a smoky grey that stared seemingly into the distance behind the head of his guests. "What problems do you think I have, Administrator?"

"Oh, I wouldn't presume to tell you your mind," Cattrine said, and it was as though Cyrus could see her gently withdrawing bait at the end of a string, waiting to see if the Oliaryn would swipe at it.

When he did, it was graceful. "We live in perhaps the wealthiest nation in Arkaria," Iraid said. "We are rebuilding from the catastrophic damage of the last war, and certainly," he said right to Cyrus, "are having an easier time of it than your fellow man in the outlying areas of the Confederation. The King ... he helps fund our reconstruction, unlike Reikonos to its orbiting ... what do they call them? Dominances? I forget."

"So the King is utterly responsive to your every concern?" Cattrine asked, apparently leaving subtlety behind. Vara's brow rose.

"And we come to it at last," Iraid said softly, smoothing his silk doublet, which to Cyrus looked less like something a general would wear and more like something to be found on a monarch. "Danay is your enemy, not mine."

"Of course," Cattrine said, nodding. "I only thought, given his ..." Her eyes glimmered and reminded Cyrus of someone brandishing a dagger, the blade catching the light, "... his claims about the growth of the Kingdom's fortunes—" Iraid's face grew stiff, "—about all the successes he has presided over, both before the war and since—that perhaps, given how much you and this province have helped shape those fortunes with your burgeoning trade, even this ruined city, you might have warranted perhaps a bit more ... recognition for your role in things."

She just buried that dagger right into Iraid's rib cage, straight to the hilt, Cyrus thought, watching the Oliaryn's stricken face. His lower lip twitched, betraying resentment turned to rage. "Very good," Iraid said when he finally spoke, every word coming out in a harsh whisper. "I always knew you were clever, Administrator, so very clever in our dealings." His voice rose closer to its normal volume as he began to recover. "Fine. You have it. We in Termina put forth our best efforts, and the King taxes us harshly from afar. It slows our recovery; we send gold to Pharesia and receive only a fraction of the value back. As if that were not vexing enough, he says nothing about Termina's place in his Kingdom's economy." He slapped his desk hard with the palm of his hand then pointed at Cattrine. "Without the two of us, and Amti, he would be bankrupt in a year. We feather his nest and he tosses us twigs. In your case, he makes ready to war upon you." An ugly resentment darkened the face of the General. "But that does not mean I am fool enough to cast my lot with heretics who come to me with some ... what do you come to me with?" He held his hands up. "Some plan to go against the king? Because to stick out my neck next to yours ... that would be foolish. More foolish than keeping my mouth shut and letting gold flow away from my city's coffers, for that injustice would matter little to me as a dead man." Both his eyebrows rose with significance as he looked to each of them in turn.

"What if," Cattrine said, suddenly pensive, "there were a way for you to cast off those chains? To capture more of that outflow of gold, and due credit, and keep it here." Her eyes glittered. "For your people ... and yourself, of course."

"I think it would be treason," Iraid said with a small smile, "against the monarchy."

Cattrine's smile grew vicious. "It's only treason if you fail. If you succeed, then you are the undisputed Lord of this province and this city, which is practically a nation all on its own, is it not?"

Iraid returned her gaze without even a flicker of emotion. "And you say this as the Administrator of a fellow province seeking its own freedom of course, I take it?"

"We have a very similar problem, you and I," Cattrine said. "We watch the gold flow out and wonder how much more beneficial it might be to keep even a small percentage of it in our borders. We think ... how much benefit does this net me? And we find those scales ... lacking in balance."

"I would rather the scales lack balance than my body lack its head," Iraid said.

"I would rather balance the scales and keep my head," Cattrine said. "And I suspect a few more of the provinces around here, the Lords and Ladies, feel exactly the same."

"Perhaps," Iraid said. "But perhaps not."

"Come now," Cattrine said, leaning in conspiratorially, "what do you really want, Lord Iraid? To be something akin to the King of your own province, independent of a monarch who bleeds you dry and steals your glory? If that were an actual possibility, something achievable, that you could reach out and take without worry—would you?"

Iraid looked past them again. "I would, were it possible." He leaned forward. "But let me tell you, without the proper help ... it is not possible."

"We have some help," Cattrine said coolly.

"The elves of Amti will hardly be enough," Iraid said with a wave of his hand, and Cyrus caught a flicker of emotion from Cattrine that suggested to him that she had, indeed, counted them among her allies in this. *It seems natural she would have opened negotiations with them; they hate*

King Danay as much or more than she does, and they all certainly have goods to trade. "You will need, by my reckoning, Lord Merrish of Traegon and Lady Voryn of the Emerald Coast, at minimum." He looked directly at Cyrus. "You would be well advised if you attempted a meeting with Morianza Yemer, as well."

"'Morianza' is roughly translated to 'Duke,'" Vara said quietly as she leaned forward. "Yemer is …"

"He was the father of your man Odellan, I believe?" Iraid asked, eyes narrowed in consideration. "He is one of Danay's closest councilors, though he is a bit … estranged from the King at the moment, as the Morianza has retreated to an estate in the north in his grief."

"His grief?" Cyrus asked and felt like someone had run a finger through his chest as it dawned on him what that meant. "Because of the loss of his son."

"Indeed," Iraid said flatly. "Mention my name to any of these individuals, and I will deny this meeting, and I will be believed. But if you can get them on board with your cause …" He tilted his head thoughtfully to the side. "I would be almost inclined to believe you could do it … supposing you could do one final thing."

"And what's that?" Cattrine asked, leaning forward.

Iraid smiled mirthlessly. "With the three of us Lords and Ladies, Morianza Yemer, the leadership of Amti, your Lord of Rockridge, the official Lord of Emerald Fields, and the Lady of Nalikh'akur," he nodded at Vara, "you will have many of the Kingdom's provinces on your side. The remaining provinces are not particularly loyal to Danay, but you will need a palatable alternative to him, and you will need the people. And for that," he said, smiling smugly, "you will need an endorsement that would prove impossible for most."

And with that, Iraid smiled broadly, looking directly at Vara, who closed her eyes in understanding. "Damn," she whispered.

"What?" Cattrine asked, clearly hesitant to reveal her ignorance. Cyrus did not need to ask, for he already suspected, and when his wife spoke the answer aloud, it was like the lightning from Quinneria's hand had been loosed in the room, a word so charged it might as well have ended the meeting right there, resonating through all of them as if it had sparked straight out of the sky itself.

19.

"Gods," Terian said at their meeting place at a disused portal in the Gradsden Savanna, the air less brisk than in the wintery north. "Iraid set a damned near impossible task for you on that one. Why didn't he just ask you to storm the upper Realms and bring some god heads back while he was at it?"

"It is hardly impossible," Vara said, speaking quietly, as if afraid Larana and Bowe would overhear their meeting from where they stood in the afternoon sun, hovering over the portal a hundred feet or so away, the Falcon's Essence spell allowing the two of them to function as lookouts. The tall grass of the savanna had grown brown for the winter and seemed not to stand fully upright in this area. "But it will require some effort on my part."

"Well, in that case," Terian said with a smirk, "see if you can perhaps carve some time out of your busy schedule, maybe skip the afternoon lovemaking with the man in black armor and get to work on it."

"The rest of Iraid's list," Cattrine said, now genuinely pensive, "the people he mentioned—I don't know them. Lady Voryn, Morianza Yemer … the only one I have contact with is Lord Merrish of Traegon. He trades in some of our crops, though I don't think I've met him more than once or twice."

"Both Merrish and Voryn have territories that border my own," Vara said, somewhat jarringly reminding Cyrus that as Lady of Nalikh'akur, Vara had something more than ceremonial duties. "I've met them both on occasion, and I have a semi-regular correspondence with Voryn. Odellan's father, though—Yemer—him I don't know."

"What do you think the chances are that he's mad at me about his son's death?" Cyrus asked.

"Everyone's mad at you about something," Terian said with a nod. "So … very good, I would think." His gaze flicked over the chain wrapped around Cyrus's chest and waist. "By the way, I grade that a total failure as a fashion statement, but probably an excellent idea for survival purposes." He looked at the others when his quip was greeted with nothing but blank stares. "Oh, come on. Someone had to speak for Vaste since he isn't here."

"I suppose we could have stopped off and picked him up," J'anda said, "if we hadn't wanted to keep our movements as mysterious as possible. Popping in and out of Sanctuary is probably not the wisest of courses, after all."

"About that," Terian said, a little darkly, "you need to use the return spell to get back home."

Cyrus frowned, then the answer came to him. "If there are spies in Sanctuary, they might post an ambush at the portal to the north."

"The topography there lends itself well to hiding," Terian said with a nod, rather sagely. "Tell no one where you're going and don't dare go back via that portal. It's *probably* safe, but I wouldn't stake my life on it, and I'm not even a heretic at the moment."

"Something I noticed in the conversation with Iraid," Vara said, "is that he … almost seemed to offer us counsel on another matter at one point."

"You noticed that, too?" Cattrine asked with a nod. "I think he is subtly trying to prod you in the direction of a solution to your problem with the Confederation but, if you'll recall, it was before he, uhm …"

"Broke cleanly in the direction of giving us aid, yes," J'anda said, nodding. "He was still being careful not to tip his hand at that point." He inclined his head toward Cattrine. "You did a masterful job of drawing him out, I might add."

"Am I the only one that missed whatever you're all talking about?" Cyrus asked, staring at each of them blankly.

"Well, of course," Terian said haughtily. "Even I understood what he was saying, and I wasn't even in the room." He snorted and then shrugged. "Joking, of course. What did he say?"

"He hinted at some of the resentments and divisions in the Human Confederation," Vara said. "He suggested that Reikonos is perhaps taking the lion's share of the resources in rebuilding itself, leaving the outlying districts—the Riverlands, the Northlands, and the Southern

Reaches rather dry."

"There are more districts than that," Cyrus said. "There's also the Western, the Mountain, and the Southeastern Districts."

"Ouch," Terian said. "I can confirm he's right, at least in the Southern Reaches, which borders us. The governor there, Reynard Coulton—well, his state took a walloping from our armies. Prehorta, Idiarna, Santir—Yartraak's armies sacked them all, stripped their crops, murdered their garrisons and their people … the Confederation army sits encamped around Reikonos, a vestigial response to a siege now more than a year over, but Coulton's meager force at arms are all sitting on our border, glaring resentfully with their skeleton defense." He made a sour face. "Coulton has nothing nice to say about me personally, I hear. Seems he thinks that I'm the same as the old boss, and he's just waiting for me to come marching through his desiccated corpse of a territory." He puckered his lips mischievously. "Apparently he doesn't realize I've got better things to do than try to squeeze gold out of a pauper."

"What about the other districts?" Cyrus asked, peering at the dark elf.

"The Riverlands are probably experiencing something similar," Terian said, wincing slightly. "If you recall, after Leaugarden they did receive a nasty shellacking from that undead army, plus Goliath. Malpravus marched them to the coast, plundering and pillaging all the way. That tends to leave a mark. As to the Northlands …" He shrugged. "Our spies don't really consider it a high priority, being so far away. The governor up there is Allyn Frost, and all I know about him is that he's a very vain man. For the other three, the war didn't much touch them, and they're all lacking governors at the moment." He made a face. "Some kind of brouhaha at the end of the war, but the details are a little muddy. Our spies pegged it as internal warring in the Confederation."

"I can verify that Allyn Frost of the Northlands is as Terian says," Cattrine said, nodding. "I've had dealings with him on trade negotiations. He's not unreasonable, but he does have an immense ego, perhaps one of the largest I've seen outside of my former husband or …" She glanced at Cyrus.

Cyrus frowned and clanked his gauntlet against the hanging chains across his chest as he pointed at himself. "Me?"

"He's an older man," Cattrine said, glazing quickly over that. "He's losing his hair and, as near as I can tell, does everything he can to hide it, though it's rather obvious."

"I'm not vain," Cyrus said, frowning. "I mean, I don't have an ego—"

"But of course not," J'anda said soothingly. "What was it you said to the trolls when you invaded their town? Something dramatic and not very humble, I recall. And then there was something about a boasting given to the dark knights at Livlosdald who rode ahead of their armies? And—"

"I do not—" Cyrus looked at Vara, who was rolling her eyes. "I don't, do I?"

"Of course you do, dear," Vara said. "There's a thin line between immense self-confidence and ego, and you stand astride it like a titan and cross handily over every time you forcefully remind those who you are about to kill of all those whom you have struck down before them. I can't say your confidence isn't somewhat deserved, though it is also curiously thin at times, vanishing like a dark elf's self-respect at the opportunity to whore around—"

Terian frowned. "Not all of us are whores. Some of us merely do the partaking." His eyes flashed around the circle. "I mean, I don't anymore … but, you know. Before."

"Taking us back to the subject at hand …" J'anda said. "So the potential weaknesses in the Human Confederation boil down to divisions of state and, much like the ones in the Elven Kingdom, fracture along territorial lines. How curiously predictable."

"Look at it from their perspective—which is really analogous to my small state's perspective," Cattrine said. "We are nominally part of the Elven Kingdom and ruled by Danay, but have almost no elves among our populace and are subject to a monarch who likely would have flooded us with troops last year after his daughter's death merely to assert his control. Now, you could argue that he runs roughshod over us because we are mostly humans, settled in his lands, but we are also one of the most-taxed provinces because of the enormous amount of production that comes out of our territory, and we have no voice in his court, he does not build roads or protect us with his troops … essentially we pay him for existing." She looked around the small group. "And so it is with the other provinces—though they receive some protection from the military, especially in the north from the trolls and in Termina from the dark elves. But they also commit their own local troops to these causes, and so they are left to question: what does the monarch do for me? Because they certainly send wagons of gold in tribute to the palace in Pharesia. And in places like the Emerald Coast, they have not seen a soldier within their borders since the days of the troll war."

"Well, we also get that most excellent caste system that acts as a virtual prison for every person in the Kingdom outside of Termina and now, Emerald Fields," Vara said acidly. "Because surely no elf should ever desire to be more than they are."

Cyrus's head was whirling. "What we're talking about here ..." He let out a low breath. "Exploiting divisions in these powers? What's the endgame if we go this route? Prying apart the Kingdom and the Confederation? Fragmenting them into smaller states that will fight each other in nasty border wars?"

"Provided they're not crushing in your walls, why do you care?" Terian asked with a careful glint in his eyes.

Cyrus gave him a leaden look. "You know damned well why I care. Because our function in Sanctuary is not to leave Arkaria torn down to its foundations." He took a slow breath, feeling as if all the hope were slowly draining out of him. "We were supposed to help people. To save this land from dire threats, not become one ourselves."

Terian gazed at him sadly. "You're really struggling with this decision, aren't you?"

Cyrus shrugged languidly. "Well, I'm not exactly like an arrow shot from the bow on it. More like—"

"A drunken donkey staggering down a mountain path with a heavy burden on your back?" Terian asked.

"So flattering," Cyrus said, "but yes. Near enough."

"Cyrus," Cattrine said softly. "You look to protect Arkaria from threats, but who started a war that killed countless of its people?"

"Pretnam Urides," Cyrus said, sighing. "The Council of Twelve. Danay, at least, had a hand in it. Yartraak."

"Well, Yartraak's dead," Terian said. "He won't be starting any more wars, and neither will the Sovereignty, so long as I'm in charge." He grinned. "Congratulations. You've saved Arkaria from the dreaded dark elven menace."

"And the goblin one," Vara said quietly.

"And the titan one," J'anda said.

"And probably the troll threat as well," Cattrine said. "And while the Confederation and the Kingdom are certainly reeling from the last war and in no mood to start another large-scale conflict, even your cautious mind must admit that they are not hesitating to throw their weight at smaller 'threats'—such as you."

"Cyrus," Vara said, taking hold of his hand, "you were there when Pretnam Urides courted the war with the dark elves. Alaric told me of his gleeful mood when it was declared. He and his fellows thought it a chance for their glory, to expand their holdings in the Plains of Perdamun. What did they do, by their hands, by playing into Yartraak's?" She stiffened. "Countless villages and homesteads in the plains, pillaged and destroyed. Reikonos and Termina, plundered. The Riverlands, sacked. Yartraak even had Aloakna, a city of his own expatriates, purged from the map with fire and slaughter. All that was begun with Pretnam Urides's happy consent. And Danay was hardly blameless; he sent troops to the plains as well, and it was mere luck that we resolved the issue before he had cause to run his forces against the dark elves as well. It bought him months before he was dragged into the conflict, one he would have happily embraced were his armies not drawing down by my peoples' aging population."

"And for our part," Terian said, standing almost silently, seething anger in his expression, "the dark elves lost one half of our young men under the age of five hundred. The poor of Sovar were ground down by the war that Yartraak started but that Urides conspired to make happen. This was not a fight of the God of Darkness's own invention; it was the imperial ambitions of powers crossed against each one another, man versus god battling for territory and control. Urides fanned those flames, and millions died on our side and the human side, and all were left ragged by its end. We'd be in the midst of a famine that would be killing the entire land if not for the timely arrival of the Luukessians in Emerald Fields." He nodded at Cattrine.

"Yes, well," Cattrine said darkly, "it was an unfortunate chain of events that led us here, but those that have survived have made the most of it and are growing more prosperous, freer and happier than ever we were in Luukessia—save for that tyrant in Pharesia who wishes to keep us beneath his boot."

"This is all about control," Terian said. "Whether it's the Leagues,

Danay, or Urides and the Council of Twelve, they seek to control the actions of their people, to keep some down and some up, through force of social constraints, magical laws or simple force." He broke into a grin. "Personally, I like that you've driven all our enemies into such a tight cluster—Derregnault and Amarath's Raiders," he nodded to Vara, "Urides and his Council brethren, King Danay," he nodded to Cattrine, "the Leagues, and ..." he broke into a bigger smile, "let's not forget Goliath, where we have Malpravus, Carrack, Orion, Rhane, my old friend Sareea ... it's almost like you've corralled them together and lined them up for easier slaughter."

Cyrus blinked. "I don't believe there's going to be anything easy about trying to wipe out that list."

"But we're going to do it," Terian said, "provided you don't lose your nerve."

"I'm starting to get a little clearer picture of how," Cyrus said, "but I still don't know if I believe it's possible."

"Oh, it's possible," Vara said. "We just have to do to them what they've been doing to us all along." A hard look fell over the paladin's face. "Divide and conquer."

"Let's just hope they don't divide us first," Cyrus said, his mind running to faraway lands, wondering about what was going on all around them, even as they planned their own moves. "Because I suspect Goliath and the rest aren't just standing around, waiting to see what we do ..."

20.

When the meeting was over, Cyrus, Vara, J'anda, Cattrine and Terian returned quietly to the portal and the waiting Bowe and Larana. Cattrine and Terian disappeared in the rushing wind of Bowe's teleport spell while Cyrus stared at the others, considering his next action. "J'anda, Vara …" he said quietly, "return without us, will you? I need to speak with Larana for a moment."

Vara raised an eyebrow at that, but held her tongue from unleashing whatever was on her mind. "I will expect you back in our quarters in ten minutes," she said instead. "We have things to discuss."

"Yes," J'anda agreed with a light smile. "Many, many things. Things of various natures, of importance … the state of the Merlots for last year, for instance …"

Vara rolled her eyes. "Brilliant cover." She glanced at Larana. "She may be quiet, but she's no idiot."

Larana's eyelids fluttered. "Thank you," she mumbled.

"Ten minutes," Vara said, twirling her fingers as she cast the return spell and disappeared in a twinkle of light.

"We will discuss the wines in twenty minutes," J'anda said with amused self-assurance, "for I doubt you will need any more time than that." And then he disappeared as well.

Cyrus stood on the empty savanna with Larana as a light wind blew through, stirring some of the long grass, lying at a forty-five degree angle from the ground, reminding him of the light slope of the Grand Span in Termina at its start. The grass, however, was a bridge leading nowhere, its thick mat a perfect cover for the south's enormous animals. Cyrus was reminded of the immense cats that made this place home, bigger than horses and able to stalk quietly through the grasses.

He shuddered and looked at the druid who stood with him. "I wanted to talk to you for a minute before we go back," Cyrus said, staring off into the distance to the south. He could see the beginnings of mountains in the distance. *Somewhere in that direction lies a city in ruins because of my actions.*

All my other enemies have died save for Goliath, Danay, Urides and ... Archenous. Perhaps it is inevitable that this moment comes, that I'm compelled to destroy them as well.

Perhaps ... this is the only thing I'm good at.

"What did you want to talk about?" Larana asked in her usual quiet voice.

"I wanted to thank you for transporting us today," Cyrus said, "and ask you again to please keep secret from absolutely everyone where we've gone."

She nodded hastily. "Of course."

Cyrus took a step that crunched a blade of grass as wide as his thigh. "Did your father ... ever talk about my mother?" He glanced sideways at her.

Larana stiffened and her eyes came slowly up, wide with worry. "Did you ... do you know anything about her?" Her face was lined with worry, but under the dirt he could see that she looked younger even than he.

"I know she's Quinneria," Cyrus said, carefully watching Larana's reaction. She flinched as though she'd been smacked in the arm. "Did he tell you that?"

"Yes," she said after a moment in which she composed herself and cast her eyes downward again. "He did."

"I find myself in the curious position of wishing like hell I'd asked Belkan more about my parents when I had a chance," Cyrus said, pursing his lips. "Now I'm left with more questions than answers, and few people to ask. If Cora was within easy reach, you can bet I'd be happy to interrogate the hell out of her at this point. Same goes for Alaric, and Curatio." He looked at Larana, who stayed very still. "Alaric killed my mother, did you know that?" She nodded. "And Belkan delivered me, an orphan, from Cora—one of the founders of Sanctuary—to the Society of Arms." Cyrus watched her carefully, and she nodded again. "Do you know why he did that? Handed me over to people who tried to kill me?"

"Because there was no way around it, he said." Her voice was soft and worried. "They knew about you."

"Who?" Cyrus asked, focusing in on her, stunned. *I should have asked her this months ago, but I just assumed, that, as with my father's sword, she knew nothing.*

"Urides," Larana said. "The Council of Twelve? I ... I don't know. Whoever controlled things in Reikonos. They knew you existed, that you were somewhere in the city. Alaric—he feared what they would do if they caught you out of the public eye, that they would kill you for certain, no chance of intervention."

"Gods," Cyrus gasped. "No one ever told me any of this."

"Because they would have killed you if you'd known, if you'd shown any inkling of remembering," Larana said quietly. "Belkan ... my father ... told me that Alaric struck the deal that saw you handed over. That he sent someone to watch over you for a time in the Society—"

"Erkhardt," Cyrus said numbly. "He sent Erkhardt. I remember him now. And when I ..." There was a tingle of loss, and Cyrus's voice cracked. "When I ran away from the Society on induction day, I think Alaric brought me back."

"It was the only safe place for you," Larana said, her eyes big and mournful. "Quinneria ... your mother ... she knew there was no escaping what was after her." Her head drooped again. "What's after you, now. They all came for her too, all the armies of Arkaria. Hounded her into the Plains of Perdamun, chased her until she ran across Sanctuary ... and into Alaric." She bowed her head. "He ... he ended her flight. Brought her down at last. As she lay dying, she made him promise ... Belkan said she died after making Alaric swear that he would ensure your safety."

"I don't really remember her," Cyrus said, voice rough, heart strangely numb. He looked into Larana's face, streaked with ash from either the cooking fires or her own blacksmithing efforts. "I didn't even know she was the Sorceress until someone told me a few months ago." He cracked a grim, mirthless smile. "My mother is the most famous person in Arkaria, outside perhaps my wife, and I barely remember a thing about her."

"It's probably for the better," Larana said, eyeing him, her head still down. "If you'd remembered—anything—of who she truly was, Belkan said they would have killed you. Alaric convinced them to take the chance because you were just a child. They were scared of what you might become. He suggested the Society, played on your father's name … and Belkan said they went for it, hoping desperately for another Rusyl Davidon … and frightened of what would happen if you ever discovered what you were capable of … What she was teaching you to be."

Cyrus flicked his fingers as he repeated a spell in his mind, and a small fire sprang from the tips of his gauntlets, the size of a torch's flame only. It was a fraction of what he was capable of at this point; he'd been practicing. "I know what I'm capable of now, but still I hesitate. My power is becoming clearer to me, but the targets … the places I'd direct it … I fear to turn loose against them, in spite of knowing they mean to kill me, to skin me away from my fellows, my friends, and end me in the dark of night with nary a witness, if they could." He looked at Larana. "You must think it strange, this … reticence on my part."

"You're a good man," Larana said quietly. "You don't want to hurt anyone."

"Oh, but I do," Cyrus said sadly. "I just know that afterwards I'll regret it. When I came to Sanctuary, I could kill anyone. I thought. But Alaric changed me. He made me consider things beyond myself, beyond those who had attached themselves to me. And yet, the more these … outsiders … come for me, the more I'm reminded of where my home is, where I belong, and who I should be fighting for. The trust, the bonds of closeness between me and my army, of those who are still standing with me as the world turns against me …" He shook his head. "It's as though I never even knew Alaric at all. As though all our talk of purpose has slipped away in the night, replaced by grinning, leering, angry faces of my enemies."

Larana hesitated. "I was … with Sanctuary before you were." She licked her lips, seemingly afraid to speak her mind.

"Go on," Cyrus said.

"I knew Alaric before you did—" Larana said.

"I doubt it," Cyrus said with a knowing smile.

Larana swallowed heavily. "Well, I've known him for a long time. I grew up in Sanctuary. You … you remember the talk, the ideals. But … I saw more. I saw it all. You forget … when Mortus hit you … Alaric was the first to strike back. When your friend died in Enterra … Alaric went there and ravaged them, killing hundreds to save us from permanent death. And when Partus barely even threatened Vara, Alaric killed him in an instant." Her head was the farthest up Cyrus could recall seeing it, and her voice was stronger than he ever remembered hearing it. "Alaric may have only had one eye, but he ... he had two hands. One was the hand of friendship ... and the other was the fist of merciless vengeance, and he used them both. He just didn't do it selfishly." She bowed her head again. "He didn't start a personal vendetta after the titans killed Raifa, but when someone went after his ... his family ... there was nothing he would not do to see it righted." She lowered her voice. "It's why he came for you on the Endless Bridge."

"The way you say it," Cyrus spoke quietly into the wind of the savanna, "he wouldn't hesitate to make war if he were in my position now."

"You didn't start the war," she said, "and neither would he. But he would finish it." Her eyes glinted. "However he had to. Sanctuary ... it was everything to him. Anyone threatening Sanctuary—they'd get the vengeance, not the friendship."

"Thank you," Cyrus said, looking down at her. She nodded once. "For ... all of this."

She curtsied, a peculiar sight in her dull robes. "I am at your service, m'lord." And she smiled ever so faintly through the streaked dirt on her face.

21.

"That was longer than ten minutes," Vara said as Cyrus reappeared in the light of his return spell, the Tower of the Guildmaster forming around him. Her tone was somewhere between worried and playful; Cyrus couldn't quite tell which it leaned toward.

"Well, she didn't try and kill me," he said, taking a deep breath of the still air within the shut tower before moving toward the wooden dummy and beginning to remove his armor.

"Always an excellent sign," Vara said with a nod. She moved to stand next to him and pulled her gauntlet off. "What did you talk about?"

"I asked her about my mother," Cyrus said, and watched Vara's frown deepen, "and she offered some insight on how Alaric might have handled our current situation."

"I shudder to think what perspective she might have gained from within the bounds of the kitchens," Vara said, removing her other glove, a sheen of perspiration obvious on her palms. "I trust her recommendation was not something along the lines of 'Burn them all to death within the confines of a good stew pot'?"

"It was not," Cyrus said, frowning at his wife. "She suggested, having grown up in Sanctuary, that Alaric might in fact have been a less kindly figure than I recalled him being. That behind his moralizing, his purpose, was a man who wouldn't hesitate to strike viciously at anyone who came after those he cared about."

"There is truth to that," Vara conceded, though she sounded reluctant. "Though he certainly preached the moral high road, I myself saw him do occasionally terrible, wrathful things when our members were threatened. Such is the life of a knight of any sort, I suppose, any protector."

"Yeah." Cyrus kicked off his boots one by one, cloth foot covers pressing against the hard stone floor. "Still ... that apparent divide between what Alaric preached and what he did ... I can't decide whether to find it troubling and ignore it as an area where his grasp fell short of his reach or admire and emulate it as necessary measures in the situation we find ourselves trapped in."

"It troubles me as well," Vara said, "but I find myself less divided about this than you are." Her eyes flashed. "Archenous wronged me terribly, and I parted ways with him quite content to never so much as look in his direction again. But now his goal brings him back my way again, and I find myself regretting not having taken the very un-paladin-like step of removing his head years ago so he would never have been able to ambush you in that market." Her mouth twisted in anger. "He has revived our hostility, not me, and the same goes for Danay, Urides, and Goliath. This is not petty vengeance, and these are not virtuous men. So long as we direct our attacks against them, no matter how subtly or surreptitiously, I find myself morally untroubled."

"I don't argue with any of that," Cyrus said, shaking his head. "It's always the consequences, though." She looked at him curiously. "Killing Mortus, for example. He was a cruel, ruthless, horrible creature," he took a breath. "And yet, the events that sprang from killing the God of Death led to Luukessia, to the Scourge. And although killing Yartraak brought Terian to the throne, it could just as easily have brought someone terrible. I worry what could happen if we charge headlong into killing Urides or Danay." He made a clicking noise with his tongue. "We may not pay that piper alone. The Kingdom, the Confederation ... we don't know how things would go in those places, even if we did manage to orchestrate the removal of our enemies. We don't know what it will cost in terms of alliances."

"That's a fair concern," Vara said, unstrapping her breastplate. With it gone, Cyrus could see the clinging cloth shirt she wore beneath, tightly hugging her curves. "And something I think we should discuss in great detail before settling on a final plan. If putting ourselves in alliance with Iraid and the others he named somehow ties us into darker action ..." She sighed. "Well, I don't want to cross certain lines any more than you do. Assassinating kings and oligarchs of dubious character is all well and good, but ..."

"But if it leads to the deaths of countless more innocents in a civil war," Cyrus finished as she nodded, "or puts one of those powers under the heel of some governor who wants to be dictator … I start to have a problem with it."

"Agreed," she said. "None of that." She slipped into his arms, the sweat of the day pungent in his nose. He pulled off the chain mail that wrapped his body and let it drop to the floor next to the long mystical ball and chain he'd draped around himself. She kissed him softly upon the lips and then looked into his eyes. "But if we can destroy Amarath's Raiders at the end of this, my conscience will not be troubled."

"I know you hate to ask for help," Cyrus said, curling her up in his arms, "but I think we both know someone who has more recent familiarity with the Big Three, including Amarath's Raiders, and who would probably be willing to help."

Vara slumped in his arms, her head thumping against his chest. "Urk. As though Iraid's request was not vexing enough."

Cyrus smiled faintly. "Would it really be so bad asking Isabelle for help? I mean, she's your sister, after all."

Vara took a deep breath and sighed, her warm breath sighing through his undershirt and tickling his chest hairs beneath. "No. And yes."

"Both?"

"She will help, surely," Vara said, moving her head around to lean the opposite direction on his chest as they stood there, her body soft against him. "But you know I don't like asking for help, and suddenly I am forced to seek out much of it, and from many quarters."

"Apparently I'm not the only one with pride," Cyrus said with a light smile.

"Ego and pride are not exactly the same thing," Vara said sharply. She paused a moment then said, considerably more softly, "But they are not so different, either. You and I are well matched for many reasons, and this is one of them, I think." She looked up at him, her eyes weary. The low winter sun had already faded beneath the windows outside the western balcony and the room was growing dark. "Shall we go to bed?" She ran a hand lightly over his chest playfully.

Cyrus suppressed a smile. "So long as you promise to start asking for that help on the morrow—"

"Yes, yes," she said, pressing herself tightly against him. He could feel the lingering hesitation in her grip, though, the desire not to let go, and as she looked up to kiss him once more, he happily let himself forget all that was weighing on him, at least for the night, in the comfort of his wife's arms.

22.

Cyrus was awakened by a pounding at the door in the middle of the night, the urgent hammering enough to snap him out of a dreamlike state. He sat up as Vara did the same beside him, her hand upon her sword, already drawn from its scabbard. He was slower to react, fumbling for his blade and calling out, "Yes? Who is it?"

"It's Calene," came a soft voice from outside. "We've got trouble at the wall, best hurry down." The sound of retreating footsteps echoed in Cyrus's ears as the ranger left without further explanation.

Cyrus met Vara's gaze for only a second before they both slipped naked out of their bed and dressed in silence, hurrying to make ready for whatever was waiting below.

Cyrus took longer to finish. The process of wrapping the chain and spiked ball carefully around himself so that the ball did not hit him in any unarmored places took some considerable care and left Vara sighing with impatience at the top of the staircase down to the door, clearly eager to descend.

When he was finally ready, they rushed down the stairs. Vara easily outpaced him, aided by the mystical nature of the enchantments on her armor. Cyrus clung to the grip of the morning star with his left hand and increased his speed enough so as not to be left completely behind by her. Their metal-booted feet clanged, the sound echoing through the central tower's immense staircase as they hurried down.

"We should learn Falcon's Essence," Vara said, under her breath. "Perhaps Larana could teach us. It would make descents quite a bit easier; all we would need to do would be to open the balcony and run."

"I'll put that on my list," Cyrus said tautly. "Though I admit, learning illusions is one of my priorities at the moment, now that I've got a good start on wizarding spells from Mendicant."

"I find 'return' to be quite a boon, personally," Vara said. "I had long wondered why paladins and dark knights were the only spellcasters who did not receive the use of that particular gem of the craft."

"It would make armies too mobile," Cyrus said, and when she looked at him in surprise, he elaborated. "Think about it—the ability for troops to move themselves swiftly from one point to another? It makes them less reliant on other spellcasters. Troops could defend two separate places almost at once. The power of an army would grow exponentially."

"Only if they had countless knights rather than the handful produced each year from each of the two Leagues that is responsible for them," she murmured, but he sensed her thoughts running away with her. "It also assumes that every member of said army could use spells," she went on after a moment's thought. "Clearly this is not so. Even now, even knowing the words to the spells, our warriors and rangers, with the apparent exception of you, with your mother's magical blood, still cannot cast a spell."

"True enough," Cyrus said as they reached the bottom of the stairs and hurried across the foyer and out the doors. The starry night above them shone like a shimmering black tapestry made of silk and punctured with tiny holes, a torch shining behind it. They climbed the stairs at the wall nearest the gate, where a knot of troops was gathered, staring over the parapets.

Scuddar and Calene waited for them, along with Menlos and a dozen other guards, all of them alternating nervous looks over the wall and then back down it, seemingly afraid to take their eyes off the perimeter for fear of breach.

"What is it?" Cyrus asked before he reached the edge. He strode forward before the answer came, the wall's guardians stunned into silence as he reached the nearest crenellations and looked out, Vara in the next gap to his. Cyrus stuck his head out carefully, as though an arrow might come launching at him. It didn't, and in the faint moonlight he saw but a single figure standing before the gate, a shadow in the dark of knight. "Another messenger?" he asked.

"Of a sort," Scuddar said in a low voice. "Light, please."

Guards above the gate extended torches out of the crenellations and the light shone down on the messenger. Cyrus made a small gasp of disgust as the orange fire lit rotted features, exposed bone, and glazed, white eyes in the dark figure.

"Gods, it's a wendigo," Cyrus said.

"No," Scuddar said, shaking his cowled head. "It is a corpse."

Cyrus frowned and stuck his head out of the crenellations again. He peered down at the thing standing expectantly before the gate. It *was* a corpse, he realized, a dead body of some sort, putrefied enough that the smell wafted up at him. "I'm not used to seeing the dead walk of late, I suppose," Cyrus muttered. "But you're right. That's ..."

"Necromancy," Vara said with a disgust of her own.

"It's a gift, really," came Malpravus's voice, high and hissing, from the corpse's mouth. Its white eyes glowed now as it looked up at Cyrus. "You of all people, dear boy, should know the value of a good display of power."

"Your power doesn't impress me, Malpravus," Cyrus called down to the vessel waiting below. *That thing is a mere conduit for him to annoy us, just a means for him to reach out and extend the sound of his voice to our ears.* "It never has and it never will."

"I hear there are dead," Vaste's voice said from behind Cyrus, the sound of his footsteps echoing on the topmost steps. He thumped his way over to Cyrus's right and leaned out of the crenellations. "Well, shit. That thing's dead all right."

"It's Malpravus," Cyrus said.

"If only," Vaste said with longing. "I'd exorcise his bony arse right now and this thing would be all over except for the crying. Well, the crying and Amarath's Raiders, the Elven Kingdom, and the Human Confederation."

"Plus all his assorted and annoying lieutenants," Vara added.

"Maybe they're all secretly dead puppets," Vaste said.

"No one is dead in my armies," Malpravus's voice rose from the decomposing corpse. "Your friend Terian—he made sure that those forces of mine did not survive the war. A tragic waste, of course, but so it goes. Now I have new armies at my disposal, new allies—but you know all that." The corpse lifted a hand, and clutched within it was another lock of dark hair, shining from the moon above. "I have many means at my disposal. Many ... threads ... to pull."

"What did you do with Imina?" Cyrus asked, a cold chill unrelated to the winter's night shivering down his back.

"She is safe," Malpravus replied, and Cyrus could all but hear the smile in his voice. "For now. Much like yourself, though, her position grows more precarious by the day."

"He's going to offer you a very bad deal," Vaste said in a whisper. "Whatever you do, don't be stupid and accept it. You know the value of his word is less than that of a letter from Terian to Pretnam Urides."

"I agree with the troll," Vara said, "Malpravus is a liar. If you gave yourself up in hopes of saving Imina, you would find yourself beside her in death."

Cyrus took a slow breath, and the truth sank in with the chill. "I know."

"Come out, Cyrus," Malpravus's voice called. "I will offer you the same opportunity that Pretnam Urides did, with an additional benefit— your former wife will be returned, safe and sound, minus only a few locks of hair."

"It seems to me that doesn't settle your problem, Malpravus," Cyrus called down to the corpse, which shuffled forward a step. "Because it's not just me that the Leagues want now. It's at least the entire Sanctuary Council, and you haven't asked for them."

"I remain unconcerned with the chaff," Malpravus said. "I wish to harvest the wheat."

"Oh, that's charming," Vaste sniffed. "I'll have you know I'm at least twice the wheat of this man."

"Come now," Malpravus said. "You must know how desperately fenced in you are. No matter how many meetings you take trying to stir up allies, you will find yourself in the same pen, like an animal, the reins growing ever tighter, until the slaughter comes. At least now you can meet it at the hour of your choosing rather than wonder and worry for all the rest of your days."

"Maybe you should be the one to worry, Malpravus," Cyrus said calmly.

"Dear boy," Malpravus said, the corpse gaping at him with a deathly grin, "I have denuded you of almost all your forces. My good friend Mathyas Tarreau took half your remaining number only last night. You have nine hundred and thirty-two remaining members of your guild in Sanctuary. Your friends the Luukessians are rightly guarding their own lands from reprisal by the elf king. Your friend the Sovereign finds himself in the same predicament, though I do not think he realizes how much his own realm would suffer from the armies of Reikonos marching upon his borders. And you and your pitiful remnant sit here, stewing in your own fear. It is like a rot, a putrefaction. With every month that passes, you will see more of the soft flesh peeled off until all that is left is the bone." The corpse extended a rotted hand, nothing but ivory knuckles remaining of the limb. "And I think you know … rotted flesh and exposed bone is my servant, not yours. Sanctuary will die, and I will own its corpse."

The chills prickled up and down Cyrus's neck. "I don't think so," he said, filled with defiance. "Vaste?"

"You're not the only one who exercises control over death, you prick," Vaste said and extended a hand. With a flash of white, the corpse glowed, and then tumbled to the ground in pieces, the power of the necromancer expelled from it.

Into the quiet night, Cyrus pushed back from the wall, his teeth gritted and bared, his cold fury turned hot.

"Are you all right?" Vara asked, seeing him as she brought her head back inside as well.

"He looks well, actually," Vaste said, flexing the massive hand he'd just cast the spell with. "Better than I've seen him in some time. More … certain." The troll's eyes flashed with extra meaning.

"I am certain," Cyrus said, feeling as though his very spine had been reforged of quartal. *There is no doubt now.*

We must destroy them.

"Think it over, dear boy," came a voice from over the wall, drawing Cyrus and the others to look back out. Vara gasped as she stuck her head out the teeth of the wall.

The plains were dotted with corpses. A dozen, two dozen, more— stood, spread evenly across the ground before the walls, wide gaps between them. Their heads were tilted at odd angles, their shuffling steps making a soft noise through the grass.

"There must be … hundreds of them," Vara said quietly.

"Consider my offer," the corpses said in unison, Malpravus's high voice echoing with mirth in a perverse chorus. "Before it becomes … too late." A soft cackle crowed over the plains outside the walls of Sanctuary, causing that tingle down Cyrus's back to reverberate even stronger.

We must kill them all.

However we have to.
Because our enemies ... will strike at everyone we care about.
They will raise the dead to get at us.
There is no other choice.
We must kill them all.

23.

Cyrus stared at the list in his hand, names upon parchment, written in clean strokes but blotched from haste. It had a distinct aroma about it, the deep scent of the ink, the rough smell of the parchment. Sniffing deeply, he remained unsure which fought harder for his attention. He knew only the urgency with which he read the names, over and over again.

Lady Voryn of the Emerald Coast

Lord Merrish of Traegon

Karrin Waterman—Governor of the Riverlands

Allyn Frost—Governor of the Northlands

Reynard Coulton—Governor of the Southern Reaches

"I would add Isabelle to that," Vara said, staring at the smudged list. "As well as … perhaps Cora. Amti's disdain for King Danay would mesh well with our efforts."

"Cattrine has already spoken with them," Terian said, standing in the shadows next to Cyrus. He smiled. "They're most definitely in for whatever gets Danay out of their business."

"Isn't this exciting?" Vaste asked, rubbing his enormous hands together. It was only a day removed from their encounter with Malpravus's undead messengers at the walls, and the troll had spent a long morning out on the plains, exorcising old corpses and having them piled up in a great pyre and burned while a bevy of archers watched them from the walls. There had been other dead lurking farther from the wall than Cyrus had wished to chance sending forces out, and they had remained there, watching. "Finally, we're scheming and starting trouble in the houses of our enemies the way that they've been loosing discord on us from the beginning."

"It is quite the relief to adopt the tactics of Malpravus," J'anda said with a dose of irony and a measured smile. His eyes flitted to the fifth member of their party, locked into the Tower of the Guildmaster with the rest of them. "I don't understand why we can't just assassinate Pretnam Urides and Danay and be done with it, though."

Aisling stood before the main hearth in the tower, her navy hands aglow with the light of the fire as she extended them over the blaze, seeking warmth. "If all you wanted was the leaders of those nations dead, we could do it." She spoke languidly, with less feeling than Cyrus could ever recall hearing from her, except perhaps on the day that he met her in the Grand Palace of Saekaj after killing Yartraak. Her purple eyes glowed in the firelight and found his. "But of course, the falling out from that would be … swift. The Council of Twelve would appoint another head, one of Urides's partisans, perhaps, or his opposition, and you would not know what direction they would take next, save that it would hardly stop their pursuit of you. Same with the King of the elves," she said with a sniff, as if testing the fire for smell, though she showed no reaction to the sweet aroma. "Kill him, and at best you get a clean succession to the next in line for the throne. While the new Queen—Roma, I think her name is? might be less experienced, she would likely follow the guidance of the Leagues to move against you without hesitation, for why would she sway from the orthodoxy? Vengeance would be swift in coming, and you'd soon find armies outside your gates instead of mere corpses." Aisling shook her head. "No. The reason for these meetings, these allies, is so that when the axe falls upon your foes, the succession goes the way you want, and those empires halt their pursuit because whoever is now at their head is either directed to reunifying their realm, or is actually a friend to you."

"We seem to have found the right advisor when it comes to basest treachery," Vara mused, but with considerably less sting in her voice than usual. "Goddess help us."

"Let's hope," Vaste said cheerily. "So how do we make these people," he gestured at the list cradled in Cyrus's hand, "do what we want, and push their nations to leave us the hell alone?"

"Kill Danay and split the Kingdom," Terian said, nodding, in thought, "forcing the Provincial Lords and Ladies to choose a new monarch. Get these few on your side, and along with Vara, you have a chance to push the succession to one of them, fates be willing to your new friend Oliaryn Iraid." His eyes flashed in amusement. "He takes the simmering heat currently on Sanctuary and douses the flames, as he suggested to you," he looked directly at Vara, "well … you know."

"That still leaves us with the Confederation," Cyrus said, staring at the top three names on the list. "And Amarath's Raiders, before we get to Goliath."

"That one's a bit more of an impenetrable trap, I'll admit," Terian said, nodding. "However, if Iraid has suggested correctly, and there are divisions, we need to find them and exploit them. The elves are much closer allies with the humans, and probably Iraid, being right on their border, will have insight gained through trade that my spies, through subterfuge, might not."

"Amarath's Raiders is as breakable as any other army," Vara said. "Once we get around to them, I might have a few ideas to halt their enthusiastic approach to us, but—as pointed out by my dear husband—my sister is more recently acquainted with them than I am. She should be able to confirm if my suspicions are still accurate."

"What are your suspicions?" Aisling asked cautiously. She sounded very conciliatory to Cyrus's ears, as though she were trying desperately to avoid provoking Vara at all.

"That Amarath's Raiders have become a cult of personality centered around Archenous Derregnault," she said, a little frustration bleeding out, but not directed at Aisling. *That's progress*, Cyrus thought. "When Trayance Parloure ran the Raiders, it was a guild top heavy with leadership, with commanding officers who could think for themselves and who commanded smaller squads, so they could operate independently in a crisis. That way, if, for example, during a fight with the Siren of Fire, she killed the Guildmaster or Expedition Leader, the war party was not utterly incapacitated." She ran a hand along the side of her hair, drawn up into the ponytail, inadvertently freeing a few golden strands. "If it is as I suspect, and Archenous has remade the guild in his dictatorial image, then all that free thinking will have melted away like ice in summer. Killing him and a few of his closest lieutenants could end the guild as an effective force outright."

"Tyrants don't like fellow leaders," Terian said, rubbing his throat uncomfortably. "They think of them as competition."

"That is Archenous exactly," Vara said stiffly. "It is why he took command the way he did, and the reason he wiped all the rest of us out who could think for ourselves. I have heard he can no longer hear so much as a criticism breathed in his direction without flying off the handle at the person who speaks it." She looked down. "More than a few have died at his hand since the betrayal."

"All personal concern or grudge aside," J'anda said quietly, "I find this all hopeful news, even the situation among the humans. Now we merely need find an entry point to their political circles and perhaps we start making headway."

Cyrus looked right at the enchanter. "I'm glad to hear you say that, because ... I think you might be that very entry point."

J'anda sighed, his very slight frame seeming to swell under the influence of a large breath. "But of course." He bowed his head in resignation. "I am at your service, as always."

"I might need you to go to Asaliere with Cattrine," Cyrus said. "She's trying to get a meeting with Karrin Waterman, and we'll need someone to present our case who doesn't appear to be a current heretic."

"Hmph," J'anda said. "I could teach you to make yourself not look like a heretic."

Cyrus shook his head. "This is a preliminary arrangement to meet, on neutral territory, with the location to be determined and teleportation to be provided by us. I don't want to chance walking into an ambush in the Confederation."

"Any territorial governor in the Confederation would have to be nuts to consider taking you up on that offer," Terian said, his hand dropping from his chin. "You're basically talking about asking them to trust you enough to have an unfamiliar wizard whisk them away to who knows where without guarantee of safe return." He shook his head. "Don't expect any takers."

"If you've got a better idea, I'm listening," Cyrus said.

"I've got a better idea," Terian said with a smirk. "Cattrine offers a tour to the three governors you're looking to meet with. They all do some nominal amount of trade with her, so she makes a conference of it, and holds it in the Emerald Fields—"

"Which are our known ally," Cyrus said, frowning.

"It's not a perfect plan," Terian said, "but again, there's trade between these parties. The threads of war are not tightly wound between Emerald Fields and the Confederation just yet. They're far too reliant on the Luukessian farms to want to cross that line. If things break to war, the humans are going to come for the Sovereignty, or possibly bypass us and head straight for you while the elves deal with Emerald Fields. Count on it." He folded his arms in front of him. "Thus, Cattrine has the ability to call that meeting with a just little finagling. She can get this done, she's already told me."

"It's a shame she's not here to speak for herself," Vara said, a little acerbically.

"Having all of us meeting together every time is a dangerous game," Aisling said, "regardless of how careful we are. Too many eyes are watching the people in this room; it's helpful to vary the lineup of this shadow council so that we can at least try to keep Malpravus and the others from guessing at who might be conspiring against them."

"He already knows we're up to something," Cyrus said, feeling that tight sensation inside once more. "He alluded to 'meetings' when he sent his dead to our doorstep last night."

"He sees to the motives of people more clearly than most anyone I have ever met," J'anda said quietly.

"All he cares about is power, though," Terian added. "That's his weakness. I don't think he can conceive of people acting for reasons outside their self-interest when it doesn't align with his beliefs. Honor, decency, loyalty—these are the things we can blindside him with."

"Meanwhile, he can blindside us with treachery," Vaste said. "Well, that and a hundred and seventy five thousand swords, spears, axes and spells." He paused as if to think it over. "I know which one I would bet on right now."

"Well, let's get to whittling that number down," Terian said, looking at the parchment in Cyrus's hand. "I'll start sending messages through Bowe and Cattrine."

Cyrus held the parchment a moment longer than he had to before thrusting it into Terian's waiting hands. "Be careful with this."

"As though it were my own life in my hands," he said, nodding once at Cyrus. His smile drew down, a wistful look taking shape under his long nose. "Because really, if you bunch of mummers get taken out ... it won't be that long before they come for me."

24.

The note from Isabelle came back the fastest, a few days later, a simple missive on a small scrap of parchment that provided Cyrus and Vara a time and place, and was written in her own hand. It said, simply:

Mountains of Nartanis Portal—Tonight at the fall of evening

Cyrus and Vara settled in to wait, spending a quiet day lost in thought, neither speaking much. The air was thick with tension that Cyrus had no words, no weapon, to cut through.

When the hour came at last, Cyrus and Vara descended to the foyer. The last of the dinner crowd was waning, and Cyrus realized for the first time that he had not eaten today. His stomach rumbled slightly as they walked across the circle of the great stone seal, casting looks around for a druid or wizard.

"Shall we ask Larana?" Vara asked quietly, her eyes following two of the new trolls as they wandered toward the lounge, large flagons clutched in their hands.

"We may have to," Cyrus said, looking around. Once again, warriors and rangers were the only members in sight. *I wonder how many spellcasters we have left? We need a count on that, not just total members.* Motion close to the ground caught his eye. "Mendicant!" he called, and the goblin moved swiftly toward him. "I need a teleport spell."

The goblin stared at him. "I could teach you, you know. Then you'd never have to ask again. Though," he lowered his voice, "it is a lot of dull memorization and subtle changes in syllables for the last part of the spell. Most wizards end up sending themselves to the wrong locations for the first year or two. Personally, I have ended up in Fertiss instead of at the Pharesia portal more than a dozen times—"

"Not the sort of mistake I can afford to make right now," Cyrus said dryly. "Can you take us to the Mountains of Nartanis?"

"Certainly," the goblin said with a nod as a small group of Sanctuary adventurers wandered past, watching Cyrus and Vara with undisguised curiosity. "Mountains of Nartanis it is." He held up a hand and it twinkled with green light all about his claws. The foyer's high stone walls, enormous stained glass window and crackling hearth vanished, only to be replaced by a mountainous wasteland, hills of black dirt and rocky terrain. Across the red sky in the distance swooped the shadow of a small drake, dragonkin the size of a vulture.

"Here you are," Mendicant said, bowing.

Cyrus cast a quick look around, ducking his head around the portal to make sure they were alone. There was no one in sight. "All right, Mendicant, thank you." He glanced back at the goblin. "You can go. We'll use return when we're ready to come back."

Mendicant hesitated. "Are you sure? I can wait."

Vara gave Cyrus a careful look before composing her own response. "Yes, thank you, Mendicant," she said, "but we have some private business out here if you don't mind."

"Very well," the goblin said, shrugging lightly. "If ever you need me, you know where to find me." And he faded in the light of a return spell.

Cyrus stared at Vara in the empty space between them. "How many people do you suppose heard where we were going?"

She had a worried look. "The few that were walking past. Perhaps a handful more in the lounge. The question is, how many could they tell, and is any one of them a spy for Malpravus?"

"Mendicant could be a spy for Malpravus for all we know," Cyrus said, drawing a deep breath through his nose. The air here was a little thinner and smelled of sulfur from some of the lightly erupting magma geysers in the distance. Cyrus stared straight ahead. The dark, ashen soil was pitted with innumerable footprints, most of them wending off toward the goblin city under the mountain, Enterra. A few headed in other directions, however, seemingly randomly, and Cyrus fixed his gaze ahead, toward a path he'd walked more than once …

"Someone's coming," Vara said as a light flickered on the portal, a spell casting green energy that illuminated the darkening grounds. Night was almost upon them.

Cyrus waited the second before the spell dispersed with bated breath. A blond elf with a commanding presence, draped in white robes, stood there along with a wizard of dark elven origin in her shadow.

"You may go," Isabelle said—a little imperiously, Cyrus thought—and the dark elf vanished in a return spell of her own, leaving the three of them standing in the silence of the mountains, the sun sinking below the peaks on the western horizon. "Well," Vara's sister said. "Here I am. You call and I appear. What can this humble officer of Endeavor do to be of service to the most wanted people in the land?"

"You didn't tell her in the message?" Cyrus asked, frowning at Vara.

"I did not," Vara said, a little impatiently, "possibly because I felt that exposing our plans in an easily intercepted letter would be dangerous to both her and us."

"Dangerous?" Isabelle's smooth nose wrinkled. "I realize you're heretics, but surely you can't think anyone is coming after you? No one would be fool enough to risk it."

"Oh, but they are coming after us, sister mine," Vara said. "Goliath, Amarath's Raiders, the Confederation and the Kingdom all."

"The Kingdom at least would not be fool enough to come for _you_," Isabelle scoffed.

"Danay tried to kill her a year ago," Cyrus said.

Isabelle's eyes widened. "If that is the case," she said, sounding stricken, "then you are right, and as they say—all bets are off. I wish I had known this before I came."

"Because you wouldn't have come?" Vara asked.

"Oh, I still would have," Isabelle said, eyeing the empty ground surrounding them as the darkness continued to creep in around them, "but I might have been more careful in my discussions about those plans."

"You weren't careful about mentioning where you were going?" Vara asked, her voice rising with every word.

"I was not careful, no," Isabelle said, creeping ever closer to the two of them, suddenly wary of their surroundings, "and now that you have mentioned Amarath's Raiders, I am especially concerned as several of our officers have recently been poached away to join them, leaving us in something of a delicate position regarding our security. Spies are a concern ..."

"Dammit," Cyrus said, beckoning Isabelle closer. "We need to—" Cyrus started to say, but spell-light lit the portal once more as a flurry of teleportation spells began to crackle into existence around them.

With a flash, they were surrounded, the crackle of magical energy dispersing to show the faces of dozens of members of Amarath's Raiders, their distinctive livery of a horse's head stitched onto their surcoats and cloaks, their boots crunching on the ash-covered ground. A quick survey told Cyrus there were at least thirty, mixed between warriors, rangers and spellcasters.

And standing at their fore was Archenous Derregnault, with his scarred face barely visible in the day's fading light. His sword was already in hand, as were those of his guildmates, and he met Cyrus's eyes for only a second before tilting them toward Vara as his lips twisted in a grin of triumph.

25.

"Dammit!" Cyrus shouted as he grabbed the handle of the chain entwined around him and felt the small burst of speed and strength it gave him. He ripped his blade free of its scabbard to find himself facing thirty more members of the Raiders and countless arrows beyond that. A quick try at the return spell told him what he had already known— the Raiders had wizards who were casting cessation upon the field of battle. It was a good maneuver, one Cyrus himself would have insisted on had he been in Derregnault's position.

"Vara, we need to—" he started, but already his wife was in motion. Her sword was free of its scabbard and she was bellowing a cry loud enough to be heard on every peak around them. She came at Archenous Derregnault with a fury, and he barely got his sword up in time to block her, his face showing surprise even in the dark. "Dammit, Vara!"

"She's lost her mind," Isabelle murmured, pressing her back against Cyrus's as warriors of Amarath's Raiders began to press toward them. Cyrus could see the wicked grins of humans, dark elves, trolls— massive, hulking creatures, even the humans and dark elves— advancing with malice in their eyes, clearly keen on the opportunity to take down both a heretic and a warrior of Cyrus's reputation.

Every one of them was equipped with a mystical steel weapon, though perhaps not with the boosting power of speed and strength that even the modest chain and morningstar gave him. He considered that fortunate as he parried the first strike and jabbed his blade into the very slight gap above a gorget. A dark elven warrior made a *gurking* noise as nearly black blood squirted down his horsehead surcoat and darkened his livery beyond recognition. He pitched forward and Cyrus moved to the side to let him, knocking away two other attacks, including one pointed past him at Isabelle.

"Here!" Cyrus said and kicked the fallen warrior's blade back to Isabelle. He counted himself fortunate that they were not surrounded yet, and that he could keep himself between his sister-in-law and the horde of mercenary adventurers who were coming at them with murder in their eyes.

"Thank you," Isabelle said, scooping up the blade and holding it expertly before her. A warrior came charging at her from Cyrus's side and she met him with a perfectly timed counter blow that opened his neck as she sidestepped the foolishly aggressive attack. Cyrus gave her a curious look and she shrugged as her foe sank to death, doomed by the very cessation spell that was pinning them in place. "You don't live as long as I do nor climb as high as I have without taking some secret swordsmanship lessons at some point."

The rest of the masses were taking their time now, trying to close in around Cyrus and Isabelle. From his height, he could see Vara pummeling Archenous Derregnault with unceasing fury, driving him away from his forces faster than his own warriors could catch up to stab Vara in the back. Derregnault looked rattled, even from this distance, but he continued to fall back from Vara's furious assault.

"Do you think she'll be back any time today?" Isabelle asked. A wizard and a dozen warriors were trotting off behind Vara, scrambling to keep after her as she drove Derregnault farther and farther away from them. "Scratch that. She'll run him right into the Sea of Carmas before she lets up."

"Yep," Cyrus agreed as two spears came at him simultaneously. It was almost clever, what these two warriors had done, but it wasn't quite sufficient to the task. They both thrust at exactly where he was standing, and so he moved, pushing Isabelle back easily. Their blades clashed in the space that Cyrus had occupied only a moment earlier, and he smacked the hafts of both spears, letting momentum drive them down into the dirt. It had little effect other than to halt the warriors while they paused to pull their spears out of the black ground, but it gave Cyrus another moment to step back as a few arrows began to rain toward him. "This has not been the best year of my life."

"Don't let your new bride hear you say that," Isabelle fired back, hiding easily in his shadow as arrows spanged off his armor. He lowered his head and let his helm protect his face. There were only five rangers, and fortunately none of them were as good a shot as Martaina. *They won't miss forever, though,* Cyrus thought, as an arrow snapped against his shoulder and a splinter stung him in the cheek. "Even after all this, the year of your marriage should indeed be the happiest ever."

"It will be if she kills Derregnault," Cyrus said, driving his new blade against a mystical steel weapon thrust at him by a leering troll. He knocked the troll's enormous blade aside and jabbed his own up under the troll's breastplate as steaming, stinking breath wafted on him from above. The troll moaned in pain as Cyrus gutted the bastard and took his revenge by slamming a fist upon Cyrus's helm.

Cyrus felt as though someone had tried to hammer him into the ground as a farmer might drive a post to fence a field. The blow dulled his senses and slowed his reaction. He ripped his blade free of rancid troll guts, the smell of feces from shredded bowels overwhelming him, and he staggered back. Isabelle caught him, only barely, giving him a moment to recover before she started to collapse under his immense weight.

Cyrus blinked. The world had grown rather fuzzy around him, and eight swords were driving toward him now. He threw his own blade up and swept across, hard, knocking every one of them off course. His vision cleared, and suddenly he realized that he'd only hit four swords, that he'd been seeing double, and that he'd thrown his defense in a very awkward way that had tipped his numerous foes to his temporary weakness.

They were all charging at him now, or at least it seemed that way. There were grins of triumph, hot breath that stunk of old meat, and they were all piling in on him on both sides and in front. Cyrus staggered back under the assault, trying to swing his sword to block them, but knowing there was no chance that he would manage to fend off all of them before one managed to strike the lucky blow that would kill him.

26.

A half dozen blades clanged against Cyrus's armor as he blocked at least four others, finding himself at the center of a vigorous pincushioning attempt to impale him. Isabelle grunted behind him, trying to block her own particularly vicious attacker, a human in full armor with a faceplate down to hide his features.

The smell of battle was thick now with the scent of death and rot, and Cyrus was hard-pressed to tell which kill had tainted the mountain air the most. The sky was barely lit around them, red highlights over the mountains to the west shedding their last light on the scene of the fight. Cyrus was a good hundred feet from the portal now, driven back by the unceasing efforts of some twenty warriors and five or so rangers that were dedicating their lives to ending his. Thus far they were at least doing a fair job of it, though he knew they were closer to killing him than they probably realized.

All they need to do is score one good attack on my face, slip one arrow in an eye, one sword into the cheek, and I'll stop for a second, stunned, and they'll plunge five more in, and that will be the end of it. He'd lost track of Vara by now, his attention focused on the fight before him. Isabelle's sword was clanging as she labored against her lone attacker, one man who'd swept past Cyrus on the side to try and flank them both. *She's good,* he conceded. *Better than any healer, forbidden by the Leagues to even use weapons, has any right to be …*

But how long can she hold out against a professional warrior, whose job is the wielding of sword and steel against his foes?

The answer seemed evident, but the sound of the pitched battle between the two of them behind him gave no sign of flagging, even as he struck hard at the shoulder joint of an attacking elf in grey armor.

He pushed his blade through the chainmail below and a scream pierced the night, the elf hurling himself backward, off the tip of the sword, to avoid any follow-up by Cyrus.

That suited Cyrus just fine; had he committed his sword to finishing the elf, it wouldn't have been available to block the next three attacks, which came immediately after his blade cleared the elf's wounded shoulder. Thick, black liquid ran down the silvery sword like oil and spattered off as he clashed his weapon against the next weapons.

"Cyrus!" Isabelle called, and he spared a glance to see her continuing to fall back, driven farther from him by the need to avoid the armored warrior's unceasing offensive. She looked strained, beads of sweat running down her face, her cheeks red with exertion.

Shit, Cyrus thought. *If I turn my back on these to save her, they'll pounce and I won't achieve much of anything. Turn my back on her to save my own arse, and that bastard will finish her off and then come at my back with impunity.*

Damned if I do.

Damned if I don't.

Cyrus drew a long breath, prepared to turn and sprint, hoping to catch the warrior on Isabelle with his back turned, when he heard a hard rumble tear through the air behind him. Metal rattled, armor clanked, men screamed, and the earth itself shook.

Cyrus, for his part, did not dare turn around and look, in spite of greatest temptation. He suspected he knew what had happened, but he had one singular task at hand, and he threw himself into it with reckless abandon.

He caught the warrior attacking Isabelle as the man's head was turning to see what had caused the rumbling. Cyrus drove the point of his blade under the massive helm, up under the point where the man's jawbone rose to meet his ear. One the blade was driven in, Cyrus yanked hard upon the hilt, pushing it forward while leaving the blade anchored.

Blood rushed down from beneath the helm and a choking noise spurted from behind the mask. Cyrus kicked the man in the chest and ripped his sword free, reaching under Isabelle's defenses and pulling her close to him in very much the same manner he regularly did to her sister.

Isabelle's eyes went wide with surprise as she landed against his side, but Cyrus was already turning. Vara was charging up the field toward them, her force blast spell having cut a wide canyon through the group of Amarath's Raiders who had been attacking him. His eyes flicked into the distance and he saw Archenous Derregnault stumbling after her, blood running down his breastplate and a retinue of warriors in his wake. The wizard who had been following along with him, however, was not anywhere in the group, and Cyrus knew instantly what his wife had done. She'd drawn them away from the wizards maintaining the cessation spell around him and Isabelle, somehow killed the one tasked to keeping her from using magic, and then hammered the bulk of the Amarath's Raiders party from outside the range of the remaining wizards' cessation fields.

She scrambled toward them now, eyes wide, her gambit clearly having paid off. "Go! Go!" she called and a twinkle of light appeared at her fingers.

Cyrus did not hesitate. The damage done by her blast was already dissipating, ashen soil drifting down upon them where it was stirred by her attack. The warriors who had been so keen to attack Cyrus were picking themselves up, and somewhere, presumably, so were the wizards who had trapped them here. Cyrus thrust his hand up, Isabelle tight to his side, and mirrored his wife's spell, casting a return spell and letting it carry the two of them away from the site of the ambush.

27.

Cyrus shoved his sword roughly back into the scabbard. A thousand little aches settled over him the thrill of combat faded. He took a breath of the familiar air in the Tower of the Guildmaster and sighed as Isabelle pulled herself from him and Vara sparkled into view as the magic faded.

"That was a very near thing," Isabelle said, beads of sweat dripping from her chin. She wiped her face with a heavy sleeve, and Cyrus noted that the white fabric was stained with wetness where it had caught some blood from her first attacker. "I didn't realize quite the peril you were in."

"What did you think happened to heretics?" Vara said with a familiar dash of contempt as she slung her own blade back into its scabbard with excessive violence, the sword rattling within the confines. "Did you expect them to receive perhaps a good wining and a four-course repast in the presence of the kings and ministers throughout the land? We're *heretics*. They hate us and want us dead."

"Well, I hadn't heard anything about *you* being a heretic," Isabelle said, taking her sister's insults as though she were well used to them by now. She nodded at Cyrus. "Only him."

Cyrus glanced at Vara. "Maybe they're holding off on declaring you because you're the shelas'akur."

"That doesn't explain why they wouldn't have declared the rest of the Council," Vara huffed, her arms crossed before her and her face sullen.

"Still, we made it out of the jaws of that particular death," Isabelle said.

"Barely," Vara said.

"But we did make it out," Cyrus said and caught a withering glare from her that prompted him to look at Isabelle.

Isabelle's full lips quivered, trying to hold back a smile. "My dear sister, are you perhaps reacting to what just happened?" Vara narrowed her eyes at Isabelle, but the healer went on. "Something akin to ... a memory, perhaps? Like a not-so-gentle reminder of your retreat from Termina?"

Vara stiffened, her eyes blazing as her sister drove the blade to the heart of the matter. "I nearly watched my sister, my last surviving blood, and my new husband murdered in front of me. Indeed, you both would have died had I not had the presence of mind to divide the fools so I could break them."

"I think you mean 'so that you could give in to endless rage and remember yourself just in time to save us,'" Isabelle said. Cyrus, for his part, cringed, anticipating a response worthy of Vara's attack on Archenous.

"But I did come," Vara said, and her reply was tempered like steel, cooled and stripped of some of the anger, and Cyrus knew that Isabelle had spoken true. "And in time to save you."

"You did well," Cyrus said softly. "I just thought perhaps in addition to losing your head at the sight of Archenous, you were of a mind to settle our question for Isabelle without having to ask it."

Isabelle frowned. "What was this question?"

"How would Amarath's Raiders fare if we were to kill Archenous Derregnault?" Vara let the question out almost loathingly, as though reliving the events at the portal as a personal failure.

"Not well," Isabelle said after giving it a moment's thought, "but not as poorly as they would before they scooped several of our officers. Not dunces, any of them, and perfectly capable of stepping in should Archenous fall." She frowned. "If they've cast their lot in on hunting you, they must be getting something for it ..." Understanding dawned. "Of course. That's why they've been allowed to return to their old guildhall in Reikonos."

"Same with Goliath?" Cyrus asked, drawing a furrowed brow from Isabelle. "Because they seemed to be somewhat paired up, at least when they came at me the first time."

"They came at you before?" Isabelle asked with a quiver of concern.

"In the markets in Reikonos," Cyrus said. "They laid a trap."

"Ah, that was the commotion a few days ago," Isabelle nodded slowly. "It all begins to make sense now."

"Well, at least someone understands," Vara said fervently. "They are coming at us with all they have."

"Then I do not envy you, sister," Isabelle said after a long pause, concern shadowing her chiseled cheekbones.

"No one does, at this point," Vara said, settling in.

"I am afraid I am going to be of little assistance beyond information," Isabelle said, shrugging.

"I assumed as much," Vara said, "and would not have involved you in heresy in any case. I had intended our meeting to be secret, though obviously that failed. I do hope the consequences will not fall too harshly upon you."

Isabelle smiled faintly. "I will decry your name if need be, though if you need my further assistance, I would be glad to render it." She waited a long moment, looking curiously at Cyrus. "I suppose I should not be surprised you don't immediately ask for Endeavor's aid in this."

"I wouldn't presume to involve your guildmates in our mess," Cyrus said, shaking his head. "Enough of our own have left to convince me that very few people indeed wish to become sunk in this particular mire."

"Well, I would be willing to be mired with you, if it should come to it," she said, her lips faintly puckered with regret. "If you find you have need of me, send word again and I will come, even if it is only as a healer."

"It would have to be truly desperate for us to wish to put you through that," Vara said quickly, and in her words Cyrus could feel the specter of Chirenya over the room and Vara's fear of losing her last family member.

"It seems you are headed that way," Isabelle said, the regretful look turning into a small smile. "And if you should reach it and find yourself in need, do send word, sister." She twirled her fingers and disappeared into the return spell, but Cyrus could swear the afterimage of her smile lingered behind, like an invitation for them to call her back at any time.

28.

Time passed slowly, like drips of ice melting from a rooftop. And the ice did melt, as winter turned to spring, the thin frost that had sparkled on the windows and rooftop of Sanctuary becoming liquid and running off, turning the well-trodden ground wet and muddy. The New Year came, a month passed, then another, and another.

"The Governors of the human states put me off," Cattrine said in one of their ever-less-frequent meetings. The frustration was palpable in the room. "Perhaps if I could give them a more solid reason to arrange this—"

"Yes," Vara said acidly, "let's tell them exactly where and when the heretics whom their government hunts will be out of their stone cage."

"I hate to say it," Terian eyed her and Cyrus with muted pity, "but it may come to giving them an opportunity and hoping you can spring free of any trap they may attempt. Whatever we want to accomplish among the humans, we're not going to get it done without these people. Even if we killed Pretnam Urides somehow right now, we have little reason to believe anything would change in the Confederation's stance toward you."

"Little is changing regardless," Cyrus said quietly, feeling a little self-pity of his own. He had not left Sanctuary since the ambush in the Mountains of Nartanis, and the grounds behind the walls were starting to feel restrictive.

Imina lingered guiltily in the back of Cyrus's mind. Sometimes he would wake in the night, cold, in fear of what Malpravus might have done to her. Vara, for her part, remained reassuring in these moments, but none of the corpses that ringed the Sanctuary wall had approached to deliver any further messages regarding her fate.

Nearly two hundred more members left in the months following the arrival of the New Year. They left in a trickle, in ones and twos and threes, and Cyrus felt each departure keenly, for there was little else to focus on, trapped as they were.

"We're going to slowly bleed to death," Ryin had said mournfully at a Council meeting two months after the ambush in the Mountains of Nartanis. "This is our fate. We will draw down slowly over the next year, until we do not have sufficient numbers to even defend the wall, and then the armies of our enemies will come in and crush us."

"They could have done that by now if they truly wanted to," Mendicant said. "So why do they not?"

"Because we promised them an army of heretics in opposition to their every attempt," Vara said sharply. "And thus far, we are delivering on that promise. We may only have fifty spellcasters left, but they are fifty who know how to cast spells across almost every discipline."

And that much was true; Cyrus had learned the destructive magic of the wizard and the druid, throwing fire and ice, the illusions of an enchanter, though he struggled with mesmerization and charming ("If it were easy, every enchanter would be as good as I," J'anda had said with a smile), and teleportation. Particularly easy to him, though, had been the ones that Vara had taught him.

"You must visualize the power flowing forth from your hand," she had said as they stood upon the archery range, a half dozen scarecrows standing out down the line. "Imagine the power blossoming forth, exploding, driving forth your foes like sand in a typhoon."

When he had released his spell, it had not hit as hard as what he'd seen done by his wife, but it had knocked down three of the scarecrows, and he had only improved since.

Their missives to the elven contacts went unanswered. Lady Voryn of the Emerald Coast appeared to be gone, according to the messenger sent by Cattrine, and the first communiqué to Lord Merrish went unanswered, as did a second. Cyrus felt a small tinge of desperation grow ever larger as spring cemented its hold on the Plains of Perdamun with drenching rains that finally began to turn the grass green, and as the sun came back out one day he finally felt ready to send a message to Odellan's father, Morianza Yemer.

"Cattrine says he's still at his northern estate near Javeritem," Vaste said as Cyrus scrawled words upon parchment in his own hand. "Why do you have to write this letter again?"

"Because Cattrine doesn't know him," Cyrus said stiffly, looking down at the yellowed paper. It looked like aged skin to him.

"I didn't realize you did," Vaste said, loitering in the tower as Cyrus sat hunched over his desk. The balcony doors were all opened, and blue skies were visible outside for what felt like the first time in months.

"You know damned well I've never met the man," Cyrus said, signing his name with impatience. He considered adding "Heretic" in bold letters underneath as a title, but signed it "Lord of Perdamun, Guildmaster of Sanctuary" instead, even though he knew that the former title had likely been revoked by both Reikonos and Pharesia by now.

"Yes, you should have sent him personal correspondence after his son died in glorious battle," Vaste said, thumping a sandaled foot against the wooden chest Cyrus kept in the corner. "Might have been a more appropriate time to open ties."

"I would have, but the King of the Elves overreacted a bit when I had to deliver the news of his daughter," Cyrus said, neatly sealing the parchment in an envelope with a blob of wax that he stamped with the Sanctuary seal. "It didn't leave me feeling free to send even a messenger to Pharesia to deliver any such missive."

"Always an excuse with you," Vaste said, sounding more like he was jesting, but weakly, as though the energy had left him over the last few months. "What do you expect to get out of this contact if he does agree to a meeting? Because it seems to me if you come to him suggesting some sort of revolt against his King … I mean, assuming he's a loyal subject, it's going to go poorly for you."

Cyrus stared straight ahead at the stone wall. "Vara has a plan to stir some loyalty in the kingdom, but … it requires some help we haven't been able to get just yet."

"Oh, right," Vaste said, nodding. "These travel embargoes, they're really hell on us. No one can come to our gates without Malpravus's little watchers seeing, and who knows who's watching within the walls?" He paused to think it over. "Why, if it's as Ryin suggested, and we're doomed to watch our numbers sink to two hundred, or a hundred before they move in, I think I'd find it ironic if it turned out that ninety of them were spies for Goliath waiting to turn on us at an opportune moment."

Cyrus froze, the envelope cradled in his bare hands. "I don't think that 'irony' is what I'd be feeling at that moment."

"Well, you wouldn't have time for much else with a betrayal of that scope," Vaste said. "Irony and then a flurry of blades piercing you, that's about all."

"You're so damned cheerful," Cyrus said, pushing his chair back. "Why don't you go torment someone else?"

"Because there's really no one left," Vaste said seriously. "It might as well be you and me here."

"We have seven hundred and twenty-one members remaining—" Cyrus began.

"Siewart George left last night," Vaste said. When Cyrus did not react but to frown, the troll went on. "He was a ranger. Gnome. He came after Enterra, one of that lot—"

"Oh, yes," Cyrus said with a nod. "Short fellow—" He stopped. "Obviously."

Vaste gave him that pitying look again. "Yes, obviously. Anyhow, near as I could tell, he was one of the few gnomes your fetching bride did not despise. She even told him that he was 'quite skilled' at one point."

"So he was a very good ranger, then," Cyrus said, staring a little forlornly out the open balcony.

"My understanding is that his small size made him one of the greatest sneaks in our entire guild," Vaste said, a note of mournfulness in his tone. "He was apparently an impressive scout and hunter. Calene told me that, while he was not indispensable, he was one of our best."

"How many of our best have we lost?" Cyrus mused.

"Nine thousand or so," Vaste said with a little more energy. "More if you count Leaugarden, but my memory doesn't stretch back that far, and let's face it, those were mainly Luukessians, who, technically, are still part of our army."

"True," Cyrus said with a nod. "Though it's hard to feel that way when they're encamped in Emerald Fields." He paused. "You know they built permanent barracks before the winter to quarter those troops?"

"Hard to miss buildings that size," Vaste said with an arched eyebrow. "It's like walking into Council and not seeing me standing next to my chair."

"I often don't see you in Council," Cyrus said, "but it could be that I'm ignoring you."

"See, that's the Cyrus we need again," Vaste said, clapping his massive hands together. "I know you can't lead as well as you might want to, since so many of our plans are secret, but walking around dour and down is not helping anyone. Even if you can't share what we're doing with others, you should at least act like you're confident in the direction we're going."

Cyrus stared at him blankly. "The direction we're going is down." He held up the envelope in his hand. "I'm sending a letter to a man whose son died under my command, hoping that he'll decide to betray his own king and help us murder him."

"So we've nowhere to go but up!" Vaste said.

Cyrus cocked his head at the healer. "Well ... our enemies haven't encircled us to squeeze us to death, so ... no, we could sink farther."

"Ungh," Vaste said, putting his face in his massive, paw-like hands. He peeked out from between immense green fingers. "You know why these people are leaving, right?"

"Because all Arkaria is against us and they don't like the thought of being invaded and killed?"

Vaste let his hands drop, and his face turned serious. "Because without leadership and hope," he said, "why would you stay? If you don't believe in the chance that we'll come out of this, why remain and fight? You could go get yourself killed much easier elsewhere."

Cyrus started to open his mouth to reply but stopped. "That's true," he conceded after a moment's thought.

"We need to give these people a direction," Vaste said. "We need to find hope for them. We need them to believe we're doing something, even if the Council doesn't believe it, even if they don't see anything but us walking tall, sure of ourselves."

"Gods, Vaste," Cyrus said, sitting back down. "I don't know how we even ... how do you do something like that? Find certainty in yourself at a moment like this?"

Vaste stared straight at him and there was a not a trace of humor when he spoke. "If I die at the hands of Goliath and their allies, but I do so with my remaining friends here in Sanctuary at my side ... I would consider that a better death than if I lived to be a thousand and croaked in my bed with a fine, intelligent, beautiful trollish woman beside me."

"Well, the former is certainly more likely to happen than you finding 'a fine, intelligent, beautiful trollish woman' or living to a thousand—" Cyrus said with the glimmer of a smile.

"Stop stealing my dreams."

"You make a fair point, as you do in your times of sober reflection," Cyrus said. "All right. I will try to walk tall again."

"Walk like you've got a purpose," Vaste said. "Like you're always going somewhere, and with a hint of a smile on your face. People will see it, and they'll take heart. Life without hope is just death."

"Fair enough," Cyrus said with a nod, and he stood, pushing a smile onto his face. "Better?"

Vaste cocked his head and studied him. "You still look hideous to me, but perhaps your fellow repulsive humans will derive some comfort from it."

"Mmhm—"

The door at the base of the stairs clicked open and Cyrus froze, listening. Metal boots tapped their way up, and he could tell by the sound that it was Vara, and she was in a hurry. When her head emerged from the stairway in the floor, she was wearing a smile of her own.

"See, that's the look, right there," Vaste said. "Purpose, optimism, mischief—"

"We've just gotten a letter from Lord Merrish of Traegon," Vara said, raising a parchment of her own in triumph. "He wants to meet—immediately."

29.

Cyrus, Vara, Vaste, J'anda, and Larana appeared in the whirlwind of the teleport spell at the portal outside the city of Traegon, the northernmost city of the Elven Kingdom. There were towns to the north that Cyrus knew, such as Nalikh'akur, which was nominally still Vara's holdfast, but Traegon was a massive city, probably one of the largest in the Kingdom. Even outside its walls Cyrus could see the minarets extending into the deep blue sky. The air was colder here than at Sanctuary, and Cyrus drew his cloak tightly around him.

They wore the illusions of elven travelers. A lone elven woman waiting for them scanned them carefully before nodding once and beckoning them follow. She was ahorse, as were they, and they all rode together south in her wake.

They followed the road for almost an hour in silence, Cyrus afraid to make conversation with his companions. He felt reassured because Windrider was beneath him and they were under the influence of J'anda's strong, persistent illusion rather than his own somewhat limited versions of the spell. He was getting better, but the duration of his spellcraft was considerably less than the more practiced master enchanter, and he was quite content to leave this particular deception to the expert.

The wind blew intermittently out of the west, the nip of the air causing Cyrus's flesh to pucker beneath his armor. He watched the trees carefully as they rode, fearing ambush from all sides, from any side. His small party were all dressed as highborns, and the lowborn laborers they passed along the way did not dare gaze their way for long.

Finally the woman guiding them left the road at a small path, her horse at a canter. Ahead, Cyrus could see a mighty plantation house, a sprawling estate behind low walls that would not have stopped a goblin from scaling them. They were ornate and beautiful and entirely for show, he decided, like much of the rest of the Kingdom.

The horses whickered and whinnied as they came to a halt just before a massive field. Workers were out there in it, plowing and breaking the ground with horses and hoes. Most of the workers were using animals, but one was breaking the stubborn clumps of earth with just a tool. He was shirtless and standing in the middle of the field, far from any others, and he worked the earth as though he were expert at it, moving swiftly in a row.

Their guide pointed at the man. He was bronzed, and his long dark hair flowed over his shoulders, untamed. He looked young from what Cyrus could see, even by the standards of the long-lived and barely-aging elves. His muscles bulged, straining from his labor.

Cyrus glanced at the guide, who nodded, and started to make his way across the plowed field, his boots sinking into the loose earth with every step. It looked as though they'd turned up frost within the ground and were breaking it up. He frowned at the labor, thinking, *Won't it just melt on its own?*

Vara followed a pace behind Cyrus, and he could hear Vaste and J'anda after her, the troll grunting with particular effort as his weight sank him into the dirt with each heavy step.

"Hail," the young, shirtless man said as he paused in his labors. He was sweating and dirty, traces of black earth dusted along his chest and caught in the runnels of perspiration that gleamed on his chest. Cyrus caught Vara looking for a moment too long and frowned more deeply.

"Lord Merrish?" Vara asked tentatively, slowing her advance.

"'Tis I, Shelas'akur," Merrish said, leaning against his hoe and flashing a ready grin at them. "Though you would not know it to look at me, any more than I would know it simply by looking at you."

"You've got a sight spell on you, then?" Cyrus asked, staring at the young man.

"I'm a wizard, yes," he said, and the gleam of magic lit his hand as a skin of water was conjured out of thin air. Lord Merrish pressed it to his lips and drank deeply, then poured it out over his muscled chest, washing off the perspiration and dirt.

"Thank you for inviting us out here," Cyrus said, looking around the plantation fields. The other elves laboring were stopping for a break of their own, wandering away in all directions, far from the conversation going on at the center of the field. He glanced back; J'anda and Vaste were keeping their distance, apparently content to let Cyrus and Vara do the talking.

"Do you always work your own fields?" Vara asked with undisguised curiosity.

"Frequently, yes," Merrish said, still grinning. "I'm quite the abnormality, I'm aware."

"May I ask why?" Vara stared at him, at least now keeping her eyes on his face. Cyrus still felt a rush of annoyance that he could not quite pin down.

"You were born and raised in our Kingdom," Merrish said, still cradling the conjured skin of water. "Still, perhaps you didn't see it, given your birth ..." He frowned, mouth turning down. "Our Kingdom ... is at a ripe moment, one waiting to be plucked by the appropriate hand."

Cyrus felt a blanket of cynicism fall over him, an old suspicion that had long served him well. "Your hand, I suppose?"

Merrish grinned. "Doubtful." He worked the hoe left and right in the dirt, nervously, to little effect. "I spoke to Oliaryn Iraid a few days past when I was visiting Termina. You've been there, of course." He looked at Cyrus. "Marvelous city, isn't it?"

"Less so than it used to be," Cyrus said, drawing a sharp look of rebuke from Vara.

"It's the jewel of our Kingdom," Merrish said, and if he was insulted by Cyrus's remark, he did not show it. "A place where one can go and be unworried with the constant demands of caste. Lowborn, highborn, those between ... it matters not in Termina. Some in my station see that city as infection, a pustule of the spreading contagion of the humans." His eyes gazed into the distance; Cyrus thought he was being exceedingly dramatic. "I have been to the Confederation many times. Reikonos, Santir, Asaliere, Isselhelm, Montis, Taymor, Wardemos—I have traveled those lands and found them ... very admirable, in their way. The distinction of caste, of birth, swept away? The ability for someone born in a stable to poverty-stricken parents to rise, to ascend to heights in the capital, as did Pretnam Urides?" Merrish's eyes gleamed. "I can hardly imagine the same tale being told anywhere in the Kingdom."

"And not just because you people aren't having babies anymore," Cyrus said, feeling a little like he was channeling Vaste. This caused Vara to roll her eyes once more then glare at him subtly.

"It's true," Merrish said with a nod. "No point disguising it or flowering over it—we aren't. But even if we were, they would be born into a system where they would never rise on their own merit or fall because of their own failures. They would be locked firmly into the path of their ancestors." He glanced at Vara and smiled. "You are the only one to ascend beyond her class of birth anywhere outside of Termina, in this Kingdom—"

"Well, she is *from* Termina," Cyrus muttered, drawing another ireful look from Vara.

Merrish favored Cyrus with a patronizing smile. "You don't see it, because you have grown up within the bounds of the Confederation with all its wondrous opportunity for ascent. Why, you, most disfavored of them all, son of a heretic, have now become one of the most powerful men in Arkaria, and still you reach forth the hand." He leaned on the hoe, crooking his elbow around it, and lowered his voice conspiratorially. "You, Cyrus Davidon, could be the kingmaker in this land, if you should use your opportunities right."

"And would I be making you the king, should I follow that course?" Cyrus asked, trying to take some of the sting out of his question now that they'd come around at last to what he wanted to know.

"I don't want to be king," Merrish said with a fervent shake of his head. "I'd rather no one was king, that we chose not to bend the knee to one person, for fear that they might end up a singularly vain and insecure, petty person caught up in their own self."

"So you're one of the ones that longs for the fragmented days of old," Vara said, drawing wearily to her conclusion, "before the union of the Kingdom. Admittedly, I wasn't there, but all the tales I have heard of those days indicated that there were still hierarchies of birth, but there were also internecine battles between the various lords who considered themselves kings of their own lands."

"I'm not opposed to a king or queen," Merrish said, seeming to reverse himself. "I would prefer not to have one, but I am hardly the lone decider of these matters. But at the very least, I would like the distinctions between class destroyed."

"No more nobility?" Cyrus asked with undisguised amusement. "I don't think your fellow lords are going to like that much."

"There can still be lords," Merrish said, "since trying to wrest their hereditary lands out of their corpulent hands would prompt a war in the kingdom unlike anything seen since before the union." He sighed impatiently. "I only wish to see the distinctions of caste washed away. It is a prison, more odious than some idiot who four generations ago swore service to Danay and received land and title for it. Lords can parcel off their land and sell it to a highborn, if so possessed. But a lowborn cannot rise above their station in life regardless and can never hope to own a parcel of land outside of Termina. This needs to change."

Vara's skepticism was well buried. "This is the price for your help in our ... endeavor, then? Promises of reform?"

"Yes," Merrish said with a hard nod. "A promise of reform, and also a guarantee."

"What's the difference?" Cyrus asked, watching the elven lord with a smoldering level of irritation.

"One can be empty words," Merrish said with a glint in his eyes, "the other carries with it some level of enforcement." He lifted off the long wooden handle of his implement. "Say I help you put together this ... this *conspiracy*, call it, for I can give you the key to unlock the door to Lady Voryn, whom I know you seek." He smiled. "Let us assume we bring her together with Oliaryn Iraid, and perhaps a few more, for I'm sure you have others aiding you. You could promise in front of all of them that you would try very hard to garner what I've asked for when it is all done and whatever—hmm, change, let's call it—has been made to the Kingdom in your favor. But when it is all said and my part is done, what assurance do I have that the others, whose faces I can imagine at my mere suggestion of this to them, will not simply speak with you quietly and convince you that a try is all that is required? 'Oh, we have tried, but no one wishes to make this change.'" Merrish's voice went high, and his eyes settled into a knowing look. "Of course no one wishes to make the change. It is not in their favor and will surely cause them to lose support among their highborn friends as their stations are swept away."

"What assurance could we possibly give you that would mean a damn?" Vara asked, frowning.

"The only one that matters," Merrish said, eyes agleam once more.

"One bound by the authority that no one would deny."

Vara's face became a stiff mask. "That is not an assurance I can make at present."

"I recognize that," Merrish said, still smiling pleasantly. Little droplets of sweat were falling off him now as he shivered, his time spent resting apparently causing him to grow chilly. "But when you have the means, I expect it. I will not move without it, and should you try to bypass me, you will find me a swift enemy of yours."

"Lovely," Cyrus said, his blood chilling. "We didn't have enough of those before, obviously ..." Cyrus gave a long sigh. "Why not one more impossible task? Amidst so many already, this one won't be much more of a burden."

Merrish grinned. "I'm certain that for the man who freed the slaves of Arkaria, upending a simple caste system can be done with greatest ease. But in lieu of a reciprocal promise of my own, I offer this." Merrish nodded his head in seeming concession. "Two things I will do for you in order to show my sincerity in this matter. The first—Lady Voryn. She has received your missives but sent them back, yes?"

"Yes," Vara said cautiously. "She is absent, according to her retainers."

"Lady Voryn is the most faithful woman you will ever meet," Merrish said, eyes still gleaming. "She is devoted to her beliefs, to the Goddess of Life, beyond anything else. That is her key."

"I see," Vara said quietly.

"I expect you do," Merrish said, smirking. "The second thing I will do for you is arrange an introduction to another friend of mine. His name is Allyn Frost, and I was told you that you might need to make his acquaintance."

The Governor of the Northlands, Cyrus thought, suddenly frozen at the Lord's admission. *Did he hear that from Iraid? If not ...* Cyrus's blood ran cold. *Well, there's nothing for it, now. If what we're planning is widespread knowledge outside of our little shadow council ... we're going to be absolutely burned.*

"Power speaks to power, you see," Merrish said, looking straight at Vara. "I've known Governor Frost for many years and have had more than a few dealings with him. When you leave, you'll be given an envelope with the time and date of your meeting. It will have to take place at his keep in Isselhelm, for he will not journey to you and you would not want him to in any case."

"Of course," Cyrus whispered, suddenly ashen with worry at the thought of more of his secrets exposed. *This is a pox of a thing, trying to hide your intentions and worrying when anyone roots them out. I miss open battle, open war, charging enemies fearlessly knowing strength will decide the contest.*

I hate being weak. It's like hiding at night at the Society again in fear that someone is going to prey on me when I'm sleeping. I thought I'd left those days behind me, but it's like they're back, only now my enemies are more fearsome than ever before.

"Thank you most graciously for meeting with us," Vara said, nodding politely to Lord Merrish, who bowed, his bronzed chest dipping with the rest of him and raising Cyrus's ire as he did so.

"It was hardly an imposition on me," Merrish said with a smile gentler than he'd yet shown. "I wish you all the best in these endeavors, and I hope to hear from you very soon in regards to that guarantee."

"I shall work on it with the utmost effort," Vara said, though the words seemed to stick in her throat. She bowed her head once more. "Lord Merrish."

"Shelas'akur," Merrish returned.

Vara turned on her heel and started back across the field, each step hindered slightly by the upturned soil. She took an envelope extended by Merrish's dark-haired servant and then she gestured to Vaste and J'anda, each of whom nodded and began to cast the return spell. Larana, in the distance, did the same, shimmering into the light before any of the rest.

Cyrus, for his part, glanced at his wife but held his tongue as he cast the spell for himself and the chilly field disappeared, replaced by the stone walls and open doors of the Tower of the Guildmaster.

"That was unbelievably rude," Vara said before she'd even finished appearing from the spell. "Merrish consents to meet with us after untold waiting—"

"About three months, really," Cyrus grumbled.

"And you go and make a fool of yourself by butting heads with the man—"

"I saw you looking at his chest, I don't think I'm the one who made a fool of myself—"

"Well, it would have been hard not to notice, and it's not as though I sat there with drool dripping out of my mouth as you once did in the Temple of Vidara over a group of bare-chested priestesses several thousand years your senior—"

"Excuse me," came a soft voice, drawing both of them out of their spat. Terian stood in front of the west-facing balcony, undisguised amusement stretching his lips into a broad smile. "Ahhh. Marriage. Isn't it grand?"

"What the bloody hell are you doing here?" Vara snapped at him, pivoting as she folded her arms over her chest, making a fortress of herself.

"I," Terian said, very slowly, very dramatically, "have most excellent news … and something to show you."

"Marvelous," Vara said acidly, "show us, then."

"Can't do it here," Terian said, smirking. "You have to come with me to Saekaj." His eyes danced with unfathomable excitement. "I would tell you what it is, but really … it's the sort of thing you need to see in order to believe it."

30.

They huddled awkwardly closely to Terian for his return spell ("I never wished to be this near to you," Vara said. "I know," Terian agreed with a knowing smile, "that's why it's so marvelous."), carrying them back to the Grand Palace of Saekaj. Cyrus cast the spell of Eagle Eye upon his vision, the fine wood appointments to the palace becoming visible under the light of his spellcraft.

"Kind of a relief to be able to do this for myself now," Cyrus said as they strode out through the main doors under a large portico. The sound of rushing water heralded the two enormous waterfalls that emerged from either side of the palace's facade. A small moat ran in front of them, underneath a bridge that led to immense, wide-open gates. Cyrus could see movement beyond as a carriage rattled to a stop in front of them.

They boarded the carriage wordlessly and it rattled along the dirt and rock path of the cave. The seats were padded but the interior was dark. Cyrus sat next to Vara, both of them staring at Terian, who lazed in Alaric's old armor against the backrest as though he were ready for a nap, smile of satisfaction draped across his face like he himself was draped across the seat.

"When are you going to tell us what we're here to see?" Vara asked, more than a little snappishly.

"I'm not," Terian said with a grin. "I want to see the look on your faces when you lay eyes on my surprise."

"Hmph," Vara said, making a snorting noise as she once more folded her arms against her chest. "Months of inaction and now suddenly we have two meetings in one day. Why do you suppose things happen like that?"

"Who else did you meet with?" Terian asked, sitting up straight in his seat.

"Lord Merrish," Cyrus said, a frown suddenly upon his face. "My wife thinks he's a tasty morsel."

Vara focused her eyes on the ceiling of the carriage. "I think your brain would be a tasty morsel for some hungry troll, and your senses have become inflamed by not only your outsized ego but also your raging insecurity."

"What did he want?" Terian asked.

"For Vara to gawk at his physique, apparently," Cyrus said.

Vara let out a grunt of distinct impatience. "Goddess, husband, this is not an attractive side of you."

"Much like your arse," Terian said, nodding at Cyrus. "Sorry. Maybe it's just me, but it just doesn't seem proportioned properly. Too long? I don't know, maybe it's the armor—"

Cyrus looked at Vara. "Is it my arse?"

Vara turned her head to stare at him incredulously. "Yes. Yes, it's your arse. That's the reason I was looking at a very fit man with his doublet off. But by 'your arse,' I mean it as Niamh meant it, that it is the entirety of you, not a singular part of your anatomy which I normally find to be a wonderful handle with which to grasp you—"

"Ooh, I think this carriage ride is suddenly making me queasy," Terian murmured. "No. No, wait, it was that little revelation, not the ride."

Cyrus looked out the window as the carriage came to the end of an avenue lined by enormous manors walled off from the street and rattled past smaller row homes all built together. A market lay off to the other side, filled with immense numbers of haggling people and a raucous crowd. "So this is Saekaj. You know, I don't think I've ever really had much chance to look around here. Last time we just sort of marched through, army behind us ..."

"And you won't get much of a look right now, either, except as we pass," Terian said, seemingly eager to turn the discussion away from Cyrus and Vara's little spat. "But I will tell you, the markets now are the busiest I've ever seen them in my life. Now that we've got regularly commerce between Saekaj and Sovar—"

"You didn't before?" Vara asked, her face pinched.

"Long story, but no," Terian said, shaking his head. "Anyway, things have changed. They're better, more stable, less violent and oppressive. The lower chamber, Sovar, is finally starting to prosper after thousands of years of the Sovereign smashing them down. And," he said brightly, "we've begun to open up surface settlements again, reclaiming some of the open territory above and farming it with our own people rather than the slave labor of before. People are establishing homesteads up there, and we've got five towns growing under the sky." He puffed with pride. "Give us a few years and we won't just be sustaining ourselves on root vegetables, mushrooms, and spiders."

Cyrus exchanged a tempered look with Vara, whose face was now squeezed with disgust. "Uh ... that's good," he said, as delicately as he could.

Their reaction did not escape Terian. "I know," he said. "It sounds bad. Hell, it was bad. But it's getting better. We're finally coming out of the dark."

The carriage rattled as it took a turn and suddenly ran down a steep slope, as though traveling down a mountain. Cyrus braced himself against the sudden force of gravity at his back, threatening to push him toward Terian, who looked quite relaxed. "What the ...?" Cyrus muttered.

"Oh, right," Terian said with a grin visible in the thin slit of his helm. "I knew there was a reason I picked this side of the carriage." He smiled at Cyrus and Vara's obvious discomfiture. "So ... what did Lord Shirtless want? Surely not just to inflame Vara's loins?"

"My loins are quite cold at the moment, I assure you," she said in a tone that left them in no doubt that it was the truth.

"He wants us to dissolve the elven caste system," Cyrus said, pushing aside the bitterness that he'd felt toward Merrish throughout their discussion. "Also, he knew we were angling for meetings with Lady Voryn and Governor Frost—"

"Whoa," Terian said in sudden alarm, bending to lean forward even against the weight of gravity, "how'd he know that?"

"I'm not sure, but it worries me," Cyrus said tightly.

Terian leaned back against the carriage. "That is worrying. Our plans are supposed to be secret."

Vara sighed. "Did it not occur to you both that he might simply have been led in that direction by Oliaryn Iraid, who in fact pointed us toward the Confederation territories specifically?"

"It occurred to me," Cyrus said with a nod that Terian matched, "and then I rejected it because worrying about the other ways he—and who knows who else—might have heard about it is so much more ulcerating."

"Cyrus speaks the truth," Terian agreed, looking unsettled. "If you're right, Vara, it presumably costs us nothing that Iraid might have hinted at our plans to a kindred spirit. But imagine for a moment he wasn't talking to a kindred but someone who would sell us out in a heartbeat to the Leagues. All our planning, all our scheming would come to naught. Goliath and the rest would have ample time to counter us."

"There seems little we can do about it at present, save for send a message to Iraid asking him if he divulged these details, and requesting he keep his tongue still in the future," Vara said, "though that might deprive of us of further allies which we sorely need."

"And might reach the ears of spies, which we sorely do not," Terian said, settling back in the carriage once more. "So, this thing Merrish wants …"

"Dissolving the elven caste system," Cyrus said, shaking his head. "Seems the lord is a bit of an egalitarian."

"It seems the lord is a bit of a fool," Vara said. "Dismantling the caste system is well nigh impossible."

Terian smirked in the dim light. "So was the thought of killing a god only just a few short years ago."

"Not so," Vara said. "Requiem's Guildmaster did that very thing, if you recall, some ten thousand years ago, and apparently others did as well, if Alaric and Curatio were to be believed."

Cyrus frowned. "But that guildmaster used a godly weapon to do so—Ferocis, the Warblade of Bellarum." Something prickled in the back of his head at that thought.

"Yes, well, there were quite a few of them lying around Arkaria until just a few years ago," Vara said with a helping of sarcasm as they rattled over a particularly hard bump. "We're not even traveling past houses anymore. Where are you taking us, exactly?" Her voice rose in mild concern.

"Oh, stop with the suspicion already," Terian said, shaking his head. He thumped his axe's haft against the seat behind him. "I'm taking you to our prison, the Depths."

"And you think that will allay our suspicions?" Cyrus asked him.

Terian shrugged. "Do you need my axe again to feel safe, Davidon? Where's the trust?"

"I must have left it on the surface," Cyrus said dryly as the carriage took a turn and Vara bumped against him at the sudden change in direction.

The carriage came to a halt as words were exchanged between the driver and some other party ahead. Cyrus could hear the shouts but could not discern what was being said. After a minute, he heard heavy gates creaking open and the carriage began to move forward again.

"There's a cessation field over this area," Terian said, sniffing. "We have some magical prisoners. Using magic in this area would be a bad idea in any case. Guards tend to frown on it because, well, they think it might be an escape attempt, naturally."

"Naturally," Vara said without amusement. "Tell us again that you're not leading us down to our deaths or imprisonment?"

Terian snorted. "If I wanted to do that, I'm pretty sure I could come up with an easier way to go about it." He pushed the door open as the carriage rattled to a stop. "Assassinate you naked in your bed, perhaps. Call you to a meeting and have warriors sneak invisibly up behind you to cut off your heads before you could draw weapons." Terian frowned. "Actually, that reminds me—we should start casting cessation spells around us before our meetings in the future. Break invisibility of whoever might be lurking nearby."

"Clever," Vara said, giving Cyrus a sidelong glance as she stepped out of the carriage ignoring Terian's proffered hand. The Sovereign of Saekaj grinned and offered Cyrus a hand down as well. He ignored it as he stepped out of the carriage.

"This way," Terian said, taking a lantern from one of the guards standing nearby just as Cyrus's Eagle Eye spell faded and left him straining against the darkness.

Terian led them through exceedingly dark passages, the only light cast by his lantern. They passed guards in light armor who stood to attention as Terian passed. The Sovereign of Saekaj returned their salutes with nods and walked on, boots clanking against hard, tunneled stone.

"This is the mining section of the Depths," Terian said, leading them forward. "They have a farming section as well, for mushrooms

and bitterroot, but this is the place where we put those we loathe most."
He paused, seeming to think it over. "On the other hand, the dung
smell in the farming area is … overpowering, at best. Maybe the miners
get the better end of the deal, come to think of it."

"Such a charming nation you lead," Vara sniffed. "So civilized."

"How do they punish criminals in elfland?" Terian fired back.
"Make them join the unicorn mounted patrol where they're forced to
ride all around your magnificent and bounteous kingdom without a
saddle?" He mimed grasping at his hindparts. "'My overly long arse
aches after a hard day's ride upon the bare back of that ivory beast'!"
He grinned at Cyrus. "That's my impression of you if the elves capture
you before the Leagues."

"We have a prison of our own, you know," Vara shot back a little
hotly. "It is at sea, an island off the coast, and is very isolated, I am
told."

"Yes, I can imagine a temperate island of you mild-souled elves
being a real hell," Terian said. "Probably has a gaming room and
everything." He paused at a crossroads. "Ah, here we are." He knocked
upon a wooden door that Cyrus had not even seen.

The knocking resonated through the passage, much farther than the
light cast by the dim lantern. Cyrus squinted, feeling as if there were
things just beyond the failing light that were moving in the dark. He
could hear the trickle of water and other faint sounds; footsteps in the
dark, Vara's steady breathing. The smell of musty air was ever present
in this prison, and it threatened to choke him.

The door rattled open and Terian started to move in. Light filtered
out from the open portal as the Sovereign stepped inside. Vara followed
cautiously, and Cyrus, annoyed at being last, came in after she had
cleared the door. It was shut immediately behind them by a grim-
looking guard and locked with a loud click before the guard pocketed
the key.

They were in an immense courtyard-like area, probably half the size
of the Sanctuary foyer. Tunnels were plowed into the walls around
them, mining tunnels held up by wooden supports that ranged from
looking very aged to very new. They stood upon a high shelf of rock
and looked down upon faces that stared up at them. He saw
innumerable dark elves squinting at him, the faint light of three lanterns
mounted on the walls shining down on them. Every single one of them

was dirty, dirty as if they'd been scrubbed in black over every bit of their faces. There were tables laid out on the floor of the room and steps cut into the rock that descended to them.

The prisoners seemed cowed, not a sign of defiance on any of the faces looking up at Cyrus. In fact, one by one, after they'd taken a short gander at the newcomers, the prisoners began to look back down at their tables and the small plates before them. They were eating, Cyrus realized. He didn't recognize a single thing they were consuming, but the plates were full.

Two sets of eyes did not break from staring up, though, he realized at last. He honed in on each one at a time. The first belonged to a shorter prisoner, whose face was as blackened as the others, covered with the dark dust. *Do they mine coal here?* Cyrus wondered, almost sure of the answer. That particular prisoner had a long beard that was as dark as his face, perhaps darker, his eyes the only light spot on him.

Cyrus cast his gaze to the other prisoner staring up at him. This one … this one was a she. Her hair was also black, though he saw a glimmer of some other shade beneath the dust that caked her. Her face was a study in desperation, even beneath the filth. She was thin, waif-like, and at the sight of them, her shoulders slumped.

"I can't believe this," Vara said in a quiet whisper.

"Yeah, this a dirty, dirty place you have here," Cyrus opined as he looked down at the scene before him, prisoners at dinner.

"Not that," Vara said. "The—those two."

Cyrus stared back down at the two prisoners who looked back up at him. "Maybe it's just my failing human eyes, but they're so covered in coal dust I can't even tell who they are."

"Cyrus Davidon," the male prisoner said, voice scratchy, and yet somehow familiar. He stood, and Cyrus realized it was a dwarf.

"I know you," Cyrus said, staring over the ledge at the dwarf below. He cast his gaze to the woman; she still stared at him as well, though with considerably less enthusiasm than the dwarf. She seemed frozen, stunned into immobility, her plate forgotten in front of her.

"Aye, you do," the dwarf called up. "And I know you." He looked down the line at each of them. "Vara. Funny to see you here."

"It's not so funny to see you here," Vara said quietly. "Or you, either," she said to the woman who sat below.

The woman rose haltingly to her feet. She looked exhausted, as though she were about to fall over from the mere effort of standing. "Hello, shelas'akur," the woman said, and now Cyrus saw the points of her ears, nearly lost in her filthy hair.

"You're going to need to give these two a bath and parade them into the daylight if you want me to recognize them," Cyrus muttered to Terian. "Because right now … they might as well be two of the gods for all I can tell."

"They're not gods," Terian grinned, entirely too pleased with himself. "They're far more useful than that."

"Maybe if you need miners," Cyrus said, shaking his head. "But I can't recall any need for a broken-down elven woman and a daft-sounding dwarf in my life currently—" He froze mid-sentence, as a thought came to him. "Wait …"

"Yep," Terian said, nodding as Cyrus tumbled to the identity of first one, and then the other.

Cyrus shook his head, feeling stupid for not recognizing them sooner. "It's really them, isn't it?"

"Freshly captured from where they'd run, hiding out in Taymor," Terian pointed to the elven woman, "and Montis, respectively," and drew his thin finger to the dwarf. "Said they'd run from Goliath, didn't want to be part of it anymore."

"Who could blame them?" Vara asked, staring down at the prisoners below. "I can't imagine any reason I'd want to stay with those bandits."

"Well, she did have a husband who I believe is still causing you quite a few problems," Terian said with a smirk. "Apparently, her loyalty lost out on that one."

"Hello, Tolada," Cyrus said, calling down to the dwarf, who nodded his head in greeting. And then he swiveled his gaze to the elven woman, who looked positively broken as she stood there, staring up at him, all hope lost. "Greetings, Selene." He felt a wicked smile split his lips. "I have … so many questions for you both."

31.

"The thing you have to understand about Goliath and Malpravus," Tolada said, chewing idly on what looked to be mushrooms swimming in some kind of fat, "is that everything that comes out of that necromancer's mouth seems so damned reasonable when you're hearing it. It's only later, when you're separated from the rest of the herd and you get a little time to reflect, that things start to unravel."

"He casts a hell of a spell is what you're saying." Cyrus stood next to the long table, the courtyard emptied of all the prisoners save for Selene and Tolada, the guards having ushered them down the tunnels and back to work in order to give their Sovereign and his guests their privacy. Cyrus suspected there weren't many options for interrogation rooms in this cool, damp warren of mines.

"No spells," Tolada said, shaking his head, Cyrus's subtle pun soaring over the dwarf's head. "He doesn't need a spell, because he tells people what they want to hear, and he does it so well that it took me years to realize exactly how bad he was putting me on." He nodded at Selene. "She left before I did, maybe she got it quicker. Malpravus ... he hones in on what's important to people and then just holds it over your head, dangles it whenever he starts to sense your loyalty might be fading ... 'Oh, don't forget, you're so close to getting those mystical daggers you always wanted ... I heard tell of a hammer that could make you a match for Cyrus Davidon ... '" Tolada harrumphed. "Meanwhile, behind our backs, he's arranging goblins to raid plains shipping and striking pacts with the Dragonlord and the Sovereign of Saekaj, anything to increase his power a little."

"Or a lot, in most of those cases," Vara said, watching the dwarf eat with mounting disgust. She eyed him uneasily, his blackened beard

169

coated with greasy residue. "What do you know of his most recent attempts at alliances?"

"I've been gone for years," Tolada said, shrugging. "He tried to make inroads with the titans again, but that's an old story. We killed a lot of dragonkin trying to turn their heads."

"I suppose we should count ourselves fortunate he did not have any luck in that regard," Vara said, "else it might have made our endeavors last year in the south much more arduous."

"Indeed," Cyrus said, shaking his head. "Anyone else, Tolada?"

Tolada shrugged. "Malpravus kept a line of communication open with Amarath's Raiders. He and, uh ... whathisface ... the pretty boy with the scar, looks a little like you," he nodded at Cyrus.

Cyrus frowned. "Tell you me you don't mean Archenous Derregnault."

"Yeah, that's him," Tolada said, cramming a piece of blackish bread in his mouth. "You're like the spitting image of each other," the dwarf said, speaking around the immense, partially chewed lump of food.

Cyrus cast his eyes sideways to Vara and found her still staring across the table at Tolada, her arms still crossed, but her cheeks burning in the lamplight. He started to say something, but Terian, perhaps sensing the direction he was going, spoke first.

"Selene," Terian said, and the elven woman looked up at him with a timidity that reminded him of Larana, "when you last saw Goliath, what were they doing?"

She stared at them in frightened silence.

"Come on, now," Tolada said, licking his lips. "What are they going to do if you tell them? Goliath probably already wants to bloody kill you for desertion. Can't get much worse than that."

Selene clamped her mouth shut, her lips pressed so tightly together that they turned white.

"Is that true?" Cyrus asked, watching her. Her eyes swiveled around to look at him. "They're out to kill you?"

"Of course they are," Tolada said, using a dirty finger to mop up some of the slop left on his plate. "Malpravus doesn't truck with any sort of desertion. Disloyalty he'll tolerate to a point, especially if you're entertaining a better deal elsewhere, but none of us could get a better deal than safety in the belly of Goliath. We were all cast-outs from Reikonos and Pharesia, after all, and even the Dwarven Alliance looked at me askance last time I visited. Guards told me to leave, that I wasn't welcome there. Goliath is a hated name all around Arkaria. Made me wish I'd gone with Partus when he asked me to."

"Well, Partus and his entire group are dead," Cyrus said, watching Tolada's eyes widen at the mention, "so I'd say you dodged an arrow on that one."

"Aye," Tolada said with a nod. "I'd say so." He licked his lips again. "Well, if there's nothing else you need me for, there's a tunnel caved in that I need to see to excavating." He sniffed, seeming to enjoy the air. "I should have been a miner. It's only after all this drudging madness these last few years that I see how good they've got it back home. No worries about where you're going, who you're going to have to fight ... just good earth on your hands and in your beard, and honest labor to be done."

Cyrus frowned at him. "You can ... clear a cave-in?"

"Of course," Tolada said, getting up off the bench onto his stubby legs. "Or at least a good miner can." He grinned at Cyrus, white teeth gleaming beneath his black beard. "I wouldn't recommend you try, you'd just get buried." He laughed at his own joke and waddled off down a tunnel without looking back, humming some tune as he went.

"That is the happiest prisoner I've ever seen down here," Terian mused as Tolada disappeared into the dark. "Remind me to cut rations or something."

"Oh, you're a bloody wonderful holy warrior," Vara said.

"Well, I'm also a Sovereign of a nation of—let's just say it—angry, bitter, vengeful elves." He smirked. "It's in our very nature, the darkness, and while I'm trying my best to be better, I take my role as ruler here very seriously, including the crime and punishment segment of my duties."

"What did Goliath's members do to deserve this internment?" Vara asked stiffly, looking at the silent Selene, whose eyes were now back upon the table.

"Didn't you know?" Terian spoke acidly. "Malpravus tried to take over Saekaj Sovar. After the Sovereign left, he took over the army of the undead and attempted to invade us so he could seize power. Almost succeeded, too. Goliath is an enemy of the state here, as are all its past and present members." He glared at Selene. "I doubt she was around for that, but I can't be sure, and she won't talk. I'll let Tolada go if he wants to, once Goliath is finished, but her … she's going to be in here forever unless she cooperates, because we lost a lot of lives in my nation thanks to Goliath's efforts."

"I wasn't around for that," Selene said quietly, her eyes unmoving. "I wasn't around for any of the war. I wasn't even in Taymor for long before your people dragged me away. I was just trying to get back to the Kingdom."

"Where you could … serve out a prison sentence there?" Terian asked.

"I don't think they would have caught me," she mumbled. Her tone was muted. "The Kingdom isn't looking for former Goliath members, they're more focused on the officers. I could have made it."

"I'm more than happy to arrange transport for you," Terian said, leaning back a little. "But if you can't even answer a question or two, I think you might be here for quite some time." He grinned at her. "How's the food?"

She looked up at him with desperate loathing. "Terrible."

"Good," Terian said, nodding with satisfaction. "Maybe I won't cut rations after all. I think Tolada's just a weirdo, probably the exception to the rule that gets a strange charge out of being here, like Grinnd—"

"What can you tell us about what Goliath is up to?" Vara asked, causing Selene to stare down at the table once more. "Why did you leave?"

"Why wouldn't I leave?" Selene asked, speaking like her mouth was full of food even though Cyrus hadn't seen her put so much as a speck in since his arrival. "Dragging myself through the Bandit Lands with them was not exactly the life I sought when Orion and I joined them."

"What were you expecting?" Cyrus asked with no small amount of amusement. "You and Orion made a failed pact with the Dragonlord, and then he helped scheme to dishonor Sanctuary—your former guild, I might add, you traitorous—" Cyrus stopped himself before appending a judgmental title, and took a moment to breathe and get control of himself. "What did you think was going to happen?"

"I thought we were going to best you," Selene said, looking up at him with hatred in her eyes. "I thought we were going to get what we wanted when we let the Dragonlord free. But we didn't. You saw to that. You left Orion so ripped apart, his face—" She shuddered. "I couldn't even look at him after that. He expected me to share a bed with him, looking like—like a monster." She shook her head, and dust fell from her hair, puffing in the dim light. "I didn't even know about the plan with the goblins. We barely spoke by then. When you and your friends forced us into exile, Malpravus led us into the Bandit Lands." She looked at him with loathing. "Do you even know what it's like down there? A hundred of our people died in an old temple when the Avatar of the God of Death rose up and killed us."

Cyrus felt unbridled amusement break across his face. "Did he now? That was … fortuitous."

"Yes, he did," Selene said, her voice thick with revulsion. "We were always hiding in out of the way places, combing the swamps, squatting in the ruins of the ancients. Do you know why they call it the Bandit Lands?"

"Because you were there, obviously," Vara said.

"Because it's all banditry, all the time," Selene said, her hatred whispering out in the quiet cave. "No guards save those you bring with you. Small settlements that prey upon one another with feral savagery. Do you know how many villages we came upon that had been burned, ruined, their people murdered or ripped away to be slaves for some other group?" She shuddered. "When I left, I traveled by night, sleeping hidden during the day as I made my way north out of that hell. I heard so many footsteps, so many shrieks, so many cries of war. I ate plants, I foraged and got sick off bad water in the swamps and counted myself lucky the day I found the coast. It took me three months to make it to Taymor. I was skin and bones when I got there." She held up her arms, and for the first time Cyrus realized that within her blackened robes her wrists were minuscule, almost no meat upon them. "I've gained weight since I got here, and the food is horrid."

"Truly, no one has suffered as you have," Vara said with a little acid of her own. "Except the people caught in the war that your guild helped start. Famine, sackings, countless murdered and killed in the war … yes, you precious little soul, you have truly been handed adversity that no one else could possibly understand."

"I don't see you starving," she said, "shelas'akur." She said it as a curse, and her eyes fell upon the small band of gold upon Vara's fingers where she'd removed her gauntlets and hung them upon her belt. "It would appear even your cold heart has found room for love." She looked at Cyrus. "Are you the lucky man who finally melted that heart of frost?"

"Some days I'm the lucky man," Cyrus said, drawing an annoyed look from his wife, "some days ... not so lucky."

"Count on today to be one of the latter," Vara said matter-of-factly. "Selene ..." She stood, looking down on the healer. "I hope you enjoy your stay here, and I hope it lasts the rest of your long life."

"I think we can count on that," Terian said with a nod. "I know the guy in charge, see, and he's got something of a grudge against Selene here." He smirked down at her as he stood. "Something about ... oh, I'll let you remember, but it's to do with that one day where you and Orion got into a squall that blew half of Sanctuary out the doors. Including me," Terian said, tapping his breastplate with his finger.

"I see you're wearing the armor of Alaric now," Selene said sullenly. "I suppose it'd be too much to ask for you to adopt his forgiving nature."

"Alaric was very forgiving," Terian said, nodding. "I could be forgiving, too, but not if you're going to continue to be a shit and tell me nothing useful about Goliath."

"What do you want?" Selene screeched, her patience clearly at its end. She folded in on herself as if she were besieged on all sides by enemies. "I have nothing to give you. I didn't even sleep with Orion for a year before I left the guild."

"Why was he so keen to stay?" Terian asked.

"Because he hates Cyrus," Selene said, looking at Cyrus with utter loathing. "Malpravus is perpetually egging Orion on with talk of revenge, even though it's obvious he doesn't really mean it. I couldn't handle being around my husband any longer. He's totally consumed by his hatred, his anger. I didn't bed him, we didn't trade confidences, and Goliath moved, and moved, and moved constantly, Malpravus driving us forward until we could barely walk." Her voice cracked with self-pity. "I don't even know where they ended up, they kept going deeper and deeper into the jungle, and I couldn't take it anymore. Others left, too, obviously, and they never even sent anyone to look for us. I didn't know the guild even came back, that they were welcome here." She was speaking in choking sobs, tears rolling down her black cheeks and exposing pale flesh beneath them as they washed away the coal residue.

"Surely you must know something," Cyrus said, rising to his own feet to join Terian and Vara. "Why were they plunging into the jungle? No one would have come for them if they'd just traveled a few days south of the last portal in the southeast."

"It's not the last portal," Selene said miserably. "The one north of the old bridge? It's not the last." She let this revelation out painfully, as a crackling sob. "There's another one, in the jungle. I heard Malpravus talking about it once when I was resting near Carrack."

"Where is it? This other portal?" Cyrus asked.

"I don't know," Selene said, shaking her head. "I have no idea, just that it's—it's in the Bandit Lands somewhere, and that he was trying to get us to it. He didn't tell us why. He didn't exactly share his plans, if he had any, with the members. It's why so many of us left, because we didn't know what we were doing." Vara gave Cyrus a look of significance. *Leadership*, Cyrus thought, trying to interpret her look. *Looks like it's a plague that affects us all in desperate times.*

"Is there anything else you can tell us?" Vara asked softly.

"I don't know," Selene said numbly, now looking as though she were going to collapse on the table. "Nothing you don't already know except ... perhaps ..." She looked up. "Malpravus ... he hates you."

"Tell us something we don't know," Terian said.

"Not you," she said, shaking her head at Terian.

"I know he hates me," Cyrus said.

She shook her head weakly again. "Not you, either. He always hoped you could be swayed to his side. That's why I was sure he was lying to Orion with his talk about getting his revenge; Malpravus spoke out of both sides of his mouth constantly. I heard him talking about you when Orion wasn't around, and ... he seemed certain you'd fall to his way of thinking sooner or later." She turned her eyes to Vara, and they were filled with a loathing all her own. "No, it was *you*. Malpravus hated you. You and Alaric, he couldn't shut up about how much he despised you both."

"The feeling was mutual, I assure you," Vara said, sounding a bit affronted. "But I must, I'm curious ... what did he say in reference to this hatred? What was its source?"

"I don't know," Selene said, collapsing, her head falling onto the table lightly as the elf seemed to give up. "All I know," her voice came, muffled, "was that he wanted you dead ... and I presume, given exactly how much his lifeless eyes lit up when he talked about your death ... that it has not changed since I left their fold."

32.

"Well, this is all very interesting," Vaste said as they all stood around the Tower of the Guildmaster—Vaste, J'anda, Cyrus, Vara and Terian, hashing over both the meetings. "And here I thought you two had just decided not to come back at all, or that you'd bound your souls elsewhere, or that you'd been ambushed and captured by Lord Merrish in some ill-advised, possibly brilliant scheme, but no! No, you've been to the dark elven prison and spoken with former idiot members of Goliath being held captive." His onyx eyes flicked to Terian. "And you, Terian … you're imprisoning people now?"

"I run a nation, Vaste," Terian said, giving the troll a pitying look. "Yes, I imprison people, it's practically a requirement for a functioning society. And in case you've already forgotten, it was less than two years ago that you people imprisoned me in the dungeons here in Sanctuary."

"Oh, yes," Vaste said, staring off into the distance. "I recall that now. The time really does speed along, doesn't it?"

"What do you make of this portal beyond the last?" J'anda asked, thinking carefully over what they'd covered.

"Sounds as though it's a perfect place to set up your secret and evil base," Vaste said. "Especially if no one knows how to cast the spell that gets you there."

Terian nodded slowly. "True. I'm still trying to get my wizards and druids to figure out the spell to the portal Yartraak had secreted away in the Grand Palace of Saekaj. They seem to think it's written in the runes, but unfortunately, someone—Yartraak—killed a great many of our scholars, including the people who might be able to read the language of the ancients that it's all written in." He shrugged. "Turns out the elves would finally be useful for something. Too bad they're allied against me right now."

"We have many uses," Vara said archly, "scholarly works and intelligence being but one of the boons of our society."

"The other being Pharesian brandy, I think," Terian said with his usual smirk.

"Oh!" Cyrus said, blurting out as he looked at Vaste with an amused smile of his own. "I almost forgot! Selene said that Goliath lost a hundred people exploring an ancient temple in the Bandit Lands when they ran across the Avatar of the God of Death."

Vaste's eyes widened as he broke into a smile of his own. "HAH!"

"I know!" Cyrus doubled over, beset with laughter. "I honestly never thought ..." he cackled, "... any good would come out of our little mishap there, but ... haha ..."

Vaste slapped his knee, eyes closed as he guffawed. "Couldn't happen to a more worthy guild. Oh, my, that does my heart some good."

"I was thinking the same thing," Cyrus said, the laughter finally fading. "Shame Malpravus didn't get eaten by that thing."

"Too bony," Vaste said with a shake of the head. "Not nearly enough 'blood of sacrifices' for the Avatar of the God of Death to find sustenance."

Vara wore a look that showed her patience clearly worn thin. "I assume that was referring to the two of you and your ill-fated expedition with the gnome who-must-not-be-given-name into the jungles down there?"

"Annoying as he might be, Brevis is not quite as terrible as I used to believe," Terian said.

"Yeah," Cyrus said, sighing. "It was a frightening time, but the things we've seen, that we've dealt with since—including the actual God of Death, not just his physical manifestation on Arkaria—well, the fear I felt then pales in comparison." A sober look crept across his face. "That temple down there, though ... I wouldn't be surprised if there were more like it. I mean, what with the Endless Bridge being built in that area, who knows what other remnants of ... the ancients, presumably ... well, who knows what else is down there? I could easily believe Malpravus found another portal beyond the remembrance of anyone else and has been using it to keep himself well out of striking distance of Arkaria's armies."

"It is a clever solution, really," J'anda said. "Anyone who wishes to reach you must undertake a journey of months, but you may reach anyone else in a matter of seconds."

"I'd like to yank that feeling of safety away from him," Terian said, wrinkling his long nose. "Just tear it right out of his skeletal fingers."

"I understand that." Cyrus nodded and cast his gaze off the balcony. "In fact … it makes me think about your warning about the portal just north of us."

"Are you thinking of trying to close it as well?" Vara asked, stiffening.

"I'm more than thinking about it," Cyrus said. "We need to do it."

Terian made a face. "That's going to make it really hard for me to get here, Davidon, which means our little meetings are going to get a lot more complicated."

"Not that hard," Cyrus said. "You can just bind your soul here."

"I have to go home sometimes, too," Terian said. "And as much fun as it is to barge into your bedroom uninvited, I like to be able to approach from the balconies so that I don't accidentally wander in when you two newlyweds are intimate."

"I, too, enjoy that privacy," Vara said acidly. "Let us keep that."

"I don't think we're going to have a choice much longer," Cyrus said. "That portal is five minutes from our door. The next nearest gives us at least a couple days of warning. Plus, we get it shut, we can clear out Malpravus's little army of dead without worrying about him sending in immediate reinforcements to kill our people. It's going to have to happen."

"And our meetings?" Terian asked sourly.

"We'll have to find another way," Cyrus said. "We'll have to find someone whose soul can be bound in the garderobe over there, or something—"

"Marvelous," Terian said, unimpressed. "Some poor soul is going to have to show up in your toilet every time they cast the return spell?" His eyes moved swiftly as he thought. "Perhaps I'll save that honor for Mrs. Lepos …"

Vara rubbed her hand against her forehead. "Or we could just have them bind outside the door …"

"No good," Vaste said, shaking his head, "what happens when Mendicant hears hammering and comes wandering up?" He grinned, his underbite showing those enormous lower teeth. "Might as well just cast the binding spell right in your bed. They can slip in in the middle of the night and nudge you awake."

"I am not slipping into anyone's bed in the middle of the night save my own," Terian said. "But I will talk to my wife about coming here to bind before you shut the portal. At least then we'll have a direct conduit easily available to reach you without being seen. She mostly spends her time in Saekaj and Sovar in any case, so she's really ideal for it."

"Perfect," Vara said in a tone that indicated she thought it was clearly anything but, "and now our bedroom will be a sanctum which you can enter at any time, regardless of whether we have the doors shut or not. Beautiful."

"Hey, it's not exactly my idea of a good time, either, seeing the warrior in black's elongated arse—" Terian said.

"I do not have an elongated arse!" Cyrus said.

J'anda peered at Cyrus, eyes creeping down. "It does look rather long in those greaves … I don't think I ever noticed that before …"

"I have," Vaste said. When he had drawn every eye in the room, he explained, "I've often compared it to my own and found it … lacking. Not nearly as full or luscious."

"Which is exactly the comparison I make between your wits and those of a gnomish child," Vara said, giving him an evil glare. "In any case, drawing back to the point and away from our upcoming security precautions, unless we wish to mount an expedition in the far jungles of the Bandit Lands, I do not see how knowing this detail about Malpravus's secret portal is any advantage for us."

"It's not," Terian said, "unless we can find someone who knows the spell."

"That's likely to be highly guarded information," Vaste said. "After all, the moment anyone else knows it, it ceases being a secret base. Recall how badly we were compromised when the dark elves figured out how to send war parties directly into our foyer during the war."

Terian's brow furrowed. "Hmm. I wonder how Yartraak did that?" He puckered his lips in thought. "That bears some investigation."

"Yes, you go investigate that," Vaste said, flicking his fingers at the dark elf. "Meanwhile, we've got—what? A meeting with a human governor?"

"In two weeks," Cyrus said, turning his head to look for the piece of parchment Lord Merrish had given them at the end of their interview. "I guess 'immediately' would be too much to ask."

"It's not as if we're in an urgent hurry, under dire threat or anything," Vaste said, shrugging broadly. "Why, we're practically on holiday out here, without a worry in the world—"

"Just give me some warning before you seal that portal out there," Terian said, standing upright. "And about that meeting with Frost ... I think I should send Aisling with you. In disguise, of course."

"Of course," Vara said icily, "for even a glimpse of her slattern face as it is will surely result in them being driven from the Northlands at the head of a mob with pitchforks and torches."

"That's what I like about you, Vara," Terian said, "you just don't ever give up a grudge."

"I'd be prepared to give up a few, actually," she said, "like I did with you, provided there was reason to."

"I'm afraid in this case," he said, starting to cast his return spell as the glimmer of light consumed him, "that these grudges aren't going to be settled by anything less than the death of at least one of the participants." He disappeared in a blaze of white light.

The former dark knight's last words left them all in a grim and silent mood, seemingly fearful to talk, and the night began to close in outside.

33.

The arrangements to shut the portal north of Sanctuary took two days to make; Terian arrived with Kahlee on the evening after their meeting, slipping up to the balcony under cover of darkness in their usual way. Cyrus tried to take note of which direction they approached from in order to discern who among his guildmates might be in Terian's employ, but he did not see their arrival until they came in behind him.

"Don't try and out-sneak me, Davidon," Terian said with a broad grin, clearly cottoning to Cyrus's intent. "I was a dark knight, you know. There's a not a dirty trick out there that I haven't perpetrated. Hell, I invented most of them."

The binding was done in no time at all, just inside the door down the stairs, which all involved felt offered the greatest amount of privacy for Cyrus and Vara. "I promise," Terian said, "I will knock hard on the inside of the door when I arrive and will not ascend the stairs until I know you're either aware we're here or I'm certain you're not at home."

"That's damned decent of you, Terian," Cyrus said dryly, "but I think we both know that the truth is that you're afraid your wife will see my long bottom and become enamored of it."

Kahlee frowned at him and did not say a word. However, her eyes drifted down almost surreptitiously, as if to check on Cyrus's assertion.

On the morning after, once he'd eaten, Cyrus gave the order to Mendicant to close the portal, and the goblin went out under cover of invisibility spell to carry out his will. It was done in moments, and the wizard reappeared at the wall moments later, casting a cessation spell that revealed nothing before he slipped in through the front gate.

"What's to stop them from reactivating the portal themselves?" Mendicant asked nervously as he rejoined Cyrus and the small war party forming just inside the gate.

They stood under a grey spring sky, the wind blowing harshly across the Plains of Perdamun. "Hopefully, the arcane and lost knowledge of how to do it," Cyrus said. "While it's hardly secret, neither is it a commonly taught spell in the Leagues." He looked back at his group, which included Vara, J'anda, Mendicant, Samwen Longwell, Erith, and Fortin, as well as roughly one hundred others, and gave them a reassuring nod. With the exception of the rock giant and Mendicant, they were all mounted on horses. "We're going to ride out, at guard, ready for anything. I don't think there's an army lurking out there, and should we find ourselves alone, our mission will be to run down the corpses dotting the plains around us."

"We used a gnomish spyglass to get a rough position and count," Vaste said, holding a parchment with a crude map of Sanctuary and the surrounding area on it. Small, crudely drawn skulls with X's to denote the eyes and tongues stuck out marked the locations of the dead. Cyrus stared at the map with a raised eyebrow as Vaste continued to speak: "We've seen about fifty."

"Reanimated corpses make for poor eating," Fortin rumbled. "All in all, warlord, the meals since I have come back to guard this place have been exceedingly poor."

"We apologize for the lacking in your culinary experience," Vaste said with undying sarcasm.

"Your apology is accepted," Fortin said.

"That wasn't a—" Vaste began, then sighed. "Never mind."

"All right, then," Cyrus said with a thin smile, "let's get started."

They rode out onto the quiet plains, Mendicant casting cessation on a constant basis as they went. Cyrus had been torn when the strategy had been proposed; taking magic out of their defense seemed a poor decision to him. Vara had argued that it was their only true way to be certain there wasn't an invisible army lurking, so he had acceded to her argument.

They rode without incident for nearly an hour, in a careful ring around the wall. The early kills were easiest, and they caught many of the dead unawares, riding them down with little trouble. Soon enough, though, the corpses began to run, and finding them via the map was becoming an increasingly difficult proposition.

"None of these seem to be where you say they are," Longwell

complained, putrid chunks of meat and flesh trapped on his three-pronged lance.

"Yes, it's almost as if a necromancer is controlling these creatures and is now fully aware we're slaughtering his pets," Vaste said, eyes fixed on the map as though trying to decode some great secret from within the parchment. "It seems obvious he would start moving them to avoid that, doesn't it?"

"How far away do you suppose he is from us?" Mendicant asked, on the back of a pony that struggled to keep up with the other horses.

"He could be a thousand miles away for all we know," Cyrus said, looking for their next quarry. He spotted it in the distance, ambling off on rotting legs toward the horizon. "There." The war party turned in that direction, hooves thundering. "Or he could be lingering near the river. Who knows?"

"If he's a thousand miles away," Mendicant said, bumping along to the uneven plains, "that's impressive magical control." He looked to J'anda. "Could you control someone that far away?"

J'anda nodded. "I have done something similar a few times. I can recall influencing people in Reikonos after teleporting back to Saekaj. The distance does not seem to matter in control, though proximity was required to set the original spell." The enchanter stared off into the distance, clearly contemplating something.

"If the same holds true for necromancy," Vaste said with a sour look of his own, "that means Malpravus was here at one point, in order to establish his control over these corpses."

"That's hardly surprising," Cyrus said. "Someone had to drop these bodies here, after all." He rode up on the next corpse and took its head off in a slashing motion. The body fell to the ground, its momentum and fall causing it to break apart. The stink made him blanch, the strong odor of rot creeping down his throat and threatening to start him retching. "It's not as if they're local."

"Where do you suppose he got them?" Vaste asked. "And who do you think died in order to make the soul rubies that allowed him to revive them?"

"I don't even want to know," Cyrus said, sheathing his new sword with a rattle in Avenger's Rest. The blade had acquired a deathly stink in the course of their hunt, but putting it away seemed to help.

They rode for another hour and killed half as many of the corpses as they had in half the time before. The next two hours produced similar results, until finally, some five hours later, they felt reasonably assured that they had rid the area of all of the undead spies left behind by Malpravus. The horses kept their distance while Mendicant cast a fire spell upon the last body, consuming it with flame. Lines of black smoke still puffed up on the horizon in all the places where they'd found a corpse, like signs of a war that had been waged and lost.

"Urnnnnnnngh," Fortin said, grunting low and wheezing, shifting laboriously from side to side as he walked in a slow circle around the war party.

"You all right, Fortin?" Erith asked, guiding her pony nearer to the rock giant. Cyrus, having experienced firsthand what rock giant vomit smelled like, carefully guided Windrider in the opposite direction.

"I have not run this much in quite some time," Fortin said, making a low gasping noise that sounded like rocks grinding against steel. "I find myself ... unpleasantly fatigued ... and perhaps a tad ill."

Cyrus gave Windrider another slight jolt to move him away; the horse did not seem to require much encouragement. Cyrus cast an eye back toward Sanctuary. "Looks like we're a couple miles out. You going to be able to make it back all right?"

"I just need ... a minute to rest ..." Fortin said, bending at the waist, placing his enormous hands on his knees. "Every time we caught one of those things, I thought maybe ... we'd take a break ... but no, we kept moving. You people and your horses. I need a mount."

"Maybe a dragon?" Cyrus asked with vague amusement.

"I think he'd have better luck with one of those savanna cats," Vara said, watching Cyrus edge ever farther from Fortin and taking a cue from him. She was following only a dozen feet behind him.

"Yes ..." Fortin said, nodding. "A savanna cat ... those creatures the size of three of your trolls. Those would be a worthy mount for a Grand Knight such as myself."

Cyrus raised an eyebrow at the rock giant's use of the title. "I'm not so sure they'd let you ride them, Fortin."

"I would tame one," Fortin said, taking a breath and seemingly inflating himself back to standing upright. The sound of rock rumbling rolled over the plains. "I would show it my fearsome strength and it would be cowed at my power. Yes ... when this task is over, I will go to the Gradsden Savanna and find myself a worthy steed."

Cyrus thought about replying. Any number of possibilities sprang to mind, most of them detailing exactly how fatal such an expedition would play out for the cat. He caught a look from Vara, though, and said nothing. *Let him dream.*

And so he said nothing, and the war party rode back to Sanctuary quietly, for no one else had the heart to quash the dreams of the rock giant, either.

34.

The time between the sealing of the portal north of Sanctuary and the scheduled meeting with Governor Allyn Frost of the Northlands was another dragging series of weeks, time spent unproductive and stale, with few breaks in the routine.

One of them was a meeting that Cyrus scheduled even before he'd begun the process of sealing the portal. This one took place in the dead of the night, and was made possible by Mendicant undertaking a journey to Emerald Fields on Cyrus's behalf. A day earlier he'd sent word to Cattrine by a different messenger requesting her to deliver a sealed missive into the hills above Emerald Fields, into the mines of Rockridge. This she did, and as a result, Mendicant appeared moments after he left, twinkling back into existence at his point of bind, the return spell carrying him back with a dwarf clutched tightly to him.

The dwarf was of medium height, hair and beard braided carefully, his face cleaned for the meeting, lacking the dust and dirt with which it had been covered when last Cyrus had met him. The dwarf looked around nervously as he appeared in Mendicant's quarters. Cyrus was awaiting them both, leaning against the wall, the torch fires and the hearth burning. As they appeared, Cyrus looked out into the hall, checking to see that it was empty. "Hold on," Cyrus said and then practiced his illusion spell by transforming the dwarf into J'anda, whom he knew to be in his quarters, asleep. "All right, let's go."

"So much secrecy," Mendicant said softly, under his breath, as if in awe of what was being done.

"Come to my quarters in five minutes, Mendicant," Cyrus said. "Knock softly on the door, and I'll let you in as soon as our meeting concludes." He smiled with reassurance at the goblin. "And thank you."

"You're welcome," Mendicant said, bowing, his robes dragging the floor as he stooped. "I am happy to be of service."

"Follow," Cyrus told the dwarf, who was now disguised as J'anda, complete with the staff. The dwarf, whose hands had been empty when he'd arrived, stared in wonder and pushed the illusion into the floor. It disappeared when it made contact with the stone, as if it had somehow been thrust into the floor and wedged there. "Don't do that," Cyrus warned, and the dwarf jerked the staff out again and followed him as he opened the door.

"Shh," Cyrus said, beckoning the J'anda illusion forward. They ascended the stairs with only minor incident—the dwarf nearly tripped over his feet while trying to figure out how to reconcile what he saw of his taller dark elven self with his actual, shorter legs. When they arrived at Cyrus's quarters, he opened the door and led the dwarf up after locking the door and then dispelling the illusion behind him.

"Hello," Vara said as they both reached the top of the stairs. She was waiting on one of the chairs, a book beside her, clearly put down when she'd heard them approaching.

"Vara Davidon," Cyrus said, making the introduction, "this is Keearyn."

"Lady Davidon," Keearyn said, quickly kneeling, "it is a very great honor to meet you."

"No need for any of that," Vara said, rising to her feet. She was dressed in her full armor and her sword was on her hip, clearly prepared in case the dwarf proved something other than compliant. Cyrus had met the dwarf before and considered the likelihood roughly equivalent to Vaste shutting his mouth when presented an opportunity to insult someone or Ryin passing up a chance to argue. "It's a pleasure to make your acquaintance, Keearyn."

"This isn't the first time we've met, ma'am," Keearyn said, bowing his head.

"It's not?" Vara asked, her brow furrowing lightly. "I have to apologize, as I can't seem to recall—"

"Keearyn is one of the slaves we freed from Gren two years ago," Cyrus said, feeling a curious reserve tugging at him. "He was captured by the dark elves when they sacked Aloakna—"

"Caught me and my family on the road outside town," Keearyn said, burbling with excitement. "And sacked is the right word for what they did to us as well—stuffed us in canvas and took us to the Depths, that hellhole—"

Vara frowned. "I recently had cause to visit the Depths, and I met one of your fellow dwarves there."

Keearyn's large brow rose up. "Truly? I pity that poor bastard. I could not conceive of a worse fate than being stuck there for any stretch of time."

Cyrus and Vara shared a look. "Tolada seemed like he was enjoying himself," Cyrus said, prompting Keearyn's eyes to seem to grow wider than his stubby fists. "Anyhow," he went on, explaining to Vara, "I met Keearyn when I went to … uh … fight with Fortin. He's the foreman at the mines up on Rockridge."

"Ever at their service, yes," Keearyn said, stooping again, quickly. "And yours, if you need me for something."

"As it happens," Cyrus said, smiling weakly, "I do."

Keearyn stared up at Cyrus with wide eyes, struck with awe. "You have … need of a humble miner?"

"I have need of an excellent miner," Cyrus said, "which I have heard you are. I have a task for you, one which must be carried out in absolute secret, and which I can pay you and whoever else you need a significant sum of gold to undertake."

"I … I … no gold is necessary—" Keearyn began.

"I think it is," Cyrus said. "It's likely to be an extended bit of work. You'll need workers you can implicitly trust, and from what I've heard … they'll need great skill."

Keearyn nodded. "Whatever you require and request, I shall make happen. Many of my workers are members of my own family, and I trust them with my life. Whatever you need, we can accomplish."

Cyrus let out a long breath. "You might want to hear the task I'm setting forth before you agree so readily." He took another breath, and then told the dwarf exactly what he wanted of him. The fire crackled in the hearth, shading the dwarf's astonished face in orange tones, highlighting the braided beard that hung down below his belt. After Cyrus had outlined in broad strokes what he needed, he asked, "Can you do that?"

"You weren't making a jest at all," Keearyn said, rocking back on his haunches. "I—I'll have to see it to be sure, but yes. It could take quite some time, though. And you're right … I'll need gold. To do something of that scale ... I couldn't fund it out of my own accounts."

"We've got some time," Cyrus said. "And I've managed to accumulate a reasonable fortune as Guildmaster of Sanctuary." He pursed his lips. "Some of it is here, and you'll have it before you leave. Some of it's in banks in Reikonos and Pharesia, and getting to that will be a bit more difficult under present circumstances. For now, though, I'll make sure you have plenty enough to get started."

"If it's as you say, this could be the work of years," Keearyn said, his rugged face struck with worry.

"As I said before," Cyrus said, smiling lightly at Vara, who met his with a much more concerned look, "we've got some time ..."

35.

The day of the arranged meeting with Governor Frost seemed to come more swiftly than other events Cyrus had waited for of late. The spring air had turned warm, the skies had cleared and any trace of winter had been left far behind. In the distance, from the top of the tower, Cyrus could see the fields of the nearest farmers to the north going about their labors, if he chose to spend his time watching. Sometimes he did, for lack of anything else to do, leaning against the stone rail that lined the edge of the balcony, staring hard out at the far distance, watching a small spot on the horizon tread across the fields. He knew it was a beast of burden of some sort, its master an imperceptible speck, gradually turning the ground a deeper shade of brown as he tilled the way that Lord Merrish had been doing in his own fields.

"Only an hour to go," Vara said, easing up on him. They were both already in their armor, waiting for nothing more than the appointed time to arrive. There was quiet below, the silence of Sanctuary a difficult thing for Cyrus to get used to. Time was, there would have been peals of laughter from the lawns, activity on the archery range, people wandering about the gardens or taking horses out for a ride from the stables. Now the lawn was empty, though he'd been across it enough of late to know that it was getting saturated from some of the recent torrential rains.

"Not that we're counting," Cyrus said, turning his head to glance at her.

"It has been a long, difficult few months," Vara said, staring past him. "Perhaps now that spring is here—"

"Perhaps if we can get what we have set out to accomplish done," he corrected, and she nodded. "Because the simple change of seasons is unlikely to reduce the pressure upon us. If anything, the steady atrophy of our numbers will only make it worse."

"Are you still obsessed with our numbers, then?" Vara asked, quirking an eyebrow at him.

"I haven't asked and no one has told me," Cyrus said, turning to look back at the horizon. "That seems the wiser course, since we're already reduced to the barest minimum to allow defense of the wall."

She nodded once and did not press the point. "Do you think—?" she began, but a hard knock from the door down the stair halted her in the middle.

"Come in," Cyrus said, looking back as he called out. He waited, Vara at his side, the gentle breeze blowing between them as footsteps sounded. Calene appeared a moment later, an envelope in hand, and went straight to Vara, offering it to the paladin without a word.

"Thank you," Vara said, taking it, staring at it with a frown. She opened it and began to read.

"How goes it among the rangers, Calene?" Cyrus asked as he waited for Vara to finish.

"It goes," she answered. "We're scheduled for an archery practice later today, just to sharpen our skills. Seems leaving hands idle too long causes problems, and since a stealth march practice would require us to leave, and that seems unfeasible at the moment ...."

"I couldn't have said it better myself in relation to the idleness," Cyrus said. "Are you ready for your first council meeting?"

"Aye," Calene said, reddening. "I'm ready. Not sure what I can possibly contribute, but I'm ready as I can be."

"Thank you for this, Calene," Vara said with a nod, her face as blank. Cyrus gave her a frown at a glance; there was a burgeoning excitement behind her eyes, though she was clearly trying to contain it.

"You're welcome," Calene said, nodding. "If there's nothing else ...?"

"That'll do it," Cyrus said, giving her the nod of dismissal. The ranger gave a small salute and walked back toward the door. Cyrus followed her with his eyes and did not stop watching her until she'd closed the door behind her. He turned to face Vara. "What is it?"

"I have to go," Vara said, her face suddenly split between hope and agony. "Right now. The meeting we've been waiting for has been arranged, but it's now."

"Damn," Cyrus said, leaning back against the balcony rail, the metal of his greaves scraping against the stone. "How are you going to get there?"

She gave a shrug. "I need someone to teleport me."

"You should take J'anda," Cyrus said seriously.

"J'anda is to take you to Isselhelm to meet with Frost."

"I can have Larana do that," Cyrus said.

"That's daft," Vara said, rising up, cheeks heated. "We can't have anyone knowing about the Frost meeting."

"We can't have anyone knowing about yours, either," Cyrus said. "That'd be a more definite guarantee to set tongues wagging than me taking a meeting with the governor of the Northlands."

Vara sighed, turning to look out over the balcony. "Weeks of pointless waiting and then once again it all breaks loose at once. Do you get the feeling sometimes that we're meant to be divided?"

"Only insofar as us divided is the easiest way to take us apart," Cyrus said, facing in toward the tower, staring into the shadowed interior. "If we were at the strength we had even a year ago, before the battle in the jungle with the Avatar of the God of War—"

"But we aren't," Vara said quietly. "You might as well wish for us to be back in the time before we had to suspect half the members of our own council of betraying us to Goliath and the others. The sundial's shadow does not move back, dear husband, it only goes forward. We remain trapped in these unyielding circumstances until we wriggle free of them by our own ingenuity or until our enemies foist death upon us."

Cyrus felt a small smile take root on his face. "Which one would you bet on right now, if forced?"

"I would always bet upon us," Vara said, leaning up to kiss his cheek. "Are you sure about taking Larana to Isselhelm?"

"No, but she wouldn't be the only one coming with me," Cyrus said, and he saw the flicker of distaste across his wife's face as she recalled.

"Ugh," Vara said. "The harlot. You should take Vaste with you."

"No. Someone should remain here, just in case," Cyrus said, shaking his head. "Aisling ... she's saved our lives more recently than she tried to take mine. And if she kills me ..." His smile turned rueful. "Well, she'll be beating out a long line of people for the privilege."

"I don't like this," Vara said, staring out over the plains. "I don't like this at all. The line between enemy and ally has become far too muddled for my taste. All of the people we face now ... they were all friends at one point in time." A flicker of emotion ran over her features. "In some cases, much more than that."

"Things change," Cyrus said, nodding. "It seems to me that it's these times, these ... trying times ... that you find out who really matters most. Who you can count on. It's not when your tide is rising that you can test the loyalties of those around you; it's when the tide has gone out and left you stranded in a long waste of empty sand ... that's when you find out who'll stand with you."

"There aren't nearly as many people standing with us as I would have thought given everything we've been through," Vara said quietly as the wind whipped stray strands of her hair around her.

"Aye," Cyrus said, a slight choking feeling crawling into the back of his throat. "I thought we'd bought more loyalty by our service, too. But apparently we haven't, and so this is the price we pay. Once again, odds against us, backs to the wall." He nodded at the note in her hand. "But if things could change ..."

"I'll be back as soon as I can," she said and kissed him on the cheek. "You should consider taking Vaste. At the least, take Larana along with you for the meeting? She's trustworthy. She adores you, after all."

"I'll consider it," Cyrus said, ignoring the last bit, "if Terian doesn't provide us with a wizard or druid for transport."

Vara sighed as she walked back toward the tower entrance, leaving him behind on the balcony. "You know, I feel as though I am growing immensely as a person right now. To let you go off into a hostile realm with her by your side and without launching into a rather hearty fit ..."

"It's good that you're growing," Cyrus said, afraid to look back. When he did, he tried to put as much humor into his expression as he could. "We need to be bigger, after all, in order to face these problems ..."

"Not one of your best," she observed, and with the scrape of boot on stone, she began to turn away. "If I were a lesser, more grudging person, I would tell you to watch your back, as the likelihood that anyone else with you will is lower than I would care for."

"I will," Cyrus whispered, confident that she would hear it, even as he listened to her steps fade down the stairs and the door shut softly behind her. "Believe me, I will."

36.

When the knock sounded at Cyrus's door a few minutes later, he half expected it to be another messenger. His ears pricked up, and he realized that the heavy thudding was coming from within the tower, not without.

"Come up," Cyrus said quietly, tearing his attention away from the far horizon, from the sun hanging lazily overhead in the sky and shining down with just enough warmth to make him want to stay outside, on the balcony, for a time longer.

Footsteps sounded, soft and gentle, as Kahlee Lepos, her hair now a stunning scarlet color, led Aisling and the druid Bowe up the stairs. Cyrus watched the dark elven triad with a strange sense of resignation. *Curious bedfellows,* he thought, and then mentally slapped himself. *Vara would not be pleased to hear that verbalized.*

"Greetings, Lord Davidon," Kahlee said with a faint smile and a respectful bow of her newly colored head.

Cyrus stared at the bright hair, then bowed his own. "Lady Lepos," he said, realizing he still didn't know her title, even as he made to pay his respects.

"Good enough," she said, her smile widening just a touch. "You know Bowe and Aisling, I believe?"

"I've made their acquaintance," Cyrus said with a trace of irony.

"Where is your lady wife?" Aisling asked, a little stiffly, as if expecting ambush from behind. She was strangely still, unmoving just below the top step.

"Called away to a last minute meeting that, well, that she needed to attend," he said, arching his eyebrows. He could see that at the least the women got his message. Bowe, for his part, remained inscrutable, his

194

long white hair queued over his shoulder, his posture relaxed yet somehow attentive.

"And J'anda?" Aisling asked, biting at her lip, not relaxing one whit.

"I sent him with her," Cyrus said. "He's learned the teleport spells." He took a sharp intake of breath. "I assume Bowe can provide transport?"

"Yes," Bowe said simply.

"But not illusions," Aisling said.

"I can handle that," Cyrus said, drawing himself up to his full height. Aisling managed her surprise well. "Truly?"

"I've been practicing," Cyrus said with a smile. He lifted his hand, visualizing the results desired in his own mind as he said the words under his breath. He closed his eyes in concentration, and when he opened them, Aisling bore the very image of a Northlands woman, clad in furs and leather rather than her finely crafted armor. Bowe looked like a dark-haired human with a facial tattoo, and Cyrus glanced down to see his black metal armor transformed into a bloodstained tunic of the sort a butcher might wear.

"Impressive," Aisling said in a neutral tone of voice. "I admit, even knowing you're an outcast heretic, I find your abilities … surprising."

"I find them surprising as well," Cyrus said, coming in off the balcony only with great reluctance. It was as though he could feel the warmth of the sun fading with every step he took, crossing back into the dark shade of the tower. "Since only a year ago, I couldn't have cast a spell if my life depended on it." He frowned as his own words sunk in. "Or perhaps until my life depended on it, given how things unfolded."

"I will leave you three to it, then," Kahlee said with a nod. "Unless you desperately want to drag me along to your adventure."

"Are you just going to sit here and await their return?" Cyrus asked with a frown.

Kahlee glanced around the room and her eyes fell upon the table by the bed, where Vara kept her favorite book. "I'll read that, if it's all the same to you. Unless you have something more interesting, or you'd prefer I just poke around your personal possessions." She smiled thinly, as though goading him.

"If *The Champion and the Crusader* whets your appetite for entertainment in our absence, have at it," Cyrus said. "The only other volumes you're likely to find here are old histories of wars and battles that—although I find them appealing—are rather dry for most."

Aisling peered around the room with great interest. "I always found it interesting that none of Alaric's books were here when you ascended to the seat of Guildmaster."

Cyrus paused, thinking. "How do you know Alaric had books?"

"He spent so much time in this tower," Aisling said with a faint smile on her pale, illusioned face, "I can hardly imagine he spent all those hours staring at the walls or out the windows."

"It's what I do," Cyrus said quietly. "Though I suppose it's possible I have more on my mind than he did before he … well, you know."

"I'm sure I don't," Aisling said with that same smile. "And I suppose he could have just faded into the ether and wandered around the world when we all assumed he was up here. There's really no way to be certain."

"True enough," Cyrus said, and he glanced back at the sun. "The hour draws near." He looked to Bowe. "Take us to Isselhelm?"

The druid nodded subtly, even in his Northman guise, and the power of his teleportation spell whipped around them with a rising wind. Cyrus's eyes found Aisling, and hers his, and there was a flash of discomfort between them in the storm as they caught each other's gaze and then looked away swiftly as the tornado of magic swept them away and far to the north.

37.

Isselhelm was a city of mud roads and wooden houses, crude structures that looked quite a bit like Santir to Cyrus's eyes. It was just out of the mountains, a mere handful of miles off the border of the Dwarven Alliance, and situated on a river that flowed south, carrying all the minerals and metals of the dwarves to markets in other lands. One enormous, domelike mountain stood close at hand, nearer to the city, like a foothill against the backdrop to the north, and the howling of wolves in the distance reached Cyrus's ears even over the city noise.

The smell of manure hung heavy in the air, along with the burning of coal, dark smoke clouding the sky. Cyrus took a few steps away from the portal to see suspicious guards in boiled leather. They had the look of local men rather than of the human army, and they watched him and his cohorts closely as the wind of the spell faded around them.

Cyrus gave them a nod, checking to see if his illusion had held through the teleportation. It had, but it was only then that he realized his error; Bowe did not look anything like a druid, and neither did he or Aisling. *Shit*, he thought. *Let's hope these guards are morons.* While they watched suspiciously, they did not look unduly alarmed, and Cyrus beckoned Bowe and Aisling to follow him and struck out to the north, where he remembered the local keep being.

He cast a look back, ostensibly to check on his party, and then waved them into an alley. "I made an error," he said, once he was sure the guards gathered round the portal had remained there, on guard, and safely out of earshot. "I forgot to make Bowe look like a druid." His words echoed down the quiet alleyway, the dripping of water off the eaves into a muddy puddle punctuating his statement.

"Oops," Aisling said mildly.

"Yes," Cyrus agreed, "a potentially costly mistake should they dwell on us. We need to throw off suspicion immediately."

"Three wanderers gives them a definite number of us to look for," Aisling said. "Perhaps we should reduce our number to two."

Bowe stood very neutrally, casting his gaze to Cyrus. "I will accompany you if you wish, but if you would prefer, I will leave you here."

"I can get us back to the tower," he said, turning to look at Aisling, "but if anything happens to me at any point—"

"I'll be stuck on my own in a potentially very hostile city, yes," she said, taking it all in and giving a nod. "If Bowe leaves, we'll be a lot better able to blend in here."

Cyrus frowned. "How so?"

The amusement in her eyes showed through the illusion; they practically sparkled. "Because almost everywhere in Arkaria, including here, two is a couple and three is a crowd."

Something prickled down Cyrus's back, ending in a twinge at a scar just to the side of his spine. "You want us to pretend we're together?"

"I'm not exactly aflame with the prospect," she said, "but it gives good cover. This city is large enough to guarantee that not everyone knows each other. With Bowe beside us, we're stuck looking like traders or something of the sort. If he leaves, we can walk along giving the illusion of lovers on a stroll in a different part of town, all the way up to the keep. Throw a little overly affectionate acting in, the sort even you humans find sickening in your young lovers, and the guards will avoid us out of sheer discomfort." As she spoke, the amusement dried up. "I don't find the prospect appealing, just to be clear, but I am here because when it comes to deception, you are a fool and I am the expert. Trust me on this if nothing else, and we'll make it to our meeting without arousing suspicion."

That tingle in Cyrus's scar seemed to flare, not in pain exactly, but more as a reminder. His reluctance found its own voice in that unease, and he took a long breath. "Fine," he said at last. "Bowe, thank you for bringing us here."

Bowe gave him a sharp nod and was gone in the twinkle of a return spell a moment later, without saying a word.

"He's a taciturn one," Cyrus said, staring at the waning light where the druid had been.

"He's a pleasure to work with," Aisling said, all business. "No pointless conversation. Now, give us a different illusion. Drape yourself in heavy furs, and give yourself a short sword here," she tapped him at the belt, "and reduce your height by at least a foot."

"I can understand the height reduction," Cyrus said, frowning, "but the sword?"

"Northmen all carry swords of a shorter length," she said, eyes darting about the ends of the alley as if she were expecting trouble. The alley was mud and half-melted snow, and it made a sucking sound with every motion they made. "All but the traders, and they carry their daggers hidden, as though everyone does not know they're hiding them. If you want to blend in, be the rule, not the exception."

"All right," he said, visualizing his own illusion in his mind, trying to hew closely to what he'd seen on the countless Northmen he'd known throughout his years. When the spell-light faded, he found himself in heavy furs, with a sword of the length Aisling had suggested.

"Good," she said with a nod, looking to either end of the alley again. "Now, for me—make me taller. The women of this land have at least six inches of height on me, on average. Give me a bulge here," she patted her waist, "and furs over it. The women here carry their blades out of sight as well. Red hair seems to be commonplace in Isselhelm," she waved at the darker shade that crowned her current illusion, "so use that. Also, these," she pointed at the sandals barely visible, exposing her feet, "are not a great choice for this land or these streets. Boots would be more advisable."

"You really do have an eye for detail," he said, shrugging, trying to visualize a Northlands woman in his mind. He twisted the illusion and then let it loose, and when he opened his eyes again, Aisling had turned into the very image he'd imagined, taller and less willowy, thicker with muscle on her arms and chest, her slender biceps replaced by muscular ones hidden under furs.

"Details save your life when you're in my position," Aisling said, feeling for her dagger, which Cyrus noticed was in the opposite position of the one cast into illusion, bulging slightly at her waist. She leaned in and pretended to kiss him, but this appeared to be all for the illusion because he knew her actual face was practically upon his neck, though when he looked out she appeared to be right up on him, pressing her lips to his illusory ones. There was no contact between their faces, but it was still a strange sensation, and he closed his eyes, even though the only actual touch he could feel from her was her body against his armor, lightly.

She broke away, eyes darting to the left. "There was a guard passing," she whispered in explanation.

"It's all right," he said, looking down at her in faint amusement. "That was, perhaps, though, the most false kiss we've ever shared, and that's truly saying something."

She smiled faintly, though he would have sworn he saw danger behind her eyes. "Come along."

She took his hand and led him out of the alley in the opposite direction. She led him, and when he came around close enough to see her face, an illusion of its own sort was pasted upon it. She looked satisfied, an odd glow on her cheeks, a coy smile upon her pale, human face. "Try to act like you're young and in love," she muttered. "I know it won't be easy—"

"Doesn't seem to be a problem for you," he observed, still feeling quite cold at the way she was conducting herself. *It's as though every fear I ever had about her—heartless, soulless, able to shed who she really is like a snake in an instant—is all true.*

"I spent years throwing myself at you," she said, under her breath, that same pleasant smile poised on her lips, even though the tone she was letting out was dark, coupled with a slight hiss, "on the orders of a god and his closest servants, in order to try and save the life of the man I loved. Once I finally got you, I had to maintain that hold by any means necessary." She glanced back at him, her pleasant disposition making a strange contrast to her soft, menacing words. "However wounded you were by my 'betrayal,' realize that I didn't want to be trapped where I was, a dupe in someone else's game, forced to subjugate everything about myself—my mind, my body, my damned soul, if such a thing even exists—to seducing you." Her bitterness bled out around her happy expression, and Cyrus's blood ran colder than a frozen river. "I'm sure you devoted endless thought to how horrific what I did to you was, and it certainly was, no doubt. But realize that I wanted to do *none of it*. Not one bit, and that includes being with you in the first place."

Her harsh, remorseless tone felt like a hard slap to Cyrus's face. "Well," he said, cheeks burning, "I didn't know I was with someone who didn't want to be with me, or I assure you I wouldn't have been."

"And that's why you need me now," she said, all trace of the bitterness gone. "Because I'm the sort of person who will do whatever is necessary, no matter how horrible … and you're not going to survive without that."

"I notice you don't seem too torn up about what you did to me," Cyrus said.

"I did what I did," Aisling said, still smiling, but now he saw the hollowness there as they passed a public house, its windows shaking with drunken singing. "I became what I am. Looking back is pointless. There is no time for regrets, even if I had them."

"Do you have them?" Cyrus asked.

Now there was an undercurrent of danger in her reply. "I regret more that I was forced into my position with you than anything I did to you as a result of it."

It took every bit of will he had not to rip his hand out of hers. "So that's a convenient way of saying that if you had to do it all over again, you'd screw me and stab me and still not worry about it."

"You seem to have come out of it all right," she said with a shrug, and now her smile was maddening, and Cyrus clamped his mouth shut tight to prevent a hasty, nasty reply.

They wended their way through alleys and down side roads, Aisling leading him. He had a vague sense that they were still heading north, but the rage in his mind was clouding his concentration. *She did what she did because she got backed into a corner and because she cares more about her own skin than that of anyone else caught up in her whirlwind.* He tried to conceal the look of fury that he was sure stuck out on his face even through the illusion, but concentration was impossible beyond the bare minimum he was using to maintain their illusion. Even that much was a strain.

"Get your head out of your ass," she muttered, and he saw the flicker of his illusion fade, her skin turning a shade darker.

"I'm sorry," he said mildly, barely containing his anger, "I'm just trying to wade through what you just said. I suppose I'd assumed remorse on your part after I let you walk away in Saekaj."

"Don't assume," she said, her voice still dark. "And why would I be remorseful now? You're married to the woman you always wanted, you're fit as a boarhound, and all your recent adversity and setbacks have nothing to do with anything I did or put you through. Why should I waste time feeling bad? I'm here helping you, aren't I?"

"I still have a scar on my back thanks to you," he said, resisting the urge to yank her around.

"Does it ache in the cold?" she sneered. She did not slow her pace. "I still have scars of my own, courtesy of you and others, but you don't hear me carping about them."

"My people died at Leaugarden thanks to you," he said, his anger rising, the thin threads holding him in check breaking as they stepped into another alley, this one blocking the sun with thatched roofs overhanging on either side. The light dripping of water into puddles on the muddy ground echoed under his whispered accusation.

"Your army suffered a loss at Leaugarden because you underestimated both the Sovereign and Malpravus," she said matter-of-factly, finally stopping, turning loose his hand, and coming around to face him with blazing eyes. "You are blind, Cyrus. You walk in the world of battle and war and miss all else, including spying and subterfuge. Even now you want to ignore the fact that there are undoubtedly people in the midst of Sanctuary doing far worse things than I ever did. You want to believe that your people are all good people, that loyalty runs thicker than blood, but you should see by now that this is a lie. There's a reason you've had an exodus, and it's not all down to greener pastures elsewhere. Malpravus and his allies are taking you apart a piece at a time, and you still fret about wrongs I did to you in years past. Well, I got wronged, Cyrus," she pressed herself up in his face as he lost the concentration to maintain her illusion, and her navy skin was almost purple with rage. "My own body got used to try and keep you on the hook even as you tried to wriggle away like a caught fish." Her cheeks blazed dark and her brow arched. "You and I got stabbed in different ways, in different places, with different weapons, by the same damned culprits—Yartraak and Malpravus and all their various and sundry servants." She slammed her fingertips into his chainmail at his side and it rattled, his illusion falling. "But always in the weak point. When I was with you, against my will, the life of my only lover up to that point—my only love—hanging in the balance ..." Her voice trailed off, her fury finally coming out after a pause to build. "When the day came when I got the word to do it ..." measured loathing marked her words as her dark blue skin faded, "I actually felt a prick of conscience. I did you wrong, but you became the reminder of everything I'd let Yartraak and Dagonath Shrawn do to me, every piece of dignity I let them strip, every last bit of … hope, of belief that I was a person rather than just an object that you could pour your seed and your secrets into." She drew up, short once more, her fury seemingly spent. "I was never less alive than when I was with you. I took every bit of myself and threw it into a deep, dark hole inside. So, no, I suppose I don't have much remorse. I did what I had to in order to survive, and the way I see it, you're fine. There are others that got in my path, got killed … they'll never have the chance to be fine." Her lips twisted in a sullen way. "You didn't die. I didn't die. It all worked out. And now here we are." She blew out a low breath. "I can help you, if you'd stop living in the past and put all your bitterness aside. We both got screwed." She looked sick and angry as she said it. "You got the better end of the deal, in the end. You got your great love. Mine …" She looked away, but there was an unmistakable flare of emotion that she did not manage to hide quickly enough.

Cyrus was struck to silence. "What happened to him?"

"I killed him," she said, cold, almost malicious, her violet eyes caught somewhere between shedding a tear and issuing him a warning.

The chill wind ripped through the alley, hard out of the north, the bare breath of winter reaching out of the mountains ripping through the spring day. "Why?" Cyrus asked quietly.

"Because he …" She stared back at him, seemingly stunned, as though … shocked, he realized, that he'd asked the question. "He wasn't …" She choked off her reply. "Because he … because he had scars of his own, after years spent in dungeons," she managed to get out at last. "And because unlike you—hopefully—he couldn't let them heal and move on with his damned life after being wronged."

"Well, that seems like a cautionary tale," Cyrus said, pulling his arms tight around him, his armor silent as practically hugged himself, the chain wrapped around his chest rattling, exposed now that his illusion was gone.

"I wouldn't worry about it if I were you," Aisling said, and he saw the faint sparkle of glassy tears in her eyes. "I don't really care about your part in my … whatever. It's over now."

"Then I suppose I'll let go of your part in my humiliations," Cyrus said, and the wind whipped between them again.

"Wonderful," Aisling said, in a voice that implied it was nothing of the sort. "Can we get on with this, then?"

"All right," Cyrus muttered, trying to visualize the illusion he needed to cast again. "In a hurry to get away from me?"

"I just want to go home," Aisling said, twisting at the waist, as though repelled by his mere presence.

"It's getting to the point," Cyrus said, still trying to summon up the will to cast the spell, "when I begin to wonder what's going to be left of my home when this is all done." He took a breath and cast the illusion, opening his eyes to find Aisling returned to her taller, paler, human state.

She adjusted the furs draped over her, as though the illusion could protect her from the bitter wind rolling between them. "It'll never be the same," she said. "Speaking from personal experience," she added a moment later.

"Of course not," he said, feeling oddly choked as he let her take his hand in hers once more. He consoled himself at the reminder that there was a thick layer of plate gauntlet between his fingers and hers, armor all over his body and hers, but it was the chill wind out of the north that seemed to be the greatest division between them. She led him out of the alley, her patently fake smile just a little less bright than it had been before their argument, and onward toward Isselhelm keep, wolves howling in the distance over the drip of melting snow.

38.

Isselhelm Keep was a squat structure built in the style of the Northlands, all stone, rising out of a brown moat replete with refuse and human waste. Little chunks of ice and garbage lingered in the water, causing Cyrus to shudder lightly as he stared at it as they approached. The keep stood in the center of the sprawling city of Isselhelm, a proper home for the governor of the territory, a fortress that could withstand at least small-scale attack, though Cyrus doubted it would last through a concerted siege that included druids and wizards.

Whoever defended the keep must have had that thought as well, for the walls were patrolled by men with bows, watching the approaches carefully. Any force coming at them with the Falcon's Essence to lighten their steps would be greeted with enough arrows to give the governor time to decide whether to run or fight.

There were audible howls in the distance. Cyrus listened to the wolves and wondered how far out they were. *Can't be more than a few miles outside the city walls,* he decided.

Cyrus walked a little closer to Aisling now as they approached the drawbridge, which was extended over the moat. It was a long bridge, consisting of heavy wood and strong chains that stretched back into the keep. As they neared the wooden guard outpost at the end, they were scrutinized by armored Northmen with at least as much suspicion as those who had been stationed around the Isselhelm portal.

"We have a meeting with the governor," Cyrus said, presenting his letter, his breath misting lightly in the air. Spring had not taken full hold in the north, at least not yet.

The guard before him read the page once, then regarded Cyrus and Aisling with a heavy-lidded glare, as though he could see through their illusions. For all Cyrus knew, he could. "Go on," the guard said in a rough voice. "Present your letter again at the guardhouse across the bridge. Try anything funny and they'll riddle you with arrows."

"Such hospitality," Cyrus remarked, drawing a sharp look of rebuke from Aisling, exactly the sort of thing that Vara would have done were she here. He lingered on that thought but a moment before deciding that it was not the sort of comparison that would win him any favor from either party. He started across the drawbridge, decoupling his hand from Aisling's. "No need to maintain that illusion any longer," he said.

"Indeed," she said, a little coldly.

The drawbridge shook beneath them, just slightly but enough that Cyrus wondered at how much it would move when a fully laden cart crossed it. "This is awkward," he said just before they reached the arch of the keep's gate. The teeth at the bottom of the portcullis were visible where it had been withdrawn, and guards were lurking in the shadows under the arch that entered the bailey. "You and I being here, I mean."

"I should say so," Aisling said as they reached the next set of guards and Cyrus presented his letter of introduction. They stayed still and silent until they'd gotten the go-ahead from the guards and were pointed toward the keep across the bailey courtyard. There, they were met with another round of guard inspection as Cyrus stared up at the keep's central tower.

It was almost a castle in and of itself. It extended up behind the walls and moat surrounding it, a blunt, squat tower that had either been designed as a concession to the fact that a good Falcon's Essence spell could place invaders on any roof, no matter how high, or because building a taller tower would have cost more money than the governor who built it had at the time. It looked like it had been around for at least a hundred years, the mortar falling out here and there between the stones.

The whole bailey stank of hay and horses and worse, and Cyrus presented his letter for the fourth time and once more waited in silence until finally the guard opened the door to the tower and beckoned him forward with Aisling, leaving his post in order to escort them inside.

Cyrus stepped into the waiting dark, Aisling just behind him, and let his eyes adjust. There was a fire burning in a nearby hearth, and he realized he'd stepped into a small version of Sanctuary's foyer, with much less space, much less natural light, and a single narrow staircase that hugged the wall, disappearing into the next floor.

"This way," the guard said, metal boots clinking as he led them up the staircase. He wore metal gauntlets and a breastplate, but leather beneath that and very, very thin chainmail. It was the mark of an elite guard who did not possess actual elite equipment. *With Praelior in hand, I could carve through a hundred like him in the space of minutes*, Cyrus thought. *But now …* He let the thought die out, not wanting to pursue it.

They followed the spiraling staircase for quite some distance. It seemed to encircle the tower in much the same space-efficient way as the stairs in the Citadel in Reikonos, leaving the center of the tower open for rooms. They passed several, including a kitchen, a very large dining room, and what appeared to be a large war room with a map table. Cyrus tried to see what he could in that room, but he glimpsed the table for only a minute before someone just inside shut the door, foiling his attempt to look further.

Cyrus realized it when they reached the top of the tower because he had been counting the floors they passed and knew that there couldn't possibly be any more between him and the roof. Here they were led into a large circular chamber with a desk, the only natural light coming from a small window behind it. The desk was gargantuan and looked to be of elven make, with its careful and intricate designs. It was at least as long as Cyrus on its widest side and was covered with depictions of armies of Northmen in their furs and leather battling against the dark elves. There was no sign of a dwarven army anywhere on it, though Cyrus supposed the north had not been at war with the dwarves in hundreds of years.

"You look different than I expected," the man behind desk said, long hair flowing out from under the thick fur cap that covered the top of his head. If he was indeed balding, as Cattrine had said, his hat was hiding it well. The grey, however, was impossible to hide, and to Cyrus it almost seemed like an extension of the wolf fur that Governor Allyn Frost's hat was made of. His cloak was made of the same fur, and though his raiment was much finer than that of the people Cyrus had seen walking the street, it felt very much like variations on the same theme. Cloth was impractical here; furs were the fashion. "You look like us," Frost said, considering them carefully from under a wrinkled brow. "I don't like it."

"My apologies," Cyrus said, bowing to the governor of the Northlands, "I assumed you'd like it even less if everyone in Isselhelm knew you were taking a meeting with a heretic."

"I wouldn't care for that, no," Frost said, drawing to his feet, smoothing out his fur cloak and vest. "But …"

With a snap of his fingers, the room around Frost seemed to spring into motion. Guards poured forth from a door hidden in an armoire, the clank of their plate armor and squeak of their leather filling the room. A spell drifted through, stripping Cyrus and Aisling of their illusions. Aisling reached for her blade even as a host of bows were drawn behind them; Cyrus could hear the twine straining and knew that Aisling, at least, would be dead if they were loosed.

Armed and armored guards swarmed around them, filling the space between Frost's desk and Cyrus and Aisling, swords drawn, pointed right at the guests in his keep. A wizard filled the air with the sound of mumbled chanting as he cast the cessation spell, as clearly part of the plan as the freshly polished swords in their faces.

"… Then again," Allyn Frost said, a broad grin on his wolfish face, "perhaps it's not as a big a problem for me as you might think."

39.

Allyn Frost stared across his desk at Cyrus, a smile of triumph pasted across his face, which was pale under his wolf fur hat, white like a man who'd been through a long winter. "All right," Frost said, and motioned to his troops. "Take their weapons, and then you can go."

"We can go?" Cyrus asked sourly as guards stepped up and made to grab for his sword.

"You stay," Frost said with great glee, "we haven't had our meeting yet."

One of the guards started to put a hand on Cyrus's sword, and he began to jerk his hand toward his chain, but Aisling slapped it away. "Don't," she said, her eyes afire, meeting his. She withdrew her dagger from her sheath and handed it, hilt-first, to the nearest guard. "That would be rude," she said, her eyes twinkling just slightly. She blinked and looked down, and Cyrus saw her weapon in the guard's hand—

Except it wasn't her weapon. It didn't look anything at all like her godly dagger, in fact. It was ornate, certainly, but when she'd held it in her hand, it didn't cause her to fade out of sight in the slightest.

Cyrus found something reassuring about that and held utterly still as the guards confiscated his new sword and unwrapped the mystical chain from around his chest. *At least I've still got my armor*, he thought, trying not to show his anger as the guards began to filter out of the room.

"I want you to remember who's in charge here," Frost said, still standing behind his desk, the complement of guards down to only a half dozen, two bowmen still drawn on Cyrus, one on Aisling, and the other guards with their swords out, watching for the slightest sign of intransigence. The wizard still lingered in the corner, his low murmuring a reassurance that a return spell wouldn't save Aisling before she was run through. For his own part, Cyrus felt fairly confident he could pummel all six men plus the wizard and kill Frost before any of them could land a killing blow on him, but he didn't feel the need to share that, nor the fact that he'd learned the resurrection spell. "I find many a problem comes in negotiations when one party fails to realize how much at the mercy of the other they are," Frost went on. "You're a heretic," he said with a look of superiority, "I'm the Governor of the Northlands. You're an outcast; I'm practically a king. At my word, you'd be turned over for execution. At your word ..." he chuckled, "well ... I think we know nothing would happen."

Cyrus glanced at Aisling. Beneath her cool, seeming indifference, he felt as if he could pick up on what she was saying with just a look, as if somehow all the time they'd spent together, even though it had all been a lie, had given him an insight to her thoughts. *Do nothing*, she was saying. *Let him have his sense of power, see where it leads.*

Or perhaps he was just imagining it.

"Nothing would happen," Cyrus said, and he caught an almost imperceptible nod from Aisling of approval.

Frost's grin grew even broader. "Damned right. You're at the lowest rung now, Davidon."

"So why does the governor of the Northlands want to meet with a man on the lowest rung?" Cyrus asked, folding his arms in front of him. Perhaps it might have looked to the guards like he was just putting up a defense, but he wanted his arms closer to action, in place where he could throw them quickly behind him while the rangers were discovering that their arrows didn't do a damned thing against his armor. "Seems like a man in your position could have conversations with any number of more ... useful? ... partners. More powerful ones, at least."

"Aye," Frost said, nodding. "I could. But you know ... they are lacking something critical that only you possess." His canines poked slightly out of his lips, and Cyrus could see yellowing upon the teeth. "Do you know what that is?"

"No," Cyrus said, shrugging. "Why don't you tell me?"

"Desperation," Frost said. "Everyone else—they're rebuilding after the war, timidly consolidating their power, afraid to reach out and make a move, but you—you're backed into a corner." He raised a finger and pointed it at Cyrus. "You're desperate, because you're fighting to survive right now. You can feel the boot about to land on the back of your neck."

"I've generally heard it referred to as an axe," Cyrus said, "but yes, your meaning is taken."

"We don't waste an axe on executions up here," Frost said with a cruel smile. "We lay a man down and crush his spine with a few good stomps. Break the neck, you end the man."

"Is that what I have to look forward to here?" Cyrus asked. "Or do you have use for my … desperation?"

"Desperation can be very useful," Frost said. "You were a citizen of the Confederation at one point. You know how they constitute the Council of Twelve?"

"One member from each district," Cyrus said, "plus six from Reikonos—"

"*Nine* from Reikonos," Frost said, and there was a sliver of irritation in his voice. "Time was, we in the outlying lands of the Confederation, we had a voice that could be heard. Now Reikonos, now Pretnam Urides … he rules the whole roost. He's folding the western plains, the Mountain District and the southeast and dividing them among we who remain." Frost's eyes glittered dangerously. "Now at first that sounds good to Reynard Coulton in the Southern Reaches, to Karrin Waterman in the Riverlands, and me over here, increasing the size of our territory but then we realize—we're three against Reikonos's nine. We're rump states in servitude to the capital. Who grows the food? Who gets the lumber, who mines the ore, and who gets it all sucked away at whatever price they're offering in the name of rebuilding Reikonos?" He thumped a thumb into his chest. "Yeah, that's us, we few who will remain."

"Boy, if only there was some way a desperate man could help you with that problem," Cyrus said, coolly.

"Well, as it happens," Frost said, cruel satisfaction on his lips, "I think you just might, and we might be able to do something for you in return."

"You don't say."

"Be a smartass all you want," Frost said, starting to show the first sign of ire, "but you'll either agree to this at the end or die."

"Well, tell me what you want me to do, and we'll see which I pick,"

Cyrus said, staring him down.

Frost's expression became sullen. "I want you to kill Pretnam Urides. While you're at it, I want the rest of the Council of Twelve dead as well."

Cyrus stared at the stone wall behind Frost. "If I do that ... it seems to me that the Human Confederation is going to come at me with every man at arms they've got, and probably quite a few that aren't under arms with them. Mercenaries, I mean, and other guilds."

"They could," Frost said with a nod and a smirk. "But without a council, most of the power falls to us Governors. The other three districts aren't quite folded in yet, but it's coming." He nodded. "We have a common enemy."

"You're desperate, too," Cyrus noted. "You know damned well the dark elves didn't assassinate the Governors of those other districts."

"I can't say for certain," Frost said with a grim smile, "but you could probably find out from your good friend the Sovereign." His amusement vanished. "If his people had anything to do with it, I'll eat a block of ice without a pick to break it up first. The dark elves were in turmoil, fighting among themselves for control of Saekaj when it happened. This Confederation of ours is being tugged closer together all the time, and all the expense of those of us who aren't in Reikonos." His smile faded.

"So I somehow arrange a similar fate for the Council of Twelve as has befallen some of your fellow Governors," Cyrus said, thinking it over, "and suddenly my problems all disappear?"

"Your problems with the Northlands do," Frost said, smiling again. "You're going to have to work a little harder to convince the other two governors to get on board with this mad plan of yours, though. Assassinating people?" He put a hand over his fur-covered chest. "I don't know, that's so ... dodgy." He grinned like a predator. "I wouldn't want anything to do with it, personally. Might sully my reputation."

"How do I know you won't just turn your dogs loose on me after I do this?" Cyrus asked. "I wrap things up nicely for you, maybe you decide you don't want to take any chances with me opening my big mouth and telling anyone?"

"You know what's going to happen after you do this?" Frost asked, looking at him warily now. "We're going to break away from the Confederation. Reynard Coulton and Karrin Waterman will want to follow, and the Confederation could find itself in a fair amount of chaos. Into that chaos, a few clear voices are going to start shouting, trying to pick up the pieces of what's left. I'm going to call my part of the army camped around Reikonos home. My fellow Governors would surely like to do the same. Do you know how much of that army is our men?"

"I have no idea."

"Ninety percent," Frost said. "Because these are the ones we held back to defend our own territories until after Reikonos got sacked. So— you strike your bargain with me, you manage to squeeze one with Waterman and Coulton, you're not going to have to worry about the Confederation army." He flashed Cyrus a toothy smile. "In one fell swoop you're going to lose two-thirds of the raw force that's threatening you right now at the Leagues' behest, because my boys will come home when I call, and the rest of the Confederation will be in too much upheaval to go after some heretic with the little they have left."

"Why not just yank your troops right now?" Cyrus asked, his gaze flicking around Frost's office. An enormous bearskin hung on one of the stone walls. "If you and the other two remaining governors own that much of the army?"

"Because then we'd get assassinated," Frost said, looking at Cyrus as though he were a moron. "You've met Pretnam Urides, yeah?"

"Many times."

"He's a powerful wizard," Frost said, looking around with something approaching nervousness. "Head of the Commonwealth of Arcanists. The only thing more powerful than the man himself is his ambition, and in this you'll be doing us both a favor; I wouldn't put it past him to have done those other governors himself."

"Seems like a cessation spell would fix him right up, then," Cyrus said, nodding at the wizard in the corner. "Lure him in for a meeting, do the job."

"But then everyone would know he was assassinated here," Aisling said softly.

"The dark elf gets it in one," Frost said, pointing at finger at her. "The point here, Davidon, is to get out of the Confederation while it's in confusion and no knows what the hell is going on. I don't want to tell my troops to come home and start a war with Urides and his cohorts in the process. I want Reikonos to be stewing in its own leaderless chaos so that my fellow Governors and I can go on our merry ways. I want to be so far removed and independent by the time they find themselves marching in the same direction again that it's not even a thought to try and drag us back in. We'll be their number one trade partners, and they'll know that if they come roaring at our doors, that trade's going to stop and their precious city's going to starve."

"All right," Cyrus said, looking at Frost's desk. "I guess I don't have much choice."

"Don't play like you weren't already casting about for a way to kill Urides," Frost said sourly. "I've heard what he's said about you before; there's no love lost between you two."

"No," Cyrus said, "there's not. I just want to be sure I'm not starting a bigger fire than the one I'm already in." He smiled faintly. "Desperation does funny things to people, you know."

Frost rolled his eyes at this. "Kill the Council of Twelve and strike pacts with Waterman in the Riverlands and Coulton in the Southern Reaches and you'll walk out of this with a little blood on your hands and the Confederation in such a mess that even if they had an army, they wouldn't be able to point it at you." He knocked once on his desk and guards began to re-enter the room. One of them slipped Cyrus's sword back into his scabbard while another hung his chains back around his neck, but loosely, shoving him a little once finished. Cyrus looked back and saw grinning faces as well as drawn bows pointed at him. "Oh, and Davidon?" Frost asked, smiling like his men. "Don't forget who brought you in to do this. Because if you bollocks this up, if you try and drag my name into it … I'll throw you to the bloody wolves." The thin howling outside in the hills beyond the keep assured Cyrus that Frost was not bluffing.

40.

Rough hands shoved Cyrus and Aisling along, out the path of the keep, scarcely allowing them to walk under their own power. He watched the guards, the smiling pack of jackals that paraded behind them, poking at him lightly with their swords. They were being somewhat kinder to Aisling. He wondered if perhaps it was because she was a dark elf, or if it was because she was an unknown quantity to them. He was, after all, the man in black armor, known throughout Arkaria. Something he'd noticed since his fall was that no shortage of people seemed happy to take a poke at him now that he'd been brought low. *They wouldn't have dreamed of it before,* he raged, forcing his anger not to show.

He and Aisling were dumped out on the long drawbridge, the guards halting their escort at the edge of the long wooden path to the other side of the moat. Cyrus gave them a glance back, trying to commit their faces to memory in case he ever had to come back. They were truly pack animals, braying and laughing at him from within their safe little grouping. The next howl of the wolves in the distance seemed somehow even more appropriate to him now.

"Come on," Aisling said, taking him by the elbow and pulling him toward the other side. "This is no place to get caught out, and smashing their faces will do nothing but give you a short-lived rush of satisfaction."

"Don't underestimate a short-lived rush of satisfaction," Cyrus said, casting another hostile look behind him. The guards were still there, jeering now, laughing to see the back of him.

"I never have," Aisling said, steely and resentful, "especially as relates to the appetites of men."

Her remark killed his desire for a fight and drew his ire from the men behind him back onto her. She seemed to have done it purposefully, walking quickly ahead of him and forcing him to hurry to catch up.

She halted in an alley just on the other side of the bridge, shivering, her dark blue flesh exposed to the chilly air, a patch of dirty, half-melted snow a slushy mess beside her. "We can't wander through town like this."

Cyrus cast a resentful look back. "That bastard. I have half a mind not to go back and—"

"Why?" Aisling asked with some force, slapping him on the gauntlet, drawing his attention to her dark and furious purple eyes. "Put aside your pride. He gave you everything you wanted and needed except a sop to your ego."

"What the hell are you talking about?" Cyrus asked as she stood, breathing hard into the cold alley. "He threatened us—"

"Because he's an impotent weasel who needs to do that in order to feel in control." She rubbed her leather-clad shoulders. "Stop paying attention to his threats and look at what he did for you—he's opened the door to the Confederation. Personality of an angry badger aside, he's set up a very viable way for you to remove the Human Confederation from your list of worries. Stop feeling insulted. He slapped you in the face with one hand, but he gave you a bag of gold with the other."

"Apparently I don't let insults pass as easily as you do," Cyrus growled, looking right at her. "Among other things."

"You'd be wise to learn," Aisling said, looking down the alley. They seemed to be behind another inn, and there was commotion within, carousing and singing. "When you're in a position of power, say, running the largest guild in Arkaria, carrying the most powerful sword, there are things you can do and say that you can't when you're—oh, I don't know—unarmed, for all intents and purposes, and a heretic, with everyone turned against you." Her gaze flicked spitefully at him. "You're under the wheel, Cyrus. Ignore the jeers of the crowd and get the damned wagon off your chest." She turned and started to walk away. "*Then* get your revenge, if you have to have it."

"Wait!" Cyrus said, almost spitting into the cold air.

"I don't really want to," Aisling said, her back to him. "I think I've said about all that needs to be said at this point, and far more than I think you'll listen to."

"I …" Cyrus began, feeling suddenly quite humbled, as though the ground had dropped from beneath him. "Thank you."

She stiffened. "For what?" she asked without turning around.

"I know you didn't have to help me," Cyrus said, the chill frosting his breath into mist against the white wall of the inn, a shade of grey like a cloud blowing past. "And I'm sure you have other things you'd rather be doing. Other people you'd rather spend time with."

"Yes." She nodded once and then bowed her head. "And you're welcome." She turned her head. "I don't hate you, you know. I did, for a while, after it was over. But it wasn't you I hated, any more than you'll end up hating Frost once this is all over." She turned, taking a deep breath, her deep blue skin flushed in the chill. "He's a symbol of your powerlessness, a reminder of how far you've fallen since this began, just like you were a reminder to me that I was … not in control." She nodded once, to nothing in particular. "You're trapped, and to feel so powerless … I know that feeling. You're surrounded by enemies. I know that feeling, too," she said, looking at the ground.

"Thank you for taking your time to try and show me the way out," Cyrus said, standing very still.

She nodded once. "You should return us to your tower before anyone sees us here. If Frost had been smart, he would have let us recast our illusion before sending us out."

"I don't think he cares who sees us here," Cyrus said, shaking his head. "You heard the man. He thinks he's a King in this place, not a Governor. He might mean to be, once this work of ours is done."

"Does that matter?" Aisling asked softly, shivering in the cold. "If you get what you want?"

Cyrus opened his mouth to say yes. *Putting Allyn Frost upon a throne here in Isselhelm feels like folly, like giving Bellarum more power, or handing Pretnam Urides the elven kingdom. And yet …* "I suppose it doesn't matter," Cyrus said, shrugging his shoulders and drawing forth the memory of the return spell. "All I can do right now is steadily work on removing my enemies."

"A worthy goal, if not a laudable one," Aisling said softly. The magic of the spell consumed them both, and they disappeared, leaving Isselhelm's dirty, snowy alleys behind them for the Tower of the Guildmaster. Cyrus's skin felt immediately warmer as he appeared, the chill gone from the air and replaced with a light breeze that felt positively tropical as it swept around him.

"Ah, you're back." Cyrus turned to see Vara sitting upon the couch, Kahlee Lepos across from her, the two seemingly engaged in a quiet conversation before he and Aisling had appeared.

"And you as well," Cyrus said expectantly, though Vara's eyes widened as she looked from Cyrus to Aisling. She looked almost insulted, but the disquiet died in an instant on her lips. "How did it go?"

"We have what we needed," Vara said, a little less energetically than was normal for her. "I have sent a messenger to Lady Voryn already, and I suspect we will have an answer back from her within the day." She looked from Cyrus to Aisling. "And for you?"

"Frost is a prick," Aisling said, before Cyrus could speak, "but he laid out a way to remove the Confederation from your path."

Vara's gaze flicked to Cyrus. "Is this true?"

"It is," Cyrus said, nodding slowly, ignoring Aisling's rolled eyes at his side. "All of it. Frost suggests that the Governors of the Southern Reaches and Riverlands are ripe for withdrawal from the Confederation, and that ninety percent of the army around Reikonos is theirs and will return when called."

Vara's eyes narrowed. "Then why do they not simply return home?"

"They surely fear Pretnam Urides, yes?" Kahlee asked, stepping up into the conversation. When Vara looked at her curiously, she went on. "He has such ties to the Leagues in Reikonos, I've heard it said he might even run them from far, far behind the scenes."

"Alaric once told me he's tied to it all, but I'm not sure how deep," Cyrus said, nodding. "It's a mystery to me how the Leagues operate, and who exactly is in charge. I mean, we know they're tied to the gods somehow, but they're somewhat shadowy in how they do things—"

"That is not so," Vara said, shaking her head. "I mean, each League, in and of itself, has a master, as I'm sure your Society of Arms did—"

"Yes, but the Society of Arms had its strings pulled from without," Cyrus said. "Recall, they were handed me, and after I made it through their gauntlet of near-death, they wanted me to languish in poverty, with not one guild to pick me up. Those dictates came from somewhere." His jaw tightened. "And that somewhere is the top of the Leagues, I suspect."

"They're our shadowy opposites, then," Kahlee said quietly. "For in

Saekaj, the Leagues were run by their heads, as Vara said, and then reported to Yartraak. Presumably there is some similar conduit between the patron gods of the Elven Kingdom, the Human Confederation, and the dwarves and gnomes."

"But the dwarves and gnomes aren't coming after us," Cyrus said.

"Yet," Aisling interjected, a little harshly.

"Does that mean that their leadership is less predisposed to get in a fight?" Cyrus asked, thinking out loud. "Or that their 'patron' gods are less invested in seeing us knocked flat?"

"Well, I don't think Vidara is much invested in seeing us 'knocked flat,' as you put it," Vara said with undisguised sarcasm. "My bet would be on Danay pushing the issue in the Kingdom because of his grudge with us."

"Which means perhaps Pretnam Urides is pushing the Confederation, perhaps for much the same reason," Cyrus said, nodding.

"Urides was not as personally motivated to see to our downfall," Vara said. "We've not killed any of his children."

"That you know of," Aisling said with a cocked eyebrow of amusement.

"I don't believe he has any," Kahlee said.

"Whatever the case, motives be damned at the moment," Vara said. "If this Governor Frost has opened up a path to removing the Confederation from our plate of troubles, I say bravo. If we can sweep clean the Confederation and the Kingdom from coming after us, it is unlikely to spur the gnomes or dwarves to come make trouble. That will leave us with only Amarath's Raiders and Goliath to contend with."

"And whoever is pulling the strings at the Leagues, whether here on Arkaria or up in the realms," Cyrus said. "Lest we forget, Amarath's Raiders and Goliath are still no pushovers."

"But without enormous armies to help back them up, they are less of a threat, especially if it came to a siege," Kahlee said. "Why, with Goliath and the Raiders as your only foes, our little alliance might be able to stop them."

Cyrus frowned. "I question that. Goliath and the Raiders are highly trained, and the dark elven army is … well, it's very inexperienced. And while I respect the skill of the Luukessians and their dragoons, Malpravus has proven he can stop them cold."

"Still, we move closer to our goals," Vara said, looking straight at him. The tower smelled of cold air now, as though Cyrus had brought the winds of Isselhelm with him in the return spell. "You're going to need to write to Morianza Yemer again, and soon. Tonight, if possible."

"If you do it now, we can take the letter with us and have it brought to Cattrine for delivery in the Kingdom," Kahlee said.

Pain struck Cyrus's chest, almost as though he had received a spear to the heart. "All right," he said at last. He glanced at the desk in the corner. "I just ..." He sighed. "I wrote to him before. There was no reply."

"What did you say?" Kahlee asked.

"I requested a meeting," Cyrus said tightly. "I kept it formal."

"That's the entirely wrong tack," Vara said, staring at him as though he were bereft of brain. "Did you even acknowledge his son in the missive?"

"No," Cyrus said, swallowing heavily. "I didn't think I ... I didn't know how to broach it."

"You don't know how to write to a man to talk about his son dying?" Aisling asked, deadpan. "Don't they teach that in the Society of Arms?"

"I doubt they teach it anywhere," Cyrus said, walking the short distance to the desk. The quill and inkwell loomed on the flat, golden-wood top of the desk, and he pulled a spare length of parchment out of the drawer, listening to the squeak as he shut it.

"Would you like some help?" Vara asked, easing up behind him. "This is necessary. Whatever you write, it has to capture his attention. Perhaps we should—"

"I think ... it's best if I write this myself," Cyrus said, staring at the blank page before him, wondering what he could possibly put upon it with quill and ink that could express everything he felt roiling in that hole in his center. *Odellan was one of the bravest men I have ever met, and if not for trying to save me from my foolishness, he might still be alive, and Sanctuary might still be whole.*

The thought stung, a bitter slap to the face harder than the wind in Isselhelm. He turned to Vara, standing behind him, and then looked past her to Kahlee and Aisling. "Would you mind ... waiting out on the balcony?"

It was Vara's turn to raise her eyebrow. "Two of us have seen you naked, yet you object to us witnessing you drafting a letter?"

Cyrus's face reddened. "I ... I know it sounds ridiculous, but ... I feel like I need to be alone for this."

His wife stared down at him, looking as though she wanted to argue. Behind her, out the balcony door, the sun was sliding lower in the sky; in a few hours it would set. "Very well," Vara said after the determination to argue seemed to have passed. "Ladies ... perhaps we can watch the empty sky for a time."

Cyrus listened to them walk outside, heard Vara shut the door behind her, leaving him alone in the Tower of the Guildmaster with only a deep sense of grief and responsibility, which he tried his best to pour out onto the page.

41.

"The room looks so much less empty than when last we met," Cyrus observed to the Council Chambers a few days later, the officers, new and old, stood around the circular table. Cyrus had left his helm on the wooden surface, black quartal against the dark wood, and glanced at the faces arrayed around him. Vara, straight and silent, sat to his immediate right, then J'anda, Ryin and Mendicant sat in unbroken succession, only Ryin showing any emotion. The druid looked strained, though he put on a polite smile for the newcomers. Menlos had taken Andren's old seat, and Erith sat to his right. Beside her was Odellan's old chair, still empty. Longwell came next, looking distracted but with his hand still on his lance. Vaste, next to him, looked around with his usual humorous expression, though he said nothing yet, and Scuddar had chosen Thad's old seat to Vaste's right. Calene sat next to him, leaving Vara's old chair at Cyrus's left empty. "We're moving in the right direction in terms of filling the Council," Cyrus said, trying to push a smile of his own onto his face, which was resisting him.

"And in the wrong direction in terms of our other numbers," Ryin said, softly but loud enough that everyone heard it. When he was sure he had everyone's attention, he spoke once more. "We are down to five hundred and twelve members as of this morning." He looked slowly around the Council. "We now are at the bottom threshold for defending the wall. If we lose any more, they will be able to overwhelm us given but time, numbers, and effort."

"And Malpravus surely knows that," Vaste said, entirely too cheerily for Cyrus's taste. "What? They've got a hundred and seventy five thousand troops to their names, we've got five hundred."

"They know we still have allies," Cyrus said, putting on the brave face. "That's got to figure into their calculations."

"They're surely not sitting idle while we watch our numbers dwindle," Ryin said, leaning forward. "I know our plan was to wait this out, but ... when we decided that course, we did not know how bad things were going to get in terms of desertions. We need a new plan."

"I'm open to all manner of possibilities," Cyrus said glancing around, "if anyone's got an idea."

"You're telling us you don't already have a plan?" Erith asked, a faint accusation in her voice.

"I have the plan we agreed upon," Cyrus said smoothly. "But as Ryin said, it was essentially to try and wait it out, hoping none of our enemies would march on our walls and trusting that the threat of total war between them and the dark elves plus Emerald Fields would keep us in a state of truce while we waited for things to improve."

"I agree with Erith," Longwell said, seemingly ignoring Cyrus, not even looking at him. "Some of you have gone to meeting after meeting. If I were the suspicious sort, I'd be accusing some of us of either backroom scheming or flat-out treachery."

"Hey, hold on now," Menlos said, leaning forward. "That's a bit strong, don't you think? Who would you be pointing that accusation at?"

"I think if anyone's been leaving regularly lately, they know who they are," Longwell said, finally looking at Cyrus. "I don't see a need to drag names through—"

"Cyrus," Erith said quietly, staring straight at him. "Vara." She looked at the elf. "J'anda, Vaste."

"Well, there they are anyway," Menlos said, looking a bit flustered.

"Are you accusing us of anything in particular?" Cyrus asked, holding still in his seat. "Or just ... leaving Sanctuary from time to time?"

"I think you've got something else going on, now that they bring it up," Ryin said, squinting, concentrating, looking at Cyrus. "And I want to know why we weren't included."

"What would I be including you in?" Cyrus asked coolly.

"Whatever you're in," Longwell said, staring him down.

"What if it's group sex?" Vaste asked.

A deathly silence fell. "Well, it'd be nice to be asked," Longwell said finally.

"What if it included me?" Vaste pressed, now leering.

"Then it would not include me," Vara said, shuddering.

"Or me," J'anda said.

"Fine, it's just Cyrus's long arse and my supple one, then," Vaste said, shrugging. "Small group, I suppose, but still—"

"This is ridiculous," Ryin said.

"I agree," Vaste said, "I mean, have you looked at his arse—"

"I meant this story," Ryin said, lashing the room with his voice. He turned to look at Cyrus. "Are you working on something? Some plan that you're not sharing with the Council?"

"I don't know where you would get that idea—" Cyrus began.

"You can't even lie well," Ryin said, thumping his hand down upon the table and then cringing from the sting.

"Ancestors," Longwell said in a quiet whisper. "I wouldn't have believed it possible, but you're cutting us out. Right now, you're cutting us out of whatever you're doing."

"I'm not—" Cyrus said.

"Let's all just hold on a minute," Menlos said, raising a hand. "Cyrus is Guildmaster, and I'm sure, whatever he's doing, he's leading—"

"Leading us into a ditch to die," Ryin said, laughing mirthlessly. "We stood and …" He dragged himself to his feet, his robes sweeping around him. "We proclaimed to a messenger of the Leagues that we were standing together as heretics, joining … gods. I feel such the fool." He looked right at Cyrus. "Did you even wait until that meeting was over before you started scheming behind our backs?"

Cyrus sat there, trying to hide his shock, feeling as though he were back in Allyn Frost's tower, his weapons ripped away and the Governor lording his powerlessness over him. "As Menlos said, I'm the Guildmaster of Sanctuary. And you should all know by now that both the holders of this position that you've known have had their secrets."

"You were never like this before," Longwell said in quiet accusation.

"Well, it's my first time being declared heretic," Cyrus said.

"We were supposed to be in this together," Ryin said, incredulous. "We said we stood as one to the Leagues."

"We *are* in this together," Vara said.

"No, we're not," Longwell said, staring around the table. "If you're hiding things from us—I mean, *now* of all times—this is the moment where we should be united like never before, especially if there's hope of a plan, because I see him—" He pointed at Cyrus. "I see him walking around now with a little more power in his step, and I see people leaving, and I think … maybe he just still believes. But now I'm thinking he's got something to believe in, and I want to know what it is."

"Why?" Cyrus asked quietly, looking right at the dragoon.

"Because maybe I'm worried your plan's going to leave me in the dust," Longwell said, more viciously than Cyrus would have ever expected from the dragoon.

"That's unfair," Menlos said.

"We're all together on the gallows," Erith said, her own words a quiet accusation. "We're the Council. We were supposed to be united."

"I thought we were," Cyrus said, looking to his right to see Vara staring at the table, seemingly stunned into silence. "But now I'm not so sure. You're all leaping to rather remarkable conclusions, given the circumstances. We have some allies, and the key to maintaining those allies is to make sure that we have regular communication with Administrator Tiernan and the Sovereign of—"

"No," Ryin said, shaking his head. "I'm sorry, but that's just not so. I know Mendicant has taken you places, and so has Larana. If you wanted to go see either of those people, go visit our allies, you could use any wizard you desired—"

"No, I couldn't," Cyrus said, a line of attack dawning upon him at last, "because Vara and I have already been ambushed by Amarath's Raiders and nearly killed once; I have no interest in giving them further opportunities."

Silence fell over the room, as though Cyrus had blown an immense fire spell in the middle of the table. "What?" Ryin asked, aghast. "What did you say?"

"Just before the start of the year, Vara and I went to meet with her sister," Cyrus said, searching his Council's faces for signs that they might have heard this before. "We picked the Mountains of Nartanis portal. Mendicant spoke the destination aloud in the foyer and dropped us off there. Almost immediately, we were set upon by a nasty little war party from the Raiders. They cut off our retreat with a cessation spell, and if not for Vara's quick thinking and forceful attacks, we would be dead." He paused for effect. "Someone told them we were coming." He neatly left out the admission by Isabelle that her guild had been rife with defectors to the Raiders. *They probably did find out from her, but there's no need to spread that around when I can simply repurpose it to quiet this crew for a little while—hopefully.*

"You don't think this is the sort of thing you should report to the Council?" Ryin asked, eyes narrowed. "For all we know, one of the people passing by when you left is a traitor."

Mendicant was flushed a deep green. "I am so very sorry, Lord Davidon," the goblin said, practically gasping, breaking his silence for the first time in the meeting, "I apologize—"

"It's not your fault, Mendicant," Cyrus said. Clearly the goblin did not consider himself a traitor. *Which is good,* Cyrus thought, *because I don't think he's a traitor either.*

Or maybe I just don't want to believe anyone in Sanctuary—especially in the Council—is a traitor.

"Gods, I hate to bring out the pitchforks and tar," Menlos said, "but do you know who was around you when you this happened? Might be nice to get an idea of who among us could be a traitor."

"You think there are traitors among us?" Calene asked, her wide eyes large as teacup saucers. "Oh ... oh, gods."

"It is a natural assumption in times such as these," Scuddar said in his quiet voice. "Especially after what Malpravus's corpses said to us at the wall."

Ryin's eyes nearly popped out of his head. "What did the corpses say?" He turned an accusatory look at Cyrus. "And why did we not hear about it?"

"He just suggested, in his lording-it-over-us sort of way," Cyrus said, struggling to stay as casual as possible, "that Mathyas Tarreau, who walked out with half our guild, was doing his man-of-the-people act at Malpravus's behest."

"That cost us half of what we had left here at Sanctuary," Longwell said in quiet desperation. "It's all people have been talking about since. At least half of what we've lost since is attributable to that, people saying they should have gone with Tarreau—"

"Yes, it comes as a real shock to me that Malpravus would do something so sneaky and malignant," Vaste said, nodding soberly. "Oh, wait, no, it actually does not. I was thinking of someone else. Malpravus would do anything to screw us, and planting dissenters in our midst is probably one of the least vicious things he would do."

Ryin set his accusatory gaze on Cyrus. "You truly have been hiding things from us."

"Oh, I'm sure you would have found them all out," Vaste said, mockingly, "you know … in the fullness of time."

"These are not small things you've been holding back," Longwell said, and Cyrus could see the sense of betrayal in his eyes. "You've … You suspect us, don't you?"

"That's another strong accusation," Menlos said, starting to sound a little desperate. He turned his head to Erith. "Are all the Council meetings like this or did you save this for my first time?"

"I can recall only a very few that have gone anything like this," Erith said.

"I don't suspect any of you," Cyrus said, raising his voice and quieting the chamber. "I don't. I think Goliath is doing what they always do, sowing the seeds of discord. I don't believe any one of you is working with them. But … that doesn't mean I don't have suspicions." He shifted uneasily in his chair. "We've had a problem with Malpravus getting word of happenings in our Council meetings for as long as I can remember. Whether that's because some of us just talk too loosely outside this chamber or something more sinister, I can't say." He looked right at Longwell. "I don't suspect you."

"Good," Longwell said, sounding insulted even so.

"I don't suspect any of you," Cyrus said, glancing about, "and if I had some actionable plan, something I could direct our guild toward, I would include you." He shrugged. "But we've got—what was the number? Five hundred and twelve souls left to our army? I don't know what kind of plan I could orchestrate with that amount of force, and if I did have one …" He sighed. "I'd need you all, that much is certain. You, plus all the force our allies could muster. I'm a General, after all, and while battle is my forte—this sort of battle? It's not one we can win." He looked around the table again. "If I knew a way to shift those odds, be assured I would. But that's not the sort of plan I'm any good at."

"You are a 'pointy tip of the sword' sort of fellow," Vaste agreed.

"You lack a certain degree of subtlety, it's true," Ryin said reluctantly.

"Exactly," Cyrus said, nodding a little sadly. "If I could craft some grand battle plan that would work, don't you imagine I'd do it?" He waited for a reply, any reply. "And if anyone sees the way to fight our way out of this, I'm more than willing to listen. But for now, all I've got is ... well, a secret or two, but they're tilted toward keeping things from getting worse, or attacks coming without us knowing it." He tossed the last bit in, secretly hopeful that it would make its way back to Malpravus. *If he thinks I've got spies of my own, maybe it will give his bony stomach an ulcer or two of the sort he's been sending my way.*

"I just don't see why you can't—" Ryin started to ask, face still clouded with suspicion.

He was interrupted by a hammering at the door which stopped all conversation. "Come in," Cyrus called, wondering who would be the messenger now.

Larana slipped into the chamber, looking as though she'd rather just drift right back out the door. "Sir," she said, not meeting the eyes of any member of the Council, "we've ... we've had word from Emerald Fields."

Longwell stood, his chair skidding he got up so fast. "What word?" There was no disguising the bare edge of fear in his words.

"They've ... had a skirmish with the elves," Larana said, barely looking up, and there was a stir among the Council, "the messenger ... he says that the war has begun."

42.

The officers of Sanctuary appeared at the portal of Emerald Fields to find themselves surrounded, at least a hundred spears pointed at them. The tips remained pointed at them even when it was clear who they were. "Move!" The order was directed at them in a brusque, unfriendly tone. "Clear the field, please."

Cyrus moved, and Vara, Longwell, Vaste, Ryin, Menlos, and Mendicant followed behind him, through a narrow gap in the wall of Luukessian men standing guard over the portal. The faces of their former guildmates were set in grim lines, and the stink of sweat and tension was in the air. Cyrus marched his way down a well-worn path toward town, the guards at the portal already seeming to have forgotten about them.

"I think we can safely say something drastic has happened here," Vara intoned, low and quiet. "I have never seen the guard this tense, especially considering they knew who we were."

"This is the easiest avenue for a sneak attack," Longwell said, the dragoon walking stiffly, carrying his lance upright at arms. "They're right to be worried and on their guard. The portal is our greatest lane of trade, and we can't afford to close it under anything less than the direst threat."

Cyrus saw the town of Emerald Fields ahead in the distance, brimming with activity, bustling on the streets lined with wooden buildings. The clean lines and newly constructed dwellings gave the entire area a very different feel even from Termina. *Emerald Fields is not a part of the Elven Kingdom*, Cyrus thought, *not at all. They're no more a part of Danay's ancient and traditional land than I am.*

Cyrus plunged ahead with his party toward the center of town, keeping his eyes sharply peeled for familiar faces. "We need to get to Cattrine's office, see if she's even there."

"What do you imagine we'll be able to do?" Vara asked softly, walking beside him, their motion kicking up dust on the dirty roads.

"Not a thing," Cyrus said, keeping his eyes fixed on the town ahead, "but we need to hear what's happened directly from her—and then we need to figure out what's next."

They walked through the turbulent streets, people yelling, running about. Still, it was hardly a panic, and nothing compared to the night over a year before when they'd turned out to defend this place against the titans rampaging through its streets while the citizens fled before them in fear. This was a near-calm by comparison, the occasional loud yells balanced by anxious whispering among the denizens, as though death had come to pay them a visit and some were fearless while others were merely stunned.

Cyrus made his way through the streets as carefully as he could; most of the citizens moved when they saw him, the crowds parting so that he could push his way through. He passed countless settlement buildings before he finally caught sight of Cattrine ahead, speaking with a knot of soldiers who wore the steel armor of the Luukessian dragoons. She had a drawn look on her face and was paying very close attention to what they were telling her.

Cyrus stopped, suddenly, lingering just down the street from where she stood. He made a small motion, taking a slow walk across her field of view. She acknowledged him with a flick of her eyes, shading herself with a hand from the sun-drenched day, and gave him a subtle nod toward her office. Cyrus returned the gesture and walked down the side of one of the wooden buildings to the base of a staircase that ran up to a second floor. He started to climb, his officers following behind him.

They waited in the Administrator's office in strained silence for ten minutes, then fifteen, then half an hour. The quiet nearly defied belief in Cyrus's view; Ryin and Longwell were, after all, present, but both waited in the stewed silence, clearly unwilling to retread their earlier quarrel in the Council. Instead they all stood, simply waiting, until the door creaked open and Cattrine Tiernan made her way inside, her eyes alight with an indignation that the usually placid Administrator displayed only rarely.

"Well, they've gone and done it," she said without preamble. "A group of elves from the detachment that's been prowling our northern border crossed over last night and got into a scrape with our cavalrymen. Naturally, our enemy was unprepared, and our alarm rang out quickly, so the elves were run down inside fifteen minutes, all thirty of them."

"You didn't lose any people, then?" Cyrus asked.

"Not a one," Cattrine said with a tight smile. "But I think we all know that this is not the end, but a beginning. Danay will claim we've entered a state of insurrection, and he'll have to answer our fire with his own. And so it will begin."

"How long do you reckon?" Ryin asked, crestfallen.

"Not long at all," Cattrine said, any trace of humor vanishing as the lines of her face went slack. "I'm sure they've already heard in Pharesia. He'll be marshaling his forces in minutes. Terian just sent me a notice saying that he was preparing to send us more dark elven soldiers." She smiled tightly, humorlessly. "This is how it begins, you see. They'll tie us up and—"

The door slammed open, and in came a breathless Dahveed Thalless, the healer's white robes trailing behind him, the druid Bowe in his wake, his long queue of hair whipping behind him. "We have a problem," Dahveed said, his blue skin particularly flushed, as though the heat were getting to him.

"Other than war?" Cattrine asked.

"No, it is still war," Dahveed said, trying to recapture himself as he stood, panting slightly. Bowe's eyes were even more narrowed than usual as he stood behind the healer. Cyrus watched the druid. *He seems ... angry?* "We were preparing a troop movement out of Sovar in reaction to this attack when something ... happened," Dahveed said, an interplay of emotions rioting across his face. One moment he seemed angry, the next, weary, until he finally settled somewhere between them. "Someone ... brought a shipment of Dragon's Breath into the main tunnel into Saekaj and Sovar ... and somewhere, about a hundred feet from the surface ... they lit it."

"Dear gods," Erith breathed. "That's ... the main passage into both cities. Without it—"

"Yes," Dahveed said, with a short nod. "Without it ... Saekaj and Sovar are cut off from the surface ..." With a rueful look, he brought his message to its crashing conclusion. "And with that ... we are effectively out of this war before it's even begun."

43.

Cyrus looked over the hill toward the entrance to Saekaj Sovar. He and the others, minus Longwell and Mendicant, who had remained in Emerald Fields, had teleported to the Saekaj portal and made their way toward the entry. There was a frenzy of activity, soldiers running to and fro to little point that Cyrus could discern. Dahveed and Bowe walked with the Sanctuary officers, allowing them to pass hostile soldiers and guards, all of whom watched the outsiders suspiciously. Cyrus saw a whole platoon of dark elven women glaring at him as he went past, and he tried not to stare, having never seen dark elven women in warrior armor before, at least not in those numbers.

"Well, this has been a day," Ryin said, a few paces behind Cyrus and Vara as they stared down at the hill where stood the entry to Saekaj Sovar. On either side of the darkened entry stood guard towers, but the outlines were only barely visible through the dust-clouded air. A billow of dirt had dispersed into the atmosphere outside the entry tunnel, and little was visible beyond it. It hung there, like a pall, an impenetrable shroud that hinted at what waited in the passage below.

"So no one's coming in or going out in that direction," Cyrus said quietly. The air was a little colder here than it had been in Emerald Fields. The sky was clouded, and the sun was sinking lower on the horizon.

"And we have no portal accessible below," Dahveed said. "That's going to severely limit what we can bring in and take out."

"I know there are other ways into Saekaj," Cyrus said, looking at the healer.

"There are," Dahveed agreed, "but they're smaller tunnels, not designed for the heavy capacity of the main entrance. So while we'll be able to move armies out with wizards and druids to some extent … food going in will be a problem. You can't transport wagon loads of grain with the return spell, after all, and those other tunnels are inadequate to the task of carting things in."

"So your army isn't entirely cut off," Cyrus said, "but your food supply to the civilians is." He shook his head, staring down at the disaster. Soldiers were rushing in and out of the collapsed tunnel like ants coming out of a hill. "In other words, you're about to have bigger problems than fighting a war."

"It entirely fouls our logistics," Dahveed said, eyeing Cyrus. "We'll need labor in order to clear the tunnels and to carry down food in long marching chains. Guess where that labor will almost certainly have to come from?"

"Your army," Cyrus said tightly.

"If we had deeper coffers," Dahveed said apologetically, "or there wasn't a hint of war brewing over us, we might hire this task to dwarven miners. Or the goblins, potentially. But with our gold going in other directions, mostly to keep the people fed …"

"I need to talk to Terian," Cyrus said, feeling a throbbing behind his eyes.

"I can pass a message along," Dahveed said, straightening up. "As you might imagine, he is somewhat occupied at the moment."

"Are you going to have to withdraw your forces from Emerald Fields?" Cyrus asked, his voice taking a sour turn.

"I will convey your question," Dahveed said, nodding, with a bow. "I wouldn't care to answer for him." He bowed and stepped closer to Bowe, and both of them disappeared in a return spell, leaving Cyrus with his officers on the overlook below the now-sealed entry.

"Damnation," Ryin said. "This … this is …"

"It's not quite damnation," Vara said, "but we're drawing nearer, it seems."

"What do we do now?" Menlos muttered in quiet awe, watching the aftermath of the destruction through heavily lidded eyes. "If the dark elves have to pull out of Emerald Fields … the Luukessians won't stand a chance against those damned elves."

"This is a blow," Ryin agreed, his face slack, numb with shock. "And well calculated, at that."

Cyrus, for his part, stared down at the hill, at the entry to the city beneath the earth. "Goliath scores another hit," he whispered, sure that Vara would hear him. He saw her nod subtly, and he knew that something had to be done, and immediately.

44.

The return to the Tower of the Guildmaster was a quiet affair, their twin spells carrying Cyrus and Vara back to the silent sanctuary atop the keep, nary a hint of breeze coming through the open doors to greet them. They had stayed, along with the other officers, until past sundown at the overlook to the entry to Saekaj, but no progress seemed to be made, only an endless cavalcade of soldiers going into the aperture beneath the hill and coming back out again covered in black dirt.

"Again everything comes at once," Cyrus said, speaking into the quiet. He could not hear anything from beyond the balconies. When he walked out to look down at the wall, he saw the fires burning, but remarkably few figures moving about atop the thick grey line that divided them from the plains.

"We are in the midst of a storm, aren't we?" Vara said, stepping out to stand with him on the balcony. The air was completely still, almost stifling, even out of doors.

"So it seems," Cyrus said, looking out into the approaching hints of dusk. "Goliath and the elves seem to have moved their pieces forward today. Almost as if they could sense us gaining some small ground of our own."

"Perhaps they did more than sense us," she said, wrapping her shining steel gauntlets around the stone railing with a creak. "I know you didn't want to say it in Council, but it is entirely likely that Terian is right, that they have us well and truly riddled with spies."

"'Didn't want to say it'?" Cyrus let the words drip out like a foul drink. "I don't even want to think it." He looked at his wife, feeling like he was beseeching her for something he knew she couldn't provide. "These people have been with us for years. Have been our *friends* for years. Have fought with us through … through gods. Through the death of a land. Against titans and dragons and everything imaginable." He bowed his head, staring down at the ground far, far below. "No, I don't even want to contemplate it. I've conceded to the point, and I'll keep our circle tight for these plans, but I see no path to ferreting out a traitor and thus no reason to dwell on it."

"Fair enough," she said, arching her back slightly as she stood next to him. "But if you did see a path to uncovering one … would you be willing to walk it?"

"I don't know," Cyrus said. "Ask me when you've found that way."

They stood there in the silence until a knock once more sounded at the door. "Come in," Vara called, beating Cyrus by seconds. She caught his eyes sadly, and hers flicked to his scabbard, a subtle reminder once more than he was not all that he once was.

The messenger was Calene again, though not nearly as out of breath this time. "We had two missives," she said, holding up envelopes, "from Emerald Fields, both."

"Thank you," Cyrus said, catching the ranger's curiosity in her bearing, the way she inclined herself as if to watch them open the messages. "You may go, Calene."

He caught the hint of disappointment from the ranger, but she departed swiftly enough, closing the door behind her without more than a look back. Cyrus watched her, waited until she was surely out of earshot before he turned to his wife, who was already tearing into her envelope. "This is a good example. What if, for instance, the traitor was Calene? Newly appointed to the Council, but she's been with us since before Luukessia. She followed me all through that godsforsaken land, fought in every battle, saved the lives of her guildmates. What if she turned out to be a traitor?"

Vara glanced up at him from the parchment in her hands. "What if she were?"

"How would we even handle it?" Cyrus asked.

"Execution is the standard answer." Vara's eyes flew back and forth across her letter.

"Dammit, Vara," Cyrus said. "We've lived with these people. They've been our friends."

"If there is a traitor," Vara said, "then any friendship has been pretense, and they have lived here only in order to provide information to Goliath in order to make us suffer at an opportune moment. Anyone who does that—and I'm thinking specifically of that dark elven whore you spent the morning with—"

"Knew that was going to come back to haunt me later."

"—is a deceiver of the worst sort," Vara said. "At least Aisling has the excuse of a god threatening someone she loved. It's a motive I can almost understand." Her expression hardened. "Almost. Anyone indebted to Goliath has no such excuse, and I would behead them myself if I should find them out. I would actually prefer to disembowel them and let them bleed, but my paladin ethics compel me toward a quicker, more merciful end."

"Thank goodness for that," Cyrus said, clutching at the envelope in his fingers almost uselessly. "Who wrote to you?"

"Lady Voryn," Vara said, glancing back up. "She is receptive to meeting, having gotten my letter. I need to go to her now. I think given recent events, she'll be easily persuaded to back us."

"Back us in what?" Cyrus asked, throwing his arms wide. "We still don't have an actual plan for dealing with Danay or removing him. For all the doors he's opened, Iraid still hasn't shown us one that leads into the royal palace."

"No," Vara said, finishing her letter and folding it crisply in half before stuffing it carefully back into the envelope it arrived in, "but he has set up the chain for afterward. Do you realize that we now have the ability to determine the course of the Elven Kingdom should it fall to discord after Danay's death?"

"What about the current heir?" Cyrus asked. "Nyad's older ... whatever."

"With myself still installed as Lady of Nalikh'akur and all else we have allied with us," Vara said, her cold blue eyes piercing in the approaching eve, "we might be able to disqualify the heir. Even if we can't, the sheer amount of chaos we'll be introducing, coupled with the sudden insurrection in Emerald Fields—it will put a squeeze upon the incoming monarch." She smiled thinly. "If Cattrine is right and Amti can be persuaded to throw in with the uprising, I daresay the Kingdom will experience a very sudden shift in priorities—away from us, and away from waging a war in Emerald Fields. They'll need a conciliator in charge, and quickly. Whoever takes the throne will have to sue for peace among their suddenly warring constituencies or face the break-up of their empire."

"Wonderful," Cyrus said. "Now we just have to find a way to kill Danay, and we can watch the Kingdom dissolve. Too bad he's protected by guards every single hour of the day and hidden away in a fortress of a palace." He pursed his lips as he clutched the envelope thinly in his fingers.

"What?" Vara asked.

"I had a thought …" Cyrus said and then his eyes fell to the envelope. "I haven't even read this yet. Any other day lately, getting a letter would be cause for hurried opening."

Vara sighed. "Well, don't let something as insignificant as having a thought keep you from taking heed of a message sent directly to you." She paused, as if waiting for something. "Well, what is it?"

"My thought or the letter?" Cyrus asked, breaking the wax seal.

"Either," Vara said impatiently.

Cyrus stared down at the words on the page, and skipped directly to the signature. "Well, the letter … is from Morianza Yemer, Odellan's father …" He looked right at her, feeling a strange clawing in his belly. "And he wants to meet with me. Immediately. Tonight, if possible."

45.

Cyrus appeared in the darkness of a portal outside Javeritem, in the far north of the Elven Kingdom. He was clad in the disguise of an envoy of the King, concentrating on the illusion upon him and Windrider and trying to make them as close to real as he could manage. Larana had teleported him here and now stood at Windrider's side, upon the ground, seemingly waiting for something.

"You can go," Cyrus said to her, not really sure what was on her mind and equally uncertain whether he wanted to know it. "Thank you."

His words apparently decided her on her course, for she did not vanish in the light of a return spell but spoke instead, softly but clear. "You're taking a meeting with Morianza Yemer."

He stared down at her in muted surprise before he gathered his words to reply. "You ... that's supposed to be a secret. How did you know?"

She looked out into the darkness around the portal and put a hand aloft. Nessalima's Light flowed from her fingers, casting the ground around them in a soft white. She pointed her hand up and the light drifted into the air as if caught by an upward wind, wafting above them. When it had risen to a height some twenty feet up, she muttered another spell under her breath and opened her eyes, looking around.

"What are you doing?" Cyrus asked, glancing around.

"Making certain no one is lying in wait," she said, casting her gaze around in a slow circle. "Making sure no one is invisible, in ambush, seeking an opportunity to strike you down."

He peered down at the druid, her tangled hair a rat's nest that barely allowed her tanned face to peek out from beneath it. "How did you know where I was going, Larana?"

"Yemer's estate is the only thing of interest within a hundred miles of the Javeritem portal," Larana answered quietly. "What if he blames you for the death of his son under your command?"

"Then I guess I'll have a fight on my hands," Cyrus said, smiling though he did not much feel like it.

"I should go with you," she said, quietly but firmly.

"You should get back to Sanctuary," Cyrus said. "You don't even have a horse."

"I can walk," she said, and with quiet whisper, she floated into the air on a Falcon's Essence spell. "I can run if need be. I can follow behind you. I won't be any trouble."

"Any trouble I expect to run into won't be from you," Cyrus said, starting to move Windrider into a canter. The horse did not move, steadfastly ignoring his command for the first time, ever. He looked down at Windrider, who whickered and ignored Cyrus's attempt to spur him into motion. "Not you, too?"

"You could be walking into danger," Larana whispered. "You need someone to go with you. To watch out for you."

"If I wanted someone with me," Cyrus said, casting an irritated look back at her, "don't you think I would have asked Vaste or J'anda or Ryin or one of the other Council members?"

"They're busy," Larana said quietly. "And you're worried Goliath's next move will come at Sanctuary, since their last two hit our allies."

Cyrus took a breath, raising an eyebrow at the druid. "So now you're a blacksmith, a cook, a druid, and in your spare time you've been studying strategy and tactics?"

"I've also been studying heresy," she said, blushing as she looked away. "At your command."

"Windrider ..." Cyrus said, but the horse did not move. "What the hell is wrong with you?" Windrider whinnied, and to Cyrus it sounded like pure obstinance. "Fine," he said at last, "come along, then." The horse made another irritable noise. "I don't speak horse, but I think he's suggesting you should get on his back." Another surprising whinny, this one somehow slightly more accommodating, suggested to Cyrus that he'd read Windrider's intentions correctly.

Larana got onto the back of the horse with little difficulty, her Falcon's Essence spell allowing her to avoid any climb. Once she was on the back she clung loosely to Cyrus and said quietly, "Are you in a great hurry?"

"Almost always," Cyrus said, feeling he'd gotten the worse of this particular bargain. "Even when I'm not, I'd rather hurry up and get where I'm going so I can do my waiting there."

The soft glow of a spell spun around them, and Windrider's hooves lifted off the ground under the influence of Falcon's Essence. Cyrus clung tight to the reins in surprise. "Whoa! I don't think—"

"He can handle it," Larana said, and Windrider leapt into motion, charging into the air. They gained altitude quickly, soaring a hundred, then two hundred feet up as Larana's spell of light faded, falling back to the earth. They rose up above the copse of trees that shadowed the portal to the west, and the horse ran steadily into the night, clearly at ease, without fear of the empty space beneath his feet.

The night deepened as Windrider galloped beneath a rising crescent moon. Cyrus held tight to the reins, a sense of beleaguered worry clawing in his stomach like an animal scrabbling to get out. He did not dare turn to say anything to the druid at his back, though he could tell even through the barrier of his armor that she was far more at ease with this state of affairs than he was. The land was laid out before them, dark treetops, the occasional farm, a river that glistened in the silvery moonlight, and there, in the distance, a manor house with many lights lit in its windows.

Windrider began to descend without Cyrus even telling him to, approaching the house in the distance as though he knew full well where they were going. "You seem awfully certain that's our destination," Cyrus breathed into the chilly air, and the horse responded with a whicker that left Cyrus once more in no doubt that his horse was something more than ordinary.

Windrider's hooves hit the hard-packed clay of the estate's road like some Pegasus soaring down from the heavens. The power of the Falcon's Essence spell seemed to subside all at once, though whether it did or the horse simply steered them so low as for it to be pointless, Cyrus could not say. Windrider took them right up to the front door of the house where a well-dressed elf in a silk doublet waited, eyeing them upon their approach. Cyrus did not know whether he had seen them make their landing down the drive, but knowing what he did of keen elven eyesight, he would not have bet against it.

"I am to see Morianza Yemer at once," Cyrus said, dismounting and offering the envelope to the footman, who hurried down to take it. He read it while Cyrus offered a hand to Larana, still covered in the illusion of an elven woman in highborn attire, a spell she had cast without him even noticing. She took his hand and he helped her down, though he had a sense as he was doing it that she did not require any assistance at all.

They stood, waiting for the footman to finish reading the letter of introduction. When he was done, he said, "Of course," and bade them enter. Beyond the doors to the manor was a well-lit entry hall, all marble and finery, with banners hanging and art that would have pleased Oliaryn Iraid hung upon the walls. It was clearly the country estate of a landed lord, a man of power and refinement, and when the footman led them into a door to the right, Cyrus felt certain that based on what he had seen of the house from the air, they would be wandering for quite some time before reaching the Morianza.

His assumption proved false mere seconds later when Cyrus found himself in a sitting room with a man who was unmistakably related to Odellan. His hair was silver where Odellan's had been blonde, but the chiseled features looked very much the same. The only difference was that this man wore a silken doublet rather than armor, and he had considerably more wrinkles around his eyes. *He has age about him*, Cyrus thought, *and it is more rare to see that among elves.*

"Morianza Yemer," Cyrus said, using the man's honorific as he waited for Yemer to stand and acknowledge him. Yemer was still seated, one leg crossed over the other, a leather-bound volume placed upon his knee. He'd heard them upon their entry, Cyrus knew, but he seemed to be biding his time, his eyes unmoving, as though steeling himself to do something he did not particularly want to.

"Leave us," Yemer said to his footman, who bowed and exited the room, shutting the door behind him. Yemer still did not look up, staring stiffly at the page of the book in front of him.

"Larana, can you—" Cyrus began.

"It's all right," Yemer said and closed his volume with a rich thump. He took another deep breath and sighed. "She can stay. But if you wouldn't mind removing your illusions … I don't care for those types of spells. Never have."

Cyrus nodded and swept them away in an instant. "I didn't have much use for them, either, until I suddenly found myself hated and hunted in places in Arkaria where I need to tread. Now I find it hard to part with them."

"You cast them yourself, now?" Yemer asked, standing up but still not looking at Cyrus. He smoothed the silken doublet as though he were at court and then clasped his hands behind his back.

"It became important to learn," Cyrus said, feeling as though he were excusing a weakness.

"I would imagine," Yemer said sedately. "You have been seeking my attention for some time."

"I would have sought it even sooner," Cyrus said, "but ... I'm afraid your monarch has made me unwelcome in the Kingdom, and I didn't want to tempt fate by bothering you at a time when I felt certain I was the last person you'd want to hear from."

Yemer looked at him at last, and Cyrus saw even more of Odellan in him, the careful, surveying gaze, the hints of warmth beneath that had so distinguished his son. "I did hear about your ... unfortunate altercation when you came to deliver the news of our heirs' passing. The King was much aggrieved to lose his youngest daughter."

"Were you not much aggrieved?" Cyrus asked, watching carefully for the answer. "For as I understand it, he has countless more heirs. You ... had only the one."

"Yes," Yemer said, his head sagging as he drifted away into introspection for a moment. "And no." He looked up at Cyrus, and there was the hard edge of a General in his gaze. "I raised my son to be a warrior, as I was. I have seen so many die, as I'm certain you have. He made me proud in Termina, even though politics went against him. When the news came ..." He paused. "I took it better than Danay, curiously. I shouldn't have, for as you pointed out, I certainly felt as though I'd lost more. He had a new heir appointed within the day, and it wasn't as though he hadn't disavowed Nyad from the line of succession before. I ... lost my only son. My only child." Yemer straightened, his military bearing obvious even under the fine clothing. "Since then, here I remain. Not in exile, but ... certainly not eager to return to Pharesia. I find I enjoy the peace of this place, but lately, the whispers ... the rumors ... are like maddening voices in my ears."

Cyrus swept his gaze above the crackling hearth, fire dancing within its stone confines, and saw a portrait above the mantle like in Iraid's manor in Termina. This one was no battle landscape, however, though he was also well acquainted with its subject. It was Odellan, in a heroic pose, in his winged helm and with his blond hair flowing out from beneath the steel that protected the sides of his face. Cyrus stared at the portrait; a handsomer bit of brushwork he could seldom recall seeing. It captured the essence of the man he'd known, fully and completely, from the bold nose to the pronounced chin. "Rumors?" Cyrus asked, coming back to the moment, to the words Yemer had spoken.

"Yes, rumors," Yemer said softly. "That you have met with Oliaryn Iraid in Termina and found blessing there. That you have talked with Merrish in Traegon and found his favor as well. That just this eve, as we sit poised on the precipice of war, your consort, the shelas'akur—"

"She's my wife," Cyrus said.

"—is meeting with Lady Voryn of the Emerald Coast and will find her quite willing," Yemer said. "If these words have reached me, solitary and distant, you may be assured they are swirling through Pharesia even now."

"Damn," Cyrus said under his breath. *That might just be the end of the game, then, if Danay already knows we're maneuvering an alliance against him.*

"Take heart," Yemer said, looking at him sadly, "for all is not lost yet."

"It's not?" Cyrus asked cautiously, looking at the older man. "And why would it not be? Are you not a loyal subject of your King?" He watched for reaction, but Yemer did not stir, merely stared straight ahead. "Are you not a man who has served Danay the First for more years than I have lived?"

"I was loyal, I did serve," Yemer said, nodding slowly. His eyes moved slowly to Cyrus. "Perhaps you might answer for yourself why I would not be loyal any longer."

Cyrus looked at the painting above the fireplace and noticed something he had not before—it was draped in a sheer layer of black fabric. He cocked his head and saw that it extended from above like a funeral veil and covered the portrait. It was barely visible in the firelight. "Because of him."

"Because of him," Yemer croaked softly. "I gave all to this kingdom. My son ... I heard tell that even in his exile he fought bravely, and in his death he sought to protect the land I served."

"He did," Cyrus said, staring at the painting. "He died in an attack on the dragons so we might bring them into the war against the titans, which, I'm sure you know, were on the verge of overrunning the southern end of the Kingdom last year. He believed in what we were doing, and fought to his last breath so that we might stop them—what he considered to be the greatest threat the elves had faced in ... well ... quite some time."

"I heard the rumors, of course," Yemer said, lowering himself back to his seat. "The whispers of spies in your guild." He waved a hand at Cyrus. "They were filtered, through the mad grief of another father, one who lost a daughter he barely knew." Yemer looked at Cyrus. "I *knew* my son. I knew my boy. I raised him, I was there for it. I had him very late in life, and I lavished all the time and attention upon him I could. The way among elves of my birthright is different than among your people, I know. We give over our children to nursemaids who raise them while we go about our lives. Not my boy. I raised him. His mother and I did, happily inviting the ridicule of our friends." Yemer laughed bitterly. "I did not care, for I had a child, a son, in a time when few did, and I was determined to raise him to be strong and proud and fearless, and I would not chance him failing to learn these things from some nursemaid." A ripple of emotion ran across his face. "He did me proud in Termina, defending that bridge. He did me proud once more when he took his exile in stride, as a man should, though the cause and fact of it made me sick in my bowels at the cowardice of my king." Anger flickered across Yemer's face. "When first I served Danay, he was a man of courage, determined to do right by our people. Now he has become a man of increasing cowardice, worried less about what is right for our people and more about what keeps him comfortable."

Cyrus listened intently as Yemer told his story. There seemed to be no deception in him, but the words reaching Cyrus's ears sounded too good to be true. "That's a peril of ruling, I'm told," Cyrus said.

"You want to kill him," Yemer said bluntly.

"He very nearly did the same to me when I came to deliver the news about his daughter," Cyrus said. "He had guards surround us, archers fill the top level of the throne room ... he was going to ambush me, have me dismembered and my body destroyed. He threatened the same to my wife and another officer of my guild. If not for the actions of one I called friend and another I felt sure was my enemy, I would not be here now, not be heretic nor anything else save ashes and dust, sprinkled in the gardens of the palace in Pharesia."

"I don't fault you for your anger," Yemer said. "Danay pursues you because of Nyad." He looked up, then away again. "Not because he knew her or loved her, I think, for he did not do either, not in any way a normal person could conceive of it. He loved the *idea* of her, the youngest of his impossibly large brood. She was a symbol, something more to him than a mere person, which allowed him to ignore the person herself with her failings and rebellions."

"He never did seem to know her," Cyrus said, thinking of the time that Nyad had come face to face with her father in the palace and had not even recognized him, dressed in the garb of a simple steward of the house. "Or she him, at least."

"How could he?" Yemer asked softly. "He had countless children, many wives." Yemer lowered his voice. "I had one of each—my wife died in an attack by the trolls during the last war, thanks to the King's lack of vigilance against our enemies, and my son was exiled for his courage, for his bravery—for the vigilance our King lacked. For his virtues, he was cast out of his own homeland. It's as if Danay said bravery was not welcome here in the Kingdom any longer, not under his rule." He looked up at Cyrus calmly. "What about you? Is it as I've heard? Do you favor bravery?"

"I've often said that we accept none but the brave in Sanctuary," Cyrus said. "Though we are not now what we once were, I still count every man and women among my company brave."

"All Arkaria is against you," Yemer said. "Or so it seems to me."

"It seems that way to me, too," Cyrus said quietly. "Often."

"Well, not all Arkaria, perhaps," Yemer said, standing once more. "My son sent me letters, frequently, which I was obliged, by my station, to ignore." He sniffed. "I now find myself hating my station, hating my King, and realizing, as an old man, that I have no one but myself to blame for either. If I'd had the courage my son exhibited, I would have stated my mind before my king, and I would have gone into exile with my son or blocked it by my action. Either way," the old man once more stirred with emotion, "he might not be dead now."

Yemer looked up at Cyrus, barely holding himself together. "Danay surely knows of your plans to gather allies against him. If you mean to assassinate him, to end this war against your allies in Emerald Fields before it begins, you must do it now. Tonight."

Cyrus felt as though a dagger had been plunged into his belly. "I would, but ... for all the plans we've made, for all the support we've had pledged, the one thing we don't have is a way into the palace in Pharesia. We have no way to kill the king."

"You do," Yemer said, nodding slowly. "For I am, this very eve, right now, going to the palace in Pharesia to see Danay, his old advisor returning to him on the eve of war." He smiled grimly. "And I will bring you, in disguise, as my aide. I can get you into the palace, but not into a meeting with Danay. From there, you will have to make your own way." His smile faded as the darker considerations of what he was proposing seemed to settle over him. "You will have to find him yourself ... and you will have to end him with your own hand."

46.

Despite wearing both an illusion and a heavy cloak and cowl, Cyrus half expected to be killed the moment he appeared at the portal in Pharesia, but he was allowed to pass, riding at the old man's side on a borrowed horse, with nothing more than a cursory look from the guards surrounding the portal.

He'd parted with Larana and Windrider with great reluctance on the part of both horse and druid. Larana had insisted upon casting his illusion. "I'm a practiced spellcaster," she'd said, "and I will think of nothing but maintaining your illusion from now until you return to Sanctuary. You'll be thinking of other things." He'd acceded and also convinced the reluctant Windrider to return with her, his fears threefold: one, that the distinctive Windrider might be recognized even if Cyrus was not; two, that he'd be forced to flee the palace in a manner that left his horse behind; three, and perhaps most vexing, that even if he managed to escape with Windrider using the return spell, he would have to somehow walk the horse down the enormous staircase of Sanctuary in order to return the poor beast to the ground. It seemed to be on the third point that Windrider relented, though Cyrus did not know how the horse could possibly know how many steps there were from the top of the tower to the foyer.

"Pharesia will be a city in silence at this time of night," Yemer said from beside him as they rode forth toward the walled city veiled in moonlight ahead of them. The portal was outside the city gates, a considerable distance away, as though the elves did not want the threat of invaders or easy transport at hand. "We may be approached by guards, given that we are at war."

"But they can't see through my illusion?" Cyrus asked.

"Most would not be able to," Yemer said, the hoofbeats of their horses echoing in the night. "I expect most of the spellcasters who could provide them with the ability to see through illusions are even now moving our troops south in preparation for the march on Emerald Fields. We will need to be hasty."

They rode under the massive wall of Pharesia, it taking only a few words from Yemer to get past the guards. The moonlight shone on grassy green, the color of Pharesia as Cyrus remembered it. He could not recall any other city so verdant, so teeming with plant life.

They threaded through the wide streets toward the immense trees that were planted at the four corners of the palace, trees so mammoth and massive as to be larger than anything Cyrus had ever seen until he'd laid eyes on the Jungle of Vidara in the southern lands. These were trees fit for hiding titans, and they provided shade for the palace grounds, like mountains on the horizon in these flat lands.

A sweet smell hung in the air as they rode into the palace proper, its towers glinting faintly in the moonlight. The palace itself was colossal, and Cyrus recalled rainbow colors upon its towers when they were visible in daylight. At night, they were shadows under a bright moon, the evening cool but not uncomfortable. When he turned his gaze north, Cyrus saw the disused wing of the palace where he'd once spent a month with Vara as she recovered from a grievous wounding at the hands of assassins.

And now I'm returning to this palace once more as an assassin myself, he thought. *In four short years, I've become what I despised.* He smiled grimly. *Imagine what I could be in another four years.*

They headed straight for the primary entrance, with its enormous portico. "I don't know where he'll be," Yemer said, not looking at Cyrus. "He could be anywhere in the palace."

"Could he be sleeping?" Cyrus asked.

"Unlikely," Yemer said as they grew closer to the portico, which had at least twenty servants waiting to take horses, to open carriage doors, even at this time of night. "He never could sleep when there was inevitable action to be taken, such as war." Yemer shook his head. "Sometimes he merely disappeared, and no one could find him for hours at a time. The palace is gargantuan. I presume he has hidden places where he could while away time, go to think."

Cyrus nodded as they came under the shadow of the portico and it blotted out the moonlight above them. Torches burned on every column, shading everything around them in a gentle orange light. Two footmen ran up and took their reins as Cyrus and Yemer dismounted. They started toward the entry doors, but a man in a long cloak ran to them, descending the stairs and practically throwing himself to his knees before Yemer.

"My apologies, Morianza," the man said, and Cyrus thought for a moment he was going to kiss Yemer's feet in his haste to debase himself. "No one but staff and closest advisors of the King are allowed in the palace at the moment."

Yemer drew himself up, bristling, to his full height. "And does that include me?"

"Of course," the man said, bowing his head again. When he came up to look at Yemer, Cyrus could see the man's eyes, which were wide and pleading. Cyrus scanned the face, remembering the times that Danay had dressed as a mere steward in order to move freely about his palace without being noted by the staff. It was most certainly not him; this man was pudgier, had wider cheeks, a more sloped forehead, and his teeth were entirely wrong. "But your servant—he may not enter."

"I am a Morianza of the Elven Kingdom," Yemer said dangerously. "One step below the King himself."

"I realize this, your Grace," the servant said, practically throwing himself facedown upon Yemer's mercy, "but the orders come directly from King Danay himself, and he has issued a decree that any violators will be subject to immediate death." The man brought his obsequious face back up again, and Cyrus almost imagined he saw tears there, though there was no glinting in the shadowy orange torchlight. "I would not wish you to be deprived of your servant's life."

"I can wait out here, your grace," Cyrus said, suddenly uncertain. *Damn you, Danay. You really do know we're coming.* "Perhaps ... explore the gardens for a time, until your meetings are over?" He glanced at the servant, who was staring hopefully at him at this suggestion. "Unless that also carries the death penalty?"

"No, no," the servant said, "that would be perfectly, wonderfully acceptable!"

Cyrus exchanged a look with Yemer, unsure of how much was conveyed beneath his illusory facade. "I will wait in the gardens," Cyrus said. "Look around a bit, perhaps, if that is acceptable to you?"

"I will return in an hour or perhaps two," Yemer said curtly, as though speaking to a servant. "If you need to depart before then, I release you to do so, and will make my own way, so worry not over me." Cyrus caught the hidden message in his statement—*If you find a path into the palace, do what you need to and get out.*

Cyrus bowed sharply, though not nearly so deeply as the servant, who was just now scraping himself up off the ground, and watched Yemer walk away, up the steps, the servant following him. At the top of the steps next to the entrance to the palace, Cyrus saw guards, watching him carefully, their spears at attention. He was sure that if he approached any closer, the spears would come off their shoulders and be rammed into his body as expediently as possible.

With nary a look back, he turned and made his way out from under the portico, wandering slowly toward the gardens. He paced himself, took his time, and followed as near to the side of the palace as he could, searching the entire time for any possibility of entry so that he could commit the murder he had come here for.

47.

In the dark of the night, Cyrus found himself staring at the walls of the palace of the king, searching for entry. The windows were all high up above the ground, however, and sealed, glass glittering with the reflection of the moon. Not one was open, no sign of billowing curtains on any of the floors above, and even the balconies he could see appeared to be closed tight.

Cyrus walked the silent, empty grounds, no sign of guards anywhere. The grounds were expansive, he supposed, and not a high priority to patrol. His footsteps against the soft grass carried him away from the palace as he debated his course, wondering what to do next.

What am I thinking? Cyrus wondered, pulling his cloak close to him. He could not even see himself beneath Larana's illusion, no sign of his black armor in the moonlit night, no hint of his sword at his side or the chain wrapped around his chest. He could feel them all the same, though, but there was no reassurance there.

What am I becoming? he wondered, every step carrying him further from the palace, from the king. He looked over his shoulder at the shadow of the massive structure. Up on the roof above the main wing, he could see guards on patrol, walking the edge, eyes scanning the heavens in case someone tried to storm the bulwarks to attack from the skies.

"That's not going to work," he muttered under his breath as he walked toward the shadowy north wing. The massive tree at the northwest corner was directly in front of him, standing taller than the palace itself, and a considerable walk from where he was, sprawling gardens laid out before him, between him and the trunk of the tree.

I'm not going to be able to get in there, Cyrus decided, casting a last look at the fortified palace, not sure whether the despair he felt tugging at his insides was the result of feeling as though his mission was already a failure or if it was the result of feeling that he'd come here to do something he'd never have believed he would have done. *Why am I doing this?* he wondered, his feet carrying him along as if he were in a trance, into the gardens.

The leaves of the bushes and trees looked oily and black all around him as he pondered thoughts darker than the night that surrounded him. *Would I truly assassinate Danay, if I had the chance? If they threw open the doors to the palace right now and invited all in, would I seek him out? Would I plunge my sword into his chest, look him in the eyes as he died?*

Cyrus tried to remember the king's face. He could vaguely recall the hatred, the look of fury when he'd seen him last year, leering down from the throne, his rage palpable, shaped into the form of a small army that ringed the room, ready to kill Cyrus, Mendicant, and even Vara.

Ready to kill us all, now. Cyrus took a deep breath, and the sweet-smelling air of some night-blooming flower crawled up his nose and into his mind, causing it to further swirl. It was a lovely aroma, and as he turned his head to the right it seemed to grow stronger. His feet carried him in that direction, past a line of shrubs shaped into a solid block of shadowed green.

The gardens reminded him vaguely of the Realm of Life as he'd seen it in its wildest state, with endless mazelike hedges that seemed to cut one off from the rest of the world. He followed a passage of bushes in the direction it led, wondering when he should simply give it all up and return to Sanctuary.

I would *kill him*, Cyrus realized, the King's face flashing into his mind once more. *I would absolutely kill him. And I would do it for Sanctuary.* A rueful feeling settled over him. *I was locked into it the moment my officers rose around me in front of that messenger—what was her name? Agora. Agora Friedlander. The moment Ryin defied her and threw his shawl, the moment the others followed ...* He shook his head as though he could clear the feelings shrouding his heart, but he could not. *That was when I was stuck upon this course. No surrender, no retreat, for they would accept neither from me, and those I have sworn to protect were thrust into this danger with me beyond any chance for withdrawal.*

King Danay would kill me, kill Vara, and raze Sanctuary to the ground if it were within his power. Then he would crush Emerald Fields and bury the dark elves. Cyrus bowed his head. "And that is why," he whispered to himself, "why I must."

"Why you must what?" came a soft voice from behind the hedge.

Cyrus jumped in surprise, turning his head to the impenetrable bushes with rising alarm. He stared into the darkness, following the edge of the bushes to a break, slowly, and then peeking his head through.

Within the hedge was a beautiful winter garden, rectangular water features bordering it, night-blooming jasmine planted at the corners, vines growing from stone trellises on two of the sides. It was a perfectly hidden alcove, and at its center was a small fountain, water spraying out in a slow stream.

A man stood at the fountain's edge, looking at Cyrus. He was clad in servants' robes, watching with his head cocked curiously at the apparent intrusion to his solitude.

"I'm sorry," Cyrus said, his voice rasping unintentionally. "I didn't … realize anyone else was out here."

"I am but a humble steward," the man said, turning his back on Cyrus to look at the fountain. His voice was damnably familiar, though, and Cyrus's eyes widened. *No … it can't be.* "Everyone else is closed up within the palace for fear of this war and its tidings. Should you go anywhere else in these gardens, you will find the solitude you seek."

"I'm not … necessarily looking for solitude," Cyrus said, stepping carefully into the winter garden, evergreen pines planted around its edges, keeping his voice at the unintentional rasp. He forced his pace to stay languid, his body to relax. *It is almost impossible to imagine that of all the servants in this place, this would be the one.*

"I understand the desire for company," the servant said, still staring at the fountain. "For fellowship. To be alone in the night is a worrying thing in most cases. The instinct, the fear … the idea that some evil waits in the shadows to devour you is a primal one, even among our people, removed as we are from the savage worries of the humans, or the dark elves, or the dwarves."

Cyrus kept a slow stride, afraid that any sudden movement might spook his quarry before he could even be sure that this was Danay. *If everyone else is in the palace, why would he be outside? Out of his security precautions? Away from his guard?*

The answer occurred to him just as quickly: *Because he thinks he's smarter than everyone else, better than everyone else, and beyond the reach of actual harm.*

"It is a paranoid fear," the servant went on. "We have eradicated the dangers that plagued the early elves. Wolves, bears ... the predators that torment our brethren south of the Heia mountains. Even the trolls are at bay now, fearful of our might." The servant smirked into the dark. "Our enemies are all but defeated. There is nothing left to fear."

Cyrus's eyes narrowed as the elf spoke. *That arrogance ... the trolls are at bay because Sanctuary invaded their city and stripped them of their slaves and their dignity.*

"Nothing to fear here, at least," the servant went on, running fingers through the fountain gently, the dark waters stirring at his touch.

"That's not why I would seek company," Cyrus said, taking the long walk around the square of the garden, approaching from the side of the fountain, underneath an ivy-covered stone archway. "Though it is a good point. Most of our fears are mere specters, vanishing in daylight, especially here in the Kingdom."

The servant's smile could be heard in his voice even though Cyrus could not see his face. "Who are you? And why do you wander the gardens?"

"My master came for a meeting with the king," Cyrus said, pretending to clear his throat. It sounded like a skidding boot on stone but wet. "I was denied entry to the palace, and he asked me to wait for him. He said it would be some time."

"You seek company to while away the hours," the servant said, nodding as Cyrus came back out from underneath the arch. "This I understand, for the hours are dull, especially now, when one has not enough thoughts to fill them."

"Too many thoughts, I find," Cyrus said. "Often unproductive ones that chase each other 'round and 'round the head, like hares during a hunt, moving too swiftly for you to settle your bow on one target."

Cyrus could see the steward's forehead in the moonlight now, hair draped back. The cut of his clothing suggested he was a man of some importance, not the lowliest of servants. *It doesn't look like what he wore when last I saw him dressed in this manner, but he sounds ... that's no guarantee, is it? Every servant in the palace probably wishes he spoke like the king, and any one of them would probably adopt his mannerisms as much as possible out of sheer flattery and hope for advancement.*

"That is not as common a problem," the servant said with a thin smile. "At least not in my experience. An excess of thoughts is not the thing that plagues most. Indeed, I find the opposite to be true; there is too little thought among the masses."

Snooty bastard, Cyrus thought. "True," though, was what he said. "Why do you seek solitude?"

"I find myself burdened by the same problem as you," the servant said with a salutatory nod. Cyrus could see his nose now. It was plain; nondescript, even, though his eyebrows were heavy and stood out. "My mind also races like horses chasing after one another."

"There is certainly much to worry about," Cyrus agreed, circling around the fountain opposite the servant, taking his time, not daring to approach, not yet. "These are troubled and troubling times." He smiled lightly. "There is a little left to fear."

"What does your master worry about?" the servant asked, watching him with a close eye.

"I'm not certain I could say," Cyrus said, giving the most wistful smile he could manage, and hoping it showed through the illusion.

"Are his worries your own?" The servant asked, now turning slightly away, as if paying attention to something else.

"Some," Cyrus agreed, pausing opposite the servant at the fountain, the spray of water tinkling between them. "Some are my own."

"Ah, a man who lives his own life in addition to doing his service," the servant said with a slow nod. "Here in the court we don't have many of those. Bred out of them, I assume. You see it in the highborns, of course, but to those in the low service …" He shook his head. "There seems to be only the work."

"Perhaps it is different out in the country," Cyrus said.

"Perhaps indeed," the servant said, nodding. "From where do you hail?"

"Outside Javeritem," Cyrus answered after a moment's pause in which he puzzled over the best option. If he lied, and the servant was a mere servant who walked away afterward and inquired about him, the consequences might fall upon Yemer. He settled instead on the truth, filtered through the lie that had gotten him this far.

The servant stirred at this, straightening. "Does that mean that Morianza Yemer has come to court?"

"He has," Cyrus said, starting a slow walk around the fountain, intending to thread his way just a little closer for a better look at the man, whose face he still couldn't see terribly well.

"Interesting," the servant said, staring into the distance, seemingly lost in his own thoughts for a space. He blinked as Cyrus slowly inspected the row of plants that ran in a straight line behind the fountain. They appeared to be of the flowering sort, but there was not a bloom to be found among them, the stems trimmed and pruned. "And what has he come to say, returning after his long absence?"

"I don't entirely know," Cyrus said, quite honestly. He peered at the servant, catching a closer glimpse of the man's face. Yes, it was plain, so plain that he was having trouble determining for certain ...

"A strange message for him to travel from Javeritem to convey," the servant said with a smirk. "Is it that he comes merely to show his support, fly his banner ... or is it that he views you as low enough that he has not deigned to share his feelings with you?"

"It could easily be either," Cyrus said, trying a knowing smile as he stepped closer to the edge of the fountain, leaving the pruned plants behind. The servant was only fifteen feet away now, standing with the fountain between the two of them. "You know how that is, I expect."

There was a flash of deep amusement in the man's eyes. "Only too well."

I am almost certain that is Danay in servant's guise, Cyrus thought, keeping his smile carefully in place lest it fade. He took a slow breath and placed his hands carefully on the fountain's edge, leaning forward to look into the waters, the tinkling of the spray like gentle chimes in the still night. "What thoughts race in your mind, my new friend?" Cyrus asked, looking at the man's reflection in the rippling waters.

If it is him ... do I do this?

Do I stab him through the heart?

Murder him here in his own garden?

Cyrus's breath came out ragged, and he raised his gaze to the servant, who seemed to contemplate his answer before responding. "There is much on my mind," the man admitted. "Some of it I would not feel comfortable discussing with anyone, but there is one thing that should be obvious, for it is on the mind of all elves at the moment."

"The war," Cyrus said.

The servant smiled, and it was at that moment that Cyrus realized he was unmistakably Danay. "The war," he agreed.

"Do we ponder it so heavily because it is so far above our control?" Cyrus asked, drawing a smile from the man. "Or does it ring around our heads because we fear we might have some hand in it? That we might be sent to it?"

"That latter might be a fear I don't share," Danay said, almost smirking. "I believe I'm beyond going to war myself at this point. Privilege of age, I suppose. But you're young; of course it would be upon your mind. And your other insight ... men have always feared that which they cannot control, that which they cannot comprehend. War, especially these last years, seems an unstoppable sort of monster, marching across Arkaria and consuming all in its path. It inflames the fears, even though our own danger is low ..."

"I doubt many in Termina would see it your way," Cyrus said dryly.

Danay's face rippled with subtle annoyance. "An aberration. They are comparatively few."

"I heard the titans were marching up, trying to enter the Heia pass last year," Cyrus went on. "That would seem to be a cause for concern."

"The titans are no more a worry now than an invasion of gnomes," Danay said, almost contemptuously. "These humans in Emerald Fields, though ... with their dark elven allies, and heretics behind them, nested here in our lands ... they need to be crushed. They are cause for concern." He smiled darkly. "But not for long."

"So it's to be that way, then," Cyrus said sadly, nodding as he drifted around the corner of the fountain. He tried to make it as casual as he could. When Danay looked up at him, Cyrus spoke again. "I suppose you know, being this close to the center of the Kingdom. Out there," he swept a hand to encompass the far reaches, "we don't know, not really. When the word came through of what happened today, we speculated that perhaps it was—an aberration, as you called Termina." Cyrus smiled thinly.

"They will be a memory soon," Danay said, giving a thin smile of his own. "This is a certainty you can take home, from the center of the Kingdom to your little corner. Spread the word, and when it comes true in the days that follow, you'll look like a prophet." His face darkened. "For I know this—they have gone too far, these rebels, these heretics, these invaders. They have repaid the kindness of a home with insult and intransigence."

"But they produce so many crops," Cyrus said, feigning surprise.

"They pay … quite the considerable amount of gold to the King, as I have heard it …" He crept just slightly closer, almost breathless, not daring to take one in for fear it might reveal him. He was less than ten feet away now. *Longwell did this once, as I watched. He did it to his own father, to save a land. I do it, too, to save the Luukessians, to save Sanctuary, to aid the dark elves … for this man speaks of us as beneath his contempt, animals to be slaughtered for crossing in front of him in the street.*

"Gold is little consolation for insult," Danay said, his eyes flashing with anger. "We will take all they have and make it our own, and they will be driven from our lands and into the arms of their so-called allies. Let them all band together if they wish, on their own grounds, naked and stripped of all our generosity." He smiled, malicious and dark. "Others align with us on this. Emerald Fields is a haven for heresy, for traitors, for dark elves. They have many enemies, enemies who spread across the entirety of Arkaria, who refuse to stand idly by while this scum reaches out its hand and takes—"

"'Enemies everywhere,'" Cyrus mused, only five feet away. He was just drifting now, stepping into conversational range, like a person who simply wanted to talk. "Yes. Yes … of course they do. How could they not have enemies everywhere?"

"Truly," Danay went on, nodding. "Those who oppose them are our natural allies, and these … rebels … are our enemies. I should have seen it before, but it took them allying with the dark elves to truly reveal them for what they are. The sheer number of those lining up against them now, though … this little war we've begun will see them crushed, mark my words. The wheels are already in motion. I hear." Danay added the last part hastily, as if to cover himself. "Allies will come, soon, to aid us. They will march down and help us wrest what is rightfully to be ours from the grasp of those intruders." He smiled. "If any are left to run, I expect I know where they'll go … and our forces will be right behind them." He looked right into Cyrus's eyes, now not two feet away. "No mercy. Sleep soundly in your bed knowing that on the day after tomorrow, we will take the fight to th—"

Cyrus did not wait any longer, withdrawing his blade from its scabbard with a hollow rattle, seizing hold of Danay's tunic and plunging the weapon into the king's chest on the left side. It drew a gasp of surprise, and Cyrus threw the king off the tip, then stabbed again, this time on the right. This drew another gasp, and then a rattling breath. *This is not what Alaric would do*, Cyrus thought, an acid thought at an acid moment, threatening to consume what little was left of his self-respect.

But Alaric isn't here.

"You were right," Cyrus said ruefully, quietly, as the king fell to his knees. "There are enemies everywhere, Danay."

"H-h ..." A wet, wheezing gasp emerged from the King's lips. "H-ho-w? Di-d? You ...?" He did not manage to get the last word out.

"How did I know?" Cyrus asked, and the king nodded once. "We've met before, with you in this guise." The king was slumped on his haunches, fighting for breath as his silken doublet glistened dark in the moonlight, wet with his blood. Cyrus made no attempt to disguise his voice now, and with a breath, dispelled the illusion before him.

Danay's face fell in an instant. "Im ... poss ..."

"I'm afraid not," Cyrus said, shaking his head. "Unlikely, perhaps ... and yet here we are."

"You ... won't ... s ... ave ..." Danay started, spitting up red that slipped down his chin as he spoke, the color leeched by the white moonlight. "You ... can't ..." He sank to his back, his strength fading.

"Perhaps I won't be able to stop you, your plans, in time," Cyrus said, kneeling down before the King of the Elves. "You certainly did hate us, hate Sanctuary, hate Emerald Fields. Enough that I would have known it was you with my eyes closed by the time we reached the end of our conversation." Cyrus smiled, but his expression was sad. "I think, though, without you at their head, whoever ends up in charge here might just see things differently." He brandished his blade in front of him, and pressed it against the king's throat, eating into the skin as the eyes of Danay the First widened for the last time. "And even if they don't ... at least we'll be rid of you."

48.

Cyrus was sitting on the couch in the Tower of the Guildmaster when Vara returned. He had scrubbed his skin raw and cleansed his sword of its bloody stain, and was waiting, his hair dripping onto the soft cotton shirt he was wearing, his armor already placed back upon its dummy. The torches burned around him as he stared at the stone floor, the last look on Danay's face still flashing before his eyes, that shocked betrayal at a casual conversation so quickly turned to his own death. It was a look Cyrus had seen many a time in battle, where men knew that death was a possibility, yet still it came as a shock.

Cyrus stared at his red arms, exposed, the hair rippling up and down them. He had turned the water in his shower as hot as it could go, and it had felt as though it had been heated by the breath of a dragon or a particularly strong fire spell—like the sort that he had used to incinerate Danay's body after decapitating the king and leaving his head on the edge of the fountain to be found. He had done it to guarantee that there would be no chance of resurrection. He could still feel a phantom sense of blood on his hands, even though they had been covered by his gauntlets the entire time.

"I have been assured of Lady Voryn's support," Vara said, striding up the steps into the Tower. "So that is done." She flashed a smile at him, triumphant but weary. "How did your meeting with Yemer go?"

"He informed me that Danay had surely heard we were instigating rebellion against him," Cyrus said, watching Vara's muted enthusiasm fade, the corners of her mouth pulled down by the revelation. "I also learned that Danay was planning to bring in Goliath and Amarath's Raiders as well as, presumably, the humans in a bid to crush Emerald Fields, to remove them utterly from our side of the board."

"Goddess," Vara breathed, letting the gauntlet she'd been pulling off clatter to the ground with a hard rattle. "We must warn them."

"I've sent warning to Emerald Fields," Cyrus said, nodding. "It was the first thing I did when I got back, but ... I doubt Danay's attack against them will go off as planned."

"I see no reason why it wouldn't," Vara said, sounding suddenly urgent. "If he's aware that we're plotting against him, his reaction will be swift, and our plan is almost assuredly at an end." She ran a hand over her smooth, pulled-back hair. "What now?" she breathed, almost to herself.

"In a day or two, when the convocation is called," Cyrus said, in a low, unworried, nearly dead voice, "you'll go and do what we've been planning to do all along."

Vara almost seemed to miss his statement. "My dear, there will be no convocation. If Danay is forewarned, then we will not be able to kill the king." She let out a low breath. "All our planning, all this deal-making ... all for naught."

"I think all of it will come in handy during the convocation," Cyrus said quietly, still staring at the stone floor. Wide eyes flashed before his own, and he shuddered at the thought of the blood running down the doublet of the king of the elves.

Now she stared at him. "Why do you expect they would call a convocation when the King is not dead?"

He looked up at her, and he spoke in a hoarse rasp, the same voice he'd used to talk to Danay before he'd killed him. "Because the King is dead."

Her face twisted. "I beg your pardon?"

"I killed the King," Cyrus said, lifting his hands. "Only an hour ago. Stabbed him through the chest, once in each lung, cut off his head and left it for them to find, burned his body—"

"How?" Vara asked, inching closer to him, caught somewhere between fascination and horror. "How did you do this?"

"Yemer got me into the palace grounds," Cyrus said, looking up at his wife, his own emotions flitting somewhere between a desperate sort of pride and hope for approval and sick disgust at what he'd done. "They wouldn't let me into the palace itself, though, so ... I went for a walk in the gardens ... and ran into a steward of our mutual acquaintance."

"You're sure it was him?" Vara eased down to kneel next to his legs. "Absolutely certain?"

"I am absolutely certain it was Danay, yes," Cyrus said, nodding, not looking at her. "The way he looked, the way he spoke, the way he … the way he talked about us, Emerald Fields … it was him. I know it."

"Goddess, if this is true …" Her voice drifted off. "If you've done it …"

"Then there will be a convocation called," Cyrus finished numbly. "And you'll need to put your plan into effect, because Danay very definitely indicated that he had his own plans, and they sounded an awful lot like enlisting help to destroy Emerald Fields in a grand invasion."

"Dammit," Vara said, drawing a sharp breath. "We can't even react to this news, you know. To send word announcing his death would be—"

He looked up at her. "I know. I left no evidence suggesting what happened was related to us in any way."

"But the blame will have to go somewhere," Vara said. "We always knew that."

"And you already have a solution for it," Cyrus said, not able to smile.

"Yes," she said, "and hopefully it will work." She leaned in to kiss his cheek, but it was perfunctory and bereft of the passion they'd so often shared. Cyrus could still smell blood on himself, and it left his stomach unsettled.

49.

Cyrus did not awaken so much as he was jarred out of a reluctant stupor by the echoing sound of a hand slapping against his door at the first light of dawn. Tiny hints of blue were peeking through the windows to the balcony, and Cyrus sat upright to find Vara rousting herself out of thick slumber beside him. "Hello?" Cyrus called toward the stairs.

"Did you do it?" Terian called, his head appearing as the paladin stormed up the steps, Alaric's helm crooked under his elbow. "Well, did you, you magnificent bastard?"

Cyrus wished for a moment he could deny it, here in the solitary, quiet atmosphere of the tower, which seemed so unsuited to what he was about to confess to. "I did," he said.

"Excellent," Terian said, his expression like a lion's that had just had fresh meat thrown in front of him. "All of Arkaria is abuzz, naturally. They found his head late last night, no sign of a body save for a pile of ashes. My spies got the news out this morning, after the grounds had been swept three times by an army division they brought in to help." His smirk grew broader. "They have nothing save for some vague rumblings about an elf who came as aide to Yemer and wandered off into the gardens to have a look around."

"That'd be me," Cyrus said. "Is Yemer in trouble?"

"I doubt it," Terian said, "since he's not even at the palace at this point, nor at either of his homes. Trust me, they searched."

"They're going to blame it on him, aren't they?" Cyrus asked with gnawing dread.

"They're going to blame it on us, actually," Terian said, "since we have the obvious motive." He turned his attention to Vara, who was still blinking sleep out of her eyes and had the sheets clutched against her in spite of her silken nightgown. "You're going to fix that, right?"

"Perhaps after coffee," she said with a yawn. "Yes, of course we will."

"Gods, this is the greatest news," Terian said, positively bubbling with enthusiasm. "Finally, a triumph, and especially after yesterday ..."

"How long is it going to take you to dig out?" Cyrus asked.

Terian's smile immediately evaporated. "Months. We're working on alternate routes to bring food in, but we've also begun to ask for volunteers to join our surface settlements in the interim, hoping to alleviate the problem. The fewer mouths we have to feed below, the less I'll worry over the next few months."

"But you will still worry," Kahlee called from over her husband's shoulder, slipping quietly up the stairs, her reddish hair like a fiery cloud in the morning light.

"How can I not?" Terian grumbled, turning back slightly to look at her. "They've cut off our line of supply and buried us in the earth."

"We should have expected this," Cyrus said with a shake of the head.

"Yes, just like Danay expected to be assassinated while hiding in his own garden disguised as a lowly servant," Terian said, smirking. "You can't predict the insane lengths Goliath and their friends are going to go to kill us all, Cyrus. No one could have imagined that attack."

"You're sure it was them, then?" Vara asked.

"I'm sure," Terian said, nodding. "It's not as though we have any witnesses, but it seems like just the sort of evil that Malpravus would plan."

"I suppose," Cyrus said, slipping out of bed. His feet hit the cool stone floor, and his soft cloth shirt rustled against his chest hair.

"Regardless of who did it," Terian said, "it's hampered us. Killing Danay gives us a chance to even the score, because now, as long as Vara doesn't screw this up, we can remove fifty thousand soldiers from Malpravus's hands. It's not exactly yanking the blade out of his bony grip, but it's at least like pulling away his backup dagger." He stood there thoughtfully for a moment before going on. "Where are we on the Confederation now?"

"I need to meet with their governors," Cyrus said. "Coulton in the Southern Reaches and Waterman in the Riverlands."

"When you meet Reynard Coulton, don't mention my name unless it's to curse it," Terian said.

"A very good practice for any occasion," Kahlee said with a smile.

"You're far too wise to have married him," Vara said.

"So I'm often told," Kahlee replied.

"You know, I'm quite the catch, being the Sovereign of a whole land," Terian said with annoyance. "But besides that ..." He turned his attention back to Cyrus. "I just want to remind you ... don't get complacent now that you've had one triumph. This is a war, General, and it would be best if you pounce on fighting your next battle as swiftly as possible."

"Cattrine is our avenue in with Karrin Waterman and Reynard Coulton," Cyrus said, "and I'm fairly certain she's a bit distracted at this moment, what with the impending war and all—"

"Fine," Terian said, "but get back to it as soon as you can resolve this. Hell, maybe before. You don't know, Cattrine might be looking for a distraction."

"Right now I expect she's looking for a way out of seeing elven armies charging across her fields and destroying her peoples' hard-grown crops," Vara said.

"I won't coast on my achievement of last night," Cyrus said, nodding along. "I don't feel it was much of an achievement in any case, decapitating a man and burning his corpse. We weren't in a battle, he wasn't armed, and he didn't even see it coming until the blade was in his chest."

"If only all our enemies would expose themselves in such a way, this little war of ours would be over in an hour," Terian said. "What's the likelihood Malpravus prances around a secret garden in his hidden base down in the Bandit Lands?"

"I don't see him doing much in the way of prancing," Cyrus said, thinking it over. "He's more of a glider."

"When will the convocation be?" Kahlee asked, pushing them back on the road.

"Danay is the first monarch to be killed," Vara said. "Hell, he is the first monarch, period. I expect we'll know within a few days when the summons reach us."

"And you're sure they'll still call for you?" Terian asked. "Because ... this doesn't go so well without you there. All of you."

"Even if they send no invitation to the Lady of Nalikh'akur, they will have no choice but to admit the shelas'akur," Vara said simply, her eyes narrowed in anticipated anger. "To deny me would be foolish—"

"Danay tried to kill you last year, let's not forget," Cyrus said.

"And he was the King," Vara said. "No one else would be able to manage it in public life and expect to not be murdered afterward by a bloodthirsty mob. I will be safe there."

Terian looked at Cyrus. "And you? Seems a little unlikely the elves are going to let a heretic just walk into wherever they're holding this meeting."

"He will be safe as well," Vara said, a thin smile dancing upon her lips. "For the way he shall enter the convocation … there is not a chance that anyone will dare to interfere with his passage."

50.

The convocation came a mere five days later, and Vara had received her invitation, brought to her by a servant from her keep at Nalikh'akur only hours after it had been received there. It listed the time and place of the meeting, and little else. "Just as well, that way no one will know what to expect," Vara opined after reading it thrice, searching for any information she might have missed.

Once more time seemed to have slowed its passage. Though Cyrus felt somewhat confident in the plan they had and the allies on their side, he also harbored doubts that festered while they waited. He could see how it weighed on Vara, too, in the restless way she turned in bed at night. He realized late one night that they had not so much as touched hands for several days. He resolved to remedy it on the morrow, but that day was the convocation, and they both rose early to prepare.

The convocation was held in the very same throne room where Danay had held court. The banners above the throne were black, the coat of arms that of Danay's own house. A long table had been set in the middle of the room, and Cyrus waited on its outskirts in a crowd of royals and onlookers, escorted to where he stood within the depths of a cloak that was not his. He stood, however, in similar company, next to another person so clad, at the back of the watchers that surrounded the table, which had one seat for each of the Lords and Ladies of the Kingdom.

Cyrus looked around for the presumptive heir, but did not feel comfortable asking the cloaked figure any questions about elven politics. He considered asking one of their escorts, but it seemed a strange conversation to have here, in the midst of a convocation where the next King or Queen of the elves was to be decided.

So instead Cyrus held his tongue, sniffing the varied perfumes that hung in the air. Some were pleasant, and some seemed to conspire to deny him of his breath in much the same way as he'd deprived Danay of his. Fortunately, there was a strong scent of spring in the air around him, which diluted the worst of the perfumes. Still, Cyrus's skin crawled to be in this place, at this time, and knowing full well what he had already done to make this meeting occur.

The arrival of the Lords and Ladies was a thing of pomp and circumstance. They came in a procession, all dressed in finery and looking very serious. He found himself pitying them in some small measure as they were escorted to their seats, had the wooden chairs pulled out for them, and slid back in. He saw Lord Merrish, fully clad in a doublet on this occasion, and felt an annoying rush of relief. Cyrus straightened in surprise when Cora came striding in, wearing her blue cloak, and took a seat at the far end of the table. *I didn't know she was a Lady of the Kingdom. I thought Amti was well cast out.*

Oliaryn Iraid came in toward the end of the procession, taking a seat at the head of the table and relaxing within its bounds, surveying the group before him as if it were his own kingdom.

Vara entered in full armor and to an eruption of murmurs through the crowd. She ignored the attention, even as it buzzed in a frenzy, and took her place, sitting stiffly in her seat, eyes fixed straight ahead.

If there was a buzz for Vara, there was a considerably louder and less pleasant reaction when Cattrine entered the room, Longwell at her side. Longwell did not have his lance, apparently denied the privilege of carrying it. He looked strange without either it or the spare sword he carried upon his belt, but he escorted Cattrine to the seat set aside for the Lord of Emerald Fields and allowed her to take it; he remained standing just behind her, drawing scandalized looks from all around and prompting another hum of conversation in the surrounding crowd.

The buzz quieted seconds later as Fortin stepped into the chamber, drawing gasps before the entire throne room was silenced. If the rock giant was in any way affronted or taken aback, he did not show it, walking with measured stride and great care to the seat beside Cattrine and carefully removing the well-made chair as daintily as if he were picking up a child, offering it to Longwell, who took it graciously and pulled up to the table beside Cattrine. Cyrus could almost hear the breath stuck in the throats of onlookers, every eye in the room on the

Lord of Rockridge.

"This promises to be interesting," Cyrus's companion said in a low voice into the silence. Cyrus did not reply with words; fearing to draw any attention to himself, he merely nodded. A few scattered heads turned to look at them, but Cyrus ducked his head beneath the cowl and saw his companion do the same out of the corner of his eye.

Morianza Yemer appeared in the door, apparently the last to arrive. Another shocked silence greeted him, followed by a quiet thrum of whispers, surely loud enough that the elves in the room could hear them, for Cyrus could pick up the bare hints here and there.

"... heard he might have known the murderer ..."

"... could have snuck them in himself, I reckon ..."

"... but who would do such a thing?"

"In my capacity as Oliaryn of Termina and largest landholding Lord at this table," Iraid began, leaning forward, his grey beard particularly well trimmed on this occasion, "I call this convocation to order. We assemble here today to go about the grim business of determining succession of our throne in the wake of the tragic death of King Danay the First—"

"Hear, hear!"

"Let it be war!" came a howl from the crowd, answered by many, many more.

"Now hold on, there," Iraid said, frowning, putting a hand into the air that cut the room into silence. "This is a convocation of succession for the throne, not a council of war."

"She and her bastard heretic friends killed the king!" a woman in the front row screamed, pointing a finger right at Cattrine, who turned to look back at her accuser with little surprise. Cattrine looked as unflappable as Cyrus had ever seen her; *I suppose when you've been through all she has, it takes more than a few screaming highborn elves to cause concern.*

Vara was first to her feet. "I am the shelas'akur, and I am one of her 'bastard heretic friends.'" A gasp ran through the room. She did not hold her place, coming around the table, storming right up to the woman who had spoken, hands on her hips, and leaned in to the accuser's face. "Do you want to make war upon me as well?" She stared, unflinching, and Cyrus noted the woman who had spoken seemed to be trying her utmost to melt back into the crowd. "Do you wish to defeat me, see me broken in death, and glory in the power of your kingdom to destroy life—*as Danay intended to do before he died?"*

It was as though someone had cracked a whip into the chamber, lashing nearly everyone in the throne room across the face. To Cyrus it had the effect minus the sting of landing, as though it had stirred the air before him and sent a jolt of energy through the room, and he smiled.

"Shelas'akur," Oliaryn Iraid said, still holding up his hand even though now the chamber was quiet, "it profits us little to insult the memory of a man now dead."

"I don't seek profit," Vara said, the crowd she'd nearly waded into withdrawing, giving her a wide berth, "I seek peace. Peace for the kingdom, peace for my people, peace for myself. It seems some in this chamber are of a mind that war is the better course. I can only assume they are not residents of Termina or Emerald Fields, two places in the Kingdom that have borne the brunt of war these last years and are quite heartily sick of it, enough that we wish the rest of you would damned well catch up and stop trying to start one with us."

"I, for one, would be quite happy to accept peace and get on with my business," Cattrine announced, Longwell nodding beside her. "My disagreement with Danay, distilled to its simplest form, was entirely about his threatening of our lands so that he could kill the shelas'akur and her husband."

A ripple of shock ran through the waiting crowd. "LIES!" someone shouted.

"These are not lies," Fortin said, standing up and silencing the whole room once more. "Lies are untruths; these are facts unpleasant to your tiny, soft, sensitive, pointed ears. Your King tried to kill your shelas'akur."

"This is truth," Vara said, and the crowd went silent. "He attempted to do so in this very room, only a year ago. We were saved through the intervention of the dark elven ambassador, of all people." That caused more than a little disquiet, whispering voices echoing with shock in the chamber.

"Again," Iraid said, the noise of the crowd subsiding, "we attack the memory of a man now dead. While I am firmly in favor of not retreading the ground you mention, having no interest in killing the shelas'akur, I think we should firmly focus upon the matter before us: the succession." Iraid's part in this was straight man, Cyrus knew, the one to keep the discussion on track and to look impartial, even though he was steering things precisely where he intended to.

And herein lies the problem, Cyrus thought. *Danay had his course, and it was to throw in with the Confederation, the Leagues, and Goliath. Was he the loudest voice, the deciding vote in that debate, as we suspect? For if he was not, then someone in this room will be working against us in earnest ...*

"Whoever is chosen," Iraid said, looking around at the royals interspersed in the crowd—perhaps they were all royals, for all Cyrus knew—"be it the designated heir or another, they will have a heavy task before them. I submit that peace should be a decided course before we agree to anoint anyone. This monarch's first act cannot be to carry us into chaos once more, for none of us want war—"

"I want war!" a man in the front row shouted, his face red. A dozen others in the crowd rang out with the same chant, shouting at Cattrine, ignoring Vara.

"Well, that's decided," Cyrus said, shaking his head at the outburst. "I think this is your moment."

Under the hood, the figure next to him nodded subtly and gently pressed through the crowd. The cloak was a flowing green, and the hands that extended from beneath it were golden, skin smooth and supple. They did not shove their way roughly through the crowd but touched lightly upon shoulders, causing people to turn, to be stunned, and to step out of the way with a bow, practically falling over themselves to clear a path to the table at the center of the room.

It was a short journey, and Cyrus watched it happen, even as most of the room, unaware of this passage, dissolved into shouts and jeers, calls for war, and angry dissembling. It was only when the cloaked figure reached the center of the room that the cries finally began to dissolve.

The cowl came back, the delicate hands lifting it back to reveal dark and shining hair, crowned by a vine with flowers as its jewels, and eyes as green as spring, almost alive as the grasses of the plains, that flashed as they looked over the crowd. The figure cast a slow gaze around the entire throne room, and every single voice was quelled in an instant.

"The Goddess," Cyrus heard someone in front of him say in awe.

"Life-Mother," another whispered. The room rustled as prayers were murmured and countless elves knelt in the presence of their deity. Cyrus remained standing in his place at the back of the room, as did Vara, in the center, and Fortin. Cattrine and Longwell stayed seated, but every other Lord and Lady knelt before the presence of Vidara, the Goddess of Life.

51.

"War is antithetical to life," Vidara said in a slow voice, the words dropping gently from her mouth. Cyrus was reminded of the slow bloom of a flower over the course of days, the petals separating to reveal the beauty within. "I hear calls in this chamber, among my people, for war in your own lands ... and it fills me with sorrow."

"No!" Denunciations swept through the throne room from countless bowed heads. "No war!"

That might have been the fastest an angry mob has ever turned peaceful, Cyrus thought, seeing the red-faced young man who'd first called for war now shaking his head vehemently and renouncing his position of only a moment earlier.

"I am pleased to hear you say that," Vidara said, strolling toward the head of the table, now abandoned by Iraid in his rush to get to a knee. "For you are all my children, and the thought of you fighting ... I can scarcely bear." She slowly paced her way to Vara, giving her a careful look. "Shelas'akur."

"All-Mother," Vara said with a quick bow of the head.

"This is my creation," Vidara said, running thin fingers through Vara's hair, studying the fine blond strands. "My blessing, given out for you. Danay attempted to destroy her in a fit of pique." The Goddess of Life's gaze became dangerous, Cyrus thought, like a thorny vine, or a storm that darkened the sky. "I find this ... unacceptable. This is a child of wonder, a prize ripped from the grip of Death, who tried his utmost to tear my people down into his abyss. To attack her, to kill her, would be sacrilege."

"Sacrilege," came a low, repeated mutter through the crowd.

"Your Leagues ..." Vidara said more sharply, "... they have grown wild and impetuous, like a forest undergrowth that must be burned lest greater conflagrations result. They would have you do this thing in their names, but not mine. They would have you kill my blessing and kill her husband." She gave the crowd a hard look. "I would have you *not*." She surveyed the crowd imperiously, and the green eyes glowed as she swept them. "Which side would you choose?"

There was a long moment of silence, or so it seemed to Cyrus, before the crowd answered in what sounded like a thousand voices. "No!" "Of course not!" "Absolutely not!" "No ..."

"I see I still have faithful here," Vidara said, nodding slowly as she looked into the hopeful eyes of the crowd. "I was afraid after Danay that I had lost this Kingdom forever." This pronouncement seemed to land like a barrel of Dragon's Breath, compelling looks of shock from nearly the entirety of the crowd. "Choose your leaders more wisely next time, my children. For none of you is born greater than any other—" there was another stir among the crowd, "—from the perceived low to the thought-of high, I recognize no difference. I care not for the gold you keep in your accounts, nor the estate you maintain in the country. I care about life and your goodness to life, and if you spit from on high to a beggar who is low, then I say that you, truly, are lower than the one you spit upon."

"But ... but ..." The red-faced young man seemed to sputter. "But we are ... highborn."

Cyrus couldn't help but smile. *Vara was right, as usual ... I didn't think anyone would be stupid enough to say it, but there we go ...*

Vidara's eyes flashed in anger, the green turning harder, darkening like storm clouds, and her gaze fixed upon the young noble who had spoken. "Is that all that matters to you, then? That when you were born it was here in a palace and when they were born it was in a field? The miracle of life is not less because it comes in a field." The Goddess of Life seemed to draw up, increasing in height by a full head as the anger settled upon her. "Very well, then. I see now that letting you have your titles and self-importance and trusting you would not abuse them was a foolish error." Her voice crackled like thunder. "There will be no more distinctions among my brood. Your titles no longer matter, whether you be Lord or peasant. There will be no more castes. You will live in this land—my land—as though all of you were exactly the same. The low may rise to rule and the high are not guaranteed not to fall just by birth. Am I understood?"

The silence was horror, Cyrus realized, one chubby royal a few feet away from him on all fours, mouth agape, gasps making their way out of his lips every few seconds. Another, a woman, was on her knees, back arched, eyes wide, hand in front of her mouth, staring at the Goddess of Life as though she'd just been struck.

"There will be no more Kings," Vidara said, her voice taking on a storm-like quality as she spoke. "The people in this place will choose their leader, it will not come by right of blood. Your royalty is worth no more to me or this land than the blood of a peasant, who is your brother in my name if not your own acknowledgment." Vidara whirled on the red-faced man in the front row, her cloak whipping behind her. "You understand this now?"

He nodded, once, his face an ashen grey. All he could do was nod furiously, over and over.

"No more royals," Vidara said again. "No more war against my people. You will only take up arms against those who attack you, and not against guests in this land." She took a step over to Cattrine and laid a hand upon her shoulder, stroking the chestnut hair. "For these are my people now, too, and are under my protection." She strode around to Cora and gave her shoulder a caress as well. "No matter how far you wander, you are my children, and you should care for each other, regardless of distance. All who threaten my own risk my peril. For life may be generous or treacherous, full of joy or pain, and I assure you of this: if you defy my word, you will find yourself cast out of my grace, and you will receive the latter—as Danay did." At this, she showed her teeth, and Cyrus had a vision of a predatory cat, ready to leap into its prey, her beautiful face turned ugly and horrible in an instant.

Silence reigned for almost a full ten seconds after this proclamation, and then Vidara settled her gaze on Cyrus, at the back of the room. "Take care of my precious gift, Cyrus Davidon." Every head in the room turned to follow the Goddess of Life's attention. "Let no harm come to her."

"I'll do what she'll let me," Cyrus said, and Vara cast him a look of grudging irritation. The rest of the chamber was silent, but they were all watching.

"Be in peace with yourselves, my children," Vidara said, drawing her cloak around her, "or you will find yourselves at war with me." And with that, Cyrus watched her vanish in the soft glow of white light, leaving a speechless chamber of equals behind her.

52.

"I never really appreciated the view from up here," Terian said as they stared off the north balcony of the Tower of the Guildmaster. Cyrus stood next to him with Vara on the other side, and Kahlee next to Terian. They were all looking out over the sunlit day on the Plains, nearly a week after the convocation of the elves. No reprisal had come to Emerald Fields; the new ruling council had, in fact, dispersed the elven army back to their original posts, with widespread proclamations made of the Kingdom's rejection of the League dictates against Sanctuary. Cyrus had seen them, written in the script of the elven language. He didn't fully understand it all, finding their language much easier in the hearing than writing and reading, but Vara had been smiling when she'd brought it to him, and it sounded very much like the coalition against Sanctuary had lost a rather sizable ally. "I mean, our officer quarters were only one floor down," the Sovereign of Saekaj went on, his helm tucked under his arm, "but the windows are so much smaller, I feel like it's hard to get full enjoyment of it without this sweeping balcony."

"Yes, it's a shame that Alaric never invited you up here," Vara said.

"Don't pretend you got invited up here, either," Terian said, a little sourly. "I know you two were the favorites, but—"

"I never got invited up here," Cyrus said, leaning against the railing, scraping stone against his bracers. "I'll admit it. Never really looked out my window in the officer quarters, either. It's not really the same."

"That's what I'm saying," Terian agreed, pointing toward the Waking Woods to the northeast. "I mean, look at that. You can even see the old temple from here."

Kahlee peered into the green lands ahead. "What old temple?"

"The old temple that Yartraak and Mortus's followers built over there," Terian said, leaning closer to her and pointing. "It's peeking out of the forest, just barely visible over the trees, see? It's not far from where we used to hunt ghouls." Cyrus followed his pointing fingers and saw the tip of a stone pyramid barely visible in the green sea of the Waking Woods.

"You and Cyrus used to hunt ghouls?" Kahlee asked. "Or you and Vara?"

"Both, at various depressing points in their lives," Terian said with an easy grin. He withdrew his hand lazily. "So, you're not drifting aimlessly now that you've managed this first success, are you? Because remember, I warned you about that."

"I'm meeting with Governor Reynard Coulton of the Southern Reaches in one week," Cyrus said, frowning at the light rebuke. "Haven't heard back from Waterman yet. Cattrine was trying to get something set up with her as well, but Coulton seems to have taken my offer kindly enough."

"Yes, hopefully there won't be horrible death waiting for you at the meeting point," Vara said, still staring out over the plains.

"A very real danger with all of our meetings, unfortunately," Cyrus said as a thump came from within the Tower of the Guildmaster, causing Vara to jump at the sound.

"Nothing to panic about," Vaste announced, stepping out of the stairwell. J'anda, Longwell and Cattrine were behind him, the dragoon easing his way up tentatively, as if uncertain if he were stepping into a place where he would be welcome. He had a curious awe in his eyes as he looked around, and Cyrus tried to remember if he'd ever invited Longwell up to the tower before. "It's just us."

"Plenty of cause for concern, then," Vara said, coming off the balcony railing and looking impishly at them.

"Oh, ha ha," Vaste said, adding in the measured applause of his ham-like hands thundering one against the other for a few claps. "You know, I think your poor sense of humor is the reason we're down to four hundred and ninety-one guildmates."

"Looks like we have a guest," Terian said, staring right at Longwell.

"Samwen will be joining our confidences from here on," Cattrine said, laying a hand on Longwell's shoulder. "We couldn't have pulled off the convocation success without his knowing assistance as Lord of

Emerald Fields."

"Did we also have the knowing assistance of Lord Fortin of Rockridge?" Cyrus asked, frowning. "Because—"

"No," Cattrine said, with the hint of a smile on her lips, "Fortin is merely exceptionally good at taking simple instruction and expressing righteous indignation when his friends and allies are maligned."

"We're still losing people?" Cyrus ignored everything else said as the singular piece of news mentioned by Vaste struck him hard. "Even after—"

"The Human Confederation is the largest power and they are still quite upset with us, for heresy and whatnot," J'anda said, shrugging. "And it's not as though we have announced the sudden reduction in hostilities. People here still believe all Arkaria is against us, or near enough as not to matter. I have even heard rumors that the dwarves and gnomes have been offered inducement to join the alliance against us."

"Where did you hear that?" Vara asked.

"Just rumors floating around," J'anda said.

"They're not rumors," Terian said, shaking his head. "They're absolutely true, but the neither the dwarves nor the gnomes are particularly motivated by the prize being offered."

That floated around in the tower for a moment as they fell into silence. "What are they being offered?" Vara asked, sounding quite stricken.

"The Plains of Perdamun," Terian said with just a hint of hesitation. He paused, adjusted his helm against his side with a clink, then went on. "Because if they help get rid of you, then—"

"The plains will be empty of my claim," Cyrus said, feeling like ice water had been poured down his back. "No more Lord of Perdamun, though I'm sure they've vacated that title already."

"Only the humans, now," Terian said with a tight smile, "and you've got an in for taking care of that problem. If you can remove them, it's a fair fight."

"I don't think we can call any fight in which Goliath participates 'fair,'" Vaste said. "Unless it's all of them, weighed down in full armor, hands bound and with eight anvils lashed to each of their legs, fighting against the Torrid Sea from fifteen miles off the coast. I would consider that very 'fair' indeed, and it would in fact make my day, week, month, year and possibly lifetime."

"As you can see, Longwell," Cyrus said, giving Vaste a look, "we're a very serious lot around here, just like in the other Council."

"I'll confess to being a bit unsurprised that you're doing some under-the-table plotting even after your denials," Longwell said, a guarded gaze running over the little group, "but I am a bit surprised at the scope of it. I assumed you were up to planning some great battle with our allies, some way to rain down a strategic defeat on them with a—I don't know, a bombardment with our siege machines."

"Well, Forrestant left months ago, along with most of his corps," Cyrus said, "so that leaves us in a poor position to bombard anyone who's not just standing idle outside our walls where the damned machinery is already pointed." He shook his head, placing a hand behind him on the railing and leaning back. "No, this is just us, taking treachery to new lows in pursuit of defeating the forces arrayed against us."

"Good," Longwell said with a curt nod.

Cyrus raised an eyebrow. "You think that's good?"

Longwell gave him a wary look in return. "I think it's a fair sight better than just standing around here, waiting for these treacherous arseholes to come sweeping down on us to finish things."

"Speaking of treacherous arseholes," Vaste said, "what do you suppose Malpravus and Amarath's Raiders are up to?" He looked around the small circle. "I can't imagine after this elven defeat they're going to just hold off on marching on our gates."

"They're almost entirely reliant on the human army," Terian said, watching Vaste carefully. "Without the humans, they'd be vulnerable to us on a pure numbers basis, even with Sanctuary shrinking like a nipple in the winter air."

J'anda frowned. "I don't ..." He shook his head. "Never mind. If you could mobilize your entire army, we would perhaps be on even footing, numbers-wise. But you cannot, because of the sabotage, yes?"

"You're right, we can't," Terian said with a nod, "but there are also political considerations going into deploying that human army that keep them from simply doing it. My feeling is that Pretnam Urides has been holding off because he was certain you'd continue to grow weaker, not stronger, and that he wanted you as vulnerable as possible before making his move. He did just come out of a war that ended in rather a lot of casualties for the Confederation. And he and Danay were ultimately running this show, not Malpravus. They rule countries; Malpravus rules a small army that's dependent on those countries for supplies, lest his strength waste away and his people desert like—" Terian stopped, glancing briefly at Cyrus. "Well, you know."

"All too well," Cyrus said.

"Urides was waiting for Emerald Fields to get their comeuppance, and for us, the dark elves, to be removed from the field by that sneak attack, I presume," Terian said.

"Or possibly something else still waiting to be unleashed?" J'anda asked.

"That's a frightening thought," Cattrine said.

"It's a very Goliath way of doing things," Vaste said.

"I wouldn't count on them just sitting around passively waiting for us to keel over," Vara said.

"Yeah, they have to be working on something," Cyrus said. "The question is … what?"

"I don't know," Terian said, shaking his head. "I have no inkling of what Urides is up to, other than generally managing the Confederation and possibly the Leagues in human territory. He's a very sneaky person, tough to surveil with any reliability. We have a few paid spies in his employ, but they're all very much at a distance, and word is that Urides keeps even his inner circle at arm's length. It doesn't help that he's a wizard, because he can come and go as he damned well pleases without having to ask anyone's assistance or permission." Terian smirked. "Something to keep in mind when you go to kill him."

"I'll have quite a lot on my mind when that moment comes," Cyrus said, running fingers through his own hair.

"I assumed the only thing on your mind at that point would be something along the lines of, 'This is for my shitty childhood, you bastard'!" Vaste said. "And then much stabbing, followed by a dismemberment or a decapitation, like you did with Danay."

Longwell raised an eyebrow. "You did that? Killed Danay? Yourself?"

Cyrus found his mouth opening and closing a few times before he was able to speak. "I did. But let's keep it to ourselves so that when it's Pretnam Urides turn, it comes as a surprise that Sanctuary is in the business of killing our enemies via assassination."

"I'm just glad someone did it," Longwell said with mild appreciation. "Every once in a while you get an enemy so bad, they're like a weed, defying every other attempt to get rid of them. Sometimes that's just the way you've got to go."

"Well, he certainly went that route," Vaste said.

"You seem to be killing quite a few rulers of lands," Kahlee said, breaking her long silence. "Yartraak, Danay, the Goblin Emperor, the Dragonlord—"

"Plus, Vara killed the Emperor of the titans," Vaste said. "And Cyrus's mother killed more trolls than anyone else." He paused to think. "You know, the Davidon family really has left quite the path of carnage in their wake."

"I am well aware," Cyrus said quietly. "Back to the current problem we need to wipe out—"

"The humans," Terian said, nodding.

"We're not wiping out the humans," Cyrus said with a burst of impatience. "We're wiping out Pretnam Urides—"

"And letting the Confederation fall into chaos and probable civil war," Vaste said brightly. "We're do-gooders."

"Gods," Cyrus said, tilting his head back. "We really are doing this, aren't we? Supplanting another ruler, wrecking another land."

"Now, now," J'anda said, "it's worked out really very well in all the other lands we've done it. Why, look at the goblins. They're practically ready to join the civilized world now."

"Then there's the matter of the dark elves," Vaste said, "I mean, they were nothing but a horrific, warlike people before, and now, look—they're our closest allies and can wipe their own arses on parchment letters to the rulers of other nations."

"And the trolls are even applying to your guild now," Terian said with that same smirk. "That never would have happened, trolls being civilized enough to walk upright and stop scratching themselves in inappropriate places or fornicating with goats—"

"Oh, damn you," Vaste said mildly. "I should have known that crack about your people would come back to bite me in my delicious ass."

"The point is, Cyrus," Terian said, "for all your bellyaching about the horrors inflicted, you've done some good as well."

"Our people have never been in better condition," Kahlee agreed.

"The elves do seem to be in a rather better state now that Danay is dead," Vara said. "We have our own council now rather than one man meting out whatever whim he decides. And you have long railed against the injustices of the Council of Twelve. It sounds from your meeting with Governor Frost as though other people in the Confederation have their own grievances to pursue against both Urides and the running of that entire nation."

"So ..." J'anda said, smiling lightly, "... cease this fruitless worrying over consequences out of your control and do what is right—kill the leader of your country."

Cyrus gave J'anda an arched eyebrow. "When you put it like that, you make me want to do the opposite."

"This is the correct course," Longwell said with a nod. "For Sanctuary and for the Confederation, it sounds like." He gave them all a swift look. "I know it's going to sound odd, coming from me, this being my first meeting of this, err ..."

"Shadow council," Vaste said. "I think that's really the best name for it."

"Well, anyway with it being my first meeting of the shadow council," Longwell said, "but ... we're now in a tough position with no conventional way out, not with everything against us like it is. I'm just glad you're ready to make some difficult choices, ready to do whatever it takes to get those of us still here, who've been here all along ... out the other side."

"Well, we're damned sure going to try," Cyrus said with a reluctant nod. "And at least it's looking a little better now than it did a few days ago. Still ..." He shook his head. "We have so much left before us, and our enemies are just lurking out there, waiting to do who knows what in pursuit of destroying us." He touched his forehead with the metal fingers of his gauntlet. "Something is coming. They'll throw something at us soon." Cyrus tightened his face into a mask. "We just have to hope we can knock the legs out from under them before they can unleash whatever they've got planned to destroy us."

53.

When the news of the elven desertion of the Leagues cause reached the ears of Sanctuary's members, there seemed to be a brief resurgence of hope, but Cyrus noted that it faded as quickly as the morning dew did in the early summer days. He found himself walking in empty halls, but the whispers he heard did not quite carry the desperate fear that they had before, even if they did not ring with confidence the way he might have wanted them to.

Day after day, as he waited for the appointed hour of his meeting with Reynard Coulton, Cyrus found himself creeping around empty halls and through the nearly deserted towers of Sanctuary in a way he could not ever recall doing before. The air was warm, the atmosphere thick and humid, and he found the breeze at the top of the Tower of the Guildmaster insufficient to the task of dispersing it.

And so he walked the halls like the Ghost of old. He looked for nothing in particular, simply trying to make himself seen to those who remained, greeting all that he saw with a smile and a kind word. In return he received much of the same, though perhaps a shade more tentative than he desired from some, and he knew in his heart that these were the ones wondering if they'd made a poor decision to stay.

"It's an inescapable sort of doubt," Longwell said one day as they both sat in the Council Chambers. There had been no meeting scheduled for quite some time, but both of them had found themselves outside the door and stepped in to talk. "I'll confess to having felt it myself while you were keeping me out of the shadow council." He inclined his head. "If there was a way to make what we're doing known, it'd help." He held up a hand to stay Cyrus's reply. "I know there's not, not after Tarreau's betrayal, but … I don't know how else to spread hope around here, other than what you've been doing with walking and talking and greeting."

"It's a persistent problem," Cyrus said, nodding. "When we were growing like mad, we didn't have to work to spread hope or optimism. People would walk in the front door and feel it, like it was a warm rain being poured down on the place. We were sending expeditions to distant places, we were bringing back treasure from faraway lands, filling the coffers and their pockets with gold. Our army was always on the move, always doing something, even if it was just endless rounds of the Trials of Purgatory. People had new armor, new weapons, solid reminders of what we were doing for them." He sighed. "What do they have now? Most of them haven't been outside these walls in nearly five months. The grass out there is more trampled than it was after the dark elven invaders burst in during the siege. People are walking themselves mad under the same skies, itching for something more than dull guard duty staring out at empty plains, wondering when the armies are going to start marching in on us."

"It's a shame we can't take them somewhere," Longwell said, thinking it over.

"We could," Cyrus said, shrugging. "Now that the crisis in the Kingdom is over, we could ask some of the Luukessians to come back, give our people a chance to spend some time in Emerald Fields."

"We could," Longwell agreed, clutching his lance. "Why don't we?"

Cyrus felt a strange tightness in his chest. "I don't know. Something in me resists that call, even though I know they'd come and I know Cattrine would be willing. Something about loyalties, about theirs being in their new home."

"They've got loyalty to you as well," Longwell assured him.

"I know," Cyrus said quickly, dismissing it with a nod. "I know. Perhaps I just don't want to trap anyone else in here with us. And drawing down our own numbers would be ... well, idiocy is the word that comes closest to mind, with less than five hundred defenders remaining ..."

"I think we should—" Longwell began, but the door to the Council Chambers clicked open as someone tugged on the handle, causing him to freeze, clutching his lance as he turned to look behind him.

"Oh," Ryin Ayend said as he entered, closing the door quietly as he stepped inside, "it's you."

"It's us," Cyrus said, nodding at the druid, the sunlight streaming in from the balcony windows behind him. "Just … stopped in to have a chat."

"Did you?" Ryin surveyed the two of them with a raised eyebrow. "How fortuitous."

"Well, we passed outside, he on his way up and me on the way down," Longwell said, frowning at the druid as Ryin wandered toward his seat. "Not sure you can call that 'fortuitous.'"

"Oh, I would call it fortuitous," Ryin said, smiling strangely. "Do you know what else I would call fortuitous?"

"No, but I get the distinct impression you won't be leaving me in the dark for long," Cyrus said with undisguised irony.

"That the Elven Kingdom just reversed its position on hunting us to the death," Ryin said. "Interesting that so very many of the parties involved were our own people, our allies, or the goddess we saved from torture at the hands of Yartraak." His mouth twisted. "Perhaps 'fortuitous' doesn't quite cover it, after all."

"You're right," Cyrus said with a nod, "that's really more like 'blindingly amazing.'" He paused, watching the druid's stony stare. "'Blessedly fortunate'? 'Astoundingly'—"

"You did this," Ryin said, watching him through nearly closed eyes. "You orchestrated it, didn't you?"

"Nudging our friends and allies to help us remove a knife to our belly?" Cyrus asked. "I would have been a fool not to call in a few markers once the opportunity was presented, wouldn't I?"

"This was not an opportunity merely 'presented,'" Ryin said, leaning forward on his elbow. "The King of the Elves had to die for it to happen."

"I hope you're not accusing me of killing him," Cyrus said. "Because exploiting the situation is one thing—"

"I'm not accusing you of anything," Ryin said, leaning back, "because I don't know what you've been doing. I only know that you've been up to something—"

"Which I believe you've now seen some evidence of, in the form of the elves backing the hell away from us—"

"Ryin," Longwell said softly, "you and I had conversations about our worries—"

"We had conversations as outsiders," Ryin said, waving him off, "but it would seem you're no longer an outsider, Lord Longwell of

Emerald Fields. It looks as though you're in the thick of things."

"Are you mad because of how things turned out or are you mad because you weren't involved?" Cyrus asked.

"I'm disappointed I wasn't consulted," Ryin said, staring right at Cyrus, "I'm angry that I'm apparently considered too much a risk to be trusted, when I've put my very life on the line and joined you in heresy. And I'm bitterly upset that I don't know how far you've gone to achieve the results you have." He leaned forward. "You may have deflected my inquiry about Danay's death, but consider this—I don't know what you've been up to. If you're insulted at me making the thinnest accusation in your direction, realize it's because I'm not sure what you're playing at anymore, nor how deep your considerations are running, only that things have turned out very—I'll just say it again— fortuitously for Sanctuary in this." He straightened up in his seat. "Anything you'd care to share?"

Cyrus watched the druid carefully, looking right into his eyes. *Is this man a traitor? Will he take anything I tell him and go whisper it right to the ears of Malpravus?*

How would I even know until it was too late?

"There's nothing I can think of at the moment," Cyrus said softly.

"Of course not," Ryin said, almost sadly, as he stood up, smoothing his robes as he did so. "In the first few months after the Jungle, after your spell, it struck as me as strange that so many would choose to forsake our bonds of fellowship and choose to flee." He looked right at Cyrus. "Now it does not, for while we have been granted some small victory in recent days, and you are clearly involved, I cannot trust that you will be looking out for me in all this. I imagine it's a common feeling, that hopelessness." He crossed past the empty hearth, his robes swirling behind him.

"Ryin," Cyrus said, and the druid stopped at the door. "Trust cuts both ways, like any blade. You tell me now that you don't trust I'm working in your best interest, but I would tell you in return that I don't know that I can trust anyone in this guild's loyalty when our secrets keep getting spilled to Goliath and our other enemies."

"And I imagine that is why we will lose everything—both our fellows and the coming battles," Ryin said, his voice hoarse, as he opened the door and quietly left, leaving it ajar, his quiet footsteps scuffing on the stairs as he walked away.

54.

Cyrus's walks of the following days found less hopelessness than he imagined and also found Ryin still haunting the halls of Sanctuary, though he subtly avoided Cyrus when he saw him coming. Cyrus, for his part, took some relief in knowing that the druid had not chosen to flee into the night following their conversation, but neither did it engender in him a desire to seek Ryin out to reassure him.

What would I even say? Cyrus wondered for the thousandth time following their argument. *He's right, of course. It's not because of Terian's warnings that I find myself so untrusting. This is a choice I've made, to believe that revealing these secret plans could result in disaster, in Pretnam Urides, Archenous Derregnault and Malpravus being able to counter what we do next. I have more confidence in their ability to subvert my own guild than in my ability to form trusting relationships here in these very halls.*

Then again, we have lost over ten thousand members in the last year, so ... perhaps my concern is justified.

This day's walk had carried Cyrus down all the way to the foyer. The halls and stairwells of the towers had grown stale to him, and he sought the open spaces out of doors, longing for a glimpse of the shrouded sky, blue peeking from beneath white-grey clouds that glowed with the warm summer sun.

The foyer was nearly empty, only a few souls lingering in the lounge, having a quiet discussion. Cyrus glanced into the Great Hall and saw Larana between the tables, watching him as he crossed the great seal. He raised a hand to wave at her, and she gave him a more restrained wave in return. He continued his path to the door and out rather than interrupt her or risk an uncomfortable conversation that he did not wish to have.

The sun was hot on his black armor, and as he stopped on the stairs, he took a breath of the air. It smelled of dirt and moisture, as it had rained the day before. A few brown puddles were visible, dispersed over the upturned, trodden ground in the paths near the wall. The unceasing patrols had destroyed the once verdant lawn and left the place looking much like the streets of Santir. It was hardly as disheartening as their loss of numbers, but it served as a reminder of just how much they were losing, both in numbers and in general change. *It's a constant reminder of the people we once considered family beating a path away from our door.*

Trying to put this particular unpleasant change out of his mind, Cyrus headed left, toward the archery range along the side of Sanctuary, and there found fifty rangers turned out in their green cloaks, taking their practice with a bow, Calene Raverle at their head, shouting orders in a high commanding voice. She took no note of him as he passed, nor did any of her charges, and Cyrus was once more left with the impression that he was a ghost in this place. *Fitting,* he thought. *I follow in Alaric's footsteps—at least in some regards.*

He made his way around the smooth side of Sanctuary, following along in the shadows of the immense structure. He detoured around the southwest tower where it jutted out, stretching into the sky, and laid eyes upon the garden in the distance, still a lush and verdant contrast to the paths before the steps.

Guarding the way to the bridge that spanned the garden pond, two enormous shadows stretched across the ground. Cyrus frowned, the shapes a most peculiar sight in what he had once considered a haven of peace even in Sanctuary's most chaotic moments.

Fortin stood nose-to-nose with Zarnn, the troll, only a foot or two of distance between their mammoth chests. Cyrus picked up his pace, unsure what to do. *If I had a Praelior, stepping between them would be less of a concern …*

There was no sound coming from either of them, just a low, crackling breathing from Fortin that Cyrus could hear once he got closer. There was no physical contact between them, either, just their noses a few inches from each other's. It appeared to Cyrus they were having some form of staring competition.

"What the hell is this?" Cyrus asked when he was only ten feet away. Neither Zarnn nor Fortin looked up, keeping their eyes fixed upon one another. When neither answered him immediately, he raised his voice and asked again. "I said, what is this?"

"First to look away loses, Warlord of Perdamun," Fortin said.

"That's not my title," Cyrus said.

"Is good title," Zarnn opined.

"Mine is 'Grand Knight of Sanctuary,'" Fortin said.

Zarnn made a rumbling noise. "Is good, but not better."

"He's also Lord Fortin of Rockridge," Cyrus said.

"Less impressive still," Zarnn grunted. "Should stick with 'Grand Knight.'"

"I generally do, these days," Fortin agreed.

"You're having a staring contest in front of the garden?" Cyrus asked, looking from the troll to the rock giant.

"It seemed the best place," Fortin said, not looking up from the troll's eyes. "Out of the way, hardly visited anymore. A proper staring competition takes hours."

Zarnn made a low noise of agreement. "Best to be outside, where bright light will give advantage over cave-dweller rock."

"Rock giant," Fortin corrected, sounding as nonplussed as a grumbling creature with rocky skin could, Cyrus supposed.

"I should be troll giant," Zarnn said. "Need title, too. Would go well with gold and power Zarnn intends to find."

"I suppose that search is going a bit fruitlessly at the moment, eh?" Cyrus asked, putting a little more humor into it than he might have had he felt Zarnn would fully take his meaning.

"Not searching now," Zarnn said. "Staring. But will win gold when win contest."

Cyrus frowned. "Did you ... put money on this?"

"Only a gold piece," Fortin said, squinting at the troll in front of him. "I assume that's a bounty for a swamp troll, though."

"Is very much," Zarnn agreed. "Too much. Is why Zarnn cannot look away."

Cyrus started to ask whether Zarnn had a piece of gold, but stopped himself just in time. *If he doesn't, it's just going to humiliate him and possibly enrage Fortin ... which would end badly for all of us standing within twenty feet of the fight that would almost surely break out.* "How long have you two been at this?"

"Hours," Fortin said.

"Days?" Zarnn asked. "Unsure. Stomach grumbling, but is ignored.

Riches to seek."

Cyrus blinked his eyes, trying to decide if he even had anything else to say in this matter. "Good luck to both of you," he finally decided and then steered his path away from the both of them, snaking his way to the bridge and crossing it, glancing down at the pond below, still in the windless day.

"Is good Guildmaster," Zarnn said behind him, voice a low rumble.

"A better warlord you'll not meet," Fortin agreed. "I pity Goliath and their bony leader. I bet his flesh will taste like rotten meat."

"Rock giant eat dark elf?" Zarnn asked.

"I don't think Malpravus is a dark elf," Fortin said. "I think he is in fact a very stretched and desiccated human, tainted with evil and possibly some of those disgusting elvish spices."

"Elvish spices bad," Zarnn agreed. "Taste like sweaty nethers."

"Mmm," Fortin said. "I don't think I have ever tasted sweaty nethers. Are they flavored at all like gnomes?"

Cyrus increased his speed to avoid hearing the answer to that particular question and found himself drawn toward the small shrine on the other side of the pond. He glanced into its shadowy confines, looking for the candles that had been lit within when last he'd been there. There were none, only a darkness, as Cyrus stepped up to the carefully constructed memorial to Alaric Garaunt.

"I don't think you'd believe the conversation I just overheard," he said, feeling the cool shadows embrace him as he came in out of the sun. "Hell, I don't believe the conversation I just overheard." He took off his own helm and set it on the altar where Alaric's own had rested once upon a time. He stared at the unthinking action, peering at his own helm, and drew a long breath. "Huh. I rather doubt anyone's going to be around to construct a memorial to me when I die the way we did for you. Not that you're dead," he added somewhat hastily, as though Alaric were in the air, listening to him.

Cyrus held still in the quiet, listening to the faint hum of a troll saying something in the distance and a rock giant responding. "We're on a bit of a downturn at the moment, Alaric. We haven't seen numbers this low since before Ashan'agar. And the things I'm having to do to fight this fight?" Cyrus laughed ruefully. "I know you wouldn't approve of them. Part of me is bothered by that." His face went slack in the darkness. "The other part of me ... I guess is starting to get used to the idea that you left. That for whatever reason, you left. And you didn't just leave, you kind of left me in the dark."

Cyrus raised his hands in the dark interior of the shrine. "You didn't tell me you killed my mother. You didn't tell me that she was a heretic. That would have been nice to know. Maybe you really were just guarding against what might happen if I found out." Cyrus smirked. "Fat lot of good that did. They're all after me now anyway. Supposedly you were protecting me all along, but I guess you're pretty well done with that now. Maybe not, though, since apparently you had some hand in sending Terrgenden to save me from my own recklessness. I'd thank you, but we lost a lot of good people in that fight and, well, now that I've been declared heretic and the Council has joined me, we've pretty much wrecked Sanctuary, so I'm not sure I have much to thank you for.

"Gratitude is a problem for me, I guess," Cyrus went on, running his fingers through his hair. It was starting to get longer again. "All I can see lately is what I've done, and the chain of events that's spun out of every choice I've made since I got here. I can see a line from Niamh dying at the hands of Mortus's assassins to Luukessia dying after we killed Mortus. I can draw a course from Narstron's death in Enterra to Orion betraying us to the Dragonlord to the sack of Reikonos and now to Goliath hanging over us like a hawk swooping down on a field mouse. Whether it's the first encounter I had with the titans or the goblins setting loose raiders on convoys, I feel like everything that's happening now has its roots in the past, like it's all tied together in some grand and horrifying way. And that goes for you as well, being my mother's killer, my protector, and later my Guildmaster."

Cyrus took a breath of warm, sticky air. "Most people don't live lives this complicated. There was a time I might have thought it was a blessing that I had so much to deal with, that I had found that much-vaunted purpose you always tried to tell me about." He lowered his voice to a whisper. "Now it appears my purpose is not to protect Arkaria but to sneak up on my enemies in the night and fell them in a way that you would never have condoned. The worst part is …" Cyrus felt a grim desperation settled in. "… I think it truly is the only way."

He let out a long breath and smelled the dank air, so different from that waiting just outside in the sunlight. "I don't know why I said all this just now. I don't think you're listening." He picked up his helm and put it on his head, feeling the sweat still on it. "Wherever you are, I imagine you have your reasons for being away. I just know that … I always felt like you knew far more than you were letting on. In fact, now I begin to suspect you might have seen further than any of us. That you could tell me how all these things are connected, what I'm missing, and help me see if there was some …" Cyrus paused, and a pang of sadness rang inside him, "… some way out of this with honor, some path I'm blind to. But instead I'm forced to do things you never would." The sadness fled, replaced by faint resentment. "I guess that's why I'm not you. Reason number … hell, I've lost count of them all. They're innumerable. I'm a warrior, Alaric. A warrior who casts spells, but a warrior nonetheless. An enemy presents his back to me, I stab him, just like that." He lowered his head. "If there's a way out of this, I'll take it, honor be damned. My purpose is to see my people through, and that's all there is." He raised his head once again and started toward the sunlit aperture outside, with its sweet smell of fresh air, and he stopped just before it, feeling the shadow of the shrine still cooling him, holding him in its embrace. "But if you wanted to show up, maybe point my eyes in a different direction, I damned sure wouldn't mind, Alaric." He waited for a few seconds, but there was no reply, not even the sound of the wind. Cyrus left the shrine and walked alone back to the front of the guildhall with its trampled paths leading away from the door.

55.

"Today is the day," Vara said as the sun rose over the Waking Woods in the distance, somewhere beyond the open balcony. Cyrus could see the Bay of Lost Souls faintly in the distance, a dark shade on the horizon. He strained to look, imagining that on a clear day he could see almost to the ruins of Aloakna, a ghost town wrecked by the dark elves in the war. "Are you ready?" Vara asked, snapping Cyrus out of his reverie.

Cyrus shifted, adjusting his belt and scabbard, making a face as he did so. "Ready as I'm going to be, I reckon."

"You're making a face," Vara said, glancing back at him. "What is that face supposed to mean?"

Cyrus paused, trying to think back over the last few seconds. "I ... oh. It's this belt." He adjusted it again; it was the same one that he always wore. "It doesn't feel right, I think. Probably the new sword." He didn't even look at it, just nudged the hilt. He hadn't so much as drawn it to practice since he'd beheaded Danay. He hadn't wanted to look at it, not really, and for the first time in a very long time, he had no desire to feel his sword in his hand.

"You still feel the loss of Praelior, then," Vara said, standing in the rising sun, her hair glowing in the light.

"It'd be hard not to," Cyrus said, adjusting the belt again and tightening it a notch. It rested oddly on his hips; not uncomfortable, so much as simply not what he was used to. He was aware of it dimly, but did not care to focus upon it. "Having a weapon such as that at my disposal for so long only to lose it ..." He shook his head. "I don't know. I suppose it'd be a bit like you losing your arm—or your armor."

"Yes," Vara said, sounding much more reserved. "Well, as you know, I have in fact had a treasured sword stolen from me before. And it is certainly no easy thing to cope with, though I was dealing with other emotions at the time."

"I can only imagine," Cyrus said. He paused, peering at her. "Wait … so Archenous still wields your own blade against you? When you fought in the Mountains of Nartanis?"

"Indeed he did," Vara said, sounding more than a little resentful. "I would have taken great pleasure in cleaving his hand off and reclaiming it, then turning it against his waiting neck. Unfortunately, that was not to be." Her lips were pursed with dissatisfaction.

"Well, I don't think our account with him is settled just yet," Cyrus said. "I expect you'll have another chance to remove his head."

"I do hope," Vara said. "It's truly my fondest wish, right up there with seeing Malpravus impaled upon a spear and carried forth with it jutting out of his mouth like a roasted pig."

"Not much meat on that pig," Cyrus said. "He'd look like a scrawny rat with a stick shoved up his arse."

"Regardless, it would be satisfying, no?" Vara asked, staring off into the distance. She sighed with some gusto. "When are we leaving?"

"*We're* not," Cyrus said, striding over to the desk and snatching up the parchment note upon it. "You're staying here to mind the wall."

"The blazes you say," Vara replied.

"Relax," Cyrus said, giving her a smile. "J'anda, Vaste and Longwell are coming with me."

"I suppose that makes me feel marginally better," she sniffed. "But why do you feel the need to exclude me from this?"

"Because Reynard Colton is a notorious xenophobe," Cyrus said, adjusting his belt once more and sighing when he caught himself. *I need to stop doing that. Praelior is not coming back on its own; I need to find Rhane Ermoc and take it back, but until then, I need to stop fiddling with my damned belt.* He did not glance down. *And perhaps put in some practice with this sword so as not to be utterly clumsy and incompetent with it if I find myself in need of it.*

"So you bring a dark elf, a troll, and a man from across the sea to meet with him?" Vara's eyebrow was raised. "I thought you were supposed to be some sort of strategic genius, but I'm beginning to think I had the right of you when I called you an idiot all those times …"

Cyrus shot her a smile. "J'anda will be in disguise, Vaste will be intimidating, and Longwell's a human. Colton's bile is mostly reserved for elves and dark elves, the latter because he was recently at war with them and the former because 'Those pointy-eared tree-worshippers didn't do a godsdamned thing to help during the war.'"When she looked at him with slightly more umbrage, he shrugged. "Colton's words, allegedly. Certainly not mine."

"He sounds like a true treasure."

"We don't get to pick our allies when we're trapped in a tight corner," Cyrus said by way of agreement without agreeing. "But you're right—under normal circumstances, a year ago, I wouldn't have stepped in this man's territory even if avoiding it required a five hundred mile detour."

"Well, now all it requires is failing to mention your 'pointy-eared, tree-worshipping' wife, I presume," she said.

"I have never seen you worship a tree, come to think of it," he said, pretending to give it a thought. An inadvertent grin split his face. "Though I suppose I have seen you with something a bit like—"

"Don't," she said with a shake of the head that compelled him away from the remark before he made it. She let them stew in the silence for a few seconds before she broke it. "When do you leave?"

A knock echoed in the tower before he could answer her. "Right now, I would guess," he said. "Come in!"

The door squeaked open to admit J'anda with his purple-tipped staff, Vaste with his spear-tipped one and Longwell with his lance. Vara took them all in with a glance. "Well, I'm certain that your current entourage, with their impressive collection of staves, shall surely capture the imagination of Reynard Colton, for he sounds to my ears like a man who will be impressed by a large stave."

"Mine's more of a lance," Longwell said, frowning.

"Mine's a spear now," Vaste said, holding it aloft, the pointed end with the crystal in its middle glinting in the sunrise.

"I believe we might have walked in on a conversation midstride," J'anda said, frowning, "and I don't believe that she meant that in a flattering way. In fact, I think she might have been using 'staves' as a sort of stand-in for—"

"Yes," Vara said with a pleased smile. "That's exactly what I meant." She shot Cyrus a look, one of concern thinly veiled under sarcasm. "Take great care, husband, for any man you would not normally care to have as an ally is not the sort you should trust." She leaned in and kissed his cheek then his lips, then she stepped back to allow the others to gather around him.

"I'll watch out," Cyrus said, catching her eyes. She smiled at him with obvious reservations as J'anda, Vaste and Longwell all filed in behind him.

"I'll watch out, too," Vaste said, looking down at Cyrus. "Though you should really join our club and get a tall weapon. Maybe a spear? One of those very long swords the Northmen use? You know the ones, tall as an average human man—"

"I'd settle for just getting my old one back," Cyrus said, once again feeling the need to adjust his belt, and the odd weight there.

"Watch your back," Vara said as J'anda began to cast the teleportation spell, glow lighting the Tower of the Guildmaster around him.

"I'll watch his long bottom for you," Vaste said as they began to disappear. "Mmmm. No, that just doesn't compare favorably with mine at all …"

Cyrus watched Vara's blue eyes turn green in the reflection of the spell-light and disappear as he was taken away, away from her and to a place he did not truly care to go.

56.

"You know, I've been to some lovely towns in my time," Vaste said as they made their way across Idiarna, a small southern town at the very edge of the Human Confederation, "but this isn't one of them."

"Well, it did get rather thoroughly sacked in the war with the dark elves, as I recall," J'anda said, wearing the guise of a human, illusory vestments identifying him as a healer. He had somehow cast his illusion spells between the moment they'd disappeared in the tower and when they'd arrived, or else had done so before they left, though Cyrus could not quite fathom how he'd managed it. "Very difficult for a town to look good when it is recovering from being burned to the ground … what? Three years ago? Four?"

"Somewhere in there," Cyrus agreed, scanning the town around them. It had very much the same look as Santir, the buildings wooden and plain, the architecture different from that found in Emerald Fields. It was a peculiar thing, Cyrus thought, how wildly divergent the styles of human architecture were even when they used the same building materials. Idiarna did look bigger than Santir as a whole, however, though it seemed to pale when compared to Emerald Fields. "Idiarna and the western Confederation in general has always been the poorer part of the human state. They don't have anything but crops, and they're not as fertile as the Riverlands. They lack the mines of the Mountain District or Northlands, and they don't have the ports like Taymor in the southeast. Trade with the elves and farming is about all they've got nowadays, and both took a big hit after the war." Cyrus shrugged. "Maybe if Terian opens trade to this part of the Confederation … but my suspicion is that he's not the one blocking it, since I've seen any number of dark elven merchants plying their wares in Reikonos."

They walked the muddy streets, flat ground stretched before them. Cyrus could see a keep, a wooden fort in the distance, looking much like it was new as well. It lacked the imposing presence of Isselhelm's keep, its crude design reminding him of a titan fort or the troll city of Gren. It had the same jagged pikes circling it, though at least it had a dirty moat to section it off from the rest of the city.

Even the tallest buildings were not more than two stories, and Cyrus began to wonder if there was some reason they did not build taller buildings. It was an idle curiosity, though, and one he did not intend to indulge when he met Governor Coulton. *This certainly doesn't look like a regional capital ...*

The streets were busy, horses clomping along the muddy streets, their smell heavy in Cyrus's nose, the stink of laborers, animals, and piss in the streets. One animal left droppings in front of him and Cyrus steered his party around it without comment, walking them past a boarding house that had black clouds billowing from its chimney.

The keep was straight ahead on the wide road, the avenue wider than the average streets in a town of this size. Cyrus looked back and saw the portal behind him and beyond it, the outskirts of town only a few blocks past. In the opposite direction, toward the keep, he could see nothing past the wooden fortress. At the next cross street, he looked both ways and noted that it was not particularly far to either end of town to the east or west.

"How many people do you figure live here?" Cyrus asked, mostly talking to himself.

"Perhaps ten thousand," J'anda said, having apparently taken the same note Cyrus did. "Do you suppose there were more before the sack?"

"Almost certainly," Cyrus said, whisper quiet, walking along with his illusory druid robes swishing around him. "I think Idiarna got caught by surprise. They might have lost over half the town."

"Another tragic chapter in this entire history," J'anda said with a sad shake of the head.

"It's true," Vaste said, surprisingly solemn. "Remember when we sacked Gren? And by sacked I mean, 'Only killed the people who attacked us'? And when we 'sacked' Saekaj, leaving it standing entirely and only missing its god? And Enterra—"

"I take your rather obvious point," Cyrus said, smiling in spite of himself. "And ... thank you."

Vaste leered down at him from behind the broad face of a human. "For what?"

"For reminding me that even when we're doing our worst, others do much, much worse," Cyrus said.

"I was really just reminding you how amazing I am as an officer," Vaste said smarmily. "I mean, the guild I lead is really quite tremendous, and I'm clearly a moral compass—"

"There was the time we conspired to have the titans wiped out," J'anda said with a smile of his own.

"Well, of course they deserved it," Vaste said.

The keep bridge was down, the gate open. There were no guards at the end of the bridge, but Cyrus could see them ahead, on either side of the crude gate. He proceeded with his parchment invitation in hand, ready to present it.

The sounds of the keep were quiet ones, the waters lapping at the base of the bridge below them. This bridge was a sturdier, shorter one than he'd crossed in Isselhelm, as seemed to befit the moat. This moat was slightly less dirty, though still very brown with some various floating objects in it, including a log. The guards were wearing boiled leather of the cheapest variety, and their expressions were surly.

"We're here to meet with the governor," Cyrus said softly to the first guard, who was scrutinizing him with a disinterested air, perhaps because Cyrus's illusion gave him an aura of respectability.

"In you go, then," the guard said after a quick look at his parchment, handing it back to Cyrus with care. He gestured with his spear and Cyrus went on, through the gate and into the bailey of the keep.

The bailey was no more impressive than any other part of the keep or, indeed, of the town of Idiarna in general. It was a new building, hastily constructed, and the ground was a mud-filled mess, no hint of greenery in its midst. At the center of the bailey was an old stone tower that looked a little like a nub rising out of the earth. Only three stories, it towered over the rest of the town, but at its top was a flat roof of wood that did not look strong enough to hold even a single defender.

The bailey itself had two guard towers on this side of the stone tower but circled around with the wall behind it. Cyrus suspected there would be two others hidden in the shadow of the tower, at the back of the circular wall that ringed the keep. The guard towers were all lashed-together wood, crudely made, plainly built on a very small budget. *I wonder if Governor Coulton has two pieces of gold to rub together at this point?*

Cyrus made his way toward the stone tower's doors just ahead of him, sweeping the bailey courtyard with a impassive gaze as he moved. If there was to be trouble, he fully expected it within the tower itself, where his freedom of action would be constrained, as Frost had done. *Hopefully Coulton won't get any stupid ideas about asserting himself, because I am in no mood to—*

He heard the quick steps before he saw their origin, but when he turned to look, his mind barely registered what he was seeing. A blur came from his left, a glowing blue blade held high and an ululating battle cry preceding it. Cyrus's breath caught in his throat and he stared, dumbstruck, as the blur ceased less than ten feet away from him, crisp lines resolving into a scarred mouth turned upward in a nasty grin—

Rhane Ermoc.

Marching boots behind him forced him to glance back. The dark elven woman who had been with Goliath at the ambush in Reikonos was coming around the left side of the tower with a complement of troops, all armored to the full, mystical steel covering them from boots to helm, and their weapons looking twice as dangerous as the sword that hung so awkwardly from his belt.

"Well, hell," J'anda said softly as the female dark knight held up her hand and stopped the march of her small army only a few feet from Cyrus to the left. "Sareea Scyros," the enchanter said.

"None other," the woman said in a voice that suggested to Cyrus that she was quite pleased with herself. The sound of marching boots came from behind Rhane Ermoc as well, and Cyrus turned his head to find a phalanx of armored warriors falling in behind Ermoc in neatly layered lines.

A *thunk!* at his feet drew Cyrus's attention to an arrow fired in the earth. When he followed its slant upwards, he saw Orion grinning at him from the tower behind him to his left. Spinning around, Carrack waved from the one behind him to the right, as the gates were already closed by the guards who had just let him in, the two of them chortling at what they'd done.

"We're—" Cyrus began.

"I believe the word you're searching for," Rhane Ermoc cut him off with a wild grin, brandishing Praelior and speaking so fast he was barely understandable, "is ... trapped."

57.

"You find yourself in a nasty situation, Davidon," Rhane Ermoc went on, words flying out of his mouth like spittle, "but then, I always knew you'd come to an ugly end."

"I'm not ended just yet, Rhane," Cyrus said, looking around, searching for any weakness. The illusion disguising Cyrus faded in an instant. Cyrus shifted slightly, and the mud that surrounded his boots made a soft, wet slurping sound.

"If you think you're still alive by anything other than the grace of the fact I'm going to taunt you for a while before I start depriving you of life," Ermoc said, still grinning, "you're dumber than you look."

"Says the man with the scar across his lip that probably came from poor table manners," Cyrus fired back, keeping his hand clear of his scabbard. It wouldn't do any good to reach for it in any case, because the advantage granted by his current sword was less than nothing against Praelior.

"Is that so?" Ermoc shot forward, and Cyrus felt a burning pain in his own lip before he could move. He grimaced, knowing in his heart what Ermoc had done before he even reached a hand up to touch it. *The bastard split my lip right good, probably half an inch toward my cheek.*

"Hah!" Orion crowed from behind him. "That's right, give him some souvenirs before we kill him. Make him so ugly even his wife won't recognize him when Malpravus walks his corpse up to the gates of Sanctuary."

Cyrus compelled the muscles at his mouth to rest and then, quietly, his hand behind his back, murmured a healing spell and felt the pain cease immediately. *What the ...?* He blinked as Ermoc grinned. *They can't possibly have been so stupid as to fail to cast a cessation spell, can they?* He tried not to let his eyes widen as he turned his head slightly, looking for something, anything, from the rest of his party. He got a subtle arching of the eyebrows from J'anda, and the trace of a knowing smile from the enchanter, whose fingers were glowing purple as he cast a spell.

Need to stall, Cyrus thought. *Need to give J'anda time to work. Otherwise …*

We're dead. And Malpravus really will be walking my mangled corpse up to the Sanctuary gates … His heart plunged in him. *That'd sink the guild right there, break the last bit of morale, and send Vara into a spiral of anger or sadness …*

"Take good stock of your situation," Ermoc said as Cyrus turned slightly to see Vaste frozen in place, looking quite alarmed, his spearstaff pointed to their left at the dark elven woman J'anda had called Sareea. Longwell, for his part, had his lance pointed to Ermoc's forces at the right. "I can tell you're feeling the pinch, but let me rub it in for you, salt in the old wound. Carrack is just sitting up there," Ermoc pointed to the tower behind Cyrus. "Ready to rain the fire on you. Of course," Ermoc grinned, "I'd rather make your death personal. Very up close."

"I don't know why you hate me so, Ermoc," Cyrus said, staring at him with angry eyes. *Hope he doesn't notice my lip has stopped bleeding. Probably can't see it's healed under all the blood.* "The first time I met you, you accused me of something I didn't do. The next time, you killed a prisoner I brought you—"

"And insulted me." Ermoc's eyes flashed darkly.

"I get the feeling lots of people have insulted you in your time, Ermoc," Cyrus said. "Mostly your intelligence, but—"

Ermoc lashed out again and this time caught Cyrus just beneath the cheek, but more lightly. It was a searing pain, but one that he grimaced away from as he felt the warmth of the blood running down his stubbly face. He brought his left hand behind him again and counted to five before casting the healing spell, giving the blood plenty of time to well and run before he did.

"You always had everything handed to you, didn't you?" Ermoc asked, grin fading, replaced with anger. "Big strong warrior with a big strong name. War hero's boy. I bet you said your daddy's name everywhere you went. Him just giving you that and your armor probably opened every door. He gave you everything, you're nothing without that armor, this sword," he slapped the blade, "and your name. I wish I'd known about your stinking heretic mother before, I wouldn't have wasted so much time thinking you were hot shit."

Cyrus blinked. "You … you were jealous? Of me?"

Ermoc's dark skin flushed even darker. "I'm not jealous of you, you—you—scum!"

"Says the man who betrayed his homeland and joined a guild that was cast out of Reikonos for doing the very thing you looked down on me for supposedly doing," Cyrus said.

"I—I—" Ermoc stuttered.

"Rhane, there's no point in arguing with him," Orion called down from behind Cyrus, atop the guard tower. "He'll just sit there and spin you around all day. It's what he does." There was unmistakable hatred in the way the ranger spoke.

"I ran into your wife the other day," Cyrus said, glancing back at Orion.

The bow wavered in the ranger's hand. "You're lying."

"She's not doing so well," Cyrus went on, as if Orion had never spoken. "Seems she abandoned you when you were crawling through the Bandit Lands?" *If they're going to kill me, I might as well strike them with the only weapon I have left—their pitiful insecurities.* "I guess she couldn't take the sight of your face any more—"

An arrow spanged off the chainmail at Cyrus's elbow, and he turned his face away, chuckling. "Hey, Orion, I finally got better chainmail than you—"

"Ermoc, just gut him!" Orion screamed, voice echoing with odd resonance under his helm.

"With pleasure," Ermoc said, his face stiff as a smile cracked through. He started forward—

And a blast of fire hit the troops behind him as he stepped away, flames streaming out of the middle of them as screams echoed through the wooden bailey. Cyrus saw faces of the Goliath warriors charring and blackening in their armor, and immediately he knew what had happened—J'anda had charmed Carrack and set him against his own.

In the formation behind the dark knight named Sareea, the men yelled and started to charge—right into their own numbers. Swords were plunged into their fellows, and the front lines broke as they tried to kill both the men behind them as well as Sareea, some four soldiers breaking off to attack her from behind. She managed to avoid their first attacks through a careful ballet of agility, surprising Cyrus with her speed.

Cyrus grabbed hold of the hilt of his sword as he heard a cry behind him, and he turned his head involuntarily. The world began to slow around him, as though everyone had decided to move at their most leisurely pace. He made it around in time to see J'anda standing there, painful grimace on his face, as though he'd been pinched particularly hard. Three arrows jutted from his chest, navy stains seeping through his robes.

"Damn," the enchanter said mildly, talking at normal speed.

Vaste was hit next, an arrow plunging through his neck, dark green blood fountaining down his black robes and soaking into the dark material. He looked at Cyrus with those onyx eyes, dark blood staining his chin. He tried to speak, but no words came out, only blood, and the troll sagged to his knees as he went limp in death, falling face first into the mud.

"Take Ermoc!" Longwell shouted, words slow, already surging into action, charging at half-speed at Sareea Scyros, leaving J'anda and Vaste behind. Cyrus watched him begin his charge and suddenly realized—

We're going to—

He spun just in time to see Rhane Ermoc come at him and slammed his weapon against Praelior in a hard clash of the blades. His defensive move could not win out against the strength of Praelior, and he took a step back. An arrow clanged off his back plate, and Orion shouted in rage above him.

"You'll not get away this time," Ermoc hissed and came at him again, so much more slowly than he should have, like he wanted to savor the kill. Cyrus blocked him, then blocked him again, Ermoc's face twisting in fury—

And then Cyrus heard the last cry, the one he'd been dreading.

He could see from where he stood when it happened. Sareea Scyros was no longer fighting her own men; J'anda's death had released the magic that bound the troops behind her, and now she stood with her fellows, surrounding Longwell, blades plunging in and out of him at the cracks of his armor, warm, red blood squirting—

Gods, Cyrus thought. *This is it. I'm—*

Ermoc screamed and came at him again, Praelior held high, slashing down, and Cyrus clanged his blade against that of his enemy, turning him aside again. The sun flashed on his blade as he knocked Praelior away, and something at last clicked in Cyrus's head, something he had not realized until now.

The sword Cyrus held in his hand was not the sword he'd been carrying for the last several months.

This one ... was different.

It bowed out along the blade into a curving edge along one side, like a scimitar, but was flat on the back of the blade. The hilt was wrapped with the finest leather, and clung to his hand like it was bonded with it. Even in the sunlight, it seemed to carry a faint glow of white. When he brought it around again, he realized that Ermoc wasn't moving slowly—

Cyrus was moving faster.

"How?" Ermoc screamed impotently, raising Praelior above his head again, his nose running in his fury, disgusting yellow dribbles on his stubbled, scarred upper lip.

"You said it yourself, Rhane," Cyrus said, smirking in spite of himself, in spite of his situation. "My father gave me everything—name, armor." He brandished the blade high, and suddenly he remembered a moment he had forgotten, standing in their old house, his father's voice coming back to him, resonating between the clash of his new blade against the old. "And now I've taken up his sword. Rhane Ermoc, meet Rodanthar—" Cyrus whipped the sword in front of him, feeling a warm satisfaction that reminded him of the moment he'd first taken up Praelior, and watched his new blade shine in the light, "—The Saber of the Righteous."

58.

There was no time for gloating, for before Cyrus even finished his taunt, another arrow winged him from behind, bouncing off his armor and reminding him of the precarious position he found himself in, even with his new weapon. He lashed out at Ermoc, driving him back with a violent slash. Ermoc staggered away, fear in his eyes, the blue blade of Praelior clutched tightly in his hands.

Cyrus heard the stampede of footsteps in the mud, metal slapping against wet dirt. He spun and caught the first soldier attacking him with a plunging point to the face. It splashed blood at him, but he ignored it as he ripped the sword out. An arrow skipped Cyrus's cheek and tore it open, and he felt a burning rage enter him.

"Well, that's about enough of that shit," he muttered as the blood streamed down his face.

He kept Rodanthar in front of him, fending off the attacks of the soldiers coming at him, and turned his left hand loose at the tower, not even looking. A fire spell surged out in a second, a billowing ball of flame that slammed into the tower where Orion had been practicing his craft. Cyrus saw motion out of the corner of his eye as the ranger leapt from the twenty-foot height and slammed into the mud below. The sound of bones breaking and a cry of pain was like sweet music played right into his ear as he made the same motion and destroyed the other guard tower, just in case Carrack was still atop it, waiting.

Cyrus plunged his blade into two more soldiers coming at him, in rapid succession, both in the neck, both without mercy, cutting both the heads cleanly off. His aim was such that he neatly avoided their gorgets, striking to kill in such a way that even if a healer were present, there would be no reviving them. He slashed through them as though they were straw men, no more substance than he might have found practicing against air, and when he drew the bloody, gleaming blade of Rodanthar back, he saw the others waiting fearfully, cowering behind Sareea Scyros, who watched him warily.

Cyrus looked sidelong at Ermoc, who still stood, stunned. "I guess Malpravus should have sent more men," he said and pointed Rodanthar at Sareea, who blinked as he pointed the blade at her and the men behind her. She took a step back, clearly intimidated, and Ermoc ran at her as she began to twinkle with light, a return spell clearly at work. Ermoc slammed into her as she disappeared, the spell drawing the both of them out of the line of fire the second before Cyrus let loose a billowing flame spell that struck the other rank of soldiers, immolating them in an instant.

The intensity of the heat made Cyrus flinch back. It was as hot as any spell he'd ever cast, perhaps hotter, and it had landed in a solid thirty-foot circle, scourging the men within it with flames worthy of a blacksmith's furnace. The armored figures within danced in agony, running to and fro until they fell to their knees one by one like puppets being dropped as their master cut them loose.

Cyrus felt the sweat trickle down his forehead as he surveyed the battlefield. There were no other survivors save one; Orion was grunting, trying to get back to his feet at the base of the burning guard tower. Carrack's corpse was beneath the flaming wreckage of the other tower, the wood structure already collapsed on itself. The gates of the keep were thrown open and the guards who had barred the doors had made good their escape, no sign of them on the drawbridge.

Cyrus cast a furious eye at the tower behind him and raised a hand. "Reynard Coulton!" he shouted, and heaved a fire spell at the wooden roof far above. It blossomed in flame as a meek face peeked out of third floor window, wide eyes looking up in shocked surprise. Cyrus could see a beard on the man, and hints of fine cloth in the form of a cloak draped around his shoulders. The flame Cyrus had cast would burn his roof, spread to the interior of the tower, and surely, eventually, leave the entire thing a charred mess, burning the governor out of his home. "Come out before I start a fire at your front door as well!"

Cyrus did not wait for the governor to follow his instruction. He hurried over to Samwen Longwell. The dragoon had been pierced with so many swords and blades that the mud around him ran a dark shade of red. Summoning the words to mind, he drew upon the resurrection spell and cast it, and Longwell lurched painfully back to life, blood spurting once more from his many wounds. The smell of the blood was sticky in the warm air, and Cyrus hurriedly cast the healing spell upon him, watching the sprays of red come to a halt as Longwell's wounds were healed. He breathed in and out, the harsh and ragged breaths slowing, losing their fearful urgency, as Longwell's deep brown eyes met Cyrus's.

"We ... made it?" the dragoon asked, his gaze almost blank, drifting around Cyrus.

"So far," Cyrus said, kicking the dragoon's lance back in easy reach from where it had fallen. "Get yourself together; it's not over yet."

Cyrus rushed over to Vaste where the troll had fallen. His face was buried in the mud, and Cyrus knelt down to roll him. It was not easy, even with Rodanthar in hand, but he managed it with some grunting. The first survivors from the burning keep's tower began to emerge as he was casting the resurrection spell upon Vaste. He watched them with furious eyes as he brought the troll back to life. They did not watch him nearly so closely, coughing and hacking as they cleared the smoking entry to the now-burning tower. Plumes of black were starting to reach into the sky, soiling its pleasant blue with their smoke.

Vaste surged back to life with a vomiting of nearly black blood, and when the healing spell was done, he had not finished regurgitating the blood from his mouth. His eyes were wide and panicked, as if he were choking upon his life's blood—which, Cyrus realized, he probably was. The troll groaned as he hacked up the last of it, spitting into the already saturated mud. It did not smell like human blood smelled, Cyrus reflected dimly; it was different, more earthy, perhaps. "Or maybe that's just the horse manure," Cyrus muttered.

"Wha ... t?" Vaste said through sputtering lips, strings of blood still oozing their way to the ground as he rolled to all fours in preparation to stand. "Oh," the troll said, his normally yellow-green skin looking far, far more yellow at the moment, like fresh-shucked corn. "That's horse manure, right there. My hand is in it. Gods. This is the worst resurrection ever."

"Count yourself lucky you're back," Cyrus said, hurrying over to J'anda, once more casting furious looks at the men streaming out of the tower. He was waiting for Coulton, but once the man showed up, he wasn't likely to stop what he was doing just to deal with the bastard.

As he began to cast the spell to bring J'anda back, Cyrus could feel the drain of the spells he'd cast like a hard-settled fatigue wearying him. It was like he'd done a whole day's labor and was ready for bed, but it was not yet even midday. He cast the spell, watching the light at his hands, hoping it would not turn red. It didn't. J'anda sprang to life, and Cyrus grabbed his fallen staff and thrust it in his hand. J'anda's thin fingers clung to it, hard, as Cyrus ripped the arrows out of him, chopping them neatly beneath the heads with Rodanthar and pulling them through, and then cast the healing spell. Again his fingers flashed white, though once more he felt the curious drain. He clutched tightly to his new sword, as if afraid to let it go.

J'anda seemed to take his resurrection better than the others. His eyes flashed to Cyrus, less fearful, less pained, and Cyrus wondered if it was because of the staff held in his fingers, the knuckles as pale as his face from the strain of desperation to cling to it. "Somehow ..." J'anda said quietly, "... I knew you would see us through this."

"Couldn't have done it without your help," Cyrus said and then waved his sword over the enchanter's face. J'anda's eyes caught the motion and followed the blade. "We had some other help, though, too."

"Indeed," J'anda said, rolling over to get to his feet. Behind him, Cyrus could hear Vaste attempting much the same, and Longwell's heavy footfalls as he shuffled through the mud, leaning heavily on his lance. "Goliath ... gone?"

"All but the last dregs," Cyrus said, nodding toward Orion, who was trying to crawl through the mud but making a bad show of it, crying in pain as he tried to pull himself forward on one working arm. "Fish Carrack's burnt corpse out of that tower over there, will you?"

J'anda raised an eyebrow at him, casting his gaze toward where Cyrus had pointed. "Why would I do that?"

"Because I asked so nicely," Cyrus said as he strode toward Orion, who floundered in the mud. *Time to settle a very old score ... for good.*

Cyrus walked up to where Orion lay in the mud, cradling a broken arm, his legs clearly not functioning, pointed at odd angles. His helm shielded his expression, but his head was tilted so that the thin eye slits were turned toward Cyrus. "How's it going down there?" Cyrus asked him lightly, clutching Rodanthar in his hand.

"Never … better," Orion practically spit at him. "How are you?"

"Well, since I just waltzed out of Goliath's carefully set ambush for me, things are definitely looking up." Cyrus stared down at him. "So … how long until your idiot leader lands a thousand troops in the Idiarna portal?"

"You've got hours," Orion said, obviously lying. "Have a seat, let's talk for a while, chat about old times."

"Or we could just fight to the death," Cyrus said squatting down to look Orion in the eye. "Once and for all."

Orion stared back at him, and when he spoke the loathing just bled out. "If you're going to kill me … just get it over with."

"I don't think so." Cyrus shook his head. "Since the day we met, you have consistently betrayed me and attempted to destroy everything I care about. I've been fairly magnanimous thus far, but magnanimity has run the hell out, Orion. So, no, you're not going to die quickly, but I'm going to try and make it somewhat fair, if a bit humiliating." He stood, stuck the point of his sword behind Orion's ear, and tapped the edge of his helm, knocking it up and inch and catching it on the blade. He did it twice more, taking care not to cut Orion as he did so, and took the helm off his head. With a kick, Cyrus punted it into the smoldering wreckage of the guard tower Carrack had perished in. J'anda, dragging a blackened corpse by the ankles, his robes covered in ash and soot and his staff clutched awkwardly in one hand, gave him a frown for his efforts. "Sorry," Cyrus said to the enchanter.

"Stop playing with your food and eat already," J'anda shot back, dragging the carcass toward the center of the bailey, where men were still coming out of the tower.

"No," Cyrus fired back. "All right," he turned his attention back to Orion, whose scarred face leered up at him through lips that had been peeled back from his mouth, a gaping gash running toward his cheek. "Now let's make things a little more fair, shall we?" He cast a healing spell upon the ranger. It did not fix any of the scarring on his hideous face, but his legs cracked as the bones set, and his arm straightened where it had been broken.

"There you go," Cyrus said, sheathing his sword. "Now … I think it's time we settle this like men."

Orion lurched to his feet, mud and manure dripping from his tunic. "You're bigger and stronger than me."

"Yes," Cyrus agreed.

"You're going to hammer me like old beef," Orion said, seething resentment.

"Now, now," Cyrus said, "for years you've tried to arrange my death and destruction through every treacherous means you could bring to your aid. What is that if not changing the rules to favor yourself?" Cyrus smirked at him, raw anger surging through him. "I think it's time you got a taste of your own horseshit."

Orion wavered for a moment. "It doesn't have to be like this."

"Last I recalled, you still have daggers," Cyrus said, not looking away from Orion. "I've put away my sword. This is the closest to a chance to kill me as you'll ever get, Orion." Cyrus leaned toward him. "You might want to take it, because in five seconds, if you haven't tried, I'm going beat you to death right here—no mercy."

"You wouldn't," Orion whispered through his gaping lips.

"You're damned right I will," Cyrus said. "One—"

Orion drew a blade, a short sword, from behind his back. "I've been wanting to do this for a long time."

"Die?" Cyrus surveyed him with pitiless eyes. "I know. It's why you keep coming after me, and until now I've been too decent to grant your request. But now," he let his voice fall low, fury infusing it enough that Orion's mangled eyes widened just slightly in fear, "I'm granting all the requests to die, every last one. Every single person who has crossed me, who is coming after me and mine, they are about to have it granted—and I'll start with you."

Orion came at him with skill, a lancing strike that would have done well against normal armor. It could easily have broken through solid chainmail, and his slash was perfectly positioned to sail past Cyrus's plate at the elbow. It could have opened an artery, started the bleeding—

But instead it clanged, steel against quartal, and Cyrus jerked his arm into a right angle. The edge of his vambraces pushed tight against the bracers wrapped around his wrists and trapped the blade between them. With a twist of his hips, Cyrus ripped the weapon from Orion's grasp and flung it across the ground. It plopped softly into the mud some ten feet behind him, and Cyrus was left standing only three feet from Orion, who gaped at having his weapon yanked away in mere seconds.

"What else do you have?" Cyrus asked the ranger, staring at him with undisguised fury, just waiting for him to make a move.

Orion did not answer, instead turning and breaking into a run. He was angled for the open gates, pelting along on uncertain footing, and he made it almost three steps before Cyrus reached out with a long arm, seized him by the collar and yanked him backward, ripping his balance away and slamming him into the mud. Cyrus dragged him backward, Orion kicking his feet involuntarily and flailing his arms as he skimmed the mud. Cyrus drove a boot into Orion's left shoulder and heard the cracking of his collarbone. The ranger gasped hoarsely at the pain.

"You betrayed Sanctuary," Cyrus said, looming over the ranger. "You sold us out to the Dragonlord. You conspired to steal the godly weapons from almost every nation, and to free Ashan'agar, which would have killed nearly every single person in Arkaria. And as if that was not enough, you aided Goliath in turning the three major powers against us and starting a war that led to the death of millions. You helped sack Reikonos, and you've done everything you can to try kill me and mine." Cyrus kicked Orion in the ribs and heard them break, taking sweet satisfaction at the cracking of bones. He kicked him again and the ranger jerked in pain, moaning. "I can't pretend this is justice, Orion, because that would probably come at a gallows, perhaps with some impartial hangman knocking the footing from beneath you while your neck stretched and you kicked and twisted in midair. But this is what I'm going to give to you—the vengeance of someone who has had enough of your shit."

Cyrus knelt down astride the ranger, landing his armored greaves in the center of Orion's chest and heard them crack the ranger's breastbone beneath chainmail. All the air left Orion in one hard exhalation, and his ruined lips burst comically open. Cyrus stared into that scarred face and remembered the day he'd let him walk away in the arena of Reikonos. "How many people do you reckon have paid the price for my last dose of mercy for you, Orion?" Cyrus asked. "I told you I forgave but didn't forget, and now I don't do either." He raised a gauntleted fist and brought it down on Orion's face, ripping open the ranger's cheek with the first punch. He took hold of Rodanthar with his left hand and punched with the right, and the ranger's face disintegrated with the second blow, Cyrus's gauntlet buried up to the wrist. He struck twice more, shattering what little was left, insuring no resurrection spell could ever put back together what he'd put asunder, and then he stood, momentarily contented that there was one less problem for him to worry about, and he turned his attention to the burning tower.

"This is turning out to be a good day," Vaste said, leaning heavily against his spear, as Cyrus strode past him. "I didn't think it would, you know, what with the ambush and dying and spitting up blood, and the neck injury, but you know … it's getting quite a bit better."

"Watching a man get his head burst like a ripe cantaloupe does it for you, eh?" Longwell asked, leaning slightly less heavily on his own spear, still terribly pale, either from the resurrection spell or watching what Cyrus had done.

"Watching this man get it like that?" Vaste asked. "Yes. Yes, it does."

Cyrus walked right past them to the burning tower. Flames licked out of the stone windows on every floor now, and out of the roof, black clouds climbing into the air above them, and smoke was billowing from the entrance. He turned his focus on the men lingering close to the door in a thick knot. Cyrus had seen fires before, had seen the way people behaved during them. The instinct was to get as far as possible from the blaze, to turn around and look, watch as the fire did its magnificent, horrific work.

These men did none of that; they stayed close to the tower, their fear of what lay beyond it far greater than their fear of it.

"If any of you wants to die at the end of my sword, or possibly my fist," he waved his bloodied gauntlet before him, "then stay between me and Governor Coulton," Cyrus called, catching the attention of every one of them. "If, on the other hand, you want to live … get out of my way." He made his voice low and guttural, his visceral fury pouring out.

The men scattered, circling away from him as Cyrus barreled toward Reynard Coulton, unmistakable in his lush, velvet cloak and silken doublet, a man of wealth in a city of utter poverty. Cyrus grabbed his doublet with his bloody gauntlet, smearing it red with chunks of Orion's skull and soft tissue. Coulton looked ready to faint.

Cyrus dragged him forward, lifting him into the air. Coulton was not a tall man, and his short-cropped white hair was darkened by soot. Cyrus stared into wide, hazel eyes, and felt the fear pouring out of the governor of the Southern Reaches. "Hello," Cyrus said tightly.

"I ... I'm ... sorry!" Coulton said by way of greeting.

"That much is obvious," Cyrus said, not breaking eye contact. "Give me a compelling reason why I shouldn't kill you like I just did him." Cyrus tossed a thumb over his shoulder. "After all, perhaps if you die, the next governor of the Southern Reaches will be more ... flexible."

Coulton shook his head like a leaf dancing in a strong gust, trapped by its twig. "No, no, no. There wouldn't be a next governor, and if there was, he'd be appointed by Pretnam Urides, so they'd be beholden to—"

Cyrus lifted Coulton even higher. "Plainly you're already beholden to Urides, so what have I got to lose by burning the rest of your keep to the ground and hoping for better next round? Hell, maybe this will serve as a warning to Karrin Waterman about who she really ought to fear in the contest between myself and Urides."

Coulton shook his head desperately again. "Waterman—Waterman will gladly fall in line with what you want, with what Frost wants. I—I can arrange a meeting—"

"*Like this one?*" Cyrus's eyes flared with anger and he felt the silken doublet tear slightly as he lifted Coulton closer to his face.

"NO NO NO!" Coulton screamed. "This was Urides! All Urides! He heard about your meeting with Frost, and he—he approached me! Wanted me to set this meeting. Made me do it, under threat of death! He knows you were conspiring against him!"

"Then you're useless to me," Cyrus said, "because if Urides knows—"

Coulton shook again. "No, it can still work! You can still do it! The people will follow us, the governors! But you have to get rid of the Council—"

"How am I supposed to kill Urides if I don't know where he is and he knows it's coming?" Cyrus asked, dropping his voice low.

"I—that I don't know," Coulton said. "He—he—he lives in the Citadel—"

Cyrus froze. "What did you say?"

"He and the Council, they live in the Citadel now," Coulton said, voice cracking. "I'm sorry. You're right, there's no getting to him there, you'd need an army, and—"

Cyrus slackened his grip on Coulton. "If I kill him, you'll call back your troops from the army and remove the Southern Reaches from the Confederation?"

"I want to," Coulton said, nodding with excess enthusiasm. "I do. But—but—"

Cyrus narrowed his eyes. "But what?"

Coulton almost staggered back into the flaming tower door, which was now filled with flames, the heat causing Cyrus to sweat. "He's going to kill Frost. He's sent Amarath's Raiders to Isselhelm to do it, to make sure that he puts an end to this little rebellion before—"

"J'anda!" Cyrus shouted, glancing back over his shoulder. "Grab that wizard carcass and get it back to Sanctuary!" He snapped his eyes toward Vaste. "Take Longwell and go. Assemble everyone you can when you get there—sound the alarum." He yanked Reynard Coulton toward him. "Come on, you." He cast a look back through the gates; over the drawbridge he could see the Army of Goliath marching toward him, only a minute away now. He tossed a blast of flame at the wooden wall on either side of the gates and then turned back to Coulton, who seemed to be gasping for breath.

"Wh—what—where—?" Coulton stammered.

"I'm getting your stupid arse to safety," Cyrus said, pulling the governor toward him as the roof of the burning tower began to collapse behind him, filling the air with a terrible sound of crashing timbers. He cast the return spell and watched the keep of Idiarna disappear as it dragged him and the governor of the Southern Reaches away from Goliath's impending reinforcements.

59.

When he appeared back in the Tower of the Guildmaster, Cyrus immediately began dragging the governor toward the stairs.

"You're back," Vara called from behind him on the balcony, her voice sounding slightly muffled by the whip of a wind outside. "And you've brought—"

"Come with me!" Cyrus hurled over his shoulder at her, sweating beneath his underclothes as he pulled Coulton along with him, practically dragging the man down the stairs, the governor's feet barely keeping up.

"What happened—" Vara barely had time to get out before Cyrus pulled open the door, clutched the hilt of Rodanthar and broke into a run, lifting Reynard Coulton behind him so as to avoid dragging the man to death in his haste.

Cyrus hurried down the stairs as J'anda burst out of the officer quarters with Carrack's blackened corpse heaved over his own thin shoulder, his staff keeping the body from falling off. "You look strong," Cyrus observed as he pulled Coulton past the enchanter.

"Strength seems required at the moment," J'anda said tensely as he fell in behind Cyrus and they moved down the stairs.

"Wait!" Vaste called from the landing behind them.

"What the bloody hell is going on?" Vara called from somewhere behind the troll.

"That husband of yours is in a tizzy again," Vaste said. "Apparently Pretnam Urides has sent Amarath's Raiders to kill Governor Frost of the Northlands."

"Damn!" Vara shouted, voice echoing down the stone staircase.

"Exactly," Longwell said from somewhere up the stairs as Cyrus burst out onto the enclosed space outside the Council Chambers, trying his best to plunge forward and ignore the conversation taking place behind him. "We're about to land quite heavily in the shite, I reckon."

"We might be able to stop it if you lot would just hurry up," Cyrus shouted over his shoulder, paying no heed to Coulton's pained look; it appeared that Cyrus had dislocated the governor's elbow, but Coulton was merely cringing, not saying anything.

Cyrus hurried down the stairs from the Council Chamber and into the wide-open space as the tower stairs circled the central shaft to the foyer far, far below. "Hang on, governor," he said lightly as he stepped off into the abyss before Coulton could protest.

"AIEEEEEEEEEE!" Coulton screamed as they whizzed down the center of the tower, the foyer some innumerable stories below racing closer and closer.

"This is why you should never trifle with Sanctuary," Cyrus said quite calmly as he watched the stone floor rising up to greet him. He cast Falcon's Essence under his breath, and it took hold less than one story from the end of the shaft, like a gentle landing upon pillows as their momentum abruptly halted and Cyrus began to run, angling down toward the entry into the foyer. "We're quite mad."

He tugged the governor into the foyer, which was nearly empty, and bellowed, "ALARUM!" at the top of his lungs. Somewhere, in the distance, a bell began to ring, and his call was taken up by another, and then he heard shouts in the distance mirroring his own. "ALARUM!" he called again. Faces began to appear from within the lounge, and Larana emerged from the Great Hall, staring up at him where he hovered some feet above the ground, casting aside the rag in her hands and hurrying to stand near him.

J'anda came behind him, walking on air, the body still draped over his shoulder like a strange and hideous vestment. "Have I mentioned lately that I do enjoy the benefits of heresy? If only there was some way to mingle them with the more civilized days when we could trade with the entirety of Arkaria, I think I would be quite content."

"Wine cellar getting a bit thin?" Cyrus asked as Vaste screamed gleefully before stepping out of the spiraling stairwell.

"We are down to the saddest of choices," J'anda said. "Last night I was drinking gnomish wine."

Cyrus watched Vara emerge from the stairwell behind Vaste, her "landing" a little more ungainly than the troll's or Longwell's, who had emerged a second before her. She seemed to bob in the air, as though she'd forgotten exactly how the Falcon's Essence spell worked. "How was it?" Cyrus asked J'anda without thinking.

"Very small bottles," J'anda said sadly. "I think I opened five before I filled a single glass."

"What the bloody hell do you intend here?" Vara asked as others started to emerge from the staircase. "Surely you don't mean to—"

"I do," Cyrus said, cutting her off abruptly. "J'anda," he snapped his gaze to her. "I need you to cast the resurrection spell on this corpse and then take it to Terian. Keep the cessation spell over Carrack all the while—hell, don't even heal him, let him wallow in pain, dying over and over if need be—"

"If he dies over and over," J'anda said with a thin smile, "he might forget some of the things you will want to ask him about later."

"Damn," Cyrus muttered.

"I will ensure he makes it safely to Terian," J'anda said with a nod. "I presume you mean for this man to be imprisoned in the Depths for the time being?"

"Well, we can't keep him here," Cyrus said. "Tell Terian what's happening. See if he can spare any forces for—"

"I will tell him," J'anda said with a nod, and then disappeared in the light of a teleportation spell, the green glow so bright that Cyrus had to blink away.

"Mendicant," Cyrus said, nodding at the goblin, who emerged from the staircase with Erith at his side, floating like the rest of the officers who had taken the shortcut down, "I need you to go to Emerald Fields. Tell the Luukessians—"

"Let me do that," Vaste said, cutting him off. The troll's color was almost back to normal. "I know what to say. And I've been practicing my teleport spells, I think I've got this one down." He frowned, casting his eyes skyward. "Or, wait—is that the one that leads to Verklomrade …?" He shrugged. "Only one way to find out." He, too, cast a spell, and disappeared in the light of a wizard teleportation spell.

The foyer was steadily flooding with people. Menlos and his wolves had arrived now, come in from the outside, along with Calene Raverle, her bow slung over her shoulder. Fortin, too, came in through the doors, towering, Zarnn just behind him along with the rest of the troll applicants. The one with the beard stared hard at Cyrus, but Cyrus ignored him. "Anything in sight at the wall?" he asked Calene, who shook her head quickly. "What about from the tower?" He looked to Vara, who shook her head. "Then we've got at least a day before anything beyond the horizon makes it here."

"A day to what?" Ryin Ayend asked, emerging from the stairs, ducking his head to avoid hitting the lintel as he floated over ten feet above the ground.

"Larana," Cyrus said, looking right at the druid who was standing beneath him, gazing up at him with her deep green eyes, awaiting but a word, "I need you to go to Asaliere, straight to the keep and tell Governor Karrin Waterman that Pretnam Urides has sent Amarath's Raiders to Isselhelm to kill Governor Frost. Tell her I want a word, and if she refuses, grab her bodily and drag her here. When you're done with that, feel free to join us in Isselhelm, where I'll be using my new sword to carve my way through our enemies." The timid druid nodded with a sly smile and disappeared in a rush of wind as her teleportation spell pulled her away.

"What the hell are you planning here, Cyrus?" Vara asked carefully. "What is going on?"

"Pretnam Urides discovered that Allyn Frost was plotting against him." Cyrus dragged Coulton around and soothed his cringing with a healing spell cast sublingually. "He figured out we were going after Coulton here, so he sent Goliath to ambush us. That plan came to a bad end, as did Orion." He pulled Coulton to stand at his shoulder. "We're going to go to Isselhelm and face the army Amarath's Raiders has sent, and if possible, we're going to save Governor Frost. If that's not possible, we're going to give Amarath's Raiders a beating so hard that they'll be lucky if they can maintain their guild's cohesion afterward. And if nothing else," he said, with a furious gleam in his eye as he looked around the room and saw quiet awe and silent determination creep into the eyes of those assembled, "we're going to remind all of Arkaria why they once feared the march of the Army of Sanctuary."

60.

"This is madness, you realize," Vara said as they appeared in the muddy roads of Isselhelm. The corpses of the guards for the portal lay slaughtered before them, screams in the distance echoing in the air here beneath the mountains. Cyrus turned his head north and saw the great dome of the hill for which the city was named looming in the distance behind the keep. "You mean to take our expeditionary force of less than five hundred against an army that numbers somewhere over five thousand."

"I do," Cyrus said, striking out for the keep at a run. He did not dodge into any alleyways as he had last time, instead running along the main roads and listening to the sound of the footfalls behind him, Sanctuary's army appearing within seconds of his own arrival. "And I mean to win."

"You always mean to, every time," Vara said, hurrying to keep up at his side. "But that doesn't always mean you can."

"Oh, but this time I can," Cyrus said and drew Rodanthar. It gleamed even in the shadow of the building they ran beneath, eclipsing the sun.

Vara did a double take, her face puckering as though the smell of the horses that permeated the dirty streets was affecting her. "Where did you get that?"

"It's my father's sword," Cyrus said, smiling.

"I bloody well know *what* it is," she said as they jogged through the streets and into a square that was deserted except for a half dozen bodies of townfolk and guards, some of them clearly slaughtered with their backs turned. "I was standing right next to you at the damned painting when you saw it. What I want to know is where you got it."

"It was in my scabbard when I went to draw my sword in the ambush," Cyrus said, adjusting his belt self-consciously. He frowned. "Wait … that's why I kept fiddling with my belt—the weight was wrong."

"You don't even notice when someone swaps your sword out for something far better," she said, shaking her head in amazement. "For an occasionally brilliant man, you do act rather daft sometimes."

"Too true," Longwell called.

"I hear that," Erith agreed from behind them.

Cyrus followed the road, every wooden door in the town shut tight, faces peering from behind windows, clearly scared by what they had seen come through their town. He turned his attention ahead, through the streets, the timber houses battened up for invasion. They streamed past in a blur as he ran toward the square ahead, smaller than the last one they had passed through, ignoring the corpses strewn in the roadway. Not one of them belonged to an Amarath's Raiders warrior; they were all townfolk, including the occasional woman, and only a few had been struck down from the front.

This is what we face, Cyrus thought. *This is what we've always faced. Enemies who would employ callous cruelty, who don't worry as I worry about right and wrong, who care only for the destruction of anyone in their way.* He glanced at Vara and saw the set of her jaw, the furious determination as her blue eyes swept the death and destruction around them. The smell of death was in the air, foul and disgusting, and that same determination slammed into Cyrus in a hard hit, and he clenched Rodanthar even tighter in his hand as he moderated his pace so as not to leave his army behind.

"When we come upon them," Cyrus called back, trusting his words to reach his army, "give them no quarter. If you see a spellcaster, strike them down first, without mercy, for they will show us none. Burn the life out of them with great relish and smile while you do it, knowing that your actions are not only a boon for Sanctuary but to all Arkaria, for we face none but the lowest, and we will treat them accordingly."

He reached the last square and turned north, Isselhelm's keep visible ahead. Its drawbridge was up, warning apparently having reached the keep before the army of Amarath's Raiders did. Cyrus could see arrows flying above the stone walls, and an army below and all around, swarming through the air with Falcon's Essence on some quarter to half of their number. Some of the defensive arrows were landing, and bodies were falling to their knees, held aloft by spellcraft; others took lethal hits and dropped from the sky like felled birds on a hunt. Flame and ice spells were being hurled and the battlements and the drawbridge appeared to be aflame.

"This is a mess," Vara opined as they paused for a beat before continuing their run north. She was already breathless, though whether it was from the anticipation of the fight to come or from the run, Cyrus did not know.

"Let's make it messier," Cyrus said, and surged forward again, the footsteps of his army behind him, loud in his ears as he returned, once more, to war.

61.

The Army of Sanctuary slammed into the back ranks of Amarath's Raiders without warning. The sounds of battle were simply too loud for the Amarath's Raiders lines to hear their approach, for Cyrus had kept his army quiet until they were upon them, and he tore apart some eighteen men in armor himself before the screams and shouts began to trickle through the Raiders in earnest.

Cyrus did not care. He looked for familiar faces but saw none, the enemy army pressed against the moat, their druids casting Falcon's Essence at the edge, sending forth their forces to besiege the battlements of the keep. Arrows were still flying from beyond the crenellations of Isselhelm's defenses, but they seemed to be at a vastly reduced rate, and he suspected it was because there were too many of the Raiders upon the walls now.

"We appear to have lost the element of surprise," Vara called, her blade carving a dark elf's head from his body. "I think this means we should feel free to apprise them that they face true heretics, with all that entails."

"I couldn't agree more," Cyrus said, slipping back a step and raising his hand. Down from him, he saw Vara do the same, a smile on her lips, a streak of blood on her white cheek.

In tandem, they released a fearsome volley, the force blast spell blooming from their gauntlets, plowing a clear path for thirty meters on either side of them. Armored men were flung bodily through the air as if a battering ram had swept through, knocking them back into the moat by the hundreds and leaving a clear path to the keep. The sound of splashes reminded Cyrus of a long-ago raid upon the Temple of the Mler off the Emerald Coast; the sound of Amarath's Raiders plunging into the foul moat made him think of his own army jumping off the boat that had carried them into the Torrid Sea.

Except my warriors stripped their armor off first so that they didn't drown, he thought, watching the foaming of the vile waters as panic set in upon those still conscious. He and Vara had just hurled at least two hundred warriors into the water, and he suspected less than twenty would manage to crawl out again. He spun right and fired off a blast of flame into the armored corps of Amarath's Raiders that stood there, blanketing them in fearsome fire in a twenty-foot swath. He dodged away, moving toward the edge of the moat, throwing a less magic-intensive ice spell at the water. It struck and frosted over the surface of the moat, trapping some dozen men within its frosty clutches and more than a hundred more helplessly beneath it.

"Gods, Cyrus!" Erith screamed from behind him. "You just doomed them to drown!"

"I had more or less already done that when I threw them in in the first place," Cyrus said, separating the head of a large human warrior from his armored body. "I just finished the job, that's all."

Longwell's lance plunged into the guts of a warrior, ripping through the surcoat that covered him and tearing it off as he twirled the lance in the man's guts. "No mercy, right?" He spun it free and jabbed it into a charging warrior's face. "This is a policy I can get behind; treating our enemies as they are, knowing they wouldn't give us a single kindness were our positions reversed."

Ryin Ayend streaked overhead, launching fire spells to left and right, devastating balls of flame directed at the Raiders still trapped on this side of the moat. His face was twisted with fury, and Cyrus suspected that the long-held anger that the druid had been feeling toward him was being excised from his soul like venom drawn from a wound.

The sound of wolves in the distance gave way to the sound of wolves nearby, and Menlos Irontooth released his dogs of war. They leapt into action, dragging strong warriors down as the Northman plunged his blade into the fighters of Amarath's Raiders. "Invade my country, will you?" he called, dealing death to one of them. "We'll see how you like it when my steel invades your chests!"

"I don't think they'll much care for it," Vara muttered as she edged close to Cyrus, letting loose with another force blast that sent another thirty or so Raiders, including spellcasters hiding behind their armored compatriots, into the moat. She quickly followed with an ice spell of her own, trapping more of them under than Cyrus had.

"You too, Vara?" Erith asked, closer to the front rank than Cyrus had ever seen her. The dark elven healer clutched her short sword awkwardly as she stared at the moat.

"I know some of these loathsome curs," Vara said, not taking her eyes off the battle as she laid into a trio of rangers that was trying desperately to escape her. "They were the ones who laughed and jested as I lay bleeding my life's blood out upon the soil of the Trials of Purgatory." Her eyes were dark and furious, and she swept them left and right, clearly searching for someone in particular. "It would appear that this is a day of settling scores." She turned to Cyrus. "Shall we ascend to the walls of the keep?"

"I think so, yes," Cyrus said with a nod. "Calene, Longwell, Erith, Ryin—" He caught movement out of the corner of his eye as Zarnn and the trolls thundered onto the scene. "Zarnn, too—you're with us." He threw out a hand and cast Falcon's Essence upon them, and their boots rose from the ground.

"Amarath's Raiders has trolls, too," Vara said, nodding. "They're likely at the vanguard upon the parapets."

"Then let's meet them force for force," Cyrus said, lunging into the air, leaving the ground behind him. He smiled as he ran across the empty sky, the arrows raining down only moments earlier at an end. "And let's hope your old flame is up there with them."

"Yes, let's," Vara said, icy determination fueling her, a cold smile frozen to her face. "And when we find him, I suppose I'll finally have to show him what a very big mistake he made on the day when he betrayed me."

62.

Cyrus surged through the teeth of the crenellations atop Isselhelm Keep's wall like he was jumping through a window. There were two warriors waiting on either side, their attention focused entirely on the bailey beneath, and so Cyrus stabbed through them both without much thought, ripping them both in half at the waist. There was a small army gathered around the tower, some hundred or more he estimated, and so he concentrated and lobbed a fire spell right into their midst. It hit at the middle of the ground and burst like a sheep's bladder filled with too much water, swallowing up countless men and women in armor and robes beneath its furious ire.

Cyrus ran along the parapets, ripping through the next ranger he encountered, slashing the man's arm off through his chainmail, the man staring at his bloody, squirting stump as Cyrus removed his head swiftly. *Even if they've got healers, I'm not going to give them a chance to resurrect in my wake. Let them try to bring back the dead only to lose them screaming to death once more. I hope they do. I hope they waste their magic on this, over and over.* He cut through another ranger, this one turning his back to flee, Cyrus's blade slicing through his green cloak and upward, splitting his head as the strike rose, adding a jerk at the end to remove at least a quarter of the skull with a flick of his wrist.

Cyrus swept his gaze back over the bailey courtyard and the chaos he had unleashed below. Ryin was now pumping fire spells down upon them as well, dropping in a rain that reminded Cyrus of the olden days when the Sanctuary army could bombard its foes from a distance. Ryin's spells were landing with furious effect, the druid standing at the edge of the parapet—

And suddenly Ryin was no longer standing at the edge of the

parapet; he was tumbling, tossed through the air, flying over the carnage. He slammed into the tower in the middle of the keep and then dropped like an egg turned loose. He crashed to the ground, blood seeping out of his head and face and his eyes staring toward the heavens.

"Son of a—" Cyrus had seen what had happened; it was the troll with the beard, the one that had watched Cyrus since he'd arrived, his black facial hair reminding Cyrus of a ship's captain he'd once seen in the port at Reikonos. "You!" he called as Vara tore herself from slaying a hapless warrior. She was only twenty steps from the troll, who was backed by at least six of his fellows, all hulking and standing on the parapets, staring across at Cyrus, Vara, Calene, Longwell and Erith.

"Oggran?" Zarnn called, the remaining trolls with him, trying to squeeze through the crenellations. Zarnn was the only one who had made it.

"That's not my name," the troll who had flung Ryin to his death said, slow smile splitting his lips. He waved a hand toward the edge of the parapet where the other trolls were still squeezing in behind Zarnn, and immediately they dropped, their Falcon's Essence stripped. One managed to rip down a crenellation with him, but he fell, leaving Zarnn the only troll among them, his face twisting as he looked upon the traitor and his fellows.

"You," Vara said from atop the parapet as Cyrus ran up to join them, knotting the remaining Sanctuary survivors together. "You were an officer of Endeavor ..." Cyrus tried to cast a healing spell under his breath, just to see if he was right; no light appeared. *Yeah, he's casting cessation. Damn.*

"He's not with Endeavor anymore," came a voice from down in the bailey. Black smoke rose where the spells Cyrus and the others had cast had done their work. Cyrus could see some ten or so survivors below, and at their center ... was Archenous Derregnault.

"My name is Grunt," the troll said with a toothy grin, and Cyrus remembered at last why this troll looked so familiar; he had met him once, outside the Endeavor guildhall, staring him down hard after their first trip through the Trials of Purgatory. "And I am an officer of Amarath's Raiders," the troll finished, as the six more at his back raised their weapons, ready to charge down Cyrus and the last few members of Sanctuary in the keep.

63.

Zarnn split the air with a bellow of deepest, heart-churning rage and charged at the trolls gathered behind Grunt. Grunt stepped aside, amusement lighting his bearded face as Zarnn slammed into the nearest two trolls, knocking one over and hammering at the second.

"Get them!" Cyrus shouted and charged with the rest. Erith drifted back, fear plain in her eyes. Cyrus found her conduct entirely sensible; the unfamiliar sword in her hand still shook as she gaped at what lay before them. Calene faded back as well, drawing her bow and loosing an arrow; it thudded into the back of one of the trolls now grappling with Zarnn, drawing a grunt of pain that was barely audible over the sound of Zarnn's outraged shouts and the blows he landed on the troll.

Longwell met one with his lance, extending his weapon. It was batted aside by one of the trolls surging ahead, charging at them along the narrow parapet. Vara ducked past, elbowing the troll as she went by, knocking him off balance before he could exploit and follow up his attack on Longwell. She struck out at one of the trolls and another came at her from the side. She parried deftly but was immediately in danger of being overwhelmed as a third closed in on her.

Cyrus shot ahead, lunging past her to plunge Rodanthar into the troll's hand as he swept out with an ugly mace that was made of wood with spikes driven through it. Grunt lurked just behind this one, watching Cyrus through furious eyes, backing up to the clear ground beyond the worst of the fighting. His eyes were locked on Cyrus's, beckoning him forward.

Cyrus took the invitation, removing the hand of the troll who had rushed to meet him with the mace. He shouldered his quarry hard, sending him plummeting over the edge of the parapet. He heard the troll hit the ground in the bailey below, hard, skull cracking against some unyielding surface.

"The fiercest warrior in the land comes for me," Grunt said, drawing a jagged blade from beneath his tunic. It was no makeshift weapon; this was a mystical blade, at least. "But you're not just a warrior anymore, are you? You've become more." He flexed his free hand, fingers glowing again as he recast the cessation spell. "I've become more, too, thanks to you heretics." He grinned, his lower canines jutting out of his lip like crags from a canyon. "I used to be just a dark knight, did you know that?"

"And now you're a traitor," Cyrus said, sweeping forward with cold precision, heading straight for Grunt, "and soon you'll be a corpse. It's a steady progression, and a very natural one springing from your terrible, terrible choice of enemies."

Grunt raised his sword as Cyrus came in at him. "I think I've picked my enemies wisely; whole nations oppose you, Davidon."

"Whole nations have fallen before me," Cyrus said, sweeping in. Grunt met his attack with his own sword, blunting the force of the blow sideways.

"Your ego is out of control," Grunt said with a laugh, kicking out and landing his foot squarely in the middle of Cyrus's chest. Pain shot through Cyrus's breastbone as he was thrown back five feet, and he realized that the troll's weapon was not merely mystical in origin.

Grunt laughed and brandished his sword. "It's no godly weapon, this, but I did pick it up in one of the upper realms. As good as you can get without it being forged by one of the deities." He grinned wider. "And it certainly makes me a match for you—it and my troll strength, anyway."

The troll pressed his attack against Cyrus, coming at him in a sweeping, butchering swing that would have parted Cyrus's head from his shoulders had he not ducked just in time. As Cyrus spun away, he saw the fight unfolding behind him in a flash; Longwell had fallen back, standing between Erith and Calene, driven toward them by the relentless troll attacking him. Zarnn had his back against the crenellations, both his quarries hammering at him, his arms up in front of him, bleeding from wrists to elbows under their combined assaults. And Vara …

Vara was sandwiched between two trolls with blades, both coming at her at once. She whirled between them, sweat rolling down her face, unable to get a clear advantage over either, her every motion growing increasingly desperate.

"You have no hope," Grunt said, coming at Cyrus again, swift and hard with an overhand strike. Cyrus blocked it against Rodanthar and Grunt kicked out again, this time striking him as he tried to sidestep, hitting him in squarely in the knee. Cyrus grunted in agony. "All Arkaria's against you." Grunt drove forward again and Cyrus was slower to move this time, his knee aching as he tried to put weight on it. "We will press down on you—" Grunt slammed his blade against Rodanthar and Cyrus's strength nearly failed as the pain lanced through him. "And we will continue, with numbers greater than you can muster, with strength more than you can count on, until you have nothing left to give—" He slammed his blade down again, grinning, backing Cyrus to the edge of the parapet and drawing back for a final strike. "We will win, in the end, because you will have nothing left—and nowhere to run."

With that, Grunt drove his sword forward, low, hard and unavoidable, the blade rushing to sink right into Cyrus's unguarded face—

64.

The troll's attack was fast and merciless, a blow aimed to sever Cyrus's head clean from his body. It was centered perfectly, and coming in swift with the speed endowed by the troll's sword. Cyrus saw it coming, but there was no way to duck, no direction to flee. He could only take the hit—

But he could take it where he wanted it to go.

Cyrus leapt up on the balls of his toes, a jump of six inches, and the point of the sword hit him in the center of the chest. Grunt's eyes flashed, from cold satisfaction in victory to hot rage in seeing his sure win dissipate in the space of a second.

The blow hurt; there was no denying that. Although Cyrus's armor withstood the point, it pushed the metal breastplate, padding and all, into his breastbone. It was no gentle tap, either; if it had hit him full in the face, Cyrus knew his nose, mouth and eyes would have been bisected neatly down the middle, with the point of the sword coming to rest at least a foot behind his head.

Instead, all that force ran through him, pushing him back as though he'd leapt in front of a battering ram manned by rock giants. He floundered, whipping Rodanthar around in an afterblow as if in a slow, dismal dream. It came around in his hand as he began to take flight away from Grunt, the tip of the sword catching the troll in the neck and ripping across—

The spray of green blood obscured the look on Grunt's face, which started with horror and surprise at the eyes and spread down to the mouth, his jaw dropping, though that was obscured behind the blood as it geysered into the air between them.

Cyrus felt a smile of his own spread across his face as the sword completed its cut and he watched the blade nick the other vein in the troll's throat, Grunt's eyes disappearing behind the spray of swampy green, near-black blood.

Cyrus tried to regain his footing as he flew. His toe skidded against stone for a second and then lost its grasp. He was tilting now, spinning away from the spectacle of Grunt dropping his sword to grope for his slit throat with both hands, the fear obvious in his eyes.

As Cyrus tilted away from the force of the troll's blow, he realized at last why he had not been able to touch back down upon the stone parapet.

He was no longer upon the parapet; he was now flying over the bailey, dropping precipitously, some thirty feet toward the ground below—

His whispered attempt at Falcon's Essence, muttered in haste and fear, found no purchase, and there was no soft stop to his fall this time. Cyrus landed hard, on his right leg, and the bone broke cleanly, screaming agony running all up the side and middle like someone had stabbed him properly in the thigh and knee. He felt hard points all pressed through the muscle and bone, as though they were being twisted, as though fire were being applied to every surface within and without, and it was all he could do to hold in the scream.

He had the presence of mind after a few seconds to try a healing spell, but when that failed he lost his head once more, clenching his eyes shut and crying aloud in his own head. He did manage to keep his mouth shut, but only just. The smell of mud and manure was thick in the air around him, and the ground was sticky and soft. He had landed in the wet dirt, and it was all around him; he could practically taste it.

When he opened his eyes once more, it was barely, and through tears, biting his lip to keep from letting a single noise out. The ground shook as something landed next to him, missing him by a bare foot, and he realized it was Grunt, landing face first, his body breaking his neck as he impacted the ground, up against the stone wall leading up to the parapets, his legs dangling above him, supported by the wall. It was as though he'd attempted to stand on his head but failed miserably, and now his neck was at a sickening angle, blood still spurting out at regular but slowing intervals.

Cyrus felt Rodanthar in his hand and raised the sword, slamming it into the troll's neck hard enough to sever the damned thing, the blade clanging against the stone on the other side. Grunt's body fell like a tree whose trunk had just been chopped, his immense torso and dangling legs thumping down and burying the head beneath it.

"Looks like you didn't win in the end, you treacherous shit," Cyrus muttered, pained, his leg still begging to be healed. He spat blood at the troll's carcass and then rolled to his back, scooting against the wall, wondering if any of the Amarath's Raiders survivors down here had seen his fall.

Cyrus could hear cautious movement ahead; there were at least a few of the Raiders about. His greaves were resisting his attempts to drag himself against the wall, warring against the mud that was pulling against them. Finally he won, the mud making a slurping sound as he freed himself enough to get to the wall.

He tried to cast another healing spell the moment he was against the wall, but it failed. *Grunt's cessation spell should have ended the moment he died ... which means someone else is casting it now, possibly more than one someone. I can't imagine Amarath's Raiders would like to see us return to bombarding them from on high with fire ...*

The sound of swordplay going on above him was like a focusing point for Cyrus, drawing him out of the pain of his broken leg. He blinked his eyes several times, though it did nothing for the pain, in an attempt to wake himself out of the agony-induced stupor he was feeling. He looked to his right and saw a rack emptied of swords, but it still held a few bows and quivers filled with arrows—arms for the defense of the keep in case of invaders.

Cyrus swept his gaze around the bailey; there was motion ahead. He was hidden from view behind a wagon, but there was definitely movement going on beyond. He could see one of the staircases on the far wall opposite him, carving its way up in the stone. Three armored figures ran up it quickly, clearly on their way to reinforce their troll allies above him.

Shit, Cyrus thought. *No magic means we're at a disadvantage. It means they can't heal, but ... Amarath's Raiders has to be at least our equal in fighting, and they've certainly got plenty of mystical equipment, and they've got the numbers ...*

A troll body flew over him, landing atop the wagon in front of Cyrus, at least six points of dark green blood spreading in a slow ooze through his dark leather armor. The troll wheezed, but did not try to get up, and over the next ten seconds his breathing faltered and then stopped entirely.

Cyrus jerked his head to the right. *If they come for me, I'll have a hell of a time trying to fend them off flat on my back.* He tried the healing spell again with no result and then locked his gaze on one of the bows on the rack. *Better than nothing.*

With agonized slowness, Cyrus dragged himself along the wall to the weapons rack as the sounds of battle rang out overhead. Vara's cry of war washed over him at one point, followed by another body being thrown from the parapet, but he did not see whose; he heard only a man's scream end with the hard thump of a body against the muddy bailey courtyard.

Cyrus crawled to the rack and fumbled for the bow, grasping it in his metal gauntlets with weak and fumbling fingers. "Godsdammit," he muttered through gritted teeth, holding off the pain from overwhelming him only by hard effort. It was like it was creeping up his body, threatening to drag him into the fetal position; he wanted only to curl up into a ball and make it go away. *But it's not going away, not until this is over, and this is not going to be over until I help kill every last one of these bastards.*

Once he had the bow, he needed to crawl only a few feet to reach a full quiver, and once he was there he braced his leg hard, anguish seeming to pump through his very veins as he did so. He thumped the weapon rack with his helm, causing it to rattle, but then the pain mercifully subsided, and he left the damned leg alone. He leaned his head back and readjusted his helm, blinking again to shake off the stupor of the pain, to drag his attention forward.

He was clear of the wagon now, and to his right he could see the slow-burning drawbridge, firelight visible through the timbers as it burned. Smoke pooled above him in the arch of the keep's portcullis under the parapet, gradually drifting out into the sky as though it were running toward the courtyard like water.

Cyrus took a hard breath and slipped off his gauntlets, blinking as he looked across the courtyard. There were three of Amarath's Raiders down here, staring up at the fight upon the parapets, their faces drawn. They were watching intently and apparently displeased, for their lips were tense and turned down, their jaws were tight, and their hands clenched their swords.

They were facing to Cyrus's right, so intent on the parapets that they had apparently not noticed him slowly dragging himself out from behind the wagon to the weapons rack. *Should be aware of everything going on around you, General,* he thought, staring hatefully at Archenous. He plunged his hands into the mud and then rubbed them against one another, trying to eliminate the sweat that felt as though it had puddled on his palms and fingers. He could feel the grit of the dirt as he rubbed it between his digits and pushed it into his palms.

Cyrus took a steadying breath and lifted the longbow sideways across his lap, for it was too tall to shoot upright while sitting. *Just like being back in the Society again, practicing for all occasions.* He drew back the string, the arrow between his fingers. *How long has it been since I've practiced this particular method of shooting?* He looked straight ahead, blinked once more to focus himself, and pointed at the guard on the right. *If I kill Archenous before Vara can, she'll tear me a brand new arse.*

He let fly the arrow. To his annoyance, it did not quite hit where he aimed; it struck low and to the left, burying itself in the neck of the guard on the left rather than squarely in the middle of his face where Cyrus had aimed.

"Shit," he muttered and nocked another arrow. Archenous spun in surprise, clearly caught off guard that one of his protectors had been suddenly felled. The other guard jerked to look as well, and as soon as he had settled into that position, Cyrus let fly his next arrow, correcting for what had happened last time.

This time he hit closer to his mark. The guard was sweeping back around to look for the origin of the arrow that had killed his fellow, and he found it, albeit a little too late, as Cyrus's arrow found his right eye first. The arrow sunk in halfway to the fletchings and the guard did not finish his whirl. He slipped and fell, straight to his back, making a strange gurking noise as Cyrus hurriedly put another arrow on the bow and drew it back.

Archenous Derregnault stared at Cyrus across the courtyard, his head cocked, his dark face twisted in something between rage and confusion. "You?" he asked.

"Still me," Cyrus said, drawing a steady breath and trying not to let the bow shake as he did so, "but probably not for very much longer." He muttered the healing spell under his breath once more and was rewarded with not a damned thing.

Archenous's face wavered, as his gaze moved to the parapets for a beat. A troll roared and a dark elf in armor was hurled into the stone tower behind the Amarath's Raiders' Guildmaster, who stepped aside to let his man fall beside him. "Just as well for you," he said. "I would have taken great glee in impaling you."

"As he's not a woman you professed to love," Vara called from somewhere above, "I doubt you'd get him to turn his back on you long enough to impale him—which is the only way you'd manage it." A troll fell off the edge of the bailey, Longwell's lance in his face, and slammed into the ground on the opposite side of the drawbridge from Cyrus.

"I was always better than you, Vara," Archenous replied, his face darkening further, the scar standing out like a pale line as he watched the parapets. His gaze was moving, shifting as she apparently made her way toward the stairs at a leisurely pace.

"You were never better than me, Archenous," Vara said, and he saw her now, her shining armor slick with red, blue, and green blood as she descended the stairs, Longwell behind her, his spare sword in his hand, and Zarnn a couple paces behind them. "It's why you grew to hate me so much."

"I grew to hate you because you thought you were better than me—than everyone," Archenous said, his hair whipping behind him as he stood framed by the massive door to the inner keep. "It was the same for Trayance Parloure—"

"Do not say his name," Vara snapped as she came to the bottom of the steps and froze there, the entire bailey courtyard between them. "You are not worthy to so much as whisper it, you revolting turncoat. You destroyed an entire guild for your pathetic jealousies—"

"I built one of the big three guilds—" Archenous began.

"YOU STOLE IT!" Vara screamed at him, her sword in hand. "You threw away everything you had—loyalties, friends, love—and stole everything you hold now." She pointed her blade at him. "Do not speak to me of what you built, for I am about to tear it away from you the way you tore everything from me."

"Any minute now, my people will arrive," Archenous said, shaking his head, a soft smile on his lips, "and then you'll see what happens when you go against one of the foremost guilds in the land, Vara—you were better off small with Sanctuary. It's how you started, and it's how you'll die, after all, when the rest of my army gets here—"

The drawbridge exploded into shards of wood and Cyrus cringed away, splinters clinking off his armor as he held up an arm to shield his eyes. When he looked back, an imposing, rocky figure stood framed in the smoking entry, a shadow against the glow of the fire consuming the remains of the drawbridge.

"Knock, knock," Fortin proclaimed, stepping through the smoke to enter the keep.

Cyrus whipped around in time to see Archenous Derregnault's face fall, his eyes as large as a gnome's head. He paled three shades and then straightened, as if determined not to show his disappointment.

"Sorry I'm late," Terian Lepos said, his armor glinting as he stepped in behind Fortin, J'anda's purple staff and Vaste's spear both glowing behind him as they entered. Larana followed, along with a host of others; Zarnn's trolls, Mendicant, Menlos Irontooth and his wolves, some dark elven troops in their distinctive armor. Behind them, he could hear the snort of horses and knew that the Luukessians had arrived in Isselhelm as well. "I had to stop and smear some Amarath's Raiders trash at the portal with my army," the Sovereign of Saekaj said casually.

Archenous fidgeted and backed into the tower door. He looked around at what he faced and then forced a smile. "It would appear that someone has cast a cessation spell over our little battlefield."

"That was me," Vara said, smiling with grim satisfaction as she walked across the bailey toward him, slowly, with final certainty. "You will not run away from me this time, Archenous." She raised her voice. "No one interferes in this battle, do you hear me? This is to be between he and I, to the death."

"The ice princess is going to crush this plaything as though it were a—what are those tiny creatures that play with other tiny creatures?" Fortin asked.

"Cats and mice?" J'anda asked.

"Rock giants and gnomes?" Vaste asked.

"Goblins and—" Mendicant started

"Well, from now on," Fortin said, apparently annoyed by the responses he'd gotten, "it will be ice princesses and dark knight scumthings, that shall be the saying." He looked at them all crossly. "You will say this from now on, when the situation is appropriate." He waited. "GO ON. SAY IT."

J'anda raised an eyebrow. "She's going to play with him like an ice princess with a dark knight scum-thing'?"

Fortin nodded. "Very good." He looked back at Vara, who, along with Archenous, was watching the proceedings rather spellbound, and nodded. "You may go about your play, ice princess."

"Thank you for that, I think," she said. Her shoulders tensed beneath her armor and she assumed a defensive stance as she closed on Archenous, intent on battle.

Archenous thrust out a hand and nothing happened. His face twitched, and then he smiled. "Worth a try," he said by way of explanation.

"Worthy of you, more like," she said and came at him without further ado.

Her sword clashed against his. He blocked her, but barely. He threw his broad blade up in a cross block in front of his face, but it was weak and she pushed it back to hit his breastplate at the collarbone. He'd taken a few steps away from the doors to the middle of the bailey, which was fortunate for him, for he had to dance to the side to avoid being pinned against the tower. The strain of the blow showed on Archenous's face, his cruel eyes furious and casting about for escape.

Vara came at him again and again, and he parried and blocked, losing ground slightly each time, the worry beginning to show on his face. She came at him like a woman possessed—and possessed of a singular mind to cut him to pieces. Cyrus saw no clear strategy in Archenous save to dodge the next blow and the next, and the dark knight seemed to suffer for it as the panic clearly rose within him.

"Even if I—" he said as she struck a blow so hard that the rattle of the swords against one another jarred Cyrus in his very teeth, "—manage to survive, your friends are going to cut me to pieces anyway!"

"No," Fortin rumbled. "Because unlike you, we are not lacking in honor." He sidled over to Cyrus and lowered his voice. "If she dies, I will rip his limbs off and remove his tongue while you resurrect the ice princess to deliver the final blow."

"A kind offer, Fortin," Cyrus said, straining, his leg still aching, his back uncomfortable against the weapon rack behind him, "but I don't think she's likely to lose this particular contest."

"Never underestimate the power of treachery," Fortin said.

"I doubt I can any longer, after what we've been through these last months," Cyrus said.

Vara did not let up in her withering assault, and it pained Cyrus's arms to watch her attack him with seemingly limitless strength while Archenous was battered about like a leaf in a gale. He tried to mount an offense but was forced away from it at every turn, Vara never once letting up in her attacks long enough for him to do anything but block in an increasingly ineffectual manner. It was like watching her pour out years and years of rage through the strength of her arms, beating him down by inches at a time.

"You—you can't win!" Archenous screamed. He sounded to Cyrus like the desperate voice of a man trying to convince himself and perhaps his foe in the bargain.

She struck a nasty blow overhead that he could not adequately defend against, and it once more forced his sword down from the sheer power. This time, though, the tip of her blade found his forehead and scored him from brow to cheek, a long jagged cut. Blood ran down his face and into his left eye. "I disagree," she said. She struck again, this time sideways, and he blocked her barely in time.

"You were never good enough!" he shouted, backing up as quickly as he could, stumbling, trying to blot the blood from his eye. "That's why I couldn't—couldn't stand to be with you—"

"You were never good enough, either," she said, knocking aside his next clumsy parry. "And I was always loathe to tell you, but you were endowed like that old cat they kept at the Holy Brethren in Reikonos, the poor, smallish thing. I truly did love you, to put up with all else plus that. It's a shame you weren't man enough to—"

Archenous's eyes flared, and he dodged to the side and saw his opening. "When I'm done with you, I'm going to find that damned cat and kill it, so just know—" He spun with a high slash, aiming for Vara's neck—

But failed to see that she'd goaded him and was waiting for him to open himself up. She dodged his clumsy, too-forceful attack and he spun past her, his blade catching naught but air. She had hers at the ready, though, and struck forward with a solid stab—

And caught him right in the throat.

Her blade ripped through the front of his neck, leaving it half on, half off; she slid it out like she was carving meat from a succulent pig at dinnertime and was rewarded with a geyser of blood. His jaw worked up and down ineffectually, words trying to come out with no breath—

Fortin slammed a hand against the wall. "HA HA!" He looked down at Cyrus. "First she takes his pride, insults his manhood, and then she rips his throat out! This is why I like the ice princess the best of all of you."

"You know we can hear you, yes?" J'anda called, looking somewhat nonplussed at the rock giant.

"Go destroy some terrible foe's manhood, and then perhaps I will like you best," Fortin replied.

"Give my regards to Trayance, won't you?" Vara asked, staring coldly into Archenous's eyes as he bled, falling to his knees, still gripping his sword weakly as his other hand fumbled for his gushing throat. "On second thought, you are unlikely to end up in the same place, so never mind that." She stared at his hands. "You have had my sword for entirely too long. Allow me to return yours."

With that, she spun and caught him in the back of the neck with a powerful slash that took his head from his shoulders, sending it into the air. Before it even came to rest, she twirled her sword around and drove it, tip first, into the gaping hole where his head had rested only a moment earlier, all the way up to the hilt. "Oh, and another thing—" she said, and Cyrus saw the glow run down her blade and through the crossguard—

Archenous Derregnault exploded, his armor blasting in six different directions. A boot hit the wall to Cyrus's left as he turned his face away from the spectacle. His breastplate landed in the mud a few feet away and stuck there, like a tombstone planted in the ground. Other pieces clanged off the walls of the bailey, and when the air cleared—

Vara stood there, still drenched from top to bottom in gore and blood, but with the ghost of a smile on her lips.

"On second thought," Fortin said into the still quiet of Isselhelm Keep, "*that* is why I like the ice princess best of all of you. That ... was a perfect poem of vicious excellence." He wandered forward into the middle of the mess, the bloody mud, and stooped to pick up Vara's former sword from where it lay. "Are you done with this?" he asked her with greatest deference.

"I am," she said and picked up Archenous Derregnault's ornately carved sword, which appeared to be exactly the same size as the one she'd just returned to him, sliding it easily into her scabbard. "But what use will you have for it? It's a bit small for you to wield, isn't it?"

The blade was practically swallowed up in Fortin's mighty hands. "It is," he agreed, and raised it up to push the blade into his mouth. A scraping sound caused Cyrus to cringe, and he caught Terian and J'anda doing the same only a few feet away, the high pitched screech akin to running a grater over stone. Fortin pulled the sword out of his gaping mouth and examined it; there was a chunk of something at the tip. "But it will make an excellent toothpick."

"Well ... that was truly marvelous," Cyrus grunted, the pain in his leg coming back to him now. He cast the healing spell under his breath as he felt the bones in his leg twist and knit back together. He groaned under his breath, and then stumbled to his feet, bracing against the weapons rack, which rattled as he slid up. "Now ... we need to find Governor Frost and get out of here before anyone else shows up to fight us."

"Do we?" Ryin Ayend croaked from against the keep's wall, blood dried upon his skull, Larana kneeling next to him, her hands glowing still from spell-light. "And what interest do we have in saving the Governor of a Confederation allied against us, I ask?"

"Interesting timing," Cyrus said, hobbling from the phantom pain in his leg, "I wonder why you didn't ask before, when we were stampeding through the streets toward inevitable—"

"And glorious," Fortin added.

"—battle," Cyrus finished.

"Perhaps our own troll pitching me over the battlements jarred the question loose," the druid croaked, mopping up the blood with his sleeve.

"Well, see if you can hold it in a little longer, and perhaps I'll be able to answer your question more fully in Council later tonight," Cyrus said, trying to communicate more with his look than he did with his words. Ryin peered at him suspiciously, but said nothing more. "Now we need to find Frost and—"

"I'm here," came a voice as the gates to the keep cracked open. Guards pushed them ajar and Allyn Frost came marching out, flanked by the same toadies with whom he had surrounded Cyrus at their last meeting. They didn't wear the same sneers this time, though; now they seemed appropriately cowed, clutching their spears very delicately, and pointing them behind them, slung on their shoulders, as if to avoid offending the army within their very gates.

"Good to see you didn't meet your end at the tender mercies of Pretnam Urides's mercenary army," Cyrus said, nodding to the troll corpses and the chunks of Archenous Derregnault that littered the bailey.

"No," Frost said, surveying the mess with a vaguely disgusted look. "We heard them coming through the streets and closed the gates. It would have been impossible to miss them, the savages—"

"Urides sent them," Cyrus said, cutting him off with but a word, "and he's bound to send more when he finds out he's failed." Cyrus took a deep breath. "You need to come with us. Right now."

Frost looked at the assorted forces in his courtyard, frowning. "Well—but—I can take my guard, can't I?"

"No," Cyrus said, peering at him through nearly shut eyes. "I can't take a chance that any of them is a traitor that will turn on my people while I'm off settling this. You'll be under my protection, hidden behind the impregnable walls of Sanctuary if you come with us. You're on your own if not. Make a decision quickly."

Frost opened his mouth, but the indecision went from sputtering to rage to acceptance in a blink as the man calculated his odds and fiddled with the light furs on his back. "Yes, fine," he spat, "I'm much better off with you than without, even that much is apparent to me. But how long will it be until—"

"We'll talk about it later," Cyrus said, crossing over to him and taking hold of the man. "Council—we have a meeting when we return. Mendicant—get our people out of here. We can't stay, lest Urides send Goliath or his own people are drawn after us like lightning to a tall tree." The goblin nodded, and began to cast a spell. He turned to Terian. "Might want to orchestrate your own retreat."

"Way ahead of you there," Terian said with a grin. "We'll make sure the Luukessians get home as well." He whipped a hand through the air at his troops that stood in the bailey behind him. "Come on, you lot, let's clean up this mess." With that, he walked back out through the shattered drawbridge, and Cyrus could see solid ice frozen over the filthy moat.

"Come along, Governor Frost," Cyrus said with a smirk and cast the return spell.

"What?" Frost blinked as Cyrus grabbed him. "What are y—"

But the rest was lost to the energies of magic, as they were swept back to the Tower of the Guildmaster in the crackling frenzy of the spell.

65.

Cyrus and Allyn Frost reappeared in the Tower of the Guildmaster, followed a moment later by Vara, still coated from boot to helm in vile liquids that Cyrus could no longer differentiate. There was crimson, yellow, dark blue, and many others, smearing her all the way to the exposed hanks of her hair that stuck out the sides of her helm.

"You look like you jumped in the trash dump outside Reikonos," Cyrus mumbled after looking her over.

"I don't bloody well care," she said, smiling as she pushed her hand down on the hilt of her sword, touching it in the way he remembered grasping Praelior when he'd first gotten it. "That … was worth every bit of it."

"Indeed?" Allyn Frost asked her with arched eyebrows. "I am glad we could oblige you with your vengeance, whatever your disagreement with that fellow in my bailey, but I find myself somewhat worried about—"

"Stow your worries under your hat," Cyrus said a little nastily, causing Frost to flush and grab for the fur-covered monstrosity that hid his baldness. He clutched at it then yanked his hands away the moment he realized what he was doing, and Cyrus grinned at him. "Come along; we need to talk with our Council."

Cyrus led the way, down the stairs and out of the door. Just as Vara had started to shut it behind her, with Frost between the two of them, the sound of a spell just inside the door gave them pause.

"Is that …?" Cyrus asked, frowning past Frost to look at Vara.

"Just us," Terian said, grabbing the door and pulling it open to reveal Kahlee standing there next to him. "I heard you say 'council meeting,' so of course I came running …"

"I meant the other council," Cyrus said, frowning, "but I suppose this involves you, too, so you might as well come." He looked straight at the Sovereign of Saekaj. "I think the moment has come to combine our efforts."

"Tired of secrecy, eh?" Terian asked with a smirk as they all headed down the stairs. The sound of movement below, in the officer quarters, preceded them, and when they reached that floor Cyrus saw Menlos and Calene threading their way down the steps to the Council Chamber and followed them, reaching it a few seconds after they did.

When he came through the doors, the hearths were lit and the room was near-full, with all but Mendicant and Scuddar in their normal places or about to take them.

"Calene," Cyrus said just as the ranger was about to pull out her seat, "I have need of both Reynard Coulton and Karrin Waterman, both of whom should be here in Sanctuary somewhere."

Calene froze, half bent to sit. "Uhrm ... are they anywhere in particular, or do you need me to search the entire place, from tower to foyer?"

"You'll have to go a floor lower to find Coulton," Cyrus said, "as I had one of our warriors lock him in the dungeon for safekeeping. As for Waterman ..." he shrugged. "Ask Larana. I sent her to get the woman."

"You mean to keep us in the dungeon?" Frost asked in outrage as he stood in the middle of the chamber, between the door and the table, clearly unsure of his place in all this. He fiddled with his furs, which were lighter than the ones he'd worn when last Cyrus had seen him. *Must be his summer ensemble.*

"I mean to keep you safe," Cyrus said, dangerously enough that Frost rubbed his hands against his furs to smooth them again. "Which is more than I can say for what Pretnam Urides means to do with you."

"Well, I—" Frost blinked.

"The dungeons are very comfortable," Cyrus said, waving him off. "I stayed in them myself for months, they're practically like our regular accommodations save for the isolation. Also, we'll be assigning either a rock giant or a troll to watch over you, so you should feel quite secure."

Ryin looked up at this, still grey in the face. "You ... you mean to trust the trolls? After what happened?"

"Zarnn fought by our sides," Vara said, unceremoniously depositing her filthy helm on the table. "He killed three of the traitor trolls himself, with his bare hands. Seemed to take personal offense to their betrayal."

"As do I," Ryin said a little saltily, cradling his still-bloodied head. "Where did they come from?"

Cyrus shook his head. "I should have realized it before, but one of them was an officer of Endeavor named Grunt. I'd met the bastard, but …"

"But we all look alike to you, don't we?" Vaste asked, more than a little taunting.

"You didn't know it was him either, numpty," Vara shot at him.

"It was the beard," Vaste said with a broad shrug of the shoulders. "It was very distracting."

"So …" J'anda said, "… is our battle with Amarath's Raiders at an end? Or merely a middle?"

"I can't say for certain," Vara said, looking down at the miasma of gore on her armor, "but I believe that might have been the end of it. I believe their officers spearheaded the assault on Governor Shite-for-brains's keep—"

"My name is Frost!" Frost shouted.

Vara dismissed him with a wave. "If we did get all of them, or even nearly, they might not be able to muster much in the way of leadership, which means—"

"So long as someone doesn't step in to provide it," Cyrus finished, "that might be another course off our plate."

"Or another needle-quill out of our arses," Vaste said, nodding. "I speak from experience in this matter, having once had my plump, delicious arse filled with—"

"So then what about the matter of Reikonos?" Menlos asked, looking a little flushed still from the battle. The Northman seemed to have taken it personally, and his coloration showed his anger. "What do we do here? Why are they sending these bastards into their own cities, after their own governors? I mean, they're invading their own lands!"

"There's some tension between Reikonos and the districts," Cyrus said, looking at Frost. "And, to be mercilessly frank—"

"I would prefer you be mercilessly Cyrus," Vaste said, "but if you're in the mood for whimsy, I suppose I can call you Frank. Though it's such an old-fashioned name, no one has called their child that in an elf's age—"

"—we've been aiming to exploit that to our advantage," Cyrus said, ignoring the troll. "Frost here says that the Confederation army is made up almost entirely of conscripts from his district as well as those of Governors Coulton and Waterman. If we can remove Pretnam Urides—"

"You mean … kill?" Erith asked, wide-eyed.

"—and the Council of Twelve," Cyrus went on, "then the three of them will call back their armies and withdraw from the Confederation, causing enough chaos that it's unlikely they'll be able to oppose us any longer."

"Leaving us with one problem to deal with," Vara finished.

"Goliath," J'anda said.

"Goliath," Terian agreed.

"Utter lack of intelligent troll beauties within easy traveling distance," Vaste said, shaking his head sadly. He waited for everyone to look at him. "Also, Goliath."

"And how long have you been up to this?" Ryin asked, frowning, leaning on the table. His elbow ran along the wood, leaving flecks of dried blood. "Driving wedges in the Confederation? Making pacts with its governors to split it up?"

"Months and months now," Cyrus said, and a chorus of angry voice was raised a mere moment later. "What? Before you were worried I wasn't doing anything—"

"No," Ryin said with barely concealed fury, "we were worried that you were scheming against the Council, outside the Council, which it turns out you were—"

"Because we had traitors among us!" Cyrus said, flinging a hand out. "Unless you forgot, in the midst of that crack on the head, that it was one of them that did it to you—"

"It did not escape my notice, no," Ryin said, reddening further, "but that doesn't excuse you excluding the Council because you feared traitors within the guild—"

"There could very well be traitors in this room," Terian said, lingering near the hearth behind Longwell's seat, Kahlee at his side. "I have quite a few spies in your ranks—not in the Council, because I don't need them—but spies inherited from the old Sovereign's service—"

"And what is he doing here?" Ryin asked, throwing a hand to

gesture at Terian. "He's not of the Council—"

Terian rolled his eyes. "As if being one of your staunchest allies isn't enough? Geez, Ryin, I was Elder of this guild before you'd even heard the name Sanctuary."

"And you left after betraying our Guildmaster," Ryin said, stiffening in his seat. He looked at Cyrus. "I realize we need the dark elves' help, but—I mean, really, you're taking counsel—or should I say, Council—from him?"

"I take it wherever I can get it, provided it's good counsel," Cyrus said. "For example, Aisling has also been advising us—"

"What the perfunctory hell?" Erith asked, rising to her feet. She pointed a finger at Terian and then J'anda, in turn. "I realize that these loons needed her help for Saekaj, but you? Really?" She seemed particularly blue, a darker hue than usual, and she looked at him with her eyes wide with what appeared to be surprise and disgust. "What are you playing at, Cyrus?"

"I can see you're in the middle of something rather important here," Allyn Frost said, raising a hand. "I'll just, uh—see myself out—"

"See yourself being dissolved in one of Pretnam Urides's fire spells," Cyrus shot back at him, halting Frost's motion cold. "Stand your ass right there until I tell you when you can move."

Frost blinked, insulted. "You can't talk to me like this. Why, I'm—"

"You're the rather amazing dumbass who flaunted his power over me when I stood before you not that long ago," Cyrus said coldly, and the room fell silent around them. "Now your life is in my hands, and I'm giving you a little taste of it in return. Don't fret, though, I plan to make sure you stay safe."

"So that's how it is," Frost said, pawing at his furs.

"Damned right," Terian said mildly. "This is the greatest warrior in Arkaria, right here, and until recently he had an army that would have turned your entire army into a mess like your bailey back at home. Hell, he still might." Terian eyed Cyrus's belt. "Nice hilt, by the way. Does that come with a new sword attached to it, or do the rumorers lie for once?"

Cyrus pulled out Rodanthar. It gleamed in the firelight from the torches and hearths as he waved it in front of him. "I went to grab my sword this morning in Idiarna and this came out." He watched it gleam before his eyes as it held the attention of all in the room. "Any idea how my father's sword got in my scabbard?'"

"Unfortunately, I don't," Terian said with a shake of the head. "But I heard you used it to give my old flame Sareea hell. I do appreciate that favor—"

"Sareea?" Kahlee asked, speaking into the quiet. "That cow?"

"She's with Goliath," Terian said. "One of the few officers they have left now that you've killed Orion and taken Carrack."

"We'll deal with them later," Cyrus said, waving Rodanthar once more before the council. "Anyone else care to speculate how this got into my scabbard? If anyone wants to take credit, I'll give them a warm, sloppy kiss."

"Well, that's reason enough for me to disclaim any knowledge," Vaste said. "But truly, I know nothing about it save for that it looks very pretty."

"It is a very nice sword," J'anda said, eyeing Rodanthar, "and all the better looking for having saved my skin from being peeled from my body this very day."

"This is quite a banner day," Menlos said, eyeing the sword. "Goliath takes one in the chin, Amarath's Raiders get knocked more or less out of the fight, apparently, and this on top of the elves bowing out." He shook his head. "What next?"

"He already told you," Vaste said, annoyed, "killing the Council of Twelve."

"The shite you say!" Menlos said, rising to his feet abruptly. "I thought he was kidding!"

"I didn't say that, exactly, but I'm not kidding," Cyrus said as the door opened and Mendicant came in, Scuddar behind him.

"Calene's right behind us," Mendicant said, taking his seat between Menlos and Ryin, "she had to stop on the stairs with one of her charges."

"Which one?" Cyrus asked, watching Scuddar take his seat next to Vaste, the desert man adjusting his robes as he did so.

"Coulton, I think his name was?" Mendicant's goblin face was screwed up in concentration. "The male one. I think. Did I miss anything?"

"Well," Ryin said before anyone else could speak, "Cyrus admitted he's been conspiring with some of the governors of the Confederation's outlying regions to overthrow the Council of Twelve without our knowledge. So you missed that."

"Kill them," Erith said nervously. "He said kill them."

"No, *you* said kill them," J'anda said. "He danced around it like one of the young men at the Peg House in Termina." When everyone turned to stare at him, he shrugged, tossing his grey hair, unashamed. "I don't care what anyone thinks anymore."

"You've been conspiring to kill the Council of Twelve?" Scuddar asked, his eyes squinted from where he sat.

"I have," Cyrus said, looking right at the man of the desert.

Scuddar leaned back and laced his fingers together over his stomach. "Good."

Ryin blinked. "Good?"

Scuddar shrugged. "The Confederation has never been particularly kind to my people, and it all flows from Reikonos."

Ryin's eyes widened, and he turned to Mendicant. "And what do you say?"

Mendicant looked like he'd been caught with a finger in a hard pincer. "Urhm ... oh. Uh. Well ... all right."

Calene cracked open the door and stepped in, Reynard Coulton huffing behind her and an older woman with steel grey hair following in his wake. She let them both step in and shut the door behind her.

"And what do you think of all this?" Ryin hurled at her as Calene froze as though she'd just been hit in the face.

"Uhh ... what is that?" Calene asked.

"We're killing the Council of Twelve," Ryin said. "What do you think of it?"

Calene frowned thoughtfully. "Better them than us." And she moved to take her seat.

"The hell," Ryin said, sagging against his bloody-covered hands. "Apparently no one is offended that you're scheming rebellion."

"You aren't really offended that he's planning it," Vaste said, goading the druid and causing him to look up with a little fire in his eyes, "you're really just mad he didn't trust you enough to include you."

Ryin opened his mouth to respond but then deflated. "Shouldn't we all be?"

"I don't know," Vaste said, eyes gleaming, "but if you feel like being tossed over a parapet by a troll is bad, you should see what happens when Goliath pins you against a wall while your back is turned. Because that's what nearly happened today, and that's with our plans carefully hidden to all but a few."

"Wait ... so there was scheming going on?" Calene asked, frowning.

"Yes, yes," Vaste said, "pay attention. Honestly, you people are so far behind."

"Perhaps because we were left behind," Ryin snapped, slapping his hand against the table. The sound reverberated in the chamber.

"If you feel betrayed now," Vaste said, barely concealing a smirk, "imagine how you'll feel when you find out Cyrus was the one who killed King Danay!"

Cyrus whipped his head around at the grinning troll as the chamber exploded once more.

"I should have known," Erith said, burying her face in her hands.

"—didn't need to do that," J'anda said to Vaste.

"It was so fun, though!" Vaste replied to the enchanter.

"God of Winter!" Menlos said in a thundering voice.

"I knew it!" Ryin said, pointing a finger right at Cyrus. "I damned well knew—"

"You don't know a damned thing, come off it," Vaste wheeled on Ryin.

"I miss this," Terian said to Kahlee with a deep sigh of regret. "Meetings like this, with all the jests and emotions flying across the table—"

"Excuse me," Karrin Waterman said, clumped into a knot with her fellow governors. "If I might—"

Cyrus slammed a hand against the table and quieted them all, rattling Vara's helm from the force of his blow. His own helm still sat atop his head because there were strangers in the room. "We have guests," he said.

"Sorry to interrupt what sounds like a family quarrel," Waterman said, the wrinkles beneath her eyes creasing as she spoke, "but I'm afraid I'm not sure exactly what's going on here, or what's to happen. Your, ahh, druid abducted me without giving me much in the way of context for our current ... situation."

"We're going to kill the Council of Twelve for you," Vaste said cheerily. "And you're going to withdraw from the Confederation."

Waterman pursed her lips, her face a steely mask. "And why would I do this? I mean, I can see the obvious benefit to you, but we're a key district of the Confederation. Why would I embroil myself in your conflict?"

"Because Urides is going to kill you if you don't dance to his tune, Karrin," Frost said, adjusting his hat.

"He leaned on me," Coulton said, "and threatened—well, he had no end of threats. We're going to lose everything, Karrin." He licked his lips. "Hang together on this or else he'll execute us one by one, just like Bentsen, Smoot, and Hawthorne."

Despite Frost and Coulton's words, Karrin Waterman looked utterly unflappable. "What you're proposing is preposterous."

"Without Urides and his puppet council," Coulton said, "we can do as we damned well please, for who's to stop us?"

Waterman took her time delivering a very great sigh. "Yes, Coulton, of course, but ... you fool, it can't be done." She looked right at Cyrus. "I'm sorry, but killing Pretnam Urides is—despite your obviously formidable reputation—well, it's impossible, even for you."

"Why?" Cyrus asked, putting his gauntleted hands flat on the table.

"Because Pretnam Urides is surely shut tightly up in the Citadel at the moment," Waterman said, watching him shrewdly, "where none but an army can reach him, and while I'm certain your very good friends the dark elves and the folk of Emerald Fields are quite strong, you'll need to fight your way through the streets of Reikonos while our army surges in after you in order to reach him." She folded her arms in front of her. "You'd be killed in the process. Or would you?" She raised an eyebrow at him.

"What does that even mean?" Coulton asked, clearly flabbergasted. "If he has to go through all that, clearly he'll be killed, I don't know what you're thinking—don't know what I was thinking, either ..."

Gods, Cyrus thought, his mouth going dry as he realized it at last. *She's right. Without Curatio ...*

"We can make it into the Citadel without stepping foot in Reikonos," Mendicant said. "We'll just use the portal that empties right into the Citadel's basement." He received the stares of everyone in the room. "The one that leads to the higher realms?"

"Yes, we know which one you're talking about, Mendicant," Cyrus said patiently, "but unfortunately, much like the portal in Saekaj, we can't access it now that Curatio is gone. No one knows the spell."

"We've got that portal working, actually," Terian said. "The elves helped us crack it. Turns out the spells are written in the runes on the portal."

"Still," Vara said, "unless one of us is an expert in ancient runes and would like to go and read it themselves—after crossing through Reikonos, which I assume is under heavy guard at all gates and the portal—that's not very helpful."

"I know the spell," Mendicant said simply.

Silence reigned. "You … what?" Ryin asked.

"I know the spell to take us into the basement of the Citadel," Mendicant said, nodding. "Larana does as well. We found it in a book in the library while studying."

Cyrus frowned. "We have a library?"

Vara took a deep breath, folding her hands in front of her calmly. "I will leave that alone, for I feel I have destroyed enough men this day."

"If Mendicant can get us into the Citadel," Cyrus said, "you'd better be ready to destroy a few more." He stared right at the goblin. "Do you truly know the spell?"

Mendicant licked his green, scaly lips. "I do. I've tried it, it works. I believe I also know the spell Curatio used to open the door to the entry hallway, though I didn't test that one—"

Cyrus rose and clapped his hands together like thunder. "What can we expect once we're inside?" He directed this question to Waterman, who had watched the entire exchange with steely resolve, while Frost and Coulton stood slack-jawed.

"The Citadel is staffed with a full complement of guards, including wizards, druids, healers and enchanters, trained to work in unison to halt any unexpected advance." She stood looking at them primly. "They will not, however, be prepared for an army suddenly showing up in their midst." She raised an eyebrow. "A larger question I would ask, though, were I you—how do you anticipate this turning out once you've done it?"

"Well, we'll stand over the carcass of Urides, look down into his dead eyes, and bellow, 'HA HA HA' at the top of our lungs," Vaste said. "That will probably take at least an hour. Maybe three."

"Once you're done," Waterman said, not letting up from staring at Cyrus, "you'll have killed the ruling council of Reikonos. If you're aiming to make yourself less of an enemy of the Confederation, this is not the best way to go about it."

"Urides and the Council of Twelve have been killing the district governors," Cyrus said, staring right back at her.

"Allegedly," Waterman said.

"Suppose I just let this go on, then," Cyrus said, folding his own arms. "How long do you reckon it'll be before he comes for you? Because he'll be after Frost and Coulton for sure now that they've betrayed him." Cyrus leaned on the table. "Do you suppose he's going to let that last governor slip through his fingers? Or do you think he'll just rid himself of you out of pure expediency?"

Waterman inclined her head. "You make an excellent point."

"After the Council is dead," Cyrus said, staring back at her evenly, "you will make clear what Urides was doing and enthusiastically proclaim your support for our very righteous removal of his assassinating arse along with the rest of the Council of Twelve."

Waterman, wisely, did not question this. Coulton, however, did. "What if we don't?"

"Then you'll be assassinated by us shortly thereafter, thus unable to enjoy the favor we did for you by removing Urides," Vaste said. Ryin seemed to turn purple at this, but the troll shrugged. "What? We killed Danay, we're about to kill Urides and his clowns—this is the moment when you choose to get picky?"

"I might have been picky much sooner if informed all this was occurring," Ryin said, burying his face in his hands.

"Another reason we didn't tell you," Vaste said.

Ryin's wide, angry eye glared out from between his fingers, but he said nothing.

"When will you do it?" Waterman asked.

"Right now," Cyrus said, standing up. "We have no time to waste; Urides knows he's been foiled, and for all we know, he's preparing to move to his very own super secret retreat elsewhere in Arkaria."

"You mean to invade the Citadel right now?" Erith asked, once again flushed. "Tonight? After—after all that we've already been through today?"

"I don't just mean to go tonight," Cyrus said, "I mean to go this very minute, with whatever we have left." He looked to Vara. "Check the Tower, make sure the horizon is clear, and then rejoin us here." He looked at Scuddar. "I take it the wall is secure?" The desert man nodded. "J'anda, Vaste, Vara, take the governors down to the dungeon and make sure they're secure." The enchanter nodded. Terian, Ryin, Longwell, go gather fifteen people each—people you trust," Cyrus continued. "Rangers, warriors, spellcasters. Get me the most skilled of your people, and have them outside the Council Chambers in fifteen minutes." He looked over the assemblage in front of him. "No one leaves, no one moves except those six people I just named … the rest of you—"

"Sit here and stare at each other until we get back," Vaste said, standing up with the rest of them. "Let the resentments begin to fester!"

"No," Cyrus said, looking around at them, "the rest of us are going to leave now, just to be sure we can get into the Citadel. I'll send Mendicant back for you once we're sure the spell works." He leaned hard on the wooden table. "Make sure you choose the toughest people, the ones who won't question, the ones who harbor no doubts …" He smiled grimly. "Because tonight we're going to guarantee that the biggest army pointed at us right now is wiped off the board for good." He looked over the Council. "And then we're going to figure out how to take the fight to Goliath."

66.

Cyrus stood in the wide-open chamber with only a handful of others. Kahlee and Terian huddled together, speaking quietly, the paladin smiling beneath the thin slit of Alaric's old helm. *He looks ... happy with her*, Cyrus thought. *I didn't think I'd ever see him like that, especially after Luukessia.*

Cyrus turned his head and saw Menlos and Erith huddled similarly. He was starting to grow accustomed to seeing the Northman without his wolves, but the two of them were standing at a distance from the portal, examining the broad chamber of the room they stood in, which was large enough to hold an army—and had, before, when Sanctuary had come with an expedition to see the Realm of Life.

Cyrus turned to the portal, which glowed faintly, its center not empty like the ones in fields of Arkaria, but filled with gently crackling energy.

"It is a strange thing, is it not?" Scuddar asked, standing only a few feet from Cyrus, Calene nearby. Mendicant had already returned to Sanctuary to bring the rest of their force.

"What's that?" Cyrus asked, staring into Scuddar's yellow eyes, which were glowing almost as much as the portal. They were quite easy to transfix on.

"The portal," Scuddar said, his eyes crinkling in amusement, though his mouth was not visible beneath the cowl, which wrapped the lower part of his face. "Magical artifacts, tying the entire land together from north of Fertiss to below the Inculta Desert, from Huern to the Emerald Coast."

"Plus to the realms of the gods," Calene said, inclining her head toward the portal behind them. "Can't forget them, after all." She lowered her voice to a mutter. "Not that they'd let you, sending avatars and assassins to kill you and your dear ones and whatnot."

Cyrus frowned, something suddenly occurring to him. "Scuddar, you're from the Inculta Desert—"

"That's a bit obvious, isn't it?" Calene asked quietly.

"—Have you ever been to the Bandit Lands south of there?" Cyrus asked, frowning and ignoring the ranger.

Scuddar's eyebrows crept high on his head. "A very few times, hunting those bandits that came north and struck at our settlements. Our ways demand retribution, you see. Once attacked, desert men cannot stop until vengeance has been satisfied."

"Sounds fun," Cyrus said. "How far down there have you been?"

Scuddar's face went almost blank. "As far as the jungle goes, and a little farther."

Cyrus blinked. "Have you ever seen ... do you know anything about a portal beyond the last one on the beach—"

"Yes," Scuddar cut him off, staring at him unblinking. "You speak of the old city—Zanbellish, it was called." He drew a slow breath, and Cyrus could hear it in the quiet of the chamber. "The last city of the ancients."

"I'll need to know everything you can tell me about it when we get back," Cyrus said.

"Why?" Calene asked, still frowning.

"Because that's where Goliath is hiding," Cyrus said.

"I thought they had their old guildhall back here up and running again?" she asked. "That the Council of Twelve let them back in for going after your arse?"

Cyrus thought about it for a moment before replying. "It's entirely possible, but they've got something going on at this ... Zanbellish place as well. It's where they were hiding for all these years between homes." Cyrus squeezed his gauntlet shut and it creaked almost imperceptibly at his pressure. "I mean to find them, and give them some regrets."

"Invading the home of a superior force," Calene said, "well, that's one way to do it, I suppose."

"It's the only way we've ever done it," Cyrus said as the light of the portal flared as a teleportation spell flashed, and his small army appeared. "All right ..." he said, looking them over. They were all here, now, and Vara nodded at him from the front rank. "... Let's go do this."

67.

"It's so good to be here again with you lot," Terian said as they stood upon the balcony before the blank wall that would lead into the atrium of the Citadel. The stones themselves glowed with a faint blue light, without a single torch to provide its own. "Wish I could have brought my other friends, too—"

"I must say I'm amazed you have any friends at all," Vara said lightly.

"Is everyone ready?" Cyrus asked, Mendicant beside him next to the wall. They were only waiting now for his word, and the goblin would open the doors into the atrium so that they could enter the Citadel proper. Cyrus had been through before on several occasions. "There will be guards behind this wall, so prepare yourselves."

"Last time there weren't," Vaste chirped.

"Last time Goliath had killed their way to the top before we got here," Cyrus said. "I don't anticipate that this time."

"You should be prepared for all possibilities," Vaste said.

"I am," Cyrus said, "which reminds me, should we be rushed by a herd of goats when this door opens, I'll expect you to use your unique expertise to deal with it."

"Hey!" Vaste said, and threw a thumb behind him. "That sounds like a job for Zarnn."

Cyrus looked back and saw Zarnn frowning. "Zarnn not like goats. Smell funny, make squealing noises whenever trolls walk past."

"There's a good reason for that," Vaste mumbled.

Cyrus cast an eye over his force. There were only about fifty of them, but he knew almost all of them. Every officer was present, plus Terian and his wife. Zarnn was there, as was Larana, lurking quietly near the front of the small army. Cyrus gave her a nod and she blushed, looking down at her feet immediately. A moment later, her eyes came back up once more, checking to see if he was still looking. Cyrus glanced away intentionally. "Ready, Mendicant?"

"Ready," the goblin whispered, as though they could be heard through the solid wall. "Are you?"

"Open the door," Cyrus said, clutching Rodanthar in one hand and leaving the other up, palm out. "Let's find out."

Runes flashed along the wall in an ovoid pattern that reminded Cyrus of a portal, and the wall opened. Two guards were waiting in armor, halberds before them. They did not even turn at the noiseless opening of the wall behind them. Cyrus shrugged and cast a bolt of lightning that lanced from his palm to strike one, then the other, crackling through the air as it killed them both. They clanked to the ground, smoking beneath their armor.

"I'm ready!" Vaste called quietly, clearly going for humor but trying not to be too loud about it. "Where are all of our vicious, horrible enemies? Where's the army to stand in opposition to us?"

Cyrus cast an eye toward the entrance to the Citadel. The double doors were shut and barred with a long beam of heavy steel. He strode across the atrium and stared at the doors. "Is it possible they put their entire guard force outside? In the streets between here and the portal?"

"Why wouldn't they?" Terian asked. "It's not as though they have any idea there's a back door to this place." He swept an arm in a wide circle. "They've probably got archers on every rooftop, too, in case we try an assault from the air, maybe even guards with Falcon's Essence patrolling the skies." His grin broadened. "This is going to come as quite the shock, I imagine."

"It already did, at least to some of them," Vara said, stepping over the smoking corpses of the guards Cyrus had struck with lightning. She brushed past both of them en route to the stairs that ringed the circular building. "Come on, you loafers. Let's be about this business and get it done."

Cyrus fell in behind her and they started up the steps. They climbed floor after floor, passing doors that opened into office areas, complete with desks, chairs. The torches and hearths were dimmed for the night, coals lighting the rooms. Cyrus stuck his head into every one as they passed, not wanting to be caught unawares if one was hiding a guard force that could flank them after they passed, but there was nothing but silence in each of them.

"Clearly no one here works late," Ryin said, pacing along behind Cyrus a few steps. "Appalling work ethic."

"Or more likely," Vara said, "they cleared the entire Citadel in order to place the guard and guarantee security for the council."

"Which begs the question," Terian said, frowning, "where are they? I mean, we've been here before, and the stairs end at the main Council Chambers, the ones where they deal with public debate and inquiry, and I doubt they're all just sitting there, waiting to render judgment on us as we enter."

"There are other floors above that," Mendicant said, sniffing as he hurried along, low to the ground, on all fours. "The staircase stops, but resumes behind the council desks and goes to the upper floors where the Council of Twelve keeps their quarters and private meeting rooms."

"Well, that's fascinating," Terian said. "What's more fascinating is—how do you know that?"

"It was in the same book that contained the spell for the portal," Mendicant said.

Terian frowned. "What book was this? *A Visitors' Guide to the Secrets of the Citadel?*"

"I doubt it," Mendicant said, shaking his head. "It was very old, with hand-drawn maps. And the council chambers don't look anything like what we saw when last we were here with Lord Soulmender."

It was Cyrus's turn to frown. "You were here with *me*. I was leading that expedition."

"Ego," Vara whispered.

"But without Curatio, we wouldn't have been there at all," Terian said darkly. He huffed slightly as they passed another room, which Cyrus checked and found empty. "Gods, this tower is maddeningly huge. What a shame the Guildmaster of Requiem didn't just let it get destroyed when the ancients fell; maybe the Council of Twelve would have built something with fewer stairs."

"And likely something less vulnerable to our current attack," Kahlee said, very sweetly.

"An excellent point," Vara said. "Clearly, this woman has all the reason in your marriage."

"I hear that's a common thing among the married," Kahlee replied.

"I couldn't agree more," Vara said.

"Why don't you just marry each other, then?" Terian said with a roll of his eyes. "Then you could both be 'reasonable' together and cease inflicting it on the rest of us."

They passed the next few floors in silence. Gradually, Cyrus became aware of a sound behind them not unlike the snorting of a pig. He turned around and looked back, catching Vaste with his hands on his knees. When he saw Cyrus looking at him, he said, "It was Zarnn."

"Not Zarnn!" Zarnn called from a little ways back. He was taking the stairs in stride. "Zarnn run around lawn every day, climb many stairs, not huffing and puffing over this."

"Oh, fine, it's me," Vaste said, standing back up straight. "I do stairs every day, too, it's just I don't have to do them in quite this hurry most of the time. Clearly I need to have assassinations in mind when I climb back up to the officers' quarters after dinner, so I can run up them instead of just leisurely making my way up."

"Don't get lazy on us now, Vaste," Cyrus said, "we've only got about ten floors to go." He poked his head into the next room on his left and saw display cases lining the walls, and a long empty one in the middle of the room.

"Hey, is that where—" Terian began.

Cyrus looked out the wide window built into the stairwell to his right, big enough that someone small could squeeze through. "I believe it is. Kind of surprised they've kept it as it is. I mean, Amnis was stolen … what? Six years ago now?"

"It's not as if they have any other godly weapons to put in its place," J'anda said, huffing along, his staff shedding purple light faintly in the hallway.

"We didn't think the dark elves had any other godly weapons, either," Cyrus said, staring at the enchanter's weapon, "but then you showed up with that one."

"Yes, but it's hardly as well known as Amnis, Ventus, Torris, Terrenus, Letum or Ferocis, is it?" the enchanter asked with his usual enigmatic smile. "No one even knows what it is, in fact, save for a very few. And that is its strength, to walk unknown." He sighed, moving quickly up the stairs without complaint. "In fact, its aid is the only reason I can even join you on these endeavors anymore. Without it, I'm afraid I would be reduced to walking a few feet and needing a break, like Vaste."

"Oh, rub it in, why don't you?" the troll wheezed from behind them. "Apparently I need a godly weapon, too."

They climbed the next few floors in silence, reaching the main Council Chamber to find it empty, though they could see that the old wooden furniture that had been destroyed when last they'd been here had been replaced with new, carved very finely in the elven style.

"I guess we know what the Council of Twelve did with those millions of gold pieces we gave back to them after the war," Vaste said, staring at the new wooden furnishings, the rails and seats throughout the room beautifully carved, visible under the faint glow of the tower's stones.

"Honestly, that was probably only a million of it," Vara said, giving it a quick glance. "Elven craftsmen are so proficient that it doesn't take them nearly as long as you'd think to do something of this sort."

"Mendicant, where is this—" Cyrus began, but the goblin scampered ahead, through the rail that separated the Council of Twelve's long wooden desk from the gallery where the spectators sat. He rushed past and suddenly Cyrus saw a door hidden against the wall that he had not noticed before. It was paneled in the same style as the wooden backing, though more obvious now, somehow, since he was looking for it. The goblin pushed on it and it opened without a sound.

"And here we go," Cyrus said, charging through first. What he found on the other side was more of the same: a narrower staircase than the first, threading around the back of the council room in a tight spiral to the top of the dome that crowned the Citadel.

A full orbit later he found another of the ubiquitous doors that led to the interior of the Citadel. This one did not open into one large room but rather a small area centered around double doors that were presently open. Beyond he could see a long table with twelve chairs headed by a large one at the end, twin hearths on either side of the room.

Vara frowned as she looked in but shook it off as they continued to climb up the stairs another floor. This time the door opened into a long hallway that looked vaguely familiar. Cyrus paused at its entry and counted the doors before him; there were eleven, with the last being directly ahead and five others on each side.

"This is ..." Vaste muttered quietly, peering down the hall. "Does this ..."

"This looks like the officer quarters at Sanctuary," Terian said, staring in, his brow furrowed. "And the floor below ... it was like ..."

"The Council Chambers," Vara said, frowning.

"This will be the Council of Twelve's living space, then," Cyrus said. His eyes followed the staircase. "And if the pattern holds, then—"

"Then someone totally copied someone else here," Vaste said.

"It would explain why a book in our, uh, library," he glanced down at Mendicant, "has the layout for the Citadel in its pages, I suppose."

"I never noticed the similarities in design on the maps," Mendicant said, staring down the hall, "but truly, seeing it like this ... the resemblance is remarkable."

"Well, we find it an efficient enough layout, don't we?" Vara asked, shaking her head. "Shall we split and do this, or strike first at the council members and then go on to the top floor?"

"Split," Cyrus said, his voice croaking slightly. "Four to five people per door. Kick them down when—"

"Wait," Mendicant said, and his hand glowed orange. "The doors will all be unlocked now."

"Well, that's a handy spell," Vara said, frowning down at him. "Can you use that anywhere?"

He shook his head sadly. "Only upon buildings constructed by the ancients. They made their designs with magic and—"

"We'll talk about it later," Cyrus said, nodding to Terian. "You want Urides or the chaff?"

"I'll supervise down here, make sure it gets done right," Terian said, his axe in hand. "You take Urides; you've got more personal business to settle with him, I suspect."

"True enough," Cyrus said, and started up the stairs. Vara followed him immediately, and he beckoned for J'anda and Vaste. "Also—"

"I'm coming with you," Larana said, plunging ahead, scooting around Vaste and J'anda and ensconcing herself in the middle of their party before Cyrus could protest. She kept climbing, and he was forced to hurry to keep ahead of her.

"Thirty seconds," Cyrus hissed back down the stairs, trusting that one of the elves who had come with them would make the necessary announcement to the war party.

"I don't think we're going to have thirty seconds," Vara said, and her eyes widened as she heard a thump below as someone opened a door loudly. "I think we're going to need to do this immediately."

Shouts and cries echoed through the stairs and Cyrus pounded his way up the last few steps to a door set squarely in the middle of the staircase. He reached for the handle and it opened with a turn. He plunged inside and found himself in a narrow stairway, exactly like the one in the Tower of the Guildmaster.

"Curious," Vaste said as Cyrus ran up the stairs into a room with balconies at each of the four compass points, a small outgrowth at the top of the immense Citadel, barely a wart upon its apex.

There was a bed in roughly the same spot as in his own quarters, and someone was emerging from it, clad in a robe, a staff in hand. Pretnam Urides did not look like himself without his wire-framed spectacles, although there was a curious spot on either side of his nose where they normally rested.

The walls glowed blue and the hearth blazed, and the head of the Council of Twelve stood looking at them furiously, leaning on his staff, his own eyes afire like the hearth. "How did you get in here?"

"We invaded your city and destroyed your army," Cyrus replied with a smug smile.

"I doubt that very much," Urides said with contempt, and his nostrils flared as he took a deep breath. "But if it's so, I'm sorry to tell you: your journey here has been fruitless."

"Oh, I don't think so," Cyrus said, smirking. He listened for just a moment, heard the screaming below. "We're killing your council even now, and you—well, you're just standing here …"

Urides did not smile; in fact his lips turned even farther downward. "You don't think I'm defenseless against heretics, do you?" And he extended his staff so quickly that Cyrus doubted he could have countered it even with Rodanthar. From its tip came a burst of pure wizard flame, aimed right at Vaste, and from his other hand, druid lightning raced toward Cyrus without so much as a word spoken or a second of warning.

68.

Cyrus caught the lightning on Rodanthar unintentionally; it arced toward his blade and hit the metal, crackling against the surface and dispersing harmlessly as Urides looked on, the lightning flashing back in his eyes.

The fire Urides cast, however, shot toward Vaste like dragon flame, the helpless troll staring openmouthed at it—

A blast of water like a torrential flood met it, fountaining from Larana's hand and dissolving into a burst of steam that billowed around them like smoke. Cyrus saw another glow from her and the sound ceased, both water and fire. "Cessation spell is up!" she shouted, louder than he'd ever heard her speak.

"I should have done that first," Cyrus muttered as the last of the lightning crackled away to silence on Rodanthar. "Who knew that the head of the Commonwealth of Arcanists was also secretly a heretic?"

"My faith in the Leagues is at an all-time low, I think," Vaste shouted through the hissing steam, "and I'm including in this the fact that they booted me from training for being a troll."

"Their hypocrisy does suddenly seem rather blatant," J'anda said, inching toward Cyrus, his staff before him, the purple glow lighting the steam that obscured their view. "It seems very 'It is for me, not thee' of them. Very superi—"

The clash of metal upon metal drew Cyrus's attention, and he saw J'anda holding up his staff as Urides slammed his own down upon it with tooth-rattling strength. "It is not for you," Urides hissed, much like the steam, "for you are trash. Worthless—"

"You didn't feel that way about us when we were saving your Confederation from the dark elves," Cyrus said, moving to attack him.

Urides took a few steps back and vanished into the cloud.

"I didn't say 'useless,'" Urides called from somewhere within the cloud. "You certainly had your uses. I said worthless, for you have lost any value you once had."

"Stick close together," Cyrus said in a low voice and watched Vaste and Larana draw nearer, Vara circling around behind them to take the left flank opposite him. J'anda moved to the middle, clutching his staff before him, clearly ready to use it to physically attack Urides. "When we see him, we swarm."

"How like a pack of wolves you have become," Urides called. "Seeking any vulnerability in larger, stronger prey."

"You were the one trying to make us prey," Cyrus said.

"You will find no easy prey here," Urides said smugly, almost gloating, from within the white cloud that engulfed the quarters. "I can practically hear your co-conspirators dying below."

"You're awfully confident for a man who's outnumbered five to one," Cyrus said, peering into the shadowy mist around them. The voice of Urides was echoing off the walls, and it was impossible to tell where he was. The humidity of the steam flowed into Cyrus with every breath, hot and burning, filling his chest with muted fire, the air thick like that of a place in the Northlands he had once been where they poured cold water over rocks warmed by fire, or a valley he'd visited there that smoked from the earth itself.

"I do not find your odds compelling," Urides said, and he swept in from the side in a blur of speed, his staff smashing against Vara's helm, knocking it aside and drawing blood, sending her sprawling before he faded back into the mist, his staff twirling before him.

"What was it you were saying about godly weapons earlier?" J'anda muttered, stepping out to take Vara's place. Cyrus looked at her wide-eyed, but frozen in place, knowing that to step out of his position was to invite attack against this flank. *Urides will sweep through Larana and Vaste on this side the moment I'm out of the way; the cessation spell will drop and he'll blast us with fire before we can even figure out where he's coming from ...*

J'anda nudged Vara with the end of his staff and she stirred, moaning, blood trickling down from the side of her head and soiling her golden hair. "She'll be all right."

"She'll die," Urides said in a taunting voice. "You all will perish, one by one."

Cyrus's eyes darted around the mist. Cries and screaming were still audible below, echoing from the stairs. *They must all be heretics, and likely good fighters as well. I suppose it would have been too much to hope for that this would be an easy matter of assassination—as though there's ever an easy kill. Should we all make it out of this okay, I think I'll be grateful that they put up a fight. It'll make it easier for me to square with myself about coming to kill these people in their beds.*

Urides dashed out of the steam and struck, slapping the end of his staff against J'anda's hand. The enchanter gasped in pain as Cyrus darted forward to join the attack, but Urides was too quick; he brought the other end of the staff around in a blur and J'anda could not counter it. The staff struck him in the head, a hard whack in the temple that sprayed a line of blood that spattered Cyrus's breastplate as he charged after Urides.

I have to take him now—I can't let him slip away. Vaste and Larana are easy prey for him in this, without the benefit of a godly weapon. He charged after the leader of the Council of Twelve, who grinned at him through the white mist, fading into shadow, looking less and less clear with every step backward, even as Cyrus plunged ahead.

"Do you know what they called this staff?" Urides asked, smiling with satisfaction as Cyrus charged at him, Rodanthar held in front of him. "Philos, the Burden of Knowledge. Care to guess who held it first?"

Cyrus struck out at Urides with a high overhand strike. *He can't be that good of a fighter. He's an old man, and I'm bound to be quicker—*

Urides lashed Cyrus across the knuckles as he stepped out of the way of his attack. The blow rattled Cyrus's gauntlet, even through the padding, but Cyrus retained his hold as Urides stepped away. "If you guessed Eruditia," Urides went on, lecturing like some teacher at the Society of Arms, "you would have it right. You, being a fool, though, probably guessed wrong."

"I heard you were a General once upon a time," Cyrus said, pulling Rodanthar back into a defensive guard even as he pursued Urides into the fog. "That you led men in battle."

"Oh, yes," Urides said, eyeing him through the mist between them. "In fact, I commanded your father, did you know that? I know that sword well."

"I did know that," Cyrus said as Urides sidestepped, bringing them back around as Cyrus chased after him. "I heard you were the one responsible for the near-defeat at Dismal Swamp, in fact."

"Dismal Swamp was a victory," Urides grinned, "thanks to your father's noble sacrifice. Why, if he hadn't killed that troll shaman, it might have lost us everything. Shame he had to die there, but it was a price well paid. Even better when it drew out your mother, in her rage and grief, to lead our forces to victory with her at their head. Two Davidons won us that war, and now, years later, another spared us from full wrath of Yartraak. Why, your family has been indispensable so far—or at least, your weapons have." His eyes flashed. "I'd thank you, but obviously trying to behead us now rather cancels out past good deeds."

"Our service to the Confederation never seemed to carry much weight with you before," Cyrus said, slashing down. Urides blocked him, sending his sword off to the side as the leader of the Council of Twelve stepped sideways again, his staff clutched before him. "It certainly didn't stop you from declaring two of us heretics."

"But you are a heretic," Urides said with a gleam in his eyes. "Just as your mother was before you. Heretics and heroes—it's a fine line."

"You're a heretic," Cyrus said, slashing at him but missing entirely as Urides stepped back once more, as quickly as Cyrus could advance.

"I am not, in fact," Urides said with a cackle. "Do you know what makes you a heretic?" His smile broadened. "The fact that I say so. Nothing more, nothing less."

"Then I guess when I kill you, I will be a heretic no longer," Cyrus muttered.

"You can't kill me, fool," Urides said with a laugh. "You can't even lay a hand on me with everything you have. You will fail, you will die, and then your little bride—the last hope of the idiot elves—will follow, and so will your friends, for you have no idea what you face with me." He grinned maliciously. "You've been practicing these magics for a year; I've been practicing them for a lifetime. A very long lifetime, in fact. I have forgotten more about single combat than even you know, Davidon."

"Then why haven't I ever seen you fight?" Cyrus slipped forward, dodging around a chest, and came at Urides with a leading strike, a stabbing lunge pointed right at the old man's heart. It struck true, crashing into the man's ribs—

And stopped cleanly, shock reverberating back up the hilt to Cyrus as Urides grunted, his smile widening as he locked eyes with Cyrus.

"Because only a true fool like you would announce to everyone that he had a godly weapon," Urides said, and brought the end of Philos around so quickly that Cyrus did not see it coming until it had knocked the helm cleanly off his head. There was a flash behind his eyes, and pain at his left eyebrow, shocking and agonizing, and Cyrus hit his knees without realizing he had even lost his feet. The sound of his greaves rattling as his knees impacted the ground was a dim in his ears, barely audible over the rushing of blood.

"And because no one who ever challenged me has lived to tell it, Cyrus Davidon," Pretnam Urides said, looking down at him as he raised high his staff. "Neither will you." The blow was sure to kill him, Cyrus knew, and yet there was nothing he could do to stop it as it began to descend—

69.

A soft glow lit the mist, orange, like a hearth in the distance, as Cyrus watched Urides bring down the staff to kill him. It was a certain thing. Rodanthar hung limply in his fingers, and he could barely see. His left eye was sheerest agony, pure pain, and he could not see out of it at all. *Is this how it was for Alaric …?* he wondered dimly, the thoughts coming slowly as the staff came down.

The room smelled of humidity, the sweat and stink somehow more potent for the thick air, and Cyrus could nearly taste it upon the back of his tongue. He saw the veins jutting from Urides's forehead, the smile of self-satisfaction as he brought down the killing blow, lit by the orange glow behind him, quartal chainmail peeking out from where Cyrus had rent open his robes.

The glow grew brighter as Urides's staff came closer. Its end came to a severe point, the force of a godly weapon tightly bound in a small area, certain to dash Cyrus's brains out the side of his head when it struck true. And it would strike true, for only Rodanthar could halt its sweep now, and the sword was nearly upon the ground. Cyrus's fingers clung numbly to it, but it was dangerously close to falling out of his hand altogether.

The blaze of orange grew in the light behind Urides until he was all-consumed in shadow and mist, like a dragon had loosed its breath behind him. *But there are no dragons in Reikonos*, Cyrus thought, blinking. *Not—*

Urides's hand slowed, jerking the staff's end away from its intended path. His eyes widened in pain, magnified as though he had his lenses on once more, and he convulsed, looking as though lightning had hit him squarely in the back. His lips went from the cruel smile to agonized fury in less than a second, and Cyrus was reminded of seeing a soldier stabbed in the back by Longwell's lance. The pain on Urides's face was writ large, and the glow increased in brightness until—

Flame burst out of Urides's chest in a tight circle, concentrated, and flared between the links of the chainmail as it burned the heart out of him. Urides jerked like someone had taken hold of his strings and was yanking them. He tried to speak, to cry out, but smoke streamed out of his mouth and a smell like burning meat filled the air. Cyrus rolled aside, falling to his back, unable to get his balance as the flames burning through the chest of Pretnam Urides raged hotter and grew wider, enveloping his wide paunch and cutting him in half with fire.

"So Dismal Swamp was your doing?" Vaste asked, stepping out of the mist to Urides's left as the fire continued to flare from behind the wizard. Urides's head turned, jerkily, to look at the troll, eyes nearly uncomprehending. "Then I owe you this."

Vaste plunged the spear-tip of his staff into Urides's jaw and pushed. The wizard's legs fell below him, severed from the top of his chest by the fire spell that had consumed him whole from breastbone to groin, the quartal chainmail lingering behind like a meatless skeleton as the flame stopped, dissipating to reveal—

Larana standing some five feet behind him, her face impressively red, lip quivering, eyes welling up, her hands thrust out with smoke pouring off them. She said nothing, but the way she looked at Urides's remains, which were split between his legs fallen to the floor and his head and shoulders hanging from Vaste's spear, was purest hatred.

"Care to roast the rest of him, too?" Vaste asked, dangling the dead remainder of Urides and his streaming chainmail before her. She shook her head, now seemingly embarrassed. "Fine, I'll do it, then," and the troll unleashed a much smaller flame spell that cleansed the head of his staff in a few seconds, leaving only a few smoking bones behind, hidden in the quartal chainmail. "Hmm ... they can resurrect that, can't they?"

Larana nodded slightly and then thrust out her hands. Vaste stepped back only a second before she flooded the room with another heat of such intensity that Cyrus was forced to look away, still unable to see out of his left eye. He lay there, watching, as Larana finished her spell and nothing remained save for the chainmail and a blackened scorch on the floor of the tower; no bones, no ash, not a sign that Pretnam Urides had ever even been at this place, save for—now that the mist was clearing—his mail, his staff lying upon the floor a few feet away, and his lenses upon the table by his bed.

"Hmm," Vaste said, swiping the staff from the floor. "Philos, the Burden of Knowledge?" He looked at the scorch mark that was all that remained of Urides. "I guess you've been unburdened."

"And you were never burdened to begin with. Not with knowledge, anyway." Vara stepped away from one of the nearby balcony doors, now open, wind clearing the steam from the room.

"Hah," Vaste said without mirth. "You didn't seem so smart when he clocked you from the side. You didn't even see it coming."

"Because he was using a godly weapon," Vara said, the blood staining her face and hair causing Cyrus to cringe. She laid eyes upon him and extended a hand, then stopped when she saw Larana's fingers already glowing white. Cyrus's head cleared less than a second later, the pain in his left eye fading as his sight suddenly returned.

"Speaking of which," Vaste said, looking at Philos in his hands. He glanced up, and tossed the weapon to Larana, who caught it with fumbling fingers. "I think you deserve this."

"I ..." Larana mumbled, looking down at the staff uncertainly. "You ... you ..."

"Yes, I know," Vaste said, nodding sagely, "I stepped in and neatly stabbed right through his ugly, stupid face, which, let's face it, was a service to all Arkaria. But ..." he nodded at the staff now cradled in Larana's hands, "You had him, fairly. You deserve it."

"I ..." Larana began.

"Take it," Cyrus said to her, pushing to his feet as J'anda came from behind him, another balcony door opened, the air clearing further now that a wind was seeping through the tower. "You deserve it."

"All right," she mumbled, turning the staff about in her hands. "Thank you."

"Thank you for not letting me get killed by that rank bastard," Cyrus said, rubbing his head, fresh blood still dripping down upon the day's stubble on his cheek and jaw. He stared right at Larana, who met his gaze with those vivid green eyes. "That would have been intolerable."

"I could probably tolerate it for a while," Vaste said, "but I suppose sooner or later I'd get lonely. You know, because of the—"

"Utter lack of troll beauty, yes," Vara said.

"I said 'intelligent troll beauties within—'" Vaste began.

"I know," Vara said, cocking her eyebrow through the smear of blood on her face, "and I meant what I just said ... entirely."

"Why must you hate us so?" Vaste mused idly.

"Perhaps she simply does not appreciate you," J'anda said, frowning at the blood on his robe's shoulder. "At all."

"Few do," Vaste said, shaking his head sadly as the night breeze blew through the tower.

Cyrus looked around the room. "This really is quite similar to—"

There was little sound from the stairs below now, and a clatter of feet on the steps came loud a second later, as Terian came up. "Well, that was no easy thing," the paladin said, brandishing his sword. "How did you f—" His eyes fell on the chainmail and the scorch mark. "I hope like hell that's Urides."

"It's what's left of him," Vaste said. "We thought about saving you some, but figured it was just best to be done with it."

"We did a similar thing to the rest of the Council of Twelve," Terian said, nodding at the scorch. He frowned at the chainmail. "Is that quartal?"

"I assume so," Cyrus said, "since it resisted all our efforts to burn it to ash."

Terian looked at it for a moment and then pointed. "Is anybody going to take that? Because if not, I could use—"

"I doubt it would fit me," Vara said, turning away.

"I doubt it will fit him," Vaste said, waving at Terian. "Did you see the paunch on Urides? Better start eating more if you want it to fit comfortably, Lepos."

"We should leave," Larana whispered, still turning over the staff in her fingers. She spoke normally, though still hushed.

"Good advice," Terian said, scooping up the chainmail under his arm. He looked right at Cyrus. "Unless you can think of any reason to stay?"

Cyrus's mind was muddled, his eyes drawn back to the blackened place where Pretnam Urides had met his end, a thousand thoughts warring for his attention at once. One won out over the others. "I think we've done enough for today," he said at last, nodding. "Let's get the hell out of here."

70.

"You have a lovely home," Isabelle said after appearing with Vara in the Tower of the Guildmaster a few days later. Vara had left with a heavy escort, under illusion, meeting Isabelle with an escort of her own at the portal outside Pharesia. Cyrus had been waiting nervously for them to return together, and now that they were here, both sisters standing before him, he felt relief wash over him after hours of tension.

"You didn't see the tower when you were here for the wedding?" Vara asked, taking a step away from her sister, her boots echoing against the floor. A placid breeze swept through with the breath of summer, as lovely a day as Cyrus could have envisioned, from across plains clear of so much as a convoy.

"I did not," Isabelle said with the trace of a smile. "I think we were rather busy, you recall, with the wedding and all the festivities it entailed."

"Well, here you are now," Cyrus said, sweeping a hand around to encompass the four open balconies around them. "If you ever get to the top of the Citadel in Reikonos, you'll find a very similar bit of architecture."

"Will I?" Isabelle arched an eyebrow. "I suppose there's a story behind that?"

"Not one that I know," Cyrus said, feeling like he was standing as an island in the middle of the room. He took a short walk over to the sitting area and lowered himself onto the seat. "Would you like to sit down?"

Isabelle smiled gracefully. "I wouldn't mind at all." She threaded her way over and took the seat opposite him, lowering herself into the chair as she smoothed her robes and vestments.

Vara followed her and seemed to hesitate, torn between the choice of sitting on the couch next to her husband or in the chair next to her sister. Finally, she moved to squeeze in next to Cyrus.

Isabelle watched them with amusement. "I recall a time in a carriage when you would not sit next to him, and so I had to."

Vara made a noise of impatience. "It wasn't that I wouldn't sit next to him, it was that squeezing two people in armor next to each other in a confined space is unpleasant. Better you than me, at the time."

"And now?" Cyrus asked, looking askance at her.

"Well, now I'm married to you, so I can no longer foist that responsibility off on others," Vara said with a straight face and a twinkle in her eye.

"I see the honeymoon is not yet over," Isabelle said, adjusting her robes again.

"If you can call being declared heretic and set upon by the largest armies in Arkaria a honeymoon, then no, hopefully it is over," Cyrus said dryly.

"It seems to be drawing to a close," Isabelle said lightly. "I have been listening as you asked in your last letter, and I have many things to report from Reikonos."

"Oh, good," Vara said, "and I was worried that you would have nothing more than idle gossip of washerwomen in the fountain at the square."

"I have that as well," Isabelle said, tapping her long ears idly. "But more than that ... Amarath's Raiders is done. Their guildhall is nearly emptied, and almost all their number have come to us or Burnt Offerings."

"Oh, good, treachery divided," Vara said.

"There are no surviving officers save one," Isabelle said, plowing onward, "and it was a warrior of my acquaintance that came to us only two days ago. He seems genuinely repentant, or at least his ambition hides his feelings on the matter—"

"You didn't accept him as an applicant," Vara said.

"We did," Isabelle said with a shrug. "It would be foolish not to; it's not as though Amarath's Raiders remains anything approaching a cohesive whole any longer. They have no goals, no purpose. They're utterly incapable of causing further trouble for you, like a headless man." She smiled once more. "But they have very well-equipped people."

"Now I see your own ambitions laid plain," Vara said.

"I didn't turn away Sanctuary members who have applied to us in past months, either," Isabelle said, without a hint of shame. "Endeavor needs all the help it can get."

"For what?" Cyrus asked, watching his sister-in-law carefully.

"We still mean to return to the upper realms, of course," she said. "While the war and our part in the defense of Reikonos may have distracted us, we are still one of the top guilds, and our reason for being is … well, is obviously not so altruistic as yours." Vara rolled her eyes, and Isabelle caught her. "Sister mine," Isabelle said, gently chiding, "recall that before you ran across the virtuous halls of Sanctuary, you pursued the same purpose as I do."

"Indeed," Vara said, "and now I do not." She stiffened in her seat. "So Amarath's Raiders is done, then. What of—"

"The Confederation?" Isabelle asked. "The outlying districts have announced their withdrawal and the army is essentially gone from where it had been camped outside Reikonos. What remains is barely enough to defend the city were it invaded, which, fortunately, seems unlikely."

"I'd heard Frost, Waterman and Coulton were living up to their part of the bargain," Cyrus said, nodding. He'd spoken with the governors when he'd returned from Reikonos after killing the Council of Twelve. Their relief had been obvious, save for Karrin Waterman's, whose reaction was hidden under her steely veneer. "That they broke the Confederation army is also welcome news."

"Not for the Mayor of Reikonos, I daresay," Isabelle replied with a smirk. "The poor chap is trying to hold the Confederation together through diplomacy."

"How goes that?" Vara asked, tensing in her unease.

"Better than I would have expected," Isabelle said. "He is approaching it from a considerably weakened position, after all, pledging to considerably loosen the hold the capital had been exercising, returning power to the Governors, remaking the Council of Twelve in a much more egalitarian fashion, as they were started, rather than as the tyrannical oligarchs they had become under Pretnam Urides."

"What's the likelihood he succeeds?" Cyrus asked, leaning down, elbow clinking against his greaves.

"I don't rightly know," Isabelle said with a light shrug. "The Confederation is tied together tightly through trade, interdependent, so I can't see the districts making war upon each other even if they broke apart. I expect we won't see that matter settled for some time, but one thing I can tell you is that the Leagues," she smiled delivering this news, "seem to have forgotten about you for the moment. I have friends in the Healers' Union, and you have gone from top priority to … well, no priority. Whatever drive there was to apprehend you seems gone, and I doubt you would find yourself in peril even were you to set foot in Reikonos right now."

"I don't intend to test that assumption presently," Cyrus said, letting out a breath as he leaned back in his seat. "Not that I have much reason to go there at the moment."

"Plus," Vara said grimly, "there is still the matter of Goliath, and let us not forget they have returned to their guildhall in the city."

"Oh, but they haven't," Isabelle said, raising an eyebrow.

"Beg pardon?" Cyrus asked, straightening in his seat.

"They haven't returned at all," Isabelle said, "in fact, they've withdrawn; their guildhall in Reikonos sits empty once more." She looked at them both, her features stiff. "Goliath has disappeared."

71.

The rest of their visit with Isabelle had been awkward, made so by Cyrus and Vara's hesitant glances at each other. Cyrus, for his part, knew what was in his mind as Isabelle tried to make pleasant conversation for over an hour with little response from either.

Goliath is still out there, he thought. *They're out there in the weeds, hiding, waiting to come back at us like the snakes they are.*

When Isabelle finally disappeared in her return spell, presumably having had enough of their terse, unsociable conversation, Cyrus stalked off to the northern balcony, Vara just behind him.

"Dammit," Cyrus said under his breath as Vara drew up beside him, taking position next to him at the rail.

"My sentiments exactly," Vara said, leaning over on the rail. "This leaves us in something of a bind."

"Twenty thousand troops, and their leaders filled with nothing but enmity for us," Cyrus said, shaking his head.

"We outnumber them now, though," Vara said. "And apparently Malpravus hates only me."

"Rhane Ermoc despises me," Cyrus said, shaking his head. "And I'm not fond of him, either." He put his hand on Rodanthar's hilt. "Praelior belongs to me, and I mean to have it back." He stood there for a moment, staring over the deep green plains, summer taking hold of the lovely grasses with its wind. "I wonder why Malpravus hates only you?"

"Perhaps he finds in you a kindred spirit," Vara said, a smile crooking the corner of her mouth as she stared out across the Plains of Perdamun. "Regardless, it seems like they have retreated beyond the bounds of the map to their jungle hideaway."

"Scuddar knows where they are," Cyrus said, looking down at the wall far below. He could see the red robes of the desert man against the grey stone barrier between Sanctuary and the plains. "He told me so on the night we were waiting for you under the Citadel," Cyrus said in response to Vara's curious look. "I meant to have him draw out a map as best he could remember it, but in the wake of those events—well, there's simply been too much else on my mind."

"Such as?" Vara asked. They hadn't had a proper talk in the days since everything had broken loose, having been too busy watching the wall and holding meetings of the Sanctuary Council, most of which seemed to hinge on Ryin still being upset at being uninformed about the course of their plans.

"When I was in the ambush in Idiarna," Cyrus said, nodding absently to the north, "that dark knight of Goliath's—Sareea—she used the return spell." He flashed a look at her. "I think we can expect heresy from Malpravus when next we meet as well."

"That's ... concerning," Vara said. "Or at least it concerns me."

"It should concern anyone who worries about Goliath," Cyrus said. "I haven't mentioned it in Council because ... well ..."

"We've been busy hashing over other matters and bearing the brunt of Ryin's ire," Vara said with a nod.

"I was going to say, 'Because I'm not looking forward to Vaste launching out of his seat as if he had a water spell cast out of his arse,'" Cyrus said, shaking his head. "They're not short of spellcasters. If they've taught theirs as we've taught ours, it'll be a fearsome battle when next we meet."

"Aye," Vara said. "And here I thought you were merely worried over what Pretnam Urides had goaded you with on the night we confronted him."

Cyrus frowned. "You heard that?"

"Dimly," she said, her hand coming up to feel the side of her head where Urides had bashed in her skull. "It was all very dreamlike, as though I were in a stupor, nothing but black before my eyes."

"What did you catch?" Cyrus asked.

"Some uncharitable taunting about your father and mother, and how he ultimately claimed no small amount of credit for their deeds before turning the entirety of Arkaria against Quinneria," Vara said, looking down. "Something about a long life, as well."

"Yes, I wondered what he meant by that," Cyrus said, frowning.

"But not about the taunting?" she probed, and he noticed.

"You think I let him—" he looked around, as if to reassure himself that Vaste was not present, "—get my goat?"

Vara smirked. "Urides presented himself to us as both friend and foe at various points in our acquaintance. And yet at the end, he made no more pretense—he had used us until we no longer suited any purpose, and then discarded us—"

"Except that doesn't make sense," Cyrus said, reaching under his helm to scratch his forehead. "We weren't a threat to Reikonos just because I could suddenly cast spells—because the rest of us could suddenly cast spells—"

"You don't have to be an actual threat or have ill intent for someone to assume such."

"I suppose," Cyrus said, not quite mollified by that. "But he didn't even try to use us. I mean, we didn't leave on terribly bad terms when last he parted; he might have had need of Sanctuary once more in the future, but he called us enemies and turned loose everything on us."

"Danay was against us," Vara said, ticking off her fingers one by one, "Goliath and Amarath's Raiders were easily swayed in that direction as well, and by the time they all made their lurching declaration of hostilities against you, we were down to some two thousand active guildmates—"

"But we still had Emerald Fields and the Luukessians in our pocket," Cyrus said, shaking his head. "And Terian. I just can't see it from Urides's position why he would have opposed us, even with the wind shifting against us from the Kingdom and those other two guilds. He was the lion's share of their force; without him, they would have had a much harder time opposing us, and it's clear now that Urides had internal political turmoil to deal with in his own borders." Cyrus frowned. "I just can't understand why, as head of the Council of Twelve, he'd go out of his way to make an enemy of us."

"You're choosing your words very carefully, husband," Vara said slowly. When he looked over at her, she went on. "'As head of the Council of Twelve.' But you see it making sense from his other role?"

Cyrus nodded. "Perhaps ... if the directive came to the head of the Leagues. From elsewhere."

"You think the gods themselves turned the Leagues against us," Vara said, "and Danay leapt on eagerly, and Urides went along, sweeping Goliath and the Raiders along in his tide."

"I know Bellarum wasn't too pleased with me when last we spoke," Cyrus said, shaking his head. "Though you'd think Vidara or Terrgenden would mention it if their friends were aligning their forces against us—"

"I did not have much of a conversation with the All Mother when I enlisted her aid," Vara said. "She made her communication to me through her servants. I did not even see her until she arrived with you at the convocation, and she said as little to me as she did to you, and entirely publicly."

"Still, you'd think she'd say something if she saw them moving against us," Cyrus said. "Maybe you're right. Maybe Urides just acted opportunistically, not expecting us to be able to marshal the strength to remove him from his comfortable office."

They stood like that for a few minutes, Vara looking down at her gauntlets, which had been cleaned carefully since the night of the battle when they had been covered entirely with ichor and gore. "So ... what do we do now?"

"I have it in my mind to question Carrack," Cyrus said. "And we'll need to talk to Scuddar about the base in the jungle, but ..." He let out a long, slow breath. "For now? I have a hard time imagining either Cattrine or Terian being thrilled about staging our troops in an invasion of Goliath's base where we could easily be struck down as we appear at the portal, even if we could get Carrack to part with the spell."

"Or conversely," Vara said, "having to march from the portal north of the wreck of the Endless Bridge. Selene and Tolada implied it was a journey of months. Removing the Luukessians from Emerald Fields and the dark elves from Saekaj for a period of months seems—"

"Foolhardy," Cyrus said, nodding along, a bitter taste in his mouth. *It's like defeat, the flavor of ashes.*

"Or just foolish," Vara said, staring off into the distance. "Perhaps even petty on our part."

"Yes," Cyrus agreed, but there was a feeling like worms crawling about in his belly, thrashing about to tell him how wrong he was. "At the very least ... we need to wait. Give it time. Gather information."

"The prudent course," Vara agreed, but she shifted at her place on the railing, and he could tell that she, like himself, was not entirely convinced.

72.

"Welcome back to my humble abode," Terian said, greeting Cyrus and Vara with a wide grin as they appeared in a blaze of green wizard teleportation magic in an enormous chamber filled with carriages and wagons. There was little light save for that of spells being cast, and as they appeared Cyrus caught a glimpse of a portal standing in the middle of the room behind them.

"Have we been here before?" Vara asked, wheeling around to take in the whole of the space they were in. Cyrus cast the Eagle Eye spell upon himself and then her in turn, the world brightening around him as the effect settled on his eyes and gave him vision in the dark.

"This is what I call the Courtyard of Saekaj and Sovar," Terian said, turning to encompass the whole chamber with a sweep of his hand. "It's where we used to stage carriages, bringing them down from the surface pulled by horses and oxen and whatnot, then transfer them to our vek'tag-pulled conveyances." He pointed to a carriage nearby hitched to two enormous spiders larger than any ox. "They can see in the dark, but horses, oxen, they can't, so ..."

"So here's where you moved your portal," Cyrus said, turning to look at the stone oval standing in the middle of the chamber, spell-light flashing around them as more wizards and druids brought in wagons and carts from outside.

"The one Yartraak hid in the palace for his own use, yes," Terian said, beckoning them toward the waiting spider-drawn carriage. "And now I've got our wizards and druids working every hour of the day to bring in food and take out our exports, all while the army continues to dig us out of this mess." His eyes gleamed in the dark. "I'm pleased you came today." He opened the door to the carriage and gestured for Vara to get in first.

"Glad we could oblige," Cyrus said, stepping in next and seating himself next to Vara on the comfortable bench.

"I hear your numbers have stopped shrinking," Terian said as he fastened the door closed and braced himself against the front of the carriage on the forward bench and then clanked his gauntlet against the wood. The carriage's wheels squeaked into motion after the sound of a whip crack split the air. The sounds of the courtyard, as Terian had called it, faded now that they were in the carriage, the windows covered over with velvety curtains.

"Yes, we're settled at four hundred and eighty-five members," Vara said, not amused. "Though I suppose you knew that number already, didn't you?"

"I did," Terian said with a nod. "But it's always nice to have your information confirmed." He glanced at Cyrus. "My question is—did you know that number?"

"Yes," Cyrus said, nodding, puckering his lips. "No point in not, and it's not as though it's moved in the last week. We seem to have recaptured at least a small sliver of our old reputation, and perhaps given a breath or two of hope to our members. Hopefully that'll be the end of that." Terian gave him a pitying look. "So," Cyrus said, "I take it you'd be of the same opinion as Vara when I asked her if she thought any of our wayward former members would come wandering back?"

Terian did not blink, but he cocked his head curiously. "What did she say?"

"I said," Vara spoke rather pointedly, clearly annoyed by Terian's failure to ask her directly, "that decisions, once made, are funny things, and require one to justify them constantly. Pride, in my opinion, precludes any returns. But hopefully," she finished, sniffing slightly at the damp underground air, "we will not lose any more soon."

Terian nodded slowly. "Yes, I think she's quite right. Anyone disloyal enough to leave when they thought you a loser—" Terian grimaced at his own inelegant word choice, "—is unlikely to come back now that you've been proven a winner once more. Also, you're not technically clear of the Leagues' ire, at least not from Reikonos. Nor the dwarves or gnomes, if it comes to it, though I doubt you'll find anyone pressing you about it. Carefully neutral, that'll be everyone's stance in regards to Sanctuary."

"Is that so?" Cyrus asked. "Why do you think that?"

"Because pissing you off carries a high price," Terian said with a grin as the carriage rattled along down the tunnel.

They sat in silence for a time, until Terian spoke. "So … I take it you jackasses are still sweating about Goliath being out there?"

"You're not?" Cyrus asked.

"Of course I am," Terian snapped. "Did you see what they did to the entrance to my capital? If I could personally insert my axe into Malpravus's rectum, be assured I would do so, and then twist the blade enough times to ensure that every meal he ate would become a bowel movement within a second of consumption." He bristled, shifting in his seat. "Cattrine feels things have worked out more or less equitably, but I doubt her soldiers would blink before following you off to war wherever it leads, because they're not the forgiving or forgetting types."

"That feels like it would be a lot to ask of them," Cyrus said cautiously, exchanging a look with Vara.

"It is," Terian said, staring at Cyrus through half-closed eyes. "You know where they are, then?"

"I have a suspicion," Cyrus said. "That place Selene told us about. The old ruin in the jungle. Scuddar said it's called Zanbellish. He called it the last city of the ancients."

"Never heard of it," Terian said with a frown.

"I have a map," Cyrus said. "He drew it out for me, and in good detail—the portal, the basic layout of the place. It's a city all right, or the ruins of one at least. But it's a six-month march into the Bandit Lands, through swamp and jungle, and without a recognizable road." He shook his head. "Any army walking that path will have to deal with all the diseases you could imagine—"

"And I suspect given your sordid history, you can imagine quite a few," Vara said, drawing a baleful look from Terian.

"—and of course, months of living on conjured rations," Cyrus said. "It's either that or attempt an assault through the portal, and based on what Scuddar mapped out for me," he shook his head sadly, "it's a perfect place to be slaughtered."

"I don't like the sound of desperation on you, Davidon," Terian said. "It sounds like giving up."

"The cost of vengeance in this case is going to be ludicrously high, Terian," Cyrus said, shrugging. "I have an army of—as you pointed out—less than five hundred. You have thirty thousand, of which—how many are currently involved in digging you out of the collapse?"

"Half or so," Terian grudgingly admitted. "We're digging every hour of the day presently, and making certain that our people are well rested so as not to, uh … work them to death, as the last Sovereign might have—"

"Truly, you are a wonder of progress," Vara said with a smirk.

"—but that'll be done in a few months," Terian said. "And I'd be open to another mission."

"Assuming the Luukessians wanted to toss in their lot with us," Cyrus said, going onward, "then we'd have another eight thousand … but they're almost entirely dragoons in a land where horses are going to be of no use. Scuddar said the swamps are impassible for equines. Even your spiders would have trouble," Cyrus added, stopping Terian before he opened his mouth fully to speak. "So … we could do this, but …"

Terian made a deep rumbling sound in his throat. "But you don't want to."

"Oh, I *want* to," Cyrus said. "Personally, I'd love to make a scarecrow out of Malpravus's corpse, and give over Rhane Ermoc to the trolls so I could watch them cook him and eat him—"

"I don't think even the trolls eat people," Vara said.

"—but that's me," Cyrus said. "*I* want to go. I don't want to drag my army along on a journey of six months through the wilds of the Bandit Lands. Scuddar guaranteed we'd lose several hundred just to incurable diseases of the swamps, to say nothing of the heat. And if you travel in the winter, you'll see torrential, freezing rains which will inflict a different sort of toll. No beasts of burden to carry tents, which means you're left hauling your own equipment—"

"Sounds like a job for the Army of Sanctuary that went into Luukessia," Terian said sourly. "Too bad the last year has seen that stripped away entirely."

"Isn't it?" Vara asked as they thumped over a particularly hard bump in the road. "Indeed, I find myself wondering, if we did strike out … what exactly we would find at the end?"

"And with Malpravus able to flit back and forth between the inhabited lands of Arkaria and that base of his," Cyrus said, drawing to the largest sticking point he had found, the one he'd turned over in his mind again and again, "imagine the havoc he could wreak with all of us gone for months, unable to receive so much as a word of warning in our absence. He could invade Reikonos, or Saekaj, or Huern—"

"That last one might be an improvement," Vara muttered. "A small one, but still."

"He's not known for sitting idly by," Cyrus said, giving Vara a sidelong look. "Whatever he's been up to this last year, he's been driving the events in some way, large or small, and as soon as he knew we'd won the fight in Reikonos, Goliath was out of there entirely. I don't fancy giving him a free hand to do whatever he wants in Arkaria while the bulk of us are away with our armies trying to hunt him down."

"Ugh," Terian said, his head sagging, "I hate that you're making a good point here. I was so dreaming about placing that bastard's head on a pike and dipping it in tar so I could keep it around for inspiration on rough days."

"It's not as though I'm enthused about leaving Praelior in the hands of Rhane Ermoc," Cyrus said, his jaw clenching involuntarily. "In addition to that ..." He paused. "That dark knight of yours? Sareea?"

Terian straightened, his head coming up. "What about her?"

"She used the return spell to escape me at Idiarna," Cyrus said, and Terian immediately slumped forward.

"Goliath, entirely heretic," Terian said, closing his eyes tightly. "All right. I don't want to chase them in the jungle swamps, either, now." He leaned against the carriage wall, taking slow breaths until he seemed to have regained his composure.

"Has Carrack told you anything?" Vara asked.

"I haven't had time to talk to him," Terian said as the carriage hit another bump. He smiled, but it was forced. "I was waiting for you two, truthfully. For you, I can clear my schedule and make the time."

"I feel so honored," Cyrus said dryly.

"You damned well ought to," Terian said, "but honestly, I wouldn't give this bastard one solitary moment if I didn't hold out at least some hope that he might be able to tell us something ..." Terian paused, and the resolve showed on his face, "... something that might let us still catch Goliath with a sword to the heart." And they fell into an agreeable silence as the carriage rolled deeper into the tunnels of Saekaj Sovar.

73.

"I'll tell you anything you want to know," Carrack said with a soft smile, his eyes already dimmed by his time in the dark elven prison. Once more the common area where the prisoners ate had been cleared by the guards, leaving Cyrus, Vara and Terian alone in the dank, musty air with the human wizard.

"Huh," Terian said, staring at him, "that went ... a little easier than I expected."

"You should know how Malpravus is," Carrack said, smiling broadly through his rotten teeth. "He understands power. This conversation? You have me wrapped up, trapped—you have all the power. If he were in my position, he would tell you anything you want to know." Carrack leaned forward. "That's how he is, see. In order to get what you need, what you want, *everything* is fair game. No loyalty; just alliances of convenience."

"That's an exceedingly poor way to live," Vara said, in a tone of barely repressed horror.

"But it's good way to rise," Carrack said, shrugging his thin shoulders. "And that's what Goliath was always about—climbing." He looked at Cyrus. "It's why he always wanted you, you know. Orion told him about your ambition, about how you wanted to move up in the world. He was sure you'd see it his way sooner or later."

"I assume the converse is why he hated me, then," Vara said under her breath.

"Maybe," Carrack said. "I don't know. But you're right, he hated you."

"All right, fine, you want to sing to ... what? Save your own skin?" Terian looked right at Carrack. "What do you think you're going to get out of this? Freedom?"

"I'd settle for not being flogged," Carrack said. "Can we can come to an accord on that? Because this is something I'm not keen on. The Confederation, when I went to prison there, I knew I was safe from beatings and floggings. Here ... I get the sense if I make things too difficult on you, I'm going to end up regretting it."

"You have good instincts," Terian said. "All right, then. Tell us everything."

"Where would you like me to start?" Carrack asked, waving a hand across the table between them.

"Malpravus's base in the Bandit Lands," Cyrus said, before anyone else could say anything.

Carrack frowned at him. "Okay. It's called Zanbellish, and it was a city of the ancients. We went there after Reikonos booted us out of their gates. Took months to get there."

"Do you know the spell that can carry us to the portal?" Vara asked.

Carrack looked at her blankly. "I do, but ..." He hesitated. "Let me put it this way ... I will gladly tell it to you, if he," Carrack pointed at Terian, "gives me assurances that he's not going to have me beaten to death if you use it and die. Because you will die if you go there."

"The defenses are that strong?" Cyrus asked.

Carrack nodded, brows lifted up. "Oh, yes. Goliath has more than twenty five thousand troops at our—well, their—command, and they're always watching the portal, just like all the other armies. Malpravus doesn't like to leave things to chance."

"If I teleported in," Cyrus said, watching Carrack carefully, "are you saying he'd kill me immediately?"

Carrack made a hmming noise. "The guards would, but odds are Malpravus would resurrect you to try and persuade you to join him. He's got a soft spot for you in that necromantic heart of his. I think it has something to do with your mother."

Cyrus frowned. "My mother? Wait, did he know who she was all along?"

"I couldn't say for sure," Carrack said, "but probably. He knows more than anyone I've ever met, but he doesn't share it unless he sees the benefit to him in doing so. It's why he's so good at what he does. He'll leave off important information while he's trying to coax you toward an outcome he desires—"

"This explains why he is your trusted leader," Vara said.

"—and not think a thing of it," Carrack said. "So, yes, he probably knew your mother was the sorceress, but why would he share it with you? To do so would have exposed you, making you less useful to him if you did see his version of the light." He chuckled. "And it's not like your knowing about it has been much of a boon to you. I mean, it's not as if the knowledge would have set you on the path to heresy and breaking down the class barriers more quickly than you did it anyway." He shrugged.

"Why did Malpravus seek out Zanbellish after you were exiled from Reikonos?" Terian asked, inserting himself back in the conversation and rapping his knuckles on the table as he did so. "You could have gone … well, not anywhere, but closer places, at least."

"Because he wanted to," Carrack said, leaning forward. "Haven't you been listening? Malpravus steers the ship that is Goliath, all right? Other officers are just lackeys. We take his orders because he's either holding something we want over us or he's cajoling us forward with promises. That's it. No one else runs that guild, and whatever his plans, he makes them happen regardless of what it takes." Carrack settled back in his seat. "It's why he beats you."

"Yes, he's doing an absolutely marvelous job of that thus far," Vara said, staring at Carrack through narrowed eyes. "We've escaped every ambush he's set for us, killed several of his officers and deprived him of all his allies—"

"And he still doesn't care," Carrack said. "I mean, I'm sure he's disappointed that his allies are out of the picture, because, again, you know how he feels about power, but … it doesn't matter. He'll come back." Carrack shuddered slightly, either from the cold or something else. "He always comes back."

"What did he want in Zanbellish?" Cyrus asked. "He had to want something specific, or else he would have stopped long before—"

"Secrets of the ancients," Carrack said, putting his hands palms up, their backs flat on the table. "That's what he was looking for. He had us scour the ruins for old books, for runes hidden behind vines, anything that came from the days when the city was a city and not a bunch of rock covered over in moss." Carrack licked his lips. "He did the same thing in Gren when we went up there for an expedition, too, walking around, having slaves tear vines off some of the old artifacts."

He shook his head. "I know he found something, both in Zanbellish and in Gren. But I don't know what he found there."

"Where else did he look?" Vara asked.

"He didn't take me everywhere, you have to understand," Carrack said with a sly smile. "But ..."

"But what?" Terian asked. "And keep in mind as you answer that I feel a beating coming on."

"Calm down," Carrack said, holding up his hands. "I'm going to tell you." He smiled again. "I was in charge of the wizards and the druids, so as it happened, anytime he asked to go somewhere, I was able to circle back around afterward and ask the individuals who teleported him about the destination. Only two others were ones where he seemed to be looking for signs of the ancients." He held up his hand and started ticking off points. "Reikonos—specifically the tunnels below it, where the portal to the higher realms is. He also visited the arena and the Citadel."

"Both constructed by the ancients," Cyrus said, frowning. "Where was the other place he went?"

"Aloakna," Carrack said, this time a little more smug. "But when I tell you this next piece ... you've got to understand ... this one's huge. I'm going to need a little special consideration in exchange for it."

"I solemnly promise I will not decapitate you as a traitorous enemy of every sentient being in Arkaria if you tell us," Terian said. "If you don't, well, I hope your future plans don't require a head, because I'm feeling a little itch to do an overhand swing with my axe."

"I'll start with the enticement, then," Carrack said, his smugness fading, "and maybe once you see the value, you'll come around."

"My axe will come around, yes," Terian said. "In a downward arc, and then plop! Around will come your head, as it falls to the ground, freed from the constraints of your neck."

"He went to Aloakna when it fell," Carrack said, eyeing Terian with obvious nervousness.

"When it was sacked, you mean," Vara said. "Four years ago."

Carrack shook his head, looking smug once more. "It wasn't sacked."

"Bullshit," Vara said. "Everyone in that city died, the buildings were pulled down stone by stone—"

"Oh, the people died," Carrack said, "but there was no sack."

Terian stared at him blankly. "What are you talking about? The dark elven army marched on Aloakna, and they did their—well, their thing, that they did, under Yartraak—"

"Except they didn't," Carrack said, sitting back.

"I don't think I believe you," Cyrus said.

"You don't have to," Carrack said, "but …" His eyes gleamed. "Aloakna is still standing. If you wanted to, you could go and see it for yourself. The city is still there. It's the people that are gone."

"How the hell did that happen?" Terian asked, shaking his head. "When the dark elven army hits something—and I know for a damned fact they were there—"

"As do I," Vara said stiffly, "for immediately thereafter they came and laid siege to Sanctuary."

"—it gets sacked," Terian said, removing Alaric's old helm and putting it on the table. "It doesn't get gently … not burned or whatever you're suggesting. The dark elven armies under the last Sovereign were not merciful to their enemies. They wrecked—"

"And yet Aloakna still stands," Carrack said, arching his eyebrows in amusement. "Do you wish to know how?"

"Very much so," Cyrus said, holding up a hand to quiet Terian and Vara as they started to speak.

"Well, as it happens, I can tell you what I know—" Carrack began.

"And in exchange, you will live and get no beatings," Terian said. Carrack looked at him, disgusted. "I'm willing to add in a single apple, slightly bruised," Terian said, then waited a second. "Fine. No bruises, but that's my final offer."

"I'll take it," Carrack said, sounding greatly put out, "but mostly for the lack of beatings."

"All right, so spill," Cyrus said. "Was it Malpravus that destroyed … err … killed … the people of Aloakna? Since he was there?"

"No," Carrack said, shaking his head. "He didn't do it. The wizard who took him said it was something else. He didn't see it all that clearly, but he said it was something … big. Grey skin hiding under a cloak the size of a tent. We're talking taller than a troll—"

"Yartraak," Terian said, slamming his hand against the table. "Yartraak did it."

Carrack shrugged. "If you say so. I never saw him and neither did my wizard."

"But that doesn't explain what Malpravus was doing there," Vara said, pondering it. "Unless he was there to look at the city after it was over."

"I don't know," Carrack said, now leaning back and looking exhausted, as though he'd depleted all his energy along with everything he'd told them. "I just know that the wizard who saw it said he watched the whole damned thing ... and that Malpravus was practically drooling when it was over with."

74.

"Cyrus, where the hell are you going?" Terian asked, struggling to keep up with him as they strode down the narrow, dark corridor that led out of the Depths. A guard in full armor slammed himself against the wall with a fearful noise in order to avoid Cyrus as he barreled through.

"I'm getting out from underneath this cessation field and then I'm going to Aloakna," Cyrus said, taking a breath of the dank air of the underground.

"You'll need a wizard or druid for that, you know," Vara said, calling after from a few steps behind Terian.

"Also, a horse," Terian said. When Cyrus paused to look back, he explained, "Aloakna's portal is on the far outskirts of the city. You'll regret it if you walk."

"What do you think you're going to find there?" Vara asked, staring past Terian at him.

"A big sign saying, 'Malpravus was definitely interested in this ancient rune that my tiny warrior brain can't even interpret,'" Terian said, catching up to him.

"You realize that this could be a trap?" Vara said, keeping up with Terian. "That Carrack could be baiting you to go to Aloakna alone, knowing that Malpravus and his ilk are waiting?"

"Good point," Terian said and stopped, calling back to the guard behind him. "You! If you hear that I died in an expedition to Aloakna, you make sure and beat that prisoner Carrack every single day and tell him I ordered it. Understand?"

"Yes sir!" reverberated down the hall in accented dark elven.

The Sovereign walked toward Cyrus again. "Well, I've covered that possibility."

Vara looked at him pityingly. "You've covered it in case we die. You didn't really address what to do in order to allow us to live through an ambush at Aloakna."

"Pfft, that's easy," Terian said, shaking his head. "We just bring an army."

"And if they have the portal under guard?" Vara asked, not blinking away from him.

"I have no answer for that," Terian said. "Are we going or not?"

"Yes," Cyrus said.

"No," Vara said.

"Well, I'm foolishly on the side of 'yes,' and here's why," Terian said. "Because the likelihood that Malpravus and company are setting up a permanent ambush on the off chance that Carrack would get captured—"

"It could have been given to any of the Goliath members in the Idiarna ambush," Vara said.

"—well, whatever, it's still a very intensive thing to set up, manpower-wise," Terian said, frowning. "They'd need at least a few hundred, probably closer to a thousand, just to be sure, and they'd need to keep them there for … well, at least two weeks now." He shook his head. "I don't buy it."

"But you buy the possibility that Yartraak annihilated the dark elven populace of Aloakna with … a spell or something, rather than it being sacked by the dark elven army?" Vara asked.

Cyrus frowned. "When the dark elves came for Sanctuary after Aloakna, did you have any warning?"

"No," she said with a frown of her own, "but then we were hardly expecting an army to come marching in on us from the east—"

"Did you see smoke?" Cyrus asked, and Vara froze. "Like Santir? Like Termina—"

"No," Vara said, and her voice caught. "But we might not have, would we?"

"You would have," Terian said. "Provided the days were reasonably clear, provided you could see to the east. You should have seen a big pillar of black smoke in the sky. You should have known without doubt."

"No," Vara said, shaking her head. "The sky was clear when the dark elves came the first time. It … it had been for days."

"You sound certain," Terian said.

Vara looked right at Cyrus. "It was a time of great duress, but I remember it well. But it still does not answer what you expect to find in a ruined city?"

"I expect to find not a ruined city," Cyrus said, "if Carrack didn't lie."

"And if it is not ruined?" Vara asked. "What does that tell us? That a god used a spell to destroy his people? That he involved himself in the affairs of mortals? As though we don't already know that happened with Yartraak."

"I don't know," Cyrus said, shaking his head. "But I need to see it. I need to see Aloakna, and maybe once I've seen it—I can get some idea of what Malpravus was after."

"Better bring someone who can read the runes of ancients," Terian said. "Also, a horse. I'm serious. It's a walk, and if no one's been cleaning the streets—"

"Fine," Cyrus said. "I'll get a horse. A horse and someone who can read ancient runes." He looked at Terian and nodded. "We'll meet you there in one hour."

"Fair enough," Terian said with a hint of a smile. "Don't be mad if I show up first with some friends, just to be sure the town is safe. It is nominally in my territory, after all."

"I won't be mad as long as you don't get yourself killed," Cyrus said, turning to stalk back off down the tunnel toward the prison's exit.

"But if I do, you're absolutely going to resurrect me so you can kill me again yourself, right?" Terian fired back.

"No," Cyrus said, grinning, "I'll let her resurrect you," he chucked a thumb at Vara, "and she'll tell us both, 'I told you so' for the rest of our lives, and probably say it over our gravestones after we've died of old age."

"Don't even joke about that," Vara said, whispering in the dark passage. "But I would be bloody right."

And the three of them chuckled all the way out of the prison.

75.

"What are the odds that both J'anda and Mendicant are at the wall right now?" Cyrus asked as he and Vara swept into the foyer a few minutes later, light shining through the circular stained glass window above the massive doors.

"They could honestly be anywhere," Vara said, "but as they're definitely not in their quarters, I would say—"

"Excuse me," Larana said, halting them both in their tracks. Cyrus spun around and so did Vara, at his shoulder. The druid stood in the entry to the Great Hall, clutching Philos in her hands, the wood of the long, cherrywood staff gleaming. Larana's robes looked cleaner than usual. "Did you ... did you need someone to teleport you somewhere?"

"Ah, well," Cyrus said, exchanging a look with Vara, "yes, but ... uhm ... can you by any chance read the runes of the ancients? Because we need someone who can—"

"Yes," Larana said, blushing furiously. "I can read them."

Cyrus stared at her. "You're a very talented woman, Larana."

She blushed even deeper as she bowed her head to avoid his eyes. "Thank you."

"Well, now all we need are horses," Vara said, breaking the awkward tension as she whirled to lead the way to the door. Cyrus followed her, not daring to be left behind with Larana, and when they reached the massive doors, he waited as she threw one open, stealing a glance into the lounge. Zarnn was sitting inside, a tiny book in his massive hands, his eyes squinted as he concentrated on the page in front of him.

"Huh," Cyrus said, nodding to Zarnn. Vara paused and looked back at him. "What are the odds he's reading *The Champion and the Crusader*?"

"Very good," Vara said, doing a little blushing of her own, "as I lent my copy to him." And she ducked out the door. Larana, blushing similarly, as usual, followed.

When Cyrus stepped outside, the skies were cloudy, and to the south and east he could see dark skies, almost black, like night itself was moving in upon them. "Shit," he said, pointing to it, "is that the direction of Aloakna?"

"Yes," Vara said, giving the gloomy skies a glance of her own. "I suppose we're going to get wet."

"More than that if you're meaning to go to Aloakna," Larana said quietly. They both looked back at her. "That's a typhoon coming off the Bay of Lost Souls," she said. "It'll be torrential rains and winds powerful enough to level houses, tornadoes will come out of the sky and leave great swaths of destruction behind them; thunder and lightning ..." Her voice drifted off.

"I am becoming more certain that this expedition is a poor idea, poorly timed," Vara said sourly, looking right at Cyrus. "We should delay."

"We should hurry and go now," Cyrus said, looking once more at the dark clouds. "That way we can come back before the storm hits, and if we don't find anything, we can return and look again after the worst passes. But we might find something before it hits."

"What ... are we looking for?" Larana asked, her voice a little higher than usual.

"I don't know," Cyrus said, shaking his head as he stalked toward the stables. "Carrack said Yartraak—presumably Yartraak—killed the city with a spell, that it wasn't sacked like we'd heard." He glanced back at Larana and gave her a reassuring smile. "I wouldn't worry about it, though. It's not likely to be anything lingering, is it?"

"Why are you going there, then?" Larana asked.

"Because Malpravus was there when it happened," Cyrus said as he reached the stable door and tugged it open, "and I want to know what he was looking for. Dieron!" he called.

There was no immediate answer from the stableboy, however, as the horses were going wild within their stalls. Whinnying echoed through the massive stables like screams, and there was much rustling, the smell of horse heavy in the air.

"Sorry, Lord Davidon!" Dieron Buchau came running down the row nearest the door, out of breath, and stopped before Cyrus, panting.

"Got a bit of … well … it's a little mad here this afternoon, as you can tell."

"I can tell," Cyrus said as a horse snorted, head sticking out of a stall at him. "What the hell is all this?"

"The storm," Larana said, almost too quietly to be heard.

"It's the storm," Dieron said, nodding. "It's got them all riled, they can feel it coming."

"I need Windrider and Vara's horse," Cyrus said, "and also a horse for Larana."

They stood in the wild and unruly stables, listening to the horses stamp under the wide rafters of the stables while Dieron Buchau saddled the three horses and readied them, bringing them out to their riders one at a time, looking as distressed as his animals. "I can't recall ever seeing anything like this, not at Enrant Monge and not here, I tell you …"

"We'll be back in a hurry," Cyrus said, nodding at him, "hopefully before the storm breaks."

Buchau looked out, holding open the door of the barn for them as it fought against him, trying to slam shut in the rising wind. "That'd be a real sound idea, sir." He turned his eyes southeast, toward the black formation of clouds rolling across the sky. "I don't think I'd care to get caught out in that, m'lord. No, I wouldn't."

"Nor would I," Vara said as they left the stables, stopping about twenty feet away, in the shade of the yew tree whose branches were blowing like mad, the three of them all on horseback.

"We'll hurry," Cyrus said as a drop of rain plopped on his wrist, finding a gap between the rings of his mail and wetting his skin.

"We'd better," Vara said, the concern obvious in her voice as the druid spell whipped up around them with a wind all its own and carried them off to their destination.

76.

A gale lashed at Cyrus as the spell faded, rattling the helm upon his head and causing Windrider to let out a ferocious whinny. "Calm down," Cyrus said, stroking the horse's neck, "your name is Windrider; you should be right at home here."

They had emerged in a green and overgrown place, the ground around the portal covered in tall grass, untended and untidy. From where Cyrus stood he could see the Bay of Lost Souls and an old port, with collapsed docks and crumbling stone block quays, white-capped waves washing over all that remained. Not a single boat was in sight save for a few broken boards that might once have been one, pulled up on a beach at the end of the port.

"I'm thinking scavengers have stripped the place bare," Terian called, his horse cantering up to Cyrus. The paladin was squinting under Alaric's helm's eye slits. There was a steady tap-tap-tap of the rising rain against Cyrus's own helm, and he found it distracting. The salt air was thick, so heavy Cyrus could taste it. "Came in after the fall and took every seaworthy boat."

"You'd think word of this would have gotten out," Vara said as Cyrus looked north to see the city resting behind forbidding stone walls. He could see nothing of the structures beyond, but there were the remains of a thousand shanties blown down between where they stood and the wall of the city, timbers sticking up at odd angles and in different directions, the remains of more hovels than he could count.

"I asked some enterprising friends of mine," Aisling said, appearing behind Cyrus atop her smaller horse, her cloak whipping in the fearsome wind, "and they said it was all whispers and rumors, Aloakna surviving. Said everything of value was plundered years ago by a few bands of thieves, nothing left here now but bones and ash."

"Because when you find a promising treasure trove and you're a thief, you don't tell anyone about it until the carcass is picked clean," Cyrus said with measured disdain.

"It is the smart move," Aisling agreed. Cyrus looked past her and saw Dahveed and Bowe on horses of their own, as well as a massive dark elven warrior taller than himself. *I've met him before, but I can't remember his name ...*

"We should hurry," Larana whispered, apparently loud enough that everyone heard her, for they all started their horses forward at roughly the same time. Cyrus guided Windrider toward a cobblestone road that had weeds sprouting all through it, almost like the stones didn't stop them much at all.

They rode ahead, past the endless fields of collapsed hovels, through the wreckage of more lives than Cyrus cared to think about. There were bones aplenty, that was sure, no flesh left to rot. "I suppose four years in the sea air doesn't leave much of anything but bone," Cyrus said under his breath.

"This is quite the atrocity, isn't it?" Terian scanned the field, and though Cyrus could not see his face beneath the helm, he could tell the Sovereign's mood from his voice—grim, dark and angry.

"Doesn't make me sorry we killed your predecessor," Cyrus said.

"*I* killed him while you stood there and let him swat you around like a clumsy servant," Vara sniffed.

"I provided valuable distraction," Cyrus said.

"Yes, thank you for being his whipping boy while I did the real work."

They settled into silence as they approached the gates. Cyrus could see where the stones had begun to fall out of the wall, and the great wooden gates that had once stood in place had rotted and been battered, holes appearing throughout their tall structure. The rain was steadily coming down now, and the rhythmic tapping upon his helm had increased. One of the doors had been ripped far enough off its hinges that Aisling was able to ride through without doing anything other than ducking. Cyrus, Vara and Terian were all forced to dismount in order to lead their horses through.

"Looks clear," Aisling called from the other side as Cyrus emerged into the ghostly ruins of a dead city. The rain had ceased to tap at him for a moment as they stood under the stone arch to enter Aloakna. He could see it coming down ahead, though, and felt the chill carried on the wind, drops splattering in his face as he looked out over the ruined city.

There were bones in the street ahead, a road that curved off to his right toward what he reckoned was the center of town. Bare skulls grinned at him, rib cages stood out on the weed-riddled cobblestone street. Houses had collapsed on either side of the road, skeletons of a different sort, made of stone but lacking their roofs after so many seasons bereft of care and maintenance. Other dwellings were made of wood and had collapsed; two that he could see were clearly burned, blackened timbers sticking up, remainders of an untended fire within gone wild.

"This is quite possibly the grimmest damned thing I've ever laid eyes on," Terian said, looking over the city ahead. "What are we looking for here again, other than our own tears?"

The wind picked up, nearly jarring Cyrus's helm from his head. "I don't know," he called against the wind, which howled through the gap in the gate behind them as the big dark elven warrior struggled to pull himself through while Dahveed, Bowe, and Larana looked on.

"But you'll know it when you see it, right?" Terian asked drily.

"Well, right now I see a lot of death caused by your god," Cyrus said, returning his reply with only half the irony that he felt it deserved.

"Not mine," Terian said, "I helped orchestrate his death, all right? You don't have to convince me of his utter lack of decency. I knew him firsthand. This is very much within his power to do and most probably something he would do, just out of spite."

"If he had this much power," Cyrus said, shaking his head at the carnage, "why didn't he use it on me and Vara when we fought him?"

"A spell of this magnitude would take time," Larana said, surprising them all, "and concentration." A hard gust blew through but she didn't move, Philos clutched in her hand. "He would not have been able to fight you while casting it."

Cyrus frowned at her. "Did you learn that in your studies with Mendicant?"

She looked right at him. "No."

"Movement ahead," Aisling said just as Vara was opening her own mouth to speak.

ROBERT J. CRANE

"What is it?" Cyrus asked.

"I would have told you, had I not been outshouted," Vara said. "It is some small mammal, a furry one. Smells a little. Possibly a muskrat, a beaver, raccoon, or a dark elven harlot." She smiled icily at Aisling, who rolled her eyes.

"Wow," Terian said, shaking his head, "it never ceases to be awkward with you two, does it?"

"I would have restrained myself in the event of it being something of consequence, such as a Goliath ambush," Vara said, "but as there is no apparent danger, I feel no compunction not to afford myself the occasional arrow to sling at her."

"I'm such a lovely pincushion," Aisling said.

"Much like Vaste's arse, yes," Vara said, urging her horse forward on the street, hooves brushing aside the tall weeds as she rode.

Cyrus spurred Windrider after her, the skies blackening overhead. The relentless attack of the rain against his armor was back and twice as fierce now. It rattled against the metal, splattered through the holes in his chainmail and began to soak his underclothes. It was coming down sideways, in torrents, the wind picking it up and hurling it in his face like thrown buckets of water. Cyrus tried not to flinch away, but it was exceedingly difficult.

He looked back and saw Terian's eyes blinking furiously, water cascading down his helm and streaming off onto his pauldrons and down his breastplate. "I'm the damned Sovereign," he muttered, "I bet the rulers of other nations don't have to ride through typhoons on insane expeditions."

"You're so special," Cyrus said.

"I'd rather be dry," Terian replied. "And warm."

The black clouds pulsated above them, lightning flashing through the apparent valleys in the clouds, illuminating the depths and striations in the heavy sky. Thunder cracked hard, rattling Cyrus's helm harder than the downpour. They were passing larger buildings, wooden structures that had collapsed in on themselves, fresh green springing from beneath their ruins. Cyrus saw a tree fallen into the middle of an old pub, its roots an enormous circle, torn from the ground.

"Please tell me Yartraak didn't do that with his spell," Aisling said.

"He didn't," Larana said, riding quietly behind Cyrus. "The spell killed the people but left the town untouched. All this damage is four

402

years of the bay's relentless, pounding weather."

"You seem very sure of that," Vara said, turning her head at the fore to look back.

"I'm getting more sure by the minute," Larana said and then lapsed into silence.

They rode on another ten minutes as the wind picked up harder, blowing twigs and leaves along with the torrential rains. Now Cyrus was wet and soaked, cold all the way to the bone. A piece of parchment blew across the road in front of him, twisting and dancing in the strength of the wind. He could hear Aisling trying to keep her teeth from chattering as she rode, her leather armor glistening. Even Vara seemed to shudder here and there, sitting straighter in her saddle than was usual for her.

When they reached the center of Aloakna, they found only more death. The remains of at least a hundred bodies were strewn about the area, just as clean of flesh as any of the others they had seen. Here, though, in the middle of a circular road, there was a monument of some sort formed something like a rectangle sticking out of a short cylindrical mount. Cyrus steered toward it, Windrider now being buffeted by the winds that had picked up in intensity to the point that Cyrus was beginning to fear he would be thrown from his mount.

"We need to get out of here!" Terian called, struggling to keep from falling over himself as another loud crack of thunder echoed through the empty streets of the dead city. "First time since my youth I can recall being eager to get back underground."

"Just a minute!" Cyrus called back, trying to reach the monument. When he got closer, he stared at it; there were definitely words there, but inscrutable ones, written in a script he couldn't make sense of. "Is that the language of the ancients?" He looked over the monument, plain and granite and completely unlike the portals that dotted the land or the interior of the Citadel.

"It's dark elven," Larana said, moving close enough to see for herself. Her cowl was whipping behind her, and the rains had washed the dirt from her face. Cyrus stared at her, realizing he had perhaps never seen her this clean. She looked even younger now, he thought as she concentrated on the monument. He frowned. *She looks ...*

"It's a declaration of principles," Terian said, leaning hard against the wind threatening to topple him, "for the free people of Aloakna By the Sea." He strained, staring against the hard rain and buffeting winds. "It's … I mean it's properly insulting to the Sovereign, I can see why he might have been offended enough to come destroy this place himself, there are swipes against him couched in every line … 'We pledge ourselves to always stand in the light, eschewing the darkness …'"

"So very insulting," Vara said. "Practically a suggestion that he go fornicate with his mother."

"If you knew his ego," Terian said, staring, "you'd realize that for him, it was probably so much worse."

"There's nothing of the ancients here?" Cyrus asked, hurrying Windrider in a quick loop around the monument. He stared at the other side, trying to make sense of it, wondering if it simply said the same thing as the reverse. Larana came around to join him, and after giving it a look, shook her head at him, wind whipping her hair around to cover her face, strands blocking her mouth and cheeks from view.

"Nothing but a lot of high-minded ideals that these people apparently died for," Terian said, peeking around, the water on his helm beading and running off in small rivers.

Vara peered around as well, her own helm dripping furiously. "If there's anything here, I don't think we're going to find it now. Not in this." The sky flashed once more, momentarily illuminating the scene around them before it relapsed into a darkness like night. "If you intend to keep searching, we need to come back later."

Cyrus threw a look around again as the next flash lit the sky and the town. It all looked like ruins, like the bones of a once-healthy city laid out for vultures the way the corpses of its people had been. He looked at one of the buildings that ringed the square and as the lightning faded, he saw a tall tower in its midst that reminded him of Sanctuary. He cocked his head and stared at it as the lightning flashed again, revealing it as an old chapel of some sort, decaying and falling. He was struck with a sense of horror, imagining Sanctuary decayed and falling, and he was seized with an urgent desire to return home.

"All right," he said, his throat suddenly thick, as though he'd swallowed something too wide for his gullet. "We'll go. We can come back some other time."

"If the town's still here," Aisling muttered between claps of thunder.

"I'll take your horses," Larana said, beckoning Cyrus and Vara forward, "so you don't have to walk them downstairs in this."

"You think it's this bad at Sanctuary already?" Cyrus asked, a burst of wind blowing water into his eyes as he blinked away while he dismounted, holding the reins up for Larana to take.

"Almost certainly," the druid replied, taking the reins. The lightning flashed again, revealing a new assurance in her expression, her mousiness all gone. He stared up at her as the light faded then shook his head, catching a glimpse of something familiar in her face. *You give a girl a godly weapon, I suppose maybe she develops a little confidence ...*

"We'll talk on the morrow," Terian said, waving his hand before disappearing in a twinkle of light from his spell.

"We'll talk ... never, I hope," Aisling said to Vara, riding close to the tall warrior and Bowe, who cast his druid spell and vanished in the ensuing gust, a barely noticeable stir in the heart of the storm. The healer, Dahveed, followed in his own return spell.

"The feeling is mutual," Vara said as she cast her own return spell, disappearing in a twinkle of light.

"You should go," Larana said, staring down at Cyrus as she drew the horses all tight together in preparation to cast her own spell.

"I know." Cyrus gave one last look at the town of Aloakna in all its dead glory. The wind blew hard and rattled the timbers that stuck into the air. In the distance, he heard a building collapse, the distinctive sound of wood falling in, coming to the ground hard, and he sucked in a salty breath of sea air.

There's nothing here, he thought and looked at Larana once more. She nodded at him, and the lightning lit her calm face once again. He stared at her for only a second before averting his gaze, embarrassed to be caught staring so blatantly.

With nothing more left to do, Cyrus cast his own return spell and left the dead city behind him to rattle, like bones, in the winds of the storm.

77.

"What idiot left the balcony doors open in a bloody gale?" Vara asked in clear annoyance as Cyrus reappeared in the Tower of the Guildmaster, the rain slapping hard against the stone floor, blowing in from all directions.

"If I recall correctly," Cyrus said coolly, the doors rattling hard against their bindings in the furious wind, "we both left at the same time, neither of us much paying attention to the state of the weather as we did so."

"Well, that was all down to your daft mission to soak us to the bone to little profit," she said, her ponytail absolutely drenched. She reached back and squeezed it, and water sluiced out of her hair. She had to speak loudly in order to be heard over the chaos outside, the storm's rising fury.

"I thought there'd be something there," Cyrus said, watching the rain blow in from outside, rolling across the uneven stone floor, finding the cracks, turning the grey stone a darker slate shade. A distant part of him wanted to close the doors, to lock them against the fury of the typhoon. But the floor in the tower was already well soaked, and the spread of the water could do little more at this point. Little droplets blew in and found his face, but he hardly noticed them against what was already there from his time out in the storm in Aloakna. "I guess I was wrong."

"I suppose you were," Vara said, more grudging and less gloating. A wind howled particularly hard, drawing Cyrus's attention to the hearth, the flames within billowing at the fury of the gust. He looked back at Vara as the balcony doors rattled hard once more against the ropes that lashed them in place. "In truth," she said, standing very still and speaking loud over the chaos around them, "I had hoped we would find something there."

"So I wasn't the only one, then," Cyrus said, smiling wanly, "in spite of your protestations that it was a fool's errand?"

"Well, knowing you as I do, I expect some foolishness now and then," she said, walking calmly over to him as the sky outside flashed once more, and the torches blazed and burned, stirred by the wind that once more shook the tower with its fury. "I married you knowing you were occasionally a fool, after all." She blinked against the gust that ran through just then as she stared up at him. "You try, in spite of everything. It's why you long to lead a party to war in the Bandit Lands, to go conquer Zanbellish even though you know it's bound to be fraught with peril. It's a reason I love you." She leaned up and kissed him on the lips.

He felt the warmth of her kiss, the salt air from the sea still in traces upon them as she opened her mouth to him. The storm without seemed to mirror the one within him as the very tower quivered in its fury. He kissed her more deeply, ignoring the sound of nature's primal anger, and lost himself in her for a moment, forgetting all about Goliath and Malpravus and all else as his fingers found his wife's wet hair and ran through the blond locks as he shed his gauntlet—

"Ooh, isn't this cozy?"

Cyrus broke from Vara's embrace to find Menlos Irontooth rising the last steps to the top of the stairs, looking around, taking in the Tower of the Guildmaster. The Northman had an appraising look on his face, but he was dry as could be and when a hard gust brought in a rain he blinked at the intensity of it. Cyrus watched the three wolves follow their master up the stairs.

"Menlos, what are you doing here?" Cyrus asked, flexing his hand. "News from the wall?"

"I haven't been out in this," Menlos said, shaking his head and pointing at the dark skies beyond the balcony. Movement at the stairs drew Cyrus's gaze back; this time, Erith Frostmoor was rising up them, looking a little tired, as though she were forcing herself up the last steps only through great effort.

"What's going on?" Vara asked, voice heavy with concern. She was coiled tightly beneath her armor, watching the two officers of Sanctuary as they stood, Menlos still examining the tower, Erith staring at her feet as though she had news of the worst sort to deliver.

"You haven't heard?" Menlos asked.

"Heard what?" Vara asked.

Menlos glanced around once more then gestured his hand toward the fire. "Heard … anything?"

Cyrus stared at the hearth, the flames blazing hot and high, and a sudden chill ran down his back, unrelated the weather or the soaking. He cast his eyes around the room swiftly, saw the torches burning high, and then the doors rattled hard once again, in the wind—

"No …" Cyrus muttered, "not the wind …" The gust's timing was wrong, it came after the rattle, the balcony doors struggling to burst free of their bindings, trying to warn the occupants of Sanctuary in the manner that they always did when they were—

"Dear boy," Malpravus said, his head appearing at the top of the stairs as he strode up into the Tower of the Guildmaster as though he owned it himself. The necromancer's cowl was draped behind his head, and he looked like a thin shadow rising up the stairs into this place where he so definitely did not belong. Cyrus's mind screamed its alarm at the mere sight of him, his muscles tense at the invasion of his home, and it only worsened, turning to rage as Rhane Ermoc followed a pace behind, grinning as his master spoke, Praelior held ready in his hand. "I must say …" Malpravus grinned, standing tall in the Tower of the Guildmaster, casting his shadow as the hearths violently spat fire all around them at the intrusion, "… it is so very good to see you again."

78.

"Let us not be hasty in our action," Malpravus said, holding up a hand as Cyrus grasped for Rodanthar's hilt, "for it would be a shame if your new bride were to have her soul ripped out irreparably before your very eyes." He twisted his thin fingers in front of him, and they glowed with dark light. "I can do it, but I would be loathe to harm you in such a manner, dear boy. Please don't force me to."

"How did you get here?" Cyrus asked, his fingers dangling above Rodanthar's hilt, seemingly a mile away. There was a bitter taste in his mouth, the shock at seeing Malpravus here, in this place, almost as immediate and powerful as a punch to the jaw from a rock giant.

"Oh, that was simple," Malpravus said, "I had my good friend Erith open your portal to me and my friends." He smiled, beckoning Erith forward, and she came to stand next to him, still staring at her feet. "Even now, my army is swarming into your keep, paying their respects to your noble defenders." He raised a thin eyebrow and then looked back at Erith. "Did you know I've had her watching you for all these years?"

"I had no idea she was a lying traitor, no," Cyrus said. Erith blanched but said nothing.

"Why, she joined Sanctuary at my behest," Malpravus said. "She came to Goliath first, wanting to leave the Daring behind, but I persuaded her that she could do so much more good by watching you lot here, making certain that you never got yourselves into too much trouble without me knowing about it." He glanced at Menlos, who stood with his wolves arrayed tightly around him, all faced toward Vara. "Of course, Orion recruited our other friend here to come join you, keep a watch of his own. He came to join us but we sent him back to you after he told us he'd met you during your little trip through the north, and hasn't he been just invaluable in keeping us apprised of everything?" Malpravus waved behind him, and Sareea Scyros emerged from the stairs with another figure—Mathyas Tarreau. "And this one, of course, has earned his due from Goliath. He is an officer now as well, having served us truly and faithfully."

"You've done a marvelous job undercutting my every action these last few years," Cyrus said, unable to take his eyes off the horror unfolding before him. Lightning flashed outside, illuminating the shadowed trenches in Malpravus's skull-like face.

"I have undercut very few of your actions, in fact," Malpravus said with the air of a lecturer patiently correcting a student. "It was not I who got you declared heretic, who turned the King of the Elves or the Council of Twelve against you. You did all that on your very own, without any of my assistance. Only when absolutely necessary to my goals have I brought you low, and you have done the same to me, I might add. Except that I have actually tried to help you on several occasions—why, I even had Orion extend an offer to you to join us, and you should have taken us up on that generous overture, or the one I made after it. This rift between us is quite senseless. You are powerful, there is no doubt of that. There is no need for constant clashes betwixt us."

"I've never sent an assassin after you, Malpravus," Cyrus said, staring the necromancer down. "I can't say the same for you."

"Surely you understand that was not my doing, not truly," Malpravus said, sounding offended. "The Council of Twelve sanctioned your death; I sent only the barest minimum I could get away with and look convincing. If I'd intended you to die I would have sent far, far more than I did, I assure you." His eyes glinted as he smiled like snaked. "If I wanted you dead ... you would be dead."

Cyrus started to turn his head to look at Vara, but the necromancer spoke again, drawing his attention back. "Ah ah ah!" Malpravus said. "Don't get any terrible ideas for heroic maneuvers. Your bravery is already well known to all, and I have no interest in hurting either one of you. I haven't hurt your last wife, after all. She's been my honored guest these last several months."

"Where is Imina?" Cyrus asked, staring back at Malpravus's smug face.

"Safe, of course," Malpravus said. "Under guard, naturally, at my home." Cyrus debated throwing the name out, but Malpravus beat him to it. "Of course by now," the necromancer said, "you know how to get to Zanbellish ... but you haven't come to visit." He smiled thinly. "I think I know why, but I can assure you, you would be met with a warm welcome."

"That's why I don't visit," Cyrus said. "I've enjoyed enough of your hospitality."

"Such an unpleasant sentiment," Malpravus said, walking to the wall and running his hand over the wet stones. "I only wish to educate you, to give you a chance to live up to your ... potential." He appraised Cyrus carefully as his thin hand slid over the wet surface of the stone wall. "You don't even realize what you have at your own fingertips. But I could help you. Aid you. Be the counsel that you have lacked these last years, stagnant, barely stumbling toward the greatness you once sought—"

"I doubt I'd find much greatness at your side," Cyrus said, fixed on the necromancer.

"You need all the help you can get," Malpravus said, almost sadly, "and I have studied the paths of power and advanced greatly since last we met, when your compatriot, Curatio, awakened me to possibilities, some of which I had not previously considered—power you sorely need, for I know you know," he nearly whispered, "in your heart of hearts ... that Bellarum is hardly done with you."

The chill in Cyrus's bones became a hard freeze that spread to his skin, cold all over him as he stood there. "What do you know?"

"It is not about what I know," Malpravus said, "at least, not all that I alone know. If you have spoken to Carrack, you will know the power that I seek." His bony face remained intent upon Cyrus. "The power you should be seeking."

"The power to destroy a city?" Cyrus asked, barely controlling his face, his fury. He longed to look at Vara, to seek her counsel, but she was just out of his view. He could still feel her touch upon his lips and wondered at her silence. "The power to level Aloakna, for instance?"

Malpravus breathed, almost silently in the storm, his nostrils flaring slightly. "Your dear mother understood that power. She left you behind to seek it, to exercise it ..."

Cyrus's right hand clenched, still so far from Rodanthar's hilt that the sword might as well have been in Fertiss. Menlos, Mathyas, Rhane and Sareea all stood before him, their weapons already drawn, and Erith stood a step ahead, as withdrawn as Larana had ever been. *I need help,* Cyrus realized at last. *This is too much, too much for Vara and I. The power ...*

He blinked. *Perhaps ... perhaps Malpravus has a point about power ...*

"Together we can take our first steps to ensuring your triumph in your next meeting with the God of War," Malpravus said, stepping back over to him, eminently reasonable, an island of calm in the middle of the storm. "We can take them right here, in this place, today ..." He stood before Cyrus, backed by his small army, the rest of his force surging through the halls of Sanctuary, drowning every floor in the blood of the last defenders. "Put aside the maudlin sentimentality," Malpravus said, taking another step toward him, smoothly and slowly, "this weak and craven desire to seek out a home and a family to make up for the one that you never knew as a child ... Walk in your mother's footsteps, as you were always meant to, the way she wanted you—"

The spell-blast hit Malpravus from behind and knocked him forward as though a barrel of Dragon's Breath had exploded behind him. The necromancer flew into the gap between Cyrus and Vara as Cyrus whipped around to see him rolling to a halt on the soaking balcony, his robes drenched within an instant of being hurled into the storm. Cyrus snapped his head back around in time to see—

Larana floating with Philos in hand, just above the stairs, officers of Sanctuary flooding up behind her—Vaste, blood running from his forehead; Ryin, hands aglow with lightning and fire; J'anda, his furious face lit by the purple glow of his staff's orb; Scuddar In'shara with his scimitar at the ready; and Mendicant scampering up at the last, looking more furious and feral, teeth bared, than Cyrus could ever recall seeing him.

"You strike hard, witch," Malpravus said, coming back to his feet, his robes smoking beneath him, "but my army will see you finished—"

"Your army is gone," Larana said, all trace of meekness gone, "and I have sealed the portal on them. Some, as they were coming through, in fact—" Her cheeks quivered with fury, alight with the glow of her hands, one burning a furious crimson and the other blue. "They didn't quite make it, at least—not all the pieces of them did. Those that made it before them are dead to the very last."

Cyrus turned his head back to look at Malpravus, whose own lips were quivering now, though whether in disappointment or fury, Cyrus could not say. "Very good, then," the necromancer said, drawing himself. "You always escaped my notice before—the cook, the smith, the tailor—always trifling with silly things ... but now I see you plain, the last secret that Alaric Garaunt hid in open sight." The necromancer laughed, but it was dry and sounded sick. "I cannot believe I missed it. I should have known ... he was far too soft-hearted to have done the thing ..."

"Done what thing?" Cyrus asked, the Tower of the Guildmaster turned as still and silent as if there were no storm, the sound of wind and thunder replaced by the crackle of the magics convulsing upon Larana's hands.

Malpravus lifted off the ground, gliding, his own hands springing to life in a mirror image of Larana's, golden-green coruscating on one, glowing black crackling around the other. "A brilliant deception, really. I never would have guessed him capable of it, but that was another of his little games, I suppose. To think that *he* did not know that you were hiding before him all the while ..."

"Oh, Goddess," Vara murmured, breaking her silence at last, transfixed upon Larana, her eyes wide with awe. "It's you. It's ... it's really ... *you*."

"It is me," Larana said, but as Cyrus stared at her, the Larana that he had known since he had come to this place seemed to fade before his eyes; not an illusion, but something else. There was more of what he had seen from her earlier, in Aloakna—the confidence, the straightness in her bearing, the strength that he had thought endowed by Philos, still gripped in her hands, spell-light burning around it stronger than anything he'd seen from anyone other than Curatio. Her eyes, though, were locked on him, a dazzling green and pained, watching him in fear. Even through her youthful appearance—so much younger than she should have been—now it was obvious, and he recognized her at last, as he had known her ... as he had last seen her, before she had left him, some twenty-odd years earlier.

"It is you, indeed," Malpravus spat, hatred lining his words.

"Quinneria."

79.

The fight had begun before Cyrus even realized it, and without him even knowing what had started it. Before he even had a full accounting of what was happening, Menlos Irontooth's wolves set upon Vara and she met one of them with a sword stroke that cleaved one cleanly in half, the top portion flung out the nearest balcony and over the edge while the other two snarled and snapped their teeth, dragging at her arm and her leg. Menlos himself screamed in fury and came at her with his short sword while she was distracted with his animals.

Vaste now joined the fray, his spear held aloft as he plunged toward Menlos from behind, but still several feet away; J'anda had his staff in the air and it glowed, purple light streaking toward Erith, who stood staring, her eyes aglow with magic. Scuddar was attacking Sareea Scyros and she was attacking back, her hand glowing black as she cast a spell and Scuddar's scimitar and hand alight with some magic of their own as he struck Sareea's sword, seemingly unmoved by whatever she had cast.

The fight in the middle of the room had divided Cyrus from Vara, the spellcraft of his mother—whom he could scarcely believe was there, standing in front of him—matched against Malpravus. It was a blur of color, a glow of horrible magical power, their spells clashing and forcing Cyrus back from the pure energy blasting between them. His mother looked like a fury unleashed, more power pouring off her than he could ever recall seeing from Curatio, and Malpravus matching it, his lips drawn back in an angry rictus, his dark magics surging forward as Cyrus moved aside—

He nearly had his head struck from his shoulders as Rhane Ermoc surged toward him, Praelior in hand. The warrior came at him hard, but the hearth exploded in a timely blast of fire, distracting Ermoc just enough to send him charging past Cyrus, the heat bellowing out of the fireplace strong enough that Cyrus could feel it on his cheeks as he grasped for Rodanthar and drew his sword at last.

He saw Ryin surging forward, spell-light in his own hands, fire burning forth and consuming Mathyas Tarreau, the human completely enveloped by the druid's blossoming fire spell. Tarreau was gone in an instant, but the flames lingered, casting shadows in the chaotic tower as the air was rent by the frenzied heretical magics being flung about around them. The whole tower shook, and Cyrus saw the contest between his mother and Malpravus explode skyward, ripping an immense hole in the ceiling—

"You can't evade me!" Ermoc screamed over the magical release behind him. He came back again at Cyrus, who was dazed by the sheer overload of activity around them. Cyrus offered a half-hearted defense against Ermoc, barely turning him aside, but Ermoc's own anger and overzealous attack cost him far more than Cyrus's defense. He stumbled, but Cyrus was in no position to exploit the mistake; his stance was weak, and he had been caught off balance in his last-ditch attempt to defend himself.

J'anda stepped forth and turned loose a blast of magic all his own toward Malpravus, who was still standing out on the balcony, strangely untouched by the rain hammering down around him. It was as though the magic being flung from his bony fingers was evaporating all the liquid before it touched the ground. Magic streamed from his spell-lit hands like smoke from a fire, colored faintly in the same green-gold and near black as his spells, still pouring out at Quinneria, who continued to match him with her own, their powers pooling and wrestling with each other in a miasma of colors in the center of the room.

Cyrus caught a glimpse of Vara cutting another wolf down, stabbing with her sword while Vaste was sparring with Menlos, barely keeping the Northman, his face red with anger, at bay with his staff-turned-spear. Vaste's own face was a deep shade of green, Cyrus saw between the flashes of the magical bout occurring in the center of the room.

Ryin stepped up next to J'anda and poured a fire spell in next to J'anda's casting; they seemed to run together, twisting with Quinneria's own contribution to the fight, and pushing the magical maelstrom closer to Malpravus. Cyrus blinked away from it, scarcely believing what he was seeing. *That's ... that's not how magic works, is it?*

Well ... it's how Curatio did it in the Citadel ...

Ermoc's scream of rage brought Cyrus back to himself in time for the warrior's next attack. Cyrus was staggering, so rattled about by the fighting around him, by the thoughts in his head that he could not get a full grasp of what he was doing nor what he was supposed to be doing. Ermoc came in low with his attack and Praelior clanged against the lower part of Cyrus's breastplate, making him grunt from the impact, like a weak punch to the stomach. It caught him by surprise, but by pure reflex he reached out with a riposte of his own, catching Ermoc squarely in the mouth with the tip of his sword.

Ermoc squealed and spun away, trying to drag Praelior with him, away from where he'd just clashed with Cyrus. Cyrus fumbled with his free hand but grasped Ermoc's wrist with clumsy fingers and yanked, causing the Goliath warrior to extend his arm farther than it was meant to go. His weight warred against his own shoulder, and Ermoc yelped in pain as his bones cracked and he began to fall. His fingers let loose of the blade—

Cyrus let go of Ermoc's hand ... and caught Praelior's grip in his fingers.

The feeling was immediate and fierce, like a sudden splash of water to the face on a hot, lethargic day. The world spun down even slower, the magical battle before him turning into a contest of light, pulses of energy running out of the hands of all the combatants, meeting in the center in an ever-expanding emanation of spells that was now throwing off its own blasts in seemingly random directions. One streaked across the wall behind Ermoc and left a black, burnt scorch mark as it blasted a balcony door to pieces. Mendicant had joined the fray, pouring his own spells into the fracas, but Cyrus could see no advantage being had by any side, just a steadily worsening storm of magic that seemed to be eating the roof of the Tower of the Guildmaster whole as its fury blew skyward.

Through it all, Cyrus saw Vara run her sword through Menlos Irontooth's chest once, then again, tearing through the Northman's leather armor, dark liquid rolling down his bearded chin as he slumped, just before Vaste plunged his own spear through the warrior's guts. There were no more wolves moving over there, just the healer and the paladin, finishing their task as the roiling torrent of magic crackled beside them.

Cyrus turned to see Ermoc scrambling away from him, holding his shoulder at a pained angle, his lips split from nose to chin and blood pouring out like magic from Quinneria's fingers. The Goliath warrior ducked a surge of magical energy and hid himself behind Malpravus's billowing cloak as the energy seemed to begin turning against him, the overwhelming power directed toward the necromancer apparently too much for even him to handle.

A scream drew Cyrus's attention toward Scuddar, who held out a hand and sent Sareea flying as though he'd just cast a force blast spell. This one was different, however, with no shuddering effect to the air around her. Sareea disappeared in the twinkle of her return spell as she passed through the balcony doors, apparently removing herself from the battle.

Malpravus locked eyes, covetous and angry, with Cyrus through the currents of magic eddying around him, and then the necromancer disappeared in his own return spell, dragging Rhane Ermoc unwittingly with him as Ermoc hurled himself upon the dark elf at the last moment.

Unblocked any longer by Malpravus, the magical pool of light that had been gathering in the center of the Tower shuddered once and then blasted through the space where the necromancer had been standing, then faded as the casters let their spells die one by one, Mendicant being the last to quit.

There was silence for a moment once it was finished. J'anda leaned upon his staff, the purple glow still alive on the orb, his breathing loud and labored. Rain began to pound down through the immense hole in the roof; the battle of magics had left less than half the tower's ceiling in place, and the storm outside was raging still, lightning flashing above them.

"Heinous shits," Vaste said, leaning on his own spear, looking right at Quinneria in their midst. She hovered above the ground a foot or so, staring at the place where Malpravus had been. "It's really you."

"It really is," Quinneria said, and when she spoke, Cyrus recognized her voice. It was not the muted, hushed whisper of the druid she had pretended to be for so long, and she carried none of the age he would have expected from her. She looked younger than he did, but he knew it was her nonetheless.

"Amazing," Mendicant whispered as the sky outside rumbled with a hard peal of thunder. The smell of burnt ash was in the air, and a piece of the tower's roof came fluttering down like parchment. "The sorceress has been among us all this time ..."

"The guild," Cyrus said, coming back to himself at last. Even with both Praelior and Rodanthar in hand, he felt as though he could scarcely think quickly enough. The world was moving slowly, painfully slowly; Ryin, too, was eyeing Quinneria warily, and Scuddar had come back to the center of the room, his scimitar dark with navy blood along the edge, the sword still held lightly in his grasp, ready to be employed if needed.

"They are safe," Quinneria said quietly, still staring after Malpravus. "I killed the Goliath invaders when I returned and saw them teleporting in. Still ... there were probably some losses; I did not check any other floors before coming straight here."

"We need to ..." Cyrus lost his voice; it left him as surely as anything—anyone—had left him before.

"Yes," Vara said, taking up for him, her forehead smeared with red. "We need to go floor by floor, ensuring that Sanctuary is clear of any remaining—"

"It is," Ryin said quietly, and nodded at the hearth, which was burning normally. The torches, too, had returned to their normal levels. "Or so says Sanctuary itself."

"Still," Vaste said, straightening up to hold himself awkwardly, "perhaps ... perhaps we should do a search, floor by floor. Make certain that we deal with any stragglers. Resurrect any of the fallen. And, uh, get the hell out of here before Arkaria's most awkward conversation, possibly ever, occurs." He fled toward the stairs, not once looking back.

"I ... am with you on that," Ryin said. Scuddar followed after looking curiously at Cyrus and receiving a nod. With that, the desert man seemed to recuse himself, leaving at once.

"What would you like me to do with her?" J'anda asked, brandishing his staff.

Cyrus blinked, and realized that Erith was standing beside him, her eyes still glazed, clearly under the influence of the enchanter. "I ..."

"Put her in the dungeon," Vara said sharply. "Under guard and cessation. We will deal with the traitor on the morrow ... in the manner her crime demands."

"I will watch over her myself," J'anda said with a grim nod of the head. He took a fortifying breath and marched away toward the stairs, leading Erith with his staff almost poking her in the back. She walked without will, without resistance, and Cyrus watched her go with a trace of regret and little more.

"The sorceress …" Mendicant whispered, still looking up at Quinneria in awe, rain washing down on the goblin. He did not seem to notice the drenching he was receiving, too busy was he looking up at her with something akin to worship in his eyes.

"Mendicant," Vara said quietly, "would you mind terribly leaving us be?" She spoke into the storm that broke through around the shattered tower, pouring in through the open doors and shattered roof, like emotions daring to rush into Cyrus—

Except … he did not feel anything. There was faintest hint of an emotion, like a trace of something he'd known once, but it was more akin to shock, than anything else. He simply stared at the sorceress Quinneria and dimly wondered if perhaps he was gaping like Mendicant.

"Oh …" the goblin said, stirred by Vara's words. "Of … course," he said, not sounding entirely like himself. He loped along toward the stairs, though, and disappeared down them a moment later. Cyrus listened, but did not hear the door shut. Part of him wondered if it had survived the battle and all the endless parade that had come before.

Quinneria floated down to the ground, her robes parting enough that he could see her bare feet touch the stone soundlessly as the wind roared around them. The rain was tapering, but the thunder continued, a flash of light followed by the deep rumble some seconds later. So it was when she spoke; he heard her, but the meaning only came after an interval of time. "So … I suppose you have questions."

Cyrus felt parched, as though he'd not had anything to drink in a year. He licked his lips; they felt chapped, cracked. He took a breath and it hung in his chest, ached inside him where Ermoc had slapped his breastplate into his belly. He clutched the two swords, one in each hand, but said nothing.

"I see you found your father's sword," Quinneria said at last. "I left it for you. I was wondering if you were ever going to check your scabbard."

"I …" Cyrus said, dimly, blinking, the vision before him clearly not right. He could see Vara beyond Quinneria's shoulder, staring back at him in silent support, her wet golden hair once more streaked with red from battle, and he had a moment's remembrance for what they had been doing, the small intimacy shared before Malpravus and his cohorts had appeared.

"Say something," Vara urged him quietly, her voice almost lost to the wind. "Cyrus …"

Cyrus looked upon Quinneria with faint disbelief. Before him stood a woman that he had thought he had known, that he had steadfastly ignored, and hidden beneath her veneer all this while had been something he never would have believed. It came rushing in on him all at once, the realization that this was her, that the meat pies she had fixed him always, since the day he had arrived, were the ones she had fixed when he was a child, and that the way she looked at him—that everyone always swore was love—actually was. It was her love for him as she watched over him, that her fear when he was injured or died was a mother's fear … that she had been here all along, had been with him, within feet of him … and had never said a single word to make him wiser.

It all hit him at once, like the largest war hammer dropped upon his head, and he felt it in a rush, every emotion across the spectrum, and it threatened to choke him as he spoke at last. "Hello …" he whispered, and she looked at him with those green eyes, the ones he had never once recognized until now, "… Mother."

80.

"I should start," Quinneria said, standing in the middle of the Tower of the Guildmaster, rain pouring down through the immense hole in the roof beside her, the tapping of water on stone almost as loud as the occasional cracks of thunder rumbling outside, "by saying I'm sorry."

Cyrus stood there, the fire in the hearth behind him casting warmth upon his back, the chill of the wind seeping in through the cracks in his armor and over his drenched underclothes. The two extremes battled for a moment before warmth won out in the form of a crackling fire in his belly that burst out of him in long peals of laughter that doubled him over. He laughed long and loud, amazed at the absurdity of her statement. She watched him until he settled, the mirth fleeing with its warmth and allowing the cold its victory. "You're … *sorry?*"

"I am," she said, bowing her head, the familiar mannerisms of Larana the near-invisible druid returning.

"For what?" Cyrus asked, causing her to lift her head in surprise. Vara, too, looked surprised from her place opposite him, Quinneria between them. "For … abandoning me?" That one struck true, and Quinneria bowed her head again. "For letting me be raised by animals?" He nodded at the corpse of one of Menlos Irontooth's wolves, lying close by its finished master. "For letting me forget what sleeping in a warm bed, safe and sound, felt like? For having others teach me, in most dramatic terms, what it was like to fear for your life every single day of it?" He chuckled under his breath, but it was a cold and crackling sound, all warmth gone. "Sorry for that?"

"I am … so sorry … for all of that … and so much more," she said, looking up at him with those green eyes, the ones that had feared to meet his for so long.

"How did you survive?" Cyrus asked then stopped himself, slamming Rodanthar into his scabbard. "Never mind. Alaric. Like Malpravus said, just another secret." He looked hard at his mother. "I guess the question is … how did you pull it over on Pretnam Urides?"

"It wasn't easy," she said faintly.

"But it was necessary, I assume?" Cyrus stared right at her. "I mean, I presume it was, unless you just … didn't want to be a mother anymore—"

"I never—" Her head snapped up. "I was a heretic, Cyrus. You know the pain that comes from the whole of the land turning against you, but you knew it with a guild at your back—"

"A much-reduced, constantly shrinking, schisming-with-perpetual-betrayals guild, but I suppose, yes—"

"You weren't alone," she said quietly. "But when I left you … when they turned on me … I didn't see it coming, and I was alone. My friends couldn't help, even the ones who wanted to—Cora, Pradhar, Erkhardt, Raifa—"

"Your friends are curiously symmetrical with the founders of Sanctuary," Vara said, her voice quiet, almost displaced, as though it did not belong in this tower at all. She sounded small, Cyrus realized.

"They were my friends before they were the founders," Quinneria said, taking her eyes off of Cyrus only long enough to answer Vara's question. "I knew them before Alaric did. I brought them here—"

"I don't need to hear this," Cyrus said, shaking his head. "Not now. If you want to share the history of Sanctuary, you can do at a Council meeting on the morrow." He took a sharp breath that felt like a dagger in his lungs. "We need one anyway, to try and figure out what to do next, how to handle Malpravus—"

"I can help you with that," she breathed, loud enough to be heard over the wind, only barely.

"Wonderful," Cyrus said, thinking it was anything but. "We'll see you in the morning, then." He gestured at the stairs.

"Cyrus, I—" Quinneria began, but a great cracking sounded above them, and only too late did Cyrus realize it was not thunder at all.

A wooden beam that ran the length of the roof came crashing down, dragging the top of the tower with it. The cracking and moaning of the shingles and wood in the wind had been disguised in the fury of the storm. But now it had reached its end, and collapsing, Cyrus could see it all rushing down at them, falling precipitously—

Red spell-light blasted forth, consuming every bit of the ceiling as it fell, all save for that large beam that had held it all together. It hit the ground between them, splitting neatly between Cyrus and Quinneria as it landed. The rest of the roof was swept away in the coursing magic of destruction cast by his mother, the only remains ashes that fluttered down from the heavens with the drenching rain.

They stood there, exposed, the rain pounding the completely uncovered Tower of the Guildmaster, Cyrus breathing steadily in and out as he was showered with the downpour, staring across the fallen beam at his mother and beyond her, his wife. "Thank you," he said coolly, without a trace of actual gratitude, for he found he could not even find that particular emotion in himself at the moment. There were others absent as well, but he did not care. "Now … if you'll excuse me …"

Cyrus went for the staircase, the rain rattling him as much as the events of the evening, but his name, called out forcefully in a voice he had not heard in twenty-seven years, stopped him. "Cyrus!"

He turned slowly and saw the face of his mother, the disappointment in her eyes. "What?" he asked, softly in the storm.

"Ask it," Quinneria said as Vara eased past her. "I know … I know you feel it … just … ask me the question on your mind … the one above all others."

Cyrus stared back at her, his mouth still dry. He turned his face to the heavens, letting the rain soak him, hoping it would bring him back to life, but it did not. He stared at her through the falling water between them. "Why …" he began, and his voice cracked partway through the question, "… why did you leave me?"

"Because I thought you would be better off without me," she said, and the profusion of emotions melded together in her voice and upon her face left him in no doubt of her sincerity.

"Well … I wasn't," he said simply. Vara came to his side, and they walked down the stairs together, leaving his mother, and the storm, behind them.

81.

"Cyrus," Vara said as they circled the stairwell back down to the officer quarters, torchlight dancing orange and yellow upon the stone walls, "we should talk about this."

"Can we not?" Cyrus asked, letting his feet slam down upon each stair. He did not intend to stomp, but driven by his slowly emerging emotions, each step became more forceful. He stopped abruptly and she nearly slammed into him, her face leaning down to his as she halted. "Two of our officers just betrayed us and opened our halls to Goliath. For all we know, the rest of the guild is dead."

"And yet," Vara said, patiently as if talking to a child, "your mother has just returned from death—"

"She wasn't dead," Cyrus said, "she was hiding all along, right among us. She could have said something at any moment in the last seven years. But she didn't." He pulled himself up tall and found himself looking his wife straight in the eye on her higher step. "I don't want to deal with … this … at the moment." And he turned and started back down the stairs.

"Then what do you want to deal with?" she asked, trailing behind him.

"Absolutely anything else," he said, almost running into Vaste as he came round the corner at the landing.

"Oh, there you are," Vaste said. "I was hoping to run into you post-argument."

"And you usually are so very interested in the dramatic interplay between our members," Vara tossed down from above. "I find it hard to believe you wouldn't want to be present for a conversation between Cyrus and his long-lost mother."

"You forget that his long-lost mother killed some ten thousand of my people," Vaste said, staring up at Vara with little amusement. "I don't really want to be in the same room with her at all, and while I'm certain I'm not feeling it the way Cyrus is, he's not the only one stinging from her betrayal." He rubbed his stomach. "I've been eating cooking prepared by the sorceress ever since I got here. I think my stomach is objecting." He shook his head in disgust. "She lulled me with those luscious fruit pies. Why, she could have been poisoning me all along, for all I know."

"You are still with us," Vara pointed out drily, "thus it seems unlikely she was poisoning you, unless it was the sort of poison that slowly kills the brain ... which I might find believable."

"She's your mother-in-law," Vaste said, "aren't you supposed to hate her on that basis alone?"

"Vaste," Cyrus said, "the guild?"

"Oh, right," Vaste said, deflating slightly. "It seems Erith and Menlos weren't the only traitors that rose up against us tonight. There were some pitched battles in the north towers while we were battling things out in your quarters. I just got a runner back from the wall, and it appears we're down to four hundred and fifty two." He sighed. "We lost a few in the fights as well. No resurrection possible."

Cyrus punched the wall with Praelior still clutched in his fist and it left an indent in the stone. "Godsdammit."

"You're angry," Vara said.

"And you're beautiful and terrifying," Vaste said, and when they both turned to look at them, he said, "Sorry. Thought we were just stating obvious facts."

"Damned right I'm angry," Cyrus said, pulling back his fist, still clenching the sword. "We lost a lot of good people tonight, and all to treachery." He looked down at Vaste. "Tell J'anda to bring Erith out onto the lawn. Assemble the guild."

Vara leaned forward and placed a clinking gauntlet upon his shoulder. "Wait. We shouldn't do this now."

"Now is exactly the time we should do this," Cyrus said, turning about. "Do you imagine the resolution will be different tomorrow? Or the day after? Ten weeks from now? A year?"

Vara withdrew her hand, her eyes falling. "No. No ... it ... it wouldn't." She nodded once. "I suppose ... we might as well, then."

"You're serious, aren't you?" Vaste said, standing stiffly on the landing, as though all the breath had gone out of him. "You want me to ... to gather everyone together and ... and tell them—"

"Tell them it's time for an execution," Cyrus said, far more calmly than he felt on the inside. "Tell them it's time for Erith Frostmoor to die for her crimes against Sanctuary."

82.

The rain poured down in the muddy yard around them as Cyrus stood steadfast against the winds. The big doors to Sanctuary were wide open, the bloody remainder of the great battle still obvious on the floors around the great seal within. The steady rattle of the rain, absent the earlier lightning and thunder, suggested to him that the worst of the storm was now over. The chill remained, however, as members of Sanctuary filtered out under the night sky in small groups, clinging tightly together and muttering among themselves.

The officers were clustered around Cyrus, silent as he was, and every last one of them stood tall and proud, unbowed. The only one absent was J'anda, who Cyrus knew was waiting, waiting until everyone had time to gather to bring the prisoner out.

"We're actually going to do this, then?" Vaste asked, quietly, as a distant rumble echoed across the sky.

"We are," Cyrus said.

"Far be it from me to argue," Calene Raverle said, shivering beneath her cloak, "but are you sure she betrayed us?"

"Malpravus brought her up to our quarters and she as much as admitted she opened the portal for him," Vara said in a dead voice. "Menlos was more enthusiastic in his admission of betrayal, but I don't think there's much doubt she was betraying us."

"I can hardly believe it," Calene said. "And I especially can't believe all that happened while I was on the wall. We had no idea anything was even amiss until the tower exploded." She shook beneath her cowl, rain dripping around its edges. "What a night."

"This is a good choice," Longwell said, his voice shaking as he spoke. "I can't fathom it, either, but if you say she's guilty, I believe you."

"She's guilty," Cyrus said, standing immobile in the rain, feeling the cool streaks running down his face. "You'll see."

In the great doors came another shadow, a familiar silhouette lit by the illumination within. For a moment, it stole Cyrus's breath, seeing that helm, the armor, and then he remembered that it was not Alaric Garaunt within it.

Terian came down the steps, Dahveed Thalless and Kahlee both behind him as he hurried over to Cyrus. "Gods, Davidon," he said as he came up, "Mendicant just delivered the word to us. You're all right?"

Cyrus frowned. "I'm fine. Why did Mendicant come to you?"

"Because I told him to," Vaste said. "I figured our allies ought to be made aware that we'd been attacked from within our own walls. Give them a sporting chance in case Malpravus planned to do the same to any of them."

"My guards are on highest alert," Terian said, nodding his thanks to Vaste, "as are the ones at Emerald Fields." He leaned in to speak to Cyrus. "Is it true? Did Erith let them in?"

"She did," Cyrus said dully, water sliding coldly down his spine. "We're about to deal with it."

Terian pulled back and removed his helm, his face creased with a heavy frown. "Deal with it how?"

Cyrus stared back at him blankly. "How do you usually deal with traitors?"

"Well, I kill them, personally," Terian said, breaking into a weak smile, "but you—you usually let us traitors go after we try and kill you, giving us plenty of opportunity to do the same again. It's something of a pattern with you."

"The pattern is now over," Cyrus pronounced. "Erith is going to die … right now." He saw J'anda leading the prisoner out, Zarnn and his trolls providing a guard.

Terian spun around, helm still in hand, his hair soaked through after only a few seconds with his helm off. "I don't know whether to be impressed or depressed at this change, Davidon."

"Just be glad it didn't come two betrayals ago, I'd say." Cyrus kept his eyes on the condemned as Terian took a place beside him, Dahveed and Kahlee maintaining their position behind the Sovereign.

Vara leaned up behind him and whispered in his ear. "You can't be the one to do this." When he half-turned to hear her out, she went on.

"Let me."

"Why?" he asked, blinking away his surprise.

"Because I'm the Elder," she said.

"Why ... really?" he asked.

"Because you have enough on your mind," Vara whispered, "and you don't need to add this—and possible regret later, once you've cleared it somewhat."

"I doubt I'll regret this," Cyrus said as Erith was led down the steps. J'anda kept poking her in the back with his staff, hard, and she was resisting him all the way. Clearly, the mesmerization spell was no longer in effect.

"All the same," Vara said, "I should be the one to do it. The Elder is the Guildmaster's right hand; that's why I sit where I do at the table."

Cyrus opened his mouth to protest, then stopped himself. *Why not? I won't feel a thing if I do it anyway—not anger, not satisfaction, nothing.* "All right. Have at it."

Vara stepped forward, and her voice boomed out over the storm, over the rain falling in the great puddles standing all around them. "Erith Frostmoor ... you are accused of treason against Sanctuary. Malpravus himself named you responsible for opening our portal to invasion by our enemies, Goliath, and you yourself did willingly acknowledge him to be truthful."

"I ... I did not!" she cried. "I was—I was under the influence of a spell!"

"That is not so," J'anda said from behind her, nudging her once more with his staff. Zarnn and his trolls were flanking her on all sides, looking particularly enraged, even for them. *Must be something about treachery,* Cyrus thought, *perhaps after Grunt, it hits close to home for them.* "If you had been under the influence of another enchanter, I would have felt it when I cast my spell upon you during the battle."

A ripple of conversations spread through the assemblage; Vara cut it short by speaking again. "Your excuses are like this sodden ground— they hold no more water."

"Please," Erith said, and now she was speaking directly to Cyrus, "I've been here for years. I came when no one else would—"

"At the behest of Malpravus," Cyrus said quietly, "and to spy for Goliath."

Erith's face was in shadow, but her whole frame was tense beneath her robes, her hands shaking at her sides, either from cold or fear. She looked to Terian and drew a sharp breath. "Terian! Terian, during the revolution, I—I helped you when no one else would! Please! Have mercy! Help me!"

Terian stared at her, hard, his jaw working. "All right," he said finally and tossed Cyrus a look. He reached back and unslung his axe as Cyrus watched, and then flipped it so that he was gripping it just beneath the blade. He extended the haft to Vara, who took it cautiously. "Make it clean and fast," Terian said, and Erith gasped. Terian looked straight at the healer and said, "Our debt is now squared; I've done all that I can for you."

"There is no mercy to be had here," Vara said, advancing on Erith, who ran into Zarnn and another troll as she tried to back up. Zarnn shoved her forward, and the healer stumbled. "Kneel, and I'll do as Terian asked, and make it quick. Resist, and I will tear you apart one piece at a time with a thousand swipes."

"No—" Erith gasped. Cyrus could still not see her face, but she stood frozen for a moment, clearly looking out at the crowd. She held up a hand, presumably to cast a spell, but nothing happened; a cessation had been cast by J'anda before he had even put her in her cell. She locked on Dahveed. "Dahveed! You—please, you can't just watch—I've known you since—"

Dahveed spoke in his low, clear voice. "I have given you every opportunity I could, Erith, but apparently your own choices have led you down a terrible path. I am sorry I ever took you out of Sovar; you would have been better served to stay there, I think."

"No," Erith whispered, but she sank to her knees, white robes drooping into the mud, already soaked from the rain. "I ... I can't ..." she raised her head, and Cyrus could see the glare of wetness on her cheeks, and not just from the rain. "It wasn't supposed to end like this."

"You should have known it would, when you betrayed us," Vara said, stepping beside her and lifting the Battle Axe of Darkness above her head. "You can find no more faithful friend than Sanctuary ... and no more relentless enemy, either—"

The axe fell cleanly and the deed was done, hints of dark blue staining the puddles of mud lit by the torchlight falling out of the front doors to Sanctuary. "Someone needs to burn the body," Cyrus said, and turned to detour around the place where the traitor had fallen.

"What about the head?" Vaste asked, not moving. After a moment, Cyrus realized he meant to do the task himself.

Cyrus froze on the bottom step, rain falling all around him. "Burn that, too," he said and walked away from the execution, no more cold or numb than he was when it had begun.

83.

"Well, this is a slightly different Council than the one we had a few days ago," Ryin said sourly on the next day, "and we even have a new table. Will the reckless pace of change around here never cease?" Light streamed in through the windows behind Cyrus, illuminating Council Chambers in which every single seat was full.

Cyrus had entered the chambers after Erith's execution to find the old round table burnt to ash during the battle. A new one sat in its place, rectangular, dragged up from the Great Hall by some of the survivors. Cyrus sat at its head and stared down at the grain of the wood, unfamiliar and uncomfortable, then at the black soot that stained the ceiling above it. He ran his fingers over the slightly rougher surface, looking up at the black stain upon the ceiling with steadily smoldering fury. *It's almost as though Malpravus couldn't countenance the thought of leaving that particular symbol of Sanctuary alive. Truly, I cannot picture many more spiteful swipes at us he could have taken than this.*

Terian sat to Cyrus's immediate left, followed by Calene, Scuddar, Vaste, Longwell, Quinneria down that side of the table. The end opposite him was unoccupied, but Aisling sat across from Cyrus's mother, Cattrine Tiernan to her left, followed in turn by Mendicant, Ryin, J'anda, and finally Vara at Cyrus's right, his wife more serious than he could recall ever seeing her. She too was staring resentfully at the new table and the scorched ceiling in turn. Malpravus's fire had consumed the chairs save for Cyrus's, and now the rest of the officers sat in heavily padded seats.

"Speaking from experience," Terian said, rubbing his own gauntlet over the new table, "while change is seldom comfortable, it is almost always preferable to the still peace of death." He looked around the room. "And I think the new faces are a nice touch – speaking as one of them, of course."

"And this is more representative of who's been making the decisions around here of late," Scuddar said in his low voice.

Cyrus shifted in his tall chair, feeling not for the first time that he was utterly out of place. "We've been in a very … tight space this last few months. Seeking outside help was advisable, and we wouldn't have made it through in even the poor shape we're in if not for Terian, Aisling, Cattrine and …" he cleared his throat, "… Quinneria."

"Yes, so very nice to meet you for the first time, truly," Vaste said, overly loudly. "I can't thank you enough for all those pies … that had no poison in them."

"That you know of," Quinneria said, pointedly not looking at him.

Vaste's lips puckered. "Oh. Dear."

"Yes, very nice to meet you," Cattrine said, adjusting herself in her seat. "Who is this again?"

"I'm Cyrus's mother," Quinneria said, leaning across the table to offer a hand.

Cattrine and Aisling both snapped their heads around to look at Cyrus. "You told me your mother was dead," they said in unison.

"This is why I stuck to whorehouses," Terian said under his breath, so low that only Cyrus and Vara could hear him.

"I thought she was," Cyrus said. A night of restless turning had left him without much in the way of clarity, nor anything, truly, save for heavy eyelids. *I can't decide which of these developments I'm most disturbed by; the return of my mother, the betrayal of Erith and Menlos, the invasion of Sanctuary by Goliath, or…the damned table.* He looked down once more at the rectangle of wood in the center of the room. *Perhaps this is simply the most obvious reminder of all the other changes.*

"And all along you've been here," J'anda said, staring at Quinneria. "If I might … you look so very young. Younger than he does—" he pointed at Cyrus.

"This seat ages you, I'm just going to say it right now," Cyrus said, thumping his arm rest a little mournfully. "There's a reason Alaric was all grey, and I'm not convinced it was his age. He was probably like twenty-five before he took this chair—"

"Alaric Garaunt was older than you think," Quinneria said, interlacing her fingers in front of her. She looked back at J'anda. "And you're too kind. Yes, I'm older now, for a human. Over sixty."

"But it's not an illusion," J'anda watched her carefully. "I would be able to see—"

"It's not an illusion," Quinneria said with a shake of the head. "It is magic, though. It's—it's tied to ... well, to what Malpravus is doing now, to some extent—"

"Which, coincidentally, is the reason I asked you to speak to the Council," Cyrus said, interrupting her, "so perhaps you could just slide past the explanation for why you look so young and launch right into how you went nose-to-nose with Malpravus last night with spellcraft of the like I've never seen outside of what Curatio did last time he faced Malpravus."

Quinneria nodded slowly. "Why don't I start at the beginning and work my way up because there are things you need to know," she looked very pointedly at Cyrus, "in order to understand what Malpravus has become ... and what he's doing now." She sat almost as far away from him as she could without taking the seat at the other end of the table. *Intentional?* Cyrus wondered. *Perhaps she's played the role of Larana for so long she still feels the need to hide...*

"Things it might have been useful to know months or years ago, but that you didn't want to tell us," Vaste said. When Quinneria looked across Longwell at him, he held up his hands. "For very, very good reasons I'm sure."

"Because Alaric didn't want anyone to know," Quinneria said. "So good or bad, the reasons were his, and I have been here in Sanctuary as his guest, thus it was not my place to say, nor to expose any secrets he wished me to keep." Once more she looked at Cyrus, but he kept his gaze pointed at the table in front of her.

"But now that Alaric is out of the picture, shall we say ...?" Vara asked.

Quinneria shifted in her chair once more. "Now that Malpravus is moving, and Curatio is no longer here ... there are things you need to know. So. The beginning ..."

"I wish I had something to eat while listening to this story," Vaste muttered. "It just feels like it's going to be a long one, as though she's about to make up for not speaking all these years."

With a spin of her fingers, magic danced out of Quinneria's hand and a pie appeared in front of Vaste. He peered at it suspiciously. "I can't poison a conjured pie, Vaste," she said with mild annoyance, "and if had any objections to you as a troll, I would have killed you long, long ago." She paused. "I like you. You're … funny, and warm, and kind. Nothing at all like what I ever thought a troll would be, based on my … limited experience with them."

"Your son had similar notions I had to disabuse him of," Vaste said, digging into the pie with his bare hands. "I see it runs in the family."

"When I married Rusyl Davidon," Quinneria said, speaking into the room, which was quiet except for the sound of Vaste slurping and chewing, "he was a young warrior and I was a new graduate of the Commonwealth of Arcanists. We set up our homestead in Reikonos, and I stayed there with Cyrus after he was born, reading obscure texts from the library in the city in my spare time and improving my skills while my husband worked at various points as an instructor at the Society of Arms, as a guardsman for Reikonos, and finally, when the troll war broke out, as a soldier in the army."

"Those damned trolls," Vaste muttered, his mouth full of pie.

"I often have that same thought," Vara said crossly.

"Rusyl left to go to war," Quinneria went on a little sadly, "but Cyrus was growing brighter every day. I started to teach him the fundamentals of magic, the building blocks that you all learn in the early days at your various Leagues; all the simple things—"

"Such as …?" Longwell asked, peering intently at her.

She took a breath. "If you'd like, I could teach you. It would make you a heretic, but you could learn—"

"Whoa, whoa," Calene said, her lips froze in an O. "I thought it wasn't possible for folk with no magic to learn magic."

"Yeah," Terian said, "that's another League lie."

Cyrus blinked, looking sideways at Terian. "You knew this?"

Terian looked right back at Cyrus. "I thought you knew it, too, given that with no prior magical experience you threw a fire spell in Talikartin the Guardian's face a year ago."

"But she just said she trained me before," Cyrus said, pointing at Quinneria. "And I found out she was my mother right after it happened, so I just assumed—"

"Knowing the building blocks I taught you allowed you to use the fire spell Mendicant gave you the words for," Quinneria said, looking right at him. "It saved your life. Without that training, the words are just empty words. You have to know how to discipline your mind to bring the effect into being, and that takes practice. There are also different aptitudes." She looked nervously around the table. "Some people start better at magic than others. Natural talent. Almost everyone can learn at least some with practice, but like anything else, some people start out ahead."

"This is all very interesting," Vaste said, still munching, red berry juice spilling down his chin like blood. "If that's the case, why don't more people use magic?"

"Because the Leagues don't want them to," Quinneria said. "Or more accurately—"

"The gods don't want them to," Terian said darkly.

"Because using multiple disciplines makes us more powerful as spellcasters?" Ryin asked, seemingly genuinely curious.

"Because magic taught along League lines not only sterilizes and eliminates the more dangerous, frightening elements and spells," Quinneria said, "but also because the Leagues are utterly under the control of the gods. They are part and parcel of the gods' efforts to hold back the study of magic in Arkaria. Magic of the sort Curatio used, the kind he called his 'heresy,' was an absolute threat to the gods. He, Alaric, and I used it in the Realm of Purgatory on the day we rescued you." She turned her gaze to Vara.

Vara met her eyes and stared back, blinking. "You were there, too, then."

"I was," Quinneria said. "They needed my help; my spellcraft was not as refined as Curatio's, because I haven't lived as long, but I was a stronger spellcaster."

"So fascinating," Mendicant said in quiet awe. "The spell you used at Thurren Hill …"

"Yes, let's bring up the dead trolls again," Vaste said, "so fun … and while I'm eating, no less."

"Shove the rest of the pie in your mouth and be done already," Vara snapped at him.

"I can't," Vaste said, slipping a piece of crust in his mouth. "It's so moist! So succulent! It's jubilation given fruit and dough form, and I can't believe it's been conjured out of air!"

Cyrus looked at Scuddar. "You knew magic wasn't a thing limited just to the chosen of the Leagues, didn't you?"

The desert man nodded slowly. "My people ... dabble. And I have heard the way your League members talk about magic." He shook his head, chuckling. "So very ... limited."

"I learned similar truths in Gren a few years ago," Vaste said, indicating faded scars on his forehead. "Shamanic magics taught by the elder trolls are a far cry from the League dribblings. The shaman I learned from suggested things like curses that could be placed on, uh ... entire cities." He looked nervously at Quinneria, who smiled benignly back at him.

"Like the scourge?" Cattrine asked, looking lost.

"Like Aloakna," Aisling said next to her, rolling her head back against the seat.

"What happened in Aloakna," Quinneria said, "ties very closely with what I think Malpravus is after. The ... the ancients, as you call them," she looked a little embarrassed, "they didn't use magic with League constraints. That's why they were destroyed, that's why the gods put forth the Leagues, to keep what happened ten thousand years ago from happening again."

"What happened ten thousand years ago?" Cattrine asked, putting a hand to her head. "Other than the breaking of the three kingdoms of Luukessia when Lord Garrick failed to claim the throne of Enrant Monge?" Her eyes flashed in triumph. "See? I can refer to things none of you have any idea about."

"I knew what you were talking about," Longwell said with a touch of pride.

"As did I, for I knew Lord Ulric Garrick," Quinneria said, staring sadly at Cattrine.

"I thought you said you were only sixty?" J'anda asked tentatively.

"I am," Quinneria said, "but you all knew Garrick as well; you just didn't know him by that name." Her eyes were downcast, her manner grim. "You knew him as Alaric Garaunt."

84.

Cyrus slammed his palm against the new table with a thump that stunned the whole room. "Dammit," he said mildly, cracking his knuckles. "Forgot I didn't have my gauntlet on."

"What is it?" Vara asked, voice rising in alarm.

"What?" Cyrus looked over at her. "Oh. It's ... Dieron Buchau—"

"The stableboy?" Ryin asked. "What does he have to do with this?"

"He told me about Lord Garrick when we were at Enrant Monge," Cyrus said, staring at the table, shaking his head in disappointment. "He told me about ... about a prophecy, I guess ... that Lord Garrick would save the Luukessians at their darkest hour."

"Oh, wow," Vaste said into the shocked silence. "I guess whoever predicted that one missed big. I mean, really big, since the whole damned land went down to—"

"Idiot!" Vara hissed, "Alaric saved those people on the bridge by sacrificing himself." Her cheeks burned red. "He fulfilled the bloody prophecy."

"I'm still stuck on Alaric living ten thousand years," Longwell said through narrowed eyes. "I realize I tend to be the skeptic on these ... uhrm ... mystical godly things that you people go right for, but ... uhrm ... he's not a man, then, is he? I mean, a human being would die after a hundred years. Right?" He looked around the table for support and his eyes landed on Cyrus.

"I always thought so," Cyrus said and glanced sideways at Vara. "In fact, it's been the source of a few arguments in my life."

"Well, Alaric was human, but he had some other things going on that made him less than normal," Quinneria said. "Again, this ties to the ancients in a very significant way—the ancients were obsessed with immortality, with power—"

"I bet the gods didn't like that," Vara muttered under her breath.

"Nobody likes it when you take the things they want," Aisling said, and, upon getting a heat glare from Vara, amended, "or so I've been told."

"These ancients are starting to sound an awful lot like Malpravus," Cyrus said, drumming his fingers on the table.

"And so they were," Quinneria said, nodding. "Which brings us to him. The spell I used against the trolls … it wasn't a simple curse." She glanced at Vaste, then looked away, seemingly ashamed. "I didn't just … hex their lives away."

"But they all bloody well died, didn't they?" Vara asked. "All ten thousand of them?"

"That's a number that keeps coming up today," Vaste said.

"It's very round," J'anda said. "Like you, if you keep eating whole pies."

Vaste rested his hands on his ample belly. "It would be worth it for these pies."

"For those trolls … I … stole their lives away," Quinneria said.

"WITH PIE?!" Vaste sat up.

"With a branch of magic that was long ago forbidden by the Leagues," Quinneria said as Vaste relaxed. "For I discovered a very old book in my studies, one that … well, one that I wasn't meant to see." She scratched the base of her neck. "It … there were things in there that set me upon my path to heresy, that had me experimenting with magics I wasn't supposed to know. And when Rusyl died …" she looked right at Cyrus, and once more he turned away, "… I picked up his sword and went right to the war, fighting with Rodanthar the way he'd taught me in our home—just as he taught Cyrus—and wielding my spells, the ones I'd worked on secretly, when no one but Cyrus was watching."

"This branch of magic you played with," Terian said, chewing on one corner of his mouth, "was it tied to the dark knight spells that steal vitality?"

"Yes," Quinneria said.

"I would have assumed necromancy," Mendicant said, bubbling with excitement, "something in the realm of a Soul Sacrifice."

"They're one and the same," Quinneria said. "The line between them is artificial, drawn by the Leagues to keep people from delving as deep as I did—for reasons that should be obvious. It's the same magic, the same effect. The only difference is … I didn't stop where they drew the line. I didn't use a Soul Ruby," she swallowed heavily, "I didn't bother using a blade to inflict harm first, I just reached out with the spell … and ripped the souls of ten thousand trolls right out of their bodies across the field of battle." Silence fell over the room.

"Well, isn't that a lovely bit of history," Vaste said, brushing the crumbs from his hands uncomfortably.

"It's not just history," Quinneria said, straightening up in her seat, "that's—it's essentially what Yartraak did in Aloakna." She looked at Cyrus again, and this time he could not help but look back. "It's the power Malpravus is seeking."

"And it's the reason why you haven't aged since you did it," Terian said, staring at her, "it's because you stole those souls, those lives—their vitality."

"Yes," Quinneria said with a nod, "and it's clearly what Malpravus is aiming to do. What he will do, if left alone long enough. By what he showed us in the tower … he's close. He's where I was just before I broke through, and if he's in an old city of the ancients … they were experimenting with these spells, drawing energy. It's how they powered their empire. If he's down there in Zanbellish, it's entirely possible he has access to a book or an archive of the sort that I found, that taught me how to become …" she put her hands out before her, "… what I am now."

Terian gritted his teeth and turned to Cyrus. "What do we do? Carrack told us that the portal in Zanbellish was guarded, that anyone who steps through is going to die."

"Not anyone," Vara said quietly, looking sideways at Cyrus, who looked back at her. "He seemed to be quite willing to welcome you."

"This is the thing that puzzles me," J'anda said, shaking his head. "Why does he endeavor so hard to curry your favor, Cyrus?"

"Because when Cyrus came to Sanctuary," Vaste said quietly, "he wasn't looking for bonds of fellowship." The troll stared straight at Cyrus, a sad smile on his face, "he was looking for better armor, better weapons, to move up in the world. He had the same motives as Malpravus, and Malpravus thinks …" He shrugged.

"That I can be swayed back to that same view again, given the right opportunity," Cyrus said. "That I would forsake all the bonds of fellowship I've found here and give it all up ... to be stronger."

"Is he right?" Ryin asked into the silence that followed. J'anda casually tipped his staff back and bopped Ryin lightly in the forehead, drawing an "Owww!" from the druid. He pulled his hand away, still frowning. "Fine. Forget that I asked."

"No," Cyrus said, standing and put his hand on his helm, clunking it against the table, "he's not right. Because Malpravus's very concept of what a guild is, is utterly irreconcilable with my vision of the same. He wants power, and he built Goliath around that idea; everyone there is bound by their common ambition. He even views leadership differently than we do, which is probably why he turned our table to ash on his way up to the tower." Cyrus pulled his hand from the helm and started to pace to the left around the long table. "Sanctuary was never like that. I may have come here with that in mind, but Alaric deprived me of any illusion that this was the reason for Sanctuary to be relatively quickly." He landed a hand on the back of Terian's seat. "Our reason for being here isn't common ambition."

"Damned right," Terian said under his breath, forcing a weak smile.

"Our reason for being here isn't because we're desperately seeking to live forever, to put the stopper in the sands of time," Cyrus went on, striding past Calene.

"But ... but we wouldn't mind doing that if we could, would we?" Calene asked in a small voice. "I mean, if it's not too far out of the way ..."

Cyrus continued his slow walk, pacing past a nodding Scuddar. "It's not petty ambition, it's not armor, it's not—"

"PIE!" Vaste shouted as Cyrus passed him. He shrugged with only a little contrition. "What? Pie is at least as important as armor and ambition."

"We fight for home," Cyrus said, nodding at Longwell, who nodded back as Cyrus passed behind him, the dragoon thumping the haft of his lance into the floor in approval. We fight for ... family," Cyrus said, passing Quinneria with a look that traced its way over the features of a mother he only barely recalled. He went around the empty far end and stopped behind Aisling's seat. "We fight for redemption, for the things we've done wrong in the past." She looked back at him, just a glance, and then looked away. "We fight for our people," he said as he passed

Cattrine. "For the right to be our best selves, to be known for us rather than those who we spring from," he passed Mendicant, "to be—"

"Immense, contrary pains in the arse," Ryin said with a smirk as Cyrus went by him.

"—to speak our minds freely," Cyrus said with a smile, "to not be cowed into silence because our opinions do not jibe with our fellows." He paused behind J'anda's chair. "We fight to not be afraid." He walked slowly behind Vara, trailing a hand over the back of her chair as he went by, "and we fight for those we care most about." She looked into his eyes, her blue ones shining in the summer sun filtering in from the balcony windows as she nodded.

"You should have said that when you were walking behind me," Vaste said.

"Malpravus will never truly understand any of those things," Cyrus said, coming back to his own seat, "for Malpravus only cares about Malpravus, and to hell with anyone who gets in the way of that." He thumped down heavily into his chair. "No, I won't ever go back to how I was." He lowered his voice. "Since the day I entered these halls, I've paid a price for these things I believe. I've lost ..." He thought of Narstron, of Niamh, of Andren, of Alaric and the countless others, and his throat felt too small to let his voice out. "... too much to go back. But that doesn't mean I can't go to Malpravus in Zanbellish ..." a nervous grumble ran through the room, but Cyrus only smiled, "... and pretend I see it his way."

85.

"This is a mad, terrible idea," Vara said only a few minutes later as they all stood around the Council Chamber in a nervous circle that mirrored the shape of the old table that was now replaced behind them, the long shafts of light coming through the balcony windows illuminating the deeper grain of the new table's wood. The fires crackled low in the hearths, and everyone stood silent.

"So it's like all of my ideas, then," Cyrus said with a smile, trying to reassure her.

She looked worried. "Let me come with you," Vara said.

"No." Cyrus shook his head. "This is not a fight, it's an ambush. We'll be going in at Malpravus's mercy, and I've heard from too many people that he has none for you. I can't take the chance."

She held herself out, away from him, standing at her place in the circle while he remained in the middle, and he could feel the gulf between them like a distance of thousands of miles. "But you can take the chance with him?" She pointed at Cyrus's companion in the circle.

Ryin Ayend stood next to him, frowning. "That's an excellent point. Why are you bringing me along, out of all the possible options available to you?"

Cyrus did not look at the druid as he answered. "Because you're the least threatening choice."

Ryin bristled. "I'll have you know I cut a very imposing figure in battle."

"Oh, I know," Cyrus said, "I saw what you did to Mathyas Tarreau."

Ryin settled slightly, looking a bit mollified. "Well, the bastard deserved it. Who knows how many good people he cost us?"

"So," Vaste said, staring intently at Quinneria, "you've been conjuring all of our meals, all this time?"

"Well, I did have to cook some when people brought me food," Quinneria said, "from hunting game and from Emerald Fields' harvests and such, but I used magic to do the preparation and just hid behind an illusion all the while."

Vaste was frowning. "So … what were you doing with all that free time when it appeared you were cooking?"

"Well, I learned blacksmithing," she said, "and carpentry, and continued my research into arcane spellcraft with Curatio's assistance, some of the practices of natural, medicinal healing …"

"Oh, good, then you can take over the Halls of Healing," Vaste said. "Also … this explains why the cuisine didn't suffer the year of the siege …"

Cyrus looked up at Vara and saw the fear in her eyes. "I'll be back, I swear it."

"Your return does not concern me half as much as your leaving in the first place," she said.

"Remember," he said with a smile, "I told you everyone leaves."

She gave him a look that dripped with familiar annoyance. "Your mother came back, dunce, and I am still here. Your point no longer stands."

"Cyrus," Terian said, stepping up to him in the circle, "say the word and I'll come with you, ten thousand troops at my back."

"Absolutely not," Cyrus said.

"Hmph," Terian said. "You're turning down the aid of the foremost paladin in Saekaj Sovar."

Vara made a face. "You're the only paladin in Saekaj Sovar."

"And thus the best," Terian said with a smirk. "Come on, Vara. Usually you're smarter than this. What's wrong? Is a steady diet of warrior seed killing your intelligence?"

Cyrus tossed an ice spell against Terian's helm, frosting it lightly across the eye slits. "I'm not just a warrior anymore." He stared at the paladin as Terian brushed the ice out of the way, and suddenly he knew what he had to say. "And you can't drag your nation, your people, into war to save me and my three hundred anymore, Terian."

"I can," Terian said, pulling Alaric's old helm off his head and wiping clean the face. "I will. Because as you just pointed out, that spirit, those bonds—that's what Sanctuary is." He looked around the circle.

"And while I may not be here as a member with you anymore, I wear this armor for a reason. Saekaj Sovar is governed by the principles you elucidated." He put the cleaned helm back on his head. "And I still stand with you—brother."

"Feeling a little weepy," Vaste sniffed. "Dangerously weepy."

"Would you like another pie to soothe your nerves?" Quinneria asked.

"Oh, gods, I'm going to cry," Vaste said.

"At the risk of interrupting Vaste's tearful moment," Cattrine said, "I would like to add to what Terian said—we of Emerald Fields stand with you as well, in the same way you have stood by us through all that came. If you need us, we will send every single soldier wherever you require it, at a moment's notice." She smiled warmly. "Together we stand."

"And there's not even a demonic porcupine or squirrel to blame this time," Vaste murmured, his big eyes glistening.

"Take utmost care, Cyrus," Aisling said, eyeing him with an appraising look. "I'd offer you my dagger, but it seems you have more weapons than you know what to do with." She nodded at Rodanthar, which was presently thrust inside his belt, no scabbard to call its own.

"I can—I can give you the scabbard for that," Quinneria said, voice hushed like she had assumed the persona of Larana again for a moment. "There are ..." She looked in Cyrus's eyes as he met hers, "many things I could—that I would love to tell you. The history of our family, of ... what I've learned ... or about your childhood ... anything you want to know ..."

Cyrus stared back at her, his throat tight once more. "I ... I do want to hear them."

Vaste sniffed. "This is too much." Quinneria flicked her fingers and a pie appeared in his hands. "No, wait. *Now* it's too much." He lowered his face and a falling tear sizzled against its warm, flaky top. "Why does this feel like—like the end?"

"Because our Guildmaster is about to hand himself over to the most evil necromancer who has ever lived," J'anda said.

"Nobody mentions me, of course," Ryin muttered.

"Let's get this over with, he-who-was-not-mentioned," Cyrus said, clapping Ryin on the shoulder. "When we get there, if you can, teleport out immediately. Don't wait."

"You want me to leave you there," Ryin said quietly.

"If you can," Cyrus said, "yes."

"I didn't like the sound of this when we started to discuss it," Longwell said, looking a bit stricken under his helm, "and it's not improving with time. The grapes are turning to vinegar, not wine."

"Oh … can you make a grape pie?" Vaste asked, looking over at Quinneria.

"Ryin, take us away," Cyrus said, turning his gaze back to Vara one last time.

She waited there, her expression as serious as he could ever remember. She was standing, back straight, her hand drifting toward her sword's hilt in the same manner as his, watching him. She seemed to be trying to hold it all in, to keep it together, chin up, as she watched him. With a blur of wind, she began to disappear in the power of the druid teleportation spell. It whipped hard around him, like the typhoon in Aloakna, and with a rush he was carried away from his friends, his home and his wife, and some small part of him worried, as they did, that he might not see them again.

86.

When the wind of the teleportation spell died down, Cyrus was left with an impression of jungle ruins, swallowed up by time and nature, and of little sign of life save for the greenery that sprouted everywhere. The air was hot and heavy, as though rain were coming soon and the air could no longer contain itself. Sweat started down his back the instant the spell faded around him, and he breathed deeply as he looked around for the inevitable attack.

"This is … quiet," Ryin said, bumping his back against Cyrus's as they both stood, waiting, the sound of insects chirping in the distance like some choir in an elven temple.

"I thought I told you to leave," Cyrus said. "Is there a cessation spell over this place?"

"I don't know, I haven't tested," Ryin said, voice tense. "If you think I'm leaving you here, you weren't listening to your own speech earlier."

"Damn you people for being so loyal," Cyrus said, eyes flicking over a building completely swallowed up by thick jungle vines, trees sprouting out of the strange stones that seemed to make up a road through the ground they stood upon. "I guess if you weren't, though, you'd be gone like the rest."

"True enough," Ryin said tensely, and his voice scratched as he spoke. "Do you see anything?"

Cyrus peered into the city's jungle landscape; it looked very much as though something had stood here once that had been better built than Reikonos or Santir or Isselhelm; it was almost as though one of the elven cities had been utterly swallowed by the greenery the elves so revered, as if nature and life had been given infinite license to run amok in their carefully built places. Something moved and Cyrus followed it without thought; it was a small animal, and he breathed half a breath out. "I see a squirrel. Which, unless you're Vaste, is probably not cause for concern."

"I see grasshoppers skipping through the fields ahead," Ryin said from behind him, still pressed to his back. "I see fallen buildings hewn out of the same kind of stone as the Citadel in Reikonos, stretching, ruined, as far as my sight reaches."

Cyrus breathed in through his nose, felt the heaviness of the air, sweat dripping down his face and tickling his unshaven jawline as it streamed past the hairs. "Same." He gazed into the distance; Ryin was correct, there seemed an infinite number of the box-like dwellings before him, all carved out of stone, all probably as perfectly constructed as the Citadel at one time, he figured. Now, though, rough edges were showing, chips from the sides of the blocks, a weathering effect unseen in the tall tower in Reikonos. Time had done its hard work upon this place in a way that the Citadel had not seen, and the vines that covered everything hinted at a fate that Cyrus did not wish to ponder too deeply. "I don't hear anything but nature."

"Nor do I," Ryin said, "though I find myself wishing we'd brought an elf now."

Cyrus straightened up and drew Rodanthar. He'd kept his hand from the hilt when they'd teleported, fearing to provoke a reaction from Goliath that might result in Ryin's death, but now that they'd arrived, the jungle noises and the still air worried him more than when he was certain he was teleporting into the heart of the enemy.

Four large buildings stood grouped around the portal. Cyrus glanced back at the portal itself, expecting to find it similarly covered in vines. It was not, however, and dried branches on the ground around it suggested to him that Goliath had spent a fair amount of time clearing it of vegetation since their arrival. Each of the buildings nearest to them was large; at least as large as the smaller guildhalls in Reikonos, and three or four times the size of the average home in Termina. Cyrus reckoned they were at least three stories tall, but with a wider base. He could see an entry to each of them, stationed roughly on the building where it would have been had any of the powers of the modern day constructed it—centered, and with steps leading up into the dark interiors, no hint of a door remaining.

Cyrus stared into the shadowy interior of the nearest building and reached back to tap Ryin on the arm. The druid jumped at the touch and spun to face the same direction as Cyrus. "Should we go inside?" Ryin asked.

"Well, we could stand out here all day and wait for the Goliath guards to come collect us," Cyrus said, "but frankly, I expected that would have happened by now, and since it hasn't, I'm starting to think that we should poke around, see if anyone's still here."

"What possible reason could they have to abandon it?" Ryin said, sweat streaming down his own forehead. He wiped at it with his sleeve, darkening the material with moisture. "They have an army significantly larger than our own. Even if they suspected we were coming with everything—dark elves and Luukessians—all they would need do is either shut off the portal or gather around it with spears and plunge them into invaders as they appeared, the way everyone else does."

"Malpravus seldom does exactly what's expected of him," Cyrus said, starting slowly toward the open door. He rustled the grass with a boot as he brushed over a crack that was splitting wide with green rushes. "I suspect he's not about to start just because he's chasing immortality; he's not got it yet, after all."

"Still," Ryin said, "it doesn't make much sense to leave his base behind ... unless he needed his army for something else."

That caused a cold prick of fear to run up Cyrus's back. "There's nowhere he could deploy an army of twenty thousand that he'd be able to have much effect. As you said, everyone's guarding their portals."

"Well, that's a relief, then," Ryin said with heavy irony. "Clearly they can do absolutely no harm, anywhere."

"If only that were so," Cyrus said, his boots softly tapping upon the stone with each footfall. He drew Praelior as well, just to be safe, and the world slowed to a crawl around him. More than the effect of each sword by itself, holding both the blades seemed to compound their abilities. A cricket's chirp dragged over seconds, and he jerked forward in a swift motion, leaving Ryin behind, following at a crawl.

"Good gods," Ryin said, every word proceeding slowly from his mouth, barely understandable as language. "You're so—"

"I know," Cyrus said, walking back to him with easy steps. *I probably look like I'm dashing around in a blur, worse than Ermoc did when he had Praelior alone, or like Terian does with Noctus.*

They walked together, Cyrus carefully controlling his pace, under a sweltering sun that filtered in from the green canopy above, branches reaching out between the trees that had sprouted in this place. They touched and had grown together, forming a network of branches and vines that seemed bound close to keep out the sun in places. Cyrus observed a shadowed space between two buildings, the boughs and other bindings between them so thick that the alley looked to be in deepest darkness.

Cyrus kept his ears prepared for something, anything, but over the sound of the insects and their own footsteps, he heard nothing but the occasional chirp of birds in the distance.

"This is unnerving," Ryin said under his breath. "I am becoming unnerved."

"Nothing's happening," Cyrus muttered slowly back to him as they walked, the druid only a step behind him. Ryin still squinted as though he were having difficulty understanding.

"That's the problem," Ryin said. "The tension is as thick as the air. If Goliath had just attacked already, we would know they are here, the problem would be settled, one way or another—"

"Likely ending in your death."

"But it would be settled," Ryin said patiently.

"With your death!"

"And thus I'd be free from worry." Ryin's robes trailed against sprouting grass, causing it to rustle beneath him. The druid nearly jumped out of his skin, and when he landed, his soft leather shoes clapped against the stone road. "Gyah! You see what I mean?"

"And I hear it," Cyrus said, listening carefully to Ryin's shout echoing through the jungle, the birds now silent. "As I suspect everyone else in this part of Arkaria just did."

They were only some twenty paces from the entry to the building now, the shadows pooling deeply under the arch that led within. Cyrus still could not see inside no matter how he squinted. He cast the Eagle Eye spell upon himself under his breath, but it only served to let him see the darkness closer; there was no substance to it, no shape, just a hallway lacking light from above thanks to the boughs and branches and vines hanging over the building, very much like a tunnel under a mountain.

"Come on," Cyrus whispered, and started forward again, just as silently, "and try not to get scared by your own shadow this time."

"It's not *my* shadow I'm afraid of," Ryin said, "it's all the other ones in this place."

Cyrus crept closer, and the darkness deepened, the lines of the hallway within the door becoming clearer the closer they got. Cyrus clutched both swords, listening carefully, wondering if he were missing something, Ryin a pace behind him, holding his breath as they drew closer ... and closer ...

"There's nobody in there," came a voice from behind them.

Ryin jumped again. "AUGH!" the druid called, shaking under his robes as Cyrus spun to see who had spoken—

And Cyrus froze himself when he saw, in wonder and surprise, the person standing in the entry to the building across from him.

Her hair was long and dark, though it looked stringy and unclean. Her skin was dark as though she'd been outside every day of her life, though Cyrus remembered it in exactly that shade even in times where she had not ventured much out of doors. Even from this distance he could see the relief in her green eyes, though he did not immediately recognize her face, the face of a flower girl he had purchased a glowrose from only a few years earlier—

"Imina," Cyrus whispered, and he saw the relief sag into her figure as he broke into a run toward her, cutting across the distance between them in mere seconds.

"Cyrus," Ryin said, hurrying after him, "exercise caution. You don't know—"

"I have the Eagle Eye spell upon me, Ryin," Cyrus said. "If she were an illusion, I would see it."

"Still," Ryin said, his leather soles slapping hard against the stones as they ran, "caution is never a bad thing to employ; it's not as though anyone has ever said, 'I wish I was more heedless in my actions—'"

"I've often thought that," Cyrus said, "in regards to my pursuit of Vara." He thundered to a stop a few feet away from Imina where she stood under the canopy, tiny pinpricks of light breaking through between leaves to shine upon her like diamonds on her simple cloth dress. It did not look new but nor did it look old, merely a bit weathered, as though it had seen some considerable use. She wore sandals, and her feet looked rugged, as though from long walking. "Imina ..."

"Cyrus," Imina said, smiling faintly. "He said you would come."

"Are you ...?" Cyrus stood back, afraid to come any closer, afraid he would see—a bloodless wound to indicate death, her very nature being controlled by Malpravus, something, anything to indicate the treachery he was coming to expect. "Are you all right?"

"I'm fine," she said with a breath of relief. "They all left, all of them, and he came to me before they did, told me they would leave me here for you to find."

"That's incredibly generous of them," Ryin said suspiciously, arriving slightly winded at Cyrus's side. "And a bit kinder that I would expect from Malpravus."

"He treated me decently," Imina said, looking right at Cyrus. "He seemed very fixed on not upsetting you unduly."

"I guess I didn't notice that proclivity in my dealings with him," Cyrus said, still holding back from her, his suspicions a wedge between them that he did not dare remove. "Why did he leave you behind?"

"He was done with me," she said, her thin shoulders shaking very slightly as she shrugged. "He had no further use for me, he said, and rather than march me into harm with his army, he simply left me behind … to convey a message."

Cyrus chilled immediately, the hot jungle sun forgotten. "What message?"

Imina looked at Ryin, and then at him. "He said … that he was sorry you were interrupted the other night. He said that … you will come to see it his way, before the end. That he was not done, that there is more that needs to be finished between you."

"Oh, indeed," Ryin muttered, "there's a good spilling of blood still demanded betwixt you."

"He didn't want to fight," Imina said. "He seemed … disappointed that it came to that. He wanted to show you something. 'The first steps,' he called them. He wanted to harness some power, wanted you to see it."

"Where is he?" Cyrus asked coldly, staring into the distant eyes of his former wife as she stared back at him, just a touch too blankly for his liking. She did not seem as though she were fully here, and he found it worrying. *Is it all in my mind? Or is she … different?* He watched her carefully, wondering. *All these betrayals have left me second-guessing everything.*

Imina's gaze snapped into place on his, and she shook again, just slightly, as though emotion long held back began to make its way out. "He's …" She brought her lips together and seemed to try to swallow, but choked slightly. "He'll ... be coming for you, he said. He'll call out for you when the moment is right." She looked up, and her eyes glistened at the corners. "He said so."

"I just bet he will," Ryin said softly.

"When?" Cyrus asked, taking a step closer. Imina watched him, tracking him as he approached, and she shuddered once more, in a way that Cyrus never remembered her doing, not ever before in all the years he'd known her.

She held out a hand to stay him, backing up just a step, slowly. He stopped, and she lowered her hand, then closed her eyes and nodded before opening them again. "He told me ... told me to tell you ... soon. That he would call for you very, very soon."

87.

"This is quite the surprise," Vara said as they all stood once more in the Council Chambers of Sanctuary, light waning as the sun sank in the afternoon sky. "Here I thought Ryin would be back instantly and you later, if at all—and certainly not with a ... guest." She peered at Imina suspiciously, though whether it was born of Imina's recent proximity to Goliath and Malpravus or something more personal, Cyrus was not entirely certain.

"Heh." Aisling chortled slightly under her breath, her lips tightly pushed together and her cheeks rounded as though she were holding in a laugh as she looked sideways at Cattrine. "Heh heh."

Cattrine looked back at her, frowning, as Aisling's eyes darted to Imina and then Vara. "What ...? OH." And the Administrator of the Emerald Fields flushed a deep shade of red.

"What?" Vara snapped.

Aisling still made a great show of containing her smile. She nodded at Imina, then Cattrine, then shrugged her own shoulders and nodded at Vara. "It would appear the gang's all here."

"The ... what?" Ryin asked with a frown.

"That's a pitifully small crowd, Davidon," Terian said, with a frown of his own. "The greatest warrior in Arkaria should have done better."

"What?" Cyrus jerked his head around at Terian. "What the hell are you people on abo—" He realized what they meant as the thought landed on him with the force of an axe to the middle of his head. "Oh. Gods."

"I have no idea what we're talking about," Ryin said, looking to J'anda for guidance. The enchanter, however, was a particularly dark shade of blue and pretending to look out the window.

"Oh, I get it now," Vaste said, cradling his belly in discomfort. He cringed in pain and rubbed his midsection.

"I don't," Scuddar said with a shrug.

"Well," Calene said, whispering a little too loudly, "I think we've got assembled here before us all the lovers of Cyrus Davidon—"

"Enough," Vara said in disgust.

"Oh, Cyrus," Quinneria said, putting her hand on her face to cover a blush.

"What?" Cyrus threw up his hands. "This is—a—I mean—how is this my f—you know what, we have bigger problems to worry about right now." His cheeks burned hot with embarrassment, and he tried to turn himself toward righteous indignation. "Malpravus is apparently of a mind to call me out, and soon, according to Imina."

"It's what he said." Imina looked a little flustered herself, though she was looking between Aisling, Cattrine and Vara in turn with a fair amount of dark suspicion of her own. "Also, I would rather not be here at all, if I may make it plain—"

"You're free to return to Reikonos if you'd like," Cyrus said.

"And what guarantee do I have that your enemies won't come after me again?" Imina said, her own cheeks reddening as she turned to face him down. He'd seen her like this before many times, especially at the end of their marriage. *At least she seems to be coming back to herself now*, he thought.

"Well, there are quite a few less of them now," Mendicant said, "at least versus when they last attempted it."

"That is true," Calene agreed, "we've been quite efficiently wiping them out as we go. If this keeps up, maybe we'll see Goliath's end here soon enough."

"One can hope," Terian said.

"Would you like us to keep her under guard?" Scuddar asked Cyrus, his quiet voice cutting over all else with a certain solemnity that Cyrus would not have found out of place in a temple.

"She can go if she wants," Cyrus said, "or she can stay." He looked right at Imina. "Up to you."

"I don't know where Malpravus means to have his clash with you," Imina said quietly, staring straight into his eyes with a coldness that he did not remember even in the worst of their fights, "but I want to be as far away from it as possible when it happens."

"Sister," Vaste announced, "you aren't the only one."

"Well, she has sense," Vara said.

"Don't we all?" Cattrine asked with a cocked eyebrow.

"*You* do," Vara said.

"Which means I don't, apparently," Aisling said with another roll of the eyes.

"I reserve my opinion on you for the time being," Vara said, somewhat grudgingly.

Aisling hesitated for a moment, as though trying to comb through the statement for something other than its surface meaning. "Thank you ... I think?"

"You're welcome, possibly," Vara said, plunging straight ahead. "What is the likelihood that Malpravus will choose Reikonos for his final battle with—"

"I don't think he means to have a battle," Cyrus said, shedding a gauntlet and flexing his fingers, feeling the slick sweat on his palm. "He wants me to be there when he does something to—to take the steps into this new power."

"Awww," Vaste said, "he's looking for the friend he's never had but always wanted, and it's you."

"Yeah, you can't have me all to yourself anymore," Cyrus said.

"I was always sharing you with that blond interloper anyway," Vaste huffed. "I don't even know what you see in her, my arse is so much more supple than hers."

"It's really not," Cyrus said as Vara blushed a blood red, and then turned to Quinneria, whose eyes were narrowed and who was shaking her head. "If Malpravus was going to ... I don't know, ascend to your level ... where would he go?"

Quinneria held up her hands. "He'll need magical energy."

"Well, that seems to come automatically," Ryin said.

"Not in the amount he'll need it," Quinneria said. "You recapture or regenerate a certain amount through rest and time and normal eating and drinking, but that's enough to cast *some* spells. The type he needed to even throw out what he unleashed in the Tower ..." She pointed to the ceiling. "That requires more. And there are places in Arkaria where the magics pool, and where one can regenerate that energy more quickly. Seams of power, I came to call them."

"Great," Vaste said, "so where's the 'seam of power' Malpravus will choose?"

"I don't know," Quinneria said with a shake of the head. "There are so very many, all with varying strengths—"

"Where's the most powerful one?" Cyrus asked.

"The upper realms," Quinneria answered. "But those are guarded by deities who would take a rather angry exception to him trying to access them—"

"How about the Realm of Death?" Vara asked. "That one seems perfectly suited to him, especially since Malpravus excels at controlling the departed."

Quinneria shook her head. "There's not one there, as such."

"You seem certain," J'anda said suspiciously.

"Quite," she replied. "There is in the Realm of Darkness, though, so that would be a possibility, albeit slight."

"Mortus and Yartraak aren't the only dead gods," Terian said. "At least according to Alaric and Curatio. Could he want to access one belonging to one of the dead ones? The ones that died in the war ten thousand years ago?"

"He couldn't," Quinneria said with another shake of the head. "Those are claimed by the remaining gods. I suspect Yartraak's will be taken by another deity in the next year or so—"

"Yartraak drained Aloakna," Mendicant said, speaking aloud as he thought, "taking the mortal souls for himself ... and you say these other gods sit on ... seats of power—"

"She said 'seams,'" Ryin said, a little haughtily, "get it right."

"They really are 'seats' of power to the gods," Quinneria said kindly, looking right at Mendicant. "And you have a good thought there, but of little practical application to our current discussion, I'm afraid. The point is, Malpravus will be going for lower-hanging fruit, and there are many spots on Arkaria far easier to access. He won't want to fight a god before he does what he means to ..." She lowered her voice. "He would do that *after.*"

"My stomach is rumbling even more angrily after that little piece of news," Vaste said. "So ... care to start naming these, uh, seams for us?"

Quinneria sighed, narrowing her eyes as she thought . aloud. "Reikonos sits on one—"

"Oh, hell," Imina muttered.

"—as does Zanbellish, though he's likely drained that for a time ..." She continued to frown as she spoke, "The Temple of Death in the Bandit Lands—"

Cyrus and Vaste snapped their heads around to share a look. "How do you know about that?" Cyrus asked, coming back around to look at Quinneria.

She smiled. "Who do you think trapped the Avatar of the God of Death away in that seal in the first place?"

"Uhm ..." Vaste said, "You?"

"Well, it was Alaric and I together," Quinneria said with a nod, "but yes."

Terian slapped his hand hard against his belt, rattling the axe that ran along his back. "What about the temple northeast of here in the Waking Woods?"

Quinneria straightened. "Certainly that is one. Many times, they built temples or chancels on these seams, because—"

"Gods, it's empty, isn't it?" Cyrus asked, cutting her off, staring at Terian as the Sovereign of Saekaj stared back at him, mouth slightly agape. "I mean, other than the ghouls that surround it—"

"The ghouls," Quinneria said, "are there because of that seam. It is the magic that infuses the carcasses; it is their origin."

"That's one place in a wide, vast land," Aisling said, shaking her head. "Why, of all Arkaria, would Malpravus choose that one location—"

She stopped as the atmosphere in the room changed; the light outside the windows was fading, but something about it had shifted like a cloud blocking the sun. Cyrus stood with his back to the balcony, but he could tell the change as it rolled across the shafts of light that were stretching across the table and the floor, shining in from the outside. The light had changed, was corrupted, and he saw it turn red as blood as it rolled slowly across the floor and the room began to darken.

"What the hell?" Terian muttered as they all turned to look out the windows to either side of the balcony doors.

Cyrus did not wait for the darkness to spread further; he broke into a run and from beside him Vara did the same. He went for the balcony and reached it first, one hand on Rodanthar. He threw them open into the afternoon sun and saw—

The sun was red as a butcher's floor; the sky was darkening in its grip, the shades of blue that had hung there replaced by a crimson, turning the plains an awful shade of purple to replace the verdant green of summer.

"What is that?" Cattrine asked as they all filtered out onto the balcony, watching the sky darken as the shining of the sun was muted further with every passing second.

"The beginning," Quinneria said, and her tone was mournful in a way that Cyrus found deeply, deeply disquieting.

A rumbling ran over the clear plains, like thunder without a cloud in the sky, and when it reached them, Cyrus heard a voice, plain and very familiar:

Cyrus ... come to me ... Malpravus said, his words rattling the stones in the wall above them, the whole tower shaking. Pieces of debris fell from the ruin of the roof at its top, raining down on them from above. *Come to the temple*, the voice said, *... Come and see ...*

Come ... And see my rise.

88.

"I'll send Kahlee to rally the army," Terian said as they descended on air, using Falcon's Essence to reach the ground faster than taking the stairs, descending outside of the main tower of Sanctuary, the sky still dark and red. "They can be back here in less than an hour."

"No," Cyrus said, leading the way, wind blowing under his helm. "Rally them, but don't bring them here. We need them in reserve, but committing them to the field of battle would be ..." He let his words drift off like the winds blowing past him.

"It would make it a battle, Cyrus," Terian said with urgent insistence. "Which is what we're being called to."

"No, you're not," Quinneria said, just a few steps behind Cyrus. "Don't you get it? This isn't a battle we're being summoned to; it's apotheosis."

"Apothy-what?" Terian asked, frowning as they drew close to the muddied ground, an unearthly shade in this light. "Never mind, I'll go tell Kahlee what to do." He peeled off and doubled back toward the front doors below.

"It means ... never mind," Quinneria said. "He wants you to commit an army, just like I wanted all those trolls lined up at Thurren Hill. Bring an army and you'll be marching them into exactly what he wants."

"I know," Cyrus called back as he came down, dispelling the Falcon's Essence and hitting the ground at a run, heading straight for the stables. He cast a look back at Sanctuary, all scarlet and frightening, black shadows hiding in the crevasses of its facade. It looked disturbingly wrong like this; hellish, in fact, and he turned away quickly after making certain that the others had followed him down.

"Scuddar, Calene," Cyrus called out, "you stay and mind the wall. Marshal the defenses."

"Can't pretend I'm sorry to be sitting this one out," Calene said.

"Are you certain?" Scuddar asked, pausing where he stood.

"I need someone strong to lead the defense if it comes to that," Cyrus said, looking over his shoulder at them both. "That's you."

"If they come, we will be ready," Scuddar said with a nod and a half-bow at the waist. With that, he and Calene both broke into a run toward the wall.

"This is where I leave you, I think," Cattrine said, approaching Cyrus quickly, Imina hesitantly standing a few steps behind her. "I will inform our army to stand ready as well, in case you have need."

"Close your portal when you get back," Cyrus said. He glanced at Imina. "Take her with you, please?"

Cattrine glanced at him then looked back with amusement. "Certainly," she said, clearly holding something back that she did not say. "Come along, madam," she said to Imina, "let me show you to a safer place than this."

"Gren seems like a safer place than this presently," Imina muttered but stepped aside with Cattrine.

"Ryin," Cyrus said, and the druid came forward. "Would you kindly escort these ladies to Emerald Fields and then bind your soul there?"

"No," Ryin said, shaking his head. "I'll get them there, but then I'm coming back. I won't be your messenger and miss this. I'm coming with you."

"You've come a long way since the days when you poo-poo'd everything ever suggested," Vaste said with a certain respect.

"The sky is red," Ryin said, "Malpravus is speaking in a voice that can be heard miles away, the end of civilization seems to be nigh …" Ryin smiled bitterly. "A contrarian in this case might suggest simply running, but I don't have that in me. Not for this."

"Then hurry back," Cyrus said grimly. "Because whatever Quinneria says, I expect a battle."

"I shall return," Ryin said, stepping over to Cattrine and Imina and disappearing in a blast of wind that seemed quicker than usual.

Terian came running out the front steps a moment later to rejoin them, leaping from the top and landing with a slight stagger. "All right, then, people, let's not go wasting daylight … or … whatever the hell this is." He gestured vaguely to the red sky.

"I'm with Ryin," Longwell said, falling in on the march to the stables, "looks like the end of something is coming."

"Hopefully not us," Mendicant said, scampering along, "because I was just learning some most interesting things. In fact, this last year has been easily the most fascinating and wonderful of my life."

Cyrus stared back at the goblin in wonder of his own, and then his eyes met Vara. *Has it really been less than a year since we married? It ... it has, hasn't it?* "Mine too," he said and smiled at her. She smiled back, and they made for the stables, ready to ride off into the red horizon together.

89.

They rode hard under the crimson sky, the awful light tingeing all of them, turning Vaste a sickening shade of reddish grey and J'anda almost black. Cyrus stared at each of them in turn as they galloped hard toward the Waking Woods ahead, only the nine of them remaining—Cyrus, Vara, J'anda, Vaste, Terian, Mendicant, Quinneria, Longwell, and Aisling, who rode at the back of the formation by herself. Of all of them, she seemed the most anxious, the worry obvious on her face, as though she were thinking of how to make an escape if need be.

"You don't have to be here," Cyrus said, pulling up on Windrider's reins to come alongside her.

"It's not that I don't want to be here," Aisling said, stretching in the saddle, "I just … would rather not die here, if it's going to come to that."

"Point to the one of us you do think wants to die here," Vara said.

"Probably Mendicant," Aisling said, causing the goblin to look at her cockeyed, a strange look on his small face. "You'll get hit with some unusual magic and think, 'Oh, well, if I had to go out, at least it was at the hands of a bizarre new spell.'"

Mendicant opened his mouth to speak and then thought long about it. "That sounds right," he said after a space.

"We have company," Vara said, pulling up her reins.

"Ryin, probably," Cyrus said. "Touching speech of his aside, waiting didn't seem prudent, given that Malpravus is malingering out there, turning the sky red."

"It's not Ryin," Vara said, shaking her head. "Or, I should say, it's not only Ryin."

Cyrus brought up Windrider short, the Waking Woods ahead only a few hundred meters. The horse turned, but not as quickly as Cyrus brought his head around. When he did, the spectacle behind them was such that Cyrus nearly fell off.

Tearing across the plains after them were not one, but two immense savanna cats, easily three times the length of Windrider and possessed of considerable muscular bulk. Riding high atop one was the Grand Knight of Sanctuary himself, Fortin the Rapacious, his red eyes still burning bright even with the shades of the world turned awry. Next to him, on a slightly smaller cat rode Zarnn, covered head to toe in cobbled-together armor that gleamed with the look of mystical steel. Ryin held tightly to the troll's waist as the savanna cats bounced up and down so furiously that Cyrus feared for Ryin's safety after watching for only a moment.

"He damned well did it, didn't he?" Longwell asked with measured awe. "He tamed a damned savanna cat."

"Two of them, no less," J'anda mused. "Truly, this is a day of marvels."

"Nothing about Fortin surprises me anymore," Vaste said. "But that Zarnn … he makes me think maybe I was wrong about trolls."

"Ah hah!" Quinneria said, pointing a finger at Vaste accusingly. "Even you have to acknowledge that your people—"

"Yeah, yeah," Vaste waved her off, "I still didn't kill ten thousand of them."

"If you'd been at Thurren Hill you would have," Quinneria said, her amusement vanishing in an instant. "You know why?"

Vaste just stared back at her, and there was a hint of anger in the way his jaw worked back and forth soundlessly a few times before he mustered an answer. "I don't know," he said. "Why?"

"For the same reason you're about to kill Malpravus," Quinneria said, staring straight ahead into the dark reaches of the forest. "Because if not, the consequences would be too much for your conscience to bear."

"Oh, that's not the reason you did it," Vaste said.

"No, it's not the reason I did it," she agreed. "It's the reason you would have done it … and the reason you'll face Malpravus now. Because you're not willfully blind to a grave threat." And she brought her horse around and angled it toward the forest as Fortin and Zarnn skidded their cats to a stop, ripping up great swathes of plains grass as they did so.

"What the hell is this?" Terian called in greeting. "The Brotherhood of the Savanna Cat?"

Fortin looked at Zarnn and made a grunting noise. "An excellent name."

"Mmm," Zarnn seemed to agree. "Brotherhood." He turned his head toward them. "Came to join you."

"And I as well," Ryin called from behind Zarnn, "since you didn't, in fact, wait for me."

"We were going to, but the sky just seemed so cherry red, and we decided to charge off to stop that," Vaste said. "Figured maybe by the time you got back, it'd be very blueberry again, or maybe lemony."

"You're still thinking about pie, aren't you?" J'anda asked.

"Well, I'm damned sure not going to think about Malpravus if I can avoid it," Vaste said. "Do you realize how much mental regurgitation I do every time this bastard shows up? He's like the equivalent of that piece of gristle you just can't chew through, no matter how hard you try, except he's like that for my mind. Just over and over and over again, I can't stop thinking about him."

"Admittedly it's been a while, but the last time I felt that way about a man," J'anda said, "we just called it love."

Vaste made a grunting noise more akin to something Cyrus would have expected from Zarnn. "I'd *love* to kill him, does that count?"

"I have felt that way as well," J'anda said with a smile and a nod.

"About Malpravus or your last great love?" Vaste asked.

"Both," J'anda said, "but mostly it is Malpravus I would like to kill."

"I doubt there's anyone who doesn't feel that way about Malpravus," Quinneria said. "In fact, I suspect you dealt with the last in Sanctuary who harbored those sentiments just last night."

"Well, now that we're all here," Cyrus said, turning Windrider around once more, "I suppose we should get back to it." He felt his face grow tight. "There's probably an army between us and him, after all."

"I doubt it," Quinneria said quietly. "Remember, he called you. He wants you to come."

"Time to answer the call, then," Cyrus said, and Vara came alongside him. They met eyes once more, and then they kicked their horses and raced back toward the forest.

90.

At the edge of the woods they slowed their pace, the heavy branches of the forest pooling blackness around them and hiding much of the red sky. It was like night in the Waking Woods, but the sounds were unnatural compared even to when last Cyrus had been here. The rattling and howling of the ghouls was all gone, and so, too, were the normal noises of animals and insects. The air was silent and still, neither hot nor cold, and that alone gave Cyrus a strange chill.

"I think this is actually worse than Zanbellish," Ryin said from the back of Zarnn's jungle cat. It was hard to tell which discomfited him more, their current environs or being on the back of a cat so much larger than he.

"It's certainly not as romantic as when last we were here," Cyrus muttered, and saw Vara smile slightly.

"You guys came here without me?" Terian said, faking disappointment.

"I hope you've been here since I came with you both," Aisling said, "because there wasn't much romantic about that time."

"I, uh … kind of forgot that you showed up for that," Cyrus said, cringing as he looked back at the dark elf.

"She left you in the dark to die," Aisling said.

"I did not," Vara said. "I was watching him all the while, he was fine."

"You were watching me?" Cyrus asked with a frown.

Vara shrugged. "I didn't want you to get hurt. Much," she conceded a moment later. "It was a long time ago."

"It was three years," Cyrus said.

"Practically an eternity around here."

The forest continued to darken, the trunks of the trees closing in around them. The faint red light that made its way down from above was enough to make Cyrus remember the time blood had poured down over his eyes in a fight. *Which time was that?* he wondered. *Hell, too many times to count.*

The utter silence was unnerving, and Cyrus pulled Windrider's reins to the left slightly as they passed under a small gap in the boughs above. He caught a glimpse of a pyramid in the distance, a series of increasingly smaller longwise rectangles stacked upon one another, forming an enormous triangle as they drew to the point at the top. He could see a dark entry at the topmost level and shuddered staring into it, even this far off.

"Looks like a more angular version of what we saw at the Temple of Death in the Bandit Lands," Vaste said.

"Aye," Cyrus said, "that one looked more like a cake to me."

Vaste paused. "It did look like a cake! Like the one at your wedding, but less delicious, more stony, and just a tad more aesthetically pleasing."

Vara frowned. "The cake or the temple?"

"The temple," Vaste admitted. "Sorry."

"I didn't design it," Vara said with a shrug.

"I did," Quinneria said with a deep frown. "And ..." She seemed to give it some thought. "Damn, it did look a little like that temple."

"It feels strange that you know so much," Vaste said. "I mean ... you were at your son's wedding and he didn't even realize—"

"Vaste," Cyrus said, feeling a pinch of emotion. He caught Vara looking at him and smiled back to reassure her. "Not now," he said to the troll.

"But later?" Vaste asked, splitting his look between Cyrus and Quinneria.

"Later," Cyrus said, and it carried the weight of a heavy promise in his mind when he said it.

They rode on quietly, no longer at a gallop, but instead at a canter, searching out the danger they knew to be ahead. The occasional break in the trees confirmed their position, as the pyramid drew nearer and nearer with each passing gap. It jutted into the sky, and Cyrus realized he had never been this close to it before in all his years at Sanctuary. *Never wanted to be, either.*

"I see them," Vara said, peering into the darkness between the trunks. "The army of Goliath." She snapped a quick look back at Cyrus. "They're here."

"Of course they are," Vaste said. "How else were they going to counter our might army of four hundred and ..." He made a face as he concentrated. "How many do we have left now?"

"Four hundred and fifty-two," Cyrus answered immediately, and caught Terian's eye as he said it. The Sovereign gave him a solemn nod of respect. "Four hundred and fifty-two loyal souls."

"When this is over," Terian said, "you might consider issuing a call to every city, offering any who want to return a chance to come back. I bet you'd have an enormous number of takers."

"You didn't seem to believe that'd be the case before," Cyrus said, raising his eyebrows at the Sovereign of Saekaj.

"Times change," Terian said with a smile. "You'll have utterly bested every one of your foes against impossible odds. If that's not a reason to join a guild, I don't know what is."

"I'll think about it," Cyrus said.

"If we get through all that ..." Longwell said. "I mean ... this is it, isn't it? The last enemy to be defeated?"

"Gods willing," Cyrus said under his breath. He could see the Army of Goliath through the trees now as well.

They came out at a clearing beneath the foot of the temple. The Army of Goliath was there in impressive rows, and now Cyrus could see the size of them in a way he hadn't properly since their last actual clash at the fields of Leaugarden in the Riverlands. *Where Malpravus defeated me, completely and utterly.* There was a far greater number here now, though, than then, and all turned in proper order in a way that reminded Cyrus of the halcyon days of Sanctuary when he'd led his armies of this size into formidable clashes. *If Terian's right, if we come through this, and it solidifies our reputation ... I could do it. I could issue that call, and all those fair-weather friends that fled might just coming running back to join the winning team.*

And I could lead an army again.

He took a breath and found the air still strange, still ... still. There was no movement, even with the army lined up ahead of them. He could see a couple of figures lingering at the base of the stairs that led up to the temple, and he knew them immediately.

"Rhane Ermoc," Cyrus said, pointing at one of them. "And that's—"

"Sareea," Terian said tensely. "She's mine, does everyone hear me?"

"That sounds serious," Vaste said. "I hope she at least gave you an extremely communicable disease in order to earn that ire you're carrying for her."

Terian frowned. "Actually, it was probably the other way around … but I've still got a grudge to settle with her."

"It's a shame you're no longer into that whole drinking and whoring business," Vaste said, a little too chipper for Cyrus's taste this close to what they were approaching, "I bet some of those healing spells would really come in handy for those little things you pick up in the brothels—"

"You know damned well, probably through personal experience, that healing spells don't work on natural sickness," Vara said crossly.

"There's not much natural about that particular sickness, let me tell you—" Terian began.

"Ah, it's like the good old days once more," J'anda said, "but, you know, with a little redder sky overhead." He waved a hand toward Cyrus and Vara. "And without the benefit or curse of your endless bickering."

"I always thought it was cute," Vaste said, "until I started hearing the kinky tales of—"

"Shhhh," Vara said, "or I'll regale you with one now."

"Your mother-in-law is right over there," Vaste said gleefully. "I'd like to see you do it. Keep in mind she's killed more people than even you have."

"I'll put my fingers in my ears and hum loudly," Quinneria offered.

"Much appreciated," Vara said.

"Oh, betrayed by the troll hater," Vaste said. "How could I not see it coming?"

"Cyrus Davidon!" Rhane Ermoc shouted across the field between them as Windrider cantered the last hundred meters or so to the base of the temple steps. "I was wondering if you were going to show up."

Cyrus drew Praelior and heard the sound of bows being nocked among the Army of Goliath. "I didn't have much reason to fear coming, Rhane," he said, holding the blade aloft but keeping Windrider still only fifteen or so feet before the Goliath warrior. "At least, not from you."

"Rub it on in, why don't you," Ermoc said with a sneer.

"Don't mind if I do," Cyrus said, twirling Praelior in his fingers. "Let me tell you a little secret I learned after you took my sword away

... it's the warrior that makes the blade, not the other way around. That's why I kept thwarting you even without my sword, even when you ambushed me with superior numbers. You were never going to beat me because—"

"Because you're a heretic," Ermoc said. "A cheater. A—"

"And you're a chickenshit, a coward, a thief, and a terrible swordsman," Cyrus said, staring him down. "I was known before I had the sword. I outmaneuvered you before it ever touched my hand. And now ..." he drew Rodanthar and held one weapon in each hand, "what do you figure your odds are if you keep standing in my way?"

Ermoc's face twisted with familiar hatred, pulsating with rage, but it faded into resentment. "I'm not going to block you. You're supposed to be here. He wants you here."

"Because he likes me more than you," Cyrus said, instinctively driving the blade into Ermoc's ego. Ermoc twitched, and Cyrus knew he'd found his mark.

"Because he demands it," Sareea Scyros called out, taking up the defense for Ermoc.

"He demands a lot of things, doesn't he, Sareea?" Terian asked. "But I suppose it doesn't matter to you, because every single bit of you—your honor, your loyalty, your sword—they were all for sale all along."

Sareea smiled at Terian. "I sought power. You sought ... satisfaction."

"I'm pretty satisfied," Terian said, smiling, and drew his axe. "Reasonably powerful now, too."

"You are nothing compared to him," Sareea said, shaking her head.

"Well, I'm the Sovereign of Saekaj and Sovar," Terian said. "That's not exactly 'nothing.' I mean, the last guy to hold that position was a—"

GOD.

The voice came from the top of the pyramid, as clear and strong as when it had rumbled down from the heavens above Sanctuary and rained onto the balcony like the downpour of the previous night. The ground seemed to shake under the power of Malpravus's voice, and every horse but Windrider screamed in fear.

The sky shimmered above them, and now Cyrus saw the pillar of light shining out of the top of the pyramid, thin and coruscating, like the light of a spell. He stared as the ground rocked once more, and the voice stretched out and assaulted them all, shaking their very bones.

Watch ... my ... rise ...

"It's starting," Quinneria said. "He's going to do it now."

"Do what now?" Vaste asked, nearly falling off his horse as the earth quaked and quailed.

"The spell," Vara said, sounding dead certain.

"What?" Cyrus asked. "He doesn't—we didn't bring our army for him to—"

"Don't you get it?" Vara sounded quiet in the midst of the thundering earth, as the thread of light extending out of the top of the temple began to widen, to solidify into something darker, leaving its tenuous grip on the sky behind and reaching out like spidery fingers, extending down toward them. "He doesn't need our army to sacrifice, not for this. He never did." Her eyes were wide and white, and fixed on his. "Why would he? He's brought his own."

91.

The tendrils of magical energy curled out of the top of the temple and down, down upon them. They twisted out of the sky like blood drifting in the water, lancing through the air with their own path charted, curling and roiling as they grew closer. Cyrus saw them come and was breathless. They struck Sareea Scyros and Rhane Ermoc like spears in the back and both of them shook, their armor rattling like their breath as it left them; Ermoc's skin turned from swarthy to waxy pale, Sareea's went from a deep blue to cerulean as the life was ripped from her, the tendrils of energy pulsating upward as it stole their vitality, carrying it back to the source at the top of the temple. Their screams halted in the middle, their throats going dry and their expressions of horror grew stiff and deathly, their eyes vacant.

"Hold on!" Quinneria shouted. Green spell-light surrounded them as tendrils reached in their direction. They fractured against her spell, splitting as they batted against the sphere she'd drawn around them. She held out her hands as if she could stop the coming cataclysm and it seemed to Cyrus that she did, at least in the small pocket where they stood, their horses bucking in fear beneath them as the sky started to blacken from all the twisting tendrils reaching down from the temple top.

The tendrils spread to the Army of Goliath, splitting and splitting again, until there were enough points for every single member of the army. Some tried to run, some were struck dumb and motionless as they watched what approached, but none escaped. The black spell-craft twisted into their bodies as it had Ermoc and Sareea's, and Cyrus saw the pulsation as life was drained, as every single one of them came to their unnatural end. Bodies squirmed and writhed in the darkness, screams began and ceased just as abruptly, the jerking of some twenty thousand bodies as the spell did its work was like a writhing mass upon the field before the temple.

"Was this … was this what it was like at Thurren Hill?" Vaste asked in horrified awe.

"Yes." Quinneria said, shaking with the exertion of keeping her spell around them. The tendrils of black were dancing all about its edges, licking at the barrier. The grass beneath their feet withered and turned brown before their very eyes.

When the tendrils were done with their horrible work, they held still, hanging in the air above their subjects, thin now, half the size they'd been when they started. A pulse of white glowed at the origin on the temple's top and ran down each spell thread to the bodies at the end.

"Uh oh," Quinneria muttered.

"Don't say that," Vaste said in rising alarm. "He just massacred his whole army. What could prompt an 'uh oh' after that?" He shook for a second. "Please let it be something innocuous, something despicable but harmless like—"

"Goat buggery?" J'anda suggested. When Vaste looked at him in horror, the enchanter shrugged. "Not harmless, I suppose, but perhaps less worrisome than—"

"Necromancy," Vara said as the white pulses got smaller, running to each link at the end of the spell's chain. Rhane and Sareea caught them first, being closest, and their dead eyes glowed with life once more as the tendrils relinquished their hold, turning to smoke once their dark work was finished.

Rhane Ermoc and Sareea Scyros stood unnaturally, their bodies tilted at odd angles, their weapons still at the ready. Cyrus watched the same fate befall the entire army of Goliath, the tendrils wafting away once their pulses were carried. The corpses remained upright, their eyes glowing like—

"Ghouls," Cyrus said under his breath.

"Yes," Vara said. She drew her sword, the blade bursting into flame as she did so. "They are undead." Terian matched her with his axe, the fire's light illuminating his grim expression.

"What are the odds they're just going to let us stroll on up there?" Vaste asked. "You know, without a fight?"

Only one may pass, Sareea and Ermoc said, in the same disembodied voice that had been rolling over the countryside since the sky had turned red. *And it is not you, troll.*

"Cyrus," Vara said, catching his eye, "the very minute you leave, he will send his legions against us."

"I know," Cyrus said, clutching Praelior with one hand and Rodanthar in the other. He closed his eyes for a beat and cast the spell himself, both blades lighting from guard to tip with holy flame. "Which is why I'm not leaving."

Don't be a fool, dear boy, Malpravus said in his cold hiss through the mouths of the entire Army of Goliath as it rattled forward on dead legs, lurching toward the base of the temple where they stood. *It doesn't need to be this way ... come to see me ... come to speak ... leave the others behind ... I know what you want ... what you need ...*

"By the very fact you think I would leave my friends behind to be slaughtered by you," Cyrus said, with more than a little coldness of his own, "you show me that you don't know anything at all about me— and you never have. If you mean to have a talk, Malpravus, then we're all coming up." He raised Praelior. "But if you want to have a slaughter ... well, I'm happy to grant that to you as well."

There was a moment of silence, broken by Vaste's barely calm voice. "I never thought I'd say this about Malpravus ... but please let it be the talk."

The silence reigned once more, and then all the corpses of the field rattled at once, bringing their weapons high and clinking their armor as they made to charge, Malpravus's voice crackling off the top of the temple like summer thunder.

You have chosen ... death.

92.

"I did not choose death!" Vaste shouted under the red sky. "If there's a choice, I choose pie—"

"Up the steps!" Cyrus shouted as the Army of Goliath charged forward in a shambling herd. "Dismount and climb!"

The rattle of bones and armor was loud, and Cyrus looked back just to see if somehow the skin had been stripped off the army in the process of the spell doing its work. They were all still fully clad in skin and clothes, but the rattle came anyway, and Cyrus wondered if perhaps it was inside his head.

The sky was red once more, a tendril of crimson seeping up to the sun from the temple's top, and Cyrus was left to wonder the purpose behind it, and how far it reached. *Is it red in Reikonos right now? Could they see this in Luukessia, if anyone were there?*

He turned as he dismounted Windrider, spinning as he left the saddle, pulling a leg over. "Get out of here!" he shouted at the horse, who did not spare a moment in galloping off down the side of the temple, away from the army. The other horses followed in his wake, whinnying shrilly all the way. Cyrus looked back, however, to see that the savanna cats were hissing and spitting at the army of the dead surging toward them, and he realized that they had no intention of fleeing. *Take after their masters, then ...*

"Come on!" Terian shouted to Sareea, who was charging at them, sword raised. For a moment, Cyrus thought he was going to unleash a force blast, but he did not. He swung the axe and brought it down, landing it to the side of her neck. The dead Sareea seemed to move slower than the one he'd seen in battle in Isselhelm, and when the flaming axe struck through her, she burst into flames, screaming holy fire out of her mouth as she burned up from within.

Vara sank her blade into Rhane Ermoc in a similar fashion; the same holy flames welled up inside him, crackling beneath his armor and spilling out like he'd been doused with oil. He raged and flailed, and was consumed in mere seconds, leaving nothing but his armor and sword behind in a clinking rattle as they fell to the ground.

Cyrus charged up the steps to the temple only just behind Vara and Terian, who were leading the way. He caught a glimpse of the horses turning the corner and escaping around the side of the temple, but when he looked back he saw the savanna cats leaping up the stone levels of the pyramid, hissing at the dead who were running to the base of the temple.

"Terian, Vara!" Cyrus called, throwing a hand to point back, "Take rear guard with those weapons of yours, I'm not sure if anyone else can—" He threw a look back and stopped dead in his climb.

Zarnn and Fortin had stationed themselves on the first level of the temple and the Army of Goliath was flowing into them like a river of the dead. With their cats perched to the side of the stairs, they had created a breakwater for the dead coming at them, and chaos had been unleashed. Armored dead were running up the stairs and into a cacophonous mass of screams, claws, fists, headbutts, kicks and general fighting of a sort Cyrus could not recall seeing even in his days in the Society of Arms. As he watched, Fortin ripped a Goliath warrior apart and threw both halves into the crowd, bowling over a dozen others. One of the cats was hissing around a skull it had ripped the head from one of the dead and batted away another so severely that it lost an arm and a leg. Zarnn screamed as a dead warrior clanged against his new armor. He ripped its arm off, stealing its sword, like a dagger in his mighty fist, and plunged it through three heads in a row.

"On the other hand," Cyrus conceded, mesmerized by the violence upon the step, "maybe it's under control."

"If we kill Malpravus, this stops, yes?" Vara asked, hair fallen from beneath her helm and into her eyes. When he did not answer, she looked to Quinneria. "Yes or no?"

"I've never raised an army of the dead before," Quinneria said, stooped over on a step below them, breathing hard as she watched the Goliath forces begin to surge over the bottom lip of the temple's first level like a mindless horde of ants, "but I don't think they'll survive without him, no."

"I watched Curatio exorcise a whole army of the dead once," Terian said, paused a step above Cyrus, looking like he wanted to continue charging up them without further thought. "Any chance you could do that?"

"Possibly," Quinneria said. "Did he have any help?"

"He had the Red Destiny of Saekaj," Aisling said, somewhat muted. "He channeled the souls into it, presumably so that Vidara could reabsorb them later, since they were stolen from her to begin with."

"He was also very exhausted afterward," J'anda said, casting a spell and sending purple light down into the middle of the army below. He shuddered, but an undulating line began in the middle of the ruckus as several of the dead began to tear into their own.

"So now that Malpravus has, uh … done what he's done," Longwell said, his lance pointed in front of him like it could shield him from what was ahead, "how do we stop him?"

"We get up there and kill his bony ass for good," Cyrus said, waving them forward as he leapt a step above Vara and Terian. "However we can." And he charged, his own armor rattling now as he hurried up to fight the last battle.

93.

"I see you made it up here after all," Malpravus said as Cyrus crested the last step to the top of the temple, his eyes penetrating into the dark ahead. He could not see the necromancer, but knew he was there from the voice, no longer disembodied.

Cyrus glanced backward quickly to confirm that his party was still with him. Fortin, Zarnn, and the cats had now retreated to the third level of the pyramid, the undead army swarming all around them, trying to scale the levels to flank them but failing. The four of them were holding together as a group and killing their way through the rising tide of the dead. For a moment, Cyrus watched bodies fly off the levels around them, in pieces, before he turned his attention to the others.

Vara and Terian were closest to him, their weapons still aflame like his. They stood just outside the temple arch, a simple squared lintel, after which began the darkness. Behind them were Quinneria, Vaste and Mendicant, followed by J'anda, Aisling, Longwell and Ryin. They were tightly grouped, and the apprehension was plain on every face he saw, the red light giving them all a bizarre tint.

Cyrus took a cautious step into the darkness and the sound of battle outside faded in his ears. Water dripped in the distance, echoing through the dark. The air in here was dank, as if there were a pool of water somewhere below. He saw stairs leading down and suspected there were catacombs beneath the main chamber. Another step and he could see a great seal in the middle of the floor, not unlike the one in the foyer of Sanctuary, though he could not make out the details in the dark, even with his swords shedding their crackling light.

"I really must thank you for this, my lad," Malpravus said, his voice quiet and calm. "I couldn't have done this without you." He was still somewhere ahead in the dark, and Cyrus could not yet see him.

"How did I help you?" Cyrus asked, the sound of dripping in the distance like a quiet punctuation to their increasingly surreal conversation.

"It was Mortus," Malpravus said. "Your conquest of him. Striking out against a god, you see ... it's simply not done, not these days. Bad form. Yet you did it, cleaving his fingers from his hand and proving once more a lesson long forgotten. Some looked at your victory, your conquest of a god, and marveled. *They are mortal. They are ... weak.*" A low laugh echoed through the chamber. "I looked upon it and said, *They are stronger than I. How do I gather that power unto myself?*"

"So glad I could help you in your journey for personal excellence," Cyrus muttered, taking another tentative step. He glanced back and saw the others following him slowly, all knotted together tightly in formation.

"You see," Malpravus said, taking no apparent notice of his reply, "death is the great equalizer. We all end up as ivory-bleached bones, devoid of that softness and warmth that you seem to so prize ... Except that some do not." Now Cyrus could hear the smile in the necromancer's words. "Some special few, perched upon their currents of magic as a leech unto a vein, live forever ... and I mean to be one of them."

"I don't care for that notion at all," Vaste said.

"As though I have ever given a fig for what the chattering masses want," Malpravus said with a laugh. "You were barely worthy of my notice before, troll, and you have become positively inconsequential now."

"Well, that's wounding as well as troubling," Vaste said.

"Because you are weak, you can be wounded," Malpravus said. "Words are your most efficacious weapon, aren't they, Vaste? Is that because healers were not allowed to carry swords—or is because your wit is sharp and your hands weak?"

"Why don't you just stroll on over here and find out for yourself?" Vaste slapped the length of his spear-staff into his palm and it echoed through the dark space.

"Oh, I wouldn't wish to waste my time," Malpravus said. "As I told you, you are beneath me."

"I'm actually quite a bit taller than you, short stack, which puts me above you," Vaste said. "Again, step over here and find out."

"A few of you," Malpravus went on, now ignoring Vaste, "have the aid of the weapons of gods, I see." He laughed. "I placed too little stock in those before, giving them to the Dragonlord when he asked, ignoring the benefits to myself when they could have been mine. The error seems clear in retrospect, but with so many gathered before me, now I see the aid they would bring. Power becomes clearer as one acquires more. Before it was hazier to me; now it is obvious as the nose on Quinneria's face."

Philos lit into a soft glow, and Quinneria spoke. "This is your perpetual problem, Malpravus. Now you overlook Vaste in your haste to declare yourself greater than he. Yet he might be the one who brings you low."

"Don't draw his attention to me yet," Vaste hissed in a whisper. "I wanted to sneak up on him."

"I am too high to be brought low by even you," Malpravus said. He paused, and the sounds of battle seemed to grow louder outside. "My army approaches, and your rear guard falters. I see you all clearly ... a lecher turned Sovereign—"

"I'm also a paladin now, thanks," Terian said.

"—a diseased product of an earth-dwelling race, covered in glory because he sometimes walks upright and can occasionally cast a spell—"

"Is ... is that supposed to be me?" Mendicant asked.

"—one hated and hounded in his own land as a deviant, too afraid and ashamed to even wear his own face for a hundred years—"

"You can look at my face now, if you'd like," J'anda said with silky anger.

"—an outcast kingslayer from a dead land, noble of title but lacking in any actual nobility—"

"My slaying is not limited to kings alone," Longwell said, "I've aided in the fall of gods, dragons, titans and more."

"—a thief, a liar, and a whore—"

"You make me sound so saucy when you put it like that," Aisling said.

"I think he's talking about me," Vaste said.

"—two unthinking beasts, fit more for fields with plows than fields of battle—"

"And Zarnn and Fortin aren't even here to defend their own

honor," Vaste said. "If they were, you'd already be the pile of bones you've always aspired to become."

"—a man who can't even convince those he calls friends that he is anything other than a discontented whiner—"

Ryin looked around. "Oh, that's me, is it?"

"Yes," Vaste said.

"—the Sorceress herself, so afraid of the kingdoms of men that she abandoned her own child out of fear for her own neck—"

"In fear for his life," Quinneria said hotly.

"—and then there's the so-called 'last hope,'" Malpravus said, and his voice took a mocking turn. "Born a miracle to a dying people, given everything she could ask for ... and she threw it all away. You—you fool, you smug, high-horsed—"

"That is particularly rich coming from you," Vara said with a raised eyebrow.

"You had more power than most could imagine handed to you, yours for the taking. You could have been a monarch before you reached your majority. Danay would have had no choice but to surrender the throne before the lightest of challenges from you—"

"Yes, he certainly seemed to be in a surrendering mood when last I spoke with him," Vara quipped. "You know, between the threats to kill me."

"You had everything—and you left it for nothing, to climb your way out of the abysmal depths of the Holy Brethren and join one of the mightiest guilds, only to get yourself struck down by your own foolish blindness, your—your—your love—"

Vara burned in the darkness, the fire on her blade leaping higher. "You think a betrayal by a loved one was the fault of my foolishness?"

"To not even see it coming marks you as the worst sort of fool," Malpravus breathed, "and now—even now—you find yourself with another man who has it in him to cast you aside for greater power ... and you ignore it."

At this, Vara rolled her eyes. "I've just remembered something I forgot ... you're a great bloody idiot."

"At least he took the time to insult you properly," Vaste said. "He just ignored me, like I'm beneath his notice or someth—HEY!"

"You stand in their midst, Cyrus Davidon," Malpravus said, "betrayed by so many of them, and yet you still cling tight to this notion of … *friends*, of this constructed family to replace the one that left you."

"Not all of them left," Cyrus said, bowing his head, "some of them died."

"More will die," Malpravus promised him. "Your Sanctuary will fall. Time will have its way with your little family, and you will be left alone, in the end … and all you will wish is that you had the power to make it all right again."

"This is pointless," Cyrus said, raising his sword, "because you will never understand. Not what draws us together, nor what keeps us together, nor why we fight with and for each other. You may be a necromancer, but you've always been dead inside, so hollowed out by your tireless pursuit of the one thing you think matters that you ignore all else at your own peril." He raised Rodanthar in a high guard and brought Praelior low. "And that which you dismiss … will be the thing that kills you, Malpravus."

"I see you make the foolish choice again," Malpravus said, "but have it your way, childish boy who will never have the chance to grow up. If you prize these fools so highly—" At last, he stepped forward into the light, a skeleton finally in fact, glowing eyes staring out of an actual skull, bleached clean of flesh and covered only by robes, immense, now taller than even Vaste, leering down at them all. "Then you will die with them."

94.

The battle was joined faster than Cyrus could believe, spells flung at the enormous skeleton of Malpravus and his own rejoinders sent back, crashing into the walls of the temple with bellowing fire, shocks of lightning and bursting patches of ice. Malpravus's attacks hit the floor and peppered the stone into exploding flecks, sending the entire party save for Quinneria diving for cover. Heat and cold ran over Cyrus's skin, even through the armor, and his hairs, from the long ones atop his head to those down his chest, all stood on end at the sizzle of lightning.

Vara and Terian wisely circled around the skeleton, not striking immediately, though the thing that had been Malpravus held up one hand to cast spells and the other as if keeping it in reserve to hold off attacks; that hand stayed in the air, cocked as for a punch, as the spellcasting hand unleashed a tide of something horrible that Quinneria met with a magical rejoinder of her own. Malpravus's crackled black and Quinneria's glowed green. They warred with each other in a replay of what had happened in the Tower of the Guildmaster, the conjoining spells blasting a mighty hole in the stone ceiling. The rocky pieces fell and disintegrated in the pooling of magics, consumed whole as the room pulsated with the energy of the magical union.

"This is going to get terrible quickly," Vaste shouted, aiming his spear at Malpravus and casting a beam of white out of the tip. Cyrus blinked at it, watching as the troll broke out in a sweat, enormous beads popping up on his forehead. "You mark my words!"

"Mark them with what?" Vara called, throwing a hand out and issuing a force blast that did not even move the immense, skeletal Malpravus.

"Mark them with the bodies of the dead!" Longwell shouted. Cyrus turned to see the Army of Goliath at the entry to the temple, Fortin and Zarnn standing in the way, trying to block the gaps. The dead streamed forward with screams on their lips, shattered to pieces by the hands of the rock giant and the troll, as Aisling and Longwell joined the rear guard. J'anda, too, pivoted about and began to shoot purple spells from the tip of his staff, increasing the frenzied chaos at the entry. Aisling was disappearing and appearing from place to place in the middle of it all, ripping asunder dead bodies with perfectly placed strikes then fading away again.

"We're going to need more help very soon," Ryin said, adding a blazing fire spell to Quinneria's efforts against Malpravus, blending together with her green power that was pulsating against Malpravus's black. "You don't need to mark anything for me, just believe it when I say it!"

"I believe it," Cyrus said, orbiting to the right with Vara, looking for an opening. *Leap in against Malpravus now, and all it'll take is a second's redirection of that spell for any one of us to be vaporized like the stones falling from the roof.* Cyrus looked up; he could not see the sky for all the magical energy that pulsed in the room.

"Perhaps we should try something different!" Vara called across the fray. "Terian—perhaps you should attempt some, ah ... old magic."

"I don't know any old—" Terian started, and then got it. "Oh. Well. Sure, why not?" Before Cyrus could quite suss out the meaning, the dark elf reached down and poked the pointed tip of his axe into his own wrist and then raised a hand to Malpravus. It glowed faintly, darkly, and he straightened up, the pain clearing from his face. "Uhm ... I don't think that did anything."

"You are the prick of a pin to a titan," Malpravus said, pouring more energy into the ball growing in the center of the room. "I am become greater than all of you combined, with all your weapons and artifacts and spells ..."

"He's too strong right now!" Quinneria called over the roar of the energy, which was starting to burst loose in great rolling blasts that scoured the room the way it had in the tower. "He's absorbed too many souls and too recently!"

"Perhaps a cessation spell?" Mendicant called quietly, biding his time at the floor, yet to cast a single attack in Malpravus's direction.

Quinneria shook her head, doing a little sweating herself, her hair frizzy and tangled again like when she had played Larana. "It would just leave him with godlike strength and abilities—and it wouldn't do a damned thing to stop the flow of his army, because they're already reanimated and likely to kill us if left unchecked."

"I love hopeless fights!" Vaste called. "I try to get into at least one per year! I really upped the quotient this year, though, and seriously, to do it here, in this ugly, frightening, ominous place—"

Quinneria's eyes widened in the light of the coruscating magic. "That's it."

"If she got an idea to save us from Vaste, I'm going to have to veto its use," Terian called, still holding his place on the other side of Malpravus, axe at the ready.

"No, it's brilliant," Quinneria breathed.

"Of course it is, it came from me," Vaste said.

"The seal!" Quinneria said over the crackling energies, the hole in the ceiling widening by the moment.

"NO!" Vaste called. "That's not brilliant at all! This situation will not be made better by Yartraak or Mortus's avatars being let loose!"

"Mortus and Yartraak are dead, fool," Vara said.

"They have no more avatars!" Quinneria shouted, her hands shaking in front of her. "But the seal—"

Cyrus looked down at the seal in the center of the floor, lit by the magic before him, a strange carving of two faces—he recognized them as Mortus's and Yartraak's, in side profile, with skeletons and dead bodies beneath them in the circle. "Is it ... what? Made to hold him?"

"It's a channel point for the energy that runs through this place!" Quinneria shouted, wavering. "And it can be blocked—stoppered—with him on the other side!"

"This is all foolishness," Malpravus said tauntingly, "grasping at the threads of life as I take them away from you. Power is all there is, and you have little of it remaining. I see you, Sorceress, yes, pouring out your stores to stop me, but you were already weakened, your stock depleted before you even came to me ... and I am fresh as a newly made corpse."

"So, putrid and rotting, then," Vaste said. "Okay, I like the plan better than simply being overwhelmed and dying. What do we do to make that stoppering business happen?"

"He needs to bleed on the seal," Quinneria said, straining under the attack. Her skin was wavering with light, and Cyrus would have sworn he saw a wrinkle appear on her forehead that had not been there before.

"He's a skeleton," Terian said. "They're not known for bleeding!"

"It's a—it's not an illusion, but it's a form change," Quinneria said. "Trust me, he can bleed … and you're going to have to make that happen now."

Cyrus looked to Vara and then Terian, with a quick glance spared at the entry to the temple, which was completely engulfed in a furious melee, the line growing ever closer all the time. "Okay," Cyrus said, nodding at the two of them. "This one's on us." And he let the fire fade from his sword as he leapt forward.

Cyrus swept in to attack and Malpravus shed his cloak in an instant, his rib bones splitting from his breastbone and swinging loose. They morphed and grew before Cyrus's eyes, skeletal phalanges sprouting from the tips to form additional hands.

"Holy shite! I thought he was ugly before!" Vaste screamed.

Terian came around the back as three arms swung out for him and the dark elf threw his axe up to meet them. The blade struck bone and the bone shattered, splintering and showering Terian as Malpravus screamed with laughter.

"Fools … all fools!"

Vara came at him from the side and Malpravus caught her strike with a punch of his free hand, stopping her attack mid-slice. The blade came right back at Vara and she staggered away.

The rib cage on Malpravus's right side came apart and angled six arms toward Cyrus. He saw them coming, growing digits and hands the way the bones that had gone after Terian a moment earlier had. Cyrus took it as a personal challenge. *You want to send six my way? I'll show you I'm worth it.*

With swords in hand, Cyrus could feel the effect of both working for him. The world moved slower than ever it had with only one, and he felt stronger, more sure-footed. The hands were moving at normal speed in a world that was not normal, and now he knew the truth of the matter—Malpravus was strong, but he was not invincible.

Cyrus came at the lowest arm first and cleaved it whole from the growing wrist with Praelior, the sound of bones splintering under his assault like a drumbeat in his ears. The next he caught with Rodanthar in the middle of a grasping hand and split cleanly down the middle, shearing it off and rendering it useless. He swept up with Praelior and caught two at the nubs, ripping them off before they had a chance to reach for him, and the last he got with Rodanthar, cutting them cleanly off and sending them rattling across the floor toward the altar behind Malpravus.

He stepped in to deal another blow, this one to the solid spine now exposed, but something yanked at his ankle, and he lost his footing as his leg was ripped from beneath him.

He looked down as he stumbled, and saw a disconnected, bony hand tearing at him, another climbing along on fingers behind it, scrambling for him. He started to shout to Terian but then caught a glimpse of the dark elf beset by the three hands he'd cut loose, climbing up him as he swung his axe ineffectually at them, trying to sweep them from his body—

He turned to Vara, only to see a bony, disembodied hand wrapped around her neck, her face red and her fingers tugging at the choking fingers. The veins in her temple were bulging, blood running from between the ivory fingers. Her eyelids were squeezed, only a slit of blue and white visible between them. She was dying. The panic on her face sent a frosty chill through Cyrus as the severed hands pulled him down, ripping at his armor, climbing him—as behind him, the dam burst at the door and the army of Goliath's dead flooded into the chamber.

95.

The ball of magical energy where Quinneria, Vaste and Ryin's spell had met Malpravus's was turning black and glowing, the necromancer's dark magic winning yet another fight, at least as Cyrus saw it from the floor where he lay, cheek pressed against the cold seal in the floor of the temple, defeat all around him.

Dead members of the Army of Goliath were coming into the chamber now, flowing in on both sides, even as Aisling moved around trying to destroy them and Longwell tried his best to press them away with his lance. A burst flew off the magical energy flashing in the middle of the room and put an accidental end to three of the dead, missing Longwell by mere inches as he threw himself down a set of steps to the left of the entry, disappearing over the edge.

Terian was still staggering, smashing bones with the flat side of his axe, turning them to dust while flailing wildly at his own breastplate. He was shouting but Cyrus could not hear him over the sound of the spells mingling in the middle of the room, another peal of energy bursting off and sizzling past Vara's ears—

Vara was still choking, now upon her knees, her eyes rolled back in her head and fingers wet with her own blood as the disembodied, skeleton hand sunk its fingers into her neck. She went limp and fell, her armor making a soundless crash to the stone floor as she landed.

"NOOOOOO!" Cyrus shouted, and Malpravus's skull-face snapped to look right at him, the eyes glowing red.

"And now you see your end," Malpravus said, glaring right at him, the grin leering in the flickering spell-light as the impossibly strong skeleton hands dragged Cyrus down, pressing him against the stone, "your friends cannot save you, nor can you save them. In the end, the only thing that would save you … is power."

"Or perhaps a friend with power?" came the soft voice of Mendicant.

"What was that?" Malpravus asked, the skeletal face puckered with curiosity.

Cyrus looked over to see the goblin holding out his clawed fingers. Circular blasts of red no larger than the diameter of a mead horn shot from his fingers with perfect precision and blasted the bony hands clear of Cyrus's chest and legs.

Cyrus vaulted to his feet, the horrifying pressure of the grasping hands gone, and stared right into the face of Malpravus, who was glaring back at him with a surprising amount of fury given he had no mouth with which to make expressions. "He said you're dead wrong," Cyrus said, and he leapt forward.

Malpravus was down to a snakelike spine wavering above his pelvis and legs, and he hissed as his backbone started to extend. The necromancer's speed was slower than Cyrus's now that both blades were in hand. *My strength doesn't match his, but if I do this right, I won't need it to …*

Malpravus met him with his free hand and Cyrus clashed against it as it elongated into a bone sword. Cyrus hit it high with Rodanthar and it cracked, then in the exact same spot a second later with Praelior and it shattered.

Malpravus's red eyes glowed brighter, looked wider. "You can't—"

Cyrus leapt in under the hand and struck at the one channeling the magic toward the center of the room. With two solid blows he sheared it off, but the magic poured out of the stump and he narrowly dodged the reprisal from the other stump, the bone whistling over his head as he ducked below Malpravus's empty, skeletal pelvis.

"I possess none of the weaknesses of your flesh," Malpravus leered down at him, and Cyrus struck at the left knee joint. He severed the leg and kicked it free and was rewarded by a kick from the other bone-foot, twisting around to rattle him through his armor with a glancing blow. "I need not stand as you pathetic mortals do …"

Cyrus spun and smashed the leg as it kicked at him again. Now the broken thighbones spun like wheels in their sockets. Malpravus had no legs to stand on, yet showed no sign of falling. "Dammit," Cyrus muttered.

"The head, you idiot!" Vaste screamed from behind him. "It's talking to you! Put a sword through it!"

"If only it were that easy," Malpravus said tauntingly, his spine elongating again as he stretched toward the ceiling, the glowing red eyes receding as he drew away.

That's where he's weak, Cyrus realized. *He's been bobbing that damned head away this whole battle!*

With a whispered breath, Cyrus cast Falcon's Essence and surged into the air, running. He slapped Malpravus's spine and sent a hard rattle up and down the body. Malpravus let out a bellow of outrage that shook the walls and brought down more rock from the ceiling. Cyrus dodged, a piece of stone the size of a bench clobbering him in the arm as he continued his run upward, ignoring the pain surging through him.

"Now you see me," Malpravus said, "and I see you. You see my weakness, but I have seen yours all along." The skeleton's teeth grinned. "Tell me, dear boy ... while you're chasing me, whatever is happening to that wife of yours?"

Cyrus could not help himself. His spine chilling in terror, he spun in the air and looked back down.

"GO!" Vaste screamed. "YOU HAVE TO STOP HIM FIRST OR WE'LL ALL DIE, INCLUDING VARA!"

Cyrus closed his eyes and looked away from the battle below, not daring to think, not courageous enough to look for fear he would see something that would take the heart out of him. The magic pooling in the middle of the room was cracking even harder now, black as the darkest night, and it lashed out in front of him as Cyrus jerked hard down, ducking just beneath it as it filled his nose with a singeing smell.

"This is why you will not win," Malpravus said, "why you cannot. This is your fault, your failing. You have always sought to add weakness unto yourself while I have sought to eliminate it from me. You seek softness, the touch and caress of warm humanity, of mortality, while I eschew it for the cold embrace of immortality."

Cyrus ran as the head snaked in a steady circle, drawn away on the neck like a toy on a string. It whipped around, avoiding the solid column of magic bursting up from the crackling orb of magic in the center of the room, and hit its limit.

Nowhere left to run, Cyrus thought as he charged it down.

But it did not run. Malpravus's glinting skull snapped as it hit its full extension, and then it whipped right back at him.

Cyrus saw it coming, just a hair slower than himself. He saw the small jerks that told him that Malpravus was not going to meet him squarely, was not going to crash into him with those cold red eyes, and he drew a deep breath of the dank temple air, taking in a lungful of the energy crackling through it—

And he flung his swords out to either side and charged forward into destiny.

96.

The head of the snake realized its mistake at the last, but it was too late. Malpravus bobbed to the left, desperately dodging, and struck Praelior. The blade carved an inch-long indentation into the white plate of bone, the sound of sword meeting skull like a scream piercing the night. A hard shudder ran down Cyrus's arm from the site of the impact, and he smelled acrid stinking death as he struck, tasted bile running up his throat, and it gagged him even as the force spun him around from the hit.

He saw the blood, though, black and viscous, oozing out of the wound he'd made as the skull dodged away again, trying to escape further injury. The black ooze dripped to the ground—

And hit the lines between the stones in the middle of the room—

And trickled toward the seal, just barely making it, a thimble-sized drop that seeped barely a quarter-inch into the symbol before halting, spent, too thin to carry on any farther.

"Got it!" Cyrus shouted as the skull raced away from him, red eyes watching him in fear.

"Mendicant!" Quinneria shouted, "NOW!"

The green energy Quinneria had been pouring into the union of spells at the center of the room gained a new entrant, a blazing red energy as the goblin stepped into the fight and Quinneria faded out. She took a step back, staggering like Malpravus after the hit, and then regained herself, twirling hands around her face, her body, red burning at her fingertips not from the spell she was casting, but her own life that she was using to do so. She drew a ragged breath that Cyrus imagined he could hear and then thrust out both hands under the magic burning over the seal.

The effect was immediate; there was a sound like an explosion, a rumble that shook the room.

"*WHAT?!*" Malpravus's scream was higher-pitched than Cyrus had ever heard it before. It was followed by the rushing of what sounded like wind. The black magic pouring out of his bony stump ceased in an instant. Opposite him, Cyrus watched Vaste and Ryin both collapse, face-first, to the ground, exhausted. Mendicant held steady, but only just, dipping both front hands down to catch himself.

"IMPOSSIBLE!" Malpravus screamed, the last of the spell energy blowing out the roof and disappearing into the sky, blue shining back down. "YOU CANNOT—"

A vortex of red spell-light was swirling slowly out of the seal, roiling into the air in a slow spin, twisting as it reached out for Malpravus's bony form, guided toward him inexorably until the cone had touched his skull. He tried to run but failed; it took hold of him like a firm hand, gripping him, circling his skull and engulfing him. The necromancer's shrieks filled the air as the vortex swallowed him up, yanking his long spine as it tried to flail and grow out of the tornado's grasp. He could not grow fast enough to outrun it, however, and he tipped into it as if he were falling in an unavoidable hole, the bony protrusions that were all that were left of his legs the last thing to disappear.

Slowly spinning, the vortex claimed him, dragging him down, shrinking as his screams grew quieter and quieter, the spell circling hard down to the surface of the seal until it vanished between the profiles of Yartraak and Mortus, as though it had never existed at all.

"My gods," Terian said, his face white with bone powder, his breath coming in great shuddering gasps. "Did we—"

"The army!" Mendicant said and spun, but there was silence at the entry to the pyramid, and silence flooding down from the open sky above.

"Weak and pathetic," Fortin opined from just inside the entry to the temple, a limp corpse clutched in a craggy hand. "Also ... they are no longer moving." He crushed the body's skull in his hands.

"Cyrus ..." Vaste said, lifting his head, his eyes heavily lidded.

Cyrus, for his part, was still standing several feet in the air, feeling weak, like all the vitality had been drained out of him by the tornado that had stolen away Malpravus. He dispelled the Falcon's Essence without thinking about it and came clunking to the ground only a few feet from Vaste. He shuddered at the pain as he twisted his ankle. He tried to cast the healing spell but couldn't concentrate, so weak was his mind. He cringed and staggered along to the healer. "What is it?" he asked, feeling as though he might fall down next to the troll.

Vaste looked up at him with cracked lips, bleeding between the lines, faint oozing green coming out. His eyes were bloodshot, yellow veins running out from the irises, and when he spoke, it came out in a cracking gasp. "V … Vara …"

"Oh, gods," Cyrus said, hit by the hammer of memory. He turned, and he saw her, and his whole body went cold as if he'd just had the whole north dumped upon him.

97.

"Vara!" Cyrus shouted, his voice resonating off the walls of the temple, echoing out of the hole in the roof and returning back to him as he thrust Praelior into its scabbard and then fell to his knees, skidding over stones in a mad race to get to her. He still held Rodanthar in his hand, the plates of his greaves scratching against the floor, the guard of the sword scraping in his scramble.

She lay in a corner, dead, her open eyes staring blankly at the ceiling. Her sword lay beside her in limp fingers, and the dust of bone had left the blood pooled at her neck speckled with white. Her blue eyes looked dull even as they reflected the sky shining in from above, but there was no strength in her muscles, and she did not respond when he called her name.

It'll be all right, he thought as he scrambled to her on all fours, his breath catching, the smell of the dusty dankness rising up from deeper within the temple. *She'll be fine, just fine, I just need to get to her ...*

He reached her side and threw off the gauntlet from his right hand, running sweaty fingers over her cold, pale flesh. He left a trace of wetness like a tear as he rubbed her cheek, looking down into those blue eyes with his own, trying to meet a gaze that was no longer there to be found. His hand shook as he touched her, skin like snow, and he ran his fingers down to her throat, where the damnable hand of Malpravus had done its worst.

The spell, Cyrus thought, shaking his head to bring him back to himself. *I need ... the resurrection spell.* He concentrated, closed his eyes, whispered the words—

And felt the air rush out of him but nothing else, his hand not even coming to glow.

"No no no," he muttered and took another breath, soothing, calming. "I can—you can't—" He imagined the spell, remembered the effect, spoke it into being under his breath—

And nothing happened.

His breath came harder now, in a frenzy like the battle he'd been in only moments earlier. There had been no glow, no power, nothing. His hand shook above her face as he held it over her. He took a breath, then another, trying to slow them, trying to fill his lungs with air. The smell of death was all around him, the air was still and quiet, no one was speaking—

"You can't be dead," he whispered, and he breathed the spell out once more.

His hand fell on a lifeless breast, covered over by a silver breastplate crusted with dust. He felt for movement, and when it still did not come, he felt his blood rage, throbbing in his veins. "I can't—I can't—"

"You're too agitated," his mother's quiet voice came from over his shoulder, soothing like the smell of a warm meal on a cold eve. He remembered the crackle of the fire, the pleasant, radiating warmth of the hearth, of sitting on her lap, of staring into those green eyes …

I meet you.

He breathed the words again, and the light glowed faint from his hand, the breastplate springing back to motion beneath his wet fingertips as they slid down and smeared the silver with his perspiration. Vara drew a ragged breath, blood pumping out of her neck. He gasped his surprise, his relief, and his hands shook again—

A glow behind him, red, streamed out, and Vara's neck was made whole, the pale skin knitting itself back together beneath the flowing blood, bright, snowy white beneath the crimson river below her chin. Her eyes shone, wide with panic and pain, glaring like a summer sky as they found his, and her hand leapt up to grab his in her mailed fist.

"Oh, thank the …" Cyrus felt all the breath come out of him, draining him as though it were his life's blood run out. He closed his eyes for a second and embraced the darkness before forcing them back open to stare down at his wife. "Are you … all right?"

Vara took a rattling breath before answering. "That depends," she said. "Is Malpravus dead?"

Cyrus looked over his shoulder, past his mother to the seal. The others were scattered about it, in varying states of weakness and injury.

Vaste was now sitting up, though Ryin was still lying flat. Mendicant and J'anda both looked exhausted. Longwell leaned on his lance like a cane and Aisling lurked in the shadows. Zarnn and Fortin both lingered, like statues guarding the exit. Cyrus's eyes fixed on the seal in the middle of them all. "He's ... well, he's ..."

"He's trapped," Quinneria said.

"Trapped for how long?" Vara asked, trying to sit up.

"For now," Quinneria said. "Hopefully forever."

"If someone brings him the blood of sacrifices, is he going to spring out again?" Vaste asked, looking quite sick to his stomach, head between his knees.

"That's a very real danger, yes," Quinneria said. "I think it might be best if we find a way to seal this place off somehow."

"Bury it in rock?" Mendicant looked up. "Even if we collapsed it, the sides wouldn't cover the seal, there's too little left of the roof."

"This feels like a problem that could be dealt with tomorrow," Cyrus said, taking Vara's hand in his. She looked up at him weakly, still pale.

"Well, if nothing else," Terian said, brushing off his breastplate, "I think that Goliath's done. Sacrificed on the altar of their leader's ambition for power." He stared into the silence. "I feel that's a very fitting end for them, somehow. Poetic, in a way."

"Yay," Vaste said weakly. "I'd consider it all more of a victory if we hadn't just crammed Malpravus into a vase in hopes that it never breaks."

"The seal is a little stronger than that," Quinneria said. "It's not as though most people go running around willy-nilly, bleeding on seals. Why, the Avatar of Mortus would probably still be there if you two hadn't gone bandit hunting or treasure seeking or whatever it was you did." She sighed. "No one has come to this place in years. You can feel it when you listen closely."

"All I can hear at the moment is the rather considerable thudding of my own heart," Vara said.

"Come on," Cyrus said and lifted her up as he had done on their wedding night, cradling her in his arms. She narrowed her eyes at him. "Should I not?" he asked, before taking a single step.

She looked ready to protest but stopped with a roll of her eyes. "Just this once again, perhaps."

"All right, then," Cyrus said, smiling down at her, "let's go find our horses and go home."

98.

"As usual, you seem to lead a life of constant adventure, Lord Davidon," Cattrine Tiernan said with a faint smile as she walked him down the street in Emerald Fields on the following day. It was another glorious summer day. Cyrus was warm beneath his armor, but he welcomed the heat; the terror of seeing his wife dead in the corner of the temple continued to chill him, sleeping and awake, and it had left him in a state of fatigue that was slowing his step.

"At this point, I'm just calling it what it is—trouble," he said, walking alongside her. Each of their steps stirred the dust on the dirt street. There wasn't even the slightest hint of a breeze, the air was so still.

"May I ask you something?" She waited for him to nod. "Our dwarven miners, Keearyn and his family ..."

Cyrus stiffened. "Yes?"

She smiled, and he saw a twinkle in her eye. "Well, it's been a bit quiet up in the hills of Rockridge, lately, other than the caterwauling of those damned savanna cats—"

"You can't have the Brotherhood of the Savanna Cat without the cat, I suppose."

"Well, there are a half dozen of them now," she said a bit irritably. "They've captured one for every troll in Sanctuary. I see them racing around on the hills on the backs of those monstrous things." She shook her head in annoyance. "Anyway, I was simply wondering did you send them—the dwarves, not cats—into some sort of trouble?"

"No," Cyrus said, and even to him his answer sounded odd. "Not trouble, I hope. They should be fine, just ... busy. Elsewhere. For a while."

"Trouble and mystery," Cattrine said with a faint flare behind her eyes. "It is no wonder that the women who surround you can't seem to extricate you from their lives. You're simply too compelling to fully free ourselves of you."

"Oh, you're hilarious," he said dryly, prompting her to smile tightly. "Thank you for offering her shelter, though. The kindness is appreciated."

"'Tis nothing," Cattrine said. "So ... Goliath is done, our troubles with the Kingdom are ended, and you seem to have put quite the spur in the arse of the Confederation." She smiled. "What will you be doing next, Cyrus?"

"Sleeping at night, I hope," Cyrus said grimly. "The Kingdom hasn't been giving you any trouble?"

"They've been as pleasant to deal with in the last month as ever I've seen them," she said. "They're actually very sweet now. Apparently hearing that Goddess of theirs reminding their high-and-mighties what she expected of them put them in a less grumpy spirit." She sighed. "If only I could turn her toward a few of our troublemakers to the same effect ..."

"Give me a week to rest and I'll do it for you."

"Well, I want them to live," she said, frowning. "They're trouble, but not that bad."

Cyrus shrugged. "Are you still trading with the districts of the Confederation we chipped off?"

"Yes, as much as we are with Terian and the dark elves at the moment," she said cautiously, "but I don't think they're going to break away." She looked around. "Rumor is that the Mayor of Reikonos has persuaded them to stay. Bribery of some sort, I expect, but word is that the Confederation is becoming more of a state of equals." She made a face. "Of course I suppose that could all change on the morrow, but that's the current rumor."

"I guess the veracity of the rumors depends on who you heard them from," Cyrus said as they passed the tall courthouse in the middle of the square, its wooden tower making a creaking noise as they went by it.

"Governor Waterman, actually," Cattrine said.

Cyrus felt his forehead rise. "Well ... it's probably true, then."

"I think so, too," Cattrine agreed as they snaked their way down a winding alley that led beside three small buildings to come to a stop before a cozy wooden house. "Here you go. Shall I wait for you?"

"No," Cyrus said, shaking his head. "You're busy, and I've taken enough of your time."

She smiled. "You should get some rest, Cyrus. You look—and I don't often think this of you, so pay it heed—terrible."

"Thanks," Cyrus said, nodding. "I will, as soon as I settle these last few things." And with that, he stepped onto the porch and knocked on the door.

"Come in," came the faint voice from within, and he stepped inside after turning the handle.

Inside Cyrus found a dim room, the faint light of an oil lamp shining in a wooden single-room house, dark curtains drawn over the windows. It smelled of cedar and oil, and as his eyes adjusted he cast the Eagle Eye spell, which shed the light of day into the entire place from corner to corner. He could see the bed, thin mattress crowning it, and Imina lying upon it in a new dress.

She sat up as he entered, but he could tell in the way she held herself that she was not particularly thrilled to see him. "It's you," she said quietly.

"It is," he said, his voice low in reply. He cleared his throat. "How … how are you?"

"Well enough for now," she said, dragging the trailing edge of her dress free of a snag on the wooden edge of the bed. "You seem … tired."

"I am indeed," Cyrus said, eliding neatly past the full truth.

"But you did beat him?" She sounded faintly hopeful.

"He's gone," Cyrus said. "He won't trouble you any longer."

"He was a strange character," Imina said with a dazed look. "So gentlemanly and polite but devoid of … everything." She shuddered. "I have never met anyone like him."

"And hopefully, you never will again," Cyrus said, looking uncomfortably around the room. "So … are you going back to Reikonos?"

Imina's hands ran up and down her skirt, reminding him of the time when he'd first met her and she'd seemed to paw at herself nervously. He hadn't recognized it as nerves at the time, but looking back, it now seemed plain. "I don't know. My stall in the markets of Reikonos will be gone, as will my home. Nothing stays bare there for long," she said with a note of regret. She brightened slightly. "They have no flower sellers here, did you know that?"

"I don't expect there's been much demand until now," Cyrus said, nodding. "But Emerald Fields is rising in prosperity quickly. Seems they could use some flowers. But how will you get your supply?"

"I always bought from the elves before," she said with a shrug. "I hear they do a lot of business with Pharesia here. I reckon I won't have much trouble getting deliveries."

"You have a plan," he said with a smile. "That's a good sign." He looked once more around the room and found he had nothing more to say. "I'll leave you to it, I suppose. I just wanted to check and make sure that you were doing ... well, as best you could be expected to be doing, and here I find you're doing even better than that." He started to turn to leave.

"Cyrus," she spoke into the silence after him and he froze. "I ..."

"What is it?" he asked gently, not daring to look back at her, wanting to do nothing more than get out, to return to Sanctuary. *I belong there, and this is an uncomfortable reminder of the way things used to be ... the way I didn't care for.*

"Once I told you ..." she said, bowing her head, "that you cling to your friends because you have nowhere else to go and nothing to do with your life."

Cyrus half-turned to look back at her, finding he was smiling in amusement. *Once, those words stung harder than any sword I'd ever been hit with. Now, after everything I've been through, they're rather ... prosaic.* "Yes?"

"I was wrong," she said, darting a glance at him. "You have ... done impressive things with your life, and your friends are ... most commendable people. I can tell they care deeply for you, and you have made quite the home at Sanctuary. I could see that even in the short time I was there."

A sense of anti-climax came over Cyrus. *Once upon a time, hearing these words from her ... they would have meant everything to me. Even after we parted, for years I would have given more than I had to hear her say this. But now ...* He stared into Imina's eyes and saw the sincerity there before she looked away from his earnest gaze. *Now it doesn't matter, because I've got my home, and my ... my guild. My family.*

"Thank you, Imina," he said quietly. With a short bow to his former wife, he cast the return spell and went back to his home on the plains.

99.

Cyrus strolled lazily through the foyer, making his way from the staircase toward the Great Hall, the sun shining through the stained-glass window above the great entry doors, which were both pulled wide open, inviting him out into the warm day. Tempted, Cyrus strayed from his path, scenting the smell of fresh grass and upturned earth where the well-trod ground between the door and the wall seemed to be springing into new life.

"Great day," Zarnn said, thumping past with his entourage of remaining trolls. They all stopped, executing bows at the waist to Cyrus, who paused, momentarily thunderstruck, before bowing in return.

"What are you up to this fine day, Zarnn?" Cyrus asked.

"Off to train with the Grand Knight of Sanctuary," Zarnn said with a smile, earrings rattling in his ears as he nodded, his entourage bobbing their heads in time behind him. "The Brotherhood of the Savanna Cat must be ever vigilant, ever prepared for the next threat."

Cyrus smiled. "Hopefully we're done with threats for a while."

"Hope for peace, prepare for war," Zarnn said, leading his troll brethren away toward the entrance, crossing the great seal as they thumped their way out of the foyer and disappeared out into the day.

Cyrus stood in place, not watching them go, his eyes instead fixed on the great seal of Sanctuary. "Hm," he said, more to himself than anything and took a few steps toward it. He'd never paid it much mind, thinking of it only as the place where spellcasters emerged from the portal mounted beneath the floor. He stared down at it now, at the swirling lines, the spiral of strange writing that spun toward the center of the circle, and his hand came automatically to his breastplate, thumping against it. The necklace of the Guildmaster that he wore beneath it was its exact twin, he was certain. Frowning thoughtfully at the symmetry between them, he turned and headed back toward the Great Hall.

The tables were empty, the hall silent as he made his way inside. He could hear movement in the back toward the kitchen, and he followed his ears toward the source of the noise. He looked over the empty tables with a trace of regret; a little over a year ago, this place would have been dotted with people.

But that was twenty thousand members ago, Cyrus thought. *Practically a different lifetime at this point.*

"You have that look on your face," his mother said, leaning against the kitchen door. She was clean and clad in robes of silken purple, something she would never have worn as Larana. She still looked young, though perhaps a shade older than she had only yesterday. "The one that your father used to get when he was thinking."

"Father was a warrior," Cyrus said with a somber smile. "They're not supposed to think."

"That joke is older than you are," she said. "It might even predate me." She was a little more cautious in her posture, a little more nervous, he thought, as she stepped out of the kitchen door and started walking slowly forward, drawing near to a table. She stopped, standing with one hand crossing her body, touching her elbow beneath the violet robes. "What brings you to the kitchens at this hour? Would you like me to fix you someth—"

"There are … things … I want to know," Cyrus said, finding the courage to meet her eyes again, making his way toward her slowly, pausing on the other side of the table from her. They were warm, green—and fearful, though they softened slightly when she heard his question.

"I'll tell you anything I can," she said, uncrossing her arms, stepping up to the table, faintly hopeful. Her face seemed to glow as though she were holding back a smile, the corners of her mouth twitching.

Cyrus smiled and she let loose a smile of her own. He took a breath of the warm summer air, and for once, felt it seem to seep all the way through him. "Good," he said, and they sat down in the emptiness of the Great Hall, the sunlight shining in from the windows behind them, and talked for hours.

100.

Cyrus found Vara in the Council Chambers, with the balcony doors swaying open in the glorious day, the sun bright outside them. She was huddled over something at the new table, a quill and ink in her hands, writing feverishly when he came in. Her eyes darted up to greet him, and she stopped, finishing a stroke upon the page and then leaning back her padded chair. "You look as though you should be the Elder of Sanctuary, not I," she said lightly as he came in.

"Everyone's been expressing similar sentiments," Cyrus said, "as though it wasn't bad enough that I was already destined to age so much faster than you." He pointed a finger at her as he made his way to his seat. "Just remember, you're still a year older than me."

"I expect you'll remind me every chance you get," Vara said, capping the inkwell and blowing on the page of the leather-bound book laid out on the table before her.

Cyrus sagged into his chair, feeling as though his armor weighed as much as eight trolls. "What is that?" He pointed at the book.

She blew across the pages once more to dry them and then picked it up, shut the current page, and opened it to the front. "It's this." She held it out for him to read.

"*The Journal of Vara*," he read aloud, eyes rolling across the yellowed page, "*An Account of My Days With Sanctuary ...?*" He looked up at her. "You keep a diary?"

She sighed and rolled her eyes. "Yes. Yes, I keep a diary. As did Alaric, I might add."

"No judgment here," Cyrus said, sinking back into his chair. "I've often longed for a place to express my jangling and discordant emotions—you know, before I shared my every thought with you, love."

504

"I can think of a few I wish you'd kept to yourself," Vara said under her breath.

"What's that?"

"I said I think you should absolutely keep a journal," she said, smiling brightly.

"I wouldn't know where to start," he said coyly, eyeing the book in front of her. "Maybe I should read yours ... you know, for ideas on how to do the thing properly."

She raised an eyebrow. "Is that so? You need to read mine in order to learn how to write one yourself?" She stood, taking the book in hand, and making her way over to the door to the archives. She paused and opened it, seemingly waiting for him to follow.

"Well, I'm sure it has some fascinating insights in it," he said, rising out of his chair with great difficulty. He followed her into the archives as she returned to the door. "What ... where did you put it?"

"Somewhere in here," she said vaguely, leaning in and giving him a quick kiss.

When they broke, he peered down at her. She was utterly relaxed, none of the horror of the temple still upon her. "You know when Mendicant says 'the library,' he means he and my mother were reading the books in here, right?" Cyrus asked.

Vara froze, her brow furrowing in obvious horror, her mouth falling open. "Oh ... oh ... oh Goddess," she said so very faintly.

A hard knock came at the door of the Council Chambers and Cyrus leaned back through with great effort, feeling as though he might topple over at any moment. "What?"

Calene slipped in, blinking furiously. "Sorry to interrupt you—"

"It's the Council Chambers," Cyrus said, moving out of the way so that Vara could get out of the archive. She shut the door behind her as Cyrus looked at Calene expectantly. "I don't expect much in the way of privacy in here."

"Well, I know your, uh, quarters in the tower are currently, uh, exposed to the four seasons," Calene said, flushing. "Anyway ... that little girl from the Leagues, the messenger?"

Cyrus ran through his own head for the memory, but came up blank.

"Agora Friedlander?" Vara asked.

"Oh, yeah," Cyrus muttered. "Her."

"Well, she's back," Calene said. "Brought another League representative with her. Says she's here to make peace."

Cyrus took a long, hearty breath. "Well, that's not unwanted, at least. Have her come up and assemble the Council."

"Some are here, some are gone," Calene said. "I'll see what I can do. I'll just send her up for now, then." And she left, the door cracked behind her, her soft footfalls fading down the stairs.

"The Leagues are suing for peace with us," Vara said, putting a hand on Cyrus's pauldron. He turned to look at her, blue eyes shining. "Will wonders never cease?"

"Well, we kind of destroyed everyone who was willing to fight us in their name," Cyrus said. "Plus, we stomped down pretty hard on old Malpravus, which had to be a heck of a warning if it made it to the ears of the League bosses in the ..." he frowned, "... the ..."

"Pantheon," came a booming voice from the door, and Cyrus turned to see Agora Friedlander, petite as a child, flanked by the speaker, a man in a cloak. His eyes searched their way through the room. "I think 'Pantheon' is the term you're looking for," he said.

"It is," Cyrus said coolly as their guests stepped inside. Agora Friedlander stepped back, pressing herself against the wall, a tiny figure against the stone, hands steepled in front of her, her eyes fixed straight ahead. The man with her, on the other hand, meandered ahead, looking at the hearth to the right, running his fingers over the stones of the wall, pacing slowly around the long, rectangular table. "And you are ...?"

"With the Leagues," he said, not turning to look at Cyrus. He came around the last few seats now and stopped at Cyrus's chair, running his bare fingers over the smooth wood. "Didn't you hear? We're here to end this conflict of yours. No more worries about ... heresy." He smiled, but he did not meet Cyrus's eyes, the daylight flooding in from beyond the balcony as he turned to look out.

"I wasn't overly worried about it, to be honest," Cyrus said, frowning as he watched the man step forward, taking in the view.

"I'd heard that," the man said, looking out over the balcony from just inside the door. "You know, it's an impressive guildhall you have here."

"Thank you," Cyrus said. "You haven't told me your name yet."

The man turned around and strode forward a few steps toward them, then looked right at Cyrus as he continued to walk, and any feeling of warm summer vanished in that moment. "Do I need to?" he asked, his eyes glowing brightest red.

It was as if he had seized Cyrus by the neck and hauled him to the Jungle of Vidara and back a whole year. In those eyes he saw the sights of battle, the struggle against Talikartin the Guardian, the possessed Avatar of the God of War, the screams and grunts and cries of the fight—

And Cyrus drew his swords.

Bellarum was at him in an instant, swatting him aside with a backhand that sent Cyrus through the new table and smashing into the other wall. The world tilted, splinters and boards crashing through the air around him, everything spinning until he hit the stone and cratered it neatly, crunching it and spraying gravel. Cyrus fell to the floor, the remains of the table and at least half the chairs smashing into the wall along with him, and felt the shock of the landing throughout his body.

His head felt foggy, drifting, but he forced his eyes open, to look across the room. Bellarum was there, revealed plainly now, his armor visible where it had been hidden beneath illusion a moment earlier. Vara was fighting back against the God of War, her sword drawn and held high, clashing against his bracers with every slash, but there was laughter in the room, high and jovial, echoing in the small chamber.

"I always wanted to see this place," Bellarum said, blocking every attack Vara made with ease. "It's much nicer than I thought it would be. Not a bad place to die."

"I agree," Vara said, straining with every stroke of her sword, not a single blow she'd struck having the slightest impact. "Let's kill you here."

Bellarum laughed as Cyrus tried to get to his feet and his legs collapsed beneath him. "You have so much spirit. It's a shame you were the favorite of Vidara, that weak old cow. If you hadn't fallen under her sway, I might have claimed you for my own. You have more fire than he does, anyway—"

Vara's sword struck Bellarum's bracer so hard sparks flew. "That's my husband you're talking about, and this is our home, so I'll thank you to keep a civil tongue in your head while under our roof—"

"You know what they say," Bellarum said, cackling again, "home is where the heart is." He blocked hard and checked Vara as he stepped in, slamming her against the wall. He knocked the sword right out of her hand, sending it skittering over to where Agora Friedlander stood. She stooped to pick it up, cradling in her hand. She peered down at the intricate blade with her childlike eyes then slung it over her tiny shoulder.

"And I think your husband needs to have his heart torn out," Bellarum said, his massive, gauntleted hand seizing Vara by the throat, pinning her head against the wall. He spun around to look at Cyrus, who was still trying to get to his feet and failing, the world dim around him. *Wasn't it a summer day a minute ago?* Blood streamed down his forehead under his helm, trickling into his eye thickly. "Do you hear me, Cyrus?" Bellarum's fingers glowed as he waved them toward him. "What about now?"

It was as though a suffocating blanket had been torn away from Cyrus's head, and he blinked and came to his feet.

"No, no," Bellarum held up a finger. "Don't. I'll pop her head right off and burn it in my hand before you can even make it halfway across the room." He smiled beneath the helm, and once again Cyrus found himself looking into burning crimson eyes. "I warned you ... those who do not serve will be destroyed."

Cyrus tasted blood on his lips, felt it trickling down his face. "I ... I ..."

"I know what you're thinking," Bellarum said, staring at him, still dangling Vara from his fingers. "Can you cast a spell? Could you throw your sword? The answer is—not in time. And if you throw either one of those fine swords, I'm keeping them." He peered at Cyrus. "I did give you one of them, after all. It would be only fair, wouldn't it?"

"What ... do you want?" Cyrus asked, swallowing hard.

Bellarum blinked at him, the red receding beneath them helm. "Did you not just listen? I told you. Those who do not serve ... will die. Simple enough, isn't it?"

"You want me to serve you?" Cyrus stared at the God of War. "Now?"

"I thought I healed your head wound, but still you cannot think," Bellarum sighed. "No. No. Let me explain, perhaps more slowly this time. This is why I'm a god and you're ... not." His eyes burned bright. "Those who do not serve ... will die."

The God of War's fingers glowed a deep orange, and he pivoted hard into a punch that tore right through Vara's shining breastplate, shredding the metal and boring into her center. She let out all her air in one breath and blood poured from between her perfect lips as her eyes locked on Cyrus's across the wreckage of the Council Chambers. Bellarum tossed her to the side before the balcony door, his gauntlet dripping red.

Cyrus watched Vara twist in the air and come down hard with a thud, shuddering as she landed. He watched, his eyes trapped, unable to look away from her. His breath caught in his throat, he threw up a hand instinctively, concentrating, remembering the words as he reached out to touch her with a spell from across the room, a healing caress to undo the horror he'd just seen done.

His hand glowed briefly then faltered as she landed, rolling in a twist as she came to rest on the balcony. He ripped his eyes from her and turned toward Bellarum, letting out a scream of rage and charging through the wreckage, ignoring the splinters and boards of the table as he ran toward the red-eyed beast—

Cyrus was knocked aside by a gauntlet that moved faster than he by a very great margin. He rolled, thumping along the ground, and came to rest next to something hard and yet soft, his fingers touching—

Vara.

He raised his head and stared. Her mouth moved, she lay flat upon her back, the wound inflicted by the God of War still gaping in the center of her chest, her chin covered in red and her mouth opening and closing slowly as she tried to speak, but nothing came out.

"Vara ..." Cyrus whispered, rolling over to her, crawling with his swords in hand to straddle her, shaking as he tried to cast a healing spell again—then again—then—

"Oh, it's not you this time," Bellarum said, Agora Friedlander flanking him as he stepped past them to stand on the balcony's edge. The God of War backed to the edge, smiling faintly at Cyrus. "I cursed her, you see. Didn't want you to be able to undo what I'd done." There was so much joy in his words, Cyrus thought, staring down at Vara's eyes as she faltered. She raised a hand, shaking, and brushed his cheek, but her touch was covered in her gauntlet, and the metal scraped against his day's worth of stubble, leaving a trail of blood behind.

"Vara," Cyrus said, afraid to relinquish his swords but utterly unsure of what to do. She stared up at him, breathless, making a gulping sound from her throat, desperate, trying to draw breath but failing. "VARA!"

He lowered his face to her, pushing his eyes close to hers, looking into them. He could see the light as it faded, as life left them, as the last sound passed between her lips and she sagged against the ground … lifeless.

"Oh …" Bellarum said, "Well, we're halfway done, I think." And he stepped off the edge of the balcony, Agora Friedlander following him a moment later.

"Vara!" Cyrus shoved his swords away, into his belt, seizing her face with his gauntlets, lifting her head limply off the stone. "Vara!" he shouted, his voice echoing across the plains. "No, no no no no—you were—you—you were supposed to be the one to—to live for—I was supposed to—to go—go before—" His words came flooding out in a long crawl, ripping out of his throat. "You were supposed to live, I was supposed to—you can't—you can't—YOU CAN'T GO FIRST—"

He shook her. She moved, and he felt a flare of hope. "Vara!" He shook her again, but she only danced along with his motion; there was nothing of her left. Her eyes stared blankly at the ceiling above them, past his eyes, past him. The ponytail hung without motion, flowing down, no hint of life—

"Cyrus!" The door flew open behind him, but he did not turn to look. He kept his eyes on Vara's, waiting for something, some motions, some hint—

You can't be gone.

You can't go first.

"You weren't supposed to go first." He pressed his lips to hers, but there was no warmth there, no sense of resistance, no pressing back, nothing—

Just nothing.

"Cyrus!" Vaste came down beside him, hand on his shoulder. "Cyrus, are you—" He stopped, and his hand flared with white light as he cast a spell. "Oh … oh … oh damn … dammit … I can't …"

The world shook around them and the tower lurched, dust shaking down from above. "Cyrus," Vaste said, more calmly now. "Cyrus, do you know what's going on?"

"I don't care," Cyrus said, staring into those blue eyes, like the skies he'd seen outside only a few minutes earlier … skies that held an infinity of promises …

… until Bellarum had come in …

"Bellarum is destroying Sanctuary," Vaste said, "and he's not alone. There are other gods with him. Cyrus, I've ordered everyone to leave. The wizards and druids are trying to get everyone out now but—"

"I can't leave ..." Cyrus said. The blue eyes stared back if he leaned over far enough, and he could see the promises within them if he just looked hard enough ...

"We have to go," Vaste said, shaking him again, grasping him roughly, trying to pull him away from her.

"NO!" He elbowed the healer in the belly and scrambled back to the ground, lifting her head gently, cradling the shining hair, like gold, but worth so much more to him ... "I won't leave her!"

"Cyrus! If we stay, we'll—"

A giant, armored head rose up past the balcony; Bellarum's helm was the size of one of the towers, leering down at him with eyes as large as Malpravus's skull had been in the temple. "You'll die," the God of War said in an amused sort of way. "But if you leave now, you'll have the satisfaction of knowing your home has been utterly destroyed, so ..." The helm tipped to the side. "Your choice."

"Cyrus!" Vaste hissed.

"I'm not leaving her!" Cyrus said, fighting to stay on his knees, to stay close to her, with her skin pale as a Northlands snow field.

"We have to—"

"Stay," Bellarum said in a dull roar, "and it'll all be over in a moment." The tower shook again, and that deep laugh rolled over him.

"She's dead, Cyrus!" Vaste screamed, and the words washed over him like cold water on an icy lakeshore. "I can't resurrect her! It's over!"

"It's not!" Cyrus said, shoving him back, knocking the troll into the doorframe, shattering the balcony door's window. Glass fell in sparkling shards, reflecting blue like her beautiful eyes. "It's not!" His breath caught in his throat and it took a moment to get it unstuck. When he spoke again, his words were barely audible. "It can't be."

"CYRUS!" The shout from behind him did not even convince him to look. He leaned down and pressed his cheek to Vara's, looking in those eyes, as the laughter came again like echoing thunder and—

Lightning flashed overhead and the laughter stopped, turning into a roar of fury and pain, but still Cyrus did not turn, did not look away. He wanted to lose himself in the blue, to lose himself forever, to—

"We—have—to—go!" Vaste wrapped his arms around Cyrus and

dragged him, lifting him bodily off her, pulling him in from the balcony, his helm clinking against the lintel of the door as he came up, raised high by the troll.

"NOOOOOOOOOOOO!" Cyrus screamed as Bellarum's red eyes raised up to look straight at him. His hair stirred under his own helm as he fought against Vaste's grip on his midsection, struggling, trying to get back to her as the healer dragged him away in strong arms.

The red eyes of the God of War glowed, brighter and brighter, and Cyrus could see the spell being cast, destruction about to be unleashed.

Good, was all he could think. *Good. Then this is it. It'll take me back, back to the blue ... back to the gold ... to the white ...*

To her.

The wind rose as he saw the blast unleashed from Bellarum's eye, and he knew at the last moment that it would not hit him, would not touch him. The world around him was swallowed in the howl of the wind as the blast disappeared in a whirl of druid magic and the red of the eyes was replaced by a blue sky, the noise of rushing magic by the chatter of voices and the sound of water. Vaste let him loose and Cyrus came down in a hard crash, his elbows slamming with all his weight into cobblestones.

"No," he murmured, a soft gasp. "No ... no ..."

He turned his eyes to the sky, rolling sideways, and he knew where he was in an instant. People walked by in linen and silken clothes, sandals covered bare feet, and the sun shone hot overhead as the fountain sprinkled water behind him.

Reikonos Square.

"I'm sorry, Cyrus," Vaste said, sagging against the fountain. "She was ... she was gone. There was nothing—"

"You did the right thing, Vaste," came Quinneria's ragged voice, and he saw her standing next to the troll. "Another second and we would have—" She choked on the words. "We would have ended up like ..."

"Like her?" Cyrus managed to choke out. The sky was blue. There was a wagon of golden hay rolling through on the cobblestones just ahead of him, wheels clacking as it went. A white-robed woman walked by, laughing, a companion at her side. The colors were vivid, the sounds and smells powerful and pungent. Cyrus blinked, and suddenly they were faded, along with the rest of the world, like it had lost some of its light.

She's gone.

"We would have ended up like Sanctuary," Quinneria said a moment later, her voice heavy, and her head bowed. A single tear ran down from her eye, cutting a lonely path down her cheek. "Because it's not just her that's gone, Cyrus. It's everything." The dim horror settled on him as he lay there on the cobblestones, staring up at the sky, the square swirling around him as his mother spoke. "It's all gone now ... all of it ... when they're finished, there will be nothing left of Sanctuary at all ..."

NOW

Epilogue

"This place is no grave," Vaste said, looking evenly at Cyrus, the note of sadness still there on his face, shaded by the light of the hearth. "You saw the weed sprouting. There is life here. It could live again. You don't have to spend the rest of your life mourning what you've lost in the past—"

"I don't want it to be past, don't you get that?" Cyrus asked, staring at him. "My best days are behind me."

"You could have a great many wonderful days in front of you," Vaste said, "which is the same argument you used on Vara when she tried to cut herself off from you with that foolishness about—"

"SHE WAS RIGHT!" Cyrus thundered, and as his voice echoed through the empty halls, fading the further away it carried, Vaste bowed his head again. "She was right, Vaste. She's been gone over a year and I ... it's not any better. It's not getting any better. I thought if I ..."

"I know," Vaste said quietly. "I know."

"I have fought my whole life," Cyrus said, looking out the window onto the misty plains again. The fog was creeping in, closer to the window, and now he could scarcely see the ground below at all. "Fought the odds, fought the gods, and fought everyone else on and under the surface of Arkaria at some point. Now ... I've lost everything," he said with feeling, "... and I don't want to fight anymore."

"You read this," Vaste said, and Cyrus turned around enough to see Alaric's journal in his hand. He shook it lightly. "You tell me there's no hope left, and I say you're wrong, and you know you're wrong because you know what he found, and what's inside ... is hope." Vaste smiled faintly. "Hope for a better future."

"I don't want a future," Cyrus whispered, turning back to the window, feeling the cool, damp plains air on his face. "I want my fight to be over. When I started all this, all I wanted was war and battle, to be the foremost warrior in Arkaria." He dropped his hands to the hilt of the swords at his belt. "Now that I am, all I want is peace … and to have back what I lost."

"You didn't lose—"

"I lost," Cyrus said with feeling, "I lost everything." He put his hand over his face. "And everybody left. Here we are, at the end … and it's just you and me."

"Others would have come if you'd called," Vaste said, sounding annoyed for the first time in their entire exchange. "You're not alone. And they didn't leave, you left them—"

"Everybody leaves, Vaste," Cyrus said. "That's a fact of life."

"Bullshit!" Vaste said hotly. "She didn't leave you, Cyrus, she died. It's different—"

"It's all the same in the end, isn't it?" Cyrus asked quietly.

"It's not—"

"She's not here, is she?" He turned to look at Vaste, looking hazy as the fog crept in through the window off the plains. Cyrus raised his voice and asked again. "IS SHE? Can you see her?"

Vaste's mouth twitched, his face displaying a flurry of emotion. "No," he said at last. "No, I can't."

"So she's left, too," Cyrus said, swallowing hard. "Gone on. Just like Narstron. Like Niamh. Curatio. Just like my father." He felt a pull at the corners of his eyes. "Just like Alaric—"

"Do not be so hasty to judge," a voice came, the mist coalescing into a pillar in the corner of the room, solidifying before the fire, strengthening into a figure. The mist became a cloak, covering the man from head to toe, draping him in grey, the fire casting its warmth upon his face, tired and worn, but with a voice deep with reassurance, smooth and quiet, like silk given audible form and poured into Cyrus's ear. "For some that leave might yet return, unexpected …"

"Alaric," Vaste whispered into the silence of the archive. "It's you. It's … it's really you." The smell of old parchment hung in the air, but something new was present as well, a subtle disturbance in the atmosphere that heralded a change.

"It is I," the figure said, his cloak draped around him, grey and heavy like the mist he'd just formed himself out of. "And I bring a message for you, Cyrus … one that should be very familiar to you by now …"

"Wh … what is it?" Cyrus asked, staring at the face of Alaric Garaunt, and finding himself curiously warm as well, like a sensation had returned that he had not expected, sun peeking out of the clouds on a chill morning.

"That no matter how dark things might get," Alaric said, "… there is always hope."

The Ghost of Sanctuary smiled at him, returned to his home at last, and at the sight of the knight and the sound of his words, Cyrus Davidon started to believe—for the first time in a long, long while—that what he said might just be true.

The Sanctuary Series Will Conclude in

LEGEND

The Sanctuary Series, Volume Eight

Coming June 14, 2016!

Author's Note

If you want to know immediately when future books become available, take sixty seconds and sign up for my NEW RELEASE EMAIL ALERTS by visiting my website at www.robertjcrane.com. I don't sell your information and I only send out emails when I have a new book out. The reason you should sign up for this is because I don't always set release dates, and even if you're following me on Facebook (robertJcrane (Author)) or Twitter (@robertJcrane), it's easy to miss my book announcements because…well, because social media is an imprecise thing.

Come join the discussion on my website: http://www.robertjcrane.com !

Cheers,
Robert J. Crane

Acknowledgments

Editorial/Literary Janitorial duties performed by Sarah Barbour and Jeffrey Bryan. Final proofing was handle by Jo Evans. Any errors you see in the text, however, are the result of me rejecting changes.

The cover was masterfully designed (as always) by Karri Klawiter.

David Leach did the first read on this one, and my thanks to him for it!

Once more, thanks to my parents, my kids and my wife, for helping me keep things together.

Other Works by Robert J. Crane

The Sanctuary Series
Epic Fantasy

Defender: The Sanctuary Series, Volume One
Avenger: The Sanctuary Series, Volume Two
Champion: The Sanctuary Series, Volume Three
Crusader: The Sanctuary Series, Volume Four
Sanctuary Tales, Volume One - A Short Story Collection
Thy Father's Shadow: The Sanctuary Series, Volume 4.5
Master: The Sanctuary Series, Volume Five
Fated in Darkness: The Sanctuary Series, Volume 5.5
Warlord: The Sanctuary Series, Volume Six
Heretic: The Sanctuary Series, Volume Seven
Legend: The Sanctuary Series, Volume Eight* (Coming
    June 14, 2016!)

The Girl in the Box
and
Out of the Box
Contemporary Urban Fantasy

Alone: The Girl in the Box, Book 1
Untouched: The Girl in the Box, Book 2
Soulless: The Girl in the Box, Book 3
Family: The Girl in the Box, Book 4
Omega: The Girl in the Box, Book 5
Broken: The Girl in the Box, Book 6
Enemies: The Girl in the Box, Book 7
Legacy: The Girl in the Box, Book 8
Destiny: The Girl in the Box, Book 9
Power: The Girl in the Box, Book 10

Limitless: Out of the Box, Book 1
In the Wind: Out of the Box, Book 2
Ruthless: Out of the Box, Book 3
Grounded: Out of the Box, Book 4
Tormented: Out of the Box, Book 5
Vengeful: Out of the Box, Book 6
Sea Change: Out of the Box, Book 7
Painkiller: Out of the Box, Book 8* (Coming April 12, 2016!)
Masks: Out of the Box, Book 9* (Coming July 12, 2016!)
Prisoners: Out of the Box, Book 10* (Coming September 27, 2016!)

Southern Watch
Contemporary Urban Fantasy

Called: Southern Watch, Book 1
Depths: Southern Watch, Book 2
Corrupted: Southern Watch, Book 3
Unearthed: Southern Watch, Book 4
Legion: Southern Watch, Book 5* (Coming May 10, 2016!)

* Forthcoming and subject to change